SEMPER FI

Buccari connected with the second pilot's station, where Lizard Lips had settled himself. She downloaded the aliens' icon file and pressed out a quick salutation. Lizard Lips screeched with delight and immediately made a reply.

"Check out my screen!" Buccari exclaimed. Godonov floated over her head. On the pilot's screen was written, not with alien icons but in Legion:

MUCH HERE. TEACH ME HOW.

"You have a genius on your hands," Buccari said. "We should be able to find a place for a genius, shouldn't we? Train him to be a planet survey technician or—"

"That just might work for Lizzy," Godonov replied, "but what about the hunters? They eat raw meat, for goodness' sake. They don't know piss from reaction fuel, and they get damned cranky."

Buccari laughed. "Sounds like marines."

By Scott G. Gier
Published by Ballantine Books:

GENELLAN: Planetfall, Book 1
GENELLAN: In the Shadow of the Moon, Book 2

Books published by The Ballantine Publishing Group
are available at quantity discounts on bulk purchases
for premium, educational, fund-raising, and special
sales use. For details, please call 1-800-733-3000.

GENELLAN:
In the Shadow
of the Moon

BOOK 2

Scott G. Gier

A Del Rey® Book
BALLANTINE BOOKS • NEW YORK

A Del Rey® Book
Published by Ballantine Books
Copyright © 1996 by Scott G. Gier

All rights reserved under International and Pan-American Copyright Conventions. Published in the United States by Ballantine Books, a division of Random House, Inc., New York, and simultaneously in Canada by Random House of Canada Limited, Toronto.

http://www.randomhouse.com

Library of Congress Catalog Card Number: 95-96183

ISBN 0-345-40449-7

Manufactured in the United States of America

First Edition: July 1996

10 9 8 7 6 5 4 3 2 1

In memory of:
Major Scott G. Gier, U.S.M.C.
Lt. Col. Robert C. McCutchan, U.S.M.C.

CONTENTS

GENELLAN:
In the
Shadow of
the Moon

BOOK 2

PROLOGUE

SUDDEN DEATH

"Officer of the deck, ready to relieve you, sir."

Wong looked up from the log screens. Jonson saluted smartly as she floated into a set of acceleration tethers, gracefully checking her body rotation. Her helmet was radiantly white, her boots and epaulet insignia glistening, and her matte-gray underway suit sported sharp creases, in decided contrast to his own. Jonson was a hot-runner, having been deep-selected for corvette command. She was early, as usual.

Wong hauled a shopworn hood over his egg-bald head and casually returned the salute. He made a last offhand check of *T.L.S. Hokkaido*'s annunciators. Standing mothership OOD watch in orbit was less exciting than watching oxidation inhibitors cure.

"For the log," he began, his debriefing reduced to litany. "Day twelve, Oldfather system. *T.L.S. Hokkaido* conducting colony support operations. Maintaining standoff orbit, Oldfather Three. Two point two hours from apogee. In company with motherships *Borneo*, *Luzon*, and *Crete*. Supporting freighters *Banff* and *Juneau*. Captain Ketchie is SOPO. *Hokkaido* is cell guide. HLA Condition Four. *Luzon* has broken gridlink for orbital descent to resupply station. *Borneo* is boosting from resupply orbit to replace *Luzon* in grid by 1300 hours."

"Any update on colony replenishment?" Jonson asked, interrogating the power system. The next watch filtered onto the bridge, establishing contact with their off-going counterparts. Lieutenant Sato, the oncoming junior officer of the deck, drifted gracefully past the conning station. The winsome officer glanced in Wong's direction, black eyes smiling.

"Mr. Wong?" Jonson persisted, smooth, hairless brows raised impatiently. "Any updates?"

"Uh . . . no. *Juneau*'s heavy-lifter is hard down," he replied. "Group leader deployed the Five and Six birds as shuttles to take up slack."

"I heard," Jonson grunted. "It'll take more than two corvettes hauling butt paper and dehydrates to get us on schedule. We're going to be late. Admiral Runacres will go nonlinear. What else?"

"Matrix generator number two down for preventive maintenance. Plasma blow-down at eighty percent, and thermoloading is restricted by rad-choke governors. Engineering has a dozen items on the board."

"So I see," Jonson replied, fingers playing the panel. "What else?"

"Captain's stewing in his ring cabin. The exec's planetside, taking in the scenery." Wong chuckled.

"What's so funny?" Jonson asked, intent on the pass-down logs. "OF3's not that bad. Sunsets are wonderful."

"Yeah . . . sunsets. I'll wait till we make Genellan."

"Me, too," she allowed, turning to check the status panels. "Well, if that's all, then I relieve you, sir."

"I stand re—"

A contact-alert Klaxon exploded to life.

"Fast-movers rising above the limb," the tactical officer blurted. "Exceeding orbital velocity. Polar trace."

Wong jerked his attention to the status boards. Threat alarms warbled insanely—they were being targeted. Jonson dove for the deck officer's station. Wong, the nearer, had the advantage. He slid into the acceleration stirrups and slammed open alarm covers, simultaneously shouting over the command circuit: "Captain to the bridge. Captain to the bridge. Battle stations! Battle stations."

He triggered the GQ alert. Jonson floated rigidly at his side, eyes darting across the screens. Wong looked at the situation display, searching for information.

"I've got the deck, Jonson," he said, reaching into the armor locker. "Take the conn. Clear unnecessary personnel from the bridge."

Jonson, impassive, catapulted to her assigned station.

"Good grief!" the tactical officer shouted. "Pick up button one."

* * *

With honorable abandon Destroyer-Fist a'Yerg screamed into the universe, the timeless brain-curdling battle cry of the roon, a rasping, piercing screech yodeling relentlessly up and down the scales. Fist a'Yerg seized the animal within, her *g'ort*, touching the rapture of combat—the ecstasy of fear. Blood pounded hot through distended arteries lacing taut sinews; a'Yerg reveled in the visceral convulsion of her race. Rapacious instinct honed her reactions, physical and mental; a'Yerg—savage roonish warrior—had become the blood and muscle embodiment of directed mayhem, of mortal embrace, of war.

Waiting patiently, fully cognizant in the same highly evolved braincase, a'Yerg's dominant alter ego, acute and calculating, rose preeminent, firmly suppressing the raging brute. Atavistic screaming trailed off mournfully to silence as the logical entity scanned the situation display, monitoring the disposition of enemy forces, now visible through line-of-sight detectors.

The alien ships were deployed in two groups: three units in support orbit and three more in high standoff. One of the low ships was elevating. In less than a beat cycle of her multiple hearts a'Yerg signaled for attack. She yawed her destroyer about, simultaneously rolling to keep the enemy in sight, mere specks sparkling beyond the terminator. Gravity-boosted velocity swept her past the low-orbit targets. She pulsed the main engines, checking her overshoot.

The animal in her mind asserted itself deliciously. Fist a'Yerg, embracing *g'ort*, observed more than felt her own powerful fingers clutching the throttle. With practiced self-control a'Yerg squelched the alter ego's manic impulse and set the throttle for standard attack. Her squadron deployed smoothly into attack profile, flanks setting smartly. Squeezing the throttle, a'Yerg relaxed and gave vent to the writhing within. The throttle slammed forward. Her unbridled libido howled into the endless universe. All units leapt to attack speed.

Ah, but it felt lovely to scream, a'Yerg's logical self sighed.

"Where'd they come from?" Ketchie demanded as he slammed into the command station, breaking momentum with his boots.

"HLA exit on the far side, Captain," Wong told his commanding officer. "*Borneo*'s in big trouble. They came down on her antenna farm. She had no time to rotate. Main batteries were totally masked."

"No!" Ketchie roared.

"*Borneo*'s gone," the tactical officer confirmed.

Ketchie, in full battle armor and inscrutable behind his helmet visor, thrust himself into his command station tethers.

"Jump status?" Ketchie demanded.

"Damn, they're picking off lifeboats!" the assistant tactical officer shouted. "It's Shaula all over again!"

"*Jump status!*" Ketchie shouted. "Where's *Luzon?*"

"Climbing back to grid, Captain," Wong responded. "Estimate preliminary coupling in thirty minutes, grid locks in forty."

"Weapons status?"

"Batteries One and Four manned, hot, and tagging targets, Captain. Nothing in range," Wong reported. "Batteries Two and Three are five minutes from battle temps. Kinetics armed and ready. *Crete*'s batteries are on line. *Crete* has two 'vettes in the air and two coming out. We've got three launching. *Luzon* is about to launch her alert fif—"

"Conning officer, depress your orbit. Ease *Luzon*'s rendezvous angle," Ketchie ordered.

"Aye, aye," Jonson replied.

"Captain, new contacts!" the tactical officer shouted. "Large ships reported in counterorbit around Oldfather Three, coming our way. One point three hours from engagement range."

"How many?" Ketchie barked.

"Clean returns on nine units, Captain. Fleet mothership mass or greater," the tactical officer answered soberly.

The skipper's shoulders sagged. Wong turned away. They were badly outnumbered and mismatched. There was no alternative but to retreat into hyperspace, leaving behind the freighters and marooning the colonists. No alternative—none.

"Getting emergency squawks from both freighters," Wong reported. "*Banff*'s losing orbit. She's going down. Captain's abandoning ship."

"Three waves of bug fast-movers coming our way, Skipper," the tactical officer reported. "Engagement with our 'vettes in eight minutes. Rocs have intercept position. Peregrine, flight of three, is right behind the Rocs."

"Three to one against," Ketchie snarled.

Dead meat, Wong thought, muttering a silent farewell.

"*Banff*'s gone!" the tactical officer shouted.

"Jump checks! Get hot!" Ketchie roared.

"Aye, Captain!" Wong punched up initiation sequences and felt the first ripples of acceleration. The huge ship lurched leadenly.

"Rendezvous with *Luzon* in twenty," Jonson said, her voice even. "Closing velocity category five plus. Gravity torque will be exciting."

"Exciting, my ass," Ketchie muttered, pounding his gauntleted fists together.

"*Luzon*'s launching 'vettes. Thrasher's in the air!" Wong announced.

"Recall those corvettes!" Ketchie barked.

"*Juneau*'s taking hits!"

"*Checklist!*" Ketchie roared.

"Checklist has commenced. *Crete* is synced," Wong replied, hands flying. "*Luzon*'s registering. Negative link, Skipper. At least fifteen more minutes."

"Very well," Ketchie spit. "I want this jump on minimum path. Clear all overrides. Signal *Crete* to stand by for radical maneuvers, emergency acceleration. Conning officer, all ahead flank. Direct intercept. You know the drill. Mr. Wong, keep your cannons unmasked."

"Aye, aye, Captain," Wong said too loudly, trying not to choke on his fear. A head-on, flank-speed jump rendezvous, under fire—for real! Jonson moved efficiently, setting a new course and shooting guide signals. The mothership, a spacer's faithful frame of reference, settled and pivoted. Inertial changes wreaked havoc on the huge craft's internal structures. Wong, ashamed, felt his stomach wambling.

Destroyer-Fist a'Yerg's lead triad completed weapons passes in good form, all units scoring full-weight energy strikes. The attack commander pivoted ship to watch the trailing triads coordinate their runs on the remaining low-orbit target. Scintillating energy beams rippled across the sundered structure of the dying ship. Amazingly, despite its death wallow, the alien vessel was still firing. Lifting a glove in silent tribute, a'Yerg snarled her contempt.

Communications alert sounded—battle precedence. A heavy chime signaled a secure channel engaging, preempting tactical frequencies. The attack commander's spidery hand slid to the override—a precautionary habit. Fist a'Yerg felt the cell controller's telepathic links soften in favor of the dominant's transmission.

"Victory is ours," the dominant's bridgemale droned. "Attend." More chimes, the dominant's clarion. A pause.

"Glory is yours, destroyers," Fleet Dominant Dar broadcast, hajil accents gurgling harshly. "You have made all sisters proud. All races proud. Attend."

More chimes, ringing the dominant away, and then the call to orders. The cell controller's telepathic links sharpened.

"Destroyer-Fist a'Yerg," a grating hajil voice announced, half-heard, half-thought. Shrill and brittle, Cell Controller Jakkuk continued. "Deploy to grid four. Form spearhead for diversionary attack on remaining alien interstellar ships. Honor is yours."

"Blood, but they fight, Jakkuk-hajil," a'Yerg replied. "We should collect them." The animal in her soul growled its lust, a hardening pang, like hunger, only nearer her hearts.

"You have orders, a'Yerg-roon. Obey and—" Jakkuk transmitted, her telepathic signal overmodulating with intensity.

"Eliminate them," the nasal, unmistakably slithery inflections of a lakk overrode. "There are numbers on the planet sufficient to fill our holds. Heed orders, Daughter. Honor is yours."

"Honor is mine, Mother," a'Yerg growled with obscene ferocity, the savage within instantly ascendant. Her *g'ort* would be satisfied.

The freighter *Juneau* was in extremis. Lifeboat beacons flickered magically, tragically. Panicked maydays, ever fewer.

"She's gone," the tactical officer reported. The funereal silence was deafening.

"Link signals from *Luzon*," Wong announced. "Third-order magnitude. She's coming up like an intercept booster. Massive Doppler. Way off the scope, Captain. One of us has gotta slow down big time!"

"Emergency retro!" Ketchie shouted. "Signal *Crete* to stand by for full inertial. Panic override, on my command."

"Emergency retro, aye!" Jonson shouted, disengaging governors. The starship shuddered against its own inertia, its great angular momentum causing it to pitch.

"Mind your head, helm!" Wong roared. "Meet the yaw."

"She's heavy, sir!" the helmsman shouted.

"Fire compensators, Jonson!" Wong ordered.

"Precession compensators," Jonson announced, hitting the emergency buttons. "Hold attitude, helmsman! Ease your twist."

"Well done, Mr. Wong," Ketchie shouted. "How's *Crete*?"

"Holding position within limits," Wong replied. "Maintaining hard link." Every inertial warning light on *Crete*'s maneuvering panel glowed brightly; their companion mothership struggled mightily to stay in grid formation. Another set of diodes flickered magically. "Getting tertiary link on *Luzon*! She's commencing long-range authentication."

"We're going to make it." Ketchie exhaled, steadying himself against shuddering accelerations. "Tactical, corvette status."

"Roc flight confirmed destroyed in action," the tactical officer replied mechanically. "Peregrine still has two birds in the game, sir. Two enemy confirmed destroyed. Alien fast-movers are consolidating. Leading elements are approaching *Luzon*'s main battery perimeter. Estimate engagement in three minutes."

"*Luzon* can handle the fast-movers," Ketchie remarked. "Signal recall. Let's get this link together and—"

"*Contacts! Close aboard!*" the tactical assistant screamed.

Wong jerked his attention to the tactical plot. Impossible! There, above them, in a rapidly descending trajectory, where only minutes before there had been nothing but empty space, were five ships. Starships! Completing a local HLA jump with incredulous precision.

"Emergency pitch over!" Ketchie shouted.

"Weapons free. Fire when able!" Wong bellowed. "Clear the—"

Implosion! Blast! Heat and chaos! Wong's last recollection was of Jonson braced in her tethers at the conning station, hood blown from her head, hard blue eyes wide with alarm yet jaw set with firm resolve.

And then they were dead. All of them.

The universe was filled with screams.

SECTION ONE

A SIMPLE EQUATION

ONE

GENELLAN—THIRD PLANET FROM THE STAR

She was hiking back to where humans had first landed, to Hudson's Plateau, where Commander Quinn, Rhodes, and Rennault had died, where the entire crew of *Harrier One*—her crew—would have died if it had not been for the cliff dwellers. Buccari owed it to the intelligent creatures to return. The elders had requested her presence. Unspoken in that summons but impossible to ignore was the cliff dwellers' desire to see her son. MacArthur's son. She looked down at the sprawling child, asleep in a chest harness, a solid counterbalance to her backpack.

It was spring again. The planet was awakening—expanding, stretching in the sun-star's marginal warmth. And transforming—melting, eroding, trembling in the irrepressible cycles of nature. Grimy expanses of crusty whiteness clung resolutely to north-facing slopes, and the great river, always powerful, swelled magnificently with snowmelt. The river trail was awash, but she had to make the arduous hike now. The fleet would soon return, this time with settlers, with problems. She would have decisions to make. *Too many damn decisions.*

Thoughts disjointed by fatigue, pack frame tugging at her shoulders, Buccari clambered along an escarpment. It was not warm, but exertion had soaked her T-shirt and stained her leather jerkin. She turned and checked Lizard Lips; the cliff dweller trudged doggedly behind her. She exhaled, shifted her load, and plodded forward. Ahead, Chastain had come to another runoff, a foamy cascade of green and gray.

The bear of a man, floppy cap in hand, backed off from the icy runnel, took three powerful running steps, and leapt. He flailed his arms and crashed against a damp boulder. Stones clattered down the slant toward the rushing torrent far below.

Chastain dipped his shaggy head and hunched his mountainous shoulders. A sheepish smile crinkled his soft brown eyes, swelled his fat brown cheeks, and flickered through his wild brown whiskers.

Buccari let Lizard Lips by. The cliff dweller was a guilder, a steam user, taller than Buccari but with shorter legs. His private parts were covered with a dun kilt; his vestigial talons were wrapped with stout leather. A pelt of silky gray grew from the guilder's knobby head and narrow shoulders. Creamy white fur adorned the rest of his body. The creature tossed the Legion communicator to Chastain and then threw his rucksack. Chittering nervously, the cliff dweller unlimbered atrophied flying membranes, took a short run at the tributary, and jumped. His down-stroking appendages *whoosh*ed with apprehensive energy, but the ugly creature easily cleared the impediment. Overhead an army of hunters wheeling on midday thermals whistled derisively at such feeble flight.

"Careful, Lieutenant," Chastain bellowed, brow furrowed. Beyond Chastain glacier-hung ridges heaved skyward. They had climbed to the boulder-strewn margins of the riparian valley. Isolated clumps of scraggly, yellow-barked spruce and russet-limbed rockberry flourished, but only where spreading flows of talus and rock tumble permitted.

"Kinda slick, Lieutenant," Chastain shouted.

The glacier-melt defile was not wide, but its torrent was powerful. Buccari settled her pack, sucked in a mind-clearing breath, and looked up the river valley to the immense rise of the monolithic plateau, home to cliff dwellers. Beyond the plateau were the ageless mountains, a towering snow-shrouded continental spine stark against an iron-blue sky—geologic monsters, ancient and imperturbable. She looked down at her sleeping child.

"Sir, you want to hand Charlie over?" Chastain asked. The marine placed a grimy, sandaled foot to the brink, lips working beneath shaggy mustaches. He leaned over the splashing feeder and extended a powerful arm. His pack shifted, but Chastain moderated his piston-legged stance only slightly.

Buccari exhaled. The plateau was not getting any closer.

"Here I come, Jocko," she said through clenched teeth. She pushed hard, accelerating with each step. With one hand she held her child; with the other she reached for Chastain's hairy arm. And jumped.

"Aw, Lieuten—!" Chastain blurted. Lizard Lips screeched. Chastain seized her wrist. In that instant she knew no force the universe could break their bond. She landed on the rock-udded slope and was surrounded by an iron-hard embrace. harlie stirred but did not awaken.

"Thanks, Jocko." She exhaled, tilting her chin to give the ntle giant a smile. Chastain blushed, as he always did.

She looked back defiantly at the shattered torrent, its leaping ray dancing in rainbow mists. Far below, the plummeting butary was overwhelmed in confluence with the river. The eater current, its majestic tumult exploding in brain-dulling scades, thundered downstream in boulder-rolling waves.

Lizard Lips, downy fur glistening with gems of spray, irped and thrust the communicator at her. His gruesome untenance jerked upward, long snout lifting in unbridled notion. Rows of jagged teeth glinted in the bright sun—not smile.

SHORT-ONE-WHO-LEADS ENDANGER OFFSPRING. GIANT-ONE UST CARRY, the icons on the coummunicator admonished.

She looked into the ugly creature's double-lidded black eyes d signed back: "My turn to carry. My duty. My offspring."

Chirping with agitation into the ultrasonic, Lizard Lips dely recovered the communicator and started to punch in ore icons. Buccari waved away his efforts and signed: "Talk er. Walk now. Many spans."

Lizard Lips whistled something. Buccari fixed the cliff veller with an unblinking glare. The chastised steam user wed formally, if quickly, and jumped into a rolling waddle.

Chastain moved farther from the river. Solid pillars of gran- rose between them and the watercourse, shielding them m the crashing hydraulics. Above them, on precipitous iffs, clusters and points of whiteness moved sedately— ountain goats. The hikers twisted around rugged formations. ees grew on the higher slopes, but the rugged terrain in nich they found themselves was unrelieved rock.

Shrieks! Overhead, hunters, no longer merely swirling otes, plummeted closer. Buccari glanced up at their bedlam. anger! the hunters screamed. She brought a heightened atten- n to the ground.

Lizard Lips signed unnecessarily: "Alert. Something ong."

Movement in the boulders caught her eye. A rockdog!

Slinking with feline grace, the predator emerged from dar
shadows, sunlight reflecting brilliantly from its silky black pel

"Jocko!" she whispered, pointing.

"Yes, sir," Chastain replied softly, unlatching a stubby rifl
"Two more behind us."

She unholstered her pistol as they climbed a tumble c
lichen-stained quartz. White and argent-crazed facets sparkle
in the sun's rays. The spectacle went unappreciated as snarl
reverberated in the air. Chastain eased to the crest of the scir
tillating rise. His broad shoulders sagged. More snarls. Rock
dogs closed in behind them. Lizard Lips screamed, silently t
human ears, but the carnivores heard the ultrasonic plea an
howled in vicious agitation.

"They got us in a box, Lieutenant," Chastain said softly.

She climbed beside the crouching giant. Sheer cliffs c
quartz-veined granite blocked their path. Their only option wa
to retreat. No fewer than ten rockdogs stalked their rear, mea
suring them, tasting the air. One crept steadily closer. Chastai
raised his rifle.

"Jocko, don't shoot—yet," she begged.

Buccari, pistol held high, hopped from the rocks, watchin
the predators' movements as they hungrily studied hers. Sh
felt movement. She glanced down. Charlie's gunmetal blu
eyes blinked owlishly, unsteadily trying to focus.

"No, Lieutenant! Wait!" Chastain moaned. Lizard Lip
screeched.

The near rockdog, at least sixty kilos, silver-hackled an
ears shredded by combat, slunk on its belly, cutting off retrea
Other rockdogs moved in. She shifted the pistol, hefted
chunk of quartz, took two forceful steps, and whipped th
stone sidearm. The ragged missile hit short, splintering shar
of crystal. The beast recoiled and growled magnificently, ba
ing yellowed canines and a piebald tongue of pink and blac

"Stupid dog," she muttered, shifting the pistol to her rig
hand.

Chastain, rifle butt swinging to his shoulder, jostled he
aside. The snarling predator surged forward, hackles bristlin
clawing like a bull. It feigned a charge and then settled into
coiled bundle of fury.

"Don't kill it, Jocko," she pleaded, grabbing his sleeve ar
wrapping her arm around Charlie's head. "Shoot high."

The big man sighed, twitched his weapon upward, ar
jerked off a round. The rifle's report exploded with echoi

resonance, the wasted slug singing off the rocks. The beasts re-coiled as one, many disappearing into rocky shadows. The near dog lurched but spun, silver hackles bristling. It sniffed the cordite, lowered its head, and issued a rattling growl. Charlie screamed lustily.

"I gotta, Lieutenant!" Chastain shouted. He aimed, finger tightening on the trigger. The skulking beast sprang.

Zip! A black-fletched dart struck the dog in the neck. A hail of hunter arrows whiffled the air, many sinking into the hurtling dog's body, some clattering among the rocks. The animal, pincushioned with shafts, thudded into the rocks, jerking spasmodically. The noble beast lay convulsing at Chastain's feet, whimpering.

"Now, Jocko," Buccari whispered, hugging her son's head.

The single shot echoed into the mountains, as did the screams of hunters descending. Bows drawn and arrows nocked, the host of sinewed, mattock-headed creatures fired furiously at the retreating targets, killing or maiming. The barking died. The screaming of the hunters diminished to regimented chirps. The only sound was Charlie's crying, and that, too, soon tempered.

Two hunters swooped past her and luffed into the wind, membranes billowing like parachutes. They landed at Buccari's feet. Both charcoal-furred creatures were tall warriors, yet their knobby heads barely reached Buccari's chin. Captain Two, the hunter leader, and Tonto, her old friend, wore sweat-darkened leather over chest and groin. The hideously scarred warrior chief was the second hunter she had named Captain. The first Captain had died in MacArthur's arms as Mac, too, lay dying on the rocky ridge above his valley, heroes of a great battle. She swept away painful memories and embraced her restless child.

Not in a sweet temper, Captain Two bowed stiffly. With fierce and obvious displeasure the warrior screeched and waved spindly four-fingered hands in agitated signals, his splendid ire directed at Chastain. The hunter leader dared not berate Buccari, for that would be grave insult. Even so, Tonto glared at her with fraternal impatience.

"Risk offspring! Shoot dog more quick! Stupid! Stupid!" Captain Two's blurring hand signals were emphatic. Chastain stood blinking at attention, a herculean warrior being repri-manded by a wispy Napoleon, comprehending not half of the flashing hand signals but acutely aware of being dressed down, whatever the language.

Buccari stifled a smile. She consoled Charlie back into calmness and studiously avoided eye contact with the heated hunters. Captain Two, his anger spent, turned and hopped from the rocks. Chirping nervously, Lizard Lips obediently followed the warrior. Chastain looked sideways at Buccari, smiled diffidently, and motioned for her to precede him. They walked in silence past arrow-studded carcasses, toward the river. Tonto and a butcher party collected arrows and hides.

"Dunno, Lieutenant," Chastain said, breaking the silence. "Should've had Et Silmarn fly us to the plateau."

"They don't want kones on the plateau, Jocko," she said.

Buccari understood the cliff dwellers' fear. As alien to Genellan as were humans, the kones were at once Buccari's greatest hope and her greatest apprehension. She had been on the ugly end of powerful konish weapons too many times.

Captain Two waited at a point where they could safely proceed upriver. As Buccari hiked past the hunter leader, the wiry creature bowed with grotesque formality. Buccari returned the honor.

TWO

KON—SECOND PLANET FROM THE STAR

The arching vaults of the amphitheater belied the punishing physics of the gravity-strained planet. From her cubicle on the brazenly cantilevered mezzanine Kateos studied the proceedings. The Northern Hegemonic filtering center, directly above the podium, afforded the best view in the Planetary Defense Force forum. Similar compartments patterned the perimeter of the amphitheater, all occupied by female linguists monitoring the activities of the delegates.

"A simple equation," Et Kalass summarized, cottony tufts

standing erect above murky-brown eyes. King Ollant's prime minister wore robes of dazzling white trimmed in midnight blue. His golden, grainy-skinned image was magnified on the main holo-vid; auxiliary vids scattered along the walls replicated the noblekone's ponderous bovine countenance in a kaleidoscope of movement. "Humans transfer hyperlight technology to us, and we consent to their settlement. Humans have an outpost for their civilization, and konish vessels at last travel the stars."

Et Kalass paused. A murmur rippled through the southern delegations. Kateos studied the activity. In its midst Tar Fell, chancellor of the Thullol-Ransa Compact, stared upward with inscrutable detachment. Languorously, the southerner raised a Gargantuan arm from beneath a shimmering black cloak, revealing a golden lining and the uniform of a Planetary Defense general officer.

Supreme General Talsali, commander of Planetary Defenses and presiding officer of the plenary council, recognized his glowering subordinate. Diffuse laser beams—magenta, cyan, and amber—danced across Tar Fell's bulky form. The chancellor-general's stern image, the coarse features of a commoner, replaced Et Kalass's noble visage on the holo-vid. The southerner's voice thundered from the address system.

"Prime Minister Et Kalass!" Tar Fell rumbled. The hulking warrior, thrice the mass of a large human, pushed from his grav-lounge and rose to all fours. "This is a charade."

The Thullolian spoke the ancient tongue well. Kateos crisply translated the southerner's grinding inflections into the lyrical *jodal* dialect favored by Et Kalass. She glanced at her annunciator; a shifting pattern of lights caught her attention. She selected a particularly active address and, to her consternation, detected a snippet of scrambled subconversation between a Thullolian deputy and General Krolk of the Ransa League—most rude under the circumstances. She directed facial cameras, initiated lip movement analysis, and piped the output into her decryption programs, unrealistically hoping for a cipher break. She also tripped the protocol alarm and channeled a transgression summary to Et Kalass. The prime minister chose not to register a protest.

"A charade, Chancellor?" Et Kalass replied, settling onto his lounge, the soul of injured rectitude. "Pray favor us."

"Noble Ollant is gracious with words," Tar Fell pronounced, "but in practice His Majesty maintains unyielding advantage.

Is Genellan, that miserable asteroid, to become the king's private hive, swarming with malignant alien technology?"

Kateos turned sharply at Tar Fell's undisguised contempt. The general's deep-shadowed eyes darted briefly upward and registered her presence, radiating unmitigated malice. The translator exhaled forcefully and returned to her instruments. Her physiology reacted predictably. The ventilation system in her cubicle hummed.

"That vermin-infested ball of ice," Tar Fell continued, "is like a sword poised over our heads. What does—"

"Chancellor Tar Fell," Et Kalass bellowed, rising to his hinds. "Mistake not the fragile nature of our alliance, both between northern and southern hemispheres and between kone and human. More importantly, mistake not King Ollant's resolve—"

"Ollant's resolve," Tar Fell screamed, neck tendons bulging, "but mirrors the determination of the independent nations to—"

"Order!" Talsali boomed in the brusque tongue made universal in the north during the Rule of Generals. "Gravity, there will be order! This is not a *losagoda* ring."

Interdelegation communications blossomed to an electronic crescendo. Kateos scanned for patterns of unwonted collusion. The usual suspects were busy, but so were many others—too many.

"Genellan is the king's toy," Tar Fell persisted, but softly, calming the crowd. The general's splayed features cooled. His blood-flushed complexion softened to a mottled nacre.

"The ability to travel the stars will belong to all kones," Et Kalass replied as gently. "Kon will no longer be at the mercy of marauders that come to us at their will and at our peril—while we remain stagnant, trapped and frightened in our own star system."

"Yes, of course," Tar Fell snapped. "Fine words and noble, but the Hegemony still dictates. Some would even say the Planetary Defense Force is lackey to the imperial north."

"Tar Fell!" Talsali roared. "That is an affront and insultingly inappropriate from a PDF officer. If you have issue—"

"Peace, Supreme General. I speak for my nation—" Tar Fell sighed, with well-crafted sincerity. "—as must be."

"Gravity, the aliens—the humans wish Kon no harm," Et Kalass interjected. "They have knowledge of space travel. They—"

"Four hundred years ago!" Tar Fell spit. "Four hundred years ago this planet was savaged by mysterious space travelers. Millions of kones died under evil beams, Your Excellency. Thousands of millions! That must never happen again. Remember your vows." The chamber thundered with emotional affirmation.

Et Kalass bowed elegantly, allowing the crowd noise to abate.

"The Vows of Protection demand utmost vigilance, Prime Minister," Tar Fell preached. "That vigilance enabled us to punish the latest alien attacks into retreat—twice!"

"The humans fought in self-defense," Et Kalass rumbled.

"A relative condition, Your Excellency!" Tar Fell snarled, expanding to his full breadth and height. "Aliens—humans—are again at our doorstep. What dangers will this new intrusion bring? Is this . . . this human outpost but another, more insidious invasion?"

"We gain the stars, sir," Et Kalass proclaimed.

"Pah! The stars!" the Thullolian continued. "In what form will these exotic technologies be made available? What are the waystones for this knowledge transfer? And what will be the pace and limits of settlement? Can the aliens be . . . evicted if need be?"

"Do not forget," Et Kalass replied. "Numbered among those aliens are full and true citizens of the Hegemony. King Ollant would never have lived to end the perfidious Rule of Generals had it not been for—"

"Of course, of course!" Tar Fell snapped. "The exploits of Citizen Sharl and . . . others . . . are legend." The general's malevolent glance climbed to rest on Kateos. "And the scars of Gorruk's rape may never heal. That notwithstanding, remember your vows." The chamber echoed with emotional seconds and passionate shibboleths.

"Your Excellency," Tar Fell continued, leaning on his hands. "How many aliens are on Genellan, and, truly, how many more come? Will new settlers also have this license—this *citizenship*?"

"No," Et Kalass replied, growing stern, "though I submit the planet Genellan is the exclusive domain of the Hegemony. King Ollant may please his own desires. Please push not overly hard, Chancellor-General."

"Gravity drags down the greatest king," Tar Fell replied. "Ollant will not rule forever. Alien settlement transcends his reign. The germ, once established, may never be eradicated, or should I say cured?"

"Your words are worrisome," Et Kalass replied. "Be advised that limitations and waystones have been set."

"Such as?" the chancellor rudely persisted.

Tar Fell was relentless, his truculence far exceeding his station. Using a covert interrogation algorithm, Kateos lined up the Thullolian's signal vectors. Tar Fell's staff was receiving and transmitting with nearly every southern delegation, particularly those which were not noble-governed. A grand alliance or a conspiracy? She downlinked her findings.

"There are fewer than one hundred humans on Genellan." Et Kalass sighed, lifting a finger to acknowledge receipt of her message. "Citizen Sharl's cadre—the Survivors—and children number less than twenty. The others are security and science personnel left behind when the human fleet returned to Earth for battle repairs."

"How many more come? How—" Tar Fell rudely interrupted.

"The first stage of settlement," Et Kalass nearly shouted, "has been restricted to a maximum of one thousand aliens. This will provide Citizen Sharl's Survivors with enough kindred souls for safety and society. No additional settlement will be permitted without progress toward the transfer of hyperlight technologies."

"Progress? Progress?" Tar Fell said. "What does that mean?"

"Your point, General?" Et Kalass snapped.

"Simply put," Tar Fell said, huffing hugely, "the Thullol-Ransa Compact would have diplomatic and technical representation on that miserable planet. I demand the right of emissarial domain, with full extraterritoriality and time-honored immunities." The delegations rumbled enthusiastically.

"An interesting, er . . . proposal," Et Kalass said, raising his voice above the growing bedlam. "I must discuss this with the king."

"Hear, hear, by gravity! Hold firm!" exploding pockets of dissent shouted. Southern delegations seethed with raucous protest.

Et Kalass stood and bowed to General Talsali. The presiding officer, surrendering to chaos, gaveled the meeting to a close. The prime minister surged down the aisle, dragging the Hegemonic floor delegation in his wake. Kateos routed her encrypted data files onto the net, deliberately flux-flushed local memories, and jammed the electronic portfolio into her breast pouch. Hands free, she galloped to the suborbital shuttle bays on the roof of the PDF compound.

Her facile mind grappled with the implications of Tar Fell's demands. What response was Ollant likely to give? What were the ramifications, the protocols? What negotiation tactics should be employed? What pressures could be brought to bear on the Thullolians?

A surprise, enormously pleasant, dispelled those troubling thoughts. Waiting in the passenger compartment of the prime minister's shuttle, bulbous features aglow with puckish merriment, was Master Scientist Dowornobb, her beloved mate. The prodigious creatures slammed thick masses together in a passionate, resounding collision. The pungent odor of ineffable love swirled in mingling currents about them.

"Must you?" Et Kalass gasped, slipping past the groping pair. "At least shut the hatch." The minister's voice trailed off in irritated futility as he slipped into his private compartment. Circulating fans thrummed into life and then kicked into high.

"My love!" Dowornobb caressed her cheek. "It has been so long."

"Too long, my dearest." Kateos inhaled deeply, palming moist eyes with a meaty hand. Her mate's symphony of scents was exquisitely toxic. His sinuses fluttered audibly with passion, resonating with her own.

"The old tyrant keeps you traveling," Dowornobb moaned. "Every time I descend from the power laboratories, you are busy translating for some exotic negotiation or some trade treaty."

"Twice! Twice you have come down from orbit," she sniped. "It is a good thing I am busy, or else I would be jealous of your great projects. But how come you to be here? I thought you were making progress."

"Modest progress." Dowornobb nodded, falling heavily on the lounge. "More will be known when the human fleet returns. Our sensor arrays are ready. Every emission before, during, and after their leap from hyperspace will be scrutinized."

"Have you thanked Sharl for her technical hints?" Kateos asked.

"Hints? Good friend Sharl tells us what we, as scientists, should already know. She holds back what is critical for . . .

hrrumph, negotiations. I wish she could be less reticent—but, but ... you do not know? The king has directed me to form the technical negotiating team. It is time to return to Genellan."

"At last!" Kateos exclaimed, embracing the scientist. "But I will be unable to go. How will Et Kalass possibly manage without—"

"This ... *old tyrant* will manage quite miserably," Et Kalass growled over the intercom. "You, worthless translator, have been assigned another mission."

"Minister?" Kateos queried of the disembodied voice.

"The king will elaborate," the noblekone sidestepped. "Now, indulge the shuttle captain and strap in."

THREE

CLIFF DWELLERS

Torn from mist-shrouded volcanic cliffs, gray threads of sulfurous steam tumbled skyward, obscuring the chasm and dulling the river's wet thunder. A column of sun warmed Ki's bones.

The ground trembled, or was it her heart pounding? The ground frequently trembled. Ki, widow-of-Braan, leaned against the black marble wall and ran a bony finger down a filigree of gold. A vine rife with emerald flowers twined along the wall's perilously steep perimeter. She smelled their rich perfume, but she mainly listened, sweetly anxious, deliciously nervous.

The ground had trembled. Above her a loosened stone, submitting to inexorable forces, clattered against the precipitous face of the great plateau. The matriarch of clan Soong, belying her years, darted beneath a granite overhang as the gravity missile bounded past the mist-sparkled terrace, unseen in the steamy shroud. Unseen but not undetected; the huntress

racked the spinning stone as if in slow motion, bombarding
he shard with sonic probes as it fell.

The ground would always move; the weather would never
est, freezing and warming in endless cycles. Falling pebbles
vere as inevitable as rising steam. It was a wonder more did
ot fall, notwithstanding the gleanings of the stone pickers.
above her and below, the granite face was pockmarked with
ock shelves and caves, the warrens of hunters. Lower were the
moothly finished caves of the guilders. And far below was the
rashing river. Pebbles would forever fall.

Ki returned to the brink and listened. The sparkling air, shot
vith zephyr-driven fog, resounded with an excited riot of joy-
us screams, an ultrasonic cacophony of exultation. Hunters
oared on thermals, wheeling and winging in the ecstasy of
ree flight. So festive—so unusual—for the dour likes of her
ellow cliff dwellers.

As uncharacteristic as her own sublime gaiety. That height-
ned well-being blossomed into insurmountable joy; the sleek-
urred huntress detected the distinctive sonics, the clear
manations from her own issue, the echoing pulses of her last
ving son returning home. His signal call, as distinctive as any
ignature, reverberated closer, commingling with the adolescent
witters of the girl-child. Ki hopped from the perimeter wall
nd stood taller, pickax head held erect.

Notta, the daughter, arrived first.

"Brappa returns!" the girl screeched, her membranes flutter-
ng. Notta landed with ungainly youth, tottering on the wall.
.las, a female, yet certainly Ki's favorite, for the matriarch
vould never have another, could never have another—Braan,
ne sire, was dead. And, thank the gods, she was too old.

A second presence materialized, powerful and graceful, di-
phanous airfoils beating majestically. For a cruel instant Ki's
iind played tricks—the great warrior Braan, her husband, had
eturned. Her husband, no, never again to return; her life mate
vas dead, buried as he had died, in the embrace of the long-
egs hero, in the epic battle with the bear people. No, it was
ot her husband in the mist; it was her brave and good son,
rappa, sword-hand-of-Short-one-who-leads.

"Be silent, child!" Ki hissed sadly. "Inside at once!"

Notta dutifully obeyed, jumping to the terrace and hop-
vaddling to the threshold, but no farther.

Brappa swooped onto the terrace wall with stolid grace. Tall
nd wide of shoulder, wiry and strung with sinew, the young

stalwart stowed fur-covered membranes and bowed deeply. His fur, matted and redolent of wet leather, reeked with the sour smell of honest sweat. The mother commenced the time honored ceremony.

"Welcome home, beloved son," Ki said, eyes on the ground.

Brappa, breathing deeply, bowed again, no less formally.

"Long life and great respect, Mother," the warrior replied, standing to his full height and looking over her head. "It is good to be returned to the warm mists of my mother's home. Gods grace me."

"Blessings. Thou art always welcome here, son of my husband," she spoke. "Thou art always welcome home, my beloved son."

"I thank thee, my mother. Thou art kind," Brappa responded, giving compliment for compliment.

Ceremony satisfied, the mother lifted her long jaw and smiled, rows of white teeth flashing in the sun. Membrane-draped arms held wide, they embraced most indecorously, the son's greater form enveloping the diminutive matriarch. The daughter bravely ventured from the threshold and danced with unbridled joy.

"Hast thou yet seen thy good wife and thy brood?" Ki asked.

"First duty is here," Brappa replied almost convincingly, sweeping a wing around his comely sister.

Ki smiled. "Go to them, my son. Thy duty here is done well."

"Respected mother, Short-one-who-leads is on the salt trail. She tops the plateau within the hour," Brappa chittered, pivoting to face the misty void, heavy hunter talons scraping stone.

"Of that who cannot be aware?" Ki snorted. "It echoes from the canyon walls, screamed by every sentry and even by warriors who know better." She dropped her eyes. It was unseemly to make such judgments.

"She brings the whelp," Brappa announced breathlessly.

Ki looked up sharply.

"So say the heralds," she said softly. "So say the heralds, but I would not credit them."

"In truth, Mother," Brappa said, "and she deems thee Great mother."

"Ah-h-h, an unspeakable honor, my son." Ki exhaled, look

ng up at her son. "Thine and mine. But thou must hasten to
hy lovely wife. Leave me to ponder this wondrous thing. Go!"

Brappa gently took his mother's head in four-fingered hands
nd bent to touch foreheads, softly firing sonic pulses. Ki
miled and dropped watery eyes. When she looked up, her son
ad gone silently into the mists. The daughter, shrouded in
rifting steam, perched wraithlike on the terrace edge.

Ki walked behind Notta and placed her hands on the adoles-
ent's shoulders. Bathed in warm mists, they listened. Ki's re-
ief at seeing her robust and healthy son was replaced by
irlish anxiety at meeting again Short-one-who-leads, the con-
ort of her husband's death mate.

Brappa embraced the steamy updraft and wheeled with the
inds, racing across the vent-pocked cliff face, wingtip vorti-
es swirling the roiling vapors into spiraling eddies. He
creeched his clan call, projecting ultrasonically. Replies of
elcome and long life effervesced from above and below, for
Brappa was much respected. But it was one cry above all that
esonated in his sonic detectors, one beautiful screech of re-
pectful affection that warmed his heart. Ah, the sweet trilling
f Gliss, his life mate.

Thrusting against the air with lusty impatience, Brappa saw
er. She stood alone on a lofty prominence jutting into the
iver valley. The hunter pulled in his wings and dove, gaining
reakneck speed. Gliss screeched with harsh emotion, her fran-
ic tones breaking with frightened joy.

Brappa responded with a thundering shriek. Knifing through
he wind, the warrior swooped beneath the monolithic out-
ropping and beyond, pulling up in an air-thrumming arc.
aughing with delight, Gliss pivoted to follow his flight,
rancing on delicate talons to the very brink. Brappa shot
p, high above the outcropping, eyes and sonic probes focused
n his life mate, his love. He reached the apex of his ballistic
light and lifted his encompassing span, holding the air like a
arachute. Floating down, his membranes cupped with uprising
inds, Brappa arrived at his beloved's level. Gliss, purring
ith rapture, hiked her robes and stepped into the void, into his
aiting embrace.

They touched. Brappa shivered with pleasure, reflexively
ounding the air with his great wings, braking their descent.
liss pushed away and billowed out her own membranes,
atching the warm, moist wind. Together they grounded softly

on the wall of their own cliff aerie. Brappa pulled Gliss's small
form to his, wrapping her in his membranes and crushing her
with his fervor. Gliss breathed rapidly, heart fluttering against
Brappa's hand. She was a beautiful huntress, and her double-
lidded black eyes sparkled with excitement. Her razor teeth
shone white against a crimson maw. Brappa was overcome
with joy.

It was time. Ki heard Brappa singing. She waddled with
great dignity across the terrace, hiking thin robes about her
waist. Notta followed proudly. Hesitating only to shake out
their membranes, the huntresses hopped on the wall and dove
into the mists. Escorts materializing from the fog wheeled to
follow.

Echo-ranging, Ki dove into steamy thermals, holding her
membranes close and plummeting in a tight spiral. She broke
from the veil of vapors and marked herself by landmarks on
the sheer-sided cliffs of the opposite bank. Below, the foam-
specked watercourse crashed and surged in green and gray
shadows. Ki screeched for the pure joy of flight. She checked
to see Notta cutting and shearing the air like a river swift in
her wake. Notta answered Ki's scream with an exultant shriek
of her own. The respectful escorts remained silent and kept
their distance.

Warm mists enveloped her, and Ki spread her old membranes, braking momentum against the upwelling air. She
echo-ranged. Sonic bursts from her wingmate and from the
escorts joined her own. The cliff face took definition on
her sonar mapping sensors, with the wide terrace of the assembly portal the most prominent feature. She navigated through
whirling vapors, breaking from light-shattering prisms of
mist and slowing to a graceful, slowly-beating hover over
blossom-bedecked crenellations. She lightly touched damp
stone. Notta joined her, both huntresses stowing fur-covered
membranes and smoothing their robes. Sentries landed one to
each side and waddled self-consciously ahead to take escort
positions. Ki was not nervous, for the omnipotent roar of the
great river, so near at hand, mastered all emotions.

Descending the worn, granite steps of the assembly portal,
preceded by tall apprentices bearing pennants and spirit lamps,
came the procession of eleven elders, the gray fur of their
knobby heads turned uniformly to alabaster. Guilders all, for

hunters did not live long enough to join their ranks. At their head stooped venerable Koop-the-facilitator. Jade the clarity and color of a mountain tarn at dawn adorned the facilitator's neck, for Koop was of the fisher guild. Elder Craat, penultimate in years, was next, an elder of the gardener guild. His necklace was of emerald and garnet, signifying verdure and blood. Elder Ruule followed. A stone carver, old Ruule wore a necklace of diamond and sapphire, corundum of surpassing beauty. Elder Muube, a steam user, walked at Ruule's side. Muube's necklace was of ruby and white jade, symbolic of fire and steam. Other ancients of less eminence followed sedately.

Each elder nodded with dignity. Ki held her sharp chin in the air until the procession moved past and then assumed her honored position between hunter escorts. Notta, faithful huntress-in-waiting, waddled behind her. A platoon of tall guilder apprentices bearing flapping banners and flickering spirit globes followed in their train.

The procession moved through the tunnel leading to the lift terminal, where the elders spread into a crescent. Ki stood alongside Koop at the crescent's focus, the position of greatest honor.

Screams reverberated from the moist granite, masking the grinding of lift chains. Warriors, their resonant sonic pulses filling the misty air, precipitated from the steam, membranes cupped into rigid parachutes as they descended onto rocky promontories and escarpments across the mist-damp cliff face.

A select few landed on the margins of the lift platform. Swooping through the roiling fog came Craag of clan Veera, leader of all hunters. Hideously scarred and half a head taller than most warriors, Craag was a fierce and capable battle leader. Close behind came deputies and cohorts, most notably Bott'a of clan Botto. In Bott'a's wake came her son, occupying a place of great honor for one so young, directly to Craag's left. This was his due, for Brappa-son-of-Braan was sword hand and companion shield of Short-one-who-leads.

Her son perched tall, confident and warlike, slit-eyed and alert, as a blizzard of hunters, disdaining the steam lifts, descended from the mist-shrouded ether. Leather-clad warriors landed everywhere, blanketing the perimeter of the gathering, with an entire host perched high on the surrounding cliffsides.

But attention was on the lift descending through the foggy

defile, an intricate system of return chains and gears grinding smoothly through cogs and pulleys. A soft exhaust pulsed intermittently from somewhere below as the lift settled gently, its steel-riveted and amber-lacquered wooden deck fitting flush with the granite dock.

Giant-one captured the attention of all. The tallest and widest of long-leg warriors, Giant-one towered above the others like a red-bark tree on the salt plains. Giant-one carried the whelp, who cried lustily. The waiting guilders murmured and pressed forward. A young stone carver pointed obscenely in the fashion of long-legs.

Ki maintained her dignity, forcing her vision directly forward. Steam user Toon, developer of the picture language and known to all dwellers, was the first to step from the lift. He carried the communication device. Toon-the-speaker bowed to the elders.

Short-one-who-leads strode onto stone, her cloth garment stretching across a wide and softly-swelling chest, head high, shoulders back. Dark red hair bronzed by the sun, as fine as fur only forever long, whipped in the cliff breezes, revealing ugly cartilage protrusions on each side of her head, an unbecoming characteristic of her race. She was flat-featured like all long-legs, and her sun-burnished face exhibited a handsome pearly welt running from cheek to temple, a battle scar to make any warrior proud. Large, widely spread eyes, stern and piercing, shone brightly in the mists. Ki saw strength and turmoil in those blazing emerald orbs.

Short-one-who-leads bowed to Koop-the-facilitator as dwellers bowed, deeply at the waist with hands held open at the side, palms up. The elder returned the bow. Ki remained erect, forcing herself not to stare at the alien's pink five-fingered appendages.

"Short-one-who-leads sends long life and respect, ancient one," Toon-the-speaker whistled.

"We are honored," Koop replied, stepping forward. "We are blessed."

Ki waddled at the elder's side. Toon poked at the communication device, translating the facilitator's words. Short-one-who-leads scanned the instrument, punched at it with fat fingers, and handed it to the steam user. She looked down at Ki and displayed flat, blunt teeth—a smile. Short-one-who-leads turned to Giant-one, whose great form was blocking the muted sun. She took the whelp wrapped in furs and held it tenderly to her yielding bosom. The whelp's cries lessened but did not stop.

Ki stepped forward, holding out her arms. Gasps emanated from guilders and hunters alike. Short-one-who-leads, showing teeth, bent over and placed the whelp in Ki's arms.

"Pheeee," Ki whistled, squatting to the ground and supporting the squirming mass of furless whelp in her bony lap. The pink nestling cried with increased fervor, red-faced and wide-mouthed, drowning out the protestations of the guilders. In one quick motion the huntress drew an obsidian knife and placed its cold blade against the child's neck. Ki whistled softly and slipped a bony knuckle into the babe's mouth; the screams ceased, leaving only the gasps and distressed chirps of guilders. Ki looked up and hissed, displaying rows of sharp, white teeth. Even Notta was taken aback.

But the whelp was silent. Ki opened her thin robe and pulled the child to her fur-covered breast, pressing a knuckle into its mouth. Two sharp pearls protruded from its gums, but Ki could feel other points of bone, nascent teeth, sharp edges under inflamed skin. Ki gently rubbed the tender tissue. The long-legs nestling turned in her arms and looked at her, dark blue eyes blinking owlishly. It exhaled a stuttering sigh and snuggled to her pap, its small hand pulling on her soft fur.

"Amazing," the elder Toobe said. "What medicine is this?"

"It teethes," Ki said softly.

"It grows teeth!" the elder Craat exclaimed.

"Ah," Toobe said. "There is much to learn."

"There is much to teach," Ki replied.

FOUR

HERE THERE BE DRAGONS

Bare-chested, Tatum erupted from the tent, his good arm brutalizing the twisted sleeve of his coat. Long hair fell loose around his bearded head. Yawns and curses burst in steamy condensation from the sun-bleached tangle of carrot red. It was chilly even for Tatum, but then, it was spring and he was on a ridge high above the east rim of MacArthur's Valley. Bare feet crunched frosty grass as he pushed his magnificent limb through the sleeve and struggled to fasten wooden buttons, closing the elkskin across the rusty thatch matting his massive chest. The freckled man sat on the fire-pit stones. He pulled on a pair of dirty socks and yanked on battered handcrafted boots.

"O'Toole!" Tatum bellowed, his voice booming across the mountain meadow. "I need my laces secured. Yo, Terry!"

Shaggy golden horses—Genellan horses, stubbed-nosed and knobby-legged—started at the noise, jerking their heads and staring inquisitively. Flowing tails twitched nervously.

"Yeah, yeah, I'm coming," a distant voice replied from downhill, within the tree line. O'Toole appeared from the gray-needled, yellow-barked spruce, carrying an armload of firewood.

Yawning, Tatum watched the cliff dwellers fiddle with flint and iron. A spark ignited. Smoke blossomed from grassy tinder. Spitter greeted Tatum with a cheerful twitter. The bow-legged hunter, hand signing greetings, waddled over, leaving Bottlenose fanning the glowing embers with a partially unfurled wing. Spitter's grotesque pickax face grinned up at Tatum, displaying jagged white teeth. Tatum exhaled and thrust out his left foot. The knobby-headed animal, its flying membranes double folded tightly across its back, threw a taloned foot over Tatum's shin, its skinny four-fingered hand moving in an adroit blur. Spitter chirped. The big redhead pushed out his right foot, and the hunter saddled his other knee.

"Not so tight," Tatum grumbled.

"Ah, intergalactic cooperation of the first order." O'Toole chuckled, dropping frost-crusted logs beside the fire pit. Bottlenose grabbed loose pieces of bark and fed the nascent fire.

"If you like mystery knots," Tatum grumbled. "You'll have to untie these suckers. Probably have to cut 'em off."

Tatum tried to stand, but Spitter jumped on his broad chest, grabbing at the human's hair with spindly hands.

"What the hell's he doing to your face?" O'Toole chortled.

"He's securing my frigging hair," Tatum snapped, grabbing the hunter by his luxuriant scruff and lifting him bodily onto a boulder. Tatum turned his back. With deft twists the hunter wrapped the human's thick mane in strips of hide.

"True love," O'Toole said with a laugh as he put a pot of water on the mesh grill. "Wait'll I tell Fenstermacher."

"Up yours," the redhead muttered.

Tatum grabbed the proud hunter by his leather armor and pitched him violently into the air. Spitter squawked, threw out his membranes, and swooped to the ground in a curving spiral. Landing softly, the cliff dweller danced about and chirped with glee. Bottlenose waddled over, holding out bony claws. Tatum gave O'Toole a dirty look, picked up the hunter, and repeated the process.

"How sweet," O'Toole cooed.

Tatum shouldered past the slighter man and huddled in the warmth of the sputtering fire. He chewed hunter jerky and moved a pot over the flames. Tatum stared into a brutally clear sky. The horse tenders, human and hunter, watched with silent contentment as the sun's rays bent over the ridge, illuminating cottony tendrils of fog that lay thickly across the lake and river valleys. A giant eagle sailed silently below them, black and tan pinions spreading to the rising sun.

Tatum lifted the bubbling pot, filling his kit cup with steaming rockberry tea. He brought the hot fluid to his mouth. Spitter screamed.

"What the—! Damn!" Tatum yelled. Scalding liquid dribbled into his beard. Screeching, Spitter and Bottlenose flailed at the heavy air. Both hunters set their wings and glided for the tree line. The horses stampeded into a thundering golden blur, manes streaming, tails flowing.

Tatum jerked around. Coming through the evaporation mists, silhouetted against the sun's ascent, two dragons, a male-female hunting team, rose over the grassy ridge. The predatory horrors covered ground in prodigious bounding zig-zags, one sweeping wide and the other cutting into the stragglers. The reptiles hit with savage coordination. *Thud! Thump!* A golden horse fell screaming beneath blurring claws, neck and hips broken in the instant of contact.

One of his horses!

"Bastards!" Tatum shouted, grabbing his rifle and sprinting uphill.

The rock-gray monsters saw him coming. They were the larger species, denizens of the riparian valleys to the far south, almost three meters tall, unlike the skittish, man-sized buffalo dragon that haunted the northern taiga. As one, the great flared-neck lizards reared up and roared, rapacious teeth dripping gore, yellow and crimson throat bladders billowing vibrantly. Short, thick tails twitched spasmodically, and scaly dorsals trembled beneath rippling muscles.

Tatum stalked resolutely toward the beasts, his great arm raising the assault rifle to his shoulder. The defiant dragons, jealous of their kill, held their ground. Tatum halted, legs spread wide, and fired a burst into the taller one's chest. The male reeled, staggering to all fours, but did not go down. The dragon pirouetted violently and leapt high into the air—unbelievably high—and came down screaming and flailing maniacally. In blind rage it attacked its mate, knocking her to the ground and eviscerating her with vicious clawing strokes. Rearing, the crazed male screamed in tortured victory, all the while glaring defiantly at the puny human, gibbous eyes glinting gold in the morning light. The killer jittered menacingly forward.

Tatum drew his sights on the brute's great heart and pulled the trigger. One round left the weapon, and then it jammed! The dragon leapt, seeming to cover half the distance with its first explosive step, its banshee scream warbling into a hissing gurgle.

"Oh sh—!" Tatum yelled, his voice eclipsed by the detonations of O'Toole's rifle firing on full automatic.

Despite the torrent of heavy slugs, the dragon's momentum carried it violently onward. The monster tumbled, pinwheeling rocks, grass, and dust into the air. It slid to a halt at their feet, tail thumping, jaws snapping like banging bricks. Tatum, falling backward, tossed his rifle aside and blasted away with his pistol. O'Toole retreated, pumping another clip into the reptile before it finally died.

It smelled of mildew and hot blood. Tatum rose slowly from his defensive crouch, reloaded his pistol, and retrieved his jammed weapon, maintaining a prudent distance from the downed predator. He glanced at the dead horse and exhaled fatalistically. The rest of the herd had disappeared into the trees.

"Let's go find our horses," he said, spitting at the bullet-riddled carcass.

"What the hell are superdragons doing on this side of the river and this far north?" O'Toole puffed.

"Eating horses." Tatum snarled.

"But big ones never come this far north. We—"

A hunter screamed in warning, and then another. Urgent. Frightened!

"Oh, shit," Tatum groaned. Far up the ridgeline, in golden sunlight, another pair of gray monsters scuttled across the mountain meadow, snouts in the air. And then two more breasted the ridge, closer, hardly a hundred meters away. The reptiles were headed for the trees and for the valley—and the settlement.

"Another one!" O'Toole shouted, pointing. Far down the ridge, to the north, a solitary killer pounded across a saddle of rock.

"Let's move," Tatum yelled, turning.

A different noise lifted into the calm morning air, a distant, baleful howl. Again, closer! The skin on the back of Tatum's neck crawled. A hot knife stabbed at his left shoulder, where once there had been another powerful arm.

"There!" O'Toole shouted, pointing.

The howls blended together and exploded into an echoing growl. A pack of whip-tailed dervishes, powerful hindquarters and shoulders pumping chaotically, scurried along the steamy ridgeline, their saber-toothed snouts and bristling backs silhouetted against the rising sun. Scavengers always followed dragons.

"Nightmares!" Tatum snarled, breaking into a sprint.

"Rifle fire on the ridge, Commander," Major Singh reported. "I'm sending out a squad."

"Very well, Major," Cassiopeia Quinn replied, pulling herself up the splintery ladder. The officer in charge of the exploration detachment walked across the wooden rampart and peered into the dripping mists. Night was yielding only reluctantly to gray morning. She had also heard the rifles, their reports dulled by distance and moisture. Quinn shivered. What would Sharl do?

"Thick," Singh grumbled through his luxurious nonreg mustache.

"Damn thick," the science officer agreed. It was so still that she could hear her heart beat. Stumps and crops at the foot of the palisade wall were invisible. The languid roiling of the fog forged the illusion of movement, of floating within a cloud. She touched wood to settle her balance.

"Tatum's probably shooting a bear," the marine officer volunteered.

"Too many shots, Major," Quinn replied. "Any radios working? Or intrusion sensors?"

"Only in the sunshine, Commander. Batteries are all dead," Singh reported. "Techs can't fix the charging unit until—"

"The fleet gets back," she said sighing. Quinn retraced her steps to the blockhouse, the only structure discernible in the fog. Palisade walls disappeared into grayness. A hundred meters across the settlement, oil lamps on the lodge porch provided a fuzzy, detached reference. She put her boot on the ladder's top rung. There was nothing she could do here.

"Tell your men to be careful," she ordered, taking the first step.

"Aye, aye, Commander."

"And double the guard on the walls."

Tendrils of fog rose to meet them. Tatum, pistol in hand and worthless rifle slung across his back, jogged into the cottony mist. Yellow-barked spruce, tops disappearing in wet gauze, danced by like ghosts. Too quiet; Tatum's ears strained for clues. Where were the damn nightmares?

Over his thudding heart and heaving lungs Tatum heard a horse screaming in panic, just ahead, close. Tatum stopped abruptly and listened. O'Toole, gasping, ran up his back.

"This way," Tatum wheezed, leaving the blazed trail for a tenuous game path. "The horses followed the pasture trail."

"And the . . . dragons followed the horses," O'Toole coughed.

"How's . . . ammo?" Tatum asked, sweeping through a

thicket of rockberry. They were almost to the pine glades, where the undergrowth and the cover would lessen markedly.

"One clip," O'Toole wheezed. "How about you?"

"Two," Tatum gasped. "Here . . . take them. They won't do me any good until I get this pecker unjammed. Nine shots in the pistol . . . that's it."

"Let me take a look—"

"Shhhh!" Tatum dropped to his knees. The ground shook. The wretched horse screamed again, horribly. A grinding crash, and the horse mercifully gurgled to silence. Suddenly, much closer, something huge, going very fast, pounded invisibly down the trail, mere meters away. The silence in its wake was dizzying.

"Geez!" O'Toole recoiled, the whites of his eyes huge. "Wha—"

Tatum almost backhanded O'Toole in the mouth with his pistol, pulling the other marine down. They hunkered on their thighs, a fallen tree providing meager shelter. Something moved. Something was still there, big and hulking, a gray miasma in a slate cloud. Tatum could smell it—a hissing, breathing presence, indistinct in the pervasive gloom. Tatum knew the female was there, penetrating the mists with her cruel eyes, trying to sniff out his scent in the cloying moisture.

He raised his pistol, waiting for the overwhelming charge. Blood throbbed in his veins. Perspiration ran cold under his armpit. A shadow exhaled, stirring the fog. Farther to the right than he had thought, still above them on the pasture trail. A shape moved so slowly as not to be seen, but it moved. Toward them! The stationary bole of a tree provided grim reference. He aimed at the shadow and put tension on the trigger.

Bedlam erupted. Downhill. A dragon screamed and screamed again. The prowling shadow jerked, its predatory form defined by rapid movement. Tremendous screeches and the crashing of branches echoed among the trees. What could only be a war of dragons struggling over fallen kill reverberated in the wet woods. The lurking presence roared magnificently, its fetid breath burning the fog. It exploded into motion, bounding down the hill, resolutely into battle, mists swirling in its wake.

Tatum, hand shaking, lowered his pistol. The forest resounded in cataclysm, the air vibrating with violence. The fog overhead seemed riven with turbulence, suddenly lightening with encroaching sun. The two humans were still high on the ridge and had a long way to go. The floor of the valley would be deep in fog.

"This way," Tatum whispered, moving rapidly from the path. *Where were the nightmares?*

The ground-thudding dragon battle ended quickly, with a male yodeling victory. The roaring diminished as rapidly as it had started. Instead, ripping, rending noises, liquid and visceral, penetrated the gloom.

In the distance there were other noises, answering Tatum's fears. In the wet depths of the forest a pack of nightmares bayed an unholy overture.

The squad moved through the woods, impassive fog slowing the pace. The sergeant jogged up on the point and moved ahead.

"I got it," he rasped, floppy cap dripping with condensation. The squad leader was a big man, not tall but massive. With two years on the planet, he was proud of his ability to cover ground.

"Okay, Sarge," the point man replied, falling back. The squad, twelve men strong, well trained and alert, confidently adjusted positions down the line. Just another walk in the woods.

And then came the screams—bestial roars, distant, faint, muted by the mists but unremittingly horrible and threatening. The squad leader's neck went cold, and his pace slowed involuntarily. The screams died. Moisture dripping from the leaves was dismayingly audible.

"What the hell was that?" the number two man asked.

"Can it!" the squad leader barked, racking his brain. His experience had nothing to offer. One thing was clear: Tatum and O'Toole were up there. Fellow marines and buddies, and that was enough. "Let's move," he shouted, forcing himself to jog into the cottony soup.

A half kilometer later the ground began to tremble.

"Heads up!" the squad leader shouted, standing in the trail. "Take cover. Fire teams left and right. Move! Bring up the—"

Golden horses blasted out of the fog. The herd, forced onto the trail by the encompassing undergrowth, stampeded by, boring a tunnel in the fog. In a brief lull between groups the squad leader, still conscious, was pulled into the underbrush.

"Laser Corporal!" the squad leader gasped, his face in the

mud. "Keep 'em ready. There's more coming. The ground's
... moving."

A second group of wide-eyed horses pounded past; the fog
swirled insanely but was no less thick. The marines, clinging
close to the trees, held their positions and waited.

"More," the squad leader cried, lifting his head. His eyes
were white with terror. "Feel the ground!"

"Damn!" someone shouted. The forest quaked under their
boots.

The dragons moved fast, and the fog was thick. A pair of
predators crashed through the underbrush on the left flank and
was on the marines before a rifle was fired. The male carni-
vore died quickly, but with the point man mangled in its jaws.
The female dragon ripped apart one marine and mortally injured another before yielding to concentrated rifle fire. Two
marines were wounded by fire from their mates.

A second pair of dragons, obsessed with the fleeing horses,
thundered down the path, directly through the firefight. The
horrified marines on the right flank, loath to fire across the
path at their comrades, could only potshot ineffectively at
the disappearing forms.

Large sinister shapes, wary of the explosions of man and the
pungent odor of cordite, crashed through the forest. Smaller,
more numerous shapes moved, too, but they were stealthy.

"Out and about early this morning, Commander," Nancy
Dawson remarked, wiping her nose. The tall, large-featured female, her hair an unruly explosion of fiery orange, sat at the
split-log table with her son, her pale blue eyes sparkling with
firelight. Adam Shannon, square-shouldered, jet-haired, and
large-headed like his deceased father, worked industriously at
his buffalo scrapple and biscuits. Both breakfasters were
garbed in thick leather.

"Responsibilities of command," Quinn grumbled. She tossed
her beret and Legion storm coat over a squat wooden chair.
"Governor Et Silmarn radioed in this morning from Goldmine
Station."

"More negotiations?" Dawson asked, stroking the boy's
black thatch.

"What else," Quinn replied dryly. "King Ollant's new ambassador arrives at Ocean Station in three standard months. Et
Silmarn wants us there. Sharl will be overjoyed."

"Fleet should be back by then," Dawson said.

"Let's hope so." Quinn sighed.

Quinn walked to the massive cliff dweller–built fireplace and basked in its delicious warmth. Toby Mendoza and Beppo Schmidt, on galley duty, were clearing up after the morning meal, purposefully clumping over the wooden floor, stowing pots and pans.

But their industrious racket could not mask the gunfire.

"Mommy, guns!" Adam shouted.

The kitchen clatter melted away. A muted cracking punctuated the silence. Faint bestial screams destroyed it.

Schmidt jumped to a window and threw open heavy shutters. Cold fog and gloomy morning light billowed into the common room. The noise grew more intense and frenetic. Quinn ran through the mud room doors and onto the wide porch. Fenstermacher came up the steps. The little man grabbed the iron bar hanging by a lanyard and thrashed at the metal triangle suspended from the thick eaves, raising a clanging din.

"Wait, Winnie!" Quinn shouted, grabbing his shoulder. "Listen!"

Silence, only the burbling of the spring. A single muted shot rang out. Another. Silence again, except for footsteps on the wooden floor as other Survivors emptied the lodge to stare with wonder into the fathomless fog.

"What's going on?" Chief Wilson bellowed.

"Shh!" Quinn hissed. The faint sound of running horses, growing louder, eclipsed all other sensations. Someone on the palisade shouted something unintelligible.

"Loudmouth," Dawson whispered. Wilson stuck out his tongue and leered as only a salty old spacer could, a surreal spectacle in the soft yellow of the flickering lamps.

"Winnie, get Leslie and Pepper and the kids," Quinn ordered.

"They're coming, Commander," Fenstermacher replied, pointing. The wiry man jumped down the foot-worn wooden steps to meet his ebony-haired wife coming out of the fog. Leslie Lee, china-doll countenance impassive, carried her black-haired daughter on her hip. Pepper Goldberg and her long-legged daughter were right behind them. Goldberg's swarthy tan was lightened with anxiety, her delicate features leaden with concern. Honey Goldberg, the first human child born on Genellan, frowned, reflecting her mother's worry.

"Morning, Commander," Lee said, trotting up the steps, her

short, tanned legs sharply muscled. "We heard shots. What gives?"

"You know as much as we do, Les," Quinn replied.

Billy Gordon, the only Survivor to rejoin the fleet forces, materialized out of the fog from the direction of the marine barracks.

"Commander," the corporal shouted. "Major Singh wants you to come to the guard post. Horses have come back, but there's no sign of Tatum or O'Toole. Major Singh wants to open the gates."

Goldberg moaned. Sandy Tatum was Honey's father.

"Let the horses in," Quinn ordered. "Tell the major I'll be there as soon as I get my coat."

Tatum and O'Toole sprinted through pines, zigzagging past tall straight boles, their canopy lost in yielding mists. Sunlight was turning the fog from muddy gauze to dingy cotton and visibility had risen to ten meters, but they were still heading downhill into a thickening mist. The first hardwood trees, low-limbed and sporting spring foliage, rose from a defile marking a watercourse. Tatum changed direction and made for the brush. Reverberant growls behind them were terrifying—and close.

"This way," Tatum gasped, splashing into a brook running strong with spring runoff. He stopped and looked back, peering into the fog. O'Toole hurdled the water and pulled up.

"Listen to 'em!" O'Toole hissed. "Must be thousands."

"Stay in the water," Tatum whispered, turning and jogging along the uneven streambed. "Follow me."

The overhanging brush grew thicker as the brook danced down a series of stair-stepping falls. Tatum slipped and stumbled over moss-covered rocks. O'Toole took a brutal fall, his rifle clattering. Tatum waited, helplessly looking around. The ear-shattering growls blasted through the fog. O'Toole gained his feet and limped forward, bending under a heavy low-hanging limb.

"The tree, Terry! Climb the tree!" Tatum ordered, retracing his steps and practically lifting O'Toole on his shoulders. O'Toole chinned himself, threw a leg over, and extended his hand. Tatum holstered his pistol, leapt, and grabbed the limb with his arm, while O'Toole took hold of his rifle sling. They both pulled until Tatum could get a leg over. Uphill, something splashed through the stream.

"Higher," Tatum wheezed. The men edged their way to the trunk, where the convergence of thick limbs provided easier going. They had just begun to climb when the first brutish, whip-tailed creatures darted beneath the tree, splashing explosively along the brook, howling obscenely from great upraised, underslung maws, their horrible teeth protruding like yellow tusks.

The squad, covered with sweat and dew and gore, started an unsteady retreat. The squad leader and another wounded marine were being carried by uninjured squad mates. Three uninjured marines and the one walking wounded nervously covered the rear. Four dead marines were left where they had fallen—carrion in the underbrush.

The trail downhill through the roiling fog was a tunnel into hell. The specter of bounding dragons haunted them, and the baying of stygian dogs echoed all around. Horrible creatures, creatures unseen, growled menacingly in the underbrush. A wounded marine cried in agony.

"Keep moving!" the squad leader gasped. "They'll need our help back at the settlement." It was a prayer.

Strapping her pistol over her storm coat, Quinn trotted to the edge of the porch and heard the palisade gates groaning open. Seven or eight pug-nosed golden horses, wide-eyed and slavering, thundered out of the fog, heading unerringly for the safety of their paddock. Their distraught neighing and nickering was answered nervously by the broodmares still in the corral adjacent the sprawling stone barn, invisible in the fog. Mendoza, Tookmanian, and Schmidt sprinted from the porch, spreading out in pursuit and disappearing into the leaden mists.

"Where's the rest?" Wilson asked. "Tatum took over two dozen to—oof." Dawson elbowed the chief in the ribs.

"Da's horses," the skinny, golden-haired child said, breaking the silence. Honey stuck her head between the porch railings. "Where's Da?"

"He'll be back soon, Honey," Leslie Lee said reassuringly.

"Why did I ever let Sandy talk me into staying on this damn planet? Why didn't we leave with the fleet?" Goldberg asked, dark brows knitted together. The lithe brunette moved heavily to the steps, staring at the open gates. The fog, flowing softly

ff the lake, grew thicker, dissolving the gates in whiteness.
Quinn grabbed Goldberg's elbow.

"Hold it together, Pepper," Quinn said softly, "And stay in
he lodge."

"Where's the goddamn fleet, Commander?" Goldberg
moaned. "When are we going to get out of this hell? Off this
stinking planet?"

"Not long now," Quinn consoled her, looking to Dawson for
help.

"Honey, you and Adam come with me into the lodge,"
Dawson said, collecting the children. "We can help Leslie take
care of Hope."

"You, too, Pepper. Go inside," Quinn said firmly, pushing
Goldberg toward the doors. "Honey needs you to be strong, especially now."

"More horses!" came a shout. Hooves pounding in the fog
grew louder. Goldberg pivoted expectantly, her thick braid
whipping about.

Quinn deserted the worried female and trotted downhill.
Four more horses came out of the whiteness and raced across
the settlement common. Quinn dodged from their path. No riders were with them.

"Close the gates!" The shout was panicked. *"Close the goddamn gates!"* An assault rifle opened up on full automatic.

A superdragon loomed from nowhere, thundering after the
horses. Two dragons! Rifle fire exploded into an overwhelming
din. The second beast, almost obscured by mist, recoiled er-
ratically and screamed in agony. Bullets buzzed around
Quinn's head.

The near beast, only strides away, slid in its tracks. It lifted
a fluted neck into the mists and roared with devastating fury,
eclipsing the angry rifles. Quinn pulled her pistol and moved
laterally. The hulking beast detected her movement and spun
with fantastic speed. It bunched for a split second and then
bounded for her. She crouched and grabbed her pistol with
both hands. No need to aim; the target filled her universe. She
fired and kept firing. And she screamed in fear and primal
rage.

Assault rifles erupted close by. Muzzle blasts ignited the fog
like the inside of a paper lantern. She kept pulling the trigger
and kept screaming, lips stretched from her teeth. The yodeling
dragon straightened and staggered. Quinn smelled its foul
breath, its gorge. Her pistol was empty, but rifles on full

automatic continued to hammer the beast. Turbulent air
brushed her cheeks. The monster thudded to the ground
thrashing and screaming in death throes until it made contact
with its already-dead mate. Then it trembled and expired.

The gates groaned shut. Throat dry and pained, Quinn
brought her teeth together and allowed her lips to close. She
looked down at the smoking pistol and the shell casings steaming at her feet. Her hand fell to her side, and she stood stiffly
erect. Fenstermacher, on her left, searched the gloom for more
targets. To her right was Corporal Gordon, loading his rifle but
staring at her in naked awe.

"Geezus, Commander," Fenstermacher whispered, still peering into the fog. "I think I wet my pants."

Tatum dropped from the tree and listened. The brook
burbled happily at his feet. Gunfire, frantic and prolonged,
rattled in the distance.

"Going to miss that tree," O'Toole said.

"We gotta get back, Terry." Tatum grimaced, starting to
move rapidly across the fall of the slope. "Your leg okay?"

"Yeah," O'Toole replied. "Think your piece is unjammed?"

"I have a bad feeling we'll find out." Breaking into a trot,
Tatum avoided the pasture trail, heading instead for a more circuitous route to the south. He heard a hunter's whistle and
looked up, but all he could see was unrelenting fog.

The fog, growing thicker, was luminescent with morning
sun. Grumbling howls increased in intensity on both sides of
the path. Leaves trembled with the resonance, shedding dew in
great plopping drops as if a breeze had kissed the treetops. The
winds were still.

The squad moved slower, bunching together, rifles pointed
outward, a collection of souls that had become a single orga-
nism with many legs and unblinking eyes but with a single unspeakable fear. Shadows moved through the mists about them,
keeping pace, growling in inconstant crescendo, circling.

"Keep . . . moving," the squad leader groaned, head down
over the shoulder of a fellow marine, a bleeding bag of
bones.

Nightmares smelled the blood. Their growling exploded to
an unfathomable level of insanity. A mass of thick-necked
creatures, gray-black manes rigid with bristling fury, burst
from the wetness, red-rimmed yellow eyes wide with berserk

ferocity. The rush of pelted muscle and thrashing teeth drove a wedge into the marines, separating them.

Dozens of the wide-chested, yellow-fanged monsters were blasted into eternity by an overwhelming barrage of rifle and pistol fire. But by sheer weight of numbers prognathous jaws closed on human targets. One savage creature blindsided the marine carrying the squad leader. Snarling monsters ripped into the downed troopers. Those animals, leathery tails whipping frantically, were also dispatched, but not before inflicting mortal wounds on their victims.

"Keep mub . . ." the squad leader bubbled, facedown in the muck, his last gasp. Two more bodies lay on the path.

"Let's go!" a laser corporal shouted, leaving the dead. The survivors followed, not looking back. From the forest they could hear the sounds of reckless paws, clawed feet scurrying in temporary recoil from rifle detonations. But other paws, more deliberate, still moved along the trail, following the blood spoor.

Distant gunfire echoed from the palisade walls.

"I'm going to send out the second squad," Major Singh reported.

"That leaves only one squad to defend the settlement," Quinn replied.

"Plus the science team and the—" Singh started to reply.

Ka-thunk! The palisade wall shivered with the impact of a large object. *Thunk!* Another jolt. Quinn grabbed the parapet and steadied herself. She stared along the fog-shrouded guard walk, trying to understand what had made the wall tremble.

"What?" she blurted.

"Second squad to the northeast guardhouse!" Major Singh shouted. He sprinted away along the parapet.

Horses screamed. A dragon roared. An assault rifle in the vicinity of the stables blazed into life, its angry muzzle flickering in the fog.

"Dragons inside the palisade!" a horrified voice bellowed. Marines, combat gear clanking, ran beneath her. Quinn took a deep breath and started trotting along the guard walk, eyes peering into the frightening whiteness on both sides of the wall.

A salvo of assault rifles joined the single weapon in action. *Whump!* The palisade wall shook again.

* * *

"Listen to that!" O'Toole exclaimed. "Sounds like a war."

"Yeah," Tatum grunted. The land was leveling, and the foliage was thickening. The lake was near; he could hear the crashing waters of the main lake feeders cascading to the south. There it was, green and mirror-smooth, a flock of ducks cutting silver wakes along its perfect surface. He sprinted onto the firmly packed beach. O'Toole was right behind him.

A breeze stirred the lake—and the fog. He made out the cove entrance no more than a hundred meters upwind. Something materialized from the misty backdrop, animals moving—a pack of nightmares trotting from the trees, toward the settlement, unhurriedly, almost casually.

Tatum ran faster, sand muffling his footfalls. He loathed nightmares. He ran faster. His left shoulder throbbed, more in anticipation than from the old pain.

"Oh, man!" O'Toole whined. Tatum did not look back.

Most of the scavengers had rounded the minor headland when pack stragglers perceived danger from behind them. Nightmares that could vanished into the trees; others bolted forward, tall rear ends flashing pink. The panicked animals collided with the slower-moving main body. A root-bound bank rising from the narrowing beach channeled the leaping and splashing pack along the boiling lakeshore for fifty meters.

"Take the near sonsabitches," Tatum snarled, swinging his rifle. "I'll go long." He braced himself and squeezed the trigger, praying that his weapon was unjammed. His anxiety disappeared as the riflestock hammered his shoulder in time to the murderous melody of gunfire. O'Toole's rifle joined in harmony.

"Where's that coming from?" Major Singh barked. The officer marched along the parapet, his head jerking across the azimuth, trying to locate the source of the echoing gunfire and the screaming animals.

Quinn was dizzy. She was in command; she had to stay strong. Everyone depended on her. She shoved another clip into her pistol grip, slamming it home, and took another deep breath.

The fog was lifting. From the guardhouse Quinn could make out marines posted at intervals along the five segments of the palisade. None were involved in defensive action. Six dreadful dragons lay dead within the settlement; two gray mounds lay at the main gate, and four near the stables. Gold and crimson orse carcasses were strewn about the paddock area, but no umans, a miracle considering the intensity of the crossfire.

A shaft of sunlight broached the overcast, lighting the lodge. Marines carrying ammunition cans scurried across the common. Illuminated patches of wildflowers provided a pink-and-white contrast to the funereal grayness. The mysterious firing abruptly lessened, then quickly diminished to silence.

"Who's shooting?" Singh shouted across the settlement.

"It's outside!" came the answer. Singh looked at Quinn. She glanced nervously toward the woods.

"Tatum and O'Toole!" a sentry shouted. "Coming up from he lake!"

Quinn ran to a ladder and made the ground. Singh dropped from the wall, falling heavily onto his side. The major stiffly regained his feet and limped toward the gate.

"Open the sally," Quinn ordered. "Away a fire team."

A dozen nightmares lay dead or dying. Tatum put the rifle on his shoulder and strode from the cove, along the silvery splashing brook, up the gentle slope toward the fort. A profusion of wildflowers turned delicate blossoms to the faint rays of sunlight. He raised his rifle in the air, acknowledging the boisterous hails. A section of marines debouched from the sally port beneath the near guard tower. Billy Gordon shouted frantically.

"Sounds like they missed us," O'Toole offered.

"They sound, and look, damned scared," Tatum replied, lowering his rifle and leaning into a jog. Rifle shots echoed across the clearing. Tatum accelerated to a sprint.

A dragon roared magnificently. The vibrating growls of nightmares rumbled down the gentle slope. As Tatum rounded the palisade wall, the gunfire grew louder. It came from the misty woods.

"Yo, the patrol!" came a shout from the wall. Everyone's attention was seized by the appearance of a marine partially carrying, mostly dragging a wounded buddy from the trees. The hatless marine fired his rifle with one hand, from the hip. Two other marines appeared, all firing with desperate intensity into the shadows.

"Dragon!" a guard bellowed. Pounding through the forest were two dragons, their protruding eyes lifting above the branches and glinting in unfaithful sunshine. A pack of nightmares burst from the woods at the reptiles' feet, scattering from dragon claws and cracking rifles.

Gunfire erupted from the palisade walls. Tatum grabbed a rifle clip and sprinted to support the retreating marines. O'Toole and Gordon jumped to his heels, as did other marines on the ground, spreading out in an enfilade. Major Singh's orders, shouted from the wall, were all but annihilated by the bedlam. Annihilated also were the dragons, by combined and focused gunfire. It was over. An eerie silence descended on the clearing. The fog overhead was gone, and the unfiltered sun cast stark shadows.

A hunter screamed. Another answered. O'Toole helped carry the wounded marine, while Tatum and the others retreated warily down the hill, toward the safety of the palisade. Tatum was the last through the gate. Goldberg, wan and shaken, awaited, silhouetted against the carcass of a dragon. Tatum stepped up to her, dropped his rifle, and lifted her with his single great arm.

"Where's Honey?" he asked.

"In the lodge. She's okay," Goldberg sobbed. "Sandy, I want to go back to the fleet. I want off this planet."

"Yeah." Tatum sighed, putting her down and looking away. He scanned the settlement common, noting the carnage of horses and reptiles.

"How many got back?" he asked.

"Fifteen," Fenstermacher replied. "Four mares got gutted in the corral. Sumbitches came over the wall. Right over the frigging wall."

A dozen hunters, flapping hard in the cold air, sailed across the stockade and settled on the barracks roof. Tatum recognized Spitter and Bottlenose. He whistled, and the hunters whistled back with inappropriate enthusiasm, clearly impressed by the dead dragons.

The last shred of fog blew from the valley, the sky an unrelieved expanse of blue crystal. Tatum squinted down at Quinn; the officer's eyes and forehead were pinched with worry, her blond hair a few strands grayer.

"So how's your day going, sir?" Tatum asked.

"It's still early," Quinn cried, trying unsuccessfully to laugh.

FIVE

AMBASSADOR

"As predicted," Ollant grumbled, corded neck muscles vibrating with the voluminous passage of air. The king sprang to his massive hinds and descended the multitiered throne with impatient strides, belying gravity's greater rule. "Embassies on Genellan! What next?"

"License to deploy their own interplanetaries, no doubt," Et Kalass replied. "Those overpowered lunar *ore loaders* built during Gorruk's War. Finally may we see their true purpose."

"Armed like PDF defense platforms if rumors be true," the king grumbled.

Kateos, on knees and elbows, squirmed and glanced sideways. Et Kalass, befitting a noblekone and minister of the court, stood erect beside her, ignoring her fidgeting.

"Conspiracy," Kateos whispered through her veil.

"Hush," Dowornobb, kneeling to her other side, hissed.

"Ahem . . . yes," Et Kalass affirmed, glancing down at the stirrings. "It would seem the Thullolians and the Ransa League have created an . . . ahem, joint venture. They are making plans for their own space stations and another orbiting shipyard. All in the name of commerce."

"Prime Minister, we must acknowledge the rights of the southern nations," the king said. "To do otherwise would foster yet more distrust and intrigue."

"Hrrumph," Et Kalass snorted. "For a ruler with great political leverage and considerable military resource, I sometimes think His Majesty is too generous. While I understand and share the king's heartfelt desire to foster global—"

"Spare me the double-talk, Minister," Ollant interrupted. "I wish I had a *zuct* of platinum for every sermon a certain

47

sanctimonious old noblekone has given me on the advantages of diplomacy over naked might."

"Hmm, of course," Et Kalass replied, bowing his head.

"Regardless of Thullolian intrigue, it is time for action," Ollant announced. "Scientist Dowornobb, is your team ready?"

Kateos trembled with excitement for her mate.

"Yes, Your Majesty," Dowornobb replied. "We boost tomorrow. Would that you could return with us, sire."

"Would that I could," Ollant said wistfully. "Someday I will make another pilgrimage to that cold and beautiful sphere. Ah, but for the chains and shackles of state. How goes your research, my friend?"

"Unfortunately, Your Excellency," Dowornobb replied, "progress has been limited, and I have far more theories than facts. Citizen Sharl assures me more information will be forthcoming, but she will not compromise the Legion negotiation position . . . yet."

"Our good friend is caught between worlds," Ollant said.

"Your Highness's position is hardly less challenging, sire," Et Kalass interjected soberly.

"Make territoriality concessions but do so slowly," Ollant said resignedly. "Have them provide their own shuttles. This is diplomacy, not charity. And allow the Compact to use their, ahem . . . ore loaders to boost to Genellan. The sooner they use them, the sooner we will know with what we are dealing."

"Excellent idea, sire," Et Kalass acknowledged. "It will certainly challenge their vigor."

"Ah, speaking of vigor," Ollant said. "Mistress Kateos."

Startled, Kateos lifted her head too high for court decorum.

"Oh . . . y-yes, King Ol—my sovereign!" she blurted. Her mate groaned.

Ollant chuckled. Kateos smiled largely. The king was her good and old friend. She could not help but notice the sallow circles under his sad brown eyes and the pallor of his golden complexion.

"You will be angry with me, mistress," Ollant said, clasping his large hands together, "for I give you what you have long desired."

"Your Highness?" she replied, veil fluttering with excitement.

"Your voice, Mistress Kateos," the king said somberly. "I hereby designate you entity of state for the planet Genellan, with full ambassadorial credentials. Et Kalass will elaborate on your portfolio."

Without realizing that she had done so, Kateos rolled back on her haunches and half stood, so great was her surprise.

"Your Highness!" she exclaimed, veil slipping. "I . . . I cannot. I—"

"Prime Minister, instruct your charge on court manners," Ollant said with mock severity. "Do regal decrees carry so little weight?"

"But . . . I am female!" she blurted, daring to lift her gaze. The king stared down, his eyes grown even sadder.

"Stand, Mistress Kateos," Ollant ordered. "Stand! As if you were back on Genellan and free to do so."

Trembling and grunting against the pull of her great mass, Kateos rose on unsteady hinds, awestruck—a commoner, a female, standing erect before the king at court.

"You really do not understand, do you?" Ollant said.

"Your Majesty?"

"You have broken eternal barriers. Surely you, an archaeologist and a scholar of the spoken word, must realize the implication."

"Implication?"

"Our culture knows no female heroes, Mistress Kateos. Word of yours and Citizen Sharl's exploits have spread throughout our planet, north and south. You are unquestionably a hero. It was your voice and your quick actions that halted the carnage in space. The human fleet would have been destroyed, and we would have lost our opportunity to gain the secrets of space travel."

She looked helplessly at her mate. Dowornobb's normally irreverent demeanor was a confused mask of sadness and pride—and devotion. Thoughts tumbled in her mind.

"But gravity, Your Highness, why rub faces in it? Why send me as ambassador? The very essence of diplomacy would argue against it."

"It will be different on Genellan, Mistress Kateos," Ollant replied with a determined stare. "If human females are capable of leadership, than so should be konish females."

"But—"

"Enough! I have spoken. Scientist Dowornobb, launch the science team. It is time for you and your ill-mannered mate to return to that glorious planet of blue skies. May this expedition be as exciting as the last. Stay away from bears."

With eye-clenching effort Kateos stifled her gushing gratitude, but her face glowed. She was going back to Genellan.

"Pssst," Dowornobb whispered, pushing Kateos gently to her knees.

Enraptured, she had not heard the formal dismissals. Et Kalass strolled imperiously far ahead. Dowornobb nudged her, and together they crawled from the royal chambers. Et Kalass awaited in the grand hallway.

"Mistress Kateos, you have my congratulations and deepest sympathies," the old minister intoned. "But most of all you have my greatest confidence. Your knowledge of state affairs is exceeded by few. Underestimate not your power."

"I—I serve at your pleasure, Your Excellency," she replied formally, eyes on the floor. But emboldened by her new status, she rose to her hinds and lifted her eyes, looking directly into the old minister's rheumy brown eyes. Dowornobb gasped.

"Who I am and what I know, I owe to you, Your Excellency," she said, employing the resonant power of her professional voice. "I have had the high honor of observing true genius. Worry not that I underestimate my abilities . . . or my new responsibilities."

"Yes, yes," Et Kalass replied thoughtfully, tilting his bulbous chin and looking with sober reflection down his slab nose. "Well spoken, mistress. Perhaps—just perhaps—you comprehend your peril."

Et Kalass held out his arm. With a graceful flourish Kateos took the noblekone's arm, leaving her thoroughly perplexed mate on his knees. The prime minister led her into an airy chamber off the court.

"Your Excellency," Kateos asked, "why did you not inform the king of the conspiracy? The intercepts were conclusive. General Krolk—"

"Certain things are discussed only in certain places. Ollant knows more than you realize, my impetuous friend," Et Kalass lectured. "In fact, it is old news. You will be briefed fully on matters and means of, eh, information gathering. Now, permit me to arrange your clearances. We must move rapidly, for you are to leave tomorrow."

They entered a spacious apartment that opened onto a balcony. A squad of officious lackeys crawled up to the minister to receive orders. Kateos crawled through a security veil into golden sunlight. It was a normal day, visibility restricted to little more than treble the distance one could throw a rock. The

Victory Tower, ghostly vertical lines in the smog, stretched mysteriously out of sight. Dwarfed by gravity, *kotta* trees, orange-leafed and with thick multiple trunks, lined Imperial Avenue, straight and obscenely wide. The vanishing point for the avenue and the low skyline of the capital city melded smoothly into the yellow methane and carbon-compound haze. Dowornobb crawled beside Kateos and pressed a long flank to hers. She leaned on his great mass and breathed deeply, luxuriously tasting the full-bodied atmosphere of her home planet. Her lungs would miss its tangy weight, but she looked forward to returning to the brilliant vistas of frigid Genellan.

As the king's ambassador, no less.

SIX

RETURN OF THE FLEET

Runacres, floating in zero gravity, flexed against his acceleration tethers, anticipating hyperlight exit into the Rex-Kaliph system. The gravitronic rumble dampened to null, leaving in its place the ubiquitous vibration and susurrant ambience of all powered ships. Status plots, both on his helmet HUD and on the arena screens, blinked into real time; a nav-hazard alarm sounded and was quickly extinguished. Its cause, the planet R-K Three—Genellan—an orb of swirling white, dun, and aqua, solidified on the center vid.

"Exit complete, Admiral," Commodore Wells rumbled. The burly officer was dressed in full battle armor. His gauntleted hands moved with measured pace over the operations watch console.

"Very well." Runacres exhaled, daring to relax. The Tellurian Legion fleet had returned, and a hostile welcome was not in evidence—so different from the previous two jump exits into the Rex-Kaliph system.

"No active contacts," the tactical officer reported, laboring at a horseshoe console at the foot of the flag bridge. Runacres acknowledged electronically and shook the tension from his shoulders. On the ship's command bridge, one deck below the canted flag mezzanine, the crew of *T.L.S. Eire* scurried about the business of piloting his flagship—fleet guide for a convoy of eight Legion motherships and four freighters.

"Transponders broadcasting full spectrum," the tactical assistant added. "Negative interrogation."

"What's science say?" Runacres demanded.

"Nominal," reported Captain Gray. The chief scientist's helmeted image appeared on Runacres's console. "No anomalies."

"Eagle Flight's away," announced Captain Wooden, the corvette group leader. The tall officer worked at a console next to the operations station. "Carmichael's ETA to Genellan orbit is thirty-six hours."

"Very well." Runacres muttered, staring at the digitized image of the planet, so sublime. He shook off his spacer's rapture.

"Any sign of Ketchie?" he asked.

"Negative, Admiral," Wells replied. "Rendezvous envelope's only just opened. Give him a week."

"Old sod's always early," Runacres muttered. "Time to fleet orbit?"

"Four days at standard, Admiral," Wells reported.

"Excellent termination, Franklin." Runacres slipped the helmet from his shiny head. The admiral, like all spacers, was smoothly hairless. "Stand down from jump stations. Set Alert Level Two until we figure out if we're still welcome. Relax helmets and battle armor. Formation Two-One, Grid Status Two; ahead standard."

"Aye, aye, Admiral," the fleet commodore rumbled. "Alert Two, Form Two-One, Grid two, ahead standard. Stand down from jump stations."

Wells pushed back from the operations watch station and removed his helmet, his perspiring black skull reflecting ambient light like a curved mirror. An operations watch officer slid into the vacated console and acknowledged. The boatswain of the watch piped "Attention" and passed the word, aural backup to the flurry of electronic information rippling through the fleet.

Runacres scanned the arena boards lining the curved bulkheads. On the main plot motherships broke from grid stations and commenced maneuvering to tactical stations. Icons representing corvettes debouching from mothership bays spread out from the larger units, forming a three-dimensional screen in the vanguard of the fleet disposition. More slowly but with respectable sharpness freighters slid into assigned cruise positions.

A soft surge of acceleration activated Runacres's restraining tether. He reached down and punched up the flagship captain's secure commlink. Captain Merriwether's placid, rubicund features filled his vid screen.

"Gently, Sarah!" Runacres said. "You'll run this old lady out from under her paint."

Merriwether's full lips gave hint of a wry smirk, but her twinkling, browless eyes never left the stationing plot. "Tell *Baffin* to clean up that lateral excursion," she ordered her deck officer. "Group leader, have the screen commander pay attention to drift rate. Division Two is just plain pissing away fuel."

Wooden, removing his helmet, acknowledged the admonition: "Roger, group copies." The senior corvette officer, jaw set and dark complexion intensifying, generated a sequence of signals over the screen net. Runacres monitored the group leader's actions and watched in silence as the corvette screen reacted smartly.

"Good adjustment," Runacres commented, noting the group leader's smoldering emotion. "Skipper's a little heavy-handed, isn't she?"

Wooden laughed grudgingly. "Captain Merriwether's famous for it. To her I'll always be just one of her 'vette drivers."

Runacres nodded. Merriwether had been one of his piss-and-vinegar pilots once, long ago—the unending cycle of experience. The admiral returned his attention to *Eire*'s bridge. Ensconced in its center, belying the frenetic actions of the deck watch orchestra, Merriwether floated in her tethers, conducting a dreamy waltz. He reconnected her to his secure circuit.

"Admirals are not customarily ignored," Runacres persisted.

"With all due respect," *Eire*'s captain drawled, her image intent on her instruments, "I'm a tad busy, sir. And you're forgetting, Admiral, I served on those ships you ham-fisted around. Gentle my—"

"Temper, temper." Runacres chuckled, overriding. His admin call button blinked. "Go!" he commanded.

"Admiral, Ito here," his aide replied.

"Wherever have you been, Commander?" Runacres replied.

"Ahem . . . my apologies, Admiral," Ito replied stiffly. "Envoy Stark requests permission to come on the bridge, sir."

"Granted," Runacres replied, terminating. His mood darkened.

"Poor Sam," Wells said, laughing. "You don't have to rub it in, Admiral."

"Isamu Ito's a diplomat if he's anything. Someone's got to baby-sit that bastard and his goons," Runacres muttered. "What's the latest on the plants?"

"Fleet intelligence confirms twenty operatives," Wells grunted. "They figure if they could ferret out that many, there must be at least triple that number, maybe as many as a hundred."

"One hundred security agents out of seven hundred settlers," Runacres grumbled. "Our illustrious leaders don't want our new colonists to be too independent, do they?"

"They, ah . . . designated Captain Gray as well," Wells said.

"Old news, Franklin," Runacres muttered.

"Why is he on your staff, if I may ask, Admiral?"

"He hates hyperlight duty." Runacres laughed. "I'm torturing him and I'd rather have him where I can watch him. No telling what damage he would do if I left him back in Edmonton."

The bridge hatch sighed open, and a gangling individual dressed in a khaki underway suit pulled himself through the opening, his depilated skull whiter than bone. The envoy was followed by his chief assistant, a coffee-skinned, tight-faced woman, also hairless, also dressed in civilian khaki. Commander Ito, smiling beatifically, discreetly latched on to the envoy's elbow and maneuvered him to the open area before the admiral's command station. Two burly men dressed in the black coveralls of the Legion Security Agency, their large bald heads covered with scarlet berets, followed, their awkwardness more than compensated for by raw athleticism.

"Admiral, please permit me to—" Stark began, his smile perfect.

"Good day, Envoy Stark," Runacres grumbled. "We're, ahem, a tad busy. Can't this wait? We still do not know what sort of welcome to expect from our konish friends. They may contest our arrival."

"Of course, Admiral," Stark said unctuously. "Forgive the intrusion. As Legion envoy I am obligated to be present when communication links are established."

"But Mr. Envoy," Runacres remonstrated, "we've discussed this ad nauseam. It could be hours before we establish radio contact—"

"We have a commlink, Admiral!" the tactical officer announced. "It's from our people." Commander Ito rolled his eyes.

"—hours before we establish radio contact with the konish authorities," Runacres growled, scowling at his smirking aide. "You have been provided a very adequate command center with the necessary diplomatic channels and security codes for your staff's use."

"Excuse me, Admiral," the excited tactical officer interrupted. "It's Lieutenant Commander Quinn sending her respects. They're awful happy to see us, sir."

"No doubt. All ship commanders to the link," Runacres said evenly, pulling himself back into his command station and momentarily forgetting the irritating presence of the civilians. He punched open the vid-circuit and said, "Runacres here. Your status."

The three-second transmission delay lapsed, and then the link was noisily reestablished. A burbling backdrop of exuberant voices could be heard. A metal alarm was being enthusiastically punished in the background.

"Our status, Admiral," Quinn replied. The expedition commander's digital image blossomed into clarity, her demeanor somber but relieved. She sported a disheveled crop of flaxen hair going gray and radiant blue eyes, both accentuated by a splendid tan. "Until today the mission had been merely exciting. This very morning we were attacked by a migrating horde of *Carnivorous reptilis major*. Regretfully, I must report four dead and four missing, presumed dead, all members of the marine security detachment. A detailed report has been uplinked on laserburst. Over."

"Do you need emergency assistance?" Runacres asked, bringing up the laserburst report. "Or more security? Should we sortie a medical team? Over."

"No, sir," Quinn replied after the time lapse. "All injuries are manageable, and the kones are flying in assistance from Ocean Station. Over."

"Are you in danger? Over," Runacres asked.

"No more than usual . . . for Genellan," Quinn replied. "Dragons are still about, but the real problem may be all the nightmares that followed them into the valley. Sandy Tatum says we can get rid of them if we don't run out of ammunition first. Over."

"Tatum, eh? The one-armed giant. Lost his arm to nightmares if I remember correctly. We'll bring Tatum all the ammunition he needs. Where's Lieutenant Buccari? How is she? And her baby? I trust her pregnancy was happily and fruitfully terminated. May I speak with her? Over."

"She and the baby boy are quite well, Admiral," Quinn replied somberly. "Or were, the last I saw them. Sharl departed for Hudson's Plateau five days ago. The cliff dwellers requested her presence. She took her baby . . . and Private Chastain. Over."

"Mother and babe trekking the unfathomable wilds of Genellan," Runacres replied. "With Buccari that doesn't surprise me. And if I remember correctly, Chastain makes Tatum look like a scrumwing. No doubt she also has a horde of those nasty winged buggers protecting her. Pity the dragons. Over."

"We are worried nevertheless, Admiral. Over," Quinn answered.

"No doubt. Well, we're back with you now. There'll be corvettes in low orbit within thirty-six hours. The fleet will arrive in support orbit in four days, and the first planetary habitation module will be downloaded as soon as foundation sites are uplinked. Has Lieutenant Buccari determined where she would like us to build her first city? Over."

"Sharl doesn't want any settlers on the planet yet, Admiral," Quinn replied, swallowing. "She says there are still details to work out. Over."

Stark cleared his throat too loudly.

"Permission to land settlers has not been rescinded, has it?" Runacres inquired, glancing at the envoy. "Over."

"Ah, negative, Admiral," Quinn replied. "Sharl and I have negotiated heavily with the konish technical authorities. We still have permission to put a thousand humans on the planet. Over."

Stark coughed and mumbled something to his assistant.

"What's the next step?" Runacres growled. "Over."

"Admiral, something is happening, and probably no coincidence," Quinn replied. "The kones are establishing a year-round presence at Ocean Station. Your timing could not be better. Over."

"Not soon enough, I'd say," Stark snorted.

Runacres fixed the envoy with a relentless stare. Stark closed his eyes and perceptibly bowed his head.

"I would like to see you and Buccari on board the flagship at the earliest possible opportunity," Runacres said, "to discuss settlement needs and meet with the Legion envoy. We'll set a schedule for that meeting as soon as the fleet gets close. As usual, Quinn, er ... Cassy, it is a pleasure. Runacres out."

He disconnected the link and stretched his body against the acceleration tethers. He watched the screen formations, noting with satisfaction the precise stationing maneuvers.

"Is Buccari on our side?" Stark asked.

"What side would that be, Mr. Stark?" Runacres retorted.

"The Legion's side, Admiral, and the peoples of Earth," Stark said with a metallic smile. "The same side to which you have sworn loyalty."

"My aide will escort you to your command center," Runacres said flatly. "You will have every communication service required."

"Of course, Admiral," Stark replied, pushing awkwardly down the companionway. "And I would request a moment of your time ... to review your orders, sir, and my standing on this mission."

"As you wish," Runacres acknowledged. "Commander Ito will coordinate."

Stark's entourage left the bridge. Ito remained at the admiral's shoulder. "I want out of this job," he whimpered.

"You are so astonishingly good at it, Sam," Runacres growled.

"Rather be a settler on Mag-Two," Ito muttered, following Stark.

Chancellor-General Tar Fell breasted himself on a gravity lounge and forced himself to relax. Events were accelerating. The future promised much and threatened more.

"Ollant has dispatched a ship to Genellan," General Magoon rumbled.

"It is so," Tar Fell replied, scratching his lantern chin. "Dowornobb, the astronomer-physicist, leads a team of technologists, and there are rumors of a negotiator on board."

"Et Kalass?" Magoon asked.

"Too old." Tar Fell sneered, lighting a black *wahocca* cigar. "Genellan is not for the infirm."

"Truly a forbidding planet," Magoon said.

"Adventure has a price," Tar Fell growled, exhaling fragrant green smoke. A subtle security tone sounded. Tar Fell looked to the entry.

"Fleet General Krolk of the Ransa League," the chamberlain

announced. The scarlet-robed steward, luxuriant eye tufts drooping below wattling jowls, stood at attention on all fours at the entrance to the low-ceilinged, thickly buttressed ministerial chamber.

"Gravity, the Ransan returns quickly," Magoon growled. The PDF general, svelte by konish standards, rose easily from his gravity lounge. "By your leave, General."

"Stay, Magoon. Present the fleet general," Tar Fell rumbled, also wondering what had brought the Ransan back so quickly. "The old shovel and his shipyards are vital to our plans. Krolk must know of your participation sooner or later."

The impassive steward placed a broad forehead on the polished marble, where it obediently remained. A soft gong sounded, and a massive, block-shouldered, ponderous-hipped lunar mines pilot, easily three hundred kilos in weight, appeared from the security chicane. The splayed-featured behemoth sauntered on all fours through the sterile antechamber, laser trackers locking onto his prodigious person like *molla* flies onto manure. The chamberlain, remaining on his forearms, backed unobtrusively from the chambers.

"Fleet General Krolk," Tar Fell announced, falling gracefully to well-padded elbows. Tar Fell was first a clever politician.

"Chancellor-General," the ancient ore loader rumbled in return, hesitating at the presence of a Planetary Defense Force general officer in their midst. The Ransan eased to his elbows and *thunk*ed a massive forehead against glazed stone.

"General Krolk," Tar Fell rumbled, crawling to the Ransan and touching his massive shoulder. "I present my compatriot, PDF Wing General Magoon. Excellent news; General Magoon has declared for our cause. Magoon will serve as a ship general in our first squadron . . . under your flotilla command, of course."

"Excellent!" Krolk replied, his response more formal than enthusiastic. Magoon nodded respectfully, but the Thullolian's gaze, dark-eyed and stern, locked with the bulbous glare of the old Ransan. A faint fetid hint of offal wafted into the air, preliminary to a challenge. The Ransan's eye tufts lifted ominously.

"Your rapid return portends news?" Tar Fell rumbled thunderously.

"The alien fleet has returned," Krolk reported, slowly transferring his attention to the chancellor, eye tufts relaxing.

"Ah! Returned at last," Tar Fell rumbled. He felt his own tufts prickling and stretching the skin of his massive brow.

"We have established communications with the aliens," Krolk continued, rocking back on generous haunches. "A high-level government representative, an Envoy Stark. They have even offered an encryption algorithm so that our transmissions may have diplomatic privilege."

"How considerate," Tar Fell said, making an effort to suppress his burgeoning elation. Losing control would be unseemly.

"This alien . . . this Stark solicits replies from all konish heads of state. Will you acknowledge for the Compact?"

"In good time, Fleet General," Tar Fell replied, musing. "But alas, the alien fleet has returned too soon. Yes?"

"Gravity, yes," Krolk snarled, again giving Magoon a long glare. The old space pilot's pale, grainy complexion was marbled with distended black and scarlet veins. Krolk's frustration and anger, a palpable miasma, oozed across the floor. Magoon indiscreetly lifted a kerchief to his splayed nose.

Tar Fell rose heavily to his hinds and clambered up a gentle ramp, escaping the brunt of the noxious emotions. Recirculators hummed into life, clearing the odor well of putrescent emanations. Tar Fell beckoned the Ransan and the Thullolian to join him on elevated hydrolounges.

"Fleet General Krolk," Tar Fell announced, "our venture to Genellan must carry sufficient weight."

"So it will," Krolk thundered.

"Our time is come," Tar Fell said grimly. "Tomorrow General Magoon and I resign our commissions."

"It is time, Chancellor," Krolk roared. The old spacer saluted, eye tufts springing erect. "All Ransans are anxious to serve their new armada master."

Tar Fell bowed. Even Magoon was taken aback with the Ransan's fervent display, the depth of Krolk's hate. Ransa, a nation of farmers and space miners, had suffered profoundly from the Hegemony's marauding armies. Too many Ransans had died.

King Ollant had ended the Rule of Generals, returning the Northern Hegemony to noble rule and to peace, but the scars of war remained. Tar Fell, ruler of large and populous Thullol, Ransa's southern neighbor, perceived in Ransa's hatred for the north an opportunity. Ransa had the ability to build large spaceships; Thullol had a population of *trods* available to train as crews.

"Together, the Thullolian and Ransan fleets will have no rival, our lands no enemies," Tar Fell snarled. A security laser flickered over the chancellor's features and interrogated his vital signs.

"How will Ollant react?" Magoon pondered.

"Our armada renders the Hegemony irrelevant." General Krolk burped in his elevated emotional state, emitting gas from multiple orifices.

"We have more keels than crews, General Krolk," Magoon replied.

"Trained crews, General," Tar Fell intervened. "Our conscript program is proceeding apace. I rely on both of you to develop and train new crews, using resigning PDF complements as an officer cadre."

"What of the PDF?" Magoon posed. "Should General Talsali impede resignations, it could prove disastrous."

"General Magoon suffers many apprehensions," Krolk snarled.

"Worry not, Magoon," Tar Fell consoled. "Over half the pilots are from southern tribes. I have their loyalty."

"Loyalty is a tenuous condition, Armada Master," Magoon snarled. "King Ollant may speak softly, but his reputation bespeaks a strong neck and indomitable will. The Hegemonic armies are considerable advers—"

"The southern tribes have not forgotten Gorruk's scourge of their fatherlands," Tar Fell snapped, growing impatient. "The rape of Penc and the massacre of Rouue Massif cost many PDF pilots their brothers and fathers. Fear not the southern pilots."

"Yes, my leader."

"Now is our time!" Tar Fell roared. An interrogation sensor fanned his features. Targeting lasers searched for hostile opportunities. Adversary interdiction apertures winked open. "It is time to exact retribution. Ollant spent his army and his courage deposing Gorruk. He has no appetite for war. Now is our time."

The infinite heavens pulsed with aurora borealis, shapeless waves of coral and emerald relieving a perfect blackness embedded with points of sparkling silver. Toon, vestigial talons scraping stone, led Short-one-who-leads past vigilant rim sentries.

The small moon, lumpy and brown, though full, cast dim illumination. The large moon, nearing three quarters, washed snowcapped mountains with silver, sharply defining the high rim of the plateau against the profound shadows of the river canyon. Behind them the plateau stream rushed noisily into the black void.

Short-one-who-leads bounded from the parapet and onto the uneven ledge. Toon followed nervously over the rounded edge, stepping gingerly on the flat crest. The guilder marveled at the long-legs' confidence and agility on the perilous precipice. Although Short-one-who-leads could not soar on the winds, she was a hunter, showing no fear of height or battle, yet she was as intelligent as any guilder.

They clambered through ebony shadows to a vantage point atop moon-whitened rocks. Short-one-who-leads stood erect, staring into the crystalline blackness. A vigilant sentry pointed, hands together, to the vagrant stars—tiny, faint pricks of light yet distinct and steady—a spontaneous constellation of inconstant position. Short-one-who-leads pulled back her fur-lined parka and stared into the star-strewn night, eyes glistening in the biting wind. Long hair whipped from her face, gloriously revealing the thick white scar.

"I see," Short-one-who-leads signed. She stared into the black night for many heartbeats. At last she grunted unintelligibly.

Toon pulled the communicator from his furs and typed icons: MOVING STARS YOUR PEOPLE?

Short-one-who-leads reluctantly pulled her gaze away. She took the communicator, pushed keys, and handed it back. She returned her attention to the stars.

UNCERTAIN, it read. MUST RETURN

"When?" Toon signed, chirping to get her attention.

"Now," the long-legs signed, snapping her open hand into a fist.

SEVEN

CARMICHAEL

Pressure flowing through Carmichael's oxygen umbilical eased as he dropped the EPL into Genellan's crystalline troposphere. He worked his jaws and yawned to equalize the pressure in his inner ears.

"Reentry complete, Commander," Flaherty announced.

"Roger," Carmichael replied. "Taking control."

The lander pilot placed his hand on the EPL's sidestick and blinked off the autopilot. The Endoatmospheric Planetary Lander commenced a slow roll. Carmichael, strong fingers hovering above the thrusters, permitted the excursion to continue, allowing the lander to execute a continent-sweeping barrel roll. The roll rate was so gentle, he doubted any of the passengers could sense the hypermach aerobatics. Carmichael smiled as the EPL, the "apple," carved deeper into the atmosphere. He checked skin temps, trimmed the nose, and flattened the descent, keeping within thermal tolerance.

"Never seen one of those before, Commander," Flaherty gushed. The corvette second officer, sitting in the systems operator's station, had a full instrument panel and a view port, unlike the passengers.

"You still haven't, Flack," Carmichael said patiently.

"Sure, er, aye, aye, Commander," Flaherty replied.

Carmichael hauled backstick to acceleration limits and dropped a wing. Control response was mushy at that rarefied altitude, and sustainable g-loads were extremely low. The lander plummeted from the stratosphere, corkscrewing through three complete circles. Below him was the river, stretching from its azure source in the north and winding along the great mountains until it doglegged east at Hudson's Plateau. Beyond

MacArthur's Valley the river turned south again, slipping over the horizon on its journey to the equatorial sea.

"Mr. Godonov?" Carmichael asked. "Has the river got a name yet?"

"Kones call it the East Corlia watershed," the science officer replied from the EPL's passenger cabin. "Our charts are going with that. Corlia's their name for the continent. Maybe Sharl's come up with a proper name in the last two years."

Sharl Buccari. What's it been like, Sharl? Carmichael's memories stirred, memories of a brilliant young officer, an athlete with piercing green eyes and dark red hair. Hair so dark, it was almost black—before it was shorn, sacrificed to the exigencies of space duty.

"Engines hot," Flaherty reported. "Fuel pressure's in the green."

"Roger," Carmichael replied, gently pulling the lander across a vivid horizon that was no longer purple. The planet's surface textures expanded into protruding terrain. G-loads climbed.

"Landing envelope's tightening, Commander," Flaherty ventured.

"Such is life." Carmichael sighed, giving the sidestick a last squeeze. "Compute . . . command. Auto connect," he announced.

The computer took over, and the lander banked smoothly to port. The tracking bug on the course indicator drifted smartly onto the approach course. The descent funnel flashed onto the head-up display, the signal from the MacArthur's Valley navigation beacon strong and steady, as Carmichael's thoughts returned to Buccari.

"Mach one point five, altitude on schedule," Flaherty reported. "In the groove. Passengers tucked in. Checking good, Commander."

Carmichael double clicked the intercom. They were on final. The autopilot held altitude while airspeed decayed; the EPL dropped transsonic. The glide slope indicator resolutely settled on the center, bisecting the course indicator. The apple started down the glide slope. Carmichael peered ahead. Mountains loomed ominously.

"Landing checks complete, Commander," Flaherty reported.

"Checking good, Flack," Carmichael acknowledged. The river valley came out from under the left wing, its braided channels melding into a single wide course. The endless sweeping plains to his right swirled with browns and irregular patches of gold—grazing musk-buffalo and horses beyond count.

Airspeed steadied. Terrain features sharpened; mountain peaks passed down the left side. Wingtip fences snapped erect; a growling noise vibrated through the craft, signaling movement of the articulating flaps as they warped out and down from the trailing edges of the delta wings. The lander flared, its nose elevating steadily, blocking his view of the mountainous horizon. He went to the gauges.

Airspeed fell away; the nose of the craft rotated smoothly toward the vertical like a cobra flaring to strike. With satisfying intensity, the guttural bass of the main engines exploded into activity. Carmichael was pressed into his acceleration chair. Engine gimbals started grinding. The pulsing of the hover blasters vibrated his boots, as the nose of the ship slowly fell back to the horizon. Snowy mountains looming to the south and west were suddenly blocked by rising dust and debris. As abruptly as they had started, the main engines wound down. Hover blasters screamed for a second longer. The lander shivered to a jolting halt, it's gyros winding down.

"Apple's on the ground," Flaherty announced.

Carmichael grunted. One gee tugged at his heart. Retro detritus scattered in the breeze. As he worked through the shutdown checks, Carmichael scanned the rolling terrain and spotted a squad of green-garbed marines trotting toward his ship. At their head was a slight, dark-haired man wearing what looked like a kilt. Probably one of Buccari's Survivors. He acknowledged his disappointment at not seeing her in the reception committee.

"How're the skin temps, Flack?" Carmichael asked. "Company's here."

"Won't be long, Skipper," Flaherty replied. "It's cold and breezy outside. You'll be needing a storm coat."

Carmichael jettisoned his fittings and, fighting the imperative of gravity, eased down the slanted deck, past Flaherty at the system operator's station, to the compact crew locker. He stowed his helmet and peeled off his pressure suit. Flaherty leapfrogged him and undogged the hatch to the passenger compartment.

"Another minute," Flaherty grunted, hitting the hatch release. "I'll help the boatswain with the cargo. Major Faro and her marines'll just get in the way."

As Carmichael finished changing into exploration fatigues, he felt pressure seals on the main cargo hatch letting go.

"Commander!" Flaherty yelled, "Get back on oxygen!"

It was too late; an eye-burning odor permeated the lander. Carmichael gagged and grappled with his helmet. He had forgotten the musk-buffalo. Hardy laughter roared from outside the lander.

"Wipe those goddam smiles off your faces, assholes!" he heard Major Faro roar. "Landing squad. Landing perimeter. Now! The rest of you buttheads, fall in! Who the hell's in charge here?"

Breathing shallowly, Carmichael stowed his equipment and scrambled down the ramp, sliding past the cargo pallet. Flaherty had plugged his oxygen umbilical into a crew station, as had the lander boatswain. Their faces were ashen. Major Faro and her landing squad, in field suits, had fired off their oxygen systems. Her newly landed troops were spread out evenly in a precise circle around the lander. The marines in the reception party stood at nervous attention.

"I do not share your frigging levity," Faro screamed, her gravelly voice attenuated only slightly by a breathing unit. The mountain-chested, thick-legged officer stood nose to nose with a sergeant, thumping the noncom's chest with a gloved finger.

Carmichael stumbled from the apple. Godonov, amazingly unaffected by the noxious odors, was shaking hands with the short man in the kilt.

"Let's get this cargo on the planet," Carmichael ordered, his voice trembling and his head throbbing in cadence with Major Faro's abusive shouts. It was cold; the warmth of the EPL was ripped from the snug cabin by gusting breezes.

"Chew on this, Commander," the Survivor said, his hard-featured bearded face glancing about the EPL hold. What had looked like a kilt was a baggy set of shorts, the remnant of an underway suit. The Survivor's dark thatch was bowl-cut, short around jug-handle ears but shaggy on top. He wore leather sandals laced up knotty calves, but despite the cool breeze and narrow shoulders. A rifle and a leather rucksack lay on the exhaust-blasted ground. The little man thrust out a callused hand. In it was a thick black-green leaf.

"Fenstermacher, ex-corvette boatswain second," he said matter-of-factly. "This here's thickweed. Chew it until your tongue starts humming and then put it in your pocket. You'll need it again before we get off the cliffs. Wind's not being co-operative. You can smell the crap-cows all the way to the valley. This'll clear up the pain that's making your eyeballs knock together . . . sir."

"It does the trick, Commander," Godonov seconded, chewing vigorously. Carmichael remembered his planet briefings.

"It's a damn narcotic," Major Faro said. She stared at the substance as though it were offal. "Keep your frigging helmets on, marines—those that got them." Swearing nonstop, she berated the resident marines. They wore only floppy field hats, many atop pates that badly needed shearing. Most chewed on weed without trying to disguise their rumination.

Carmichael, no longer able to speak, took the leaf and tentatively put it between his teeth. Immediately a warm, sinus-clearing sensation exploded on his taste buds. His headache, which had been excruciating, faded into mere discomfort, and that soon was gone. His senses heightened, and he noticed a dull rumbling, just perceptible, vibrating in the air.

"What's that?" he asked.

"You stampeded the buffalo," Fenstermacher replied. "Stirred up the stink something fierce. Not likely they'll be back, but we should move out. I'll take charge of the cargo, Commander. That okay?"

Carmichael could only nod as the confident little man and the lander boatswain rolled out an all-terrain truck and jacked down its undercarriage. Next they trundled the cargo pallet out onto the charred ground. In minutes, the pallet was broken down and the bulk of the cargo had been loaded onto the truck, its fat tires flattening under the strain. The overload was divided among Major Faro's marines.

"You were here before, weren't you, sir?" Fenstermacher asked idly.

"Yeah," Carmichael replied. "Didn't get down into the valley, though. Too busy running shuttles. Admiral didn't want to come in too close last time."

"Thought you looked familiar." Fenstermacher sniffed, squinting at the name tag over his chest pocket. "Shit, you're Jake Carmichael . . . er, Commander Carmichael, aren't you? The ace! You took out—"

"Looks like we're ready to move out," Carmichael suggested. Major Faro, screaming obscenities, harried her burdened marines into field patrol formation.

"Yeah . . . er, yes, sir," Fenstermacher replied. "Take that weed outta your mouth, Commander, or you'll blast off before the apple does."

"Lead the way, Boats." Carmichael laughed, removing the cud and putting the soggy mess in his coat pocket. His tongue was tingling almost to a sensation of vibration. He turned back to the EPL and gave Flaherty a thumbs-up.

"Okay, Flack," Carmichael transmitted on his multiplex. "You're cleared to orbit."

"Roger, Skipper," came the pilot's voice. "Be back with another load in the morning. Commencing takeoff checks. Enjoy the weather."

Carmichael acknowledged and turned to follow the ladened rover. The taiga was yielding, and he had to lift his feet clear of deep impressions. Full planetary gravity quickly became annoying, but he caught up with one of the heavily loaded marines and relieved her of an auxiliary pack. The gray-faced trooper smiled her gratitude. Fenstermacher begrudgingly emulated Carmichael's actions. Major Faro artfully ignored them.

"Amazing how quickly you forget about gravity," Godonov huffed, dropping back to join them at the rear of the column.

"Ain't as bad as Earth." Fenstermacher chuckled.

"In about twenty billion hungry ways," the science officer replied.

"It's bad enough." Carmichael exhaled, shifting his load.

"We got packhorses," Fenstermacher grunted. The terrain climbed slightly as they approached the river cliffs. "Waiting for us once we ferry the river. Tatum's trolling for dragons and nightmares. Using us for bait." He looked sideways for a reaction.

"Dragons hit you pretty hard, I heard," Carmichael said.

"Superdragons, big ones! Yeah. We handled 'em, but we're sure glad you're here. We're mighty low on ammo and—"

A familiar low-pitched grinding noise caught their attention. Carmichael stopped on the high ground and turned to monitor his lander, a toy spacecraft on a vast mottled carpet. In the dusty distance buffalo milled nervously, cinnamon-brown backs covering the visible horizon. Carmichael set down his load and covered his ears.

The EPL lifted on a gouting blossom of orange flame. The nose of the craft swung skyward, and then the EPL leapt from the ground, a streak of glaring flame. Split seconds later the insane explosion of primaries jolted the plains. The little ship became a meteor shooting into the heavens, climbing at a fantastic rate, trailing a brilliant, billowing white plume.

Within seconds its booming exclamations were reduced to a residual humming in Carmichael's ears. Its contrail lasted longer, but not much; high winds aloft worked persistently at shredding its ephemeral fabric. The low rumble of thundering hooves, only recently quieted, lifted back above the audible threshold with renewed intensity.

Carmichael tore himself from the man-riven sky and followed the others, treading a path that became more foot-worn and hard-packed as it neared the cliffs. The rolling terrain sprouted rocks and descended; trees and windblown bushes appeared in weather-softened defiles, and glimpses of the river appeared. Beyond the river Carmichael saw the misty, waterfall-streaked depths of MacArthur's Valley, a dramatic groove in a range of spectacular mountains that were but stairs to the titanic continental spine beyond. It was an immense vista.

They started sharply downward, traversing the open slope of a precipitous tributary valley. An expanse of river opened to their view, wide and dark green, moving with determined power past slender riparian islands. Far upstream awesome torrents pounded down from the western elevations in frothy cataracts, a faint roar on the breeze.

And then he heard airplane engines.

"What's that?" Carmichael asked.

"Abats," Fenstermacher remarked, pointing. "It's what kones call their airplanes. They'll be landing in Longo's Meadow."

Carmichael picked out two white aircraft flying along the river, coaltitude with his vantage point. He had battled konish pilots in space and had seen them from a distance, but now he was about to meet them—members of an intelligent alien race, a race of giants!

The planes came abreast of his position. They were of considerable size, with high–aspect ratio wings mounted above stubby twin-boomed fuselages. A large ducted engine was mounted above the wing. He could see pilots in the cockpits, ominous, hulking forms. One waved. Carmichael lifted a hand in return, and the aircraft rocked its wings as it rumbled past. He felt less anxious.

As he started down the steep trail, Buccari came to mind again. His remaining anxiety was displaced by anticipation.

EIGHT

MACARTHUR'S VALLEY

A thundering double explosion reverberated across the lake and echoed down MacArthur's Valley—a sonic boom, the double detonation of an arriving EPL. Yet another! Buccari had lost count. Harbingers of duty, of civilization.

She was back home. Legs cramping, Buccari breasted the sloping granite face of the valley's northern limit. Steep, glacier-carved elevations dominated the valley's western flank. Forested moraines and gentler feeder valleys patterned the eastern margin. At her feet Lake Shannon overflowed its rocky margins and gushed impatiently in a crystalline green sluice, leaping down the slanted granite she had just scaled. Behind her, and far below, the lake outflow joined the crashing cataracts of the great river.

Perched on a bleached limb protruding from a driftwood jam, Tonto waited serenely, basking heavy-lidded in breezy sunlight. Overhead, hunters swung in lazy figure eights. Buccari trudged stolidly past the outflow. Tonto's black eyes and long snout turned to follow. Upshore, beneath the steep pine-forested valley wall, she forded an energetic runoff and came to the flooded grain fens. A flock of bronze-tufted ducks exploded into the air. A herd of lake elk splashed into the hardwood beyond, their great racks of horn clattering. A calf and a cow anxiously trailed the herd.

Beached high on the granite, among the thick green vines and bladders of a moaning glory patch, sat three outrigger dugouts. The morning was well advanced. The profusion of large white flowers, except for a desultory yawning, had ended their foghorn serenade for the day. Buccari released her pack and shrugged it into the first canoe, the barrel of her carbine striking the sun-bleached gunwale. Taking a deep breath, she grunted the heavy craft into slack water. She collapsed on the warm rock and thrust sandaled feet into sun-warmed shallows. A gust of wind, a shadow across her face, and the rustling of leather wings made her open her eyes. Tonto landed softly on the canoe's bow, folded his membranes, and stared at her like a rockowl contemplating a rodent.

"You lazy dung-ball," she signed. "Why no fly?"

"You dead dung-ball," Tonto replied, four-fingered hands flashing hand signals. "You belly up. Need help." He opened a long, narrow jaw and chittered, revealing rows of white razor teeth—laughter.

Buccari chuckled and put her hands behind her head. Presently Lizard Lips arrived, wheezing and gasping. She pushed to her feet and met the stumbling steam user. She twisted the wedge-faced guilder around and removed his rucksack, careful not to snag his vestigial flying spines. She threw it atop hers, amidships in the canoe.

"Okay, Lizzy, in you go," Buccari huffed, helping the creature into the dugout. The cliff dweller lay against the packs, gasping for breath. Tonto twittered at the exhausted dweller, mostly in frequencies beyond human perception. The hunter unlimbered a wing and fanned the guilder as Buccari pushed the canoe into deep water. Tonto restowed his wings and grabbed a paddle. Buccari jumped in and matched the hunter's quick stroke. More hunters lifted on burgeoning thermals, gliding ahead.

Lake Shannon stretched before her. Towering cascades and wispy angel-hair waterfalls tumbled from the valley's glacier-hung western flank, feeding the deep and fertile alpine lake. She dug her paddle into diamond-bright water the texture of silk and pulled vigorously, relishing the strain on a different set of muscles. She relaxed into the rhythm of the water, mesmerized by the eddying whirlpools of the paddle strokes, but her fatigued mind, numbed by forced march and the monotony of paddling, gave license to mind and memory. A persistent kaleidoscope of concerns welled forth.

From the distant river cliffs came the rumble of a lander retro. Pulse quickening, she bent her back and stroked. Lizard Lips, sensing her urgency, grabbed a paddle and helped Tonto offset her impatient pulls.

She came abreast of an expansive clearing in the forest. Its dreary cinders had long before given way to emerald shoots of spring. Grasses and scrub had nearly erased the blight of Colonel Longo's landing. Now it was called Longo's Meadow. An airstrip had been bulldozed down its length. She was not surprised to see the glossy white flanks of an abat.

Buccari's shoulders burned as the canoe curved into the cove, sweeping past the headland's narrow tip. Two hunters, screaming insanely, dive-bombed them—Spitter and Bottlenose. Tonto screeched and debarked with a thunderous flap of his membranes. The hunters jousted in the air, tumbling not gently to the wooded peninsula, where other hunters screeched and whistled in welcome. Buccari's inner ears vibrated with the discordant cacophony. She lifted her hand.

Hunters had heralded her return. A cluster of disparate beings, eerily subdued, gathered on the cove beach. In noisy contrast, the children of the Survivors—skinny Honey, stocky Adam, and chubby little Hope—hopped and splashed naked along the water's edge. A clutch of nervous guilders, barely clear of the woods, stood distinct from the crowd. Et Silmarn, helmet under his tree-trunk arm, towered above the humans, waving enthusiastically. Buccari waved back. She recognized Nestor Godonov, and then she saw Carmichael.

"About time you got back, Lieutenant!" Chief Wilson bellowed. "Where the hell's Chastain?"

"Bite my ass, Gunner," she shouted, wrenching her eyes from Carmichael's. She steered between two beached boats.

"Lieutenant, where's Charlie?" Nancy Dawson cried, her shock of sun-fired hair neon red against the green forest.

"With Jocko, Nancy," Buccari replied. Guilt gnawed at her. "Charlie's with the cliff dwellers. I left Jocko behind to take care of him."

Dawson jerked erect, incredulous, hands clasped to her breast. The tall Survivor's freckled, peeling skin darkened with emotion.

"Bet Chastain loved that," Fenstermacher roared, wading into the water. "Who's baby-sitting who?" he cackled. Leslie Lee, holding Hope's tiny hand, followed Fenstermacher to the water's edge.

"Got hit by dragons, Lieutenant," Tatum said. "Lost ten horses."

"And eight marines," Quinn added, stepping forward. The science officer was haggard, but her chin was up and her voice was firm.

"The hunters announced it as a great victory," Buccari mumbled, suddenly exhausted. Eight more deaths. She looked at their faces, all staring at her expectantly as if she had an answer to all their problems. Her thoughts drifted to the solitude of a campfire high on a ridge, under a star-filled sky. Without thinking, she sent Carmichael a tight smile. His return expression was at best uncertain.

"The fleet's back, Lieutenant," Chief Wilson shouted. "We've got fresh batteries, tools, soap, clothes—"

"We got ammo," Tatum said, reaching down and hauling the canoe onto the shore. Beppo Schmidt and Fenstermacher shoved from amidships. She stood and reached for her pack, but Toby Mendoza, smiling broadly, pulled it away. Tookmanian, swarthy and gaunt, offered her a hand.

"God bless you, Lieutenant," the hawk-nosed ascetic rumbled softly. "Did your feet suffer from my workmanship?"

"Forgot I was wearing them, Tooks," she said, smiling. She looked down at Tookmanian's rugged sandals and at her hairy, dirty, and scratched legs. She wore baggy shorts stitched crudely by her own hands from elkhide, miserable handiwork compared with Tookmanian's skills. A breeze lifted from the lake, chilling her sweat-soaked body. She self-consciously tucked in her grimy, threadbare T-shirt. Her shoulder ached with the effort, the old trauma nagging at her. She was tired and sore, and she stank.

Buccari dismissed her errant thoughts and welcomed the happy crush of her crew—her Survivors. The fleet was back. She had responsibilities. Decisions needed to be made about the planet's future, her future, and her son's future. Wet little children, jumping and screaming, pulled at her clothes.

"Glad you're back, Lieutenant," Pepper Goldberg said, a crooked smile lighting her dusky face. "We were worried. The dragons . . ."

"Thanks, Pepper." She smiled, stroking Honey's tangled blond hair.

"How did you know, sir?" Wilson asked. "To come back?"

"Hunters watch the stars, Gunner." She turned to help Lizard Lips stumble from the canoe. The steam user was greeted with tentative squeaks by the other guilders. The chirping creatures sidestepped down the beach, opening distance between themselves and the kones.

She mopped perspiration from her brow and stared uphill at the fresh graves under the sugar tree and at the tilled land between the palisade and the cove, the newly turned soil in both places so similar in its rich blackness. A tardy moaning glory foghorned, spewing its pollen—the cycle of life.

Et Silmarn moved gracefully, especially for a being of three hundred kilos. The giant dropped to his fists and lowered a tremendous head. She reciprocated, touching the ground with her forehead.

"Welcome, as always, Excellency," Buccari said in passable konish, struggling stiffly to her feet.

"Citizen Sharl," the planetary governor boomed in accented Legion. The hulking noblekone blocked out the horizon as he raised up on his hinds, offering a titanic hand. "It-ah always my pleasure. Long-ah winter, yes? Your fleet-ah has returned again. It-ah exciting, yes?"

Buccari craned her neck and used both hands to clasp two of Et Silmarn's sausagelike fingers. The behemoth's hand closed warmly and gently on both of hers.

"Yes, Your Excellency," she said, switching to Legion. "It is very exciting. Now we must get down to business, yes?"

"Ah, yes! Down-ah to business," Et Silmarn replied, his grainy complexion stretched with a huge, crooked smile, his russet eye tufts vibrant with emotion. "Your fleet-ah is back. The king's . . . ah, delegation will-ah soon be on Genellan. Important-ah meeting."

"The Legion will be ready, Your Excellency," Sharl replied, glancing at Carmichael. His gaze trapped hers and would not let it go.

"Yes-s-ah . . ." the kone said, his booming voice trailing off to silence.

"Sharl, er, Lieutenant Buccari," Quinn said, breaking the lull. "This is Commander Carmichael, officer in charge of the advance team. He's carrying orders from Admiral Runacres."

"It's been a long time," Buccari said to the tall, broad officer.

"You know each other?" Quinn asked, glaring at Carmichael.

"Professionally," Carmichael quickly replied, holding out his hand. Soft brown eyes glowed warmly from his rugged countenance. Buccari had forgotten his easy smile.

"Commander Carmichael used to abuse me," she said, firmly taking the pilot's hand. "He took great pleasure in slapping me around."

"Only when you were wearing a helmet. You deserved every whack."

"This-ah is confusing," Et Silmarn growled.

"Pardon me?" Quinn blurted.

"I was Commander Buccari's primary flight instructor," Carmichael said, responding to the puzzlement. He stared into Buccari's eyes. "I came down . . . tried to see you before, Sharl . . . before the fleet left for Earth last time, but you were, ah . . . busy."

"Excuse me?" she replied. His grip lingered.

"After the fighting was over, I ran shuttles to Genellan, but—"

"You called me 'Commander,' " she said.

"It's the accepted form of address for an officer of the rank of lieutenant commander," Carmichael said, suddenly stone-faced.

"Thanks for the promotion, but I'm a lieutenant last I checked."

"You're welcome," Carmichael replied, the smile again creasing his chiseled features. "I refer to these documents: orders and promotion in grade for Buccari, Sharl Firenze, Lieutenant Commander, LSF."

Buccari closed her mouth.

"Admiral Runacres requests your presence onboard *Eire* at your earliest convenience," Carmichael continued. "He, and I quote, 'wants your posterior back in the saddle, ASAP.' The packet also includes your next assignment. How soon, may I tell the admiral, will you be returning to his flagship? For your information, Commander Quinn and I will be heading back tomorrow."

"I, uh . . ." she stammered, looking dumbly at the packet. The official seals bearing Legion serial numbers and authorization levels struck a dizzy chord. A thick gold braid slashed the black leather cover—a command emblem. She held a corvette command in her hands.

NINE

OLD FRIENDS

Buccari thought about Admiral Runacres's summons for a Genellan week—ten twenty-six-hour, twenty-three-minute days. She used the time to collect her son from the cliff dwellers and to think.

It had been a difficult week. She hung in her tethers in the survey lab of *Eagle Five*, watching *T.L.S. Eire* grow large through the wide-angle periscope. She was strangely nervous, even frightened. Her idle hands sought, needed, employment. She was a space pilot, and she was in space, in a Legion corvette making a mothership approach.

No, she was freight. She stowed the periscope and closed her eyes.

In due time berthing grapples seated with a reverberant magnetic *thunk*. She opened her eyes to the sounds of a corvette being secured to its moorings. She jettisoned her tethers. The absence of gravity embraced her like an old friend. She pushed gently toward the hatch, which slid aside. The corvette's pilot, Commander Petri Castro, stuck her docking hood through the opening.

"Ready, Buccari?" Castro asked brusquely. Once, long before, they had been in the same corvette group. "Admiral's waiting. Let's move."

"Right behind you, Commander," Buccari replied, pulling herself headfirst through the hatch, straight down through the lateral passage, and across the mess decks. The crew, in docking hoods, floated in adjoining hatches, waiting, silently watching her pass. She and Castro cycled through the corvette's EPL lock. Its pressure seal diodes glowing green, the lock opened. The mothership's brilliantly illuminated hangerbays yawned beyond, a hive of shadowless activity.

Floating along the docking ports, past towering slab-sided corvettes, she heard the ship's bell ringing an arrival. Hers? No, she did not rate quarterdeck honors. Whose, then? She cycled through the hangerbay air lock and entered the mothership's transition environment just as a boatswain's pipe pierced the thin air. Castro drifted to the bulkhead and halted forward motion, assuming a loose position of attention. Buccari returned the corvette skipper's uncomfortable smile and approached the polished brass and aluminum threshold of the mothership's quarterdeck.

Floating beyond the deck officer, a meter off the deck, was the distinctive, squat form of Captain Merriwether, black command star and rank insignia contrasting starkly with her matte-gray underway suit. Another officer, taller than Merriwether but just as buxom, stood at the mothership captain's side. That officer was dressed in the creased, Lincoln-green livery of the fleet science arm and bore the name tag QUINN, CMDR TLF. *Commander* Quinn. So Cassy Quinn had also reaped a promotion, much deserved. Behind the officers floated a tall civilian dressed in drab khaki. All wore helmets, regulation uniform this near the cycling hangerbay locks.

"Genellan arriving," the boatswain of the watch announced over the general address. A detachment of marines, slapping weapons in unison, cracked to attention. Her neck grew hot. A strange mixture of silliness and pride suffused her emotions.

Buccari pushed gently from a traction groove and moved ahead, saluting the colors and the watch officer. She used a deck baffle to kill her forward momentum and came to attention. She started to salute, but something about the tall civilian behind Merriwether demanded her attention. Something about his face—the complexion, a virulent shade of pink even through the tinted visor of his helmet—was warmly familiar.

The sky-blue eyes. Hudson! It was Nash Hudson.

Tears came, and cheek-stretching smiles.

Buccari threw Merriwether a cursory salute. Pressure equalization lights went green, and the air lock Klaxon sounded. She ripped off her helmet, her mesh-netted hair flouncing loose. Hudson removed his helmet, but more slowly. It came off to reveal a face livid and tortured, a head shiny and misshapen with hideous scar tissue, with no lips but with an encompassing grin—forever boyish. And the brilliant blue eyes. Buccari slammed her body into the much taller man, embracing him with unbridled joy. Her momentum carried both of them through the armor locks and into the mothership's primary environment. Merriwether, handing her helmet to a watchstander, followed stoically.

The corporal of the guard shouted, "At ease!" and the marines stomped in their tethers, weapon butts slamming metal. Environmental locks sucked closed behind them. A crowd of ship service ratings garbed in purple or green hangerbay suits clustered along the passageway. Buccari barely noticed the subdued cheers.

"Nash!" she finally said, holding her cheek to Hudson's chest, listening to his thundering heart. "If I'd known, I'd have been up here a week ago. Welcome home! How are you?"

"It feels good, Sharl." Hudson laughed. "To be alive, to see you. You look—and you sure feel—mighty good."

She stared up at her friend. Her helmet, attached by a lanyard, floated between them. She pulled it in and hooked it to her harness.

"Hmm, I'm feeling neglected," Merriwether grunted.

Quinn was laughing and crying at the same time.

Buccari pushed back, smiling in Merriwether's direction but keeping her gaze fixed on her old copilot. The scar tissue that was Hudson's face was uniformly slick and without wrinkles, his nose a thinly coated lump of cartilage. His tears bubbled into the air, silvery little globules. She swatted them away and pulled the ghastly countenance to her, fervently kissing the gash that served as a mouth.

Hudson came up for air, his tortured tissues blushing crimson.

"Pretty bad, eh?" the young man said, looking down at the deck.

"They'll make you gorgeous again, Nash," she said, unable to let go of his hand. "Give them time. The grafts take time."

"Yeah," he said, looking up and smiling. "I go back in two years for another patch job. They're cloning my skin because I had none left to graft. It was terrible. I was unconscious for three months. They say it's a miracle I can see."

"You're beautiful, you dumb brown-bar," she said, hitting his shoulder. The coated metal of the prosthetic device resonated like a sour chord. She jerked her hand as if it had touched fire.

Hudson laughed, his scarred face bunching grotesquely.

"My left side's like a museum dinosaur—nothing but

composite rods and bone alloy. And I'm a civilian now. No longer fit for—"

"Oh, Nash," she cried, her face wet with their mingled tears.

"Hey, hey," he said. "You know, I'd forgotten your scar. The pictures don't show it. If they can fix this mug, they can fix yours."

She felt the familiar terrain of her cheek, the thick welt running from cheek to temple, and shivered at the memories of the dragon attack and the pain. But then she remembered MacArthur's strong arms, and the memory provided sad warmth.

Merriwether cleared her throat, making a sound like a collision alarm. That was when Buccari noticed Quinn's transformation back to a spacer. The science officer was again completely hairless, returned to the discipline of twice-daily depilatories and skin scrubs. Quinn's white skull shone like a beacon, contrasting with the stubborn vestiges of a deep tan.

"Congratulations, Commander," Buccari said, thrusting out a hand.

"Thanks, Sharl," Quinn replied, her white pate flushing.

"Now I'm really feeling neglected," Merriwether growled. Buccari turned. The senior officer, eyes moist, moved uncertainly.

"You don't know how glad I am to see you, too, Captain." Buccari laughed, pushing the officer's arm aside and embracing her. Buccari was surprised at the vigor of Merriwether's response.

"Hrrumph!" Merriwether growled, finally pulling away. "Admiral's waiting." The mothership captain sailed ahead. Quinn followed.

"How does null grav feel?" Quinn whispered over her shoulder. "I chunked chow like a dirt monkey for two days."

"So far, so good," Buccari said, looking up at Hudson. She remembered something he had said.

"Pictures, Nash? What pictures?" she asked.

"Your picture's everywhere on Earth, Sharl," Hudson said, shaking his head. "Newsmags, vids. You're on posters everywhere. Even in churches. Everywhere. You're an icon."

"Wha— Why?" she asked.

"Finding the Garden of Eden's a big deal," he answered. "The Legion has used you to get more exploration funding. The media, government and commercial, won't let it go. For most people you've become a symbol of hope, practically a saint. And for some . . . evil incarnate."

"Why evil?"

"Rumor's out you're trying to restrict emigration."

They floated into an up-bore and latched on to slow-speed tractor lugs. Merriwether and Quinn opened the distance. Buccari and Hudson pushed off, diving straight up the bore.

"What are you saying?" she asked, grabbing Hudson's jumpsuit.

"It keeps getting worse on Earth, the riots," Hudson began. "But tell me about what happened here, Sharl," he pleaded.

"Oh, so much," she replied. "What do you know?"

"I know you're a mother," Hudson said. "Gee, I can't wait to see your baby. I've read the reports, but I . . . they don't tell the whole story. Commander Quinn said Longo burned the settlement down."

"Down to the stones, but it's all built back—"

Hudson grabbed a braking bungee. Buccari let go of Hudson and latched back on to a tractor lug. They neared Level Two, the end of the tractor line. Merriwether and Quinn exited the bore. Buccari followed Hudson through the exit port and kicked off the overhead, jackknifing down to the main bridge hatch at Level Two. Merriwether stayed high, floating up to the Level One entry. Security robots silently analyzed everything within their line of sight. Buccari felt a wave of null-grav nausea. She swallowed and settled her breathing. It passed.

"Wait here," Merriwether said. The hatch to the admiral's underway cabin hissed open, and *Eire*'s captain disappeared.

"Sorry about Mac, Sharl," Hudson said softly. "Wish I could have been there. I feel . . ."

"Yeah, Nash, I know," she whispered.

The hatch hissed. Four mothership captains, faces grim, descended from the admiral's cabin. Out of disciplinary reflex Buccari latched on to a bulkhead, giving the ship commanders room. They looked at her curiously but said nothing. Merriwether waved them up.

"Let's go," Quinn said, leaping to the Level One mezzanine.

Buccari followed. As she rounded the polished hatch combing, she collided with a wide-shouldered officer carrying a tactical portfolio—Carmichael. His momentum would have caromed Buccari back through the hatch if Carmichael had not grabbed a handful of her underway suit. He pushed the tactical portfolio to Nestor Godonov and pulled Buccari into the flag briefing room.

"Meet you in the ready room, Commander," Godonov said, giving Buccari a nod as he dove for the lower level.

Admiral Runacres and Commodore Wells were waiting. A holographic display depicting Legion fleet dispositions covered a bulkhead.

"Carmichael, stop bullying the junior officers," Runacres announced. The bags under his watery blue eyes were darker than Buccari remembered, his age more apparent. He was tired, but Buccari still withered under his piercing scrutiny.

"It's about the only way I can get the better of this one," Carmichael said, letting go of her underway suit. His gentle brown eyes flashed with unmistakable fondness.

"Thank you, Commander," Buccari replied.

"I'd forgotten," Runacres said. "Buccari broke Carmichael's tactical records. In this cabin are the two best pilots in the fleet."

"Ah, that would be you and who else, Admiral?" Wells deadpanned.

"Commander Carmichael took out six konish interceptors," Buccari said, cutting the laughter. "He's the ace of the fleet."

"There were other aces," Carmichael said quietly. "They just didn't make it back—Bert Higa, Denny Mitchell." He cleared his throat. "I heard you and Jack Quinn took out three before—"

"Before I marooned them," Runacres said, finishing the sentence.

"Only two," Buccari replied soberly. "Third one blew itself up."

"I'd like to hear the story," Carmichael sighed, "but I, uh . . ."

"Corvette bay in thirty minutes, Jake," Commodore Wells ordered.

"See you in two months, Commander," Runacres said grimly.

"Aye, aye, Admiral," Carmichael replied, giving Buccari a lingering look. He pushed through the hatch and was gone.

"My task group has established a link, Admiral," Wells reported. "All new grid references are established."

"Ketchie's resupply group is overdue," Runacres announced in response to Buccari's inquisitive expression. "Commodore

Wells is taking a cell to Oldfather to investigate. A precaution."

"Oh," she said. "Captain Ketchie was my first squadron commander."

"He's just running late," Wells remarked. "Probably had a material casualty. In all likelihood we'll cross in hyperspace."

"Pray let us hope so," Runacres muttered. He turned to Buccari and stared for several long, silent seconds. His gaze took in her hair, her thick eyebrows and long lashes. He looked into her soul. He knew.

"Lieutenant Commander Buccari, are you ready to take a command?"

"No, sir," she said, fighting brittle emotions.

Runacres's jaw tightened, but he said nothing.

"I . . . ah, have to . . ." she stuttered. "I can't leave my son. And I have to help establish the settlements. I feel responsible for—"

"Of course, your son," Runacres barked. "Very important to a mother. Probably something I can't comprehend. And no doubt this planet is a safe place to raise children, what with dragons, nightmares, and giant eagles. And of course the Killers of Shaula are still out there, somewhere in the galaxy, attacking our settlements. But they'll never attack Genellan. Your baby will be safe—"

"Admiral," Merriwether almost shouted. "Shouldn't we discuss fleet bunkering requirements and our negotiation position? Lieuten—er . . . Sharl will be a key player. She can help the fleet immensely."

"Ah, yes." Runacres smiled acerbically. "You haven't met the Legion envoy yet, have you? Yes, you're going to relish your new profession. Much more exciting than driving big iron."

"Admiral!" Merriwether persisted. "The negotiations. What—"

"I deal with professionals, Captain Merriwether," Runacres snorted. "This planet will be managed by a fleet administrator. Commander Quinn will be my representative. She's far more qualified to manage a planet. Mother Buccari will be too busy changing diapers."

"Dammit, Admiral," Merriwether barked, "leave her alone."

Runacres fixed his flagship captain with a murderous glare. Merriwether returned it in kind. Runacres slowly broke eye contact and returned his stare to Buccari.

"I'll not give up on you," Runacres growled. "You're a pilot. The fleet needs you; you need the fleet. When you come back, we'll start over. Go take care of that precious child . . . and your precious planet. You don't realize it yet, but they'll both grow up with or without you. I've got a fleet to command, and some of my ships may be in trouble."

"Is there—" Buccari started to say.

"Civilians aren't allowed on this bridge," Runacres snapped. "Commander Quinn, escort these . . . settlers out of here."

Buccari exhaled and shut her eyes.

"Aye, aye, Admiral," Quinn replied. "Envoy Stark is waiting."

Merriwether, her temper hot, trailed Wells and Runacres through the cabin hatch and onto the flag bridge. Captain Wooden had the watch.

"What did she say, Admiral?" the group leader asked.

"No," Runacres reported.

"Just as well," Wooden said.

"You sound pleased," Merriwether snapped.

"She's been off the pace, Captain," Wooden said firmly. "These 'vettes have been heavily modified. And how would we fit such a low-time pilot into the command list? She's a tough fit."

"You obviously don't know this officer," Merriwether retorted.

"Moot point. It appears we've lost her," Wells said.

"I don't think so." Runacres sighed. "Give her a little more time. Now, Franklin, get out of here and go find Ketchie."

"Aye, Admiral," Wells responded, grabbing his battle armor bag.

"And Captain Merriwether . . ."

"Yes, Admiral," Merriwether grumbled.

"Yours was a superb performance, Sarah."

"With all due respect, Admiral, you can be a real butt."

TEN

ENVOY STARK

Cassy Quinn disappeared into the down-bore. Buccari's emotions were in turmoil, but her relief at having announced her decision was dominant. She pushed off and arrowed for the transport hatch, passing Hudson. Hudson slapped her boot. A game—flying in null gravity. She had taken it for granted. What a rush it was to fly, something she had never thought she would miss. Hudson caught up with her.

Buccari followed Quinn out of the bore on Level Five. The science officer bounced off a thrust bumper shielding a damage control station and pushed down a radial corridor. All levels had color schemes to provide spatial orientation. Command Level Five, the communications and intelligence centers on all Island-class motherships, was known as the Pink Palace because of the anemic rosy tones of the decks and bulkheads. The logical overhead on all decks was flat gray and festooned with conduits and access panels.

"Cass, what did the admiral mean?" Buccari asked. "His reference to the envoy, I mean."

"I'll refrain from comment," Quinn said, waffling. "I'm working with the envoy in an official capacity."

"He's a dick," Hudson offered.

"Oh," Buccari said.

"Now, Nash," Quinn admonished. "Nash and I worked with the envoy's staff, translating diplomatic traffic. Nash's command of the northern dialect is amazing." Quinn was changing the subject.

"It should be. He lived with the kones," Buccari said. "Made everyone jealous, living in a dome while we all froze."

"I practiced while I was in the hospital," Hudson said. "Intel guys brought me a million hours of intercepts. It kept my edge sharp. Still have a lot to learn. It's a complex language."

"You should be extremely valuable to the envoy, Nash," Buccari said. "Stark's whole mission depends on communications."

"He was desperate for my services at first," Hudson said, "but now he's got the language in the can and a team of linguists. And Commander Quinn is quite good, too. Stark prefers working with her."

"Nash is an excellent teacher," Quinn said.

"Why have they restricted me from the comm room?" Hudson asked.

"Your attitude, maybe?" Quinn laughed.

"They don't want anyone to know what they're doing. Sharl, they—"

Two impassive black-suited men wearing red berets floated from a crossing hatch, then separated, moving to each side.

"Mr. Dee. Mr. Dum," Hudson said too cheerfully.

"Mr. Hudson," said the uglier of the two, his lips not moving. Both agents floated in position.

Buccari followed Quinn down the passageway. The science officer stopped at a security hatch and said her name. The door slid aside, revealing narrow quarters filled with banks of electronics and bustling spacer technicians. Several civilians were working together. A heavy-set, dusky female untethered and floated to intercept Quinn.

"Commander Quinn," the woman said. She studiously ignored Hudson. "This must be Lieutenant Commander Buccari."

"Sharl, please," Buccari said, putting out her hand.

"Thank you. Art Mather," the assistant replied, clasping Buccari's hand with a perfunctory grip. "Principal assistant to the envoy."

"My pleasure," Buccari replied.

"Art is short for Artemis," Mather added dryly. "Envoy Stark is in the diplomatic center. We've been receiving a steady flow of communiqués. This is really quite an exciting time for us."

The thrumming of air scrubbers was the only sound.

"Perhaps we should come back," Quinn finally said.

"Oh, no," Mather protested. "The envoy will—"

An interior hatch hissed open. An LSA colonel of middle height and vaguely Asian extraction eased over the combing. Deep-set eyes the color of oily leather clinically examined

Buccari. The security agent nodded and slipped smoothly from sight, floating through a lateral hatch.

A minute later Stark appeared, his skull glistening like white ice, his long face igniting with a broad smile. His tea-brown eyes looked old and tired, but his skin was unwrinkled, his neck and jowls as tight as any teenager's. His large ears, lobes and rills studded with precious stones, had been fashionably flattened to his skull. He wore a scarlet ascot.

A senior science officer, the silver insignia of captain's rank on his dark-green jumpsuit, followed Stark into the tight space. His physique, politely termed, was a construct of flat ovals; jowls wiggled in null grav under his flattened head like turkey wattles. Cassy Quinn stiffened noticeably.

"Ah, Commander Quinn . . . Hudson," Stark said, nodding to each. "And the famous Sharl Buccari, the avatar of all new worlds. I am honored. I feel as if I already know you. May I call you Sharl?" His diction and projection were those of a polished orator, his manner avuncular and disarming. Buccari was overwhelmed. She nodded.

"May I introduce Captain Gray, Admiral Runacres's chief scientist," Stark continued. "Captain Gray and I are old friends."

"A pleasure," Gray responded, his voice pitched high. Polite handshakes were exchanged.

"Please accept my congratulations," Stark continued.

"Congratulations?" Buccari asked.

"On your decision to forgo a fleet career in favor of helping to govern the Legion's newest colony. I look forward to—"

"But—but I only just told Admiral Runacres," she gasped.

"Good news travels fast," Stark said, smiling cryptically, "and your decision has been the subject of much conjecture. Even governments on Kon have asked about your decision. Of course we have told them nothing, but they will find out, and sooner than we could imagine. Such are the ways of diplomacy."

"So much for secrets," she said.

"Ah, the difference between event and knowledge," Stark mused. "We usually know when things happen, but we rarely understand why. Your decision was a well-observed event. It happened. Do not dwell on it. Knowledge, on the other hand, is precious. The knowledge of hyperdrives and gravitronic transmission will buy us a planet, a haven for the beleaguered of Earth. That is the knowledge that must be protected."

Hudson, floating at Quinn's shoulder, muttered something. Captain Gray, Mather, and Quinn gave him a collective disparaging glance.

"Of course," Buccari replied, noting the interplay.

"And your baby boy," Stark said, tilting his large head. "How is he? I am quite anxious to see your son and all the new children of Genellan, the first human natives. I'm told the Hegemony has declared them citizens."

"Yes," she said. "King Ollant has—"

"Ah, yes, King Ollant," Stark gushed. "A miracle! You saving the life of that most powerful kone. What providence. What amazing good luck. We have received several communiqués from his prime minister—Et Kalass—in quite excellent Legion. He has been so gracious as to provide a translation program. One of their linguists is superbly talented. Did you know all konish linguists are females? Oh, but of course you did."

"Kateos, Sharl," Hudson said. "Her conversion programs are doing much of the work. I talked with her this morning. Dowornobb asked—"

"I cannot wait to hear of your adventures," Stark said, stepping in, "but I know you must be quite fatigued. And we are being overwhelmed with communiqués. It is my duty to respond personally. I would consider it an honor if you were to join me in the admiral's mess this evening. Eighteen hundred hours. We can discuss our negotiation strategy, yes?"

"It was a pleasure," Mather said, moving to open the hatch. Captain Gray remained silent. They were being dismissed.

"I am honored to be working with you," Stark said as they moved through the hatch. "Your knowledge of the planet and your influence will greatly empower our negotiations. Welcome to the team."

They were in the passageway. The LSA agents were no longer in sight.

"Phony as space steak," Hudson snorted.

"That's enough, Nash," Quinn snapped. "It's his job. He has to pull a lot of people together. Try walking in his shoes. Just because you're a civilian now doesn't mean you have to be rude. And you'd best be careful, young man. Stark, er . . . Envoy Stark is going to have a great deal of power on Genellan."

"Not as much as Sharl," Hudson retorted petulantly.

Buccari turned, rising upward. She stared at her friend.

"Power's not what I want, Nash," she said. "Cassy's right. Let's let circumstances play out before we jump to any conclusions. Give the envoy a chance and cool your jets, brown-bar."

"Power's all he understands, Sharl," Hudson persisted. "Just—"

"Can it, Nash," she said softly. "Who was the spook?"

"Colonel Pak," Hudson replied.

"Agency liaison," Quinn answered. "Reports to Stark. Quiet man."

"Mr. Inscrutable," Hudson added. "Crawls under rocks—"

"Nash!" Buccari barked.

Hudson smiled broadly. "This is great, Sharl. You chewing my tail—just like old times. Damn, it's good to see you." He grabbed her hand.

"Let's move," Quinn said with a laugh. "I've got orders to take you to see someone, but we don't have much time."

Buccari and Hudson followed Quinn's retreating form. The science officer dropped three levels and came through the Level Nine internal air lock. Command Level Nine was group operations. Quinn proceeded expeditiously along the main radial. Interspersed at consistent lengths down the midnight-blue passageway were crew alert tubes. Across from the crew tubes were hatches leading to ready rooms. The entry alcoves bore unit history plaques and listings of past and present commanding officers. They were also emblazoned with unabashedly brutal insignia. Buccari stopped to read the plaque designating Eagle Squadron, *T.L.S. Eire*'s corvette unit. It identified Commander Joyman K. Carmichael as squadron commanding officer.

"Hey, Booch!" a voice from her past shouted. "You too good for us?"

She twisted in place, legs flailing to catch up with her upper body. Two flight-suited corvette officers bore down on her.

"Pulaski, you sack of—" she shouted, but realized that in the impending collision she was at a severe mass disadvantage. She hooked her boot on a thrust plate and prepared for ram. Lieutenant Commander Igor Pulaski's beer-barrel body, unnecessarily reinforced by the lanky form of Lieutenant Commander Bartlett Chang, slammed into her and carried her along until they collectively glanced against a bulkhead. Chang prevented a ricochet by grabbing hold and hanging on to Pulaski, who in turn held on to Buccari. Her old mates reeled her in and commenced an enthusiastic group grope.

"Too important, eh?" Pulaski chided, cherubic features laboring to appear stern. "Hanging around with admirals and cockroach kings."

"Thanks for bringing her by, Commander," Chang boomed, black eyes dancing. "Look at her! Eyebrows and hair like mud-crud! And what a tan!"

"And one serious scar!" Pulaski said, grabbing her chin.

She twisted away, covering her face, not knowing whether to laugh or cry and doing both. She realized how much she had not thought through.

"Aw, Sharl," Chang whispered, his sad-handsome face assuming a tragic countenance. "Ski didn't mean to . . . they can fix it."

"Aw, hell," she said, wiping her eyes and looking up. She put her arms around both men. "Damn, I missed you assholes."

"So what's the scoop, Booch?" Pulaski asked, his voice softening but losing no energy. "When you coming back? To the team? We'll scarf and barf like the old days. The old team. Beer and popcorn forever."

"Oh, Ski . . . don't ever change," she said, laughing with delight.

"Ski's hard as a rock and twice as smart." Chang chortled.

"Serious popcorn!" Pulaski grinned. "Serious suds! We'll get crazy. Damn, it's good to see your sorry ass. The team is back together."

I just joined another team, she thought.

"Gosh, Ski." She punched him softly. "Maybe—"

"Pulaski! Get your butt gone," came a shout. Buccari turned to see Carmichael coming through the ready-room hatch, filling its dimensions in both breadth and height. Nestor Godonov was at his heels.

"On my way, Skip," Pulaski said, blowing her a blubbery kiss.

"Chang, you're so hell-bent on following Pulaski, you might as well get fat and have a lobotomy. Now move! We got a job to do."

"Aye, Skipper," Chang said, also pulling away. Both men shot her a wink, yanked on their docking hoods, and dove for the nearest crew chute. Carmichael waved for Godonov to go ahead.

"So you're off to Oldfather?" she asked.

"Not all of us," Carmichael replied. "I tagged Pulaski for

downloader assignment on *San Francisco*, so Igor's missing out, too."

"He must be . . . disappointed," she said.

Carmichael just stared. She averted her eyes.

"I should go," he said, his voice almost a whisper. "I'm cross-decking to *Britannia*—and chopping a section of Eagles. Reinforcements, ah . . . just in case."

"Just in case," she repeated, praying silently.

"So, you're turning me down?"

"I'd never turn you down, Commander," she replied. "It'd be an honor to be in your squadron. It's just . . . I have a bigger job."

"I'm disappointed, Sharl. We need—"

The ready-room hatch hissed open, and a gaggle of curious corvette pilots floated through, all wanting to see the legendary Sharl Buccari. The faces were unfamiliar and startlingly young.

"Let's talk when I get back," Carmichael continued, pulling up his docking hood. As he started to push through the crew chute, he turned and said, "Keep your options open . . . Booch."

And he was gone.

ELEVEN

CONNECTIONS

A general quarters Klaxon exploded into life, dispatching Buccari's confused thoughts. Annunciators on the bulkheads flashed advisories. Hatches hissed shut and sealed with sober permanence. Tight-jawed personnel, dragging equipment on lanyards, flew past.

"Another drill!" Hudson shouted.

"Admiral's keeping his guard up," Quinn said, pushing off toward the transport bores. "I've got to make muster. Sharl, you can stay in my cabin. It's in Quadrant Four. Call me at flag science when you get there."

"We better hustle," Buccari said, suppressing her old conditioning. She quelled an aching urge to jump down a crew chute, to leap to an assigned GQ station, to a corvette.

Instead, she followed Quinn and Hudson amid a growing throng of crew members to the nearest up-bore, which was already flowing with human current. They plunged, jostling others and being jostled. Hudson and Buccari channeled into a queue at Level Six.

Levels Six and Seven, colored flat gray, formed the mothership's structural keel. Middeck was mass center control. Pierced by transport bores and trim sensors, the MCC hub surrounded the mothership's constantly oscillating center of mass. Within the MCC's confines technicians monitored finite element processors and laser alignment tools dedicated to tracking critical mothership stability parameters.

Buccari and Hudson streaked past ponderous thrust joints and bearing housings. Positioned at cardinal points around the MCC hub were habitation-ring transfer stations. Buccari and Hudson eased into Transfer Station Two. A steady stream of personnel moved inbound from the H-ring, clearing hub air locks in a controlled frenzy. Staging locks sealed in sequence before and behind them, metering the flow to the breech docks. Buccari and Hudson lined up for Quadrant Four.

The final lock opened. Buccari, Hudson, and ten other crew members rattled into the car. Buccari reoriented her body, placing her boots in quick disconnects on the outboard bulkhead. A soft triple tone sounded. The door curved shut, the air lock cycled, and the car settled against its pneumatic load.

They were falling, their hub car ejected outward through one of the H-ring's eight radial spokes. The surface that had been a wall in null grav became a rapidly descending floor. The car decelerated with a maglev vibration. Air locks cycled. The car door hissed open. There was a floor beneath her feet, pulling at her with one-half gee. Her helmet and equipment harness had mass, and her spine acknowledged the load. They stepped from the car, funneling through environmental locks and into H-ring Quadrant Four's transport station.

"Sharl," Hudson said, "something isn't right."

"What?" she asked, looking at him. With the floor reference established, she was reminded how tall he was.

"Stark's communications with the kones. Something's wrong. He's playing some kind of game."

She led Hudson through pressure turnstiles. Armored sheathing in the H-ring's arching ceiling slid slowly across ports, shutting out views of the sedately pirouetting bridge and of the stars.

"Stark doesn't like your warped sense of humor," she said with a laugh. She turned right, clockwise—forward in H-ring convention—and walked to the lifts and ladder wells. She hugged a radial pole and slid to Echo Ring, the "lowest" of five decks in the habitation ring. Hudson followed. She touched lightly and stepped through an armored hatch into a thwart-ship damage control station with its emergency facilities and myriad high-pressure fluid risers and valves.

"Communication traffic is extremely high," Hudson protested. "And none of Stark's linguists are good enough to handle the subtleties."

"Maybe they have it under control," she said, querying a bulkhead locator screen. Echo Deck, narrowed by the geometry of the habitation toroid, had only two parallel ring passageways. She chose the starboard passageway and walked into officers' country.

"Bull, they have to work around the clock. Something's not right. Stark needs my help. Even Quinn will tell you that. My attitude went south after Mather threw me out for no apparent reason."

"Must be the nature of diplomacy," she replied in a low voice, mocking Stark's words. She stopped and checked a stateroom registry. "Stark knows your feelings toward King Ollant and your relationship to me. He's probably waiting to see how we fit into his plans. Remember, it's his negotiation."

"I'm not sure I fit," Hudson said. "He doesn't like my act."

"Nash, you're my right hand," she said, arriving at Quinn's stateroom. "Whatever team I'm on you're on. Now, get out of here. We can't do anything while the ship's buttoned down, so I'm taking a nap. Meet you in the wardroom at 1800."

Planet Kon grew small on the main holo-vid. The Hegemonic ship captain acknowledged Planetary Defense interrogations with the requested transponder codes. PDF controllers cleared his ship. The ship captain notified the nearest Hegemonic orbiting station that he was commencing boost phase for Genellan insertion.

The Northern Hegemony maintained six orbiting stations. Those facilities were used for a multitude of purposes, including intersystem boost operations. All six of the king's orbiting stations were heavily armed, and all were used for surveillance both of the planet Kon and of the stars.

A larger constellation also orbited the amber atmosphere of Kon. Planetary Defense operated twenty defense platforms, including shipyards and interceptor stations. An additional four PDF interceptor bases orbited Kon's two largest moons, Kreta and Goho. Countless autonomous sensor arrays, some longer than the diameter of a moon, patrolled the nether reaches of the star system.

Marbled Kreta, the largest of Kon's moons, dominated the Hegemonic captain's viewscreens. His ship passed close above the brilliant body, exploiting the satellite's gravity well to secure a whipping acceleration on course. Also whirling about the moon and clearly visible was the Ransan mining collective's processing facility, an enormous complex that included a shipyard and a fuel-processing plant. Confirmed intelligence indicated that extraordinary efforts were under way, with no less than a dozen major-mass hulls in various states of construction. The ship captain directed his sensors to intensively if passively scan the facility.

The Hegemonic ship, a fat sausage with waist-segment spin set for one-half standard konish gravity to accommodate the king's ambassador, streaked outbound. An Imperial-class cruiser, ancient and past obsolescence, the ship had been heavily overhauled for its new mission. Half the complement had been left behind. Weapons and ordnance capabilities had been stripped in favor of scientific equipment.

A cabin located at max centripetal had been restructured for the ambassador and her mate. It was compact by any objective standard. Kateos awoke to the interminable surging of the circulation system. She was determined that she had had enough sleep; apparently no amount of rest was going to make the gas headaches go away.

As she rolled from the pallet, pungent vapors squeezed from her bladders, bubbling noisily free. Leaving her tiny cabin, she moved inboard and forward, leaving the zone of induced gravity. She reached the cruiser's science center, an overhauled operations area.

"Marvelous!" Mirrtis declared as Kateos floated into the room. Dowornobb flailed through the confined space like a rubbery, spastic rhinoceros. Mirrtis and H'Aare pulled the scientist down to the data terminal, all three kones outgassing with excitement. Dowornobb latched on and displaced Mirrtis from the operator's station, his attention fixated on the terminal, eye tufts splayed and turgid with excitement. Scientist Mirrtis was the first to take note of her arrival.

"Ambassador, some of the human ships have jumped!" the physicist blurted. "PDF arrays have captured gravimetric field distortions."

"Interesting," Dowornobb replied, scanning data from the Planetary Defense surveillance network. "Knowing when and where to look . . ."

"The human ships have jumped?" Kateos said. "To what purpose?"

"Ah, His Majesty's ambassador!" Dowornobb answered, brightening at the sight of his mate. "Only four. Why? We do not know. Are your headaches improved, my mate?"

"The gas is winning." She smiled weakly.

"There is too much here," Dowornobb said, turning back to his console. "So much remains unexplained. It will take many HLA arrivals and departures for us to solve this mystery."

"Will this journey ever end?" Kateos sighed.

"It has only just begun, Ambassador," said a voice. She turned to see the ship's captain standing respectfully at the open hatch.

"What is it?" she asked, endeavoring to sound assertive.

"There is another ship, perhaps several ships, joining us in the Genellan insertion, Ambassador," the captain reported. "Roughly ten days behind but closing."

Kateos leaned over and released an accumulation of gas.

"Planetary Defense?" Dowornobb asked, wrinkling his splayed nose.

"It is not transponding a PDF sequence," the ship captain reported. "We thought at first it was a Ransa ore loader cutting loose for Goho, but no, it follows us. We have signaled for PDF intercept."

"Gravity, our adventure grows more exciting!" Dowornobb chuckled, laboring at his computer console. Kateos said nothing. She was deep in thought. The captain quietly departed.

"Tar Fell," Kateos rumbled.

"Pardon," Dowornobb said, not looking up from his work.

"The Thullolians," she said. "They come to claim Genellan

extraterritoriality. Quite prematurely, but certainly a daring gambit."

"Your deductions take a fanciful leap, my mate," Dowornobb said good-naturedly. "The king made you ambassador, not royal seer."

"Not as unscientific as it may sound, my mate," Kateos replied. "I have access to information that would make even you blush."

"I dare you to make me blush, Ambassador Kateos." Dowornobb laughed, reaching over to squeeze his mate's thick neck.

"Excuse me, Ambassador," the captain said at the hatch.

"Yes," she replied, holding on to Dowornobb's hand.

"We have received an identification signal. The ship is declaring itself to be on an ambassadorial mission."

"What nation?" Kateos asked.

"Thullol-Ransa Compact, Ambassador. Should I request PDF intercept?"

"No," she said. "Send the king's greeting."

Fenstermacher, lugging a string of fish that hung to the ground, followed the path along the spring. The gay watercourse bounced and glistened over wildflower-shaded rocks. On the brook's left bank, under a broad-leafed sugar tree, were the simple graves. Beyond the stone markers was the forest through which ran the trail to Longo's Meadow and to the ferry landing beyond. On the right side of the brook, from the cove to the palisade, vegetable shoots poked through loamy soil. Two cliff dwellers—gardeners—tended the plants. Fenstermacher whistled, and the guilders acknowledged him with cheerful shrieks.

Marines stood before the sally gate next to the portcullis through which the settlement's spring exited the palisade's west wall. Fenstermacher answered their friendly hail and strutted through, inhaling the odor of freshly hewn lumber. He walked between the barracks housing Legion personnel and the nearly finished settlers' barracks, both two-story wooden structures. Across the common, below the rocky, flower-shrouded springhead, was the lodge atop its tall foundation of yellow stone. All the structures supported high-peaked roofs designed to shed heavy snow. Next to the lodge were the grain silo and the kilns. Beyond the lodge were four family cabins, all built of the same yellow, quartz-veined granite. The cabins displayed cliff dweller signatures: white marble lintels and stone planters filled with flowers.

Uphill, in the palisade's southeastern corner, were the stables and the horse barn. At the apex of the northeastern and southeastern walls, at the highest elevation inside the palisade and dominating its profile, was the new water tower, Fenstermacher's latest engineering feat. He stared at it with unchecked pride.

A work party of marines was sinking poles and stringing transmission cable from the generator shed. A cliff dweller observed their every move, making notations with a stylus.

"If you dropped a marine and a sack of shit," Fenstermacher machine-gunned as he trooped by, "which one would hit the ground first? Duh, how do ya tell the difference? Hey, grunts, which one of them wooden poles is yer officer? Hey, jar-brain, yer using the shovel bass ackward. Hey, Corporal, what's green and crawls under rocks?"

He accelerated his pace and employed his string of fish as a shield. Clods of dirt zipped around him like dark angry missiles. His path across the common was resplendent with scarlet and yellow blossoms. Leslie Lee, raven hair shining in the sun, sat on the bottom step of the lodge porch, watching the children play in the trampled grass. She held a carbine in her lap and constantly swept the skies with alert eyes.

Fenstermacher marched up and pushed out his lips for a kiss.

"Oh, Winnie, you smell like fish," Leslie said, pushing him away. "Take a shower and then maybe we can talk."

"I'm not interested in talk, my soft rounded, mounded little—"

"Take a shower!" Lee snarled, waving the carbine threateningly.

"As you command, succulent sweetness of my life." He gilled a fish to his lips and kissed it passionately.

"Oh, Winfried, no! Don't!" She burst out laughing. The kids squealed and pointed. "I'm yours," Lee gasped, blushing.

Fenstermacher gave her a lascivious wink and took the wooden steps up the tall porch with a cavalier bounce. It was a warm day. Both the heavy outer doors and the inner weather doors to the lodge were propped open, airing out the mildew and dampness accrued during the long winter. He thumped across the wooden floor into the cool, dark interior. The kitchen fires had not been stoked.

Pepper Goldberg and a fleet technician were installing more equipment. The lodge's auxiliary generator was running. Lizard Lips, head cocked to the side, stood squarely in the middle of the operation, engrossed with a multimeter. Fenstermacher started to say something, but Goldberg had a digital probe in her hands and a foul look on her face. He moved through the main room and into the galley.

Nancy Dawson and Toby Mendoza were preparing for the evening meal. Fenstermacher dropped his string of flopping, dark-backed fish on the galley's cutting table.

"I went to all the trouble of catching dinner," the wiry little man shouted. "Now who's going to clean these puppies?"

"Those are fish, you midget idiot," Dawson said with a yawn. "Puppies are what your mother spawned when she had you." The tall, big-boned redhead had no trouble pushing him out of the way with her hip.

"Yuk, yuk," Fenstermacher snorted. "Butt for brains made a joke."

"Watch it, Fensterdork," Dawson replied, brandishing a cleaver, "or I'll make Leslie a happy widow. Hey, these fish got mud clods all over them. How the hell they get so dirty?"

"Bottom feeders," Fenstermacher said, heading for the shower room.

Tar Fell peered through *Penc*'s aft station-keeping port. Positioning lasers sparked like blue novas from the flanks of the Ransan-built ships of the line. The battleships remained in an unvarying position, one on each quarter, a third looming in formation above, a fourth below, and a fifth directly behind his flagship, all tightly tucked in to frustrate PDF radars seeking to resolve their number.

The armada master let loose a metallic burp as he floated from the viewing port, one of many bubbles emanating from the orifices of his body. Even though he was a veteran PDF pilot, accustomed to null-gravity operations, space travel was anathema to Tar Fell's digestion.

Tar Fell floated through a series of armored locks and into the main longitudinal passageway. His huge body was girdled by a gravity harness. Once he was in the main bore of the ship, the induced gravitation field activated, providing the illusion of gravity by creating an attraction to an opposing field in the ship's deckwork.

Tar Fell disengaged his attraction field and glided easily along the ship's main bore until he came to the battleship's armored heart, the armada operations center. Security sensors tracked his approach, opening vaultlike hatches and flushing the environment in his stride. His staff dutifully acknowledged his entrance. On the primary holo-vid Flotilla Commander Krolk, on *Penc*'s bridge, was being briefed by Ship General Magoon, the ship's commander. His armada had too many generals and not enough crew, Tar Fell mused.

Armada! Six ships do not an armada make, he castigated himself. But then he scoffed at his own trepidation. Soon he would have seven times that number of major hulls, with complements of cruisers and interceptors adequate to the task. Power enough to defend the interests of the south. Power enough to influence the future. *Power.*

The aliens were the key to that power, and he needed to strike fast. The Hegemony must not be allowed to be the keepers of the technological keys. Tar Fell commanded the attention of the bridge.

"Armada Master," Magoon said, saluting the vid-image. "Our mission is acknowledged by the Hegemonic cruiser. Their ambassador sends Ollant's greetings, and PDF interceptors have been recalled."

"Excellent," Tar Fell replied.

"Mere gnats," Krolk growled. "Interceptors would have provided our gunners with much-needed target practice."

"From the firing drills," *Penc*'s commander said calmly, "it is apparent that both the energy weapons and the crews need much calibrating. No, we should avoid action from even such small game."

"Where is your nerve, General?" Krolk bandied.

"Come, come," Tar Fell interjected. "There is no sport here. I agree with General Magoon. Timing is everything." Tar Fell looked forward to the day when Krolk could be dispensed with. For now he needed the Ransan and his shipbuilding resources. He changed the subject. "Any intelligence on what awaits us at Genellan?"

"Other than the Hegemonic cruiser carrying the king's negotiator," Magoon rumbled, "there is nothing."

"The smallest of my battleships, even untrained and below complement, outguns Ollant's ancient cruisers," Krolk scoffed.

TWELVE

TEAMWORK

Feeling out of uniform in a civilian jumpsuit, Buccari walked into the wardroom's formal anterooms, the only compartments in a mothership where wood was permitted. Mahogany polished to a red-black sheen paneled the walls, and a breakfront of spartan simplicity and titanic dimensions housed the aging mothership's cruise trophies and unit citations.

A sitting room, incongruous with its neo-Victorian decor, sat off the entrance to the wardroom. On its walls hung oils of nautical motif. Neatly housed in overstuffed maroon leather chairs and sofas were utilitarian admin units. Elegant brass fixtures provided soft illumination. Officers dressed in immaculate underway suits looked up from their conversations. Buccari smiled nervously.

"Ready when you are, Captain," Hudson said, walking up behind her.

They entered the low-ceilinged wardroom. Table conversation silenced in a descending wave; all eyes turned. The admiral's steward pounced, escorting them up a marlinespike-bedecked companionway. Viewing port shields in the admiral's mess were drawn, revealing the slowly rotating, intricate cylinders of the operations core suspended above their heads. Providing backdrop was the star-shot blackness of space.

Merriwether, Quinn, Mather, and Stark stood behind their chairs, apparently waiting for the admiral. The table was covered with substantial linen, brilliantly white and heavily starched. Bone china and crystal stemware artfully displayed the seal of the Tellurian Legion Space Fleet.

"Ah, Sharl," Stark said effusively, "please sit beside me. And Hudson! We were not expecting you. I'm afraid we have no room."

"Mr. Hudson is my assistant in all emigration matters," Buccari said, trying to calm her intensity. "I insisted he come."

"Of course, of course," Stark said, bowing.

"Take the admiral's place, son," Merriwether offered with a chuckle, rotating her chair out to sit down. "He won't be joining us. Everyone please sit."

Stark's demeanor flashed sour.

The meal went rapidly. Even in the admiral's mess space food was space food: recycled proteins, predictable and nutritional but appealing only to the very hungry. Stark maintained a constant stream of engaging small talk. Buccari wondered how he found time to eat. As the stewards cleared the table, Stark lifted his hand.

"Ms. Mather, if you would," he directed.

Mather activated a switch, and a control panel was exposed in the table. Lights dimmed, and a painting lifted into the overhead; the bulkhead glowed into holographic life. Stark's assistant used a remote to bring up a presentation of graphs and statistics.

"Here is the Legion Assembly's plan for emigration from Earth," Mather lectured. "Logistics have been approved by the full council. Funds to build settlement freighters have been appropriated—"

"Excuse me," Buccari interrupted. "Envoy Stark, nothing's changed. We've rights to establish a settlement of no more than one thousand settlers and fleet personnel combined."

"Ah, but that's what we're to negotiate, is it not?" Stark puffed.

"You talk of freighters," Merriwether said. "What of more powerful combat units?"

"The wherewithal of the Legion can stretch only so far," Stark replied. "We're counting on the resources of Genellan to expand our horizons and our military capabilities, but first we must convert her resources into usable form. Genellan is the rawest of raw materials."

Counting on the resources of Genellan. Buccari sat back to ponder the future and did not like what she saw. Yet it was difficult to envision any alternatives. Large forces were operating.

"Sharl," Stark said, his stentorian voice assuming a patient tenor, "your opposition, er, let me say your reluctance to permit unchecked settlement is of high principle. I bring no surprises, no threats. I have nothing other than the entreaties of your fellow humans. These are difficult times on Earth—"

"On Earth times are always difficult," Hudson interrupted. "Races, nations, and religions, all breeding for superiority."

"Let the envoy speak," Buccari admonished.

"Ahem, of course," Stark said. "Difficult times. Famine is widespread; war is perpetual, genocide as common as summer storms."

"Politics as usual," Hudson sniped.

"Nash, back off!" Buccari snapped.

"But now there's hope," the envoy pressed, a gleam in his eye. "There is hope, and the hope is named Genellan, a hope for every man, woman, and child. This planet—"

"Surely," Merriwether interrupted, "you do not suggest that Genellan can promise a new life for everyone on Earth."

Reinforcements, Buccari thought.

"Of course not," Stark blurted. "But the symbolism—"

"Captain Merriwether has a point," Buccari interrupted. "The kones might take exception to . . . symbolism. We're here at their pleasure."

"Certainly," Stark replied with a flash of impatience.

"Mr. Stark," Buccari said, "tell us what you would have us do. We are, after all, on the same team."

"Yes, thank you. Where was I?" the envoy pondered.

"Stopping the emigration riots on Earth," Hudson offered.

"Yes, er . . . no." Stark stumbled. "I had not gotten that far."

'That's where you're going," Hudson added stiffly.

"Nash, please!" Buccari admonished.

Hudson turned in his chair. Quinn covered her mouth.

"We must state that we will accept everyone, eventually," the exasperated envoy said. "Without restrictions—to end the riots. Sharl, you must be our spokesman, for you are perceived by the masses as a savior."

"Accept everyone?" Buccari asked.

"Such a concession," Stark said sternly, "would have little effect. There are not enough HLA ships to make a difference. Genellan's population will be dominated by its own birthrate within two centuries. Arrivals will become, in relative terms, a meaningless dribble. Restricting immigration has no material effect other than to incite riots on Earth, killing millions of desperate people."

"If they weren't rioting over emigration," Hudson blurted, "they'd be rioting *and dying* over food or religion. Earth's an anthill that's been kicked. Genellan's an excuse for a multitude of greater sins. And that's the second thing wrong with your rationalization: it's a simple lie. You're telling people what they want to hear, not the truth."

"Nash! Dammit!" Buccari shouted, slamming the table.

The cabin was quiet. Buccari poured herself a cup of coffee. The silence in the room was burdensome. Mather cleared her throat.

"I'm sorry, Envoy Stark," Buccari continued. "We're obviously emotional about our new home. Every settler that lands is a seed that will inexorably sprout and sow more seeds."

"Of course, Commander, er . . . Sharl," Stark said, "but—"

"Allow me to finish," Buccari persisted. "Nash Hudson was harsh, but the fact remains, once an expectation is established, that expectation cannot be reversed. Who's to say the Legion will not invent a means to transport orders of magnitude more people?" She paused.

"Your point?" Stark prompted, jaw muscles grinding.

"Eventually all immigration to this planet will be shut down," Buccari said with steel in her voice. "All immigration. This planet will not be overwhelmed by a persistently breeding two-legged animal." She sat back in her chair.

"Quite idealistic," Stark said, dark eyes glowing. "Your argument begs the reality of human nature and is therefore quite at odds with my mission. But of course you are speaking in grand periods of time, which ultimately neither of us will be here to judge. Unfortunately, while you attempt to plan your species' future, I must do what I can for the living people of Earth, as must Admiral Runacres," Stark insinuated, "and his fleet."

"I see a larger solution, Mr. Stark," Buccari said. "The fleet must discover other planets, entire worlds that Earth may claim as her own."

"Ah, yes," Stark said, "planets of her own. A solution, but how realistic? It has taken us centuries to find Genellan. How soon before we discover another such haven?"

"That, Mr. Envoy, is a matter of effort and will," Buccari said. "We—that is, the fleet must have new and more powerful starships. There are great dangers out there. But there is also infinite opportunity."

"Small solace for Earth," Stark replied. "It does not overcome the reality of the riots."

"Reality has always been humanity's biggest challenge," Buccari countered.

"Yes, yes," Stark replied, conceding nothing. "Ah, but I

didn't have time to tell you earlier. We received a dispatch from Minister Et Kalass. He sends his regards. The king has granted permission to download settlers. Time and place 'at the envoy's convenience' was the minister's wording. Quite explicit."

"So be it," Buccari said, looking down at her plate.

"Then we're agreed." Stark smiled broadly. "Landings commence one standard week from today. I have authorized a schedule that—"

"The first habitation module goes to MacArthur's Valley," she said, rotating her chair and standing, "two weeks from today. No settlers will land until they have shelter. Minister Et Kalass will understand if I request a delay. I will radio him if you care to discuss the issue."

"Not necessary, my dear," Stark replied, turning on the brightest of smiles. "After all, we are on the same team."

"Right," Buccari said. "Captain Merriwether, if you'll excuse us, we'd best be getting back to the planet." She looked at Hudson. He winked.

"Of course." The mothership captain stood. "You have a corvette at your disposal. Good luck, Sharl."

As they cleared the mess, Buccari asked, "You ready for this, Nash?"

"Let's do it right," Hudson replied.

Buccari smiled up at him and walked into the wardroom. Again conversation ceased, and all eyes turned her way. Someone started clapping. A shout arose: "Booch! Booch!" The members of the officers' mess exploded to their feet, cheering and whistling.

Blood rose to her cheeks. She acknowledged the outburst with a raised hand and increased her pace to a low-grav trot.

"Damn!" was all she said.

"Would you care for a brandy, Captain?" Stark asked.

"I must decline," Merriwether replied, moving from the table.

"Please give my regards to the admiral," Stark said pointedly. Merriwether flushed, Stark could not tell whether in anger or in embarrassment. The officer pivoted on her heel and departed.

"She runs to the admiral to brief him on our little session," Stark hissed. "The gall of that man, snubbing me again."

He sat back in the plush chair and stared absently at the projections on the wall screen. "Sometime in our lifetime," he mused, "Genellan will be a monument to humanity—a major spaceport, a cultural metropolis, a center of education and human endeavor."

"Redounding to your credit," Mather replied. "Your gift to posterity."

Stark gloried in the thought.

"It would have been better had Buccari just returned to the fleet," Mather said, extinguishing the vid display.

"Perhaps," Stark said. "And yet do not overlook her considerable value to our purpose. The true art of diplomacy is using all tools available, even those that bend not to your needs. Buccari's voice will reach many ears. Somehow we must give her the proper words to speak."

"Perhaps we could simply discredit her," Mather offered.

"Not yet," Stark replied. "Her goodwill is too useful a weapon."

SECTION TWO

SETTLEMENT

THIRTEEN

DOWNLOAD

The commlink beeped. The loadmaster looked up from his metering console and cursed. It was Pulaski again, command pilot of Planetary Habitation Module One. The ruddy, heavy-featured visage of the downloader's skipper squinted from the comm screen.

"Status update," Pulaski demanded. His dog-brown eyes exploded with crow's-feet, and his bulbous nose was spider-webbed with broken veins.

"Equipment load complete," the loadmaster reported, scanning his manifest. "Corrected plenum pressurization. Personnel loading on sched. Fueling on sched. You'll hit the ground on time."

"Rog'," Pulaski replied. "Sorry to keep you guys up so late."

"All in the job," the loadmaster replied. "Loading deadheads on board the Lead Balloon Special. Have a good crash, Ski."

"Hope your snake dies," Pulaski huffed as he signed off.

The loadmaster returned to monitor the cargo control master display. Viewed on several screens from different perspectives and checkpoints, human beings floated in zero gravity, drifting through freight locks and funneling into PHM-1's loading bores. The colonists, uniformed in canary coveralls, looked like grains of yellow rice pouring in slow motion into a silo. All the settlers carried forest-green rucksacks containing emergency food and clothing. The balance of their limited belongings were loaded separately in modular containers. The loadmaster tweaked the pressure differential, increasing flow rates into the habitation module's passenger containments.

* * *

A child screamed. A siren wailed, muted by distance and dulled by its very persistence. Hatches closed, gaskets huffing and squealing. A crewman floated between the berths, checking acceleration tethers and giving the passengers perfunctory attention. Reginald St. Pierre was frightened, but he was also excited. His emotions, heightened by claustrophobia, rampaged from hope to horror. And damn his bladder.

With a sensation approaching panic, St. Pierre realized that the last of the loading crew had disappeared. A hatch clanged shut with gut-wrenching finality. Circulation systems surged; pulsing pressure changes impinged on sinuses and inner ears. The air tasted faintly metallic. The temperature cooled noticeably.

"Containment sealed and pressurized," announced a disembodied and disinterested voice—computer-synthesized.

St. Pierre pulled his arm from its sheath and dangled a hand beneath the berth. His wife squeezed his fingers, her hand clammy.

"Won't be long, Mags," he whispered, gently pulling away.

"Oh, Reggie," she whimpered, letting go reluctantly.

"Almost there, sweetness. Hang on."

The improbable irony: He was about to descend to a new planet not because of his tradecraft but because of his wife's scientific reputation. St. Pierre savored the memory of the day they had received the fantastic, stunning news of their selection. They had long before decided against bringing children into a world with no future, but now they were among the chosen few selected to propagate the human race on an entirely new vector. Now they would have children. He bit his lip with joy.

The news of their selection had been bittersweet; they would in all likelihood never again see their parents, siblings, or friends. They resigned from prestigious jobs, she as a professor at the university and he, ostensibly, as political editor of the *Edmonton Freedom*. However, St. Pierre's primary employment, as a major in the Legion Security Agency, did not terminate. Orders arrived later: subversion deterrence, passive assimilation and long-term opportunism—deep cover, a sleeper.

And then the journey: a nauseating three-day shuttle to lunar marshaling followed by an interminable loading process, with their body hair eradicated and their dignity expunged. Finally there came the four-month HLA plunge across the timeless tracks of deep space.

To Genellan, a new planet, a new home, a new future.

The orange-white glare of Rex-Kaliph flooded PHM-1's flight deck as the host freighter broke from Genellan's penumbra. Pulaski palmed the filters, dimming the stars.

"Green light. Separation in five," the copilot reported.

"At frigging last," Pulaski growled. "Number Two, clear your separation program and reverify. Don't screw it up."

"Aye, aye, sir," the cockpit engineer replied.

The crew members of Planetary Habitation Module One readied themselves for the manic intensity of their huge craft's only flight. Externally strapped to the vertical axis of *T.L.S. San Francisco*'s structural core, it was a great metal and carbon-composite lamprey. Orbital maneuvering tugs, flight decks surrounded by massive kick engines and batteries of maneuvering thrusters, trundled from their holding stations and made positive hard-point contact.

"All umbilicals disconnected," the copilot reported, studying the checks scrolling down his terminal. "Fuel pressurization good; datalinks good; OMTs in tension. Ready for separation."

"Roger," the pilot said gruffly, placing soft hands on the verniers. PHM separations were governed by an interlocking network of computers, but they were flown manually. It was safer.

"Air ops . . . One-Way One's up and ready to blow," Pulaski reported on the flight primary. "Verify green light."

"Matrix is green, PHM-1," the air boss herself responded. "You are cleared for launch. Happy landing, Ski."

"PHM-1 cleared. Single up," the pilot barked over all links.

"Roger, singling up," the copilot responded, keying in release authorizations for secondary grapples. An alarm sounded. A resonant echo rippled the ship's fabric. Red diodes on the board flickered to green; attachment points to the mothership had been severed. Three commanding red lights remained illuminated—the primary grapples: one forward, one amidships, and the massive articulating pivot at the aft attachment.

"Secondaries retracted," the copilot barked.

"Firing separation vernier forward," Pulaski broadcast. The pilot fired jets beneath the tip of the PHM's nose. "Cast off one and two."

"Casting off one and two," the copilot responded as he hit the gang release. A muted clanking vibrated somewhere far below. The nose of the PHM started to move slowly from the streaked and pocked surface of *San Francisco*'s operational core.

Ignoring his head-up display, Pulaski looked out at the parallax vanes and ranging grids that marked the mothership's flank, gauging drift rate and separation. The slanted observation ports of the air ops bridge passed from view. Blackness shot with stars replaced fragile man-made structures. Slowly, the limb of the planet descended from the top of his viewscreen. The downloader was falling inexorably onto its back. Pulaski pulsed a lateral thruster, balancing an incipient roll.

"Cast off stern," he ordered, exhaling; the worst was over. Another routine separation. He had seen the other kind.

"Clear," the copilot shouted.

"Reporting clear," the pilot signaled over the laser link. Air ops acknowledged electronically and handed him off to flight control.

"PHM-1 shows positive separation," the controller's voice announced. "Showing solid nav locks. Report switching to command mode."

"One-Way One switching to command mode now," Pulaski growled. He relaxed tension on his acceleration tethers, armed his retinal cursor, and selected the appropriate commands. Now to baby-sit the computer and enjoy the ride.

"Roger, One. You are in my control. Tugs are clear. Reentry sequence commences now," the controller announced. "Atmospherics in fifty-four minutes."

"Too cold-ah. Humans are insane," Et Silmarn said, his booming voice made metallic by the helmet amplifier. The governor, shivering in the predawn chill, trundled on all fours, his great mass plowing the taiga. "So now-ah you know great-ah secret."

Hudson was thunderstruck: Kateos was to be the king's ambassador.

"Remember, bosom friend, this is a level-one state secret," Et Silmarn thundered, reverting to konish. "You are sworn to secrecy. No one must know until Kateos has safely arrived, especially Envoy Stark."

"Why tell me?" Hudson asked.

"You are a citizen of the Hegemony," Et Silmarn replied. "And Kateos considers you as a brother. She wishes your assistance in surprising Citizen Sharl with this news. This is very important to her."

"Of course, Your Excellency," Hudson replied, wiping his nose. Ah, a conspiracy, he thought, inhaling sweet pure air. Fortified with joy, he pulled up his scarf and surveyed the landing site, the morning sun only minutes from broaching the knife-edged horizon. A breeze, hard and cold, raked the tundra, spring seemingly retreating toward winter. Hoary pinnacles sweeping the western and southern horizons wore angel-hair halos and trailed wispy streamers of crystalline ice. The night's storm had left its mark; the snow line had dropped almost to the prairie, covering the fuming volcanoes to the west with a soft mantle of alabaster—their twin cones, softly rounded and silhouetted against the dark flanks of the distant plateau, presented an image gravid with Freudian suggestion.

Visibility was compelling. First-magnitude stars glimmered arrogantly through the satin depths of a sapphire sky. The buffalo herds, harried by the persistent cacophony of lander retros, had pushed to the north and east, their musk only an uncomfortable memory.

"Sharl was concerned you would not make it in time," Hudson said.

"As-ah was I," Et Silmarn replied in Legion. "It-ah is a long flight, and the cold-ah front was severe. We had-ah to wait out storms at-ah fuel staging field. But let-ah us get-ah out of the wind."

Hudson took one last look at the taiga plain, his gaze captured by the landing pad's geometric perfection. Set back from the great river and running parallel to its cliffs, the PHM pad was graded with laser precision down to the permafrost. Robot dozers were parked on high ground closer to the river, lined up next to the heavy-lifter that had brought them down.

Two EPLs, a Legion utility helo, and Et Silmarn's abat finished the flight line. All-terrain vehicles kicking up rooster tails of wind-whipped dust patrolled the perimeter. A pack of growlers had been dispersed to the east, but most predatory wildlife had followed the buffalo herds, remaining clear of the thundering, ground-shaking activities of civilization. Hudson limped toward the prefab shelters, impending daylight defeating the flat illumination of the sodium arcs. Wind buffeted his exposed face, drawing tears. His artificial joints felt colder than the brittle air. *Ah, yes, home sweet home.*

"I still cannot-ah understand why Sharl transport-ah first

settlers to MacArthur's Valley," Et Silmarn grumbled as they neared the shelter. "Climate-ah is too harsh even for your hardy race. Sharl is stubborn."

"She requires a habitation module for the valley," Hudson answered in fluent konish. "We shall convert the PHM's secondary turbines and their housings to a hydropower station. Everything else shall be cannibalized and used for construction materials."

"It-ah damn cold," Et Silmarn replied. "Come back-ah to Ocean Station with-ah me. I know-ah your body happier in the south. Sharl should-ah bring all settlers to Ocean Station."

"Sharl is quite stubborn, Your Excellency," Hudson answered with a laugh, opening the outer door of the operation shack. He penetrated the thermal lock. El Silmarn hunched down and crawled sideways through the clinging weather baffle. Once inside the relative warmth of the ops hut, the kone removed his helmet and remained on all fours, improving his head clearance. All conversation halted. In the far corner, near a heating unit, Buccari and Quinn scanned a digital terrain mapper. Tonto, perching on Buccari's chair, glared at the kone with bald animosity, his double-lidded black eyes filled with immutable suspicion. Lizard Lips and another guilder stood shoulder to shoulder before a field workstation. Lizard Lips punched at the panel while the other cliff dweller watched, enraptured. The guilders glanced up, revealing mild discomfort, before they returned to the computer, obsession overcoming fear. Breezes scratched at the corrugated roof, and field radios babbled status reports.

"Morning, Governor Et Silmarn," Chastain boomed, grabbing the kone's hand. Chastain, a huge human, was a full head shorter than the kone and had far less than half the alien's mass.

"Good-ah morning, Citizen Jas-tain," Et Silmarn rumbled. "It-ah good-ah day for landing."

Buccari looked up and smiled, her scar wrinkling like a malformed dimple. Her green eyes were glassy and shadowed with fatigue.

"Governor Et Silmarn," she said, standing and bowing. "Excuse my manners, but we're making last-minute decisions."

"Changing landing coordinates again?" Hudson asked, forcing an idiot's smile from his face. Secrets were difficult burdens.

"Yeah, right."

Quinn, standing behind Lizard Lips, laughed loudly and looked up, brushing a strand of blond hair from her forehead. Her large eyes were rayed with wrinkles that accentuated a wide, full-lipped smile.

"What's so funny?" Hudson asked, thankful for a reason to grin.

"The cliff dwellers are, ahem, discussing our plans," Quinn said, chuckling. "They think it's quite foolish to put structures on the tundra. Lizard Lips says it is fit only for buffalo dung."

"It-ah amazes me," Et Silmarn rumbled, "to think-ah my ancestors butchered mountain fliers for their fur."

"Lizzy looks comfortable on that panel," Hudson remarked.

"Godonov downloaded the icon library into the fleet database," Buccari said. "Liz's exploring everything he can access. He opened a query line to flag science all by himself. He talks with Captain Gray more than I do. Someone in exobiology is teaching him to play chess."

Lizard Lips screeched and punched at the hand-held communicator, then pushed it at Buccari. She took it and scanned the stream of icons, her tired face brightening.

"You don't laugh much these days," Hudson said.

"What's to laugh about," Buccari snorted, poking in a response, "between getting ready for settlers and putting up with crap from our illustrious envoy?"

"Stark coming down with the settlers?" he asked.

"Yes," she said, her smile fading. "Wants to be part of the historic event." Lizard Lips and the other guilder stood like Siamese twins joined at the head, reading the communicator. Tonto, eyes never leaving the kone, hopped to the ground and eased toward the entrance.

"Why am I not surprised?" Hudson snorted, watching the hunter slink from the hut.

Everything was fluttering like a balloon pulled too fast through the air. There were choppy vibrations, and a metallic growling throbbed through the fabric of the PHM. Atmospheric reentry was under way. Children were screaming, along with many adults. St. Pierre wished the turbulence were louder to cover the unnerving bedlam. At least his bladder had stopped its urgent call; only now his sodden jumpsuit was growing cold. That would not last. They had said it would get uncomfortably warm during reentry.

He was in no hurry. It already smelled bad. His head hurt, and he was scared.

It was already warm on the PHM's flight deck. Pulaski monitored datalinks. On the navigation display the dead-reckoning tracer was being refreshed by tentative hits—meaningless data hand holding; they could have caught a pressure bounce, and the sensors would have been clueless. But they were just about through sensory blackout. A stream of synthetic-voice advisories rolled over the intercom. Pulaski killed the audio with a double click of his retinal cursor and yawned.

"Uplink on the beacon," the copilot shouted. "Fuel pressure up."

"Roger," Pulaski answered. "I want the tertiaries burning in five."

"Engineering says ready when you are, Skipper," the copilot said.

"I'll be ready in five," Pulaski snapped.

Hypermach turbulence was moderating rapidly. Pulaski looked over the PHM's blunt nose, stealing a peek at the blue, green, and gold planet. Overhead the blackness of space had been transformed, purple melding into royal blue. A wispy ribbon of haze near the horizon was widening, but there was not a cloud in sight on the visible hemisphere. A glorious day for a flight, even a one-way drop.

Brappa welcomed the refreshing pureness of open air. The smell of the long-legs was foul enough, but the odor of the bear person had been vile.

The top limb of the sun-star flared green above the perfect horizon. The emerald illusion lifted and evaporated, pulling after it a golden incandescence. Long-legs scurried everywhere. More, always more long-legs, coming from the stars. Brappa padded across the tundra, lifting his long snout into the wind, instinctively sniffing for dangerous spoor. Only the cloying odors of oil and fuel from long-leg engines came to his magnificent olfactories. Waddling alone on the taiga, far from the long-leg equipment and huts, the hunter came at last to the red and gray scab on the land. He hocked his sinuses clear and spit into a desiccated dung pile. His talons curled over the brink of the geometric gash. Brappa-son-of-Braan stared down in wonder at its unnatural perfection.

"Hearken!" a familiar whistle screeched.

Brappa stared into the sky. Plummeting downward was a brace of hunters, Sherrip and Tokko foremost. Behind them came Craag-leader-of-hunters and his scouts. All wheeled gracefully into the wind and flared great membranes, dropping softly to the ground. Overhead other hunters labored to remain airborne.

"Sword-hand-of-Short-one-who-leads," Craag sang, scarred demeanor stern yet kindly. "Thy salt be pure."

"Greetings, hunter leader," Brappa whistled. "Long life and rising winds." He bowed formally.

A double sonic boom rattled Brappa's sensitive receptors. The hunters started. More thunder from empty skies—auguries of change. A long-legs wheeled machine bounced toward them, siren blasting against the wind. Its flashing red and blue lights exceeded the rays of the flowing dawn.

"The star ferry comes to ground," Craag announced, unfurling his membranes with a mighty crack. "To the winds."

Brappa screeched a warrior's clarion. The other hunters deployed membranes, catching the insistent wind with a resounding ripple. Leaping into the air and pushing hard, the hunters shot upward and backward, the unreined wind thrusting their rigid forms ever higher. Brappa wheeled into the current and slipped against it, holding his position over the long-leg huts. Screeching, he marshaled his reconnaissance section. Good and faithful Sherrip took position on his wing. On the ground the fat-wheeled machine changed direction, returning to its circling patrol. Long-legs and bear people, trailing distended shadows, debouched from shelters. Some milled about, but most stared to the east, shading their eyes against the low golden sun.

Sherrip signaled. Brappa detected the black point in the sky, a speck growing larger, arcing in graceful descent. Brappa hauled against the breeze to gain altitude. He had seen long-leg ships land. This was the largest yet. It promised to be the noisiest.

The object slowed its descent. Its dimensions grew. Brappa struggled; the thermals were unreliable. He allowed himself to be blown toward the approaching machine, rising imperceptibly on feckless updrafts. The giant silver craft streaked soundlessly beneath him, its racing shadow losing ground as its physical essence descended to meet it. The great machine erupted with a pulsing growl, a throbbing explosion growing louder and louder, shaking the wind beneath Brappa's wings. Its shadow arrived at the scraped tundra and held there. The machine crept toward its resting place, its progress slowed to the pace of an old buffalo.

Aerodynamic lift vectors decayed smoothly. Directional thrusters gimbaled to their limits, and areas of stalled air coruscated on the planform display of the dynamic pressure distribution.

"We have stabilizers," the engineer reported.

"Roger, stabilizers," Pulaski acknowledged. The pilot checked outputs just as lateral thrusters began their explosive escalation.

"Breaking thrusters," he called, fingering verniers.

"Firing!" the engineer responded. Forward velocity decreased perceptibly. "Main thrusters are spooling."

"And mains . . . now," Pulaski announced, using his retinal cursor. He placed his hand on the heavy controls, sensing the auto-control inputs.

The mains commenced firing, perimeter banks first, followed almost immediately by the persistent trembling of the core internals. Fuel-flow indicators leapt toward gauge limits. With all banks of hover thrusters and stabilizers firing at full-rated power, Pulaski's engineering sense of wonder exulted in the effectiveness of the brutal harmonic dampening.

The PHM approached "go/no go" hover. Pulaski snorted at the ludicrous decision point. He double-checked alignment reticles, liked what he saw, and dropped landing gear—eight articulating buttresses with saucer pads. The retro program proceeded, with laser and radar probes providing billions of bits per second of altitude information over the entire footprint of the PHM. Pad lineup was true, with the wind strong, steady, and right down the landing axis. A piece of cake.

"Fuel flow peaking. Eighty percent retro thrust. Getting a wiggle on bank three," the engineer reported.

Pulaski had already seen the fluctuating thrust temps. Instinctively his hand approached the computer lockout. At that moment bank three exploded, venting a runaway thrust pattern that lifted the PHM and created a rolling moment.

"Thruster overshoot!" the copilot screamed.

"Overshoot, my ass," Pulaski grunted, twisting in his tethers and reaching for overrides. "It's a frigging blowout!"

The PHM bucked against its landing programs, everything suddenly out of correctable tolerances. Pulaski's head flailed, incapacitating his retinal cursor. He swatted at the computer lockout, slamming off the switch. His view out the window was one of hell; the PHM was far over on its beams, the horizon tilting sickeningly.

Pulaski pulled back the starboard throttles and pushed port power sticks to the wall. The horizon started to right, but not fast enough. Altitude was perilously low, and center of gravity indexes were off the scales. He eased back on the perimeter thrusters, losing more altitude. He saw the river. The lateral momentum of the PHM had drifted it to the cliff edge. The river chasm yawned. Port thrusters were up full; he needed power to maintain altitude, but it was pushing him over the cliffs. The drift rate was slowing, but not fast enough.

With a sudden inspiration Pulaski slammed the opposing nose and stern thrusters. With agonizing slowness but with dramatically increasing speed the monstrous landing craft started to twist. The huge mountains that had been dead ahead disappeared. An empty prairie sweeping to infinity took their place. Pulaski shut down the twisting pulse, anticipating the correct heading; the sun-star's glare provided a cardinal reference. Center of gravity indexes reappeared. He checked the azimuth and fired a solid counterpulse just as the river came back into view. They were over the river! Damn, they had a long way to go.

"Can we make the landing pad?" the copilot asked.

"Stuff the frigging pad!" Pulaski bellowed.

Pulaski leaned on the laterals, firing at full power. At the same time he fire-walled the throttle for bank one, the only main thruster he could trust. The port mains would slow his lateral rate and raise him into the air. He glanced at the cliffs. He did not need more altitude, just less empty air beneath him.

"Fuel twenty-three percent! Starboard thrusters overloaded," the engineer bellowed.

The big ship shuddered. Alarms screamed.

"Fuel fifteen percent!"

"Secure the goddamn alarms!" Pulaski roared, holding the PHM on its blazing column of fire.

"Six percent!"

Too far! Pulaski considered ejecting; but his thoughts went to the hundred helpless passengers squirming in the hold. He pounded futilely against the lateral thruster, wishing for more drift—demanding, pleading, praying. The cliff edge moved closer—too slowly.

"Ain't going to make it!" the copilot gasped.

"Fuel's one percent!"

Compressed air blasted Pulaski from the right. And then there was an explosion. He glanced through the gaping hole in the overhead. The copilot's station was gone—the asshole had ejected. Smart move.

"Fuel's gone, Ski!" the engineer shouted.

"Get out!" Pulaski shouted, easing the mains. His altitude dropped. Was he high enough to make the cliffs? He checked fuel; there was none. The engineer fired his seat, and Pulaski was alone on the flight deck.

The engines were still breathing. Slowly, inexorably, the rocks of the cliff migrated beneath the ship. As the starboard bank flamed out, the ship made glancing contact with a forward landing pad. The big ship lurched against the obstruction, pivoting on its stern. The port side engine's flamed out less than a second later. The PHM dropped from the sky, falling only a few centimeters before the first of five landing pads slammed onto uneven ground. The ship teetered toward the river, and then rocked back, and grounded solidly, three house-sized pads suspended over the cliff edge.

Pulaski blew out air and lifted his helmet from his sweaty head. Chilly breezes, finding the blown ejection ports, whirled about the flight deck. Pulaski reset switches and controls per post landing checks and proceeded to shut down the ship's systems, carefully monitoring the checklists scrolling across his console. The radio screamed at him and was ignored. The emergency was over; passenger containments were secure, and there were no fire warning lights. Besides, he needed to get his breathing under control.

FOURTEEN

ON THE GROUND

The corrosive growl of the PHM's main engines stopped. The sounds of babies crying and adults whimpering took their place. *Damn, the touchdown had been rough.* St. Pierre felt sick to his stomach. The effluent odor of vomit was pervasive. In the bowels of the ship the whirring of auxiliary systems wound down. After an eternity he heard the delightful measured hiss and thump of air lock hatches being cycled and purged. It was hot. It stank of burning metal.

"What's taking so long?" someone shouted.

"Goddamn VIP," someone growled. "His pampered ass gets off first."

The hatch to their containment rattled open. Spontaneous cheers exploded from the passenger racks, transforming frightened faces into joyful ones. St. Pierre's scalp crawled with the intensity of joy. His acceleration tethers relaxed. He reached over the side. Maggie grabbed his fingers with desperate strength.

"Phewee!" a crewman shouted. "This one wins the prize."

Bolts blew, and a gas seal let go with a wheeze. An icy fragrance teased St. Pierre's senses. He shrugged from his berth and slid to the deck, as did everyone else in the containment. He assisted Maggie from her tethers and held her tight. She looked at him like a sick puppy.

"Okay," the spacer shouted. "Everything's under control. Stay on the walkways. Stay clear of the ship's skin. When you get to the ground, follow the crowd to the processing tents. We'll get you cleaned up."

"Amen," a settler behind St. Pierre whispered.

"Gee, Daddy," another settler shouted, "what was the first

thing you did when you landed on Genellan? Well, son, I hosed out my skivvies!"

Cathartic laughter filled the containment. St. Pierre, holding his wife's hand, stepped through the hatch and joined a cheering throng in the thwartship passageway, everyone anxiously awaiting to descend to the new planet. Heat from the ship, pleasantly commingling with a cool, pulsing breeze, caressed his face. Hot metal popped and pinged. His turn came. He emerged onto a catwalk under gloriously blue skies and took the fifteen rungs, his euphoria rising with each descending step. But it was the final step from the ladder—his first footfall on the planet—that generated an ineffable thrill that overwhelmed all previous sensations. A tear ran cold down his cheek. He shivered and filled his lungs with cool, clean air and struggled to repress a shout of elation. Spinning like a child, he turned back to the ladder, lifted Maggie from the last rung, and collapsed with her to the ground. All around him settlers, dizzy with joy, fell to their knees in the immense blue shadow of the haphazardly grounded vessel.

"If it's not one thing, it's another," a female voice of deep timbre shouted. He looked up to see a tanned woman striding toward them, dark auburn tresses fanning in the breeze. Pointing and waving, the woman shouted orders. Spacer technicians jumped to her commands.

"This way," the woman said, her voice unmistakably firm. "Keep moving." She approached their ladder, radiant green eyes never resting. Pulling Maggie to her feet, St. Pierre examined the woman, who was undeniably attractive despite a horrific scar across one temple and cheek. The diminutive figure wore leathers and fur. *Buccari!*

"That's her," he whispered.

"Who, Reg?" Maggie asked.

"Buccari," he replied. A brittle breeze overcame his adrenaline flush, and suddenly he was envious of Buccari's thick furs. He yanked the seal-strip on his jacket and pulled up his hood. Buccari turned away to pick up a child.

"She's so small," Maggie said. "I expected a fire-breathing Titan."

"Look over there!" He gasped.

Aliens! Kones! Titans truly! In the distance huge helmeted beings clustered together, some standing on two legs, some leaning on all four. Humans walking near the kones looked

like delicate stick figures. Overhead, large long-headed birds
swirled and hovered on the wind, obsidian wings flashing in
the clean morning light. Truly a new world—fantastic. And not
a little frightening.

"Welcome to Genellan, little one," Buccari said.

She lifted the sobbing infant, its cries immediately subsiding
to a whimper. The rosy-cheeked girl cut her eyes shyly and
buried a runny nose in the soft black pile of Buccari's otterskin
hood.

The child's mother, upon touching soil, had fainted. Now, as
two spacers lifted her onto a pallet, she was coming around.
The husband stood alongside, ministering to his wife. Buccari
approached the litter. The mother's countenance shifted ephemerally from fear to relief, to joy, to embarrassment. Fresh tears
welled over the streaks of earlier emotional bouts.

"Oh, dear," she said, staring with rapture into Buccari's face.
"Bless me, it's you. I can walk. Let me—"

"Enjoy the ride," Buccari ordered, pressing the lady's shoulder to the litter. "Save your strength."

"Bless you, ma'am," the lady said, reaching for her baby.
Buccari placed the child in the woman's arms.

"Her name's Sharl," said the man, freckled and stolid. "After you."

"W-what?" was all Buccari could stutter.

"Sharl Genellan Cody," the man said, extending his hand.
He was older than his wife. "Name's Sam Cody. My wife,
Barret."

"Sam and Barret," she said, shaking the man's no-nonsense
grip and struggling with her own emotions. "And Sharl Cody.
Welcome to Genellan." She waved the pallet operator along.

A helo clattered overhead just as one of the all-terrains came
bouncing up. Hudson leaned out the door.

"They picked the engineer out of the trees," Hudson reported.
"Broken leg. Copilot landed in the river. Fenstermacher's got
him. Well, Sharl, our little corner of the universe just got
crowded."

Buccari looked around and exhaled. A cargo crane deployed
noisily from the PHM's dorsal. "It's just begun, Nash."

"Yeah." Hudson sighed. "So you want us to give Stark a
ride?"

"No," she said. "I want these ATVs patrolling the perimeter

until we get these civilians off the cliffs. Stark claims he's just another settler. He can hike down to the valley like the others. Perhaps he'll appreciate the meaning of his own words."

"Fat chance," Hudson replied.

The truck took off, and Buccari moved forward along the huge ship's fuselage. The envoy's tall form stood beneath the crew ladder at the cliff's edge. A cadre of black-suited security personnel stood near the envoy. Buccari noted with pleasure that all of them were pale and shaken. She would have to buy Pulaski a beer.

Speaking of Pulaski, the pilot had descended from the flight deck and was being confronted by Stark. Agents in red berets had Pulaski bracketed. The pilot stood uncomfortably close to the hot hull of the PHM, his mouth opening and shutting like a guppy. A sneering Major Faro and a detail of marines stood nearby, looking like they were preparing a firing squad.

"Dammit, man, you almost landed in the river!" Stark's tremulous baritone drifted on the wind. "We could have been killed!"

Buccari started trotting; a balky knee reminded her of past emergencies.

"You should thank his sorry ass you're alive," she shouted, shouldering through the tall wall of reluctantly yielding agents. "Geez, Ski! I hope you brought down some popcorn."

Her friend's hairless face burst into a radiant smile, a pink sun coming through clouds of consternation. Buccari opened her arms. Pulaski whooped at the sky and, pushing aside the nearest agent, scooped her into a bear hug.

"Nice landing," she said, pulling him through the cordon of agents. The pilot glanced furtively over his shoulder and then spit into the taiga.

"Not bad," he allowed. "Not bad."

Brappa paid scant attention to the star ferry perched with its nose over the edge of the cliffs or to the long-legs scurrying in and out of its shadow. With the keen vision of all high-flying creatures, he scanned the taiga, the forested cliffs, and the river's edge for predators, for any danger that might threaten the hapless newcomers. The coolness of morning gave way slowly, the air above the river especially cool. It was troublesome to stay airborne, yet they must.

Craag-leader-of-hunters screeched new orders. Brappa

banked into the insistent northwesterly. His wingmates wheeled with him. He signaled a tacking descent to the west, knifing through down-burbling air off the cliffs and finally over the warmer, uplifting currents above the rolling prairie. In the dust-stirred distance buffalo herds and growler packs jostled in constant movement. The creatures of the taiga plains were all fleeing the thunder of the long-legs' sky machine.

By the time they marshaled the settlers for the hike to the valley, Genellan's sun had risen high enough to provide welcome warmth. Mercifully, the biting north wind moderated and shifted to a gentle westerly. Stacks of pallets grew beneath the gaping PHM hold openings, and robot trucks scurried cargo to the helo pads in a constant stream.

Sadly, perhaps jealously, Buccari ushered Pulaski onto an EPL for return to orbit. Fur coat and leggings jettisoned, she scanned the settlers, looking for leaders—and problems. The newcomers appeared relieved, although many stared at her with disconcerting emotion. Stark recovered his composure and leapt to the task of organizing the first contingent of gravity-taxed and adrenaline-spent settlers. With Tatum as guide and a rifle team of marines for protection, the envoy headed along the steep, switchbacking horse trail from the cliff tops, seeking the banks of the great river.

A half hour later Buccari, Chastain, and another fire team moved out with the remainder of the able-bodied settlers, leaving Hudson, Quinn, and spacer helo crews to fly the cargo pallets and the remaining settlers—mostly mothers with infants and small children—across the river.

Buccari traversed the countless switchbacks, herding settlers at a lively pace. All the while the river drew nearer, its gravelly whisper growing more persistent. After an hour of knee-jarring downhill hiking, Buccari caught up with the first group, its members sitting on rocks and weather-bleached logs in the increasing shade of riparian forest. Buccari, with Chastain in her wake, trotted past the tired settlers until she came to the head of the column. She found Tatum leaning against a tree, chewing on a fingernail.

"What's the deal, Sandy?" Buccari asked.

"Envoy's taking a breather," Tatum replied. Stark, his pale complexion gone fish-belly white, sat in the cool shadows. He was not a young man. A pang of guilt sparked in Buccari's breast.

"Sharl . . . my dear," Stark croaked, straightening his tall body against the unrelenting gravity. "Afraid these ancient legs aren't holding up too well." Perspiration poured off his patrician nose. All the settlers looked spent. It had grown warm. Sunshine drenched the southern-facing cliffs, and any breeze was blocked by outcroppings and increasingly numerous rock-clinging fir trees.

"It's not far," she replied. "Jocko, give Mr. Stark a hand."

"Aye, Lieutenant," Chastain said, effortlessly pulling Stark to his feet. The envoy groaned. His perspiring agents looked uncomfortable.

"Jocko," she grumbled softly, "call me Sharl."

"Sir? Uh . . . yes, sir, Lieutenant. Er . . . Sharl, I mean . . . sir," Chastain sputtered, boosting Stark down the trail. Stark's security team plodded after them, and Tatum began rousting the others.

A settler screamed. Huge shadows flitted across the path. Horrified faces turned skyward. Buccari looked up to see hunters descending onto rocks and tree limbs, their great membranes blotting out the sun. Bottlenose and Tonto soared by, their hissing wings stirring pine-scented air. Other cliff dwellers swooped and hovered, jockeying for position. Bluenose and Spitter landed on a snag just down the trail. Captain Two landed on an outcropping above the path, his luffing membranes puffing dust into the air. Wide-eyed settlers bolted in panic. A security agent raised his sidearm. Tatum snatched the weapon from the muscular man's hand as if he were taking a rattle from a baby. Captain Two looked down at the activity with arrogant indifference.

"Don't move!" Buccari yelled, trotting up the hill, trying to calm the stricken newcomers. They had been briefed on Genellan's inhabitants, but warnings were no remedy for a first encounter with the ugly, leather-armored, bow- and pike-bearing hunters. Like monstrous mattock-headed buzzards, the talon-footed creatures leered down at the settlers as if examining carrion.

"These are friends," she shouted. "These are cliff dwellers, hunters. Don't be afraid."

Captain Two screeched mightily, baring long rows of ragged white teeth. The hunter's scream disappeared into the ultrasonic.

"Sounds like my wife," someone shouted nervously.

"Looks like her, too," another voice added, and cautious laughter rippled up the trail. The panic was over. Buccari turned to Captain Two and bowed in hunter fashion. Captain Two returned the honor.

"Long life, hunter leader," she signed rapidly. "Your presence bad. Long-legs frightened. You go far side of river. Now."

Captain Two bared gruesome teeth and chittered. He shrieked to the other hunters, and they echoed his toothy laughter. With an explosive deployment of his wings Captain Two pushed from his perch and lifted ponderously upward. The others followed, wings cracking. The creatures cleared the trees and set their wings, rising higher and higher, to join other motes cleaving the higher altitudes.

"The ferry landing is just down the trail," Buccari shouted to the settlers. "Tatum will bring you to the landing when it's your turn."

"Aye, aye, Lieutenant. Uh . . . Sharl," Tatum parodied. "Sir." Buccari used hunter sign language to insult his mother.

St. Pierre pulled Maggie to her feet. Buccari broke out a few more settlers and brought up the rear. St. Pierre fell back.

"If it's not one thing, it's another," he said.

Buccari smiled, a beautiful smile. She wore baggy shorts that revealed muscular thighs, their bronzed hardness softened by a patina of downy hair. Her grimy feet were protected by sandals secured by leather thongs wrapped around chiseled calves. A faded Legion tunic revealed the swell of her chest and a set of strong, square shoulders. Her hair, collected in a ponytail, was dark auburn beneath shimmering layers of sun-streaked chestnut. Loose wisps at her temples floated on gentle zephyrs. Green eyes, bruised with fatigue, glinted in golden sunlight. She smelled of wet grass.

"Reggie St. Pierre," he said, holding out his hand. "This is my wife, Margaret. It is an honor to meet you . . . uh . . ."

"Sharl. Please call me Sharl," she said. "Welcome to Genellan."

"And I'm Maggie," his wife replied. "Oh, Sharl, it's so . . . wild. It's going to take getting used to."

"Wait till winter." Buccari laughed. "You'll question your sanity."

"Mine's already in doubt," St. Pierre replied, studying the leader of the Survivors.

"What is it you do, Reggie?" Buccari asked, her intense gaze catching his before darting skyward.

"I'm a journalist," he replied.

Buccari glanced at him and away again. "And Maggie, what do you do," she asked, her gaze never resting.

"I'm a botanist," Maggie said meekly.

"Wonderful," Buccari said, turning and rewarding Maggie with a nova smile. "I'll introduce you to Leslie Lee. She's our plant expert. She'll put you to work. And wait until you meet our gardeners."

"Gardeners?" Maggie asked shyly.

Buccari laughed, a liquid, hearty sound. "More cliff dwellers but very different from the ones you just met. But you'll have to excuse me—" She accelerated past them to the front of the column.

The temperature dropped drastically. The impatient sound of water pushing gravel grew loud. The smell of damp rock was strong. The trail made its last long switchback through the trees and broadened to a grassy lea. The watercourse spread into view, lapping at their feet. St. Pierre gasped. Others stood openmouthed, astounded at the sight of the great river so near at hand—and of the far bank so distant.

"As high as it gets," said a wide-shouldered, heavy-featured man, his thatch of flaxen hair and sweeping mustaches intensified by the deepness of his tan. He loosened a line from around a boulder, a hawser that led to a ponderous log raft, its hewn mass straining against the worrisome silt-laden current.

"Bring in the bow lines, Beppo," a short, wiry man, standing on the ferry as if he owned it, shouted at the towhead. Despite the chill, the little man wore only sandals and shorts. His thin chest and shoulders were knotted with muscle. His whiskers shot out like sunflower petals. The one called Beppo coiled the lines.

"They're all yours, Fenstermacher," Buccari shouted back.

"Don't look worth shit, Lieutenant," the wiry man responded. "Get 'em on board, Jocko. I'll tell you when we got a load." As the giant called Jocko assisted Stark, the little man chattered incessantly, as if he could not shut his mouth even to take a breath.

"Jocko, when yer done helping that old lady, get yer ass on the port stroke. Beppo, clear that painter and fend us off."

The envoy's security team pushed on, giving ground to no one. One agent staked out a spot close to the sternpost. Fenstermacher looked up at the thick-necked officer as if he were examining a turd.

"Don't step on the lines. Yeah, you, meathead."

The agent jumped like a recruit at the little man's command.

"Sweep the stern out, Jocko."

Chastain leaned on the oar, and the raft surged against the throbbing, sucking current.

"Mr. Buccari, sir," Fenstermacher whined, waving people to their positions like a cop in busy traffic, "would you kindly expedite these dirt monkeys. This current's going to put us on the rocks."

St. Pierre clambered up the substantial freeboard and turned to help his wife. Buccari had already boosted Maggie aboard. Only Buccari, Beppo, and the marines remained on shore. St. Pierre counted nearly twenty people sitting or lying on the raft. Rowing clearance was tight.

"Where's Tatum? Ah, shit, Lieutenant, get yer ass on the starboard oar," Fenstermacher shouted.

Buccari, shaking her head, leapt nimbly aboard and threaded her way to the large oar. The little man stood by the heavy sweep tiller and leaned against the current.

"Beppo, cast off, then take over for the lieutenant before she wears out. Now lay to the oars. Full aft."

The towhead pushed the stern of the raft into the current and jumped on, bringing with him a length of line that he busily coiled. When he was done, he leapt to the oar. Buccari stayed on and worked in tandem. The raft pivoted about and surged against the current.

Fenstermacher leaned against his sweep and chattered. "Ain't got no life jackets, folks, but no matter—water's so cold and the current's running so fast, you'd freeze to death before we picked you up. We barely got that pilot outta the water in time, and he was wearing a sealed suit. Probably suffered brain damage . . . not that you can tell with pilots."

"Fenstermacher," Buccari grunted, pushing mightily on the long oar. "Shut your damn mouth."

Everyone cheered. Even Stark smiled.

"Frigging mutiny," the little man muttered.

St. Pierre, watching the cliff dwellers soaring majestically overhead, sat protectively between Maggie and the raft's edge.

The opposite bank seemed impossibly distant. The raft was pointed well into the current to prevent them from being swept downstream. Oars groaned in their leather-wrapped tholes, and the blunt bow slapped the current, tossing icy water into a brittle spray. A vibrant, muted rumbling came from upstream, a crashing and thundering of water. In the distance immense cataracts of white water exploded in foam and mist. St. Pierre looked at his wife. She smiled bravely.

Helos shuttled overhead. A big white aircraft—a konish plane, they were informed—also made the round-trip before the raft at last rounded into an eddying cove. Lines were tossed to waiting handlers who guided the craft alongside a rock quay. No sooner were the passengers off-loaded onto the smooth rocks than Fenstermacher was shouting orders to cast off. Within minutes the raft was being hauled across the current.

Marines escorted them to a robot truck. Two Genellan horses—golden, short-nosed, streaming-maned animals with thick furry hocks and shanks—also waited, one with a rider, one without. Buccari walked up to the available horse, grabbed a handful of mane, and swung herself athletically onto its bare back.

"We've got another five kilometers to the settlement," Buccari commanded. "Everyone load your packs on the lorry."

Stark's shoulders sagged. He looked longingly at the lorry. He was obviously spent.

"Mr. Stark, you may have this horse," she offered. "Do you ride?"

"Thank you." Stark exhaled, uncomfortably eyeing the burly brute. "I . . . eh, for five kilometers I would prefer to walk with the other settlers."

Buccari smiled her lovely smile and twisted the animal, using only her knees. She took her position at the head of the column. The horse frequently skittered sideways as if wanting to run.

Despite the nagging gravity, walking in shade and being unburdened of their packs made the hike over the rolling forest trail bearable. St. Pierre held his wife's hand as they rock-hopped across numerous brooks. They saw flocks of bright birds, observed marmotlike animals, and glimpsed furtive creatures gliding between trees. The other rider, a large assault rifle carried across his thighs, brought up the rear of the column. He introduced himself as Terry O'Toole and called the gray gliding varmints bat-rats. He said his main job was to keep an eye out for bears and nightmares.

Eventually the trail broached an expansive clearing that gave a view of the lake: Longo's Meadow, O'Toole called it. As they trekked by the clearing, the big white aircraft approached from over the lake and landed. It taxied to the trail near two large black tents. Marines disgorged and began unloading equipment pallets. But it was the occupants of the tents and the crew pouncing from the aircraft's flight deck that caused a nervous murmur to ripple through the settlers' column: kones, the same Titans witnessed from afar on the cliffs, but up close, all wearing helmets and thick suits. They trotted like hippopotamuses swimming underwater, surprisingly graceful and with effortless velocity. Buccari waved, and the aliens acknowledged her as if she were a great general.

St. Pierre was relieved when the walls of the palisade came into view through the trees. They stumbled past the gates, but he was not too tired to notice the armed marines patrolling the catwalks and the flocks of ugly hunters, like demonic statues, roosting on ridgepoles.

The interior of the palisade bustled with activity. Spacer engineers labored with robot lorries and balloon-tired forklifts, storing equipment pallets and food canisters in prefabs. The angry, ringing buzz of a sawmill blade came from somewhere beyond the far wall, the air redolent of resin and sap and sawdust.

But the noises that fetched everyone's attention were the happy screams of the mothers and small children who had been delivered directly to the settlement by helicopter. Yelling with joy, they leaned out the doors and windows of the steep-roofed, two-story, rough-hewn wooden structure to which Buccari led their husbands and fathers.

"This is your new home," Buccari announced from horseback, her strong voice carrying over the ambient din. "At least until you are capable of building your own. The barracks is divided into ten wards. Each ward shares a downstairs kitchen and common room and an upstairs bunk room. There's spacer rations in the general larder. Showers are up the hill. Outhouses are under the west wall."

A spontaneous cheer echoed off the palisade walls. Buccari's barrel-chested horse pranced at the outburst.

"Envoy Stark," she shouted. "You have a private billet in the marine barracks. Your staff is assigned to Ward Ten."

The envoy, still fagged from the trek, could only nod his head.

"Orders of the day," she continued. "Each ward is to choose a preliminary representative. On the afternoon watch the representatives will meet in the lodge. We'll ring the lodge alarm. It's loud; you'll hear it. Choose well. This will be the first meeting of a representative body on this planet."

"Who gets to vote?" someone shouted.

"I'll leave that up to each ward for now," she replied. "A couple of rules: Stay within the palisade walls, and no one is allowed outside the barracks unless accompanied by someone carrying a gun."

"What are we, prisoners?" someone shouted.

"Yeah, for a while," Buccari shouted back. The settlers muttered. "Until you learn how to use weapons. You've been briefed on this planet. It's dangerous. There are giant eagles that will snatch and kill a child. They'll kill a full-grown man if provoked. And there are other dangers." She looked around. "We'll talk later."

She wheeled away, leaving everyone scanning the skies. St. Pierre brought his gaze down. They had been briefed on huge bears and giant raptors and the other predators that abounded there. Animals, however large, did not completely explain the palisade walls and the guardhouses and the numerous marines carrying heavy assault rifles. *Other dangers?*

Maggie suddenly squeezed his hand.

"Reg, look over there!" she whispered, pointing into the shadows.

Against the wall and partially obscured by a tarp was a monstrous, denuded skull—reptilian, dagger-toothed.

FIFTEEN

SETTLEMENT

Bone-weary after three days on the river cliffs, Buccari let her horse trot for the stables. O'Toole followed. The children were playing outside Nancy Dawson's cabin. Dawson, pistol in hand, stood eagle watch. Startling Buccari, a hunter swished by—Tonto—gliding in ground effect. The hunter screeched. Buccari pursed her lips and did her best to emulate the cry.

Her son whirled at her whistle and started waddling through the flowers, shrieking with joy. Buccari slid from the horse, threw the reins to O'Toole, and dropped to her knees to accept Charlie's warm embrace and his wet lips on her cheek. The other children piled on, squealing and shouting. She grabbed muscular little Adam and tickled him into submission. Honey carefully put a wildflower in her hair, and tiny Hope, nose running, clung to her arm.

"Better get hot on that nursery," Dawson said, slapping the horse's rump. "There'll be a lot more babies around here a year from now."

"No kidding," Leslie Lee said, jogging up from the barracks. "Those are very, very happy wives." She grabbed her own child and hugged her with sympathetic joy.

"They've come a long way," Dawson remarked.

"Haven't we all?" Buccari replied, inhaling the sweet scent of her child's skin.

"The download manifest says we've got three university professors," Leslie Lee said. "I wonder if they knew they'd be teaching the alphabet and arithmetic to children when they signed on."

"They'll be thankful come winter," Buccari said, looking around to see where Tonto had gone. She noticed the old huntress perched on the cabin's porch, next to the stolid

Tonto—it was Great-mother, Tonto's dam. Buccari gave Dawson a puzzled look.

"She showed up at the door of your cabin this morning, Sharl," Dawson said. "Poor thing was soaking wet with dew."

"There are two of them," Lee added. "The other one's probably getting something to eat. They're—"

At that moment another cliff dweller swooped around the cabin at knee level. It pulled up, braking exuberantly with membranes outstretched; it was smaller yet. Another huntress, but young, it fluttered to a perch. Tonto, uncharacteristically agitated, chirped and leaned over to touch foreheads with each in turn. Buccari recognized Tonto's sibling, although she had grown. Buccari kissed Charlie's thatch of silky brown hair and set him down. With her son sprinting at her side, she walked up to the cliff dwellers and signed a greeting. Tonto returned the salutation curtly. The old huntress watched alertly, mimicking all hand signs.

"My honor," Buccari signed, "to have Great-mother visit." She bowed to the old one, who returned the honor with sober dignity.

"Duty," Tonto signed cryptically. "Great-mother's duty."

Pondering the implication of Tonto's message, Buccari bowed again, stepped back, and picked up her son. Charlie waved both arms at the huntress. Great-mother hopped from the rail and floated to the ground with her membranes half-deployed. Buccari leaned over and placed Charlie into the alien's sinewy arms. The huntress squatted to create a lap, and the contented child rubbed his face against the creature's silky fur.

Ki placed the grasping infant on its legs and pinched it to make its strong fingers let go of her fur. The whelp uttered a cry, but Ki chirped a sharp admonishment, curtailing the infant's whine.

"Thy presence, honored mother," Brappa chirped, "has created much concern. A hunters' encampment is no place for—"

"My duty is here, brave son," Ki replied softly, brushing the silky wisps on the whelp's pate.

"But honored mother," Brappa pleaded, "thy place is—"

The clarion call of Craag-leader-of-hunters descended from above. Ki looked up to see a trio of warriors spiraling down. Her son chirped a soft warning and politely hop-waddled away.

"Notta, good daughter," Ki commanded, guiding the infant into her daughter's arms, "mind the whelp."

Craag descended into the crowd, carefully luffing his great membranes, stirring a breeze as he dropped onto the ground. The long-legs stepped back to give the hunter leader room. Sherrip and Bott'a landed on the cabin eaves. Brappa, with a dozen breezy beats of his membranes, hoisted himself onto the roof to join them. The three hunters stared down owlishly, as animated as granite gargoyles.

Craag bowed in good form to Short-one-who-leads and then turned to face Ki, his visage fiercely stern. Ki was not intimidated.

"Long life, huntress Ki, mate-of-the-great-hero-Braan," Craag began, bowing respectfully.

"Warm rising winds, Craag of clan Veera, leader-of-hunters," Ki reciprocated, bowing equally deeply.

"The elders are much concerned for thy well-being," Craag admonished. "Wisdom dictates thy return to the cliffs."

"I am great-mother to this fledgling," Ki replied.

Craag remained silent, glaring, his fierce demeanor unrelenting. Ki countered with mute resolve, matching the warrior's unblinking stare.

"This is a hunters' camp," Craag said at last. "The presence of females disrupts the natural order—"

"There are guilders in this . . . hunters' camp," Ki spit.

Craag snapped off his angry retort with a frustrated screech that quickly trailed into the ultrasonic. Bott'a twittered a pacifying shriek to still the dozens of hunter queries lifting into the air.

"Apologies," Ki chittered, giving ground, hoping to restore the warrior's face. "Long-legs have disrupted the natural order, Craag-leader-of-hunters. My presence in their midst is as a leaf tumbling in a gale." The whelp sprinted from Notta's clutches and ran to Ki, all but knocking the huntress over. She took his strong little hand and waited.

Craag stared back, occasionally glancing down at the long-leg child. After interminable seconds the warrior chieftain bowed low and turned away. Taking three waddling steps, he pounded skyward. Brappa, Bott'a, and Sherrip pushed off to join their leader in formation, gliding over the palisade wall and downhill to their hunters' camp on the cove peninsula.

* * *

She did not understand what had transpired between the huntress and Captain Two, but Great-mother's presence gave Buccari a peculiar sense of security. She left Charlie in Dawson's care, under the unwavering scrutiny of the huntresses. After a meal and a shower she retreated to her cabin and collapsed into a dreamless sleep.

The clanging settlement alarm brought Buccari awake. She threw water in her face, pulled on a clean jumpsuit, and headed across the common for the settlers' meeting. The thick odors of the stable drifted into her senses, and she realized the weather had shifted. A high overcast forged across the metallic blue sky.

Et Silmarn and Envoy Stark, enmeshed in conversation, waited on the sunstruck lodge porch. Across the common settlers gawked from barracks windows. Two security agents stood nervously on the steps.

"The governor is explaining konish government," Stark said. "And I have been attempting to explain ours."

"Most-ah confusing," Et Silmarn replied.

"Speaking of governments, shall we go inside and start one?" Buccari said, indicating the door.

With Et Silmarn on all fours, they moved through the mud room and into the lodge's common room. Et Silmarn's heavy tread caused sturdy floor beams to groan. The eyes of the settlers moved as one, all focused on the expansive bulk of the alien. Lungs sucked in collectively as the alien rose to his hinds, his helmet brushing the rafters. The giant's breathing system whispered softly in the awed silence.

Commander Quinn and Major Faro stood before the main fireplace. The ward representatives sat on crude fur-covered furniture sturdy enough to accommodate a kone. Stark moved in, bravely taking the planetary governor by the arm. A small aromatic fire crackled in the big fireplace. The shutters of the windows were thrown wide, letting in pine scents, blue sky, and gentle breezes.

The Survivors sat at the massive trestle table: Nash Hudson, returned as ringleader, Toby Mendoza, Terry O'Toole, Tooks Tookmanian, Gunner Wilson, Beppo Schmidt, Winfried Fenstermacher, Leslie Lee, Jocko Chastain, and Sandy Tatum. Except for Hudson, their leathery tans and long hair gave them a distinctively piratical appearance next to the pale and hairless settlers, as if they were a different species. Someone was missing. Dawson was watching the children. Billy Gordon had returned to fleet duty. Pepper Goldberg.

Wilson surreptitiously dealt a hand of poker. Fenstermacher provided a muted scatological accompaniment. Buccari walked up behind Tatum and put a hand on his broad back.

"Where's Pepper?" she asked.

The tall redhead turned and gave her a fatalistic look. "She's packing, Sharl," Tatum mumbled, his voice catching. "She's going back to the fleet. She's leaving . . ."

"I'm sorry, Sandy," Buccari said, not knowing what else to say. Tatum smiled sadly and looked away. It was no surprise; Pepper had never been happy on Genellan, even during the good times. Buccari patted Tatum's burly shoulder and moved toward the fireplace, forcing her thoughts to other matters.

Major Faro was pompously lecturing about dragons. Buccari took a place next to Et Silmarn. The kone, four times her mass, smiled down at her. The behemoth was more nervous than the settlers.

"Ah, Sharl," Stark said. "Commander Quinn related the circumstances of your dragon attack. The settlers were, ahem, surprised that they had not been briefed before the landing. Major Faro is providing assurances that a repeat episode is unlikely."

"What else are you not telling us about?" a settler asked.

"I assure you—" Major Faro started to reply.

"Would any of you have changed your minds?" Buccari interrupted. She surveyed the group and recognized Reggie St. Pierre, tall and pale, alert brown eyes separated by a sculptured, if sunburned, nose, and round-shouldered Sam Cody, ruddy and somber.

"Hell, no," Cody shouted. Others mumbled their assent.

"Will there be any more . . . *surprises*?" insisted the first settler, a swarthy individual, his face locked in a perpetual sneer.

"Count on it," Buccari replied. "We've seen only a tiny fragment of Genellan. We've learned much from the konish scientists, but there are huge tracts of planet that remain unexplored even by kones."

Et Silmarn reached up and removed his helmet. The settlers shrank back in their chairs as a tart, acrid odor seeped into the air. Buccari reached over and squeezed one of Et Silmarn's fingers.

"Speaking of kones," she continued, "and konish scientists,

permit me to introduce the governor of Genellan. I present His Excellency, Et Silmarn." Buccari bowed, kneeling and touching the floor with her forehead.

"This is not-ah necessary, friend-ah Sharl," the kone rumbled in Legion, dropping onto his knees and also touching his head to the floor. The massive kone rolled back on his well-padded knees and remained at eye level with the humans.

"You speak Legion," one of the settlers blurted.

"Thank-ah you," Et Silmarn replied, his basso profundo voice resounding from the walls. "I had-ah good-ah teacher: Nash-ah Hudsawn. Hudsawn is good and-ah brave friend. His return to this planet-ah is good-ah for my heart."

"Your Excellency," Hudson acknowledged, blushing. Fenstermacher, Dawson, and Wilson let loose a chorus of rude sounds.

"But-ah I am here," Et Silmarn continued, "to wish-ah you all welcome in the name-ah of King Ollant. You have-ah come on long journey. It-ah is my wish that-ah you find happiness in your new land-ah. I will leave-ah now. Commander Quinn and I meet-ah frequently, and-ah I will visit MacArthur's Valley often. That-ah is all I have to say."

Buccari smiled her thanks, and Hudson escorted the crawling kone to the front door. The settlers exhaled and settled back in their seats, whispers slowly building to nervous chatter.

"Time to bring to order Genellan's first democratic assembly," Stark announced. "Ward Ten declares itself present and ready to vote."

"Very good," Buccari said, forcing a smile. "However, Envoy Stark, you're here to negotiate with the kones and to assist Commander Quinn in ministering to all the settlers. You will be residing in the south. The votes cast here tonight will be reserved for those settlers resident in MacArthur's Valley."

"Really," Stark blustered. "I'm a settler, too. It is—"

"Of course, sir," she replied. "But these votes will have direct significance for those who are staying. I'm afraid your vote might be overly persuasive." Her face muscles ached from artificial emotions.

Stark's countenance darkened. He started to speak but clamped his long jaw tight, impressing Buccari with his self-control.

"First," she announced, "Commander Quinn is fleet administrator for Genellan and the final military and judicial authority during phase one colonization. I'm sure her imple-

mentation of martial law will be quite painless. I asked her to
bring a log recorder so that posterity will know of our wisdom
and eloquence."

"You cheating son of a bitch!" Fenstermacher yelled. He
glanced up at the gravid silence and then melted under
Buccari's withering stare. But Buccari was thankful for the
laughter. The meeting had started off on a tense note. Hudson
returned and sat next to Quinn.

"Resetting the log," Quinn announced as the levity faded.

"Ah, Commander Quinn," the swarthy settler with the sneer
said. "During the hyperlight transit the settlers—"

"Name and ward, please," Buccari interrupted.

"Jerrad Simpson, Ward Two," the settler replied sourly.
Hudson tapped his chin. It was a signal: Simpson was probably
a Legion security plant.

"Yes, Mr. Simpson," Quinn said.

"During transit," Simpson continued, his voice flat and measured, "we held a governmental congress, with Envoy Stark's
assistance, to endorse the Legion settlement constitution and
appoint our colonial government. Why are we doing this when
our leadership has already been defined? And why were we
landed in the north?"

Buccari intervened. "Excellent questions. The Legion constitution does not consider . . . regional needs. MacArthur's Valley, by design, will be isolated from most Legion or konish
interactions."

"Why by design?" Simpson asked.

"Because the first settlers on Genellan," Buccari replied, forgetting her tact, "the Survivors of *Harrier One,* those sitting at
that table, did not participate in your congress."

The settlers stirred. Simpson averted his eyes.

"And you were landed here," she continued, "because
MacArthur's Valley needed a colonization core. You were the
first ones out the chute. The rest of the settlers will in fact be
landed in the south."

"But the Legion authorities—" another settler shouted.

"The Legion has no authority here," Buccari said. "This is
a konish planet."

The group was silent. Stark looked to be chewing on his
heart.

"Someone must govern," St. Pierre finally said. His voice
was soft, but his dark gaze was piercing. "Who governs here,

Sharl, the Legion, the kones, or you?" Hudson did not tap his chin, and Buccari was glad.

"The Legion will . . . coordinate all settlements," she continued. "Envoy Stark, Commander Quinn, and I are on the same team." She smiled a conciliatory smile in Stark's direction. "But the Legion needs to accommodate certain . . . realities. Commander Quinn may choose different methods for the southern colony. The climate and wildlife in the south are less hostile. There will be more settlers in the south. But to answer your question: In time you, the settlers, will govern MacArthur's Valley."

"How long?" Simpson asked.

"When you understand your environment," Buccari replied, "and when you are capable of surviving in it."

"Excuse me!" interrupted another settler, a plump female. "We respect what you've done, but by whose authority do you tell us what to do? We haven't elected you."

Hudson shrugged. Buccari fixed the sunburned settler with an impatient glare.

"Mrs. Jackson. Ward Two," the lady replied imperiously.

"Apparently, Mrs. Jackson, I'm not winning you over with my charm," Buccari said with a laugh. "Commander Quinn, I ask for your support."

"No one knows the planet," Quinn said, standing up, "or the kones better than Sharl. Military government will eventually give way to civil rule, but for now I am taking Sharl's advice as it stands."

"And I fully support that relationship," Stark added, smiling and nodding. "My job is to secure the Legion's foothold on this planet. I cannot do that without Sharl's help. As Sharl said, we are a team."

Buccari, surprised at Stark's unsolicited declaration, smiled and nodded back. Hudson, standing at Quinn's side, mumbled something.

"Tonight," Quinn resumed loudly, "you will elect a council and a provisional mayor. Your council will establish local civil law unless, of course, it contravenes martial law. Major Faro will sit on your council and be the arbiter for any conflict. A similar council will be created in the south. My office will coordinate the councils."

"Before we elect council members," Buccari said, jumping in, "I want to define our objectives. Legion engineers, with your help, are going to construct a hydropower plant at the head of the lake. Eventually homesteads will be established in that vicinity, when and if you are ready to leave this settlement. That won't happen until next spring.

"In addition, regardless of fleet food stocks, we will grow enough crops and hunt enough meat to see the settlement through the winter. All adults will work for the community six hours a day in construction or farming, or other suitable tasks. In addition, everyone will be assigned galley watches. Using the manifest and your background histories, Nash Hudson and I have created preliminary task assignments. We'll meet again tomorrow, same time, and, subject to the council's approval, make any necessary changes to these assignments."

"What about the children?" Mrs. Jackson asked.

"Dawson and Goldberg—" Buccari stopped. "Dawson will run the day care watch schedule from the galley detail. Children must be watched at all times. No child will venture outside without adult supervision. All children over age ten will receive weapons training. In this settlement an adult is anyone checked out with a firearm. If you can shoot, you can vote."

Mrs. Jackson's mouth dropped open.

"I encourage settlers to learn as much as possible," Buccari continued. "If someone can't build their own house and raise their own food, then they had better develop a skill that will give them the means to trade for those services."

"What happens if they can't?" Simpson asked.

"They go back to Earth."

The room was engulfed in silence. Stark stifled a cough.

"That out of the way," Buccari said, "let's vote."

"Do we have to stay in MacArthur's Valley?" Simpson asked.

"Yes," Quinn answered quickly, "for at least a year, and then you are free to choose between settlements."

The settlers elected St. Pierre, Cody, and the irrepressible Mrs. Jackson. Buccari declined all nominations. Sam Cody, exhibiting a quiet power, was elected provisional mayor. His first duty was to adjourn the meeting. Sharl congratulated the new officials and then ushered them out the door. She stood at the top of the porch, looking out at the darkening mountains. Another storm was brewing.

"Well done, Sharl," Stark said at her elbow. "I am impressed. I've always defined leadership as making people do enthusiastically what they really don't care to do at all."

"Groups don't make decisions very well," Quinn said,

joining them. Hudson walked at her shoulder, a chastised-puppy look on his face.

"That is why we are here, Commander," Stark declared. "To make the difficult decisions."

Hudson snorted reflexively and then attempted to camouflage his indiscretion with a sneeze. Quinn rolled her eyes.

"This group's decision-making ability will sharpen considerably," Buccari replied, "as soon as winter hits."

"Well, Sharl," Stark replied, "I'm anxious to try some of your methods. You'll be interested to know we've qualified the landing site for the southern settlement and have officially named it New Edmonton."

"Excellent," Hudson said, sounding marginally sincere. "I can't wait. Back to the warm south."

Buccari detected Hudson delivering a jab to Quinn's ribs. Quinn did not smile.

SIXTEEN

OLDFATHER

Carmichael pushed up through the helmet-scuffed hatch and into the corvette's darkened lab dome. Forward shields were retracted, and stars spilled across ebony heavens in milky wisps. It was dark; Oldfather, a yellow G4 star, was occulted by the third planet.

It had not taken long to locate the remnants of the Oldfather task force—a haunting echo of Shaula. Emergency beacons from lifeboats and panic buoys provided a multitude of homing references. Carmichael's corvettes penetrated the radius of destruction, while Commodore Wells's motherships stayed well back, maintaining jump stations.

"Take a look, Commander," Godonov said, disconnecting his helmet.

Carmichael squeezed by, hooked into the optics interface,

and exhaled. Dimly illuminated by search laser, the hulk of *T.L.S. Hokkaido* hung in space, grimly dark and horribly battle-damaged. Hyperlight shields were buckled, and their support trellis was carried away. The battered lady's habitation ring, shattered and askew, spun slowly. Her operations core was cat-astrophically ruptured, her communication arrays flattened like a forest of steel trees downed by malevolent winds.

"Island-class mothership, November Romeo ten forty-eight," Carmichael said, throat thick. "Flack, send an oprep: positive ID on *Hokkaido*—destroyed in action."

"Aye, Skipper," Flaherty replied softly over the intercom.

"Any more spurious signals?" Carmichael asked.

"Negative," Godonov muttered. "Just those interrogation blips."

"Keep monitoring," Carmichael ordered, giving the hulk a fi-nal optical sweep, quelling his emotions but not his memories.

"Aye, sir," the science officer replied.

"Laser burst from *Raven*," Flaherty reported. "They've found what's left of *Luzon* and *Crete*. Pretty much the same as *Hokkaido*."

"Anything on *Borneo* or the freighters?" Carmichael asked.

"Pieces of freighter scattered all over the planet," the second officer replied. "*Borneo*'s no joy. She's flat disappeared."

Carmichael grunted and disconnected his visor. He slipped past the science officer to the hatch, dropped into the main ac-cess tube, and propelled himself through the flight deck iris. He settled into the pilot's station. Chang and Flaherty silently performed their duties.

"Status on the colony," Carmichael demanded softly.

"Nothing, Skipper," Flaherty reported. "No communications. Imagery shows structural damage. Probes should be on the deck within the hour."

"Skipper, radiation's climbing," Chang reported. "Recom-mend we not go any closer or we'll be spending the rest of our careers in radtox."

"Concur," Carmichael said quietly. "I've got the ship, Bart."

The pilot hit the maneuvering alarm, smoothly powered the nose of the corvette to port, neutralized lateral drift with a burst from his starboard thrusters, and hit the axials to vector the ship on a tangent to the derelict ship.

"Let's do a lap." Carmichael sighed. "Flack, follow up: negative signals. No signs of life. Heavy radiation—transmit intensity readings and decay constants. Assessment: *Hokkaido* considered destroyed in action, all hands lost. Commencing survey orbit at fifteen kilometers."

"Aye, aye, sir," Flaherty said, keying the message for burst.

"What can we do, Skipper?" Chang asked, betraying his emotions. The copilot lowered his head as if to monitor the tactical display.

"We'll orbit until we're relieved," Carmichael replied, not answering the question, "and then we'll go where we're ordered." The realization of what had happened was registering. A part of their lives was forever missing; four motherships lost or destroyed, along with their crews—comrades, classmates, and friends no more.

"Commander!" Godonov's outburst brought Carmichael away from his morbid thoughts. "Radar returns with transponder signals! Lifeboats!"

"Say the bearing." Carmichael found himself staring in vain through the cockpit's viewscreens, staring into blackness, knowing there was nothing to see but staring and hoping nevertheless.

"I've got 'em," Chang reported, helmet visor to the radar interface. "Check one-one-four, plus one-eight. Three contacts—make that four. All on different trajectories."

"Open your scan. You might have missed some on the far side."

"Opening scan," Chang replied.

"Report the lifeboats," Carmichael snapped. "Any word on help?"

"Lifeboats, aye," Flaherty responded. "Kestrel just called in. On site in twenty minutes with full medical."

"We need to go high or low so we can see past the shadow," Chang reported. "Geez, any survivors gotta be glowing."

Carmichael hit the maneuvering alarm and pulsed thrusters. "Engineering, set up a decontamination lock. Flack, take the lander and round up those lifeboats when they clear the hot zone," he ordered, pondering. Something was not right.

"So much for having children," the second officer quipped as he unstrapped and made for the flight deck hatch.

"Mules can't breed," Chang said, reaching back and slapping the junior officer's helmet. "Good luck, mutant. We'll wait for you."

Minutes later Flaherty reported clear. Carmichael saw the silver EPL, brightly reflective in the light of the system star, accelerate past the corvette's nose and slew around to the intercept vector. It accelerated out of visual range. More minutes dragged by.

"In sight," Flaherty's laser signal announced, breaking the tense silence.

"Commander, I'm not getting any life-sign telemetry," Godonov reported. "Negative transponder. Negative stabilization. Nega—"

"*Eagle One-Alpha*, abort approach," Carmichael ordered, breaking radio discipline.

"One-Alpha aborting," Flaherty acknowledged.

Carmichael opened a laser connection. "Hold your position, Flack. It's too late to help anyone in those boats. Let's use a probe."

"Science concurs," Godonov said, joining in on the circuit.

"Roger, Skipper," Flaherty replied. "Standing by."

"Weapons," Carmichael ordered, "fire a beta drone. Mr. Godonov will take control."

Science and weapons both acknowledged. Within minutes Godonov was directing the environmental probe. After an eternity Flaherty reported a visual on the robot's strobe.

"What type of analysis we looking for, Commander?" Godonov asked. "Passives show only radiation, but lots of it."

A magnified image of a fleet lifeboat was being transmitted back to the corvette's screens. The cylindrical craft's solar panels were not deployed, and it was cartwheeling. Strobes pulsed nervously, casting bright red and blue arcs on the vid screens.

"Hit it," Carmichael replied. "Knock on the damn door."

"Roger," Godonov reported. "Ultraviolet laser is tracing . . . now. Full-spectrum radar coming up."

"Commander, we're getting a zinger from task group," the communications petty officer reported. "Interrogative unauthorized radiations."

"Talk to them, Bart," Carmichael snapped. "On-scene commander exercising discretion. Using full-spectrum probe to—"

"Jumping Jupiter!" Chang shouted, his face illuminated by an attenuated blush of frozen white light. Flash filters banged out the stars and immediately started clicking clear in stages.

"Oh, shit!" someone said over the intercom.

Telemetry images from the probe went to static. Silence.

"Detonation!" Godonov reported. "Low-yield fission."

"Flaherty!" Carmichael shouted over the UHF, his hands grabbing the corvette's controls. "*Eagle One* to One-Alpha, come in. Flaherty!"

"He's still transponding," Chang reported. "Be there, Flack!"

"Flack, dammit," Carmichael bellowed. Silence.

"Uh . . . y-yeah, One-Alpha here," Flaherty's shaken voice told them. "Damn, it blew up. Frigging booby trap. In a goddamn frigging lifeboat!"

"Flaherty, you okay?" Carmichael asked. "Get your ass back here."

"Yeah, yeah . . . uh, yes, sir, I think so, but . . . um," Flaherty replied. "Got radiation alarms going off all over the place. Uh, you'll have to bring me back remotely, Skipper. I can't see shit. Flash blind . . . I hope."

SEVENTEEN

ADMINISTRATION

After spending one night on the planet Envoy Stark was heloed across the river to catch the morning EPL back to an orbiting corvette. A fleet shuttle transported him to *Eire*. To the relief of almost everybody, his staff went with him.

The settlers' first full day on the planet was spent in survival indoctrination. Despite a chilly misting rain, a firing range was set up beyond the eastern sally gate, and about a third of the settlers were qualified with pistols. A few, including St. Pierre and Sam Cody, qualified with heavier weapons. Those who were certified were issued sidearms and rifles in a solemn graduation ceremony. Afterward Tatum awed even the other marines with a display of one-armed barrages, using actual-size, crudely painted sheet-metal targets to demonstrate the most effective ways to slay dragons, bears, and nightmares.

The settlers were separated into work details and watch teams. The watch groupings were taken under supervision by the designated Survivor in charge. Cody, St. Pierre, Mrs. Jackson, and Major Faro, in committee, visited each work detail and analyzed assignments. Buccari also toured the various watch groups, but her visits were circumspect and, as most of the watch supervisors discovered, far more critical.

The second evening Sam Cody ran the council meeting with a firm hand. Mrs. Jackson took control of watch shifts and work schedules, dispensing assignments like a field general. St. Pierre sat back and listened.

"Commander Quinn has new business," Cody announced.

"The first download for New Edmonton is scheduled for two weeks from today," Quinn reported, reviewing her admin unit. "Admiral Runacres is anxious to lift the fleet. It's too vulnerable at support stations."

"When do we go south?" Buccari asked.

"I've scheduled an EPL for a suborbital the day after tomorrow at 0900 hours," Quinn replied.

"Stark riding down with the settlers again?" Hudson asked.

"He feels the symbolism is important, Nash," Quinn retorted, her blue eyes flashing. "Why can't you take his actions at face value?"

"Which face?"

Quinn's lips tightened, her face darkened.

"Ignore him." Buccari sighed. "He's trying to get under your skin."

"He's good at it," Quinn said.

"Nash and I will hitch a ride on your apple," Buccari said. "It's time we got out of the council's way. Does the council approve?"

"We'll handle it," Sam Cody announced, eyes twinkling in his rugged face. "Any other new business? No? Meeting adjourned. Same time tomorrow, same place. Let's eat."

"Reggie, a moment of your time," Buccari said as the council members filed toward the door.

"Of course," St. Pierre said, turning with great pleasure to face the beautiful scarred face.

"I've been thinking," she said. "We need a news service. One published by the settlers, I mean. The Legion will put out their normal propaganda, but I think the settlements should have their own. Would you add that to your list of tasks?"

"I'm surprised," St. Pierre replied. "I had the distinct impression that journalists aren't high on your list of heroes."

"Perhaps you can disabuse me," she replied. "You interested?"

"Sounds like a challenge," he answered. "How do I disseminate? There's no net, no scan readers, no viewers."

She held out a piece of paper.

"You're kidding," he said. "Where—"

"Paper works best in primitive settings," she said. "It's part of the standard colony setup. I'll have the next apple bring down a hundred kilos and an admin unit. And a printer, of course."

"Damn." St. Pierre exhaled. "A newspaper." He looked up and grinned.

"I ask only two things," Buccari said, her expression hardening.

"Yes?" he asked, forcing himself to maintain eye contact.

"Be objective and be honest. I want you to look at this planet like it's your home. I want—"

"This *is* my home, Sharl," St. Pierre said.

"Convince me, Reggie," Buccari replied. She turned and walked away.

St. Pierre walked from the lodge, puzzling over Buccari's final comments. Did Buccari know he was a Legion agent? Was she playing games?

"Hey, you Maggie's husband?" someone shouted.

St. Pierre looked up. Fenstermacher and another Survivor, Chief Wilson, the galley watch supervisor, were coming up the hill. St. Pierre walked to meet them. Both men held thin wooden poles on their shoulders: fishing poles with metal eyes and crude reels.

"Yes," St. Pierre replied, extending his hand. "Call me Reggie."

"Yeah, right," Fenstermacher replied, ignoring it. "Maggie's working with my wife on some plantings. She wanted you to know she'd be late for evening meal." He turned and walked away.

"Thank you ... Fenstermacher, isn't it?" St. Pierre shouted after him. "Where might I find her?"

"Down to the cove," Fenstermacher said over his shoulder. "Where I'd be if my wife hadn't seen fit to use me as her messenger boy."

"Ignore him," Chief Wilson said, laughing. He was a portly, moonfaced man with graying beard and eyebrows. He stepped forward, hand extended. "Gunner Wilson. We met earlier. You coming our way, Reggie?"

"Sure, Gunner," St. Pierre replied, shaking hands and joining in step. "How'd you get put in charge of galley watches with a name like Gunner? Buccari angry at you?"

"Long story," Wilson replied as they approached the western sally gate where the settlement spring ran through a portcullis set under the palisade wall. Marines on the wall waved them through. "I was weapons chief on *Harrier One*. Someone had to take charge of cooking after we pranged our asses on this planet. So I—"

"Chief Cookie took over," Fenstermacher said, jumping in, "and we all just wished we'd died of starvation. Gunner's the only one that stayed fat. Funny thing, eh?"

"I'm giving myself the day off," Wilson replied. "Winfried here needs another fishing lesson."

"My fanny," Fenstermacher snorted. "I'm the king."

"King of your fanny," Wilson retorted. "When Les lets you."

The trio walked along a well-trod trail between saffron and powder-blue blossoms, the spring gurgling at their side. Fenstermacher never stopped talking, constantly castigating Wilson's heritage and fishing skills. Wilson, laconic only by comparison, returned it in full measure. The drizzly day had advanced into a beautiful evening, although as the sun disappeared behind the mountain peaks, the air assumed a bracing chill.

They followed the rill to the cove, its surface dark and mirror-flat. Two crested ducklike creatures paddled across silky water, leaving perfect, persistent wakes. An animal howled forlornly in the distance, and flocks of birds chittered in the hardwoods.

"Damn, they're rising already," Fenstermacher complained loudly. St. Pierre noticed clusters of concentric ripples along the shore of the forested peninsula defining the cove.

"Shut up, you little worm," Gunner Wilson hissed. "Every fish in the valley can hear you coming."

"Hell, I'll still catch more'n you," Fenstermacher whispered. "Can't help it if fish don't like fatheads."

"We're leaving you now, Reggie." Wilson laughed, planting his boot on Fenstermacher's posterior. Wilson pointed along the shore. "Your wife's over that way."

The duo, yakking like parrots, headed across the wooded peninsula. Hunters materialized from the brush and waddled after the fishermen. Fenstermacher flashed hand signs, and the aliens chittered indignantly. One threw something at Fenstermacher. Gunner Wilson roared with laughter.

St. Pierre forded the brook and walked along the narrow, hard-packed beach, past rows of vegetables and grains—so relaxing, so bucolic. The fertile odors were hypnotic. The opening in the cove afforded him a view of the far side of the lake and the glacier-hung valley walls. Beyond, rising in breathtaking sweeps of snow-covered granite, were the western mountains, massive and awesome. St. Pierre pondered the feeble presence of humans on this pristine planet so far from teeming Earth; they were but tiny motes of intelligence, specks of self-awareness in an unspoiled ocean of innocence.

"What cloud are you on, good-looking?"

"Huh!" St. Pierre stuttered, snapping back to reality. He turned to see his wife and Leslie Lee sprawling among the plants. They sat on a low levee, bare legs and feet in muddy water.

"Howdy," Lee said, black eyes shining behind enchanting folds. Her long jet hair was twisted into a thick braid.

"A walking daydream if ever I saw one," Maggie said, laughing, her countenance radiant.

"Aren't you cold?" St. Pierre asked, but then his attention was captured by two cliff dwellers emerging from the vegetation. Large ones, as tall as his wife—guilders. They chittered in sharp, high tones. One sampled a clod of dirt like an epicure tasting a divine sauce.

"Cold? Yeah, I guess," Maggie said, smiling at his discomfiture. "These are the gardeners I was telling you about. Meet Dirt Eater and Dirt Eater Two."

St. Pierre gawked at the ugly creatures. They wore only leather codpieces, and except for a hood of gray fur, their bodies were covered with a very dirty cream-colored pelt. They had no discernible flight membranes. Both aliens carried a many-pocketed pouch on a thick strap around their sinewy shoulders. One also wore a Legion communicator around its neck. They bowed; he nodded awkwardly.

St. Pierre reluctantly shifted his stare from the cliff dwellers to his wife. She wore a scarf under a floppy Legion expedition hat. Her clothes were profoundly soiled, and she smelled of freshly turned dirt. She was happy—and beautiful.

"They don't have membranes," St. Pierre said, trying to smile.

"Gardeners have their flight spines removed when they declare for their guild," Lee answered, her voice a pleasant alto. "Thanks for bringing Maggie to me. The gardeners love her."

"Maggie did all the bringing," St. Pierre replied, turning and staring at his wife. "I'm traveling on her ticket. And I love her, too."

Maggie blushed and wiped her cheek with a grimy hand, leaving a black stripe of mud. It was so beautiful, it brought tears to his eyes.

The quake rumbled through MacArthur's Valley at the time of night when it seemed morning would never come. Both moons were full, hanging coldly above the fantastic, dimly silvered heights of the western mountains, the large moon a perfect globe of argent, the smaller satellite golden and misshapen.

The first jolt hit with moderate force—a low-pitched *crump*. Buccari, exquisitely groggy, sat upright trying to comprehend what had happened. Charlie stirred but did not awaken. A soft shaft of moonlight slipped through open shutters; horses nickered, and in the distance a rockdog howled. Buccari swung warm furs from her body and reached out for the cold stones of the steep stairs built into her wall.

A low-pitched rumbling, growing loud, intruded on her groggy sensibilities, and then the primary shock hit, dislodging her from the attic bunk and depositing her onto the wooden floor, her hip glancing painfully off a table. Not satisfied with merely wounding her, the ground surged repeatedly, falling away and rising forcefully, frustrating her efforts to establish her legs beneath her. Rafters groaned desperately. Charlie cried. Buccari's pounding heart leapt into her throat. Her senses were sharpened by adrenaline exploding into her arteries; her night vision and hearing became especially acute. But her brain remained addled by the infidelity of the ground.

Buccari's muddled perceptions recognized a horribly loud *crunch*, but her first organized thought was concern for her son. The rolling motion refused to quiet. Her conditioning activated. She was in a seismic disturbance. Get on your goddamn feet, she fiercely admonished herself. With an exercise of will she regained her footing and grappled with the manic motion of the firmament. She placed a foot on the stairs, fighting to rescue her child.

No sooner did she push against the trembling rock than did her feckless frame of reference return to its natural state of repose. The quake was over. A muted clatter broke the uneasy silence.

Buccari scrambled up the stone ladder, dove into the bedding, and extracted her son, his complaining already abating, replaced with wide-eyed wonder. She dropped to the floor and bolted through the door into silvery darkness. A chilly, damp night greeted her.

The settlement appeared disquietingly normal. Horses' hooves thumped the dirt. She looked to the stables; moonlight danced off the swirling manes and tails of horses galloping in the paddock. People streamed from the structures, their excited voices violating the stillness. A generator kicked on. She heard arcing and saw the blue-white flickering of sparks.

Carrying Charlie on her hip, she stepped off her low wooden porch. Her bare feet sank in swampy mud. The common was flooded! She looked up the moonlit hill—the water tower was gone, carried away by the earthquake.

"Fire!" someone shouted.

Car-r-rumphh! It was a low-pitched explosion. Orange flames flickered beyond the barracks. Buccari ran to Dawson's cabin. Before she could pound on the door, it opened and Nancy's tall form stepped into the opening, her red hair exploding like a starburst of silver in the moonlight.

"Nance, watch Charlie," Buccari ordered, handing her son to the tall, blinking woman. Tatum, Goldberg, and Fenstermacher shouted as they splashed from their cabins. Buccari turned to join them.

"Get some clothes on, lady!" Dawson shouted. "You'll create a real emergency if you go over there like that."

Buccari touched her body. Nodding stupidly, she dashed into her cabin and frantically pulled on shorts, shirt, and boots. The shouting became more frenetic. The unctuous stench of burning fuel oil attacked her nostrils. Her boots unlaced, she bolted through the door and splashed across the common. An ominous cloud roiled into moonlit skies. Sheets of flame climbed the palisade next to the barracks.

The settlers, children crying, were being evacuated; the structure's foundation had collapsed, and a corner tilted drunkenly. Buccari looked around for more damage. A section of the western palisade tilted inward, one of its vertical supports sheared at the base. She spotted Tatum and Chastain in the middle of the evacuation, carrying children under their arms and herding adults before them.

"What happened, Sandy?" she shouted, grabbing children.

"Quake tumbled the fuel drums," Tatum shouted back. "Some of them ruptured. Water from the tank rushed down and sloshed fuel oil all over hell, and then the primary generator arced, lighting it off."

"Still got no power to pump water from the cove," Chastain rumbled. "Fenstermacher and Goldberg are working on the auxiliary."

Fire extinguishers *whoosh*ed into action, white exhausts luminescent in the moonlight. Major Faro and a squad of marines came running with a pumping unit. The conflagration danced high, but most areas were burning harmlessly, flames guttering on top of wet ground, the fuel being consumed rapidly. One by one the hot spots were doused. Cheers went up with the final one's demise, but Buccari's burden was not lessened; there was other damage to worry about. She turned to examine the structural integrity of the barracks.

A hunter screeched—a danger signal.

"Roof's on fire!" someone shouted.

She looked up. An orange glow limned the eaves of the barracks roof, and then a tongue of flame leapt into view. Flames! A cinder had jumped to the shingled roof. Her settlement was burning again! She had seen it burn too often.

Through the night they fought the fire. Survivors, settlers, and marines formed a bucket brigade to the cove and hand carried water up the hill, struggling to save at least the ground floor and, more important, prevent the fire from spreading. The wooden structure, its members charged with resins and wood chips, burned fast, sending clouds of glowing embers into the air. At last they cranked up another generator and were able to pump water through the hoses, but it was too late.

With the eastern sky hinting at the coming dawn, the last embers of the fire were extinguished. The building was destroyed. Buccari, hands and face blackened with soot, collapsed on the lodge porch and watched the sun flush alpenglow from the snowy peaks. With extravagant splendor the shadow of the horizon crept inexorably down the western wall of granite. Despite her morose fatigue, Buccari stared with reverence at nature's fabulous display. St. Pierre sat next to her. Fenstermacher, snoring softly, lay flat on his back behind her. One by one the council members and most of the Survivors assembled before her.

"Women and children are settled in the marine barracks,"

Major Faro said. "Marines can live in field tents for as long as it takes."

"That's the most pressing of our problems," Cody said. "What else?"

"The lake sloshed over its banks," Lee reported. "The cove broke the force of the waves, but we lost some low corn. The bucket brigade and hoses did far more damage."

"Couldn't be helped," St. Pierre said. "Shortest distance between two points."

"Should we put more people on agriculture now?" Mrs. Jackson asked.

"We'll need everyone we can get building shelters," Sam Cody answered. "What do you think, Sharl?"

"Not shelters, Sam," Buccari replied, her eyes burning from smoke and lack of sleep. "We'll build homesteads instead."

"Are they ready, Sharl?" Hudson replied.

"Building another barracks would be a waste of time," she said.

"We'll need a barracks for other downloads," Cody protested.

"If it's up to me," she said, "we've seen the last settler download for MacArthur's Valley." A mutinous muttering lifted from the council members. Buccari looked up.

Pepper Goldberg waited nervously on the periphery of the meeting. Goldberg had been prominent in the middle of the fire fighting, soot-darkened and disheveled, getting the auxiliary generator on line, chopping back burning detritus. Now she was cleaned up and wearing a creased spacer jumpsuit and gold beret. Her fine dark hair had been sheared.

"Excuse me," Buccari said, stepping from the porch. Goldberg looked at her shiny boots.

"You looking for me, Pepper?" Buccari asked.

"There's an EPL taking off in an hour," Goldberg said, lifting her chin but not making eye contact. "I'm scheduled to—I couldn't leave without saying good-bye. Sharl, I've tried, but I can't do it. I'm—"

"I understand, Pepper," Buccari said, holding out her hand. "You're a damn good engineering tech. The fleet needs you, and you need the fleet. We'll take care of Honey for you . . . and Sandy. Good luck, Pepper."

Goldberg tightened her lips and grabbed Buccari's hand, then turned for the palisade gate. An all-terrain vehicle waited there. The ATV would take Goldberg to Longo's Meadow, where a helo would lift her to the cliffs on the far side of the river. And then Goldberg would get in an EPL and blast off the planet to rejoin the fleet. Buccari exhaled and turned back to the lodge.

"Okay, council members and watch supervisors," Buccari said, striding up the steps. "Let's take this discussion inside. We've got decisions to make and votes to cast. Nash, you and Commander Quinn will have to handle the southern landings without me. Gunner, where's the coffee? How long before breakfast?"

EIGHTEEN

NEW EDMONTON

A cooling breeze redolent of brine and seaweed came off the ocean, lifting the sounds of surf and seabirds to his ears. Hudson wiped perspiration from his brow and, shading the optics with his cap brim, took a photo scan of the construction. He saved the image sequence to a file on his admin unit and checked the time; orbital uplink was not available for another ten minutes. Sharl and Et Silmarn both wanted vid-images. He felt like a promiscuous spy.

On low bluffs above the ocean industrious Legion engineers were constructing a rollout runway. Great scars of red soil scraped into mounds and tailings marred the grassy landscape. An equipment downloader yawned empty on the flats, its innards converted to an engineering barracks and materials processing plant. Large-tired trucks trundled along the road to New Edmonton, throwing dust clouds shredded by sea breezes. Some of the trucks transported sand shoveled from the dunes; others carried gravel quarried from an open pit a half kilometer to the north.

"They'll break ground for the fuel-cracking and bunkering facilities as soon as the runway is completed," Quinn said, removing her beret. "Equipment's too massive to bring down in retro landings."

"When did the Hegemony approve all this?" Hudson asked, knowing it had not. Since his arrival in the south he had been in frequent contact with both Et Silmarn and Kateos. "Sharl wants to know."

"Envoy Stark takes full responsibility," Quinn replied, her demeanor uncharacteristically evasive. "Admiral Runacres and Captain Gray concurred. The sooner the fleet off-loads the engineering crews and equipment, the sooner Admiral Runacres can download the rest of the settlers. Envoy Stark and I explained this to Et Silmarn and showed him the construction schedules. The governor gave tacit approval."

Quinn supported Stark like an able lieutenant. Deorbit roll-out runways were necessary, but this promised to be a major facility.

"I've reviewed your schedule," Hudson said, punching numbers. "It's tight. How long will it take to build the rollout?"

"Four months," Quinn replied, the corners of her chicory-blue eyes crinkling. "You know, Nash, I'm impressed with your attitude. I was worried you'd get in the way, but you've been a big help."

"Pisses me off, too," Hudson replied. "Having to come down alone. I haven't had time to go over to Ocean Station and see my konish friends. Heck, I can't even take time out to go to the beach."

"Horrors," Quinn said laughing. Her short flaxen hair, shot with gray, lifted with the breeze. Her lightweight Legion uniform blouse, sweat-stained under the armpits, fluttered against her ample contours.

"And besides, I have to report back to Sharl every evening. She's given me an action item list as long as your memory."

"Ah," Quinn said. "That smacked of a compliment."

"Especially for your age."

"M-my age . . ." Quinn huffed, whirling on the tall man. Hudson fell back, only partially feigning fear.

"Scar-faced punk," she retorted, stomping back to the foot-path.

Hudson followed, enjoying the officer's tanned legs. They left the construction site behind, traversing sandy bluffs and skirting small stands of gnarled, wind-bent cypresslike trees. They came out on a breezy point overlooking a turquoise and azure ocean. Below lay a lush strip of marshy wetland enclosed by the dunes of a barrier island. Beyond the dunes ponderous brown seabirds, heavy-billed and big-headed, glided in ground effect, swooping along waves of cresting emerald. Overhead, sea raptors, snowy white against perfect blue, wheeled and screamed. Farther inland a pair of gigantic eagles dipped and stalled in an airborne mating ritual.

"Beautiful!" Hudson said, inhaling the salty air.

"C'mon, nature lover," Quinn shouted, climbing into their all-terrain vehicle. "Tour's over. Time to head back to NEd. I've got a heavy-lifter due down."

"Nature lover, aye," Hudson replied, jumping into the truck. He gave Quinn his best smile. She laughed.

Quinn low-geared them through the dunes and put them on the rutted dirt road connecting the beach construction with humanity's newest colony, New Edmonton—officially nicknamed NEd by the spacers. They came upon a road maintenance crew. The dirt and gravel road was in abysmal condition. Quinn slowed to a spine-jolting crawl. Hudson looked out over pristine hectares of rolling grass and chaparral. In the wind-ruffled blades of yellow and green an onyx-eyed, ferret-faced countenance stared back at him. Hudson blinked, and it disappeared.

"Did you see it?" he asked, hanging on as they jolted over a rut.

"I'm watching the damn road," Quinn replied dryly. "See what?"

"Stop the truck," he said. "Poppers."

"What the hell's a popper?" Quinn asked, braking the vehicle.

"Watch," he said, standing on the running board. "They're curious as hell." No sooner had the last word left his lips than first one and then three more of the russet-furred, weasel-like animals extended flat heads above the grass like widely dispersed submarine periscopes. After a twitchy pivot in both directions the bewhiskered head dropped out of sight. But as one disappeared, another popped nervously back into view, never in the same spot as the earlier ones.

"There must be thousands," Quinn remarked. Multitudes of whiskered faces darted and dipped in the sea of grass like some bizarre effervescence. "They're cute. I've seen vid-images. The biologics report calls them *Mustela genellanus*, Genellan weasels."

"They aren't so little, and they'll steal you blind," Hudson said. "The bulls go to twenty kilos, and they'll pilfer anything shiny or colorful. Wait'll the construction crews start complaining of lost tools."

"Look over there!" Quinn shouted.

A herd of zebra-striped gazelles bounded into view over the near horizon, springing straight-legged from the grass, die-straight horns frenetically oscillating like a black forest of hyperactive parallel lines. It was a large herd. Clouds of birds exploded screeching from the grass like nervous spume before a careening sea vessel.

"They're coming right for us," Quinn said. The poppers were gone. A distinctive guttural yelping penetrated the gentle breeze, a baying.

"Something's chasing them," Hudson said, pulling his new rifle from the backseat, a heavy-gauge over-and-under. "Better start moving."

Quinn engaged the gears. The leading bucks swerved as one, darting to cross the road a stone's throw behind the truck. Gazelles emerged from the grass like dolphins from the sea, sloe eyes surrounded by panicky white, black horns clattering like a thousand drumsticks.

"Move!" Hudson shouted. The black-and-white gazelles kept coming, their dizzying patterns broaching the line of grass on an ever-widening front. The mournful baying exploded in pitch and intensity. Tall grass on the flanks of the bounding gazelles thrashed and flattened. Hudson, standing on the running board, detected the broad, rolling backs of a pack of predators.

As the truck gained speed, a phalanx of dusky, hyenalike brutes taller than wolfhounds exploded from the grass, bursting through the spot where their truck had been. Howling beasts, black tongues lolling between ragged fangs, converged on stragglers. Dozens of graceful gazelles, lithe limbs thrashing, went down in the road under throngs of thick-necked, jaw-thrashing jackals.

"First grass dogs I've seen," Quinn gasped, watching the savagery in her rearview mirror. "We lost a road crew worker a week ago to a pack. Biologists say there are a lot of them."

"Because there are so many gazelle and antelope," Hudson shouted, swinging inside and holding on as the rugged truck shimmied and shuddered over potholes and erosion gullies. "The kones changed the food chain when they eradicated all the dragons south of the coastal range."

"All the dragons?" she questioned, slowing to a manageable pace. She looked anxiously in the rearview mirror.

"Evidently it was easy," Hudson replied. "Something that big and aggressive doesn't know how to hide. The kones haven't reported a dragon sighting on the coastal plain—at least on this side of the river—in two hundred Genellan years."

"How come they didn't get rid of the grass dogs?"

"They've tried. Just too many of them," Hudson replied. "The kones tried to annihilate everything on the coastal plain that threatened them or that had fine fur. There used to be . . . mountain fliers, the kones call them. Like cliff dwellers, only simpler, less civilized. Millions of them south of the mountains. Kones hunted them for their fur. When the supply dried up, the kones went north. That's why cliff dwellers aren't thrilled when they see our large friends."

"I've noticed," Quinn replied, concentrating on the road.

They drove north. The scars and scrapings of New Edmonton came into view. Two Saturn-class heavy-lifters were on site, their bellies jacked down to the planet's surface, disgorging cargo. A tank farm was being erected for water and other drive fuels; the volatiles were color-coded shades of purple, the water silver. The distinctively unattractive profile of a materials facility rose above the graded ground. Composite extrusions, cut to size and color-coded, were stacked in rows.

They came to the helo pads and airstrip, a graded, metal-matted runway with three all-weather hangars—prestressed, lightweight domes bolted to bedrock anchors. Bright yellow aircraft in varying states of assembly squatted on the flight line.

"Let me out, would you, Cass?" Hudson asked. "I have to sign off some final-assembly gripes on my Explorer."

"*Your* Explorer?" Quinn snapped, pulling up alongside the composite brick line shack. "I believe that plane belongs to the Legion, and *I'm* allocating the plane—and a fleet pilot—for MacArthur's Valley."

"Pulling rank again, eh?" Hudson laughed, dragging his gear from the ATV. "What time's tomorrow's download?"

"It's at 0900," she replied, putting the truck in reverse.

"Thanks for the tour," he said, but she had already pulled away. "See you tomorrow morning, bright and early, then," he said to her dust.

"Hey, Mr. Hudson," came a cheerful voice. "She's topped off and ready to go. When we heading north?"

Hudson turned to see Warrant Officer Rodriguez, the fleet pilot assigned to his Explorer, trotting from the line shack.

"Hey, Johnny," Hudson hailed, shouldering his pack. "I'm ready now, but I got to hang around for the download. You know how it is. No one knows what to do unless I'm around to straighten things out."

"Yeah." Rodriguez laughed. "Heard the admiral say so himself."

"Damn straight," Hudson allowed. "Old Bobby Runacres doesn't do squat without asking me." He stowed his gear, and they walked around the canary-yellow Explorer. Rodriguez pulled and pushed on the control surfaces, rechecked fluid levels, and ceremoniously kicked the tires. They flipped for the left seat, and Hudson won.

The high-wing aircraft had seats for ten passengers and a tight cockpit for two. Hudson fired up the nose-mounted turboprop, performed preflight checks, and trundled the plane on its fat low-pressure tires to the runway. After a run-up to get all temps and pressures in limits, Hudson pushed the throttle forward. Rodriguez monitored flight test programs, recording the plane's performance parameters for final sign-off. The lightly loaded Explorer leapt against a warm trade wind, jostling on its soft tires before it was suddenly airborne.

"Yahoo!" Hudson shouted, banking the plane over the colony. Rodriguez, concentrating on his instrumentation, glanced up and smiled.

Hudson looked out at the construction, its magnitude and scope widening daily. An array of sensor stations marked the colony's perimeter, within which a road grid had been staked out and graded. Two buildings were nearing completion: the administration structure in the large central square and a four-story dormitory to the north. Large stacks of composite blocks stood at the ready, and a second and a third dormitory foundation were in varying states of formation.

Hudson lifted his gaze outward. Unlike MacArthur's Valley, New Edmonton was not geographically confined by mountains. NEd was situated on rolling highlands overlooking the ocean, twenty kilometers west of the great river delta and the transparent domes of Ocean Station. It was far enough away that the thundering retrofires of the konish orbital landers were only a distant rumble carried on the prevailing winds.

At three hundred meters above sea level and ten kilometers from the sea NEd was cooler and less humid than Ocean Station. Hudson surveyed the vast tracts of chaparral spreading between the ocean and the distant mountains. NEd lay between two river systems, each watershed providing an abundance of arable land and field game. As Hudson flew inland, he saw herds of spiral-horned antelope, black-horned gazelles, and tawny deer. Commencing at an elevation of six hundred meters, ranks of tall trees, similar to cedar, rose abruptly from the chaparral, an unlimited supply of lumber. Managed right, a planet of unlimited resources.

"Explorer niner-three-golf," his headset crackled. "This is the tower. You were supposed to ask permission for takeoff."

"Howdy, tower," Hudson replied. "Sorry about that. Figured since this was the only airplane in the air—on the whole goddamn planet—you might deduce who we were and what we were doing."

"Regulations, Mr. Hudson," the tower operator replied.

Hudson double clicked his mike button.

NINETEEN

SECOND DOWNLOAD

"PHM-2 at high key!" a controller shouted. Spacer technicians bustled about the flight operations bunker. Hudson watched the flight track of the descending planetary habitation module on a holo-vid.

"Not-ah long now," Et Silmarn rumbled softly, his inflection almost wistful, a difficult quality for a konish voice to attain. He stood on all fours beneath the low ceiling of the operations bunker.

Hudson looked up. Et Silmarn smiled through his faceplate, an uneasy smile at best. Hudson looked around for Quinn. She had been cornered by Captain Gray and Art Mather. Quinn was mainly listening, her demeanor as hard as iron. Mather, her expression placid, was doing the talking. Hudson returned his attention to the holo-vid.

"What are your feelings, Your Excellency?" Hudson asked

in konish. "More humans have traveled to your star system. Will there be regrets?"

"Regrets?" Et Silmarn replied. "I think not." But he said nothing more.

Hudson moved to an observation slit. To the south the distant ocean formed a perfect horizon, its stark juxtaposition with a cloudless, azure sky dulled only slightly by sea haze.

"Optical!" the controller shouted. Hudson looked at the main display. An optical tracking repeater captured the downloader. Through the high-power magnification, the double-delta planform of the massive habitation module was easily discernible on its sweeping turn to final.

"In the groove," the controller said. "We are go for landing."

Hudson laughed ironically. There was no way   prevent a landing; the habitation module had been committed from the moment it had left orbit. It was just of question of where it touched ground, how hard, and in how many pieces. Hudson picked up the descending craft visually, its dimensions expanding as it neared. He detected movement at his shoulder and turned to see Quinn and Mather. Quinn refused to make eye contact, and Mather smiled formally. Captain Gray had moved to the other side of the bunker. Hudson returned his attention to the landing.

Tension increased palpably. The pitch and timbre of the technicians' voices changed, and their movements quickened. Another hundred settlers, their possessions, and the equipment necessary for their survival were being delivered to the planet.

"All telemetry solid," the controller reported. "Positive glide slope, positive line up. Go for gear. Go for pad. Go for retro."

The PHM's stabilizers sparkled, spraying out shimmers in a halo of energy. Puffs of white smoke sputtered into the slipstream. The huge vessel slid down the glide slope, its nose elevating. Laterals erupted, banks of flame angling from the habitation module's flanks. Hudson felt the air vibrating. A gout of white flame shot from the ship's nose.

"Braking thrusters!" the controller reported, raising his voice.

The PHM was close enough to resolve planform geometry and reentry coloration—too big to be hanging in the sky. The perimeter thrusters engaged. Hudson's inner ears vibrated; a grinding noise elevated into his awareness, ever louder. Red flames defined the PHM's hull, projecting down and bending back in the diminishing force of the slipstream. The ship descended, its forward momentum easing to a crawl. The core internals boomed into life, blasting the ground with white-hot fury, their cacophonous report thundering into the heavily insulated bunker, making conversation impossible.

The ship settled gently downward, perfectly aligned with the geometric scar scraped into the ground, a reverse phoenix, into the flames of its old existence. Vertical motion ceased, and the last gouts of fire shot from the hull and disappeared, leaving the planetary habitation module sitting quiescent on the planet, a silent, solitary chunk of civilization shimmering in its residual heat where only days before there had been nothing but grass and soil—noble dirt, untrod by any human, unmarred by any machine.

"Fifteen minutes until hatches," the senior controller announced. "Fire trucks in position. Deploy the medical teams. Good job, everyone."

Bunker doors swung open. Ground crews hustled out. Hudson followed. Et Silmarn declared his happiness at leaving the cool shade. Receiving crews moved to stations, and cargo dollies sidled into position.

"Very different from MacArthur's Valley," Et Silmarn remarked.

"Pretty boring, if you ask me," Hudson replied.

"Boring? Ah, you make a joke—" Et Silmarn started to say.

"Et Silmarn, Your Excellency," Quinn called. Mather was with her.

"Yes-ah, Commander," Et Silmarn replied, turning his great bulk.

Quinn's expression and tone were composed, but her fiery blue eyes belied her countenance. Hudson had become attuned to her anger.

"Your Excellency," she exhaled, speaking konish, "Envoy Stark apologizes, but he has requested that your official welcome to the settlers be delayed for one week. He would like to acclimate them to their surroundings without the . . . stress that your presence might cause. His experience with the first download indicated the settlers, particularly the children, were intimidated by your presence."

"Too much competition," Hudson added.

"That's enough, Nash," Quinn barked in Legion, jaw set and face reddening. Mather's head snapped back and forth from speaker to speaker. Hudson backed down. Quinn was in a foul enough mood.

"Please, please," Et Silmarn pleaded, falling to his hands. "Do not-ah argue, my good friends. Of course I will-ah comply with your envoy's wishes. Commander Quinn, I will-ah await your instructions."

"I'll go with you, Your Ex—" Hudson began.

"No, Citizen Hudsawn, you-ah will stay," Et Silmarn rumbled, his irritation suddenly evident. "Citizen Sharl would not-ah tolerate your absence. You have a job to do, as-ah do I."

The noblekone bowed, towered to his hinds, and departed at a dignified gait. A konish land cruiser awaited him. They watched him board. The bus-sized vehicle trundled away, its balloon tires flattening a path through the tall grasses.

"That was far beyond rude," Hudson said in konish.

"Yeah," Quinn said, still refusing to make eye contact.

"Shall we attend to the settlers?" Mather prompted.

Stark was conspicuously the first person to descend the PHM's ladder. Legion vid-cam crews recorded Stark's descent from every possible angle. Captain Gray was there to take his hand, raising it like a prizefight champion's. Once the envoy was safely on the ground, the habitation module's crew permitted settlers to stream down the ladders. The yellow-suited settlers descended to the planet, many dropping to their knees in helpless joy. They blinked at the sun, inhaled the full-bodied ocean air, and hugged their spouses and children, their fears and anxieties replaced by wonder and hope.

Stark stood at the reception station through which the settlers were funneled, shaking hands and patting children on the head. Their immediate needs taken care of, the planet's newcomers were assembled on the side of a gentle swale. Stark stood alone at the focal point of the assembly and waited patiently, his tall form erect, jaw lifted nobly. Vid-cam crews scuttled about. At least one recording unit was on the envoy at all times. Members of his staff and security detail orbited the assembly.

"Welcome to the planet Genellan," Stark announced, poised like a general taking the battlefield. "Brave settlers, I give you humanity's new home, New Edmonton."

He gestured with a dramatic sweep of his arm. The settlers cheered.

"We are today," Stark continued, "privileged to witness the

reestablishment of our species. A new era has begun, and you and your children are the Tellurian Legion's messengers of hope."

More cheers, but with reduced energy. Children began protesting. Stark droned on until even he perceived the settlers' fatigued stupor.

"But we have much work to do," he summarized, pausing to let his words sink in. "Our lives, yes, our lives, yours and mine, will not be easy. We must make sacrifices, and we must work hard. Together, helping each other, we will build a new Rome, a new Athens . . . a new Edmonton."

"Yuk, yuk, I get it," Hudson tittered in a fool's whisper. "New Edmonton. Is that profound or what?"

Mather leaned over and pressed her arm against Hudson's. "Shut up, asshole," she growled.

Hudson, choosing the better part of valor, smiled fetchingly and moved briskly away, taking a position among Quinn's staff.

Quinn briefly took center stage to introduce herself and the other members of fleet administration. The ceremonies complete, the settlers were placed on lorries and driven to their dormitory. Stark, with Captain Gray at his side, came up to congratulate Quinn and himself.

"Now, that's more like it," he remarked. "No emergencies, no frightening aliens. We'll make these settlers feel at home in no time."

"We did a good job, didn't we?" Gray wheedled.

Quinn nodded. "Yes, sir." She made eye contact with Hudson.

"Two downloads on the ground and five more to go," Gray stated importantly. "The next download is scheduled for three days from today at 1000 hours. PHM-3 off *Vancouver*."

"Everything's ready here," Quinn replied. "We've made good—"

"What's this about grass dogs?" Stark demanded. "I've received reports of a fatality. And nightmare sightings."

"It's a wild planet, Mr. Envoy," Quinn replied. "It would be well to start off with firearms training."

"Why not build a wall around the settlement?" Stark shot back.

"The output from the materials-processing plant is completely allocated. Using the composite blocks for a wall will delay the building of dorms. The settlers will have to live in tents. The monsoons will commence any day."

"But a wall will demonstrate our concern for everyone," Stark replied. "The protection of the colony must be the first priority."

"Giving the individuals the ability to protect themselves might—"

"I would like a wall built around this settlement, Commander."

"But—"

"Build the wall, Commander," Captain Gray ordered. An all-terrain drove up, and the two men got in.

"Yes, sir," Quinn replied as the truck pulled out.

"Geezus, Cassy," Hudson remarked, grabbing her arm. "What gives here? Who's in charge? You're letting Stark roll you right into the ground. Sharl would never—"

"Neither you nor Sharl understands," Quinn said. "Governing a settlement this size will take skills and leadership that come only from experience. This isn't a small group of marooned survivors; it's a city being born, a nation. Captain Gray has ordered me to take the envoy's lead. Envoy Stark is certainly not perfect, but for the most part he knows what he's doing."

Hudson could only stand there. Quinn, lips tight, walked away.

"Well, Commander," Hudson said to her back, "I guess I'll head north. You don't need my advice." He turned away.

"Nash," she said.

"Yeah," he said, stopping.

"Have a safe trip, Nash."

"Thanks, Mom," Hudson said. "We'll be back for the negotiations."

TWENTY

CONTROL

"I bid thee long life, elders," Craag twittered solemnly, taking a perch in the granite dock. He bowed low, wiry hands held outward, palms up. The knotted leather amulet signifying his rank swung on its hide thong about his neck. Running water gurgled in the silence.

"Rising winds, Craag, clan of Veera, leader-of-hunters," Koop-the-facilitator replied. Eleven elders, the oldest cliff dwellers, roosted at the black marble table, five on each side of the eldest, the gray fur of their knobby heads turned uniformly to alabaster, jeweled necklaces glittering in the yellow light of the spirit lamps.

"Thee have requested an audience," old Koop stated. The ancient fisher's voice was as soft as the breezes of spring yet easily heard.

"I seek advice," Craag said.

"Such speaks well of thy wisdom," Koop politely replied.

"May thy soul find peace, old sage," Craag replied.

"Speak thou, hunter leader," Koop chirped, closing his eyes.

"Our world has changed forever," Craag stated.

"And will forever change," spoke Craat, the next oldest.

"Continue, hunter leader," Ruule chirped wearily. "Thy worries become our worries."

"I speak for the hunters," Craig screeched ritually. "Gods grace our families with many young. Gods grace our rivers and lakes with a surfeit of fish and beasts to feed our young. That is good.

"Sentries no longer perish under the burden of salt bags, for long-legs provide golden-tails and fat-tired machines to bear our mineral harvests, and all beasts of the field flee the long-leg death sticks. That is also good.

"But sentries, unchallenged and untested, become arrogant warriors who become sires of still more young. Our warrens overflow with fledglings, and our lives grow ever easier, ever softer, ever more indolent."

"Indolence is the death of soul," steam user Bool said.

"A spiral of blessings," Muube said sadly, "becomes a curse bountiful. Verily, the world changes."

"Guilders are likewise beset." Koop grimaced. "Though hunters would find abundant forage, our gardens and fish farms are hard pressed to provide sustenance. Our cliffs have become crowded. We produce prodigious amounts, yet food stocks dwindle. Our burgeoning numbers are faced with that toothless yet deadliest of perils.

"Come winter next," Ruule added, "surpluses will be consumed. Guilders will be ever more dependent on the providence of the hunt. Our medicines will be exhausted. Our weak and our aged will perish."

Craag-leader-of-hunters perched in the stone dock and remained silent. Water gurgled softly through stone viaducts overhead. The globed flames of the oil lamps burned a soft orange and without turbulence.

"The long-legs provide a solution," the elder Bool finally said. All turned to hear his wisdom.

"The long-legs are not bound by place," Bool continued. "Nay, they are not confined even by the stars. We must learn from their example. It is time we learned to live in the valleys."

The other elders shrank in their perches, all closing their eyes in concentration. Craag was taken aback.

"True," an old gardener said at last. "The long-leg grains are large and nutritious, though they require large tracts of arable land."

"Large tracts of low land," Craag remonstrated. "These are challenges to defend. It is the duty of hunters to protect guilders." He felt panic. The plateau was the impregnable citadel of their society. Hunters and guilders dwelled on cliffs, not in valleys.

"Life is a tribulation," Koop spoke. "The solution is before us."

The council chambers thundered in silence.

"Mountains ever crumble, aged ones," Craag finally replied.

St. Pierre finished cleaving the rafter. He put down his power saw, and picked up his admin unit, and recorded the scene as a vid-image. Someday he would expand this small cabin and build his own outbuildings. He wished for a way to document the sappy resins and sawdust, the sour smell of hot bodies, and the dusky scent of warm earth and foliage. And the sounds: thumping axes, birds crying in the hardwoods, elk bugling across the lake, a team of horses straining at a stump, snorting and whinnying—a symphony. St. Pierre sweated in the penetrating warmth of the afternoon sun and tasted his own salt; he inhaled, he listened, and he watched. Never had he felt so alive.

"Ah, ya dumb dingleball," Fenstermacher said, staring with disdain at the intricate scaffolding. Fenstermacher was inspecting the second section's work. That engineering section was composed entirely of guilders. More cliff dwellers arrived each day.

"It'll take more time to assemble the frigging gantry than it does to build the damn frigging cabin," the little man ranted, using hatchetlike hand signs. Lizard Lips chirped to his fellow guilders. The cliff dwellers, stone carvers and steam users, raucously expressed their opinions. A brace of hunters, perching on the gantry framework like mattock-headed buzzards, stared down impassively.

St. Pierre was fatigued, but he was anxious to finish. The foundation to his and Maggie's cabin was one of the first to have been completed. He examined the small cabin's foundation and wondered at the scale of the massive structure: ponderously thick walls, rigidly mortared and excavated to bedrock. Buccari called it a storm cellar, but St. Pierre knew it was a redoubt, their shelter against dragons and nightmares. Every cabin was built on the same plan; every cabin had a storm cellar, and every storm cellar, at the unyielding insistence of the cliff dwellers, had a rock-lined escape tunnel.

St. Pierre returned his attention to the debate. Sam Cody and the other humans stood around mopping heads and stretching backs, glad for the respite. Not so the guilders; those not involved in discussion waddled about, chipping, measuring, cutting, always moving, always adjusting. He was fascinated with their childlike innocence and unrequited assistance. Unlike hunters, who wore leather armor, and gardeners, who wore next to nothing, stone carvers wore dun-colored tunics and talon coverings of heavy leather. Their tunics were belted with harnesses holding tools and other appurtenances. Steam users wore similar garb, but usually in darker shades of brown. Their tunics had big pockets, and nearly all steam users carried a folding sextantlike device for measuring angles and distances.

"Fur for brains has enough mechanical advantage here to build a bridge," Fenstermacher said. "They ain't never heard of muscle."

Lizard Lips screeched and pointed with both hands together. Buccari and her foundation crew approached, evidently finished with site four, which was visible down the slope. The goal was to finish twenty homesteads before winter, laid out in support clusters of four cabins each. Each cabin in a homestead cluster was visible from at least one other cabin in that cluster. Each cluster would have its own water tank and food storage barn. Each homestead was allocated a ten-hectare tract of land. How the land was used and how much of it was cleared of trees would be up to the individual settlers, working alone or with their cluster members.

"Enough squabbling," Cody said, nodding at Buccari. "Fenstermacher, do it your way on site two. We'll let Lizard Lips supervise us."

"Suit yourself," Fenstermacher replied. "His contraption will get the job done, but Mrs. Jackson's construction team'll have site two done before you even set your ridgepole."

"Sounds like a wager," Buccari said, walking into the discussion and putting her arm over Fenstermacher's shoulder. "Sam, if I were you, I wouldn't take the Fensterman lightly."

The irrepressible Fenstermacher could only smile stupidly and shuffle his feet. The cliff dwellers stopped and paid heed to Buccari's presence. She bowed gracefully to the creatures and whistled shrilly, mimicking their greeting. The guilders displayed teeth and hiss-chittered in laughter. St. Pierre was fascinated with Buccari's easy power over the kones and cliff dwellers—and over the humans.

A hunter screeched sharply!

All the cliff dwellers peered nervously upward. Hunters reflexively unlimbered flying membranes. Lizard Lips flashed hand signals.

"Airplane," Buccari said, green eyes lifting to the sunlight.

St. Pierre listened and looked but detected nothing. He glanced covertly at Buccari, his eyes drawn to her like a hapless moth to a bright flame. Her beautiful face, dirty and scarred, was upturned, anticipation illuminating her tired and drawn countenance. Her hair, bound in a ponytail, had become disheveled with her exertions; sweat dripped from her nose and soaked her thin shirt, revealing a vital and sensually powerful physique. She perceived his attentions and turned to him. She tightened her lips and lowered her eyes with delightful shyness.

St. Pierre heard engine noises, but valley echoes made their direction difficult to discern. A hunter screeched, and there it was, a bright streak of yellow racing in low over the lake. The plane banked hard, arcing overhead, knife edged to the ground. The pilot pulled his craft back to the direction from which it had come, leveled the plane for an instant, and then waggled the wings drunkenly, all the while descending in the direction of Longo's Meadow.

"It's Hudson." Buccari laughed, eyes brightening. "With our new Explorer. I can't wait to go up. I'm playing hooky tomorrow."

"Good," Sam Cody said. "Leave us alone so we can get some work done." St. Pierre laughed; Buccari had been running them relentlessly.

"Watch shift's over," Buccari shouted as she hand signed to the cliff dwellers. "Fenstermacher, go tell the other crews."

"We got an hour left," Cody grumbled unconvincingly.

"Time off for good behavior," Buccari replied, heading for the lake trail. Lizard Lips screeched with irritating intensity. Stone carvers and steam users stopped at his command and began ambling away, chirping and squealing. Lizard Lips stood, contemplating his handiwork.

"Well, you guys can stand here like stumps, but I'm going for a swim," Fenstermacher declared, skipping after Buccari. He skidded to a stop. "Cody, tell the furball we'll beat you guys to the ridgepole."

"What's the bet?" Cody asked.

"Losing team puts on the roof," Fenstermacher replied.

Cody looked at his construction team.

"Let's do it," St. Pierre shouted. With rising enthusiasm the others echoed his words. Lizard Lips looked about in confusion.

"Wager accepted," Cody shouted after Fenstermacher's retreating form. The little man raised a languid hand.

"You heard the boss," Cody grumbled. "Quitting time. I want everyone here tomorrow morning with a sweat on by the time the sun clears the horizon. Lizzy, we're going to do you proud."

Cody's crew staggered downhill, most slapping the cliff dweller on his shoulder. Lizard Lips reacted to the camaraderie with bewilderment.

"Give me that communicator, Lizzy," Cody said, leading the steam user away. "Let me see if I can explain this to you."

St. Pierre watched human and cliff dweller walk away. He captured the vid-image and then leaned against the stone foundation to add a few more bits of information to his journal. Insects clicked and hummed.

"St. Pierre!" a deep female voice hailed. He turned to the summons. It was Major Faro, her camouflaged fatigues sweat-stained and streaked with dirt. A shock of blond hair emerged from her fatigue cap. Newly grown eyebrows and lashes over muddy hazel eyes gave her bland features a focal point. Her broken nose and thick neck were sunburned. She and her marines had been installing an intruder-detection network.

"Good afternoon, Major," St. Pierre replied. "Call me Reggie."

"As in Major Reginald St. Pierre?" Faro replied conspiratorially. "Or, better, Agent Reggie?"

St. Pierre kept his composure. Faro was the last person he had expected to be his control; against growing odds he prayed she was not. The stocky marine wore shorts; her thighs were columns of hairless sinew. Bulky calves danced like autonomous creatures rising from her combat boots. She was a head shorter, but she easily outweighed him, her shoulders wide and her bosom powerfully deep.

"You're being cryptic," St. Pierre replied. "I'm afraid I don't understand. Do you have something to tell me?"

"Your orders, Major," she whispered huskily, her head turning to clear the area. "Reference alpha-one-one-two."

"Counter bravo-two-niner-charlie," he sighed, almost dizzy.

"Maintain deep cover," Faro said, smiling sexually. "Continue as before. Earn the confidence of Sharl Buccari and, if possible, become her trusted lieutenant. Do nothing to jeopardize your status. Avoid agency contact even if you have vital intelligence to impart. We will come to you. Any questions?"

"No questions," St. Pierre replied, his stomach sour.

TWENTY-ONE

ANNIVERSARY

"Wish I could paint," Hudson said, his scarred face bunched in contemplation of the sunset.

"I wish I could fly," Buccari replied, watching an eagle soaring in the distance, backlit by a pumpkin-orange horizon.

Buccari and Hudson rode along the lakeshore under the boughs of fluttering hardwoods, their golden horses nuzzling each other like colts. Buccari reveled in the silky coolness of evening as the summer sun descended beyond the mountains. The light breeze that stirred the verdant foliage fairy-danced across shimmering lake waters. Daylight still reigned, but a sprinkling of first-magnitude stars emerging from the intensely blue evening sky gave notice of impending night.

With brittle abruptness a heavy-lifter launched from the distant cliffs. Attended by the corrosive detonation of its engines, it streaked heavenward. The heavy-lifter, a stiletto of silver atop a rapier of white-hot flame, climbed to the stars, its contrail plume flashing to brilliant white as it leapt above the shadow of the mountains. Buccari swallowed and relaxed. She had been clenching her fists.

"Getting late," she said, tearing her gaze from the lancing passage. She looked at Hudson, his once-handsome face distorted with scar tissue, his wistful gaze frozen on the spaceship's trajectory.

"It's tough not flying, isn't it?" Hudson finally muttered.

"Yeah," she whispered, kicking her horse into a trot.

They approached the nearly completed structures of the first cabin cluster. Fenstermacher's engineering team and Mrs. Jackson's construction crew had won the bet, but even Fenstermacher had to admit that Lizard Lips's innovations were superb. The engineers from different species had combined their

171

efforts and designed a scaffolding gantry that greatly increased the workers' log-setting productivity.

If only hydrogenerators and processing mills could be built as rapidly, Buccari silently lamented. She and Hudson were returning from surveying the Legion engineers' progress on the hydrogenerator being built at the lake's inflow. It was going slowly both because the site was remote and because so many of the fleet's colonization resources were being dedicated to the primary settlement at New Edmonton.

"They won't finish the hydro before winter," Buccari said.

"Keep them working," Hudson said. "Legion engineers have worked in worse conditions than a Genellan winter."

Hudson's return to the north had relieved Buccari of much of her worry, if only because of his unconquerable sense of humor. Hudson also provided a wealth of innovation.

"Good idea," Buccari agreed. "I'll run it by Cassy next week."

Hudson laughed. "Let me. You'll be too busy negotiating with the king's ambassador."

"Hell, no," she said. "It's too good an idea. I want the credit, and besides, if Cassy hears it from you, she'll reject it out of hand."

"She's a glutton for my charm," Hudson replied. "Oh, I forgot to tell you. I got a message from Et Silmarn. He wants to fly us to the dome ceremonies."

"You're getting a lot of messages these days," Buccari said. "Dawson tells me you're receiving encrypted bursts from the ambassador's ship. Your eyes only."

"A couple of my old konish technician buddies," he replied. Too quickly, Buccari thought. "They missed me."

"I miss Kateos," Buccari mused. "She sounds so busy."

"Dowornobb, too," Hudson said, not looking at her.

"The negotiations would go much easier with both of them here," Buccari lamented.

They trotted into the cove. The afternoon watch was long over, but Maggie and Reggie St. Pierre, holding hands and carrying rifles over their shoulders, walked along the tall corn. St. Pierre lifted his weapon in greeting. A troop of gardeners promenaded behind the couple, chirping and tweeting. Buccari and Hudson turned from the cove and trotted up the flowery path alongside the gurgling creek. The guard saluted smartly as they rode through the main gate.

They heard voices and axes at work. An unusual number of

people milled about. Ranks of hunters roosted on building peaks. Guilders perched on logs and rocks around a pyre of lumber stacked between the lodge and the stables. A musk-buffalo carcass was suspended from a gaff spar, the ground beneath it splattered with blood and entrails. A cheer went up as Buccari approached.

"Surprise, surprise," she muttered, giving Hudson a hard look.

"Just following Dawson's orders," he replied, swinging to the ground. O'Toole took their horses.

Tatum, arm bloody to the shoulder, saluted. A collection of settlers and off-duty marines watched his butchering like medical students at their first vivisection. Chief Wilson, with help from hunters, was spitting meat over a row of cooking fires. Below the new water tower another cluster of settlers watched Mendoza stretching the buffalo hide on a tanning frame.

The smell of baking bread mixed with other aromas. Tookmanian carried an armload of sourdough loaves to a trestle table. A collection of stained wooden vats arrayed against the lodge foundation bespoke another Tookmanian industry.

"Attention on deck," Nancy Dawson shouted.

All talking ceased, and everyone turned to the tall redhead. Fenstermacher stood at Dawson's side with a torch. His hard-featured face, tanned and bearded, glowed in the sputtering flames.

"Five years, sir," Fenstermacher reported, stepping forward and handing Buccari the burning brand. "Please do the honors."

Buccari took the flickering torch and walked with a measured pace toward the head-high pyre. Settlers, marines, and cliff dwellers parted before her. A ceremony, she thought. The celebration of their anniversary had become a ritual.

"Five Genellan years. Six Earth years," Buccari shouted, spinning and holding the torch high, its embers falling in a spiral. The Survivors cheered lustily; settlers and marines joined in. She applied the torch. Flames took purchase, spreading with hypnotic inexorability, crackling and popping. Buccari threw the brand onto the pyre and took a seat on a log. The spicy aroma of wood smoke and roasting buffalo blended into a heavenly miasma. Her spirits soared, and her stomach growled.

"Here you go, Skipper," Chief Wilson said, breaking her reverie. Wilson stood there with an old wooden trencher loaded with buffalo steak, valley tubers, beans, and a thick slice of Tookmanian's sourdough.

"Is this heaven?" she asked, gingerly grabbing hot, greasy buffalo and ripping it with her teeth. Her eyes closed in ecstasy.

" 'Tis not yet heaven," a deep voice rumbled. "When it is time, you will become a saint and the angels will sing."

She opened her eyes. Tookmanian's tall, rail-thin form stood before her, gray eyes radiating from a swarthy countenance, mustaches sweeping past a long, clean-shaven chin.

"Would you honor me, sir?" the saturnine man said, holding out a steaming mug of malty cider.

"Tookmanian's pickled," Fenstermacher shouted. "Look, he's smiling."

"Will my head hurt tomorrow, Tooks?" she asked, taking the mug.

"Will the flowers bloom?" Tookmanian smiled again.

"We have cliff dweller beer, too," Chief Wilson said.

"The guilders have great fermentation skills," Tookmanian said. "But please, try my cider first."

She lifted the mug to her nose and inhaled its volatile, spicy essence. She toasted: "Five years, Tooks. Thanks for all your help."

"God bless you, my captain," Tookmanian answered, lifting his mug.

She drank deeply of the cider, and it was strong, full-bodied, and delicious. Its heady powers gave immediate notice. Her head reeled. She slipped from the log and leaned against it. The silver sickle of the large moon slid behind the western mountains, chasing the last vestiges of glorious sunset. Tookmanian grinned hugely, his black mustaches sliding apart like hangerbay doors; his face, burnished like leather, exploded in a myriad of laugh lines.

"Whew!" she exhaled, wiping her mouth with the back of her hand. "I gotta eat some more." Her tongue was numb.

"Go easy," Leslie Lee chided. The medical technician, with Honey and Hope in tow, sat down on the log. "I analyzed it. It has an octane rating like reaction fuel."

Buccari, chewing buffalo, looked for her son. Survivors, settlers, spacer technicians, and marines drew near the fire, plates and mugs brimming. Cliff dwellers, black eyes scintillating with orange flames, ate their barely warmed meat directly from the skewers. Overhead, twilight surrendered to night. The full pantheon of stars assumed its reign, refusing to be dimmed by even the brightest of mortal-built fires.

Buccari detected a familiar chirping. Suddenly Charlie was snuggling under her chin, reaching for food. Great-mother, stern features bottom-lit by flames, perched stone-still on the log at Buccari's side. Great-mother's daughter, the little huntress, was festive, her vibrant body reacting to the flurry of hunter activity.

Hundreds of gruesome warriors descended on the periphery of the fire, shrieking and keening, perching in rows like anthracite statues, black eyes and red maws glistening with reflected light. Humans and cliff dwellers ate and drank, and soon everyone displayed greasy faces and glassy eyes.

As they had every year before, Beppo Schmidt and Toby Mendoza began pounding slowly, rhythmically on a hollow log with knotty cudgels. *Boom, bum-bum-boom, boom . . . boom, boom.* Shave and a haircut, two bits—the sound pattern first used to establish communications with the cliff dwellers. Slowly. A mantra. *Boom, bum-bum-boom, boom . . . boom, boom.*

Hunters joined in, softly at first, rapping on boulders with bars of metal tuned to different notes, speeding up the beat but still relaxed. The hunters embellished the repetitive rhythm with haunting counterrhythms and backbeats, but with unerring coordination they would return in perfect unison to the basic rhythm: *boom, bum-bum-boom, boom . . . boom, boom.* The pace quickened. Tatum and Spitter started dancing, parading around the flames. Bottlenose and Tonto joined in, along with O'Toole and Fenstermacher. Soon a sinuous conga line of humans and hunters threaded around the common, circling the roaring fire.

Buccari, holding her son, sat and watched, remembering. Eventually the revelers collapsed into shrieks and laughter and contented sighs. After a while the only sound was the crackling of the settling fire. Buccari leaned back and emptied her mind.

The soft resonance of a violin lifted into the night: something classical, a fugue. She turned to see Sam Cody, deep in the shadows, playing to the stars. Hunters, black eyes unblinking, twittered with awe and gravitated toward the human.

"I'll be back," Maggie St. Pierre said, getting up rapidly.

A deeper string joined in—a cello. It was Sam's wife, Barret, on the other side of the fire, playing another voice. The instruments sang together, knitting and weaving hauntingly, beautifully. And just when it felt as if perfection had been attained, a flute joined in, raising the tones to another ethereal level. Playing with an enchanting lilt, Maggie St. Pierre strolled closer to the fire, enraptured hunters following her, an incarnation of Hamelin's piper. Sam and Barret Cody joined Maggie at the fire, and the three musicians regaled their audience. Cliff dwellers crowded in, their collective sonic organs resonating in sympathetic harmony.

It ended too soon.

"More!" the humans shouted. Cliff dwellers raised the dust with their ultrasonic approval.

Cody jumped into a lively reel. Maggie St. Pierre joined in, and then the hunters with metal bars picked up the rhythm and added their own touch. Younger hunters danced to the gay riot of sound. When the musicians stopped for wind, everyone clamored for more. After a brief conference the trio commenced a serene concerto, a piece that each player knew well, for they played with passion and control. Great-mother seemed overcome. The huntress hopped from her log and stepped forward, tooth-lined snout raised high. She started singing in piercing tones, higher than the range of any violin. The hunters around the fire became silent, freezing where they stood, mesmerized by the blending of sounds. The music of human and cliff dweller lifted into the blissful Genellan night. Too soon over.

Hudson flopped at Buccari's side, wrestling Charlie from her.

"Isn't it wonderful, Nash?" Buccari yawned, leaning against the log and staring into the star-shot heavens. Fuzzy-headed, she closed her eyes, strangely fulfilled.

"Civilization's not all bad," Hudson said.

"Not all," she allowed.

"Sharl . . . sir," a voice boomed—Chastain's.

Buccari opened her eyes. Chastain's great mass stood over her, his head and face shaved clean. He wore marine fatigues. Her euphoria was swept away like feathers in a storm.

"Oh, Jocko," she groaned too loudly. The gentle murmur of conversation ceased. She climbed stiffly to her feet.

"I'm going up in the morning, sir, er . . . Sharl," Chastain said.

"Oh, Jocko, no," she cried, fighting tears. She took his big

hand. "Charlie will miss you. Oh, God, I'll miss you, Jocko
. . . so much."

Chastain had told no one. Buccari wondered how much the
big man had agonized, how much he had suffered for his loyalty. Chastain was first a marine.

Survivors clustered around, firelight flickering from sad
eyes. Cliff dwellers moved closer, curious. Leslie Lee hand
signed to Captain Two. The hunter-leader screamed and
flapped his membranes loudly, lifting himself to the lodge
eaves. Hunters started shrieking, but as Captain Two reached
his vantage point, he raised his fists, and the cacophony was
shut off. Captain Two, lit by flickering flames, pivoted slowly,
facing the four cardinal points of the azimuth. Returning to
face the fire, the warrior dropped his fists, and the cliff dwellers joined in a chorus of vibrant, high-pitched harmony that
rattled her teeth. Buccari recognized the hunters' song of death,
a paean to Giant-one, to Chastain the warrior. The shrill cries
echoed across the lake.

"We'll all miss you, Jocko," Dawson said. "Good luck."

"Yeah, Jocko," Fenstermacher said, voice cracking.

Buccari reached up and gave Chastain a hug, her arms
barely reaching around the giant's broad back. Chastain reciprocated, his massive arms whispering about her as if embracing
spun glass.

"Harder, Jocko," she sobbed. "Tighter."

Chastain, sniffling, squeezed the air from her lungs.

TWENTY-TWO

SURPRISES

"We are in Genellan orbit," Dowornobb said.

More excited and perhaps more frightened than she could
remember ever being, Kateos looked through the port at the

beautiful planet. Genellan had been growing ever larger during their approach until it had overflowed her thick viewing port, and now she could see only a blue-green limb brilliant against the infinite blackness of space.

"Calm yourself, my mate," Dowornobb pleaded, blinking his eyes and sniffling at the overwhelming onslaught of his mate's anxiety.

"The Thullol-Ransan ships are only one day from orbit," Scientist Mirrtis remarked.

"They must be very powerful," Kateos sighed.

"I will change the subject," Dowornobb said. "Envoy Stark sends welcome in the name of the Tellurian Legion and the settlers."

"He sends messages every day," Kateos replied, "but says nothing."

"Admiral Runacres also sends his regards," Dowornobb began.

"My good friend. How soon before we land?" she asked, emotions thundering in her bowels. She was too excited to be embarrassed.

"The captain recommends we wait three orbits," Dowornobb replied, "so that daylight may come to Ocean Station."

"Three orbits," Kateos said, sighing.

"My mate, I understand why your appointment was kept secret from the king's enemies during our transit, but now that we are in orbit, why have you not told Citizen Sharl? Your status cannot remain secret much longer."

"It will be a surprise," Kateos said. "Sharl will be very happy."

"I do not see why you must surprise her. It serves—"

"It is my decision."

Vibrations were putting Buccari to sleep. She walked forward onto the abat's commodious flight deck and caught Hudson and Et Silmarn giggling like drunks.

"Your Excellency, you smile too much," Buccari said in konish. Hudson looked away. The noblekone's good humor clogged the air, a cloying bittersweet essence. The huge kone overflowed his station, making Hudson look like a child in the copilot's seat. "And you, Nashua Hudson, also smile too much. You are sharing a secret?"

"Secret? The noble governor and I?" Hudson replied in

flawless alien tongue. "Pah! It is just that flying is most enjoyable."

The long flight from MacArthur's Valley was nearing termination. Below, the continent-draining river exploded between the last towering ridges before flattening out into its final wide-banked meanders to the sea.

"It is such pleasure to bring Citizen Hudsawn back to Ocean Station," Et Silmarn boomed too quickly. "The scientists are most anxious. We shall celebrate his arrival all the night through."

"Grinning like clowns," she muttered in Legion, staring outside at the endless expanse of wild planet.

"What-ah is clown?" Et Silmarn asked as he adjusted the throttle.

"A clown?" Hudson replied in konish. "It is what we call our politicians. Envoy Stark is a clown. Actually, that is a great compliment for Envoy Stark."

"Ah, I see," the planetary governor replied, brow tufts sagging.

Laughing, Buccari returned to the passenger compartment. Three immense konish scientists in bulky Genellan suits smiled at her. They engaged in small talk, expressing amazement at her garb. She wore sandals, shorts, and a T-shirt, her legs and arms tanned nut brown. She was perspiring; the kones kept the airplane unbearably warm. She pulled her hair back, lifted it from her neck, and tied it off in a thick ponytail.

The scientists relapsed into conversation. She pulled out an admin unit and returned to her niggling duties, but to no avail. Frustrated with her lack of discipline, she tried to concentrate on her negotiation strategy but could only stare out at the passing planet. The plane droned south.

"Hey, Sharl!" Hudson shouted. "Come look."

She shook open her eyes and stumbled to the flight deck. Ahead lay a breath-taking sweep of turquoise ocean studded with emerald islands and swept by towering gray-hemmed squalls. Closer, rapidly coming under their nose, gashes of red dirt scarred the elevations above the river delta. The konish science station's original undomed structure had been augmented by two very large domes. A third dome, much smaller than the others, made an unbalanced triangle. Angry swathes of highland forest had been cleared. An open-pit mine gaped from the foothills. Near the mine a thin column of gray smoke wafted skyward from a solitary smokestack. The changes since her last trip to the south were breathtaking. The kones knew how to build.

"An Imperial lander is on the pad," Et Silmarn said, pointing. "The king's ambassador has arrived. Negotiations can begin."

"Yeah," Buccari muttered.

"Admiral's party's here, too," Hudson said. "There's a Legion heavy-lifter and two EPLs. Stark must be in ambassadorial heaven."

"A meeting of the races," El Silmarn said.

"Worse," Buccari said. "A meeting of governments. Let's hope your representatives do greater justice to your race than Envoy Stark does to ours."

The konish pilot glanced at Hudson. Hudson looked quickly away. A conspiracy, she thought, scanning the storm-blotted horizon, but to what purpose?

"Big weather coming," she muttered. To the northwest, on the highlands, she saw another blemish on the land—New Edmonton—with its blocky structures and distinctive row of PHMs.

"Summer monsoons," Et Silmarn replied. The kone's happiness was palpable as he lined up for the approach to Ocean Station's runway. "Thunderstorms every afternoon."

The abat descended to a gentle touchdown. Et Silmarn rolled it out to a parking mat beneath the landing pads. Domes and gantries loomed above them. Kones wearing full Genellan rigs galloped to the plane. The cargo door opened before Et Silmarn secured the engine. Her fellow passengers, belying their dimensions, pounced lightly to the ground.

A cool breeze carrying the salty freshness of the ocean flushed stale air out of the abat cabin. Buccari grabbed her duffel and dropped heavily to the ground. Hudson and Et Silmarn descended from the forward hatch, smiling like idiots. Silmarn slid behind the impassive armor of his breathing unit. Hudson affected a yawn.

Buccari turned toward the reception committee. The scarlet and white standard of the Tellurian Legion and the midnight-blue pennant of the Northern Hegemony flew from tall masts, popping softly in the breeze. She recognized Admiral Runacres and Captain Merriwether, both florid under the natural light of a sun. The senior fleet officers were unceremoniously garbed in floppy exploration hats and fleet fatigues. Both wore sun goggles and looked decidedly out of place. Cassy Quinn stood at the admiral's side, dressed in crisp tropicals.

Stark, garbed in a formal diplomatic swallowtail with a yellow sash, stood out sorely. The pièce de résistance was a ludicrous silk stovepipe set atop his long face, giving him a total height rivaling that of the kones. His black-uniformed entourage surrounded him like a stain.

A contingent of helmeted kones approached, walking upright, as tall as trees and as wide as mountains. The two in the lead wore silver-blue Genellan suits. The others wore the burgundy uniform of the Imperial Security Guard, reminding Buccari of the day Colonel Longo died. The contingent's leader lifted its breathing unit. Buccari's morbid thoughts dissipated like smoke in a gale.

"Master Dowornobb!" she shouted, dropping her duffel.

The kone pounced to all fours and covered the intervening distance with a single gallop. The behemoth tried to touch his forehead to the ground, but Buccari wrapped her arms around his prodigious neck and hugged him like a wrestler, her smooth cheek pressed to his grainy complexion.

"Sister Sharl," came a voice gloriously familiar, deep and mellifluous. She looked up to see the other silver-garbed kone looming above her. It lifted its breathing helmet.

"Katy!" she shouted. The kone cast her helmet to the ground and swept Buccari into the air like a babe. The giant pulled Buccari to the stiff material covering her breast and squeezed. Buccari luxuriated in the breathless discomfort, attempting to return the hug.

The giant placed Buccari gently on her feet. Buccari grabbed the great splayed face and planted a kiss on its tough skin. Kateos's huge brown eyes welled, her slab nose ran copiously, and Buccari could smell the rank power of her pure joy. Hudson and Dowornobb also embraced, the scientist's emanations adding to the bitter perfume.

And then they were all hugging, Kateos and Dowornobb engulfing the coughing humans between their massive bodies.

"You all knew," Buccari shouted, breaking clear and backhanding Hudson in the chest. "And you didn't tell me."

"Ooph," Hudson grunted. "Orders, you know."

"And Citizen Hudsawn," Kateos said, rising to her hinds, towering above the humans and holding Hudson at arm's length. "Citizen Hudsawn, our dearest friend, has returned from the dead."

"We were so worried for you, Hudsawn," Dowornobb said. The sad-eyed scientist squatted and placed a huge arm on Hudson's shoulder. "Your face is quite deformed. You have suffered greatly."

"Scientist Dowornobb, at least I am not as morbidly unattractive as you are," Hudson replied in stilted high konish.

"Ah, he has not changed," Dowornobb replied. "Too bad."

"Speaking of suffering," Kateos announced, giving Buccari a conspiratorial wink, "we must attend to business." Dowornobb sneezed repeatedly, his great body shuddering with each nasal explosion. The huge scientist shrugged and put on his helmet.

"As planetary governor it is my duty to make formal introductions," Et Silmarn said in konish. Stark and Runacres, with Quinn acting as official translator, were beckoned forward. Buccari diverted her happy stare from Kateos and glanced around, wondering at the sudden formality. Stark looked particularly disconcerted, in fact irritated. Runacres smiled graciously, but his eyes revealed profound anxiety; the Oldfather rescue cell was overdue. Buccari thought about Carmichael and all her mates suffering the dangers of space.

"Citizen Sharl," Et Silmarn began, "friend to the king and representative of those citizens of the Hegemony known collectively as the Survivors, permit me to introduce the king's ambassador to the planet Genellan, fiefdom and reserve of the Northern Hegemony."

Buccari looked around for some distinguished presence not yet perceived. Kateos smiled largely.

"I present the honorable and loyal servant of the king," Et Silmarn continued, "Mistress Tios Teos Kateos, scientist and translator. In her person recognize King Ollant's authority. Her decisions are the king's. Long live King Ollant."

"Katy! Kateos!" Buccari gasped, stepping backward.

Kateos lifted her multitude of chins. Another wave of bitter odor suffused the ether and was gone quickly on the soft breeze.

"Ambassador Kateos. Long . . . long live King Ollant," Buccari said, dropping to her knees and putting her forehead to the ground. Hudson was at Buccari's side, emulating her actions.

"Rise, bosom friends," Kateos said in perfect Legion.

"Ambassador Kateos," Buccari said loudly and proudly as she stood erect, "it is my honor to serve King Ollant, as it is my honor to serve the Tellurian Legion. May both parties be well advantaged."

Dowornobb smiled at Kateos, turned, and shouted Buccari's words, translating them into konish. The crowd cheered, Buccari and Hudson as loudly as anyone. Kateos's eye tufts sprang rigid. Her joy manifested itself as a bitter tang on the breeze. No longer was it Kateos's function to translate the words of others.

"Well spoken, Citizen Sharl, but-ah all must-ah go into domes," Et Silmarn announced. "A lander descends-ah from orbit. Another emissary to join us. It-ah is soon loud-ah. Also, there-ah is rain approaching."

Another emissary! Buccari gave Kateos a puzzled look, but the ambassador only issued a cryptic smile. Kateos was already playing the game, and well. The big female bowed and turned away, heading an entourage toward the large dome adjacent to the orbital landing pads. Distant thunder rolled up the wooded slope.

"Please-ah to follow guides to negotiation dome," Et Silmarn shouted in Legion. "Talks start-ah in one hour."

The governor set off at an undignified lope after Kateos. Humans and their konish escorts filed along the smoothly curbed roadbed toward the small dome's gaping air lock. A konish technician, an old friend of Hudson's, picked up their duffels. Buccari followed Hudson into the flow.

"Having fun?" a familiar voice drawled. Merriwether, removing her face-shielding goggles, was at Buccari's shoulder.

"Good morning, Captain," Sharl said. "Fun? Honestly, no. Baby-sitting a new colony is hard work."

"I would think Hudson and Commander Quinn could handle the planet," Merriwether replied. "And what are settlement councils for?"

"Your psychology is showing, Captain," Buccari whispered.

"Psychology, crap!" Merriwether snapped. "We need your smart ass."

"It's . . . nice to be wanted," Buccari replied cautiously, taken aback by Merriwether's vehemence.

They joined the negotiation attendees under the high ceiling of the dome's main service lock. Alarm Klaxons sounded, and doors slid into place. Pressure traps and hermetic seals squealed softly.

"How's the child?" Merriwether persisted through a sour

grin. "You seemed to have left little Charlie behind—yet again."

"For a week, Captain. I left him with Nancy Dawson and Leslie Lee for a week," Buccari replied, affecting a worried smile. Badgering was not Merriwether's style. *Something was wrong.* The air lock pressurized; temperature and humidity rose.

Merriwether's features were set with angry intensity.

"Where's Admiral Runacres?" Buccari asked, a spark of realization forming.

"Heading for orbit," Merriwether said grimly. "Rescue cell's back."

"What news?" Buccari asked. Runacres's premature departure told all. Another tone sounded. The lock doors opened smoothly. They walked beneath the vaulting curve of the transparent dome. It was hot.

"Another Shaula," Merriwether replied.

"Oh, God, no," Buccari cried, heart in her throat. "What about the rescue cell? Are they—"

"No alien contact," the captain replied, pulling Buccari to the side. "They found nothing alive and recovered only about ten percent of the bodies. Took 'em a while to find what little was left of *Borneo*."

Buccari dropped her head and covered her eyes.

"Ain't the universe a bitch?" Merriwether snarled. "I'm heading up as soon as this cluster jerk is over. And, young lady, as soon as we dump the rest of these mud monkeys, the entire fleet's returning to Sol, with or without you."

"But Captain," she pleaded, "what do—"

"You've got a week to mull it over. The admiral wants—no, I want you to look in a mirror, and I want you to figure out how you can best protect your baby and your planet. How to protect your entire species, damn it. You're a fleet pilot, one of the best to ever push a throttle."

Damn! She looked at the ground, putting her hand to her forehead, light-headed with shock. *The Oldfather task force. Captain Ketchie. And so many other pilots, friends, and former crewmates. All dead!* She felt as if she was trembling. She was trembling; the very air in the dome was vibrating, a steadily rising resonance.

"What's that?" Buccari asked. But she knew; she had heard the hellish rumble before. She shivered. They moved from the air lock frame and looked up. An obscene yellow spike of flame descended above them.

"Konish orbital lander," Merriwether replied, raising her voice above the din. "Another government decided to come to the party."

Buccari, paralyzed by the display of power outside and by her internal distress, watched the thundering explosion lower into the pad cradle. When she finally brought her gaze back to the ground, Merriwether was gone. Hudson and Quinn stood watching her.

"You okay, Sharl?" Quinn asked.

She nodded.

Kateos squeezed her mate's hand and crawled forward to confront the inscrutable air lock hatch. Dowornobb retreated, joining Mirrtis and H'Aare and the other members of the technical team. She squared her shoulders and rose to her hinds. Her anxiety glands burbled. She willed them still. The air lock to the landing gantry was cycling. She sensed movement at her shoulder and glanced up to see Et Silmarn. No fear from him; she could smell only fetid anger.

"Gravity, why the courtesy?" Et Silmarn grumbled. "They are uninvited. This should be my job alone. I would not be diplomatic."

"I have made my decision, Your Excellency," Kateos rejoined. "Let us disarm them with cooperation."

"At least make them—" Et Silmarn begged.

"Hush!" she snapped, surprising them both. Signals sounded, and the air lock hissed open, revealing kones wearing Genellan suits. Four crabbed to alert positions on either side of the entrance. Sensors indicated that they were armed. An alarm was quelled. Two kones trotted out to confront the reception party. One, much the larger, stepped forward, disdainfully removing his breathing hood and rudely sniffing the air. Kateos recognized the prepossessing presence all too well. The other kone remained a step behind. She wore the universal translator's insignia, a badge with which Kateos was quite familiar.

"Chancellor Tar Fell," Kateos said effusively, stepping forward. She resisted an impulse to grovel before the Thullolian and instead bent an indifferent knee. "Had I known, we would have had a reception befitting your station. Allow me to introduce myself. I am Kateos, ambassador of King Ollant. Please accept His Majesty's welcome."

The southerner struggled for self-control, as did she. A faint whiff drifted to her senses—fear and anger together. Tar Fell had oriented himself to Et Silmarn. The hulking Thullolian took an awkward step backward, redirected his person, and bowed extensively.

"Of course, Mistress, er, my apology, Ambassador Kateos," he thundered. "I present myself as minister plenipotentiary representing the Thullol-Ransa Compact, Ransans and Thullolians united."

"An honor, Minister Plenipotentiary," she replied regally.

"Ambassador Kateos," Tar Fell announced, again fully in control, "I am knowledgeable of your work with Prime Minister Et Kalass and of your legend on this planet. The king has chosen wisely."

"You are most gracious," Kateos answered. "May I introduce Et Silmarn, the king's appointed governor. As are you, I am a visitor on this savage and beautiful planet. Governor Et Silmarn is the true and vested authority."

"Governor, Your Excellency, then may I impose upon your hospitality?" Tar Fell petitioned, bowing fully. Rising from his bow, he rocked back on his hinds, standing, a direct affront to the noble governor. "Et Silmarn's name is more stuff of legend."

"The minister flatters me," Et Silmarn replied, exuding an overstated poise. His anger hung palpably in the air.

Tar Fell, taller and broader than Et Silmarn, stared down into the governor's eyes, taking his full measure. Kateos stood in awe at the tension generated in the collision of wills.

"Sir," Kateos said, breaking the bullnecked silence, "I must formally inquire into the purpose of your visit and ask you to explain the presence of three heavy ships in orbit about this planet."

"Actually," Tar Fell replied, smiling malignly, "there are six. We have brought sufficient wherewithal to begin construction of our new embassy as soon as we have agreed to location and scope."

Six heavy ships! Kateos found it difficult to respond. The king must be informed. She forced herself to maintain eye contact.

"King Ollant has not yet sanctioned such construction," she persisted. "Are you not guilty of a false presumption?"

"The Thullol-Ransa Compact pleads guilty only to initiative," Tar Fell said smugly. "Our governments have entered into communications with the alien emissary, an entity called Stark. While we enjoy the king's hospitality, we are here at the pleasure of the aliens, er, the humans. May I present you with the human envoy's letters of recognition."

Letters of recognition! Kateos struggled with her features. The vapors of her anger joined Et Silmarn's in a pungent blend. Her ire was not helped by Tar Fell's inscrutable smirk.

"Perhaps later," Kateos said, recovering quickly. "We have prepared apartments for you and your staff."

"Your graciousness is exceeded—" Tar Fell began.

"The governor is adamant that all weapons be returned to your ship," she said, glancing sideways. "My, er, request is most undiplomatic, but no weapons are permitted within the embassy mission."

"This is a dangerous planet," the Thullolian said.

"Outside our dome it is indeed," Kateos replied. "That is your option. The governor offers you hospitality. Under the king's dome the king's laws prevail. Your weapons and soldiers must return to orbit."

Tar Fell stood silent, the merest smile twitching the corners of his wide mouth. His eyes held little humor.

"We accept the king's hospitality," the Thullolian thundered.

"Settled," Kateos said, her voice firming. "Your timing is impeccable. We are this hour sitting down to discussions with the humans. You are welcome to join us—as an observer."

"As an observer?" Tar Fell blustered. "Is it not—"

"Enough!" Kateos barked, albeit with a smile. "Other matters will be discussed when there is time to ponder the implications."

Tar Fell stared silently for long seconds.

"History is being made, Ambassador," Tar Fell finally replied, smiling cruelly. "One should never avoid an appointment with destiny . . . even if only as an observer."

TWENTY-THREE

NEGOTIATION

Lightning flashed, and muted thunder pounded the dome. The first angry squall raced ashore, sweeping the konish settlement. Hudson stood behind his chair and watched rain splatter overhead. The atomized moisture gathered in runnels that wiggled outward and accelerated downward. His artificial hip throbbed. He watched and waited. The chair to his left, Buccari's chair, remained vacant.

"Ah, a historic occasion," Stark said, standing behind the center chair on the human side of the negotiation table. "Most historic."

On Stark's right, taking Admiral Runacres's place, stood Captain Merriwether. Beyond Stark were Cassy Quinn, Captain Gray, and Artemis Mather. In the gallery behind them sat Stark's staff and a collection of Legion scientists and technicians.

The negotiation table consisted of opposing semicircles of crimson-marbled onyx. The seven chairs on each side were designed to accommodate konish anatomy. The left armrest was a console and transceiver for speech interpretation. The right was an environmental controller; the seat had a temperature unit and breathing apparatus. Uncomfortably warm and exotic for humans, the special dome was a compromise environment. To maintain acuity, kones could settle into heated cushions and inhale pressurized air rich in carbon compounds and methane. Humans could breathe cool air from outside the dome.

Fidgeting in the gallery signaled impending activity. Dowornobb and his science team lumbered down the aisle and took places at the table, leaving vacant the seats marked for Kateos and Et Silmarn. Hudson checked his watch.

Buccari walked up to her chair, staring ahead, jaw set.

"Ah, Sharl." Stark smiled. "I was beginning to worry—"

"You've heard about Oldfather?" Buccari asked, her eyes closed.

"Why, of course, my dear," Stark replied with tragic empathy. "Captain Merriwether has given me a full account. Now perhaps you will understand why we must populate this planet and why we must avail ourselves of its strategic resources."

"Yes, but . . ." Buccari replied, white-knuckling her chair.

"We will enlist the support of the kones," Stark said. "I will negotiate an alliance of power against the marauders, a grand alliance against the Killers of Shaula and Oldfather."

"Assuming they are one and the same," Quinn added.

"In all likelihood it is also the same race that attacked the kones," Captain Gray mused.

"This tragedy may serve our purpose," Stark exhaled.

"You almost sound happy," Hudson snapped.

"If good can be fashioned from evil, then I will proudly wield the hammer," Stark said pointedly. "The kones share our apprehensions."

"Can we depend on them?" Merriwether asked.

"Can we depend on Earth?" Hudson said, touching Buccari's shoulder. Quinn shot him an irritated glare.

"Enough," Stark commanded. "We must assume our words are being monitored. The first objective is to secure our right to inhabit this planet in numbers sufficient to our needs."

Buccari's eyes remained closed; her lips tightened.

"Here comes the ambassador," Quinn whispered loudly.

Kateos and Et Silmarn, walking erect, padded down the opposing aisle. An unfamiliar kone of high rank and phenomenal proportions followed. The unmistakable odor of konish anger wafted on the currents.

Hudson glanced at Buccari. She looked up in puzzlement. The newcomer was apparently a delegate from the southern hemisphere. The glowering stranger was escorted to a seat in the gallery. Kateos moved to her own seat, where she sucked deeply from her air mask. Et Silmarn remained standing. Stark directed the humans to take their seats.

"Katy's pissed," Buccari whispered in Hudson's ear. He nodded.

"History-ah is here made-ah," the governor rumbled in heavily accented Legion. Most kones fiddled with earpieces. The humans squinted in concentration. "The delegates of-ah two galactic races, kone and human, sit-ah in concert. The middle ground-ah for this momentous occasion is the third-ah planet in our system, the planet Genellan. May-ah this and future meetings have-ah successful and profitable outcomes for all. I present the king's ambassador."

"Welcome all," Kateos, remaining seated, announced in perfect Legion, her voice deep and resonant. "I cannot help but notice your somber expressions and also that my dear friend Admiral Runacres has departed. Is something wrong?"

Stark rose. Hudson looked at Buccari, who stared at the table.

"Ambassador Kateos," Stark began. "I—"

"Excuse me, Envoy Stark, for being remiss in my duties." Kateos's smoothly belligerent tone easily eclipsed Stark's address. "Your invited guest has arrived. I have granted him observer status, unless of course you would care to elevate his standing."

Hudson heard Buccari inhale through her teeth.

"I present Minister Plenipotentiary Tar Fell of the Thullol-Ransa Compact." Kateos waved a tree limb of an arm languidly in the direction of the newcomer. Tar Fell towered gigantically to his feet and bowed.

"Minister Tar Fell," Stark replied, returning the bow. The giant tilted his head to listen to the translation from his consort. "Please accept my government's gratitude for coming so far. We beg your indulgence. I suggest a separate meeting of the parties concerned to discuss future seating arrangements and diplomatic standing."

"Bullshit," Hudson muttered.

"Stark invited a shill," Buccari whispered.

"The Thullol-Ransa Compact wishes to cooperate fully," the giant rumbled, his head like a wrinkled beer tun, his great cow eyes unblinking. The kone bowed and took his seat as his brief speech was translated by Cassy Quinn for Stark's benefit.

"Please continue, Envoy Stark," Kateos ordered curtly.

"Ah, yes ... Admiral Runacres has returned to his flagship," Stark announced, his voice assuming a funereal tone. "Tragedy has struck. It is my sad duty to report the loss in hostile action of six Legion ships and over two thousand Legion spacers and colonists."

Kateos, Et Silmarn, and Dowornobb reacted immediately, their mouths dropping open, their eye tufts springing erect. As the translation reached the kones in the arena, an acrid wave of emotional pungency drifted across the arena. The humans were reduced to coughing even as the air-conditioning ducts generated a soft swirling breeze.

"Use-ah the masks," Et Silmarn advised. Hudson sucked in air through his mask, clearing his assaulted sinuses.

"Please accept our sincerest condolences," Kateos offered.

Stark coughed his lungs clear and gamely continued: "Admiral Runacres must make the fleet ready to return to Earth."

"Of course," Kateos replied. "Should we adjourn this meeting until you have had time to consider these developments?"

"This tragedy," Stark crooned, "does not have to delay settlement progress or interfere with the transfer of technical information. I am submitting for King Ollant's approval a settlement plan that among other things authorizes indefinitely the transport to this planet of twenty thousand settlers per year, er, per Genellan year."

"Twenty thousand!" Hudson hissed, turning to Buccari. She used a hunter sign, commanding silence. She would not look him in the eye.

Kateos took note of their disturbance. The ambassador narrowed her eyes and stared. Stark darted a venomous glance at Hudson.

"What would you guarantee for this generous license?" Kateos finally inquired, noting all.

"Full transfer of theoretical hyperlight technology," Stark said, "within ten years, er, konish years."

Dowornobb leaned over and whispered in Kateos's ear. She nodded.

"Among other things, Mr. Envoy?" Kateos said.

"Bunkering privileges, orbital clearances, definition of the continental littoral, self-determination guarantees—the issues that make diplomacy interesting. There should be nothing that surprises."

"At first blush surprises are never obvious," Kateos rumbled.

"She doesn't like Stark," Buccari muttered.

"Impeccable judge of character," Hudson whispered back.

"The last settlers will be brought down from orbit next week," Stark continued. "The fleet will jump immediately after. I should like to send with Admiral Runacres an agreement in principle. Much must be set in motion."

"A week is not much time to decide the fate of a planet, Envoy Stark," Kateos replied.

"On my recommendation," Stark said, speaking rapidly, "the

admiral will request that all HLA technical transfers be accelerated. We must unite against galactic barbarism. We trust the konish race will join us in common cause against this aggressor, possibly the same marauder that once attacked your home planet."

"Of course," Kateos said. But she was staring at Buccari as if waiting for her to support or contest the envoy's position. Buccari just sat, eyes straight ahead.

"Let us forge a pact," Stark nearly shouted. "Let us unite—"

"The king is anxious to review your proposal, Envoy Stark," Kateos said, preempting Stark's speech. "Please notify Admiral Runacres that he is authorized to bring another thousand humans into our system. If, in the time it takes that interstellar passage to happen, we have achieved a tangible benchmark of technology transfer, the king will permit those thousand humans to be landed on this planet."

"A tangible benchmark, Ambassador?" Stark replied.

"Scientist Dowornobb will judge your cooperation," Kateos said, continuing to stare at Buccari, who was staring at the table. "Realize that Scientist Dowornobb has already made significant strides."

"But Ambassador Kateos, it is with the utmost—" Stark remonstrated.

"Captain Merriwether, accept my sympathies and please communicate that same message to Admiral Runacres," Kateos said, standing erect. "You have lost many brave colleagues in this disaster. It is fitting that we adjourn in respect for your bereavement."

Without waiting for a reply, Kateos bounced from her seat and walked up the aisle. Dowornobb looked at Hudson, shrugged, and then departed with the rest of his technical team, leaving Et Silmarn at the center seat. The governor proceeded to close the session.

"I'm surprised you let Stark get away with that," Hudson whispered to Buccari in the ensuing shuffle. "He's taking over. He'll have this place overrun with settlers. Why didn't you stand up to him?"

She ran her fingers distractedly through her hair. "That's your job now, Nash," she said.

Tar Fell watched the truncated proceedings with satisfaction. The southerner stood as Ollant's ambassador walked up the aisle. Kateos nodded, but Tar Fell could detect her angry emanations. The ambassador was irritated with the alien envoy, an advantage to be exploited.

Tar Fell studied the fragile aliens standing uncertainly at their stations, his gaze focusing on the famous one—the tiny, long-haired, scarred female called Citizen Sharl. She had been silent throughout, not what he had expected from one reputed to be so truculent. Seizing the opportunity, he bounded to Et Silmarn.

"Your Excellency," Tar Fell rumbled, "introduce me to the aliens."

"As is your due." Et Silmarn nodded, moving around the table. Tar Fell followed. Et Silmarn stepped into the open space between the tables and bowed, remaining on his knees. Tar Fell emulated the governor. Shoulder to shoulder they were as wide as five humans.

The alien envoy uttered thin sounds. Et Silmarn said something in the aliens' language and then turned to Tar Fell and said, "Envoy Stark sends his government's greetings."

Standing straight-legged, a stick figure of a being, Stark bowed stiffly at the waist and extended a spindly hand. Tar Fell looked to Et Silmarn for assistance.

"A human custom," Citizen Sharl said in accented but clear northern konish. The green-eyed alien held out her hand to the taller human standing next to her. That alien's face was gravely damaged by burns. The blue-eyed alien took Citizen Sharl's hand, bent at the waist, and placed scarred lips delicately on the back of her hand. Was Tar Fell expected to do the same to the ugly human envoy? He looked to Et Silmarn for guidance. The noblekone was laughing.

"Citizen Hudsawn makes a joke." Et Silmarn laughed.

"My apologies, Minister Tar Fell," the ruined face said, bowing very low. His formal konish was without accent. "What I did is appropriate only when taking the hand of a female. With males it is sufficient to clasp hands." He firmly pumped Citizen Sharl's hand.

"Ah, a custom of greeting," Tar Fell said. He reached for the envoy's desperately outstretched hand.

"Gently," Et Silmarn cautioned.

"Of course," Tar Fell said. Citizen Sharl laughed, and Tar Fell glanced up at the liquid emanation. The little alien's piercing eyes did not falter. Sad eyes.

"I am at last meeting Citizen Sharl," the monster rumbled,

dropping the envoy's hand and holding his hand out to the female.

"Minister Tar Fell," the green-eyed alien replied, taking two of his fingers in both of her hands. Her voice was like fluid gold, her accent enchanting. "I wish you and Envoy Stark much success in your discussions. May all problems have solutions." It was an old konish toast.

Tar Fell leaned over and put his massive mouth on Citizen Sharl's delicate hands.

"I am honored," she blurted, her eyes wide.

Tar Fell started to respond, but the alien envoy prattled something and spread his lips in a garish smile. The alien had very square, very white teeth. A row of gemstones sparkled along the translucent rim of each ear—a vanity, Tar Fell assumed.

An alien with yellow hair like *forga* straw spoke, translating the envoy's words—a female. Her words were well formed: "It is our pleasure to have your government represented. Is there a convenient time and place for us to meet?"

"It is appropriate that I leave," Et Silmarn said, bowing.

"Governor Et Silmarn!" Buccari exclaimed. "Please excuse me, Minister Tar Fell." She extricated her hands and bowed, gracefully falling to her knees and placing her forehead on the floor. And then she was on her feet, running. Lightning flashed as she skirted the table to hook arms with Et Silmarn, so small, so delicate. A clap of thunder reverberated against the dome. Yet she was strong. Tar Fell envied Et Silmarn.

"Please tell Kateos I must see her," Tar Fell heard her say. "I have not much time."

TWENTY-FOUR

GENELLAN FAREWELL

"Does Citizen Sharl know of Tar Fell's siege?" Et Silmarn asked.

"No, I did not tell her. She has problems enough," Kateos said, watching the yellow aircraft carrying Citizen Sharl toward the northern mountains. "We talked of the future. It was not an easy conversation. She was so proud and so happy for me but so sad about her own life."

"Farewells are the bitter price of friendship," Dowornobb said.

"She is more than a friend," Et Silmarn said. "Citizen Sharl is a symbol—strong, good . . . and tragic."

"My heart is happy for her," Kateos sighed.

"Happy, my dearest?" Dowornobb asked, inhaling the sweet scent of his mate's sorrow. "She has given up her offspring. Perhaps even a planet. For what?"

"For a greater need, my mate," Kateos said. "For duty."

"Major Faro confirms that Lieutenant Commander Buccari will depart with the fleet," Colonel Pak reported.

"Good riddance," Stark said, staring into the warm night. After witnessing Buccari's intimate relationship with the Hegemonic ambassador and her almost hypnotic effect on the Thullolian, Stark wanted her off the planet.

He leaned against the balcony of his third-story office and private quarters. The terrain beneath his open window was scarred by construction and slashed with security lights, but a soft breeze rushing across sere grasses carried the full-bodied aroma of straw and a hint of the distant ocean. A waning moon lifted from a perfect horizon, limning clouds to the southeast with argent. Distant lightning flashed soundlessly, illuminating the same clouds from within.

"Buccari will have the ear of the Legion Assembly," Pak declared.

"Of small matter," Stark replied. "Buccari's zeal has evaporated. She's carrying the weight of the universe on her shoulders. And Mather will be there to protect our interests. Art Mather knows the workings and intrigue of the Legion Assembly as well as anyone."

"You taught her well," Pak offered.

Stark glanced at the LSA colonel. Pak had served him proficiently, but there was something in the officer's tone that rankled.

"What about Commander Quinn?" Stark asked.

"Captain Gray has given her explicit orders," Pak replied, making unwavering eye contact. "She is a good soldier."

"Continue surveillance," Stark ordered. "Her loyalties are disturbingly tenuous."

"And Hudson?" Pak inquired.

"A flea."

"A very annoying flea," Pak added.

"Quite," Stark replied. "Our plans may proceed apace. Reply to Chancellor Tar Fell's communiqué: I should be honored to confer with him at a time and place of his convenience. I await his pleasure."

Short-one-who-leads was returning to the stars.

A thousand hunters sang the death song. A thousand warriors, with Craag-leader-of-hunters at their head, marched from the river cliffs and embraced the wind, black bodies swirling into the skies like burning oil.

It was a sad tribute. Many long-legs cried. Even One-arm, tall warrior and brave, wept. Short-one-who-leads struggled in vain to keep tears from staining her cheeks when she at last handed her whelp to Tall-redhead. Craag did not understand. A warrior sought solace in duty, not sadness.

Craag-leader-of-hunters wheeled on the brisk northwesterly. Thermals welling from sun-heated cliffs were strong. Hard blue skies swept clear by sharp-edged westerlies arched overhead. To the northeast towering cumulonimbus clouds billowed turbulently heavenward. Stretching to infinity on the western horizon, and capped with haloes of ice, the glacier-draped mountains rose majestically, rivaling the thunderstorms. The rest of the azimuth was spanned by the encompassing flatness of the taiga plain. It was a day for flight, for adventure, for glorious death.

The flying machine bearing Short-one-who-leads squatted on the ground, visible from great distance, a sparkling metallic gem reflecting the sun. Long-legs and bear people and guilders stood near the river cliffs, watching, waiting. A tribute.

Craag, leading the great cloud of hunters, gave the machine a wide berth. A wise choice, for as the cliff dwellers flowed in screeching, slicing masses over the broad river, monstrous yellow and orange flames flowered from the silver craft. Wavering gently, the star ferry silently elevated and accelerated in an incredible arc until it was aimed into the skies. It passed the hunters' altitude in a heartbeat, trailing a rich plume of white, roiling smoke, and then the explosive sounds of the craft's passage swept over them, battering fragile bodies with shock waves. With breathtaking abruptness, the alien machine was gone, leaving only a billowing vapor trail to cleave the clear skies, the raging sounds of its engines reduced to faint echoes in the hunters' ears. A bitter scent of burning chemicals assaulted sensitive olfactories before its trace scattered in the wind.

Short-one-who-leads was returning to the stars.

But not alone.

SECTION THREE

POWER PLAYS

TWENTY-FIVE

BACK IN THE SADDLE

The boatswain's whistle blasted over the general circuit, shrill and sharp, resonating deep within Runacres's being. With tremendous resolve the admiral expunged the horrific implications of Oldfather from his consciousness. The admiral concentrated on commanding his fleet. In battle armor, he floated to his station on the flag bridge.

"Jump stations," came the boatswain's monotone advisory, a woman's contralto, deep and resonant. "Now jump stations. Stand by for hyperlight transition."

Commodore Wells and Group Leader Wooden, bulky in battle armor, were tethered into command stations, delegating the underway consoles to their respective watch officers.

"Status," Runacres barked, sliding into his command station.

"Jump countdown complete, Admiral," Wells replied. "Holding."

Runacres pushed back in his tethers, a conductor finding cold comfort in the precision of his orchestra. On the arena master display alignment beacons of the homeward-bound fleet formed an unwavering grid.

"Last bird's aboard," the group leader announced. "All units recovered. Flight ops secured. Jump stations set."

"Very well," Runacres answered, clamping his helmet seal.

"Buccari was on that last 'vette." Merriwether's drawl, fatigued from long days of jump preparation, came to him over the flag circuit.

Runacres grunted a distracted acknowledgment.

"She's only one pilot," Wooden muttered. "We'll need hundreds like her."

"That's asking a lot," Merriwether replied.

"Group leader's right, Sarah," Runacres muttered, studying

jump preparations. "Shaula and Oldfather were skirmishes. Buccari, as good as she is, is only one pilot. We're in a war. Spacers are going to die."

"Jump sequence nominal," the operations watch officer reported. "Gravity flux at point eight. Moving past peak."

Runacres looked about. Below, on *Eire*'s tactical bridge, Merriwether's jump detail moved sharply about its business. The ship's underway circuit reverberated with checklist reviews.

"Jump the fleet," Runacres commanded, checking his tethers.

"Aye, aye, Admiral," Wells responded.

"They jump!" Scientist Mirrtis shouted.

Dowornobb trotted to his instrumentation console and displaced Mirrtis from the operator's station. He reset query parameters and displayed a collection output. Data streams poured into their tables. Dowornobb monitored ten different sensors at random and then ten more; all the stations collected data at fantastic rates. The scientist worried about sensor saturation.

"Telemetry will continue at a declining rate for several hours," Dowornobb said. "The trailing bits are as vital as the initial surges."

"Wonderful data," Mirrtis crowed.

"Worthless data," Dowornobb muttered, "until organized. It will take moon cycles to process and simulate what we are seeing here."

Buccari was bitterly thankful for the brain distortions signaling a jump. Her catharsis was complete. She rubbed her eyes dry one last time. There was no turning back. She was once again an officer in the Tellurian Legion Fleet. All other problems and dreams—as well as her son—were suddenly light-years removed.

The fleet was jumping away from universal origins, transported by curving field lines known as universal expansion radials. Moving outbound was the most "time-efficient" direction. They would see Sol system in a little over three standard months. It would be a busy transit; she had catching up to do. That was provident; she needed to be busy.

There were no honors at the quarterdeck. Feeling like a grubby civilian, Buccari saluted the deck officer and presented orders. No one waited. She was left alone, painfully conscious of curious stares. She rubbed the stubble on her brutally cropped head.

First things first. She floated into the quarantine locks and pushed through yielding membranes. She glided past radtox wards to a depilatory sequencer and placed her palm on the ID plate. A matrix of lasers and analyzers commenced scanning. Buccari jettisoned helmet, spaceboots, and pressure suit and then peeled off her thermals, securing the clothing in a convey-ored cubicle. It was the middle of the watch. There were few spacers in the depilatory queue. Buccari was relieved, for her naked body was covered with hair.

She glided through an iris. Light bars radiated her warmly. Sonic skin sloughers oriented to her anatomy. Buccari sensed the resonant tingling of fan beams digging at dead dermal cells while simultaneously vacuuming away spalling layers of epi-dermis. A vaguely green membrane clamshelled about her, pressurization interlocks clicked shut, and the membrane pres-sure filled with a snowstorm of pungent bubbling gas-liquid. Reflexively, if unnecessarily, she held her breath.

The tank emptied as rapidly as it had filled. A sensor alarm sounded—not surprisingly, for her body had follicular residual. She took a large breath. The cocoon filled again with a clap of solvent, warmer and thicker, and as quickly emptied. A techni-cian, alerted by the alarms, floated by, checking status boards. *Damn, she was hairy.*

No alarm. She was ejected from the immersion stall through a high-pressure air curtain. The last phase was the medical scan. It was quickly done; a soft tone sounded. A gentle fog of oil surrounded her, and she was through the final filtering membrane. She floated into a dressing cell, where her clothes, cleaned and smelling of antiseptic, awaited her.

As she pulled on her thermals, she looked at her body, which was marked by vivid tan lines on the arms and legs. Her hair was gone, eradicated. Her body felt perfectly clean, per-fectly smooth; her thermals slipped luxuriously over lubricated limbs. She smelled like a spacer. Her vision seemed wider and brighter with the fuzzy near image of her lashes and eyebrows removed from her peripheral vision.

A monitor mounted on the wall came to life with a dull ring.

"Ah, Buccari," a wrinkled female medico announced, eyes focused on something offscreen. "Welcome aboard. We've been waiting for you."

"Thank you, Doctor, uh . . ." she said, securing her jumpsuit.

"Flight Surgeon Tanaka," the doctor replied. "Your scans reveal a multitude of medical issues. Quite remarkable. Viral and bacterial infections, extravagant scarring, damaged rotator cuff, knee trauma, bone spurs. I've set up a maintenance program. We'll have you in shape in a matter of weeks, although the scars may take a little longer."

"Thank you, Doctor," she replied. "My watch schedule—"

"Left shoulder and knee reconstruction are mandatory," the doctor snapped. "Make time if you want to drive corvettes."

"Aye, aye." She laughed. *Welcome back to the fleet.*

"Ah, Buccari," the doctor said. "We've got some of your, er, friends in sick bay. Are you aware of their presence on this ship?"

"Pardon me?" she asked. *Friends?* The image on the monitor changed, and there in the flat light of sick bay, watched by a panicky ship's master at arms, stood three cliff dwellers. Cliff dwellers! Ridiculously devoid of fur! Captured by the vid-cam lens were a guilder wide-eyed with petrified curiosity and two hunters hunched in a defensive posture, eyes slitting to ferocious intensity.

Air rushed from Buccari's lungs. Vertigo swept her. Cliff dwellers! Lizard Lips—he held a communicator, and it was impossible to mistake his shovel-shaped snout—and Tonto with his notched membrane, and another hunter—Bottlenose. They looked like plucked buzzards. If they had been obscenely ugly with their fur, without it they were triply horrible. The muscles of the hunters were corded around thin bone structures covered with a sickly gray skin.

"*What . . . the . . . hell* are they doing here?" Buccari shouted. "We've jumped. We can't get them back."

"That we know." The doctor sighed. "I'm told they marched onto the last heavy-lifter with computer-printed orders and, in hindsight, some rather dubious authorizations."

"Orders!" she shouted.

"Apparently falsified," the doctor said. "The documents weren't issued by science, but the loadmaster accepted them and brought them up in a specimen unit. Once onboard, they slipped into the power trunks. They were discovered less than an hour ago. They get around null grav like pros. As you can see, we skinned them. Probably not a good idea, but regs are regs. I've analyzed their fur and given authorization for it to grow back. Their body temp—"

The cliff dwellers reacted to her voice. Lizard Lips screeched and glided with surprising agility to the vid station, his puckered private parts obscuring the lens's view. Buccari involuntarily recoiled. The guilder backed away and looked into the vid-cam, one black eye filling the field of view. The screeches of cliff dwellers overwhelmed the audio. The creature held the communicator's small display up to the lens. The icons read:

HELP/PROTECT HELP US/WANT HELP YOU/GREETINGS/HELP

She laughed at life's absurdities and realized how happy she was to see the ugly beasts. If it wasn't one thing, it was another.

"But how . . . ?" she asked, shaking her head. She whistled sharply to get the guilder's attention and signed into the sensor: "I come."

Lizard Lips's head cocked sideways. As he comprehended her message, his gruesome jaws opened, displaying jagged teeth in a splendid smile. He chittered to the hunters. They screamed in jaw-vibrating unison.

"Quarantine compartment four," Tanaka said.

"On my way," Buccari said, flying from the dispensary with a new set of worries temporarily displacing all other concerns.

Toon sighed with profound relief; Short-one-who-leads would soon arrive. Everything would be normal, except he had not anticipated losing his fur. They would need garments—an inconvenience. At least they had been fed. The steam user went back to the console, trying to evoke a sign-on that would get him into the general-use files.

Brappa and Sherrip hissed fear and anger—a distraction. Toon glanced up. The naked hunters perched upside down, menacing the entryway.

"Worry not, warriors," Toon whistled cheerfully.

Brappa screamed a most unmannerly suggestion. Their guard jerked nervously. The frightened long-legs huddled in the corner, hand on his weapon.

"Ah!" Toon chirped; the computer responded with a menu. Toon did not understand enough long-leg words to make an intelligent choice. He pulled his communicator and queried the long-leg dictionary and dweller icon cross-reference. It was slow going, but time was not scarce.

"We worry not," Brappa shrieked back, sounding very worried. "We are here to protect Short-one-who-leads. We cannot, unless she is here to be protected. And they have taken our weapons. We should not have allowed ourselves to be caught. Thine advice is corrupt."

"My advice is correct," Toon snapped. He still could not get past the screen menu. "We have been fed. Our presence is accepted."

"That was food?" Brappa complained.

"Thou art frightened," Toon answered.

Brappa and Sherrip blasted the steam user with shrieks of fury.

Buccari entered the compartment. Hunter screeches, floating in and out of audible range, vibrated in her skull. Tonto pushed off from the overhead, membranes partially deployed, and swam to her, with Bottlenose right behind. She put out her hands and was rewarded with warm four-fingered grips. Lizard Lips chirped a greeting but did not look up.

"I'll take them," she told the ship's master at arms.

"Welcome to 'em, sir," the man said, moving cautiously to the hatch. "Ugly little buggers, eh?"

"A matter of perspective," Buccari muttered, floating behind Lizard Lips. The guilder studied an option menu. Buccari tapped out the initiation sequence. Lizard Lips screamed with joy as the next menu refreshed the screen. The cliff dweller pushed her hands aside and started working the next sequence—successfully. He lifted his ugly snout and flashed hideous teeth—another large smile.

"We go, now!" she signed. Lizard Lips reluctantly parted from the computer. She guided the cliff dwellers across the quarantine decks, ignoring gawking stares, shepherding them into the down-bore. The creatures had little problem with null grav, using their membranes and displaying remarkable control.

"It's Buccari!" someone shouted as she floated into the rigger loft. "And the bugs!"

A thick-chested senior chief exploded from behind the stacks, scattering equipment riggers with a salvo of expletives.

"Welcome aboard, sir," the chief said, eyeing the cliff dwellers warily. "We've been, ah, expecting you. You need gear, sir."

"Full issue, chief," she commanded, displaying her orders.

"At your service," the chief replied, taking her order sleeve and inserting it in the processing log. "First your multiplex."

The chief handed her a carbon-composite box containing a spidery device and a wrist-mounted admin unit.

"Damn," she said. She had forgotten. All unit commanders were required to wear the neural transceiver.

"Stick it in your ear," the rigger chief said, "sir."

She laughed, took the delicate beetle-shaped device no larger than a grain of rice, and positioned it.

"I've activated it," the chief said. "It's going to tickle."

It moved, climbing deeper into her ear canal. She sensed its fibers seeking bony surfaces in which to implant. Reflexively, she reached for the intruding mechanisms. The rigger intercepted her hand.

"You can flush it out anytime you want," the chief said. "But turn it off first and wait ten seconds for it to disengage. You dick around while it's on and it's history. Standard adminunit instructions. You automatically transmit on the receiving frequency. You need to program your user frequency and select an encryption format."

She shook off vertigo and strapped on the wrist-mounted admin unit.

"Intel will download your clearances. Medical will bring biotelemetry up on your next body job. Now let's get you fitted."

She floated into the sizing sensors, placing head, waist, feet, and hands in the forming jigs. Lasers swept her body, and then pressure molds rotated over her limbs. The chief monitored readouts and asked the normal questions: Still left-handed? Optical or aural feedback as helmet sensory default? Battle armor joint flexibility preferences? Fluid bladder locations and capacity trade-offs? And other questions, feeding in information as it was provided.

"Chief, I need to open equipment logs . . . for them," she said.

The chief exhaled. "I was afraid of that. Wha—"

"Thermals, pressure units, helmets—"

"Will docking hoods do?" the chief begged.

"Helmets," Buccari repeated. "Class One."

"Helmets!" the senior rigger yelped. "Suckers got pickaxes for heads. Helmet molds were never designed for that aspect ratio."

"Yes, dammit," Buccari snapped, and then took a deep breath. "Sorry, Chief. Yes, helmets. Make a new frigging mold.

They're going to be part of my crew. They need helmets, battle armor, utilities."

The chief rubbed his face. He glanced at the cliff dwellers. Lizard Lips inspected a helmet jig. Tonto, upside down, and Bottlenose, floating sideways, hovered like bad dreams above Buccari's shoulders.

"Nobody's going to accuse my outfit of getting in your way, Mr. Buccari," the chief replied. "Uh, as much as I hate to request it, you'll have to leave them for . . . an hour. They won't bite, will they?"

"You'd already be dead if they wanted to hurt you," she said. "And check out their wing tendons and membrane attachment points, especially on the two small ones."

"Yeah, I noticed."

"Their equipment can't interfere with their freedom of movement."

"I can do something with their underway suits and fatigues, but I dunno about the battle armor. That's asking a lot."

"Yeah," she had to agree, punching in instructions on Lizard Lips's communicator. She handed the device to Lizard Lips, who read the instructions and chirped his acknowledgment.

"I'll be back in an hour," she said, sailing off to her next task. She used a ladder well to go up one level to Level Eight, to the supply department, where she asked for the berthing steward.

"I need two adjacent cabins," Buccari said.

"Scuttlebutt's out, Mr. Buccari," the warrant officer reported. "We heard you had some friends. Actually, Dr. Tanaka made a call."

"Can you help me?" she asked.

"Here's what I did." The warrant officer brought up the berthing schematic for the habitation ring. "I evicted a couple of ensigns and moved 'em back into a hot-rack closet. You won't be popular with them, but that's what ensigns are for. That gives you these two cabins."

"I'll bring my friends by so you can set up their IDs," she said.

"Right hand on the ID plate and say your name three times," the warrant officer said, inserting her order card. She did as she was told. "Cabins D432 and D434, Ring Sector Two. You want to pay your wardroom dues now?"

TWENTY-SIX

PILOT AND CREW

Buccari floated down Ready Room Row and stopped before the hatch into Ready One. She hesitated, her emotions rampant. She sucked in a large breath, clamped her jaw tight, and smacked the hatch entry bar. The hatch articulated, and she pushed through the equipment locker and into the ready room.

Conversation dampened to silence. Heads turned in her direction. No fewer than twenty pilots were on hand, most oriented vertically to the deck. The front of the space was dominated by a bulkhead-spanning panel. Duty postings, flight-time summaries, approach and landing statistics, ship and crew status, flight schedules, and accident safety graphs gave the digital wall a kaleidoscopic effect. Her eyes vainly searched crew rosters for her own name.

Two wraparound consoles occupied the front corners; the near corner was the squadron duty officer's station, and the far corner was the ops assistant's station. Admin offices were in the far back, opposite the coffee mess. The rest of the room was dominated by six rows of pilot briefing stations divided by a middle aisle. The seats had back covers with rank insignia and last names. The front row was for primary corvette commanders, the second row for bravo crew commanders and intelligence officers, the third and fourth for first officers, and the fifth and sixth for second officers. The standard squadron complement included six primary crews and two backup, or bravo, crews.

"Booch!" Pulaski bellowed from the coffee mess. The barge of a pilot pushed straight for her, sailing rudely over the briefing stations. He bounced off the overhead and pushed down to grab her in a headlock. "Now, this is more like it!"

"Yeah," she replied, feeling better for the mauling. Bart

209

Chang and Nestor Godonov broke out of the pack. She recognized few others, the passing years having left their mark.

"Ah, the famous Sharl Buccari!" a familiar voice said. Petri Castro sat in the front row with two other officers, all corvette command pilots by their rank and carriage.

"Mr. Buccari, can I have your orders, sir?" a deep, satin-voiced greeting came from the duty officer's desk. She smiled at Castro and nodded at the corvette commanders, trying to decipher their thin smiles, and then pivoted to acknowledge the request. "Need to log you on board, sir. I'm getting zinged by the bridge for late jump muster."

"Sorry," Buccari said, handing her order sleeve to the duty officer, a tall, slim ensign. The ebony, large-featured face was either handsome or striking, depending on whether it belonged to a male or a female. Male, she decided. "Buccari, Sharl F., reporting for duty," Buccari replied. "And you are?"

"Thompson, Ted Thompson, sir," the duty officer reported, punching her in. Buccari's name appeared on the crew roster as Command Pilot 6B. Pulaski hooted obnoxiously, jabbing her in the ribs.

"I'm a candidate for your number two, sir," Thompson continued. The ensign had deep, dark brown liquid eyes. "Flack Flaherty, Commander Carmichael's ex-number two, is your copilot."

"Where's Mr. Flaherty?" she asked, wincing at Pulaski's raucous mistreatment. "I'd like to meet my number one."

"Down in the bays, sir," Thompson replied with a smile. "He spent the last month in radtox. So he's brushing up for crew quals, and, the honest truth, he just likes sitting in the right seat."

"My kind of pilot," Buccari said, holding out her hand. Thompson smiled hugely and grabbed her hand.

"About time you got here," boomed a pleasantly familiar voice. A confusing admixture of emotions welled within her. She turned to see Carmichael and felt hot blood rising to her cheeks. Carmichael's demeanor reflected her own. The big man's rugged features were softened with an inner warmth.

Another familiar face stood at Carmichael's side. Buccari tore her gaze from Carmichael's and recognized Wanda Green. Like Petri Castro, Green had been a senior pilot in Buccari's first squadron. Her name tag said, "Executive Officer." Buccari remembered her nickname to be "Brickshitter," and not because of her statuesque build. Green could get explosively angry. Not a frequent occurrence, but when she lost her temper, the entire ship, and frequently the entire fleet, would hear about it. Perfect material for an executive officer.

Green, hand to chin, shifted her huge brown eyes like an artillery officer training a heavy field piece. Pulaski and Chang toned down their act. Thompson subconsciously snapped to attention, but slightly off vertical. Pulaski braced himself and spun the big ensign like a propeller. Everyone laughed as Thompson's flailing body floated to the overhead. Green glared at Pulaski. The pilot rolled his eyes, mimicking the XO's impatience, and pulled Thompson back to his station.

"Welcome to Eagle Squadron, Sharl," Carmichael said, thrusting out his hand. She took it in hers, her whole being focused on the innocent contact. She sensed Carmichael's body heat and his intensity. She felt safe. She let go only because Wanda Green's hand was waiting.

"Welcome aboard," Green said, her voice husky. The XO shook hands firmly and warmly. "Been a long time since our Vulture days."

"Seems like a dream," Buccari replied, old memories exploding into her consciousness—good times with good friends. She glanced up at Carmichael, who stared back with disconcerting intensity.

"You have crew call in an hour," Green pronounced, demanding her attention. "I'll introduce you to your bunch."

"To your bunch of rookies," Pulaski snorted. "You're my backup, Booch! Never thought you'd be standing in line behind me, did you?"

"A prodigiously disgusting image, that," Green said. "Ready to see your ship, Sharl?"

"Our ship, Booch," Pulaski bellowed. "No farts in the pilot's seat."

"Where the hell do you sit?" Petri Castro said archly. Ensign Thompson guffawed, and Pulaski, fingering his chin, fixed him with a burlesque imitation of Wanda Green's glare.

"Give me that hour, XO," Buccari said, looking up at the time hack. "I need to, ah, pick up a docking hood and get some . . . errands taken care of."

"Dr. Tanaka told me about your friends, Booch," Green said, grimacing. "I've assigned Nestor Godonov to your crew full time. He'll be responsible for the cliff dwellers', eh, integration. Bring the bugs to crew call. I'd like to . . . meet them."

"Aye, aye, XO." Buccari exhaled with relief and pushed off for the hatch. She flew for the transport tubes.

The cliff dwellers were getting along famously. Someone had provided rations, and the creatures gorged themselves while they waited. Despite the rigger chief's best efforts to keep his area clear of unauthorized personnel, a crowd had assembled. Buccari's docking hood and pressure suit were ready. The riggers had fabricated temporary docking suits for the cliff dwellers. They looked like squat, dun-colored pepper mills with stubby legs.

With help from innumerable volunteers, Buccari moved the cliff dwellers and their equipment canisters to the habitation ring. For the cliff dwellers the journey through the transport hub to the habitation ring was disconcerting. The resumption of gravity, even a half-gee, caught them by surprise. Lizard Lips was gripped with nausea.

Lizard Lips's failing equilibrium necessitated the cliff dwellers' becoming immediately acquainted with the ship's waste-elimination system. Using frantic hand signing, Buccari entered a sanitary pressure lock with the guilder. Despite his involuntary spasms, Lizard Lips's engineering acumen made him a quick study, and his disgorgements were mostly contained. Tonto and Bottlenose shouldered into the impossibly confined space, gawking at the guilder's plight. His siege of vertigo mostly behind him, Lizard Lips proceeded to instruct the hunters in the machinery's intended use. Under his expert direction the creatures took turns relieving themselves. Buccari hated to think of the expediencies they had employed before being discovered.

She brought them at last to their cabin. The aliens were comforted by their assigned compartment's restricted geometry. They knew immediately that the tight quarters were to be their new home. Yet as the aliens became situated, Buccari grew morose. What had she done to those unfortunate creatures? What had they done to deserve being separated from home and family, perhaps to die? Tonto chirped loudly to get her attention. She snapped from her reverie to catch his hand signs.

"Gratitude. Even fat guilder comfortable in this abode."

Lizard Lips, watching the warrior's hand signs, screeched a derisive response, and all three cliff dwellers bared sharp teeth in hissing fellowship—laughter.

"Damn glad you're happy," she muttered, checking the chronometer on her admin unit. It was time.

"We go," she signed.

The hub shuttle delivered them to the operations core. The cliff dwellers were prepared for the gravity change. They attempted to frolic in null gee, but in their docking suits they no longer had use of their membranes. After a brief adjustment period her three loose cannons regained control. She herded her charges to a down-bore and dropped two levels to the corvette bays. She pulled up the docking hood on each cliff dweller and checked it for integrity. Satisfied, she deployed her hood and crossed the quarterdeck into cavernous Hangerbay One.

Buccari, casting a spidery shadow, floated under a constellation of light bars, past puzzled stares from colorfully garbed hangerbay crews. Rising before her in a ziggurat of space engineering were the bulbous thruster-pocked noses of Eagle Squadron's corvettes, six slab-sided Raptor-class FC-2J's stacked in a towering three-by-two docking matrix. She felt like a flea before elephants. Behind her, accentuating her physical insignificance, was Hangerbay Two, which housed two Atlas-class heavy-lifters, four Rondo OMTs, and two fleet reaction fuelers.

The number six ship was berthed on the lowdeck port side. Staying in safety lanes, she and her ducklings floated along the monolithic edifice that was the hull of her corvette, past the bulge of the starboard lifeboat, to the lower crew entry. Buccari moved into the white light of *Eagle Six*'s EPL bay and admired the lines of the Endoatmospheric Planetary Lander. She stroked the apple's wingtip.

She ushered her gawking entourage into the crew lock and cycled into the upper EPL bay. The lander's service hatch yawned open to reveal a chief boatswain's mate, floating head down, working at the maintenance console. As the air lock sensor went green, Buccari slipped off her docking hood. Lizard Lips drifted up and eyed the console, putting his hooded face disconcertingly close to the crewman's.

"What the—" the chief thundered, spinning backward. The stocky, spidery-veined space dog gaped at the cliff dwellers. His right eye was an implant, and a large part of his hairless skull had been surgically rebuilt—a reasonably good job.

"Howdy, Chief," she said. "Buccari, Six Bravo command pilot."

"W-welcome aboard, Skipper." The chief deftly reoriented to her vertical, glancing nervously at the cliff dwellers.

"Sorry, sir. Foster, chief lander boatswain. I'm your lead EPL technician."

"I should apologize," she said, laughing.

"My old heart." Foster grinned. "Damn, sir. Jonesy, may his soul rest in peace, was right."

"You knew Bosun Jones?" she asked, remembering and hurting.

"Jonesy and me were like this," the chief said, holding out his crossed fingers. "Me on top, of course."

"So what was Boats right about?" she asked.

"Pardon for saying, sir," Foster replied, "but Jonesy always said you had eyes like green laser cannons. He said a lot about you, sir—all good—but a lot that it wouldn't do to repeat, if you know what I mean."

Another team, another time, she thought, fighting her emotions.

"They're waiting inside, sir," Foster said.

"You're a bit senior for this billet, aren't you, Chief?"

"Pardon for saying, sir," Foster replied, "but you're a mite junior. Sorta averages out."

"Let's muster, Chief," she ordered, smiling and pushing off from his shoulder, a spacer's gesture of friendship. She herded the cliff dwellers through the hatch.

"Aye, aye, Skipper," Foster replied, securing his station.

Skipper! It sounded good, especially from an old space dog. She floated into the crew rest area. Behind her was the galley. Embedded in the bulkhead above the galley were status instruments and vid screens. The starboard bulkhead housed a grid of sleep cells. The port bulkhead held logistic stores. The forward bulkhead contained crew lockers and hatches to weapons and communications spaces.

"Skipper on deck!" Thompson shouted. The ensign protruded head down from the overhead hatch leading to the main fore-aft passageway. The big man pushed down and did a controlled handspring from the crew deck. Another officer followed—Lieutenant Flaherty, his gaudy, nonreg name tag identifying him as Flack.

"At ease," she said, looking about. Forward hatches opened. More crew members flowed onto the crew deck, all recoiling from the cliff dwellers.

"Welcome aboard, Skipper," Flaherty said, twisting like a cat to land on his feet in the center of the rest area. Her new first officer was of average height and square-shouldered,

with a high forehead. His features were regular and handsome, but it was his mischievous golden-brown eyes that captured Buccari's attention. His was a happy countenance,
infectiously so.

"Commander Green got detained, sir," the lieutenant barked,
assuming a loose position of attention. "She asked me to do
the honors."

"Please proceed, Mr. Flaherty."

"Chief Foster is lead lander technician."

"We've met," Buccari replied.

"Nakajima is the other lander rating," Flaherty continued,
indicating a wiry female about Buccari's height. "She's small,
but she's a damn good boatswain."

"Pardon for saying, sir," Chief Foster added, "but Glory
Nakajima's even taught me a thing or two."

"I thought you knew everything about apples, Chief," one of
the ratings gibed.

" 'Tis about different technologies that Nakajima be
a-teaching that old meat," a gnarled weapons petty officer interjected to the delight of the others. The weapons noncom was
a female, judging from the enchanting high-toned lilt. No other
feature gave a clue to her sex.

"Don't start, Marigold," Foster pleaded.

"I be Gunner Tyler, sir," the seasoned spacer said, the blood
vessels in her wrinkled face given over to the excesses and ab-
sences of acceleration. "And these would be my weapons ratings: Petty Officer Second Peron and Able Spacer Sawyer."

"Gunner Tyler, Peron, Sawyer," Buccari replied, shaking
their hands. Tyler's squinty gaze was unyielding and penetrating. Buccari would have to earn her respect.

"Chief Silva keeps up the steam," Flaherty continued, indicating a horse-faced, slope-shouldered individual. She shook
hands with the swarthy, powerful man. "With Chin and
O'Grady's help of course." The engineering ratings were as different as two human beings could be: Petty Officer Chin was
a middle-aged male, stocky and flat-featured; O'Grady was a
young female, as tall as Thompson and china-boned, with large,
aquiline features.

"I've been instructing Petty Officer Goldberg," Silva said.
"She says I'm crewing for the best pilot in the fleet."

"Brownnosing ain't never increased a pay chit, Chief," Tyler
stage-whispered mirthfully.

"Aw, Mari," Silva begged, rolling his eyes.

"How's Pepper doing, Chief?" Buccari replied, smiling.

"She's moving through her standards requal real good," Silva replied. "She's being rotated onto Mr. Pulaski's crew next week."

Flaherty finished the introductions: Tasker, communications technician third, short and shy, and Catta Burl, medical technician second, a moonfaced, energetic woman.

"Let me introduce my, ah, comrades to you," Buccari said, pulling Lizard Lips from a service terminal.

"This is Lizard Lips," she said, her hands on the guilder's shoulders. "An unfortunate choice of names but one that stuck."

"Pardon for saying, sir," Chief Foster offered, "but it's not hard to see why." The crew laughed. Lizard Lips did, too, immediately transforming human laughter into wide-eyed silence. Buccari introduced the baleful hunters next. No jokes were attempted.

"My plan," Buccari summarized, "the fleet willing, is to make them spacers. That will depend on what is best for this crew."

"Am I late?" Nestor Godonov announced, coming through the EPL bay hatch. The cliff dwellers chittered their pleasure at seeing a familiar face. Godonov hand signed greetings to the cliff dwellers. Wanda Green came through on his heels.

"Everyone introduced?" Green asked.

"Like old friends, XO," Flaherty replied.

Buccari used hand signs to communicate Green's status. The cliff dwellers bowed their respect. Green smiled with embarrassment.

"You should all start bowing to me," Green said, restoring her thick armor. "Enough gabbing. You have jobs to do. This crew starts primary simulation at 0800 tomorrow. Training is my responsibility. I'll be watching. Okay, Buccari, they're all yours." The executive officer pushed off and dropped through the EPL bay hatch. Buccari saw the hatch light illuminate, indicating that Green had left the corvette.

"You heard what Brickshitter said," Buccari announced, looking at each of her crew members. "Ensign Thompson, I want the simulator schedule set at two a day until further notice."

A muttering went up. Chief Tyler hawked her throat clear and gave everyone a glare that muted all conversation.

"Mr. Flaherty, coordinate with Mr. Pulaski's number one,"

she continued. "I want you and Thompson on number six flight deck whenever Pulaski's crew's not working. And I want one of you to come get me whenever that happens. The flight deck's the weak link in this crew. We're going to change that."

"Aye, Skipper," Flaherty replied, brown eyes laughing.

Buccari looked around. "Welcome," she said, "to the best crew in the fleet."

She turned and pushed through the overhead hatch into the main axial passageway. In front of her was the flight deck iris. She squeezed the latch trigger, and the iris dilated. She pulled herself onto the corvette's darkened flight deck, the hatch iris sealing behind her. Through the corvette's forward viewing screens she looked out on the hangerbay, an anthill of activity—another world.

Without looking, she palmed up the internal lights. She was back on the flight deck of a corvette. Her corvette—she was command pilot. Burning the moment into her memory, she pulled herself into the left station—the pilot's station—and engaged her tethers. She adjusted seat coordinates and placed her arms in the acceleration harness. The controls came easily to hand, massive, laden with buttons and triggers, yet delicately balanced. She was home.

The iris cycled. She detected motion. Godonov and the cliff dwellers piled onto the flight deck. Lizard Lips went directly to the second pilot's station and attempted to make a database connection. Tonto and Bottlenose gawked and chittered, assiduously touching nothing.

"Pardon me for interrupting, Sharl, er, Skipper," Godonov said. "Mind if I ask some questions about your plans for the cliff dwellers?"

"Fire away, Nes," she replied.

"Fleet science's very excited about them being on board," Godonov said, "although Captain Gray would prefer to keep them in exobiology."

"They aren't lab animals," Buccari replied, connecting with the second pilot's station. She downloaded the cliff dwellers' icon file and pressed out a quick salutation. Lizard Lips screeched with delight and immediately made a reply.

"So what are your plans?" Godonov asked.

"Check out my screen," she said. Godonov floated over her head. On the pilot's screen was written, not with cliff dweller icons but in Legion:

MUCH HERE. TEACH ME HOW.

"I've been teaching him Legion," Godonov replied matter-of-factly.

"You have a genius on your hands, Nestor," Buccari said. "We should be able to find a place for a genius, shouldn't we? Train him to be a planet survey technician or—"

"Okay," Godonov replied. "That just might work for Lizzy, but what about the hunters? They eat raw meat, for goodness' sake. They don't know piss from reaction fuel, and they get damned cranky."

"Sound like marines." Buccari laughed.

Godonov cogitated for several seconds. "I'll talk to the commandant," he said.

"I was kidding," she said, glancing at her ugly friends.

"I'm not," Godonov said. "They get around like pros in null grav, and they fly, for goodness' sake. We hook up some sensors and telemetry and we got a helluva tactical data collection system."

"Glad you're here, Nes," she replied. "Just think, you could have been stuck back at NEd. I feel sorry for Nash and Cassy."

"It was getting interesting back there," Godonov said. "The other konish ships should be arriving any day."

"What ships?"

"That's right, you weren't cleared. The envoy's crypto group kept it top secret," Godonov said. "Several squadrons of konish ships were en route to Genellan as we jumped. Communications were scrambled, but Planetary Defense Force channels were overheating. Something's going on. Almost sounded like a mobilization."

A rush of blood heated the back of Buccari's neck.

TWENTY-SEVEN

MOBILIZATION

"Gravity, four more Ransan ships en route to Genellan!" King Ollant bellowed, wrenching his gaze from the misty ocher skies. The air wavered with the fulsome aroma of his unfettered rage. "How many more ships does the Compact have? Where is our intelligence?"

"It is not just their number, Your Highness," General Talsali said. The PDF commanding general stood at attention on all fours. "Tar Fell's armada is replete with capital ships, some of greater mass than even the largest ships of the Planetary Defense Force."

"More fruit from Gorruk's War," Et Kalass muttered. "The south has been arming all this while. All motives lead to vengeance."

"There is no choice but to mobilize," Ollant dictated. "Notify Et Anitab and the general staff that I will take command."

"But Your Highness, it is—" Et Kalass remonstrated.

"Give me information, Minister!" Ollant thundered. "Not advice."

"Your Highness," Talsali protested, "the Defense Force has already suffered grievous attrition with the resignation of Thullolian crews. The loss of Hegemonic personnel will cripple the defense stations. Remember the Vows of Protection, Your Highness."

Ollant remained silent, glaring down with redolent intensity.

"I can make no promises, General," Ollant at last rumbled.

Tar Fell exulted. His armada was growing stronger, his crews more capable. Magoon would have his own squadron, and Krolk would command the new squadrons. But when would King Ollant respond to his maneuvers? Soon, Tar Fell's agents said.

For now Tar Fell would reckon with other issues. Suit temperature dialed high, he steeled himself. The air lock slid smoothly open. He was outside the dome. Tar Fell controlled his breathing and trotted from the air lock. Genellan's vertiginous expanses disconcerted him, so different from a holo-vid or even from looking out a window. He surveyed undreamed of distances with a clarity and sharpness of color that stole his breath. He missed the comforting limitations imposed on visibility by the dun and drab atmosphere of Kon.

A land rover awaited, and he crawled aboard. The vehicle trundled over grasses and through forests until the domes of Ocean Station faded from his line of sight. A field structure, protected by sonic shields and guarded by Thullolian soldiers, had been erected. Relieved to be out from under the unending skies, Tar Fell took a heated lounge and watched the alien delegation file in. His technicians tuned a language converter.

The human envoy was accompanied by translators and security agents, their puny weapons and electronic devices registering on detectors. The fragile creatures were dressed in the thinnest garments, faces and heads exposed. Many had bared the flesh of their skeletal appendages. Tar Fell marveled at their constitutions. And their culture—males served, apparently without ignominy, as translators.

The human envoy stood and spoke, his flow of words high-pitched and choppy. The fawning stick figure of a being was remarkably ugly.

"Chancellor Tar Fell," the alien translator replied with a nasal and comically clipped accent. Tar Fell concentrated on the reedy delivery. Machines could translate words with great fidelity, but not inflection or expression. "I am honored to represent the human race in your presence. My government wishes to cooperate fully."

The translator nodded. Tar Fell glanced at the output on the language converter; it substantiated the textual translation. He stared down at the slimy-skinned envoy. The puny alien shrank under his scrutiny, its wan coloration growing improbably chalkier.

"What does your government ask of my government?" Tar Fell rumbled. "What does your government offer in return?"

Stark's translator recoiled, gulped for air, and repeated Tar Fell's words in their halting language. The aliens conversed in whispers, referring to their own language converter and entering notes on a terminal. The human envoy regained his feet and spoke again.

"My government makes no formal request," the translator relayed. "My government wishes to build a bridge of mutual respect."

"To built a bridge for your race to migrate to this planet, yes?" Tar Fell replied. The translator regurgitated his words, and the aliens again held a conference. The human envoy rattled off more words.

"My government's objectives are not secret," the translator conveyed. "Indeed, we would like to migrate to this planet, but only as good neighbors and friends. We are equally interested in enterprise and technological opportunities. We have much to offer."

"As do we, Envoy Stark," Tar Fell replied, rising from his lounge. The aliens shifted uneasily. "Let us talk about technological opportunities."

Her exertions staving off the chill, Kateos bounded on all fours over grassy meadows, chasing cloud shadows and stirring clusters of copper-winged butterflies. Would that she could chase away her responsibilities so easily. She luxuriated in Genellan's gentle gravity and relished the deep vistas and the panoply of fragrances. She came to a stair-stepping bluff sheltering stands of wind-sculpted trees. The rustling lea brimmed with amber and lavender wildflowers. She ducked from the brittle breeze and knelt in the tenuous warmth of the midday sun. Before her the great river flowed gently into the sea, silty emerald diffusing into crystalline aquamarine, the far bank blending with the horizon—a breathless expanse of ocean and sky.

"Beautiful," came the voice of her mate.

"Oh, it is so very beautiful," she exclaimed, turning.

"I meant you," Dowornobb said. He dropped their breathing units.

Their great bodies came together in an Olympian embrace. Even the insistent trade wind was incapable of flushing away the potent aroma of their affection.

"This is what I came to Genellan for," Kateos sniffled, leaning against her mate, taking his scent with gulping inhalations. "Why must I feel so guilty?"

"You have been working all hours," Dowornobb said. "You should spend more time outside."

"Ah, but I might never go back," she said, rearing to her hinds and lifting her arms. "This is what I want. Not to manage the destiny of planets and races."

"Sacrifice in paradise is the greatest of sacrifices," Dowornobb murmured. "We have both been assigned great tasks."

"I worry I am not up to it." She sneezed.

"I would worry if you did not worry, my mate," Dowornobb replied. "It is time to put on your breathing unit. Tar Fell will soon return."

Kateos slipped the helmet over her head and initiated the welcome flow of warm, high-pressure air.

"Curse Tar Fell and his battleships," she said, and stomped off toward her duties, grainy features firming with resolve.

TWENTY-EIGHT

OVERTURES

Godonov shifted uncomfortably. Every marine officer assigned to First Fleet, as well as a host of science officers, including Captain Gray, the chief scientist, were in attendance. Using Lizard Lips and the Legion communicator as well as hunter sign language, Godonov had given a demonstration of potential cliff dweller tactics. Hunters dressed in leather battle armor, posturing with bow and arrow, captured everyone's attention. Godonov thought the demonstration went well.

"I'll take your request higher, Mr. Godonov," the senior marine declared. "You have my endorsement."

"Thank you, Colonel," Godonov replied. "How soon will you be able to start integration and training? Hunters need to, ah, keep busy."

"That's somewhat problematic, Mr. Godonov," the colonel

replied. "We'll have to develop more effective communication links before we can truly integrate them into our battle doctrine."

"But if you—" Godonov started.

"We will submit a request to science to develop a field communication system," the colonel persisted. "While we're waiting, I would accede to Captain Gray's request that these specimens be made available for detailed study. In the end it will facilitate your objective . . . and ours."

"But the hunters—"

"Thank you, Mr. Godonov," Captain Gray interrupted. "Let's return to our duties, shall we."

Tatum, a damp chill between his shoulders, stumbled from the stone cabin in starlit darkness, his boots leaving black stains in the silvery dew. Fog crept up from the lake and tumbled across the low rim of the palisade. Overhead, ebony heavens were washed with brilliant stars, the eastern sky providing only a faint hint of the coming dawn.

"Da!" the little voice cried. "Wait for me, Da!" Tatum turned to see his daughter, sandals in hand, dashing barefoot from the cabin. The angel-haired pixie churned up to him and hugged his leg. His big hand stroked silky tresses that glowed gold even in the faintest light.

"Honey," Tatum whispered, trying to sound angry, "how many times have I told you not to leave the cabin by yourself?"

"I'm with you, Da," Honey mumbled, not looking up. "I'm not . . . I'm with you."

He scooped up the child with his massive arm and hugged her warm, leggy body. The door to Nancy Dawson's cabin groaned open. The tall redhead appeared in the dark doorway. A cliff dweller huntress peeked around Dawson's hip, quickly followed by another. They chittered softly.

"You guys are waking the dead," Dawson said, yawning.

"Morning, Nance," Tatum whispered. He smelled the cook fire from the lodge and baking bread. Wilson and Tookmanian were already at work. Sunrise was getting later every day, with autumn not far away. "Honey's up early this morning."

"Want me to take her, Sandy?" Dawson asked.

"Nah, thanks. I'll take her up to the barn. Honey's never seen the hunters getting ready for a salt mission. I'll give her some chores. That'll make her stay in bed next time."

"Don't count on it, Da," Dawson replied, turning to her door. "She loves those horses as much as you do, but she's got an excuse—she's a kid. You need a woman, Sandy." And Dawson was gone.

Tatum strode up the easy grade to the stone-walled horse barn. A bright column of artificial light poured from the main door. The cloying odors of hot iron, leather, and horse manure greeted him. Spitter, the watch lead, hailed him from a ceiling beam. The hunter's pickax head was silhouetted against a light bar, maw gaping, jagged teeth displayed in lusty humor. Tatum chuckled at the warrior's haughty posturing and at the furious intensity of his underlings. He set Honey down. She skipped the length of the barn, eyes aglow with flickering firelight.

Stoked fires burned high, casting dancing shadows in corners not reached by electric light. Bellows huffed, blasting hot metallic currents. Hunters screeched and shrieked, their mucking shovels scraping and grating in discordant accompaniment. Pitchforks tossed provender into stalls with the steady *swish-swish* of a driving rainstorm. Manual labor, so disdained by the warriors, was a different matter when it came to servicing the precious horses. The golden animals had lifted the burden of salt bags from their shoulders.

Not only hunters were at work. Smithy hammers provided desultory timpani as the bellows fire roared white-hot under the ministrations of apron-bedecked guilders. Steam users, comically aloof from the bustling hunters, labored at forging horseshoes, tools, and tack of iron alloy. A new caste of cliff dweller had been created, a caste that included both hunter and guilder—the horse tender.

A chesty stallion caught Tatum's scent and neighed loudly. The mustard-gold horse stood alongside a stall, being curried by hunters. Furry flanks and broad back shivered contentedly under the vigorous flurry of wooden combs. Skipping about under the stallion's imposing anatomy, Tatum's deeply tanned daughter, curry comb in hand, brushed burrs from the horse's bushy fetlocks. Her hair, fired bronze by the light of flames, whipped about like swirls of gold thread.

"Watch out, baby," Quinn called, approaching the short-nosed, pointy-eared horse. "Tank will squash you like a bug."

Honey's brown eyes rolled up in exasperation. She distractedly ran the horse comb through her own hair.

"Would not," she shouted, reaching up and patting the animal's hock. "Tank's my friend." The horse tossed its silky mane.

Tatum looked about with satisfaction. Under the relentless training efforts of the hunters, the new horses captured to replace the dragon kill were integrating well into the established herd.

The double door leading to the paddock groaned opened. O'Toole and Beppo Schmidt hurried in, pulling mounts.

"Intrusion in cluster alpha," O'Toole shouted. "Sensors show at least three bears. They're heading straight for the cabins."

"Saddle up Tank for me," Tatum ordered. "Come on, Hon. You got to go back to Nancy's."

St. Pierre had just awakened. He had a newspaper deadline to make and needed time to polish some articles. He was stoking the coals in his fireplace when the transceiver unit warbled. Maggie, still asleep in the loft, groaned and rolled over.

"Attention, cabin clusters alpha and bravo," the radio broadcast, the operator's voice a register above a yawn. "Wildlife in your sector. Remain in cabins with doors and shutters closed until hunting patrol arrives. I repeat, remain in your cabins until cleared."

"What is it, Reggie?" Maggie said, putting her legs over the loft.

"Probably bears," St. Pierre answered, turning on his admin unit and connecting to the settlement net. Bears had become frequent visitors, moving between the forests and the lake, snuffling and growling in the night, leaving Gargantuan tracks.

St. Pierre brought up the sensor output and localized to the southern sectors. The twelve inhabited cabins and the technician dorms near the hydro had active IR signatures. The cabins under construction and the church Tookmanian and Mendoza were building in the hills were shown as informational icons. The settlers were ahead of schedule, and the next council meeting would determine how many more cabins could be constructed before winter. There was so much to do. They needed more than roofs and walls to survive the winter. The council was doing well, yet everyone missed Buccari's firm leadership. St. Pierre missed more than that.

St. Pierre watched as his display mapped warm-body returns. Wildlife density was astounding; there were indicators of living creatures all around the cabins. St. Pierre adjusted the

search variables and requested a filtered search for known carnivores. The refreshed screen depicted far fewer threats but
still a disconcerting number. Three icons, indicated as probable
bears, were in his cabin cluster.

"They're outside!" a voice shouted over the radio.
"They're scratching at my door." St. Pierre recognized his
neighbor's voice—Jerrad Simpson, a settler with a wife and
three children.

"Keep calm," the sterile voice of the radio technician replied. "Bar your door and shutters and move to your storm
shelter. Take your weapon. The patrol will be on site in less
than ten minutes."

St. Pierre looked up at his wife and tried to smile reassuringly.

"Help us! They're breaking down the door," Simpson
screamed. Loud crashes thundered in the background. A
weapon detonated. The hair on St. Pierre's neck rose. More
screams, and then the transmission ceased.

"Move to your storm shelter," the radio operator commanded, his voice rising in pitch and volume. "The patrol is
on the way."

The radio was silent.

"Do you read me?" the radio operator begged.

Simpson's cabin was still surrounded by threat icons. The IR
returns of the patrol were visible, moving closer—the angry
bright spot of an ATV cruising along the lake road and what
were probably horse riders coming through the forest. It would
not be long before they arrived, but would it be soon enough?

"This is St. Pierre," he broadcast over the radio. "I'm heading over to help Simpson."

"Negative!" the radio operator shouted. "Remain in your
cabin. The patrol will be there within minutes. Remain in
your cabin."

But St. Pierre was already strapping on his pistol and pulling
on his boots. He grabbed his rifle and a hand lamp.

"Don't be late for breakfast," Maggie said, her face and tone
belying her words. He had trouble wrenching his gaze from
hers.

"Bar the door," St. Pierre said, blowing her a kiss. He pulled
open the door and jogged up the hill. The eastern sky had a
powder-blue cast at the horizon. Stars were winking out.

A large angry animal bellowed its displeasure directly
ahead. St. Pierre turned on the lamp and raised its powerful

beam until, at the very limits of its range, it impinged on Simpson's cabin. Ponderous rusty smudges moved in his beam, and two by two, three pairs of golden orbs clicked into reflective focus.

St. Pierre slowed to a walk and shouted. He shouted again, loudly enough to strain his throat but also to dispel the fear rising in his gut. He had their attention; what was he going to do with it? Two bears returned their attention to the ground. The other behemoth rose on its hind legs. Its snout, much longer than an Earth bear's, lifted, and its slavering maw yawned wide. A thundering primal roar echoed across forest and lake, reverberating along the steep walls of the valley. Huge canines and kitchen-knife claws glistened dimly in the light of St. Pierre's torch. Damn, it was taller even than a kone; its head towered above the rafters of the cabin.

St. Pierre was less than a hundred meters from Simpson's cabin. The door had been ripped from its hinges. He held his ground. Pounding hoofbeats and the thrumming of an all-terrain engine lifted to his awareness. A blue-white spotlight flickered through the trees. The bears brought their attention to the new noises. Suddenly Sam Cody, rifle in hand, was at his side.

"Couldn't let you have all the fun, Reg," Cody huffed. He must have run all the way from his cabin.

A howling siren shattered the quiet morning. From out of the woods three horses thundered. Sandy Tatum's streaming ponytail and tall, wide-shouldered form were discernible in the dim light, as was Beppo Schmidt's luminous thatch of tow. The one-armed man loosed a burst into the air. The ursine monsters exploded from St. Pierre's light beam. St. Pierre and Cody ran forward. The siren-wailing ATV passed them in a cloud of dust.

St. Pierre and Cody arrived at Simpson's porch. Tatum and O'Toole had dismounted from their prancing horses and were employing flashlights to scrutinize the ground. Schmidt, still mounted, trotted at the limits of the clearing. Major Faro leapt from the ATV and ran across the sundered threshold. Her marines unloaded and deployed into a disciplined perimeter.

"Here we are," said a voice to St. Pierre's right. It was Simpson. He and his wife and three children had egressed through the cliff dweller–designed escape tunnel.

"The door just exploded." Simpson laughed nervously. "I thought we were dead."

"Simpson!" Tatum shouted, striding toward them.

Fuming, Major Faro erupted from the cabin. The mountains had assumed a peach cast. The marine officer ran straight for St. Pierre.

"What the hell!" Major Faro screamed, thrusting her nose into St. Pierre's face and bumping him violently. Despite her generous contours, there was no give to Faro's anatomy. St. Pierre staggered back. "What the frigging hell are you doing? My radio operator gave orders to stay inside. Orders! When I give orders, you follow them. You understand?"

"Sooner or later we'll have to take care of ourselves," St. Pierre dared to respond. "That was Buccari's main objective."

"Bullshit!" Faro spit, her face radiating enough fury to chase the dawn. "It's my responsibility to protect you. My orders override all your goddamn objectives. This colony is under frigging martial law."

"Let's take it up at the next council," Cody replied, looking at the Simpson family. "The important thing is no one was injured."

"Damn right we'll take it up," Faro snarled, storming back to the ATV and marshaling her troops.

"Mrs. Simpson, you had a garden," Tatum's deep voice intervened.

"Well, yes, I did," the nervous woman replied.

"Please don't bury fish in your garden," Tatum lectured. "Use manure or night soil for fertilizer; that is, unless you want more visits in the middle of the night."

"It was my idea, not hers," Simpson mumbled, hugging his wife.

Tatum and O'Toole mounted their horses. St. Pierre told the chagrined Simpson he would come by that evening, after work shift, and help him repair his door. Cody and St. Pierre walked down the hill. The pink and peach wash of predawn on the towering mountain peaks was sublime, yet no more so than the rich serenade offered by the first birds of morning. As they came to the branch in the path leading to Cody's cabin cluster, they met Mrs. Jackson, her husband, and their oldest son moving stealthily through the trees. All carried rifles and wore ebony rockdog skins.

"Did you see the bears, Sam?" Mrs. Jackson asked.

"I'll tell you all about it," Cody said, turning them around and herding them home. As the intrepid pioneers disappeared through the trees Major Faro's ATV bounced up to St. Pierre.

"Some advice, St. Pierre," Major Faro barked, leaping from the vehicle. She ordered the driver to wait on the lake road. As the ATV trundled away, she began gesticulating.

"Agent St. Pierre," Faro snarled in an all-too-normal tone, her wide face close to his.

"Yes, Major," St. Pierre replied, straining to mask his loathing.

"That was a good play," she said, her voice dropping to a whisper. "Should make you very popular with the settlers. A hero."

"In accordance with my mission," he said, dropping his chin as if being castigated. "I appreciate your capable assistance."

"Yeah." Her husky voice dropped even lower. "Since Queen Buccari isn't around, your security mission is really a waste of talent. Let me know if you need someone to practice your . . . penetration skills on."

St. Pierre would have laughed if he had not been so infuriated. He leaned forward, his nose in Faro's face. "Not," he purred, "if you were the last marine on this planet."

TWENTY-NINE

TRIBULATION

There were noises common to all large vessels underway—the respiration of great engines buried deep within frameworks of metal. Subliminal *whirr*ings, mysterious *ka-thunks*, the unending susurrant circulation of air—and vibrations, always a rich symphony of harmonics that reflected the pulse of the mission, the ship's very heartbeat. And to that heartbeat were synchronized the pulses of her crew. The beings that serviced the iron lady and were served by her became inextricably linked to the vessel's vital signs, their collective perceptions forging the sixth sense of the ship driver.

Brappa-the-warrior floated in the subtle stew of ambient

noises, too angry to find sleep. Big-ears and Short-one-who-leads would probably be disappointed, but he refused to be prodded and pinched, pricked and poked, pushed and pulled any longer. That was not his duty. Pah! Duty!

The security device on the entry *clickety-click*ed, disrupting the aural symphony, and Brappa came fully awake. The hatch hissed open. Glaring illumination exploded, and Brappa rolled from the light, craving sleep, for sleep brought welcome emptiness. Sherrip's soft plea was overwhelmed by Toon-the-speaker's indignant outrage. Brappa burrowed deeper in the covers.

"Thou behave shamefully, Brappa-son-of-Braan," Toon admonished. "Thou art surly and shirk thy duties. Thou—"

"Admonish me not, guilder," Brappa snapped back, knowing shame. "My duties are meaningless. Thou hast much to do, and for a purpose."

"Duty is duty," Toon preached.

Brappa sat and rubbed his eyes. Sleep would not come with the guilder serving as its irascible gatekeeper.

"There is much to learn," Toon chirped. "Too much even for a thousand guilders . . . or hunters. Thou must learn other disciplines."

Brappa chirped his disgust, pounced from his bunk, and waddled from the cabin abode, seeking sanctuary with Short-one-who-leads. He was her protector. Pah, *she* was *his* protector! It was madness to come on the star journey. He was a hunter, a creature of the cliffs and lakes, not of metal closets flying between the stars.

Brappa placed his palm on the security plate and chirped his name. The hatch slid open, and he walked in, the hatch hissing to. It was dark. Only the diodes of the chamber's information machine were illuminated, but that was sufficient. His eyes dilated in accommodation, and every detail became apparent.

Short-one-who-leads was there, slumped at the table, bare head on her arms. Sobs, liquid and deep, came from within her breast. Brappa crept to her and touched a soft white shoulder. She made an utterance in her low, slow tongue—a moaning of deep melancholy. His heart heavy, Brappa wrapped his membranes about the long-legs. Her tortured face lifted, splotched and wet with tears, green eyes rimmed with lurid red. Strong arms locked around the hunter's waist.

Short-one-who-leads was sad and lonely. The hunter was ashamed of his selfishness, but he, too, was powerfully sad. In his confusion Brappa did something hunters never did before females. Brappa-the-warrior, son-of-Braan-the-hero, sword-hand-and-shield-of-Short-one-who-leads, wept.

Tall-red-hair laughed—deep, guttural noises. Blood flushed the long-leg female's freckled cheeks. She put her face in her hands, hiding her dancing eyes.

Ki observed the long-leg male's peculiar behavior. One-arm had collected a great load of wild blossoms and brought them to Tall-red-hair's door. One-arm had foolishly adorned his face fur with blossoms.

"They are in heat," Tokko twittered wryly. The hunter perched on the back of the golden-tail, waiting for One-arm. They were departing on a salt mission—five days on the taiga. A new horse tender apprentice, a sentry, perched nervously at the old warrior's side. Ki's daughter, Notta, inspected the wiry young hunter with coy glances.

Ki pushed Notta over the stone cabin's threshold and swung shut the heavy wooden door. Thunderhead ran up, hiss-whistling like a steam kettle. Notta had named the whelp Thunderhead, so often did it thunk its large round head against unyielding granite. The whelp grew stronger every day and more mobile—stronger than a hunter fledgling if not as agile. Fortunately, Thunderhead had developed a silky thatch of soft brown hair on its skull, ameliorating somewhat the effects of his collisions, if not the audible result.

Ki thought it peculiar that other than a uselessly thin layer of downy hair on its arms and legs, the only place that fur of substance could be found on the whelp's pink body was its head. The long-legs' home world must be warm, Ki reasoned, and long-legs must fall and strike their heads frequently.

"Salt missions are so dangerous," Notta warbled fretfully.

"Not so dangerous as in the past," Ki said softly.

"The new horse tender is handsome," Notta chirped.

"Mind the whelp," Ki replied sadly.

THIRTY

CHECKRIDE

Buccari was sapped; her adrenaline had run out. Her eyes struggled to focus on her instruments. Her corvette's ion drives had gone down. The circulation in her battle armor had failed. Her thermals were soaking wet. Globules of perspiration floated before her eyes.

"Bogey two thousand klicks and still coming," Gunner Tyler reported. "Engagement range in thirty seconds. Board be green."

"Very well," Buccari replied, triggering the maneuvering alarm. The bogey had chased them relentlessly, answering her every move. Buccari had been trained to avoid engagement without sufficient attack support, but now she had no option but to break tactical doctrine. "Maneuvering to engage. Lay a decoy!"

"Decoy, aye," Flaherty replied. Her copilot's gloved fingers moved nimbly. There was a muted thud in the bowels of the ship.

She hammered thrusters. The corvette pivoted sharply, activating acceleration tethers. Did she have enough power to control the tactical situation? Could she even get into position to fire laser cannons?

"Power surge!" Flaherty announced. "We now have compound emergencies! Engineering, what goes?"

"Impulse accelerators are overdriving," Chief Silva reported. "Estimate fifteen seconds until they go critical."

"Secure impulse drives," Buccari ordered, shaking her head. "Bring back number two ion thruster. Reroute coolants and divert power from number two cannon." She was cutting her firepower in half, but she had to have engine thrust to create an engagement overshoot or *Eagle Three* would not have time to get into the fight. The enemy would toast her ship. They would die.

"Lay down a saturation pattern of kinetics," she ordered.

"Firing!" Flaherty replied.

The sounds of rippling ordnance vibrated the corvette. She looked into her visor's tactical display. A second enemy symbol moved into engagement radius. *Eagle Three* was moving too damn slow.

"Solid lock," Gunner Tyler reported.

"Very well," she replied.

"Bogey, dead astern!" Flaherty reported. "Outta nowhere."

"What!" she shouted. Her cannons were masked. "Salvo stern kinetics!"

"Fire in the galley!" Thompson reported, stifling a laugh.

"The galley?" Buccari shouted. "Get serious! Tasker, get back there and douse that fire. And no coffee!"

The comm technician cheerfully acknowledged. Buccari glared at the tactical display. The blip representing the enemy ship was closing inexorably. Acquisition alarms brayed.

"Cannon number one has lost sync," Gunner Tyler reported.

"Aw shit!" she shouted. "Engineering! Cross-connect the cannons!"

"Cross-connecting," Chief Silva replied.

No way in hell was there enough time.

"*Delta Four* control says the plumbing in the head just broke." Thompson actually giggled. "And the popcorn's burned."

Buccari ripped off her helmet and stared straight ahead, laboring to control her temper and other emotions.

"Zap! We just got incinerated." Flaherty yawned. "Had to get us sooner or later, Skipper."

"No matter, popcorn's torched." Thompson laughed.

"War is truly pure hell," Flaherty groaned, lifting helmet from sweat-drenched head.

She popped her tethers and dove across the flight deck. She pushed through the hatch. Wanda Green and the simulator technicians, laughing and hooting, clustered around the master station. She noticed Pulaski and Chang and began to smell the peculiar odor of a rat. Lizard Lips was in the middle of the technicians, clapping bony hands together.

"Who's the butthead running *Delta Four*?" she shouted. "This is serious training, not an aerobic workout. What moron—"

The operator sitting at the master console pivoted to face her, removing the integration helmet. It was Commander Carmichael.

"Now, butthead, maybe," the squadron commander confessed. "But I don't know if I'll accept being called a moron."

Pulaski sniggered like a horse. Lizard Lips tilted his head at the odd noise.

"Sorry, Commander," she said, grimacing. "If I'd known it was you, I'd have said 'sir.' "

"You and your crew just gave quite a performance," Green said.

"They're a damn good crew," she replied. "But—"

"Congratulations; your team passed checkride," Carmichael said. "Not only have you hurdled the certification series, you've maxed them out. No one's done that before. No one's ever made it through without getting their ass busted—multiple times."

"So you had to bust my booster at least once," she said, the muscles in her neck loosening. Flaherty floated into her vision. She noticed that her crew had moved from simulator stations and was drifting behind her. Tonto and Bottlenose, their pelts slowly restoring, fluttered to a bulkhead buttress overhead and perched upside down.

"Consider it a favor," Carmichael said.

"Thank you, Commander," she said, begrudging him a grin. "I hope I can return the consideration."

"I look forward to it, Skipper," Carmichael said. "I've signed off your log. Crew Six Bravo is officially on flight status and scheduled for lunar fly-off."

A rowdy cheer lifted, Flaherty's voice bellowing above all others. Lunar fly-off meant two nights of liberty before the fleet's arrival and the ensuing flood of carousing spacers. The dens of iniquity in Luna and Selene would be their private reserve. Smiling simulator technicians lined up to shake hands.

"Thanks, Commander," she said, feeling her fatigued face break into a smile. She accepted Carmichael's handshake and concerned stare. He held her hand for too long. She reluctantly pulled her hand from his and looked away, heart racing.

"Give it a break, Sharl," Carmichael said, his words masked by raucous bedlam. "We've got a week until exit. I'm ordering you out of simulators for the rest of the transit. And I'm taking you off bridge watches, too. Report to Commodore Wells. Flag is preparing for postdeployment hell, and you're officially assigned to staff."

"Aye, sir," she said, feeling more relief than she cared to admit.

Carmichael checked the time hack. He slapped her back, his hand sliding slowly to her shoulder. He pushed off, heading for the transit core. She watched him depart. He had wide shoulders.

"You look like shit," Pulaski said, grinning like a drunken simpleton. His meaty hand thudded against her back.

"Congratulations, Sharl," Chang said. "Now we're all qualified."

"Just keeping up with you two," she replied, bracing her boot heel and swinging with all her might. The roundhouse left landed solidly in Pulaski's generous stomach. The burly man grunted, doubled over, and smiled as if constipated, red-faced, his breath slow to return.

"Damn, Booch," he gasped, reaching out and halting his imparted drift vector. "What'd you . . . do that for?"

"The popcorn," she said. "That was your touch."

THIRTY-ONE

TAR FELL ATTACKS

Above New Edmonton on retro-blasted ground beneath the cedar forest sat six planetary habitation modules. The huge vessels were arrayed with geometric perfection—the PHM farm. Two had been reduced to skeletons, their cannibalization contributing to the settlement's needs. One PHM had been transformed into a hospital-commissary, and one into a storage facility. The other two had been converted to power stations.

A gravel road led south through chaparral and grass. Two kilometers later it became the paved main avenue of New Edmonton. Cassy Quinn, wearing sturdy boots and a rumpled tropical rig of forest-green shorts and white short-sleeved blouse, stalked along that avenue. A spacer yeoman, making notes of her morning inspection, hustled at her side.

"Tell the engineers to stand down on the wall until the housing blocks are complete," Quinn ordered, watching a gravel truck trundle by.

"But Envoy Stark expects the wall—" The yeoman swallowed his words as his brain kicked in. Quinn fixed him with a knife-edged stare.

"I want those settlers out of the mud," she said, taking off her floppy cap and wiping perspiration from her forehead. "They work in the fields all day, and they come home to a tent knee-deep in a quagmire. That chickenshit wall of Stark's can wait."

"Aye, Captain," the petty officer replied, uploading the inspection directive. "I'll send this out right—"

The yeoman's admin unit beeped. Quinn had turned off her multiplex to escape badgering calls from Stark's mindless bureaucrats.

"Envoy Stark requests your presence, Captain," the petty officer said. "Urgent."

"I guess I've seen enough today," she muttered under her breath. She looked down the gentle grade, past planted fields, toward the distant ocean, a line of blue made indistinct by sea haze. Squalls marched on the horizon—the afternoon monsoon. She headed uphill, amazed that a place could be simultaneously so muddy and so dusty.

Dormitories constructed of yellow composite blocks were arrayed in rows within a grid of concrete. In the center square squatted the administration building. Ultimately there would be a park and reflecting pool, but for now the open space was mud and rubble. The admin building was near completion; Legion engineers had attempted to give it an architectural character approximating art deco, but the overall impression was that of a prison. Stark's yellow wall, running two-thirds of the colony's circumference and topped with concertina, only added to that affect.

Quinn walked gingerly across broken ground, trying to avoid puddles. Swirling clouds of gnats like tiny static tornadoes hovered over each miniature swamp.

"Get a work party to clean this up," she huffed. "Use the scrabble to build walkways. Grade it and set up drainage."

"Aye, sir." The yeoman's admin unit beeped again. "Strange," he said.

"What?" Quinn asked.

"There was a message that Mr. Hudson is waiting—" he began.

"About time," she snarled.

"—and then the net connection blanked out," the yeoman said, puzzled. "The carriers are all being overdriven."

"Excellent data," Dowornobb announced, checking uplinks from the Imperial Astronomical Institute. "It has taken a full moon cycle, but the simulation models have at last converged. Every unit of the human fleet was successfully triangulated and gravity indexed. Several constants and patterns have come forth. I am much encouraged."

"Excellent," Et Silmarn said. "Our negotiating position can only grow stronger."

"I think," Kateos said, "Sharl would rather we discovered hyperlight on our own, but she is too honorable to tell us how."

"As would I," Dowornobb rumbled, studying the computer. "I would rather not have to accede to the interminable whining of Envoy Stark. Stark has no loyalty, no guiding principle, no honor."

"He exploits the principles of others," Et Silmarn replied.

"It is the same with our leaders," Kateos said. "My mate, you look distressed."

"The computer models expand exponentially with each data set," Dowornobb bemoaned. "It will take years of processing to analyze the next data run unless we obtain more resources."

"I will petition King Ollant—" Kateos started to say.

"What is this?" Dowornobb exclaimed, punching buttons on his terminal. "All transmissions are being jammed."

"What?" Et Silmarn shouted.

"I am getting interference on all frequencies." Dowornobb gasped. "All satellite telemetry is disrupted. I no longer have contact with Goldmine Station. Or Kon! Even the PDF circuits are jammed."

"We are under attack," Kateos growled.

"What?" Et Silmarn shouted.

"Tar Fell!" Kateos whispered.

"What?" Et Silmarn shouted again.

"We cannot just sit here and wait for Tar Fell to land," Kateos announced. "We must form a resistance."

"With what?" Et Silmarn asked. "We have no soldiers. My scientists do not know how to fight."

"Then we must flee," Kateos said, "and preserve the king's authority. We will seek sanctuary with the humans."

"We need fuel for our breathers," Dowornobb said.

"I have created caches," Et Silmarn said sheepishly.

"What?" Kateos and Dowornobb shouted together.

"At MacArthur's Valley," Et Silmarn rumbled. "Enough for one kone to last a year. And more at the fuel-staging fields. I have already learned this lesson the hard way."

"Let us warn Hudsawn and Commander Quinn," Kateos said.

"Goldmine Station is secure, Armada-Master," Krolk reported. "There was no resistance. Governor Et Silmarn was not there."

Tar Fell grunted an acknowledgment. No surprise. Since the human landing the science facility at Ocean Station had been expanded. But Goldmine Station, halfway around the planet from Ocean Station and on another continent, housed the satellite communication and logistic centers for the planet as well as the fuel-processing facilities. Goldmine Station would be his strategic focus, for controlling Goldmine would deny King Ollant the planet.

It had been too easy. There were no military forces on Genellan, only scientists and technicians. The first lander to Goldmine carried enough troops to take over the gantries and the communication center. The second and third landers carried troops to secure all the domes. Scientists and technicians were conditioned to submit to authority.

Tar Fell stared out the circular view port on the battleship's bridge. The dun and blue mass of Genellan rolled beneath him, daylight illuminating his next target. He could see the line of the great river running north and south. On the left bank of the river, where its delta met the equatorial ocean, was Ocean Station. Tar Fell pulled on his helmet and sealed his suit. It was time to visit the king's ambassador, this time not as an observer.

Quinn trotted up three flights of stairs to her office, perspiration soaking her blouse. The elevator was not working again.

The dim orange glow of emergency lanterns provided illumination. Hudson waited on the wide balcony of her airy office. The windows and outer doors were open, and a gentle ocean-scented breeze greeted her. Hudson's large-gauge over-and-under leaned against her chair. She lugged the weapon over to the wall and sat at her desk.

"So where have you been?" Quinn demanded. "You come to NEd and pretend to be helping my settlers. We listen to what you have to say—actually start depending on you—maybe even enjoying your company—and then you disappear for three days with one of my all-terrains."

"Sorry, Mom," Hudson apologized, his scarred face red from excessive sun. The tall man moved from the balcony. Strapped to his waist was a thigh-length expedition knife. He wore shorts and a field vest over a T-shirt, revealing his beat-up prosthesis. The epiderm-plastic sheathing on his left shin was tearing off in strips.

"Found a beautiful island, Cass. It's connected to the mainland by a spit of sand. I got trapped by the incoming tide."

"Low tide comes twice a day, doesn't it?" she asked.

"On Earth," Hudson said, walking around her desk and hefting his rifle. "Tides are a little more complex here. Two moons, remember?"

"Ain't that complex, young man," she replied, feeling her emotions melting against the warmth of his eyes. "Well, I'm glad you're back. Next time take a communicator."

"Aye, aye, Commander," Hudson replied mirthfully. "Now, are you ready to go? Like to get moving before the thunder bumpers roll in."

"Give me an hour," she said. "Envoy Stark wants to see me." She had promised the MacArthur Valley settlers she would attend their meetings at least once a month. She had missed two months. The northern settlers had stopped complaining, probably thinking she no longer cared.

"Want me to go with you to see Stark?" he asked. "He and I get along so well. It might shorten the meeting. Stark could use—"

"Get off my back, Nash," she replied, struggling to sound angry.

"How're you doing, Cassy?" Hudson asked, not fooled.

"The settlers are so glad to be here," Quinn said with a sigh, "but they're finally realizing what it's like to be on a virgin planet with no place to go to, no one else to depend on. And winter's coming so fast."

"NEd's a bit depressing," Hudson seconded. "Had three settlers come out and ask if I could smuggle them north."

"There are a lot more people down here," Quinn said. "It's harder to make everyone feel at home."

Hudson remained quiet, and she was glad. They had had this discussion too many times. The breeze brought in a feathery vibration that turned into a rumble, growing louder and louder.

"That's not thunder," Quinn said.

"Hell, no," Hudson snarled as he jumped to the window. "Damn, I hate that sound."

"What's wrong?" Quinn asked.

"Orbital landers. Two of them!" Hudson said, his voice rising in pitch. "No, three! Four! Tar Fell is attacking Ocean Station."

She ran to the balcony. There—a gout of orange flame. NEd was at a higher elevation than the konish domes. She could see sinister blossoms of exhaust. One was nearly down. Higher in the dark blue sky three more blazing swords of orange and yellow stabbed downward. An attack.

"Look! Over there!" Hudson yelled. "An abat coming this way!"

The rumble of the lander retros masked the abat's engine. The big high-winged craft was almost on them.

"It going to land," Hudson said, spinning from the balcony.

Envoy Stark was at the door. Members of Stark's security team lurked in the hallway. Hudson pulled up short.

"We appear to be in the middle of a conflict," Stark remarked casually. He wore loose-fitting tan slacks and a white blouse-sleeved shirt. "I would ask—"

"Excuse me," Hudson said, moving to pass. The abat's engines were suddenly loud overhead. "The conflict just came to us."

"We must remain neutral," Stark shouted at Hudson's back, whose wake through the security agents had already closed.

"Are you in contact with Tar Fell?" Quinn asked, strapping on her holster. "You sound like you know something."

"Tar Fell is claiming rights to a share of this planet," Stark replied, avoiding the question but answering it clearly.

"Are you going to recognize his claim?"

"We must not take sides."

"Of course," she acknowledged. "I must see to our guests."

"Commander Quinn!" Stark barked, reaching out and grabbing her arm. "You will not give shelter, and you will order the marine commandant to restrict his marines to the barracks. And I would advise you to bring Hudson in line until this situation is resolved."

"I'll take your advice under consideration," she replied, pushing past the envoy and elbowing through his agents.

Quinn ran down the stairs, yelling for a driver. Hudson's ATV was parked at the front curb. The pool dispatcher was haranguing Hudson. Quinn preempted the argument and ordered Hudson in. She jumped behind the wheel and angled across the muddy central area, gunning the vehicle up the airstrip road, squirting a rooster tail of dust and mud.

"Who needs roads?" Hudson yelped.

"Dammit!" Quinn shouted. "Stark's playing both sides."

"You didn't just figure that out, did you?" Hudson shouted back.

"What's your plan?" Quinn asked, not answering.

"I'm heading back to MacArthur's Valley. I'll ask Kateos to come with me," Hudson replied, turning to see if anyone was following. "You still coming?"

She glanced at him and then stared straight ahead. "Let me think about it," she said. "Situation's changed just a bit. I'm in charge here, and besides, I left my gear back at the admin building."

"Look in the back," Hudson said. "I loaded your stuff while I was waiting. They need you up north, Cassy, now more than ever. Stark and his goons are in charge down here. You're irrelevant. You just do all the work."

The ATV's radio was blinking. She punched up the security frequency. The reception was completely garbled. They were being jammed. She threw the microphone back on its hook and sat back to think.

They arrived at the airfield. The big abat squatted on fat tires, dominating the three Legion Explorers. Kateos, Dowornobb, and Et Silmarn waited. Johnny Rodriguez was with the kones, examining their trucklike aircraft. A petty officer stood in the doorway, listening on the land line and standing at attention.

"Commander Quinn, sir," the petty officer pleaded, waving the telephone receiver. "Envoy Stark wants to talk to you."

She hailed the kones and trotted for the line shack. Hudson grabbed their gear and ran toward the flight line.

"Quinn here," she barked.

"Commander," Stark answered. "My apologies. I was overly direct. Please forgive me, but we are dealing with a critical situation."

"Yes, sir," she replied, unfazed by the chameleon's transformation.

"The airfield officer tells me Ambassador Kateos has landed. Please extend to her my heartfelt welcome. I look forward to entertaining her. Could you be so kind as to escort her to my offices."

"Certainly, sir," Quinn replied. "I'll have her driven over immediately. I'm sorry I'll not be able to bring the ambassador personally. I've scheduled a flight to MacArthur's Valley to attend their council meeting. Or would you prefer I remain behind?"

"Ah! Er . . . no, Commander," Stark answered. "Please adhere to your schedule. I'll send a driver over."

"Yes, sir," Quinn replied, fighting to quell her anger. "Then I'll see you in ten days, sir."

She disconnected without waiting for a response and made two more calls, one to the marine commandant and one to the settlement's executive officer, giving orders crisply and without hesitation. Food and water were not a concern; they had enough spacer provisions in the PHM commissary to sustain the settlement for two years, and the PHM water tanks were full. Hudson was right: There was little she could do.

She threw the phone on the counter and ran out the door. One of the Legion aircraft was taxiing to the runway. Passenger seats lay on the ground next to where it had been parked. The abat was still there, but the kones were gone. Hudson was loading equipment into the abat.

"What gives?" she asked, looking at the stack of seats. It dawned on her: Hudson had sent the kones off in the Explorer. He had made room for their wide bodies by removing passenger seats.

"We'll rendezvous with Rodriguez at staging field two," Hudson puffed. "Tar Fell is probably watching us with satellites. This might confuse the issue."

"We better get moving," she said.

"Let's go," Hudson said, grinning like a kid.

Quinn followed Hudson up the ladder. She took the right seat but could not see out the front. She found a vertical adjustment, but even at full height her forward view was severely restricted. Hudson was much taller, yet even he craned his neck to see over the instrument panel.

Hudson started the engine and released the brake. The abat jiggled softly on its big tires. He did not bother with runway or wind direction but added power and trundled over the uneven ground until the big plane bounced into the air and stayed there.

"Who needs roads?" Quinn shouted.

Hudson smiled and hogged the abat around. He set climb power and aimed for a ragged notch in the northern mountains. White, roiling cumulus clouds guarded its granite pillars.

Tar Fell lifted his helmet and inhaled the painfully clear and chilly air. His lungs protested against the icy dampness, but his sinuses luxuriated in the bombardment of fresh odors. Black-armored soldiers and brown-suited security troopers moved on his flanks. Ocean Station was secured. It had been pitifully easy.

But the ambassador and the governor had taken their leave—frustrating but hardly worrisome. There was no place to go except to the human settlements. Yet he felt the need to teach the ambassador some manners.

"Armada Master, the ambassador's plane has lifted from the alien base," a commando officer reported. "It is headed north."

"How soon before your abat departs?" Tar Fell boomed.

"Momentarily, Armada Master," the officer replied. "We are making the necessary modifications."

THIRTY-TWO

ESCAPE

"Got company," Hudson said, pushing the throttle to the stops.

Quinn followed his gaze out the windscreen. The day was

bright and sunny, the sky overhead passionately blue. To sea-
ward, however, towering clouds danced on spindly shafts of
blue-white lightning. Ahead and off to the right bursts of reflected sun glinted from Ocean Station's faceted domes. She
saw the white aircraft leave its shadow on the tree-lined grass
runway. The lifting abat banked hard to the north, taking a
course to intercept their own.

"They're closer to the pass, but we've got an altitude advantage," Hudson said, adjusting power. He looked at her and
grinned.

Minutes later Hudson's grin was gone; the bearing to the
white abat was remaining uncomfortably constant, and the altitude and range differences were inexorably decreasing.
Clouds guarding the ridge grew closer. The snowy pinnacles
also grew closer, but not fast enough. Both planes would enter
the rugged pass at the same time.

Quinn saw something high. She half stood to peer out the
front. In the distance, backdropped against livid blue, she saw
another aircraft, a glint of yellow, slightly above them but descending through the pass.

"The Explorer!" Quinn shouted, pointing.

"Yeah," Hudson muttered. The abat's nose lifted, and the
plane banked hard right. She fell into her seat.

"What're you doing?" she asked.

"Let's go play. We'll buy Kateos a little time."

Hudson horsed the abat until it was pointing at the other
white plane. Seconds later the intercepting abat turned directly
into them. A point of light coruscated under its left wing.

"What's that?" Quinn asked.

"Oh, no!" Hudson groaned. He pulled into a slow barrel roll
to the left. The other abat pulled up to follow.

"What?" she asked. The light pulsed again.

"They've got a blaster mounted on their wing." Hudson grimaced. "They're trying to kill Kateos, er, us! If they hit a fuel
tank . . ."

"They didn't hit us!" she shouted, checking her wing.

"Bad shooting, I guess."

Their abat jiggled violently. The landing gear on her side of
the plane fell out of its fairing. The fat tire had exploded, and
what remained was shredding in the slipstream. Hudson fought
desperately to control the yaw, continuing to roll the abat. As
they rolled inverted, the mangled tire and its strut slammed
back into the wing fairing. The other abat whisked beneath

them. Hudson held the nose of the abat on the mountains as he slowly finished the roll. They held their breath, waiting for the landing gear to fall. It remained wedged in its well.

"Gotta get through the pass," Hudson snarled, his head swiveling violently, trying to find the other plane. "We go down here and we're dead. There's nothing on this side but vertical granite."

"Shouldn't we call Kateos on the radio?" Quinn asked.

"What good would that do?" Hudson snapped. "They're trying to kill her. This way she might get away."

"Maybe we should turn back," Quinn offered, "to Ocean Station. That will give Kateos enough time to get out of reach."

Hudson gave her a quick look.

"I've been their prisoner before," he snarled. He yanked the nose to the right of the pass. A boiling cloud filled the windscreen.

"So it's into the clouds," she deduced, pressing her face to the window, trying to find their pursuer. They droned forward. The clouds appeared to recede; the mountain ridges seemed to be at an infinite distance. Quinn wondered what they would gain by entering a cloud that was also obscuring immovable rock.

Hudson jinked right, then right again, and then left—small, quick course changes. Wispy tendrils of cloud reached out to them. Their plane shimmied.

Hudson jerked in his seat, pumping his legs.

"What's wrong?" she asked.

"Rudders are gone!" he groaned, looking desperately forward.

He dove for the clouds, sacrificing precious altitude for airspeed. At last they were obscured by implacable, turbulent whiteness. The plane bucked and rocked violently. Hudson banked to the left, toward the pass. They emerged into bright sunlight, the pass not far ahead. Hudson chose not to wait. He pulled the nose up and angled for the ragged battlements. Updrafts boosted the plane like an elevator, and its wings skimmed between rocky tors, desperately close to the unyielding escarpments. The southern face of the ridge was less precipitate. The mountain's features softened and became brilliantly white. They raced across an expansive bowl of crystalline snow.

"Maybe we'll blend in," Hudson grunted. "Are they still behind us?"

"Can't tell," Quinn replied, pressing her face against the cold window. "Bank to the right."

"Roger," Hudson replied, twisting the heavy yoke. Without a rudder the plane's flight was unbalanced. The high wing dropped in an unsteady turn, obscuring her view. When Hudson leveled the wings, Quinn's heart leapt into her throat.

"Nash!" she shouted. The other abat was less than a hundred meters behind them, coming out of a turn. She saw the flicker.

The laser beam stabbed the wing's trailing edge like a hot poker through butter, leaving an oblong hole in the flaps, a sword thrust straight through, revealing blue sky.

Hudson banked away, seeking the brilliant, billowing clouds.

"Serious downdrafts on this side." Hudson grimaced. Turbulence chopped at the abat, jerking it violently up and down.

Clouds enveloped them. Hudson steered blindly along the ridge, or where he thought the ridge was, and toward the valley of the great river. Quinn, eyeballs shaking with the jostling, peered through gauze-shrouded windows, desperately trying to detect the presence of mountain ridges. Downdrafts hammered their craft, its long wings flexing like those of an arthritic bird. They broke out of the clouds several times, the rocky, snow-dusted ridges breathtakingly close. Hudson immediately steered for another turbulent cloud and plunged in, flying perilously close to the rocks. Finally they emerged into the open, between layers of chalky-gray altostratus. The burbling cumulus clouds were behind them.

"We should be approaching the river," Hudson said, checking his instruments and starting a slow descent. The plane skimmed above milky stratus and then plunged into creamy nothingness.

"Maybe we lost them," Hudson said, peering out his window.

"No one in their right mind would have followed you," Quinn said. As they slipped beneath the cloud layer, she saw the river, its powerful course narrowed and channeled into frothing white by cruel terrain.

"The river," she yelled.

"Look!" Hudson yelled louder. She saw the other plane. It was below and ahead of them. Hudson's hands flew for the throttle, pulling it back to idle. He pushed the nose over.

"What're you doing?" she asked.

"Get my rifle!" Hudson ordered, not taking his eyes from his quarry. "There's ammo in the brown bag."

She understood. Unbuckling her seat belt, she climbed the slanting deck. The plane dipped into a gentle turn. She rocked against the bulkhead as she crawled into the passenger cabin. Their gear was in cargo netting, behind the flight deck. She extricated the hefty two-barreled weapon. There were two kinds of ammunition in the brown bag: ominous black-jacketed bullets and large-diameter shotgun shells. She grabbed a box of each and stumbled forward, laboring under her burden.

"Load it," Hudson commanded, nose pressed to the window. She could no longer see the other plane. She fumbled the jewellike, sharp-pointed bullets from the box, chambering one and pushing another half dozen into the over-and-under's magazine. Hudson stole glimpses at her progress.

"Shotgun, too," Hudson grunted. "It'll open up some serious holes. Hurry!"

She broke open the other box, spilling large-caliber shells; they rolled crazily across the flight deck. She stuffed the bright red cylinders against the stiff spring of the magazine. Hudson yanked the massive weapon from her and slammed it against a side window panel. The thick plastic separated from its frame in one piece. The slipstream roared turbulently into the flight deck.

"When I tell you," Hudson screamed, "Hold the controls. Keep the nose up!" She nodded violently. Hudson smiled, but he looked as frightened as she felt.

Hudson turned away, squinting against the blasting slipstream, and positioned the rifle barrel, pointing it out the open window. He moved the plane smoothly into a right bank and then pulled the nose up and reversed the bank, standing the plane on its left wing. The other abat filled Hudson's window. Quinn could have thrown a rock at it.

"Now, Cassy!" Hudson shouted. "Hold the nose right there!"

She grabbed the controls. The nose tried to fall. The bank angle jittered nervously. She jerked it steady.

"Hold it! Nose up!" Hudson yelled. She complied. Explosions from the shotgun made her jump. Again and again Hudson fired at the other airplane. Fascinated, she watched pieces of forward fuselage peel back and fall away. Hudson was firing the rifle, its imperative bark very different from the hollow explosions of the shotgun. The konish plane wobbled and then flipped into a hard left bank. Hudson fired one last round into its belly. The abat rolled onto its back and beyond, diving in a tight spiral. She could not take her eyes from their adversary's death throes. Nor could Hudson.

It was suddenly quiet—too quiet. Slipstream noises diminished to a whispering breeze. Their plane was stalled.

"Nose down!" Hudson bellowed. The controls were yanked from her hands as Hudson pushed the nose forward. It was too late. The plane shuddered and wallowed violently onto its back; its nose oscillated up and down and then whipped around in a tightening circle.

"Spin!" Hudson shouted, frantically moving the control column. His legs pounded useless rudders. The whirling planet leapt upward.

A loud wrenching noise commanded Quinn's attention; the spin rate increased, and the airplane's nose made larger, more violent circles. Fighting the centripetal forces, she glanced out to see the gear strut and shredded tire flailing with the airplane's tortured flight. She looked at Hudson. The pilot's face was deathly pale, but his hands were busy flipping switches. Swallowing panic and fighting dizziness, Quinn stared at the swirling ground with frustration and anger. She did not want to die. Not yet.

Mountain peaks rushed upward and past them. Ugly slopes, steep and littered with jagged prominences, leapt to meet them.

"Dropping . . . other landing gear," Hudson shouted, groping for the overhead lever. He pushed the control column forward and twisted the ailerons hard over. Quinn heard gear motors working. The plane's nose wobbled and then lifted, its frenetic oscillations slowing.

"Yeah-h-h!" Hudson shouted. He pulled the controls to his chest and slammed them forward. Blood rushed hotly to Quinn's head. Her inner ears argued with her brain. Abrupt changes made it feel as if she were spinning in the opposite direction. Hudson leaned on the control column as if his body weight could make the difference. The plane's nose halted its upward motion and fell downward, straight for the surface, with no spinning motion. Impact was only seconds away.

"Pull up!" she screamed, reaching for the controls.

"Need speed!" he yelled, his white-knuckled grip holding the plane's precipitous attitude like iron.

A shoulder of granite loomed before them. With agonizing

slowness Hudson pulled back—too slowly. Boulders expanded to fill the windscreen. Hudson twisted in some aileron, and the wing lifted just enough as the craft cleared the adamantine hurdle. They were diving into a narrow valley, with another ridge just ahead. Hudson pulled harder. The nose eased upward. The ridge blurred beneath them.

A mountain valley opened before them, and there was the wide river, gray and riven with foreboding white water. But their pursuer was gone, and their course to the north was clear. Quinn slumped back into her seat and dared to exhale. Hudson pushed the throttle forward. The roar of the engine filled the void in her being, a void created by her fright.

The engine coughed twice and died.

"Nothing, Armada Master," the commando officer said. "There is nothing on satellite radar other than the alien plane."

"Transmissions from our pilot?" Tar Fell demanded.

"There have been no transmissions," the officer reported. "It would seem both planes have crashed."

Tar Fell stared through the dome window at the distant mountains, so clear yet so far away. It mattered little whether the ambassador had escaped. He had captured the Hegemony's bases. Genellan was his.

"The alien airplane." Tar Fell sneered. "What of its progress?"

"Satellite imagery reveals the alien aircraft proceeding north along the river. Its transponder code verifies its identification and destination, although its pilot has been transmitting with some urgency. The transmissions are being processed."

Tar Fell looked through the dome at the falling rain. A wonderment. So much rain and so cold. He shivered. Even under the dome it was cold. The conqueror replaced his helmet and turned up the temperature on his suit controls, relishing the warm, pressurized air flowing to his lungs.

Quinn looked at Hudson, who groped frantically around the instrument panel, pushing on controls and banging on gauges. She looked down. The curving edge of the river passed beneath them. The shore they were crossing was steep and rocky and formidably uninviting. The far bank was lower, less steep, and mottled with forest. Narrow river islands provided protection from the turbulence of the main channel. The far shore beckoned.

"Fuel's gone," Hudson confessed. "Fuel line, I guess."

The rush of air past Hudson's open window was the only noise.

"What are you doing?" she asked.

"I'm going for the other side," he said, staring ahead, his hands firmly on the controls. "Nothing on this side but vertical rock. No shelter, no wood, assuming we survive the landing."

Quinn looked out her side window, downstream. The great river was necking down. In the distance she saw the first of the tall granite-pillared gorges that funneled the watercourse into a twisting, heaving maelstrom. Beyond that constriction there were cataracts beyond the dimensions of any earthly Niagara.

Hudson tried to restart the engine without success. He tried raising the landing gear, but only the left gear retracted. Without rudders to hold the nose, the asymmetrical gear configuration caused the plane to yaw. Hudson elected to leave the gear down.

Halfway across she said, "We aren't going to make it, are we?"

The texture of the river was sharp below them. It was too quiet; Quinn could hear her lungs rasping.

"It'll be close," Hudson said. He was gliding slightly upstream, toward the closest island. She began to imagine that they would make it. A small rock jutting from the river and creating a frothy wake passed down their starboard side, more tease than hope.

"Come on," Hudson begged, and she prayed. She could hear the river.

Quinn looked out the side window, past the gear strut and its demolished tire. The river, constantly moving and changing, welled upward, reaching for the plane. She untied her harness and stretched to peek over the instruments. The first island, an isolated gravel bar with a small stand of trees, drifted off their nose, coming down their right side. They would make it that far, at least. Maybe.

"Get back in your seat!" Hudson yelled, his harness loose so he could see over the nose. "And tighten your harness—tight!"

Quinn hunkered in her seat. The first island floated by, the tops of its trees at eye level. They would never make the far bank.

"I'm going to stall it in," Hudson said, his words knife-edged. "The gear struts will flip us if I hit too fast. We gotta get out quick. This plane will float. The current will carry it by the islands."

Another narrow island floated by, larger. Its trees towered above their altitude. Green-gray waves raced past her window, mere meters from contacting the deformed tire.

"Okay, hang on!" Hudson said. He was almost standing to see over the nose. The plane wallowed and shuddered.

"Strap in, Nash!" she yelled.

THIRTY-THREE

CASSY AND NASH

"Hudson, talk to me!" the human pilot begged over the radio. Kateos, strapped to the floor like cargo, rolled over in the cramped passenger section and closed her eyes. Dowornobb, lying next to her, placed a ponderous arm over her shoulders.

"Hudson! Commander Quinn," Rodriguez persisted, shouting.

"It is better if-ah you stop-ah transmitting, Johnny," Et Silmarn said. The governor was wedged into the flight deck opening. "Continue north. Your fuel-ah is limited, yes?"

"Yeah, we'll head for the fuel-staging field," the human mumbled. "Hudson will rendezvous with us there."

"Perhaps," Et Silmarn replied.

Kateos started to cry.

Quinn regained consciousness, her ribs aching with every labored breath. Precious seconds gurgled away before she realized she was upside down, suspended from her seat harness. The bright daylight of only seconds before had turned to green-gray darkness. Icy water *whoosh*ed through the open window. It grew darker. The bobbing plane was sinking. Adrenaline surged through her body. She released her harness and fell, splashing painfully on her back and shoulders. She was immediately soaked. Something warm and heavy rolled against her—Hudson.

"Nash!" she screamed. "Help me!"

There was no answer. Hudson needed her help! She felt for a pulse; he was still alive. She found the man's head and wrapped her arm around his chest, grabbing his armpit. She strained against Hudson's weight. He was like a wet sack of sand. Rising water quickly buoyed his mass, and Quinn was able to drag the lanky form to the hatch. She released its latch and was carried into the aft compartment by a gushing current. The cabin windows were above water, and the compartment was dazzlingly bright. She forgot the plane was upside down and turned the wrong way. As she spun about, the floating plane jolted sharply, knocking her down in a pile. The rush of waters abated. She struggled to the crew hatch and pushed it open.

Standing on the abat's ceiling in waist-deep water, she squinted into breezy sunlight. Icy river water ran down her face. The wind immediately made her shiver. The abat was held precariously against a reef of boulders. The current surged persistently around her, washing against and into the abat. She craned to look at the narrow headland of a river island. The clifflike prominence blocked her view of the main shore, and a shoulder of precipitate rock obstructed her view of the island. She knew there was only one way to go—with the current. What lay beyond the shoulder of rock, if anything, would have to be discovered the hard way.

She shook away cobwebs. Icy water made her alert. *Hudson had a coil of climbing line in his pack.* Hanging on to his collar, she struggled against her panic and retreated into the sinking abat. The cargo netting was just behind the flight deck. She found Hudson's gear and grabbed the rope. Once again attaining the open hatch, she secured the line around both of their waists. She would get Hudson to shore, and then she would think about salvaging their equipment.

Quinn held Hudson's bristly chin above the water, stepped into the current, and sank. Hudson's deadweight mass, laden with prostheses, pulled her down. She kicked frantically for the surface, debating whether to kick off her boots and jettison her pistol. She pulled Hudson's head to her belly and frog-kicked with desperate effort, fighting to keep above water. The current slammed her against the rocks. She made her way along its smooth hardness, thankful for even the most meager handholds above the water's surface. But the cold was winning. Feeling slipped from her fingers, and her bare knees ached. Each inhalation of her lungs was a burning fire. Her heart pounded. She scraped Hudson along the unending wall of current-splashed rock and around the jutting promontory, expecting to find nothing but the end of the island and no way to climb from the clutching current.

Her relief was boundless. Another shoulder of steep rock fell into the river, but between the two monoliths there was a sun-washed inlet. A sandy bottom accepted her stumbling feet. She waded doggedly from the river, chilly waters pouring from hair and clothes. Out of the water Hudson's unbuoyed bulk was immovable. She dragged his torso from the river's edge and collapsed on her back, lungs heaving, ribs burning, heart pounding.

Hudson groaned. She sat upright too quickly and became dizzy. Hudson blinked. His hand moved to his brow, where a watery runnel of blood trickled to the sand.

"Ouch," he moaned, rolling on his side.

Her relief was offset by a wave of nausea. She vomited. The wind was brittle. Her adrenaline was gone. Goose bumps rippled through her back, legs, and arms. She shivered uncontrollably.

"Y-you okay, Cassy?" Hudson mumbled, holding his head and crawling beside her. He looked about, dazed.

"Great," she retched, trying to lift her head. She wiped her mouth with the back of her hand and collapsed on the warm sand. Heat seeping through her drenched blouse was exquisite. She closed her eyes.

"You look . . . like crap, Mom," Hudson said, his voice firming.

"Thanks," she managed, waiting for the world to stop spinning.

"The abat. What'd you do with the abat?"

"Left it . . . where you parked it," she managed.

"Oh," he replied. "We should get our gear."

As if in answer, the sound of groaning metal dominated the river noises. The abat drifted across the narrow mouth of the inlet, only the glaring white twin tails visible above the blue water. Hudson stumbled halfway to his feet. The rope around his waist hobbled him to the ground. Quinn watched helplessly as the abat shuddered against the rocks and held, briefly, as if to tease. Then the river swept it away, grinding it along the island's flanks.

Hudson dropped his head into his hands and groaned softly. Quinn looked down at the rope around her waist and worried the wet knots loose. The line fell free.

"Cassy," Hudson said hoarsely.

"Yes, Nash," she replied, staggering to her feet.

"Thanks," Hudson exhaled, "for saving my life." He touched her leg. She smiled and coiled the rope, ignoring her bruised ribs.

A shadow blocked the sun.

Quinn jerked her head up. A giant eagle flying low over the river wheeled into the wind. Quinn's blood ran cold. The bird's fantastic wingspread blotted out the skies. Its head canted sideways, a terrible yellow eye fixed with primal concentration.

The great predator, black and tan pinions spread wide, prodigious talons swinging out, wheeled again and swooped straight for them, coming directly into the cove, its wings spanning the inlet. She looked for shelter. The steep-sided cove ended in a tumble of boulders above which could be seen trees and underbrush, but there was no time to scale the rocks. There was no place to run, no place to hide.

"Get into the rocks, Cassy!" Hudson shouted.

Hudson stumbled forward between her and death. The eagle adjusted to his movements, preparing to accept his sacrifice. Quinn did not remember unsnapping her holster and drawing her pistol, but the weapon was in her hand. She crouched low. The huge target loomed ominously larger, its talons curling open. Holding the pistol steady with both hands, she snapped off a shot at the eagle's head and then two more into its view-spanning breast.

The eagle wavered, its wings encompassing infinity. The great raptor fell from the sky, hitting the water with a prodigious splash. Hudson stumbled back with a yelp, wallowing frantically. The echoes of gunshots and the odor of gunpowder blew away in the wind. Hudson fell to his knees and stared at the floating carcass. Quinn lurched forward, pistol ready, a scream on her lips. Still on his knees, Hudson wrenched his stare from the predatory bird, his sandy hair dripping and lank across his scarred face.

"Cassy," the young man rasped, "you are one tough son of a bitch."

"W-what are we going t-to d-do?" she asked, teeth chattering. Her dripping blouse clung to her heaving chest. Scudding clouds blocked the sun. She shivered uncontrollably. Hudson staggered from the water and held his wet body close to hers. He was shivering, too. She looked across the slate gray river. Thunderstorms poured over the mountains, dark-bellied and fast-moving.

"Let's find sh-shelter," Hudson said, whipping his arms and looking up at the tumble of rock. His lips were tinged with blue.

The climb was steep but short. They scaled the spine of a narrow tree-studded island. They found giant trees in a confined grove on the lee of the island, like Earth redwoods. Big-leafed hardwoods grew in tight clusters at the water's edge, and delicately needled pines marched at stately intervals across the higher ground. What appeared to be an even larger island, about four hundred meters away, lay between them and the rising elevations of the mainland.

Cassy followed Hudson to the water's edge. They stared wistfully at the other island. Distant thunder rolled across the water. Leaves and pine needles whispered with greater urgency.

"We'll make camp under these low trees," Hudson said. "Keep moving, Cassy. Start collecting wood. I've got an idea. I'll be back."

"What are—" she started to say, but Hudson was trudging up the island's spine, pulling his big knife as he walked.

Activity warmed her, but she was still cold. She could feel bruises and aches from the crash. Her ankle was tender, and her neck was going stiff. She collected a respectable pile of deadfall before she heard Hudson returning. She looked up to see him lugging something dark and huge—the wing of an eagle!

The appendage was the length of three men, some of the pinions easily her height. Hudson dragged it into the branches, placed the butt end in a tree crotch, and braced the other end against another tree. Quinn understood immediately—a lean-to. She grabbed the rope and helped lash it down. Lightning strobed the treetops. Thunder boomed.

"I'll collect more firewood," she said. Raindrops splatted heavily against the leaves. "I think I can get a fire going."

"Good." Hudson's eyes had dark shadows, looking sinister in the growing dusk. "I'm going back for the other wing."

All she could do was nod. Raindrops fell with greater frequency.

She stumbled up to the pine glades and collected armloads of fragrant needles, spreading them beneath the feathered awning. Hudson returned with the other wing. They lashed it down, creating a tent, just as a squall unburdened itself. Gusts of wind flayed the trees. They scurried around the tent, tucking feathers under logs and rocks.

Near the butt on each wing was an accumulation of downy feathers. Quinn plucked them and added their padding to the pine needles.

"One more trip," Hudson said. "How's that fire coming?"

"As soon as I get more wood under cover," she replied, grabbing another armful and running for shelter. Icy rain quickly soaked her still-damp blouse. Under the feathered tent the wood and pine needles were dry. Tree boughs broke the force of the storm, but a steady drumming of rain and leaf drippings pattered over her head. Nothing came through the feathers.

Shivering, she swept wet hair from her face, took off a boot, and removed a lace. She made a loose bow and looped the line around a straight stick. After piling pine needles and dried leaves on top of a piece of wood, she pressed the sturdy stick into the middle of the tinder and spun it with the bow. After a few attempts the stick broke. She tried again, with even less success. At least the exertions were keeping her warm. On her third try she saw a curl of smoke, but the stick snapped. She tried again, with the same result.

"Damn," she grunted, falling off her haunches. She looked up to see a grinning Hudson squatting at the tent's entrance. In one hand he held a large chunk of bloody eagle skewered on his knife; in the other was a field fire striker. Rain hammered down. Lightning flickered nearby, and she realized how dark it had gotten. Thunder boomed.

"Didn't know you were doing it the hard way," Hudson said.

She grabbed the big knife, ignoring the friction starter. She impaled the meat on a thick stick and used the knife to hack out two wedges and a short stick. Wrapping the bowstring around the stumpy stick, she spun it vigorously between the wedges, adding needles and shavings. The tinder flared, and she nursed the smoldering into a campfire. Feathers near the flames gave off a sweet smell. As they cooked the eagle, they hunkered close to the fire, trying to warm their wet and thoroughly chilled bodies, their stomachs growling in unison.

They devoured their meal. The downpour slackened and became a desultory shower. The temperature dropped, and cloud gaps racing overhead revealed a moon that was nearly full. Quinn moved back from the tent opening and removed her boots and socks. She next took off her blouse and bra and hung them near the fire. Hudson turned his back and edged away. When she took off her shorts and underwear, he coughed.

"Your clothes won't dry on your back," she said, lying down and pulling the downy feathers around herself. "It's going to get cold. We'll be warmer together."

"Okay, Mom," Hudson muttered, throwing another log on the fire, "but this is only for survival purposes."

"Some caveman," she said, laughing. "Hurry up. It's cold."

Hudson removed his boots and stripped off his shirt. He rolled on his back to remove boots and shorts and then, silhouetted against the fire, hung his clothes next to hers. He paused and turned to look at her, face and eyes deep in shadow.

"Move," she ordered, "and I'm not your mother."

"Tell me about it," he said, kneeling beside her. She felt the metallic chill of his artificial knee.

She rolled on her side. Hudson, shivering, fitted his long body to hers, pulling feathers over them. It grew still and slowly warm. She felt Hudson's breath on her shoulder. The fire flickered hypnotically. Water dripped from the leaves; the river whispered a gravelly serenade.

A primitive and horrible scream broke the calm. Its horrible yodeling echoed along the river islands.

"A dragon!" Hudson whispered, sitting up. "A big one."

"Somewhere on the mainland," Quinn said, her body chilled by Hudson's movement and by her memories. "We're safe here."

"We can't stay." Hudson lay down and rearranged the feathers. "We need food and furs. No one will find us here. We should hunt our way north, to the next fuel-staging field."

"I agree," she said. "It will be quite a hike."

"A month, maybe more," Hudson muttered, putting a hand on her shoulder. His eyelashes blinked against her hair. She reached up and took his hand, pulling his undamaged right arm around her.

"A long time," she mumbled.

"Better not be much more than a month," Hudson said, "or we'll run into the first snows."

"I meant it's been a long time for me, Nash." She sighed, closing her eyes. "I'd forgotten how good a man can feel."

She felt his warmth. He was young and very much alive. They were both alive. She drew a deep breath, luxuriating in the pressure of her lungs. The dull pain made her feel alive. She pressed her body into Hudson's and felt his racing heart.

"I'm sorry I got us into this, Cassy."

"Don't be sorry, Nash."

THIRTY-FOUR

REACTION

"By Jupiter, we've done it," Stark gloated, standing on the balcony of his suite. He looked over the construction scars to the sea, over a rolling ocean of tall tufted grass. Breezes from the south advanced across the verdant pampas in rippling phalanxes of green and white.

"Sir?" Colonel Pak inquired.

"We've changed the equation," Stark said, turning and stepping inside, closing out the humid air. The air conditioner hummed into high. "Human emigration to Genellan is no longer at the mercy of an individual, human or konish. This planet will become a free territory. And the race most suited to its soil will own it."

"It seems chaotic," Colonel Pak replied.

"Chaotic, yes. The essence of realpolitik," Stark replied. "Confuse the issue and then exploit the confusion."

Pak's admin unit warbled with an urgent incoming. The agent inserted an earpiece and listened.

"Major Faro has reported in," Pak scowled. "Governor Et Silmarn, Ambassador Kateos, and Scientist Dowornobb arrived in MacArthur's Valley fifteen minutes ago in Hudson's Explorer. It seems Commander Quinn and Hudson were in the missing konish abat."

Stark stared silently at the ceiling.

"Unfortunate." Stark exhaled. "The equation just became more complicated. Of course Tar Fell will be disappointed. Notify the chancellor via diplomatic channels. Any other news? Any bad news?"

"No, Mr. Stark," Pak replied.

Tar Fell stared through thick glass at the inhospitable planet. Tall green trees thrashed in the wind. Another bright day; cloud shadows raced up from the great river. His mood was dark.

The entry hissed open, and his chief intelligence officer entered.

"We have received word from the human envoy, Armada Master," the officer reported. "The king's ambassador has arrived at their northern settlement. And the planetary governor."

Tar Fell pivoted at the news.

"And Scientist Dowornobb?" Tar Fell demanded.

"Yes, Armada Master," the intelligence officer replied. "Scientist Dowornobb also."

Tar Fell shuddered with relief, his rancid discharges blending with the acrid emanations from the cowering Hegemonic scientists. If he had known about Scientist Dowornobb's advances in hyperlight theory, he would not have ordered the ambassador's plane shot down.

His holo-vid chimed, interrupting his thoughts. The image of his military adjutant appeared.

"Armada Master," the adjutant barked.

"Yes!" Tar Fell snapped.

"Generals Krolk and Magoon request a command conference."

Tar Fell pondered the implications of Scientist Dowornobb's work. Since the takeover of Ocean Station Tar Fell's technicians had uncovered a wealth of Hegemonic hyperlight data, but the brilliance of Scientist Dowornobb was the missing ingredient.

Tar Fell also had a war to fight.

"You are dismissed," Tar Fell rumbled at the timid Hegemonic technicians. "Continue your research or you will be of no value." Scientists Mirrtis and H'Aare bowed obsequiously and crawled hurriedly from Tar Fell's Ocean Station command center.

Tar Fell turned to the holo-vid and signaled for the transmission to connect. General Magoon, aboard Tar Fell's flagship *Penc*, was the first image to appear, followed immediately by General Krolk. The old Ransan had moved his flotilla flag to the battleship *Rouue Massif* and taken command of two newly constituted squadrons.

"Armada Master," Magoon stated evenly, "King Ollant has deployed his fleet. Two understrength Hegemonic battle squadrons have boosted from marshaling orbit." Magoon's eye tufts quivered.

"At last," Tar Fell replied, relishing the abolition of uncertainty. Battle was in the offing.

"Three more Hegemonic squadrons are being fitted," Magoon amplified, his eye tufts lifting, "but they will not boost for three moon cycles. By then our forces will outnumber them two to one."

"Will our crews be up to the challenge?" Tar Fell pondered aloud.

"Our numbers and weapon systems will more than compensate," General Krolk spit, eye tufts rigidly erect.

"The battleship *Samamkook* carries the king's flag," Magoon offered. "That is their most formidable platform."

"We can match her," Krolk growled. "And with the king on board it is unlikely she will be put in harm's way."

"This noblekone is different," Tar Fell muttered. "What else?"

"Three ancient Imperial-class battleships and six battle cruisers, mostly tired old all *coddan* drives," Magoon replied.

"Estimated time to orbit?" Tar Fell demanded.

"Three moon cycles," Magoon replied. "They must conserve fuel."

"He who controls the fuel bunkers at Goldmine owns Genellan," Tar Fell preached. "Continue your training. Integrate the new ships into maneuvering drills as soon as possible. I will join the armada within the moon cycle. I have tasks remaining."

Kateos and Dowornobb huddled close to the lodge fireplace, its huge firebox crackling with burning wood. Et Silmarn stood not far away, glowering. The humans were asking a great many questions, especially the female officer, Major Faro. If it had not been for the Survivors, Kateos would have doubted their welcome.

"Are you sure about Hudson and Quinn?" Chief Wilson asked.

"We think-ah they crashed," Et Silmarn said mournfully.

"It takes a lot to kill Mr. Hudson," Fenstermacher said quietly. "We got to send out a search party."

"I've radioed Ocean Station," Major Faro said, coming from the communications room. "There are Explorers on the way. They will fly the length of the river."

"They should-ah concentrate on the area north of the mountains," Dowornobb rumbled. "Searching farther north is a waste of effort."

The meeting room fell silent. The settlers shuffled with uncertainty; the kones stared into the flames; the Survivors sat with tight lips, shaking their heads.

"Ambassador Kateos," Major Faro said, "your request for asylum has been passed to Envoy Stark for consideration."

"Horseshit," Chief Wilson blurted. "This is their planet, Major."

"Who the hell do you think you are?" Faro shouted, shouldering her way through the Survivors.

"Let's take this discussion outside," the settler called Sam Cody ordered.

Glaring and tight-jawed, Major Faro stomped out, leading the group through the weather doors. As they departed, Leslie Lee and Nancy Dawson led in another group—children.

"About time the windbags left," Lee said, guiding two miniature female humans, both fragile and tiny. One, taller than the other and frighteningly skinny, had long honey-gold hair. Kateos recognized Goldberg and Tatum's daughter, named Honey. The other girl-child, shorter and darker, had straight ebony tresses that were clipped short. It was Lee's own offspring, Hope, sired by the amusing Fenstermacher.

"Kateos," Dawson said, "look who I have." Dawson brought in two males. On one hand was her own son, jet-haired Adam Shannon—strong, thick, and growing tall. On her other hand was a smaller child with silky wisps of brown on his round head. He ran to the heavy trestle table and scaled the wooden bench as if it were time to eat.

"It is Sharl's child?" Kateos rumbled, trying to whisper.

Standing on the bench, Charlie was startled by the kone's

sonorous words. His gunmetal blue eyes widened with amazement.

"Oh, he has grown so," Kateos exclaimed, trying to control her emotions. She removed her breathing unit and inhaled the freshness of the cold northern valley. Her anger and fear at Tar Fell's violation of Hegemonic sovereignty and her sorrow at the possible death of her friends were held in abeyance by fascination.

She removed her gloves and held her breath. Dawson lifted Charlie from the table and into Kateo's hands. The human child was tiny. Charlie squirmed. She felt his muscles knotting and pulling. His thin voice expanded with surprising volume. He grew red-faced and frantic. Kateos quickly returned the child to Dawson.

"He's frightened," Leslie Lee said. "You're so big, Kateos."

"I am also frightened," Kateos replied. "He is so small."

Dawson put the child on the ground. Charlie darted behind her, peeking from between her leather-covered legs.

"I'm not a-scared," Honey said. "You're my friend."

"We are old friends," Kateos said, lifting the reed-thin child into her great arms. The golden-haired child had doubled in size since Kateos's last visit but was still frighteningly fragile.

"Kateos," Honey said, looking up with soft brown eyes and wrinkled nose, "you smell bad."

Ki was frantic. There were bear people in the encampment, less than a stone's throw distant. Ki had glimpsed the odious creatures and smelled their stink. And Tall-red-hair had taken Thunderhead to them. Ki and Notta skulked about, desperate to determine the condition of their charge. As Ki drew stealthily near the long-legs' lodge, she observed Craag-leader-of hunters circling overhead. She heard his signals, commanding her to return to shelter. Frustrated in her efforts, she retreated to the stone abode of Tall-red-hair and waited.

"I see him!" Notta shrieked at last.

Ki flew to the heavy door. There, coming across the grass, was Tall-red-hair. Trotting on fat legs in front of her was Thunderhead. Ki restrained herself, but as Thunderhead scrambled onto the wooden porch, Ki leapt to meet him. The squirming whelp snuggled in her arms, but he reeked of evil stink. Ki had Notta collected warm water and soap plant. Both huntresses scrubbed the whelp until he was red and screaming. Tall-red-hair seemed particularly agitated this day and left the whelp with the huntresses. Ki moved to the open door and watched the long-legs in turmoil, like ants boiling from a kicked anthill. A whispering of membranes caught her attention. Craag-leader-of-hunters and the warriors Bott'a and Croot'a descended. Ki bowed in good form.

"Ki, wife-of-Braan," Craag-leader-of-hunters beseeched, his return bow barely perfunctory. "Thou must leave this camp . . . now."

"My duty—"

"There will be trouble," Craag hissed rudely.

"Trouble is life," Ki replied sagely. "Life is trouble."

Craag exhaled in exasperation.

"We will bind and carry thee if we must," the hunter leader chirped rudely, "but thou and thine must return to the plateau."

Ki looked at the stern-faced warriors. She looked down at Thunderhead and considered the facts. She nodded.

"Notta," Ki shrieked, "collect our possessions." As her daughter scurried away, Ki stooped to lift the heavy long-legs whelp.

"What dost thou?" Craag hissed.

"If it is not safe here for me," Ki huffed, "then it is not safe for this one. Thunderhead comes with me."

"Thunderhead cannot soar."

"Then I will walk with the guilders," Ki said.

THIRTY-FIVE

EVACUATION

Stark watched from his balcony. The dun-colored konish land rover plowed the grasses, motoring on six fat tires, its midsection articulating with the vagaries of the terrain. There were no hints as to its purpose. A message from Tar Fell came precisely as the vehicle hissed to a stop—a burst transmission summoning Stark. The summons was void of diplomatic pretense.

Despite the sweltering temperature in the vehicle, the twenty-kilometer trip over rolling savanna would have been pleasant if it had not been for Stark's needling trepidation. Konish soldiers forbade him any human assistant, and their demeanor was ill tempered. The capacious land rover handled the uneven terrain comfortably, and Stark was afforded a superb, if unappreciated, view of his environs. Gazelles, antelope, and other grassland creatures bounded before panoramic windows. Great hunting birds swooped low over the ocean veldt. At one point the land cruiser shuddered down a ravine and passed beneath a delightful cataract to ford a wide, scintillating brook. Yet Stark's mind, clouded with concerns and maneuvers and annoyed at his usage, perceived little of nature's splendor.

Eventually the land rover settled onto a curving road that climbed gently to the domes of Ocean Station. Beyond the station was the wide and fecund valley of the great river delta. Of that also Stark took little note, for a reception committee awaited: Nearly two dozen helmeted kones stood before the main dome's primary lock.

The land rover hissed to a halt, and a clutch of giants boarded. Tar Fell, foremost among the Titans, removed his helmet and spoke in a thundering voice. A smaller kone translated, its voice an octave higher, a female. Its rendition of the chancellor's words was clear and marred only slightly by an accent.

"It is time for your government to demonstrate its support," the translator announced.

Stark looked about with no little confusion. The game was under way. Tar Fell had made another move. Stark wondered when he would get a turn.

Tar Fell rumbled.

"Winter nears," the translator relayed. "It-ah will be impossible to deal . . . uh, communicate with the Hegemonic ambassador as long-ah as she is in your northern settlement. My government-ah insists the ambassador and-ah all kones in her party be-ah returned to Ocean Station."

"If it is in my power," Stark replied.

Tar Fell rumbled more words.

"Also, you will take this translator and these technicians to your scientists," the translator said. "If you cannot deliver the ambassador, then you will-ah provide more information on star drives."

"But—" Stark replied.

Tar Fell thundered.

"When-ah your government has given us something," the translator said, "then will-ah my government reciprocate."

Without further word Tar Fell departed in the land rover. Within seconds the vehicle was trundling toward New Edmonton.

Sam Cody, his radio transmission frighteningly somber, had issued an urgent summons to all settlers, calling for an immediate meeting at the lodge. St. Pierre and his wife jogged along the lake. Behind them, filtering down from fields, forests, and cabins, the bulk of the settlers converged. Mrs. Jackson, rifle over her shoulder, stomped resolutely at the head of the main body.

"Where are the cliff dwellers?" Maggie asked as they hiked past fields of vegetables and grains. "Even Dirt Eater and Dirt Eater Two weren't in the fields this morning."

St. Pierre looked at the tall snags on the peninsula and at the settlement structures. It was a rare moment when hunter sentries were not perched on ridgepoles or in trees around the cove. In the distance he heard the distinctive sound of abat engines.

"Something's happening," St. Pierre replied.

"Reg," Maggie said, grabbing his hand, "something really big is happening."

"You know something I don't, Mags?" he said, searching the trees.

"Only that I'm pregnant, Reg," his wife said.

St. Pierre whirled to a halt, kicking sand and gravel as he spun to his wife. She looked up, her joyful face illuminated in the utter perfection of a Genellan evening. A waxing moon glinted in her eyes.

"Oh, Mags," he said, hugging her.

"Come on," she said. "Sam Cody said to hurry."

"Oh, Mags," he mumbled, stumbling after his wife. His happy spirits welled warm within him, followed almost immediately by a rush of worry. The future again. He worried about their future.

Cody and a small group of settlers, most armed, waited outside the palisade gate. Cody, jaw set, was giving orders.

"What's going on, Sam?" St. Pierre asked, putting a protective arm around his wife's waist. She held to him tightly.

"Major Faro shut down the hydro," Cody replied. "She wants all settlers mustered for a goddamn briefing. Where's Mrs. Jackson?"

"Right behind us," St. Pierre replied. As he spoke, a troop of settlers came marching up from the cove.

"Faro damn well better have an explanation," Cody shouted.

Cody and St. Pierre joined Mrs. Jackson at the head of the procession. The settlers streamed through the palisade gate and across the common. Major Faro, wearing a helmet and full battle armor, waited for them on the lodge porch. Armored marines guarded the doors.

"What the devil's going on?" Sam Cody shouted. "You can't—"

"Listen up!" Major Faro bellowed. "All Legion personnel and settlers are being evacuated. The ambassador will be given sanctuary, but not here. Envoy Stark has ordered the kones moved to New Edmonton."

After a stunned silence the crowd exploded with angry disbelief. St. Pierre looked about for reactions from the Survivors. Not a Survivor was to be seen.

"On what authority?" Cody demanded.

"Martial law," Faro snapped. "Konish governments are engaged in hostilities. When winter comes, this settlement will be untenable. Airlift of settlers begins tonight. A schedule has been posted. My marines will assist you in transferring your essential belongings."

"We're not leaving our homes!" Mrs. Jackson shouted.

The crowd roared. St. Pierre grabbed his wife's hand and yelled with them. Major Faro stood, arms akimbo, on the porch, helmet visor glinting with the sunset. Suddenly that helmet jerked upward. A low-pitched vibration climbed into St. Pierre's awareness.

The vibration grew to a rumble, rising in a steady crescendo. A commotion came from within the lodge. St. Pierre turned at the sound of floor timbers groaning under a heavy tread. The massive forms of Kateos, Dowornobb, and Et Silmarn bolted through the doors and onto the porch. St. Pierre lifted his eyes to follow their searching gazes.

Two konish orbital landers, each a stabbing sword of flame, approached from the west on a parabolic track, their vertical movement decelerating as they neared touchdown—apparently the cliffs beyond the river. Even at that distance the obnoxious noise was painfully loud. As the explosions of exhaust neared the planet, black cylinders became visible atop stupendous retro explosions. The noise was suffocating. St. Pierre covered his ears. Retro flames, partially obscured by intervening trees, met the cliff tops. A glow blossomed, and retro shocks bounced from the planet. With heart-seizing finality the earsplitting bedlam halved and then ceased.

The silence was unnerving. Into the sensory vacuum rose the awed muttering of the crowd. Those uncertain noises were eclipsed by the frightened neighing of horses. St. Pierre looked toward the stables. A procession of horseback riders and pack-horses came from the stables, Tatum and Nancy Dawson trotting at the head. Tatum's long ponytail and Dawson's wiry explosion of hair flashed red-gold in the evening light.

"Where the hell do you think you're going?" Major Faro asked.

"Where we want to," Dawson replied, sitting tall on her shaggy golden horse. "We're citizens of this planet. No one tells us what to do. We've come to collect our fellow citizens."

The sound of an electric engine downshifting filled the void. A robot lorry trundled across the common, parting the settlers. It pulled up to the lodge, stopping centimeters from Major Faro's unwavering knees. Fenstermacher leapt from the lorry, controls in hand.

"This crowd will disperse immediately," Faro shouted, the cords in her neck protruding magnificently. "Return to your cabins."

"Ambassador Kateos," Dawson commanded softly, "Governor Et Silmarn, friend Dowornobb, get on the lorry." The kones moved uneasily from the lodge porch. Tatum and O'Toole plowed their horses between the aliens and the closest marines.

"Like hell," Faro snarled, raising her pistol threateningly. The kones halted on the stairs. "My orders say these kones go south."

"Uh oh. Bad idea, Major," Fenstermacher said, ducking behind the lorry. Moving as one, the Survivors raised their weapons, each barrel directed unwaveringly at the marine officer.

"Marines!" Major Faro snarled, undaunted.

Marines stationed around the palisade raised weapons, most with apparent reluctance. Few aimed at living targets.

"Settlers!" Sam Cody suddenly shouted. Every settler with a

gun in his or her hand raised it, finding a convenient green-garbed target. The hopelessly outnumbered marines quickly lowered their weapons.

"You will obey my orders," Major Faro shouted.

"Major Faro," St. Pierre pleaded, walking forward. "We can't be fighting among our—"

"I'm taking the kones into custody," Faro screamed. The major pivoted sharply and pointed her pistol at the konish ambassador.

"Please do not fight over me," Kateos begged.

St. Pierre reacted on reflex, his long arm blurring out. He slapped Major Faro's arm upward and stepped in close, leveraging her thick forearm backward and smoothly disarming her. Faro struggled mightily. St. Pierre had no choice but to twist the muscular arm behind Faro's back, locking her bull-strong body in a painful restraint. He wrapped his other arm about Faro's rigid bosom and thick throat and pulled her hard body against his. He placed his mouth delicately next to her ear.

"Duty calls, darling," he whispered, lips caressing Faro's neck.

"You're . . . frigging dead meat," Faro rasped.

"Time to go!" Fenstermacher shouted, pounding on the lorry's bed.

The kones bounded from the lodge steps and into the back of the truck, testing the limits of its suspension. Fenstermacher signaled with the lorry's horn. Tookmanian came running with Hope in his arms and climbed in after the kones, followed by Toby Mendoza with Adam. Beppo Schmidt, carrying Honey, came next. Schmidt lifted the child into the lorry and ran to the horses.

Suddenly Leslie Lee was running toward them, screaming.

"Charlie's gone!" she shouted, her voice liquid with grief.

"No!" Kateos thundered, standing. Her great mass rocked the lorry. Dowornobb pulled her down. A cry of distress lifted from the crowd. Dawson started issuing search orders. Tatum and O'Toole pranced their horses through the crowd and took off at a gallop.

And then they heard the sound of abat engines. Two white aircraft circled to the north, heading for the cliffs and the konish landers.

"Fenstermacher, get the lorry out of here," Dawson shouted.

* * *

"Find him! You must find him!" Kateos keened, her full-throated bellowing overcoming the noise of the vehicle's gears. "It is all my fault. I bring nothing but problems."

Fenstermacher rounded a curve and pushed the lorry's throttle to maximum speed. The vehicle's electric motor screamed at high rpm. It rocked on its big tires as it bounced along the lake road, its all-wheel drive grabbing dirt and throwing it into the air. Fenstermacher worried little about the overloaded suspension. It was his wife he worried about—and little Charlie. He glanced back. Lee sat in the well of the lorry hugging her own child, a fall of ebony hair masking her sobs. Next to Leslie Lee, Dowornobb held Kateos in his gigantic arms, trying to console her. Behind the lorry, in a cloud of dust, a string of golden horses galloped, manes and tails streaming. Chief Wilson and Beppo Schmidt rode the lead horses. Nancy Dawson brought up the rear.

Fenstermacher arrived at the far end of the lake and drove past the sprawl of construction that was the deserted hydro project. As they slowed to a crawl, the northwesterly breeze swept them with their own dust. The lorry shuddered to a halt.

Wiping grit from his eyes, Fenstermacher stared down the considerable length of Lake Shannon. In the dusky distance an abat turned for Longo's Meadow, its landing light shining bright.

Back on the lake road Dawson had reined up. Two more horses came pounding up—Tatum and O'Toole—to join her. The three riders continued, riding hard. A hunter screeched. Fenstermacher looked up to see two cliff dwellers circling downward. As the riders pulled their mounts to a halt next to the lorry, the hunters settled onto a snag hanging over the lake, warily watching.

"Did you find him?" Kateos pleaded, rocking the lorry as she pounced from its bed. "You must find Sharl's child."

"Spitter says the cliff dwellers have him," Tatum reported.

Leslie Lee looked up hopefully.

"Cliff dwellers are running from the bear people," Tatum said, glancing sideways at the kones. "Going back to the plateau."

"You must find Charlie," Kateos begged. "This is my fault."

"Me and O'Toole will go find them," Tatum said, pulling his horse's head around. "They can't have gotten far."

"No," Dawson ordered. "Stick to the plan. Charlie's the safest human on this planet."

* * *

When the last Survivor had disappeared through the palisade gate, St. Pierre pushed Faro away. She wheeled on him.

"You're under arrest, you bastard!" she roared, ripping off her helmet. "Marines, put this—"

"Shut up, Major!" Sam Cody shouted, stepping between St. Pierre and the murderous major. Several settlers, rifles up, joined Cody. The officer turned on her heel and marched toward the barracks. Cody mounted the lodge steps and turned to the crowd.

"I want all settlers back in their cabins," he announced, his voice calm but authoritative. "Sit tight and listen to the radio. Mrs. Jackson will radio-muster all cabins. Report any strange or unusual happenings. Right now St. Pierre and I are going to meet with the kones. We'll make a radio report in one hour."

St. Pierre and Cody jogged for the palisade gate. Major Faro and a squad of marines were waiting in two all-terrain vehicles.

"Get your dumb asses in the truck," she ordered. "Let's find out what the bugs want, and then we'll settle our differences."

They arrived at Longo's Meadow. Two abats were on the ground, their cargoes of soldiers disgorged. A trio of black-uniformed officers turned at their approach. All wore breathing units.

"I'll do the talking," Cody insisted. St. Pierre was not inclined to argue. Major Faro shot him a look of utter disgust.

The kones were huge. A mountain range of soldiers deployed around the humans. The three officers stood shoulder to shoulder, wider than any eight men. The one in the center rumbled the flowing, turbulent noises that made up their language. Another kone galloped forward, smaller, probably a female but still more than twice the size of a human.

"Chancellor Tar Fell has sent us to collect-ah the Hegemonic ambassador," the translator conveyed, her voice trembling, whether with fear or cold, St. Pierre could not tell. "Who-ah are you?"

"We are ... the leaders of this settlement," Cody replied. His ruddy complexion had turned white. He swallowed several times as the translator did her job. The kones were immense. Their breathing sounded like steam pistons, and the very force of their communication was intimidating. St. Pierre, by far the tallest of the humans, was dwarfed. An officer bellowed. The small one translated.

"We demand that-ah all kones be brought-ah here."

"That cannot happen," Cody replied nervously. "We are free men. We respect the freedom of others. The kones do not wish to come here."

The translator delivered his response. Silence. The kones stood and stared. A minute went by, then two. St. Pierre attempted to peer through their faceplates in the gathering dusk. All three appeared to be trembling or shivering. Their commander exploded with a sonorous burst and then spun away on all fours, galloping to the waiting abat.

"An orbiter will-ah remain here for Ambassador Kateos and-ah her party," the translator said, her voice revealing a tremor; she was debilitatingly cold. "Tar Fell wishes to conduct-ah peace talks with Ambassador Kateos. Tar Fell cannot-ah conduct diplomacy in the wilderness."

"We will convey that message," Cody replied.

The translator galloped to catch up with the officers. No sooner was she on board than the abat commenced rolling. The white craft made a climbing right turn over the lake on its way back to the cliffs.

"Now we have to find Kateos," Cody said.

"That will be my pleasure," Major Faro snarled. She glared at St. Pierre. "Get in the truck."

The humans returned to the palisade. The truck stopped in front of the marine barracks, night nearly on them. St. Pierre was not surprised when four burly noncoms materialized. An additional platoon of hard-faced marines formed a cordon around the trucks.

"What's going on?" Cody demanded, trying to force his way between St. Pierre and the marines.

"Tell Maggie I'm okay, Sam," St. Pierre said.

"St. Pierre's under arrest," Major Faro announced, pushing Cody aside. "Throw him in the brig."

"What the hell do you gain, Major?" Cody pleaded.

"Just shut up and deliver that supersausage's message to your pet kones," Faro snarled. "I've got my orders. I want those bugs out of here, and I want your civilian butts on planes south."

On the cliffs beyond the great river a bear people star-ferry thundered into the sky. Layers of rock spalled from the cliffs. Boulders tumbled into the river valley. White-hot exhaust created sharp shadows, momentarily eradicating the dusk. Ki turned to watch the cosmic spectacle, a globe of energy elevating on a column of fury, accelerating with a violent imperative. The corrosive detonations quickly diminished to irritating vibrations, and finally the horrible blade of fire was reduced to a point of light, a white star moving laterally through the constellations. And then it was gone.

Two machines landed; only one departed.

The whelp's whine replaced all other noises. Ki shook the buzzing from her ears. Ki ignored the whining and pointed her snout upstream. Thunderhead's cries dropped to a whimper.

"I will carry the whelp," Craag-leader-of-hunters commanded.

"It is my duty," the stooped old huntress replied, plodding onward through misty gloaming. "Heed thine own, hunter leader."

Craag walked silently at Ki's side. The river thundered, its liquid ragings a constant companion to her pain. Ki sang soft songs to Thunderhead. The long-legs whelp, bound tightly to her back, made an effort to mimic her. Notta walked behind, chirping in harmony.

The river path looped upward around a headland of massive boulders, giving Ki a view up and down the river. In the moonlight, before and behind her, she observed a caravan of guilders and hunters plodding over the smooth river rock—refugees once again. Refugees from the bear people. In the liftless air of night all the hunters hiked on the ground, guarding the guilders and helping to carry their tools and belongings. Those behind her had closed the distance, while those ahead were stretching away. She was slowing the pace. The plateau and the cliffs of the dwellers were still far away.

"Thou have the stiff pride of a foolish sentry," Craag admonished.

"Everything stiffens with age," Ki shrieked in return.

"Thou speak for the female, of course," Craag retorted.

Ki, grown silly with fatigue, giggled like a pup at the warrior's unexpected jest, bawdy and unmannerly as it was. But what could she expect? She had intruded on his dominion.

"Thank thee for thy good counsel, honorable warrior," Ki replied, signaling her obeisance with a compliment. "My soul commends thee."

"I will carry the whelp," Craag ordered.

Ki sighed and looked up at the scarred warrior. His hard black eyes stared down at her with unflagging respect.

"It is my duty," she said, "but we would travel faster if thou were to carry the whelp. I accept thy generous offer."

"Thy wisdom flatters us all," Craag replied too quickly.

"Gloat not, arrogant spear thrower," Ki replied, turning her back to the warrior, "or I will not relinquish the whelp."

"Humble apologies, fierce huntress," Craag replied, mercifully lifting the squirming burden from her tired old shoulders.

THIRTY-SIX

COLONEL PAK

The MacArthur's Valley brig was a jail in name alone. What made it a prison were the bands of bulletproof alloy that ringed St. Pierre's ankles. His leash was long enough for him to pace the room or lie down on the cot, which was what he was doing when a black-uniformed officer marched through the door.

"Sleeping late, Major?" the officer asked.

"Colonel Pak!" St. Pierre shouted, jumping to his feet. A marine followed Pak through the door and came over to release his leg hobbles.

"We've got work to do," Pak said, turning and walking from the cell. St. Pierre followed his old commander's erect form. St. Pierre greatly respected the colonel. Han Pak was the consummate professional, efficient and, if necessary, deadly.

"What are you doing here, Colonel?" St. Pierre asked, stretching the muscles in his legs. "This isn't your line of work."

"Let's concentrate on your mission," Pak snapped. "I've been scanning Faro's reports. She's made serious accusations regarding your loyalties. Are we on the same side, Major?"

"Major Faro and I are not on the same side, Colonel," St. Pierre replied. "I'm a settler on this planet. I've come here to live."

Pak riveted St. Pierre with an implacable glare. St. Pierre

was almost a head taller, but Pak's indomitable will gave the taller man a childlike feeling of subordination.

"Another sentimental asshole," Pak mumbled. "Come on, settler!" he shouted. "I need your help. We do not have the luxury of time."

St. Pierre jogged to catch up with Pak, squinting at the bright sun as he left the shade of the marine barracks. The settlement was eerily deserted. He saw only two marines on the palisade catwalks. Two ATVs waited in front of the barracks. One truck was full of uniformed LSA agents. In the other, two men sat on the passenger bench; one was a uniformed LSA agent, and the other was his neighbor Jerrad Simpson. The truck was loaded with expedition supplies and weapons.

"You drive," Pak commanded, getting in.

"Where to?" St. Pierre asked.

"You tell me," Pak replied. "I must talk with Ambassador Kateos."

"I've been locked up for two days," St. Pierre replied. "Give me a hint."

"Major Faro's a loose cannon," Simpson reported. "After you were jailed, she tried rounding up the settlers, using force. She secured the intruder-alert systems and jammed the networks to keep us from watching her movements. She managed to send a couple of planeloads of settlers south before it got ugly. Mrs. Jackson got shot."

"What?" St. Pierre shouted.

"Arm wound," Simpson said. "I think she's okay, but that's when a half dozen of Faro's marines mutinied. They went into the hills with the remaining settlers, including your wife, Reggie. Major Faro and a bunch of real confused grunts are out there, trying to haul the mutineers back to town. It's a mess."

"And likely to get bloodier," Pak added. "I don't give a damn whether you settlers go south. I came here to talk with the kones. I want you to find them for me, Reggie. Tell them I want to talk. While you're finding the kones, my agents and I are going to bring a certain marine major under control."

"I have a hunch we won't be very far apart," St. Pierre said, getting behind the controls.

"That's why you're driving, Major," Pak replied.

"Tookmanian's church," St. Pierre mumbled, shifting into gear.

* * *

St. Pierre knew the Survivors had fled to the hunting camp at the southern end of the valley, high up, beneath the glaciers. Tatum had taken St. Pierre to the remote caves on two occasions. The Survivors called it High Camp; they had hidden from kones there once before. But there was not enough room at High Camp for the Survivors and the settlers, too. The settlers would probably be at Tookmanian's church.

St. Pierre hiked across a steep traverse below the church. He had separated from Colonel Pak and his cell of field agents hours earlier, taking the most direct trail to the church, a steep and arduous hike. Pak and his agents, pursuing Major Faro's marines, had headed farther north, along one of the parallel ridges leading to the valley's southeastern rim.

Tookmanian's church was a sturdy structure of yellow rock and thick beams situated high above the southeastern end of the lake. The tall, high-peaked roof was complete, lacking only a spire for its soaring two-stepped steeple. Tookmanian and Toby Mendoza had started the chapel as a memorial. A kilometer higher on the ridge, at its zenith, was a tumble of rock topped by twin soaring pinnacles. It was on that ridge that kones, humans, and cliff dwellers had fought and died. Cairns of rock served as monuments to the fallen. It was a sacred place.

It was a bright day, crisp and perfectly clear. St. Pierre looked down on the lake vista. Rugged, snow-capped mountains, fantastically proportioned, so tall as to seem illusory, reared skyward beyond the jeweled water. Glacier-hung peaks, their lower elevations bleached with new snow, were reflected with awe-inspiring fidelity. Adding to the glorious reflections, exquisite swatches of yellow and crimson foliage adorned the lake margin, heralding autumn. Despite his anxieties, the surreal vista stole his breath.

"Maggie's right," a woman's voice said, startling him. "You're a dreamer." St. Pierre caught his balance and looked up the steep slope. Standing on a rock, her explosion of red hair contrasting against the deep blue sky, was Nancy Dawson. Higher up perched two ugly hunters. That meant Tatum was also near. Dawson waved him up and disappeared behind the rocks. The hunters followed her.

He found Tatum and Dawson lying on their bellies, peering over the ridge with field glasses.

"Stay low," Dawson said.

St. Pierre crawled up the gentle slope through thick bundles of lavender flowers. He noted one area in particular, a sunny spot that had been emphatically flattened. He wondered what else the two lanky redheads had been doing. He came even with Tatum's sprawled form. A hunter, perching on a low limb above their heads, twittered. Tatum whistled softly, and the hunter waved spindly fingers in a rapid sign. Above them another cliff dweller flew lazy figure eights.

"What are you doing here?" St. Pierre asked.

"We brought Kateos down from High Camp to talk with Sam Cody," Dawson replied. "They're having a conference at the church. The hunters told us about Major Faro, and we wanted to check it out." She and Tatum exchanged glances. Dawson blushed and looked away.

"Below the ridgeline, just past the tall stand of trees," Tatum said, handing St. Pierre the field glasses. St. Pierre scanned the terrain on the next ridge. Hiking up the ridge was a platoon of marines. Major Faro's tanklike form was prominent at their head.

"Déjù vu," Tatum muttered.

"Huh?" St. Pierre said.

"Second time someone's tried to yank our tails outta this valley," Tatum growled. "Kinda gets you riled up. Sure wish the general was here to see us kick ass."

"'The general?" St. Pierre asked.

"Buccari," Tatum replied. "The Booch. She's something else. I remember . . ." His voice trailed off sadly.

"Let's get back to the church," Dawson whispered, pushing away from the ridge.

Colonel Pak's agent cell made visual contact with Major Faro's marines high on the ridge ahead of them. Pak pressed forward with renewed purpose. On the ridge to their right was the church, a bright luminescence surrounded by deep green forests.

"We're not far behind, Colonel," his cell leader reported. "She's still ignoring radio calls."

A hellish growling rolled up the wooded slope. Off to the left a rifle fired. Another burst followed. The growling changed to a banshee scream. A final shot echoed against the valley's sides. The growling diminished to nothing.

"What was that?" Pak barked. A moment went by as the cell leader listened to his helmet transceiver.

"Scout on the left wing ran into some nasties," the cell leader replied. "Nightmares. Scout says he scared them off, but there must be a couple dozen animals downwind from us. The scout thinks they're following us. He sounds pretty scared."

"As well he should," Pak replied.

Faro heard the rifle fire echoing between the ridges. She spun toward the noise and searched the lower elevations. She could see nothing, but she knew Pak was there. His radio calls were a nuisance. She had a mutiny to take care of. Mutinies took precedence over security games.

"We've got them, sir," the corporal reported. "We've got body locks on at least four mutineers."

"Excellent," Major Faro replied. She labored to catch her breath. It had been a long uphill hike from the valley floor. They were almost to the tree line. Across the narrowing defile separating the ridges, less than four hundred meters away, stood the church. She could see people moving around. Faro moved to the satchel battery, a backpack missile system capable of firing 20-mm antipersonnel homing lancets. She bent to its powerful targeting optics.

St. Pierre, Dawson, and Tatum started sprinting when they heard the distant gunfire. They arrived at the church winded and sweaty, passing through a guard post manned by maverick marines. A baby-faced laser corporal, the senior marine among the mutineers, hailed them.

"I'm telling you guys to march back to the palisade," St. Pierre gasped. "Right now! There's a senior officer here. He'll protect you from Major Faro. If it goes to a court-martial, we'll all testify. As long as you stay up here, you're fair game."

"We've been talking about that, sir," the marine replied. "If there's one Major Faro, there's probably dozens. We decided we'd like to just stay here and become civilians, like Tatum."

"Shit," Tatum grumbled. "You got both your frigging arms, marine. Use 'em to pull your head outta your ass so you can hear the man. He's talking sense." Dawson put her hand on Tatum's shoulder.

"Talk to them, Sandy," St. Pierre said. "My wife's waiting for me."

St. Pierre walked from bright sunlight onto the dirt floor of the church. His eyes and skin adjusted to dark dampness. The only light came through openings that one day would have glass windows. A circular opening, not large but beautifully positioned on the chancel wall, framed a glorious segment of mountain vista. Beneath the window in a column of sunlight, on the only section of wooden floor that had been installed in the structure, sat the kones. With them were Sam Cody and Mrs. Jackson, her arm in a sling. A dozen children of varying ages sat nearby on the rough-hewn planking, talking and playing with the gigantic konish ambassador. Maggie was with them.

St. Pierre was silhouetted in the bright door. His wife looked up and tilted her head, registering his backlit presence, uncertain. She rose tentatively to her knees, peering into the glare.

"Maggie," he said, stepping forward onto soft dirt between massive floor joists. Maggie's eyes opened wide; in the beat of a heart her face transformed magically from uncertain anxiety to unbridled joy.

She pushed to her feet, ran to edge of the flooring, and leapt into his waiting arms, her lips pressing against his with exquisite pain. They embraced passionately, kissing fervently in the middle of the unfinished church. The delightful sound of children giggling captured St. Pierre's attention. He lifted his eyes over his wife's head and stuck out his tongue, making them laugh all the harder.

"You're looking particularly beautiful today," he said.

"Reg, I was so worried," Maggie said.

"I have not thanked you for interceding on my behalf," a thundering voice announced, dominating all other noises. St. Pierre looked up. The konish ambassador crawled rapidly to the floor's edge. "Nor have we properly met, although I have talked at length with your intelligent wife. I am Kateos." The floor beams groaned under the creature's mass.

"We all thank-ah you," another of the giants boomed. Both of the others, larger still, approached the edge, one walking on his hinds, his grainy visage towering over the nave, truly a behemoth. St. Pierre reflexively pulled Maggie backward.

"I-ah am Dowornobb," the largest one said. "Kateos is my mate. I-ah owe you the greatest of debts."

"Ah . . . I am here to ask you to do something," St. Pierre stuttered.

"Yes?" Kateos rumbled, her great head tilting.

"There is a man, a Colonel Pak," St. Pierre said. "He wishes only to talk to you."

"About what—" Kateos started to say.

"Save that for later," Tatum shouted from the door. "Major Faro's just across the ridge. Let's get out of here."

"Oh, Reggie," Maggie moaned. "When can we go home?"

"Soon, babes," St. Pierre replied. "Colonel Pak will stop this insanity." He pulled her to him and hugged her. She was trembling. Her heart was pounding.

"Come on," St. Pierre said, pulling her toward the door.

Major Faro put her eye to the viewing scope. There in the reticles were three of her marines. Target ranging and acquisition indicators on the firing console verified lock-on. Faro also spotted Tatum, the tall one-armed Survivor. And next to Tatum, coming from the church, she observed the distinctive profile of the agent St. Pierre. Hot blood rose to the back of Faro's neck. She used the sighting vernier to adjust the aim. The reticles centered on St. Pierre. She depressed the sensor ID, designating a new target.

"Stand by to fire," Faro ordered.

"But Major," the battery tech protested, "snipers report seeing women and children inside."

"Fire on my order, mister," Major Faro commanded, stepping back from the sight and glaring at her subordinate.

"But sir—"

Faro walked up to the noncom and stuck her nose into his face. "I'm getting real tired of this shit," she growled. "Consider yourself relieved. Now, get out of my way." The marine stepped hesitantly aside. Faro snatched the remote firing mechanism from its housing.

Colonel Pak used hand signals to deploy his field agents. The marines were less than a hundred meters away. Pak heard Faro reprimand the sergeant and then walk to a sighting scope and retrain the weapon, her intention suddenly apparent.

"What are you doing, Major!" Pak shouted, pushing into a sprint.

Faro turned. The major's severe demeanor was accentuated by bruised-eye fatigue and hollow-cheeked intensity. She smiled, an evil, vindictive smile. With her hand held at waist level, Faro flipped off the trigger guard of the remote device and depressed the firing mechanism. The missile battery mechanically propelled a unit from its bore. The homing round's reaction fuel ignited a split second later.

* * *

St. Pierre stood in sunlight, too happy to be worried. Child-like, he skipped a few steps and turned to look at his wife. The young marine corporal stepped aside. A shrieking came and went in a heartbeat. The marine, his angelic face distorted with immense surprise, flailed into St. Pierre, knocking him to the ground. Stunned, St. Pierre struggled to push the marine away. They were both covered with blood. The corporal's chest was eviscerated, his sternum and ribs blown through.

St. Pierre rolled away and struggled to his feet. He tore his eyes from the marine, trying to find Maggie. She was sitting down, twisted sideways against the church, her eyes open, staring far away. She was too still. He noticed the blood first, running down the wall where the side of her head was pressed. He fell to his knees and crawled to her, needing to touch her but frightened to do so. He knew she was dead.

Pak had the sergeant tie Major Faro's arms. The noncom performed his duties with relish. Major Faro stared unblinking into space, the hint of a sneer on her thin lips.

"Sergeant," Pak ordered, "lead the marines back to the barracks. I'm taking the major into custody." The sergeant saluted and gave orders. Pak directed his agents to return with the marines.

Pak, slapping Major Faro on the back of the neck with his pistol butt, pushed her into the clinging underbrush. They started down and across the thicket-choked defile separating them from the church. Halfway up the opposite slope, scratched and bruised, they were met by settlers, Survivors, and marines, all with murder in their eyes. Pak pushed Faro forward. The armed mob fell back silently, following him and his prisoner up the hill. When Pak reached the shadow of the church, he realized the full extent of the tragedy.

"Oh, God, no!" he exclaimed.

St. Pierre turned at the sound of his voice. His eyes locked on Faro, and rage transformed his countenance. St. Pierre let his wife's broken body slip gently to the ground. Once clear of his burden, the distraught man advanced slowly.

Halting his prisoner, Pak swung his pistol around by the barrel, offering it to St. Pierre. At the same time he kicked Major Faro's legs out, pushing the stocky officer to her knees. St. Pierre took the pistol, distorted features blackened with rage. Pak stepped backward.

"Why didn't you shoot me, you bastard!" St. Pierre cried,

brandishing the pistol, hate filling his eyes beyond mortal capacity. "Why her?"

St. Pierre put the automatic's big barrel on the bridge of the marine's nose. Major Faro sat silently, stiffly erect on her knees, waiting impassively for death. Her sneer was gone, but no hint of remorse shadowed her eyes. St. Pierre looked up from the major's face and into Pak's eyes, his rage melting to anguish. The tall man sobbed grotesquely and threw the weapon aside.

"I can only make her die once," St. Pierre cried, putting his face into his hands.

Major Faro's lungs moved generously with a sudden exhalation. St. Pierre turned, slump-shouldered, to look again at his slain wife. One of the settlers had thrown a shroud over her supine form. St. Pierre, shoulders trembling, walked toward the lake.

"Terry, you and Beppo," a tall one-armed redhead shouted, "get your horses and stay with him. There's nightmares all around." Two men ran to the other side of the church and reappeared at the far end, riding golden horses down the hill.

The one-armed man stepped forward and yanked Faro to her feet.

"Nightmares," the tall redhead snarled. "Ever go trolling for nightmares, Major?" Faro's pale blue eyes widened, and her mouth dropped open. She looked around for intercession as the one-armed man pushed her down the hill. No one moved to stop him.

"Colonel Pak, my name's Cody."

Pak turned to see a ruddy, thick-shouldered man. Behind him towered three konish giants.

"This is Ambassador Kateos, Governor Et Silmarn, and Scientist Dowornobb," Cody said. "St. Pierre said you wished to talk to them."

Pak stared, gathering his courage.

"Envoy Stark asks that you return to Ocean Station," Pak finally managed. "Chancellor Tar Fell wishes to discuss diplomatic matters. The Thullolians have provided an orbiter for your transportation. Envoy Stark will personally guarantee your safety and sovereignty."

"We will go," Kateos said, "if only to prevent more of these innocent people from being harmed."

THIRTY-SEVEN

STARK'S REIGN

Ki plodded to the threshold. Gliss, wife-of-Brappa, stared into the night, seeking starlight where there was only dismal darkness. Wisps of steam driven by the north wind fluttered past the entry, mixing phantasmically with snowflakes in the orange glow of spirit globes.

"Come inside, Daughter," Ki pleaded, clasping her marriage daughter's robe. "Come inside and be warm."

Gliss lowered her eyes and accepted Ki's gentle guidance. They retreated through the entry baffle, dropping heavy tapestries behind them, and entered the abode's antechambers. A runnel of steaming water flowed across heating rocks. A wood fire crackled. Gliss removed her fur cloak and followed Ki into the abode's main room.

Under the eyes of old Upolu, Gliss's fledglings frolicked with the long-leg whelp, their play competitive and earnest. Soon even the despondent Gliss was laughing at the innocent mayhem.

Thunderhead, a name given in jest, was an excellent name for the whelp. He displayed a resilience and spirit that would have made any warrior mother proud, along with a tremendous alertness—certainly not the acute range of hearing or the sensitivity of smell of hunter fledglings but a wonderful curiosity and cunning, an ability to anticipate. Rokko and Broon, Gliss's offspring, had initially dominated the helpless long-leg child, nipping and clawing its smooth and tender hide, but that had changed quickly. The whelp's indomitable nature, raw cunning, and greater strength soon gave it the dominant position in the nest.

The peltless whelp wore otter and growler hides fashioned with great pride by the huntresses of the cliffs. Thunderhead screeched and hissed after the fashion of the fledglings, developing a nascent comprehension of simple signals.

"Ah, Mother," Gliss sighed with profound emptiness. "What does life bring?"

"Blessings, my daughter," Ki replied, looking around for Notta, her own beautiful daughter. Ki chirped a summons. Notta dutifully appeared, coming from the kitchen, bringing with her a cold draft. Notta's lovely black nose glistened with moisture. Notta, too, had been outside, Ki deduced, and knew why.

"A hunter's life is not easy," Ki spoke the old words. "Thy husband suffers in his loss for thee, as thou suffer in thy loss." The old huntress nodded at the tumbling young ones. "But look about. Pay heed to thy blessings."

A bitter breeze dried Hudson's eyes. The great river curved gently, its far shore distant. Hudson and Quinn, using tall staffs as walking sticks, trekked upstream along the river's edge. The stout staffs, points forged with fire and blood, had served them well. Both hikers carried bundles of thick fur—river deer, marmot, and rockdog—insulation against the chilly and lingering nights.

The river sang, pushing fine gravel and gurgling over larger stones. The stony river margin was only a few paces wide before it climbed abruptly into chalky cliffs too steep to scale. Hardwoods with foliage bronzed and yellowed by frosty mornings hung over the cliffs, providing a bright visual border to the monotonous topography—the sparkling blue river on their left, the gray rocks on which they walked, and the white, yellow-fringed cliffs on their right, all below hard blue skies. For days they had been imprisoned in that single dimension, that linear realm. Far ahead a wooded promontory descended to the water's edge, marking a reversal in the river's gentle curve. Closer, two hundred meters up the shore, the cliffs were at last notched to river level with a brush-filled defile.

"Wonder if anyone is looking for us," Quinn said.

"We would have seen more planes," Hudson replied, turning and staring back the way they had come. "I'm glad these cliffs are finally ending. I'd rather not be so pinned in."

"We're making good time—" Quinn's words were clipped to silence.

"What?" Hudson asked.

Quinn peered into the distance. Hudson looked up the rocky

shoreline. Distorted by the rise of rock-warmed air, motion could be detected, as if the gray-black rocks were animate. Only different. There was something familiar about the nervous movement. And then he heard the growls, ending all doubt.

"Nightmares!" Quinn gasped.

"How many bullets are left?" Hudson asked.

"Not enough," she replied.

"We can't run from them," Hudson said, striding forward. "We've got to beat them to that notch."

"Then what?" Quinn asked, jogging at his side.

"One bad option at a time," Hudson replied. "Run!"

Quinn moved with surprising speed. Hudson's damaged joints severely restricted his sprinting ability, and Quinn slowed to his pace.

"Go ahead," he gasped, pounding over the loose gravel.

"Yeah, sure," she huffed back. "I run ... interference, and you ... run up the hill while they ... have me for lunch."

He put his head down and pushed harder. The nightmares were clearly visible, sprinting with their peculiar stiff-legged gait, their tails whipping in a hectic counterrhythm. The pack was three hundred meters beyond the defile, galloping like the hounds of hell. The brush-shrouded notch was less than a hundred meters away.

"Come on!" Quinn screamed, moving ahead, arms pumping.

At ten meters from the notch the nightmares were less than fifty meters away, their great underslung jaws raised in exultation. Their growling lifted to a frenzy. Hudson winced at flashes of saber-toothed fangs. His heart pounded in his chest, and his lungs heaved for air. He threw off his bundle of furs.

A runnel of water flowed from the notch, dancing over pebbles on its steadfast journey to the great river. Quinn's feet raised fountains of water as she hit the little tributary. His feet thrashed the water seconds later. Before their splashes had hit the ground, the pack of nightmares were at the stream, churning up fountains of mist, their horrible screams drowning all other sensations.

Quinn hurdled a low branch, her head exploding golden foliage from overhanging boughs. Hudson followed, leaning through the cascading leaves, tracking Quinn's footfalls in the trickling stream, climbing higher, scrambling onto larger and sharper rocks. The sides of the notch narrowed; the foliage disappeared. Rock-rattling growls echoed obscenely in the narrowing confines, vibrating in the air. Hudson felt hot breath on his back.

"Duck, Nash!" Quinn shouted.

He looked up to see Quinn's pike stabbing past his shoulder. She straddled the brook, legs planted on boulders. Behind her the defile narrowed to a crevice, a chimney. Hudson dove, splashing between Quinn's legs, wriggling against unyielding rock. He struggled to stand and turn sideways. An animal screamed.

Quinn's shoulders spasmed violently as she was thrown into Hudson's chest. At the end of her staff, impaled through its throat, was a writhing nightmare. Another beast frantically scratched and clawed atop its dying brother. Hudson, off balance and soaking wet, lifted his pike over Quinn and thrust at the predator's head. The beast, blinded in one eye, retreated screaming. Another raging nightmare replaced it. Other nightmares, growling with thunderous resonance, scrambled high on the rocks overhead.

Hudson forced the beast against the rocks. Another nightmare came roaring at its side. The manic beasts, struggling viciously, wedged themselves between the unyielding rocks. Hudson retracted his pike and stabbed desperately at the frothing, yellow-fanged maws. Quinn used her boot to pull her pike from the maw of the first animal, joining Hudson with her own thrusts and parries. They retreated. The crevice widened, giving them room and footing to defend the gap. Suddenly a beast fell from the rocks overhead, crashing to the ground behind them. Snapping and spitting, it bounced and sprang. Too close to stab with a staff, the nightmare seized Hudson's knee in iron jaws and wrenched him to the ground.

"Help me!" Hudson screamed.

Quinn's hand moved. Her pistol aimed right at the creature's head. The detonation in the close quarters was deafening. Hudson felt the bullet blast through the beast's thick skull and shatter what was left of his knee. The nightmares, startled by the report, retreated momentarily and then came back with full fury. Hudson, dead nightmare still mangled into his knee joint, picked up his staff and staggered to his good leg.

The Thullolian orbital lander touched down at Ocean Station. Pressurization systems equalized, and Kateos felt the welcome surge of warm, high-pressure air. The suborbital flight from MacArthur's Valley had lasted barely thirty minutes, but her body struggled with the pressurization cycles. She did not belong in space; the glands and membranes of her body searched for equilibrium.

"I go first," Dowornobb said, breaking loose from his restraints.

"I am the governor," Et Silmarn argued. "It is my place."

Kateos pushed to her feet and stepped in front of both. A Ransan crewman opened the hatch and brusquely directed them toward the air lock.

"The irony," Et Silmarn rumbled. "Tar Fell deigning to receive us under our own dome. What impudence."

"We should not have fled," Kateo moaned. "A mistake. One among many."

"Do not berate yourself, my mate," Dowornobb said soothingly. "It is better to make mistakes than to do nothing and die. Remember, the monster tried to kill us."

"What is to stop him from killing us now?" she asked.

"We have the human envoy's promise," Dowornobb replied.

"Is that an answer," Kateos snapped, "or are you trying to make me miserable?"

"Oh, my mate," Dowornobb moaned. "Be not bitter. Be strong—"

The air lock alarm sounded, and the interior doors hissed open. Tar Fell stood waiting, his face calm with malignant satisfaction.

"I apologize," Kateos whispered contritely, squeezing her mate's hand before she stepped through the air lock.

"Ah! Ambassador Kateos," Tar Fell exclaimed, neglecting to bow. "Now diplomacy can finally begin."

"Chancellor General," she acknowledged, bowing but not touching her head to the floor. She rose to her hinds and walked imperiously into the terminus. As she moved across the floor, a squad of troopers scuttled behind her, cutting her off from her mate and Et Silmarn. Dowornobb shouted in futile protest and struggled violently into their midst. The scientist, a very large and powerful kone, was pinned with considerable difficulty to the floor by six brutes. Et Silmarn, exercising the better part of valor, held his ground.

"I demand to see Envoy Stark," Kateos declared. "He has granted us sanctuary."

"So he has," Tar Fell replied, watching as Dowornobb's struggles abated. The scientist was hauled before Tar Fell.

Kateos, held tight by one of Tar Fell's officers, could only look on helplessly.

"Do not . . . harm my mate," Dowornobb snarled and sputtered. His lips bled, and the fetid emanations of his anger welled about him in exploding waves.

"Master Dowornobb," Tar Fell said, waving a hand before his gloating countenance. "Never have I seen a scientist behave so aggressively. Calm yourself. I have a diplomatic proposal."

Dowornobb's breathing slowed, his fury softened to mere hate. Tar Fell nodded to his captors, and the big scientist shook off their grip. Dowornobb was every bit as large as Tar Fell, but his rage seemed to inflate his person to even greater proportions. Kateos wanted to run to his side but could not escape her keeper.

"Much better," Tar Fell said.

"What is your proposal?" Dowornobb demanded.

"Your advances in hyperlight theory," Tar Fell began, "have come to my attention. I should like that research to continue right here in your own laboratories with your own assistants. Does that sanctuary not appeal to you? You will be free to come and go as you please."

"I am a citizen of the Northern Hegemony," Dowornobb replied. "I am loyal to my king."

Tar Fell laughed. "Take him to his lab," he roared, stepping forward to the waiting orbiter. "We will see how cooperative he becomes."

"Outrageous! We came here in good faith," Et Silmarn protested. "You have no right to—"

"Let the governor govern his planet," Tar Fell scoffed. "Put him outside." A platoon of troopers closed on Dowornobb and Et Silmarn, subduing their struggles. Once the area was clear of disturbance, the armada master held out his arm to Kateos.

"What is to become of me?" she asked, refusing his arm.

"I must return to my armada," Tar Fell replied. "Therefore, you and I must conduct our diplomacy in space."

"You . . . you are making me go back into space?" she asked.

"There is much to discuss, Ambassador," Tar Fell replied, pushing her toward the air lock.

Pak was tired. They had flown through the night, the Explorer buffeted by unending turbulence. Rodriguez had done a remarkable job flying them to New Edmonton and getting down through the gusting squalls. The whole continent was socked in.

Escorted by one of Stark's assistants, Colonel Pak and Sam Cody climbed the stairs to Stark's office. The administration building's elevator was not operating. Battery-powered emergency lights provided dim illumination. The windows on the stair landings, misted with drizzle, revealed lead-bottomed clouds scudding up from the ocean.

"Weather's ruined our solar power storage," the assistant prattled. "They should get the PHM generators back on line this afternoon. And the heaters, thank goodness. This dampness goes right through you."

As they neared the third-floor landing, they heard Stark's voice coming through the open door of his office suite.

"To hell with them," Stark shouted.

"But, Mr. Stark," a familiar voice replied. Pak recognized the voice of one of his agents—Clancy, New Edmonton's mayor.

"Am I supposed to tell you how to manage this settlement?" Stark roared. "Do I have to do everything for you? Take some initiative, man."

"The wheat harvest was destroyed by rain . . ." Clancy moaned. Pak walked into the office without knocking. Clancy jumped to his feet.

"And insect infestations," the mayor continued in a much firmer voice, "took care of just about everything else."

"Are there not enough space rations in the PHMs?" Stark sighed, acknowledging Pak with a nod. "I was told we had ample stocks."

"Yes, Mr. Stark," the settlement's mayor said, glancing nervously at Colonel Pak. "It's just that spacer food is not the most palatable."

"We can bring down five hundred kilos of grain—corn and wheat," Cody said bluntly, looking down at his list. "We'll trade for generator fuel and medical supplies."

Stark looked up imperiously, as if Cody were a child.

"There would have been a great deal more," Cody added, "if the harvest had not been disrupted."

Stark turned away and said, "Why don't you gentlemen take your issues downstairs? Colonel Pak and I have other matters to discuss."

Clancy nodded in salute and led Cody from the office. Stark was careful to shut both the inner and outer doors.

"I'm disappointed, Colonel," Stark remarked, sitting at his desk.

"How so, Mr. Stark?" Pak replied. "Has the ambassador not arrived?"

"Yes," Stark replied. "I commend you on that most excellent outcome, but I wanted MacArthur's Valley shut down. It's foolish having settlements so far apart. Most untenable."

"Closing down MacArthur's Valley would have required killing people," Pak replied. "I did not come on this mission to kill settlers."

"You saw fit to sanction the death of Major Faro?" Stark inquired.

"It's in my report, sir," Pak replied. "I take full responsibility, under LSA mortal license regulations."

"Yes, yes, quite gruesome. Extreme prejudice." Stark sighed. "How does it feel to have the power of life and death, Colonel? Godlike?"

"I would ask you the same thing, Mr. Stark," Pak replied softly. "I kill men, but I don't start wars."

Stark turned slowly to face the shorter man.

"Insolence does not become you, Colonel," Stark said, sneering. It was a hollow gesture. Pak saw fear in the man's face. "You are here to support my efforts, Colonel, not to judge them. That is for others more qualified. We are not playing petty games of espionage, Colonel. We are gaming for whole planets, nay, for the very future of the human race!"

As Stark ranted, the mortal fear in his face was displaced by fanatical righteousness. Pak had too often seen that manifestation and realized that no amount of rational discussion or physical threat would penetrate its armor of delusion.

Someone knocked on the door. It opened.

"The planetary governor is here," an assistant interrupted.

"Et Silmarn?" Stark said, his fervor broken with surprise. The envoy went to the window. "How did he get here? I see no land rovers."

"I believe he ... walked, sir," the assistant said, glancing nervously behind him. A large animate mass thudded up the stairs.

"Please send him—"

Et Silmarn, Genellan suit dripping, ducked under the lintel and pounded across the floor. The giant ripped off his helmet and stared. The stench of the kone's anger permeated the building.

"Ah, Governor Et Silmarn," Stark blustered, staggering sideways to use the desk as a barrier. "What—?"

"Envoy Stark-ah," Et Silmarn roared. The kone inhaled deeply and fell back on his elephantine haunches as if to spring. Colonel Pak moved to the doors, perversely enjoying the envoy's panic while at the same time worrying about his own safety. The kone was mere emotional threads from running amok. Pak's hand moved to his pistol.

"Envoy Stark-ah," Et Silmarn rumbled. "It-ah is not-ah clear to me what-ah evil arrangement you have-ah made with Tar Fell."

"I-I assure you—" Stark garbled, leaking saliva.

"I will say just-ah this," Et Silmarn growled, his decibels falling but his intensity rising. "If-ah Scientist Dowornobb or Ambassador Kateos is-ah in any way harmed, I will-ah kill you dead-ah."

Et Silmarn spun like a cat for the door. The giant glared malevolently. Pak jumped to the side.

The kone whirled again and took a surging lunge at Stark. Stark looked to Pak for salvation. Pak unholstered his pistol.

"And," Et Silmarn thundered, "I will-ah do everything in my power to-ah keep more humans from ever stepping foot-ah on this planet. Is my diplomatic language clear enough?"

The kone did not wait for an answer but stomped out, his tread shaking the building. Stark stood blinking, knuckles white on the back of his chair.

"Envoy Stark," Pak inquired, "where is the konish ambassador?"

"Tar Fell has taken her from the planet," Stark replied.

"What?" Pak shouted, his iron control nearly disintegrating.

"Tar Fell played his hand," Stark added. "At least we now know what horse to bet on. We have no choice now, do we?"

Pak remained silent. His rage and his intellect struggled mightily. His intellect won by small margin. In his career Pak had been party to subversion and devious plotting, but never so unwittingly. He reluctantly holstered his pistol.

THIRTY-EIGHT

THE COMING WINTER

Spitter brought word of Charlie's safe arrival at the plateau. Subsequent messengers delivered more comforting news, but finally a last messenger summoned all the hunters, including Spitter and the remaining horse tenders, to return to the plateau. Winter was on the wind.

Bringing in the harvest consumed the settlement. Dawson's request for an Explorer flight to retrieve Charlie was given low priority, for there was no assurance when the weather would change. As long as the weather held, the Explorers were used to make the long haul between MacArthur's Valley and NEd, returning settlers and ferrying trade goods.

St. Pierre, profoundly disconsolate, was strong-armed by Tatum and O'Toole into a scouting expedition into the high wilderness. They had camped in caves, huddled around campfires. They had prowled under frozen night skies exploding with stars so profligate and brilliant in some arcs as to be milky streaks of silver. They had hiked on glaciers, leaping over blue crevices and walking beneath surreal arches of water-formed ice. And St. Pierre had seen a snow cat. Pure white, with tufted ears and huge feet, it had moved like smoke, flowing to the top of an ice ridge. It had stopped to look back, long tail twitching languidly. Tatum slowly, very slowly, had raised his rifle, sighted for an eternity, and then lowered his weapon. The cat had disappeared. They had seen the soul of nature.

When he returned to the valley floor, tired and hungry, St. Pierre discovered that Nancy Dawson had moved his possessions into Buccari's vacant cabin inside the palisade. A grateful family of settlers, not yet assigned a homestead, had already moved into his and Maggie's vacated cabin, preventing a retreat.

His fellow settlers, with good-hearted insensitivity, gave St. Pierre no time for bereavement. The newspaper became the settlement's priority, second only to bringing in the harvest. St. Pierre sank himself into his task and tried to begin a new life. He was not sure whether living in Buccari's tiny cabin, among her artifacts, made the task easier or more difficult. The crushing agony of his wife's memory clashed too frequently with unfathomable dreams. St. Pierre understood the workings of his emotions well enough to realize that he was transferring his affections to a new target. Too soon, he chastised himself.

He had been in only one church in his life, and that was the yellow-stone church where his wife was murdered. He had never sought spiritual solace. Now he prayed for his wife's soul and for the soul of his child never born. And for his own soul.

But he dreamed of Sharl Buccari.

"Hey, Reggie!" someone shouted as they pounded on his door. St. Pierre opened the heavy wooden door. A razor-sharp wind fanned the fire on his hearth. Dawson stood on his porch. In her boots she was almost as tall as he was. Tatum loomed behind her.

"Johnny Rodriguez is back from NEd," Dawson shouted, her cheeks crimson with cold. "He's flying us up to Hudson's Plateau."

"What?" St. Pierre asked, not comprehending.

"To the plateau where the cliff dwellers live," Dawson said. "Get your boots on. We're waiting for you." She reached in and pulled the door shut. St. Pierre, already wearing his thermals, pulled on his insulated overalls and boots. He grabbed his admin unit, gloves, and Legion storm parka and stepped outside.

The first gentle snowfall had come, layering the valley with a virgin mantle. The Survivors had held a silly ritual in the lodge, saying farewell to the ground. It would not be seen again for many months. St. Pierre pulled on his parka and drew the hood tight. Except for the vivid blue sky, everything was brilliantly white. The mountains, glaciers, and cliffs in all directions were uniformly tinted; evergreens had become sugar trees, and settlement roofs were frosted like cakes.

Dawson and Tatum, rifles looped over their shoulders, waited, cold-blushed faces close together, breaths blending.

Neither wore a hat or hood. The fresh sun gilded their gaudy red hair with golden highlights.

"You doing okay, Reggie?" Tatum asked, his bushy orange beard and eyebrows not hiding his concern.

"Yeah," St. Pierre replied, trying to smile. He pushed cold hands into his gloves. "Damn, it's cold."

Dawson answered with a condescending grunt.

"Hell," Tatum said, hefting a large backpack. "Winter won't start for another month."

"Come on," Dawson said, striding across the snow. "Let's rescue Charlie while the weather's cooperating."

"He should come to rescue us," St. Pierre said with a laugh.

They trudged across whiteness. The spring rill was a line of blue-black darkness slicing through the settlement. Fenstermacher stood in the common with a lorry-load of ice blocks carved from the frozen lake, supervising construction.

"Looks like they're making igloos," St. Pierre said.

"Yeah," Dawson replied. "Long narrow ones."

"Tunnels," Tatum added. "Snow gets so deep, we tunnel under it."

Chief Wilson brandished a laser alignment tool. A wide path had been staked between the lodge and the palisade gate. Smaller paths radiated to various structures within the palisade. St. Pierre captured a vid-image on his admin unit and trotted after the redheads.

Under Sam Cody's supervision a robot lorry was being unloaded of fuel oil drums. Dawson confiscated the controls. Leslie Lee was also waiting, carrying a medical kit. Tatum threw his load into the lorry's empty bed. Lee, high cheekbones blushed with chill, smiled at St. Pierre. The cold gave her perfect complexion a silky glaze. She brimmed with nervous excitement.

"How'd it go at NEd, Sam?" St. Pierre asked, hopping on.

"Never stopped raining," Cody puffed. "Not trying to be flip, Reg, but it's awful nice to see happy faces. They're mighty demoralized."

"They should have stayed on Earth," Dawson muttered, climbing into the operator's station. Tatum jumped in at her side.

"Some of them might agree with you." Cody sighed.

"Let's go," Lee barked. "Charlie's probably grown wings by now."

"I'd go with you," Cody said, "but it's time for me to hibernate."

"You deserve time off, Sam," St. Pierre said, waving to Cody.

Dawson maneuvered out the palisade gate, the lorry's fat tires squeaking in the snow. They arrived at Longo's Meadow, its pure swath of white blending with the expanse of frozen lake. The meadow was delicately stitched with tire and ski tracks. A bright yellow Explorer on skis stood ready, its engine under a warming hood. Settlers with another load of cargo waited for the lorry. They huddled around a fire, trying to stay warm. Johnny Rodriguez was with them. He came over to the plane.

"Take the copilot's seat, Reg," Tatum shouted. "You should get some good vids." St. Pierre did as he was told, while the others took seats in the passenger compartment. The plane was started and warmed up, and then it taxied to the smooth center of the meadow.

After a last set of checks Rodriguez added takeoff power and headed across the meadow, pulling off the ground quickly. The pilot banked gently down the lake. A herd of elk dashed along its frozen margin, seeking sanctuary in snow-frosted trees. Rodriguez climbed slowly toward the lake's northern end. The river valley opened before them. Frosted hoary white and gleaming silver with spikes of frozen spray, kilometer upon kilometer of exploding cataracts still ran wild, their icy torrents dancing downstream to the implacable demands of gravity.

"In a couple of weeks the whole thing will freeze solid," Lee shouted. "In the spring, when the ice melts, it absolutely explodes back into life." She had squeezed forward to look out the front. St. Pierre peeked into the passenger cabin to see Tatum and Dawson snuggling close, interested in other terrain. He returned to the natural scenery and collected more vid-images. Adjectives did feeble justice to the power and scale of the river vista.

Rodriguez climbed above the river cliffs. The endless taiga spread to infinity to the north and east, a vast mantle of white, shaded and tinted with subtle swales and downs. Ahead on the right was the valley of the twin volcanoes, their softly rounded forms spewing thin spumes of ash into a west wind, their lees dusted to charcoal-gray. Steam vents and discoloration in the snow marked the path of the valley's watercourse, starting at the base of the twin volcanoes and gravitating into the larger river valley. As they flew abeam the tributary, a string of geysers rippled steamy fountains into the air.

"Look ahead," Lee said. "Hudson's Plateau."

Monolithic and huge, the plateau was like a great basalt piston risen from the firmament, a dark stone cake fifty kilometers in diameter, its top frosted white and decorated with a ridge of cruel and rugged karsts.

Beyond the plateau were the western mountains, great vertical spires, granite behemoths ranging from horizon to horizon, an insurmountable wall cleaving the continent. The tiny yellow Explorer droned onward, the artificial noise of its angry little engine daring to echo in the greater natural void. Onward they flew, spanning the unconquerable river, flaunting their mercurial power before eternal mountains. St. Pierre glanced at his fellow passengers: five minuscule souls, five motes of arrogance—the seeds of human civilization.

Hudson's Plateau seemed to hang in the distance, to get no closer, only to grow larger, to spread laterally, gradually encompassing the horizon. The plateau took on a hazy definition. Cliffs changed shade and tone as he watched. Tendrils of whiteness flowed upward, veils of gauze twisting ephemerally against the darker mountains.

"Steam," Lee said, reading his squinting eyes. "The whole plateau is riddled with volcanic vents. It's even more spectacular in early summer, when the river's running high."

"Look down there!" Rodriguez shouted. "In the chasm." He banked right. St. Pierre blinked his eyes clear. Deep within shadow, at its narrowest point but still at a formidable width, a jewel-like suspension bridge spanned the frost-crusted river.

"You can't see it in the summer," Lee shouted. "Too much spray."

"Fly down the cliffs, Johnny," Dawson shouted.

Rodriguez flew along the rim and then circled back. The plateau's top was a tremendous expanse of white, offering the pilot an infinite selection of landing options. He brought the Explorer down on its skis, within two hundred meters of the cliff edge. Rodriguez positioned the plane for takeoff and then shut down. It was a different world, a flat expanse of whiteness, the horizon at one's feet.

The loading door opened. A cruel blast sucked all warmth from the plane's interior. St. Pierre pulled on his gloves.

"Forgot how cold it gets up here," Dawson grumbled, tying a scarf around her face and pulling up her hood.

St. Pierre was last out. He jumped into the snow and went in up to his waist.

"Ever use snowshoes?" Tatum asked, throwing a pair his way.

"It's time to learn," St. Pierre replied, watching the others secure snow webs to their boots. He was soon shuffling across white powder, too excited and working too hard to feel the bitter chill. The edge of the world was only meters away. His hands sweated.

St. Pierre heard hunters chirping before he saw them. They wore white fur. He saw them only because the grim-visaged warriors broke cover. Other hunters, red-rimmed eyes glaring, appeared over the edge of the cliff; they wore leather armor and carried pikes, bows, and crossbows. St. Pierre took a vid-image.

"Everybody bow!" Tatum shouted, initiating a greeting by bowing from his waist, hands out, palms up. St. Pierre emulated the others. The hunters reciprocated. St. Pierre recognized the horribly scarred hunter leader. Captain Two and Tatum exchanged hand signs.

"Stay close," Tatum ordered, following the hunter over the cliff edge. Dawson went next and then Lee. St. Pierre's stomach lifted into his throat as he followed in Lee's cautious, sliding footsteps. The trail turned sharply right, the snow yielding sickeningly. There was nothing on his left side but misty streamers lifting from the void. He turned his head and leaned into the snow. He edged downward along the curving path, waiting for his footing to fall out from under him.

"Look down," Lee said.

"Huh," St. Pierre said, opening his eyes. The others stood on bare rock under an ice-crusted overhang, their snowshoes already removed. Behind them a rough-hewn tunnel led into the cliff. Sheepishly, St. Pierre stepped onto solid rock. His knees buckled, but he concealed his infirmity by collapsing into a sitting position, intent on removing his snowshoes. Beyond the toes of his boots, far below, through wisps of steam, he could see the curve of the river. He considered taking a vid-image, but his hands were shaking.

"Leave your snowshoes," Tatum ordered, walking into the tunnel. "We'll come back this way."

"Wonderful," St. Pierre said, pushing from the abyss. He

followed the others into the tunnel. After fifty meters the interior changed from rough-hewn to finished rock. A runnel gurgled through a bermed gutter. Wicks floating in transparent globes burned candy-orange, although large sections of the tunnel were darkened. In those murky sections St. Pierre perceived slitted murder ports and other ostensible mechanisms of ambush.

After three hundred meters the sides of the tunnel opened, and they came to a metal-edged wooden deck supported by chains suspended from an intricate block and tackle. It was a lift platform—an elevator! A brittle breeze swept crystals of snow over St. Pierre, but wonder dominated all discomfort.

"Take vids," Dawson whispered, elbowing him. "That's why we brought you, so you can tell everyone else."

St. Pierre snapped out of his amazement and took several views as he gingerly stepped aboard. It was as solid as the rock he had stepped from. He saw chain links moving before he perceived vertical motion. His frame of reference slowly moved downward, but his attention was captivated by the vista. In front of him was the vast taiga, covered in white. The twin volcanoes, their shrouded peaks still far below St. Pierre's elevation, dominated the view. The river valley, heading due east from the plateau, created a dramatic visual division. South of the river were mountains, somewhere in which was nestled MacArthur's Valley. The visibility was infinite; in the far distance the great river made its sweeping turn to the south for its continent-spanning run to Ocean Station.

The lift settled delicately, flush into another stone dock. Crowds of guilders parted from their path as they were led down a corridor to another lift station. Another elevator ride ensued, with the same breathtaking vista. St. Pierre's senses were saturated. He had seen reports on the cliff dwellers' world, but his intellect was not prepared for the scale, robustness, or polished elegance of the environment.

Another globe-lit corridor awaited them at the lift terminus. This time they walked for hundreds of meters, passing numerous trunks and offshoot passages, all filled with curious cliff dwellers. They were led into a low-ceilinged chamber. A sheet of water arched over the entry door, although the room was quite warm. They walked under the glistening waterfall and were met by a collection of guilders.

"The ones with necklaces are elders," Lee explained. "The

one in the middle wearing green jade is the head guy. Bow whenever Sandy bows."

Tatum and St. Pierre hunched down to avoid bumping their heads on the uneven ceiling. St. Pierre concentrated on taking vid-images. A small commotion caught his attention, and little Charlie, garbed in supple hides, run-skipped across the room, hiss-whistling and shouting. The rosy-cheeked child leapt into Dawson's arms. St. Pierre, his neck warming with emotion, captured the image.

"He's been eating good," Dawson grunted.

"We need to go," Tatum said, bowing deeply to the elders. "The weather's changing." He hand signed to Captain Two.

The hunter leader nodded emphatically. They turned and retraced their journey. When they arrived at the lift station, the huntress called Great-mother, wearing a hooded fur cape, stood alone on the middle of the great wooden deck. Wind gusts ruffled the ebony fur of her cloak. A pitifully small rucksack lay at her feet. As Tatum approached, she hand signed with painful deliberation.

"She's coming with us," Tatum said.

"Where's her daughter?" Lee asked. "Sandy, ask her."

Tatum flashed more hand signs. The huntress watched carefully and attempted to respond. Captain Two chirped with the female. She screeched with bald intensity. The warrior turned to Tatum and waved his fingers with resigned clarity.

"She says she is blessed," Tatum explained. "Her daughter has been taken as the mate of a warrior."

"She's crying," Dawson said.

Neck muscles protesting, Hudson lifted his gaze into a slate sky. A soft whisper of wetness caressed his nose—a snowflake. Not snow! No. He climbed another step and swung his wooden crutch, his left leg and foot dragging disinterestedly after him. He had lost count of the days. If it had not been for the inarguable presence of the river, he would have lost all reference. The planet was a wilderness. As often as he had flown down the river's length, his comfort with geologic landmarks had evaporated with the change of perspective. To fly over land was to make an abstraction of reality—the reality of distance and fear. On foot one became all too intimate with planetary scale, physical danger, and, worst of all, pain and hunger.

The river defined their longitude, but they were still lost, if only in the single dimension of latitude. How much farther?

They had seen and heard airplanes, Explorers, and abats, but they were unable to attract attention; the planes' tracks were too far west, or their altitude too high, or the clouds too thick.

"It's snowing," Quinn said, turning to check on him.

"I noticed," Hudson mumbled, making an effort to catch up.

"Need to keep moving, Nash," Cassy exhorted. "It's snowing."

"Dammit, I can see," Hudson snarled.

Quinn, lips tight, turned and resumed climbing. The ridge's peak was less than a hundred meters away. Hudson jammed his crutch forward one more time.

Quinn waited at the top. They had been forced from the water's edge by sheer cliffs, and navigable terrain had led them higher and farther inland. They had crossed many ridges. The river, flat gray under an overcast, could be seen over the tree-tops, spreading to a distant far bank now hidden by tumbling whiteness. From their lofty position they witnessed the advancing squall, a tidal wave of winter rolling straight for them.

Hudson tore his eyes from the swirls of gray and white. He did not wait for Quinn; he descended haltingly. Ahead was another ridge, and beyond that more ridges to climb before they could return to the river's edge. And return to the river they must if there was to be any hope of rescue. It was huge planet, and they were so small.

A gentle breeze brought the first sifting tickle of white. And then came flurries. Large snowflakes swirled into Hudson's face, flicking his eyelashes and sticking to his beard. He opened his mouth and stuck out his tongue. The flakes only teased his want. Soon he would have far more than his thirst needed. His mind drifted into a robotic delirium; his working foot moved, his crutch moved, his dead leg dragged behind.

Someone was shouting. Not shouting, whispering.

"Nash!" Quinn hissed.

He stopped and turned. The ground was covered with whiteness even beneath the trees. Quinn was not walking under the trees. She was in the open, next to an escarpment. The wind blew hard, the snow falling with a purposeful slant. Quinn's fur-covered form was obscured by a riot of tumbling snowflakes.

"Come here, Nash," Quinn called, her voice louder, impatient.

Hudson shook off his malaise. Quinn's tone was urgent.

"What is it, Cass?" he asked, ignoring his pain.

"A cave," Quinn replied, kneeling and peering into a shadow.

Hudson staggered to the entrance and fell to his good knee. He crawled past Quinn and examined the ground. A faint musty odor of rotten meat and wet fur wafted to his olfactories. The markings in the ground were unmistakable: large pad impressions with horrible claw extensions. He backed out into the false brightness of the blizzard.

"It's a bear cave, Cass," he whispered.

They stood there, looking at each other through swirling flurries.

"We'll need a torch," Hudson finally said. He hobbled to the trees and started collecting deadfall. Quinn joined him. Soon they had two faggots bound with hide. Hudson collected larger pieces of wood and started a fire, which he used to ignite a torch.

"Only three bullets left," Quinn said, checking her clip.

"Give me the pistol," Hudson said, leaning on his crutch and holding the white-smoking torch. Quinn looked at him.

"You going to grow a third hand?" Quinn said. "Or another leg? You're not fast enough, Nash. I'll do it." She grabbed the brand from his hand, its flames hissing with snowflakes.

Hudson started to argue, but he knew she was right. Quinn strode resolutely for the cave entrance. Winter was on them. They were not going to be rescued. They needed shelter. He grabbed the other torch and pushed it into the fire. With the torch guttering in his hand, he dragged himself toward the cave opening and prayed.

Crack! A pistol shot. A roar, liquid and enraged. *Crack!* Another shot. *Crack!* Silence.

"Cassy!" Hudson shouted, edging closer to the cave mouth.

The glow of the torch came first. Quinn, tight-lipped, pistol at her side, stumbled into the snowstorm.

"It had a cub," Quinn said.

"Kill or be killed, Cass," Hudson said.

"There's about five hundred kilos of stinking dead bear in there," Quinn said, jaw set. "Let's get to work."

THIRTY-NINE

RETURN TO SOL

Brappa's ill humor dissolved as he clamshelled his helmet over his knobby head. The prospect of the journey's end charged the cliff dweller with uncharacteristic excitement.

"May thy talons find soft rocks," Sherrip twittered.

Brappa could not help but laugh at the young warrior's joke. Hatches clanged shut as the long-leg crew members sailed to launch stations. Brappa and Sherrip sealed their helmets and dutifully tethered down. Toon-the-speaker, puffed up with his own importance, took his station behind a machine next to the long-legs they called Big-ears.

Brappa watched disinterestedly as Toon-the-speaker communicated with Big-ears. Big-ears talked aloud as he hand signed or punched symbols on a machine, his voice activating the intercom circuit. Even though cliff dwellers could not speak the words, many of the long-legs' rumbling inflections were becoming understandable. Big-ears had taught them the meaning of "go," "stop," "right," "left," "up," "down," and other commands. Big-ears sounded his own name: "Nes-tor."

Big-ears floated next to Brappa and tethered down.

"Greetings," the long-legs signed. Although comically slow, Big-ears had picked up much hunter hand sign.

"Greetings," Brappa signed back. The long-legs showed happy teeth through his helmet.

Alarms sounded. Brappa felt nauseating vibrations in his brain, the same stomach-churning sensations he had experienced at the journey's start. The motions lasted an eternity. Brappa sensed the very fabric of their ship protesting, sharp screeches at the limits of hunter hearing. Sherrip and Toon shrieked, Brappa glanced sharply at the long-legs.

"Starship nears end of journey," Big-ears hand signed.

301

For that Brappa was thankful.

The trembling ether calmed; hyperlight exit was complete, a routine jump. But Buccari's excitement was high; she sat in the command seat of her corvette, her first launch as skipper. She had just jumped back into Sol system. It had been almost seven years since she had walked the soil of her home planet, yet it would be a while longer before she trod on earthen soil; fleet crews were slated to spend weeks at the lunar grav docks before Earth leave was granted.

"What're they waiting for?" she asked.

"Holding for passengers," Thompson reported. "And guess what? They're boarding us. I'll go back and help Nestor get them in harness." The big junior officer pushed through the flight deck iris.

"Hope they enjoy sharing the crew deck with cliff dwellers," Flaherty remarked.

"Tough," Buccari muttered, concentrating on her instruments. The hangerbay pressure dump was complete. A grating foghorn resonated in the metal around them. The mothership's massive outer bay doors, telescoping slabs of composite and alloy, slid open with astonishing speed. Buccari's attention was wrenched from the instruments. Hanging in the infinite blackness of space beyond the gaping doors was a graceful limb of silver: Earth's moon. It was large and close, and beyond it, daintily opalescent and halved perfectly by its terminator, was Earth.

"Damn," she said aloud.

"Concur," Flaherty replied.

Minutes dragged by, and then Thompson reappeared.

"Geez," Thompson said. "It's Admiral Runacres and his aide. And Captain Gray and that civilian, Mather."

"What the . . . ?" Buccari remarked.

"Hope the *admiral* enjoys sharing the crew deck with cliff dwellers," Flaherty needled.

She let loose a lungful of air and used her eye cursor to select the general intercom. "Welcome aboard, Admiral," she broadcast.

"Thank you, Skipper," the disembodied voice of Zeus responded.

"Admiral Runacres has directed a change in your flight plan," came the voice of Commander Ito. "I'm feeding authority codes and orbit priorities into the nav box."

"Yes, sir," she replied, assuming they were advancing her moon base docking priority. "Admiral, would you care to take a position on the flight deck?"

"Not today, Skipper," Runacres replied. "I need some sleep, and besides, I'm getting acquainted with your crew members. Mr. . . . Lips seems quite insistent on my society. He's brought up your icon translator for my elucidation. No thanks, I'm having too much fun. Enjoy yourself."

"Aye, sir," she replied, switching back to the flight deck circuit. "What does that mean, not today?" she puffed.

"Sweet moon cheese!" Thompson blurted. "Check out navigation and you'll see. We're being cleared present position direct, priority one trajectory, Boost Station Two! Earth orbit!"

"Earth orbit! What the . . . ?" She stared at the nav HUD, trying to reconcile the updating screens. Thirty hours to Earth, to crowds of people, to civilization. She closed her eyes and swallowed.

"Eagle Six, Eagle One," Carmichael's voice came over tactical.

"Six here," she said, returning to the moment.

"You've received new orders," Carmichael said.

"Affirm," she replied. *No shit,* she thought.

"I'll be following you down with the rest of the staff," Carmichael continued. "Heavies are anxious to see you, and the exobiologists are demanding to see the cliff dwellers. Admiral Runacres will give you the full brief. Good luck. One out."

She double keyed her mike. *Heavies? What the—*

"Hope you guys brought a change of skivvies," Flaherty snorted.

"Skivvies, heck, what's the month?" Thompson said, punching his console. "November! We'll need storm coats and—"

"Can it," Buccari snapped. The diodes on the screen command panel flashed green. "Counting down."

Lockdown interlocks cleared. The launch officer designated her first to go—no surprise, considering her passenger. Buccari activated the maneuvering alarm, counted to three, and hit the kick switch. The ponderous corvette was propelled down its launch guides by a massive low-pressure launch piston and thrown into yawning blackness. Acceleration pushed her firmly into her seat.

"Corvette away," Flaherty announced to no one in particular. Her ship cleared the bay doors. Clearance lasers flickered from amber to green. With the mothership falling astern, her tensions melted away. Bright stars welcomed her into the black vacuum of free space, a pilot once more. It had been too long. She gave the port quarter thrusters a smart pulse; the corvette's tail slewed to starboard.

"Clear angle," Flaherty reported.

"Mains," she barked, firmly setting throttles. "Three gees." The corvette jumped. Thompson hooted.

"Shit hot!" Flaherty grunted. "Your own ship, Skip."

"*Our* ship," she replied, engaging the autopilot. "My crew."

Buccari pivoted in her tethers. Both flight deck officers turned to face her, inscrutable, gold helmet visors catching the white-yellow fire of Sol. She knew they were smiling.

She laughed. "Ain't it grand!" She looked forward, past the magnificent crescent of the moon. Earth lay fine on her nose.

FORTY

STATISTICAL DISTRIBUTIONS

During their dash all fuel-reserve regulations for arrival in Earth orbit were ignored. En route they received information summaries, including exciting news about a formative alpha-one-minus orbiting G124—designated Hornblower Three—discovered by Second Fleet units commanded by Admiral Chou. Although no high-order intelligence was evident on the steamy planet, Chou's geologists had determined that the resource-rich and life-abundant ecosystem was evolving similarly to Earth. The habitability rating of the jungle planet would continue to improve. The admiral had left behind a seed colony.

Other news was not as sanguine: Indo-Australia, the last viable civilization in the southern hemisphere, had imploded after a desperate spasm of nuclear war. The Asian Cooperative, in decline since before Shaula, had been savaged by religious schism. The TGSR, under siege from the east and south, its technologies and resources dedicated to warfare, was defending itself by annihilating its enemies, real or potential, on a genocidal scale. Its armies were marching across central Asia, exhibiting the worst tendencies of Attila and Genghis Khan.

The Tellurian Legion pursued neutrality in those greater conflicts, but Albion-Gaul and the Nordic Protectorates were hard pressed to avoid conflict. Nor were the Legion's hands clean in conflicts with the hapless People's Republic of the Americas. The Legion had retreated from the eastern seaboard, its southern border now delineated by the geography of the St. Lawrence Seaway/Great Lakes/Missouri River/Sacramento River Delta. San Francisco, Buccari's birthplace, had become a neutral city-state.

Buccari was given highest approach priority, leapfrogging a half dozen stacked-up vessels. Admiral Runacres made a respectable approach to the outer marker. Buccari brought the big corvette into the bustling docks, disdaining tug assistance. A VIP shuttle was waiting. She left Flaherty in command and was whisked into Earth's milky atmosphere. Destination: L.S.S. Alberta, the space station closest to Edmonton, capital of the Tellurian Legion.

That had been yesterday. She had since survived a parade and a press conference.

"This way, please." An attendant attired in stocking breeches and powdered wig took her parade cap and escorted her into a paneled chamber. Her medals chiming dully, Buccari walked down a sloping floor into a high-ceilinged, mural-bedecked room past rows of empty audience pews. The room was dominated by a mahogany bench behind which sat fifteen men and women—the Legion Council. Several wore military uniforms. In the middle of the gilded bench, seated in a high-backed thronelike chair, Socrates Duffy presided, red-nosed and leonine.

"Please be seated," the president announced, his gravelly voice filling the room.

Before the bench was a green baize-covered table at which were seated Fleet Admiral Runacres, Admiral Chou, commander of Second Fleet, and Vice Admiral Klein, commander of fleet science and intelligence. They had changed from their parade uniforms. The other participant, a crew-cut, white-haired civilian, turned in his chair. Buccari recognized Dr. Jean-Marie Thoreau, the architect of Legion hyperlight exploration. A fifth chair, the middle seat between Admiral Runacres and Dr. Thoreau, was vacant. A page led her past a row of crowded staff tables; she made eye contact with Merriwether and Carmichael. Dr. Thoreau rose halfway to his feet as the page slid back the empty chair. She smiled at the old man, took her seat, and was thankful to be seated; gravity was having its irrefutable effect.

"Good afternoon," Duffy rumbled. She glanced up and down the green baize; the gold braid resting atop the table was disconcerting to the point of dizziness. They were all waiting for her to speak.

"G-good afternoon, Mr. President," she exhaled, turning forward, the movement chafing her neck. Her stomach rumbled hollowly. The chaotic press conference had pre-empted her lunch.

"Nice of you to find time for our hearing," Duffy continued.

"Ah ... my pleasure, sir," she answered, indecorously scratching the stubble on her head.

"Hearings on space exploration were precipitated by Admiral Chou's discovery," the president said. "But your return, bringing the horrible news of Oldfather, rendered our discussions irrelevant. We have reviewed Admiral Runacres's burst summaries as well as Envoy Stark's findings and recommendations. While you were at your press conference, Stark's assistant, Ms. Mather, gave a rather excellent administration briefing and Captain Gray presented an entertaining science update. Now to focus on operations. The tragedy at Oldfather is foremost on our minds."

Dr. Thoreau shuffled his notes. The notes were handwritten. The manager of the greatest technical asset in the history of mankind used a gold-nibbed foundation pen. And he shaved poorly.

"Dr. Thoreau," Duffy continued. "Would you lead the discussion?"

Dr. Thoreau cleared his throat. He smelled of rosewater and tweed.

"Thirty years ago," Thoreau began, snowy eyebrows bunching, "the space fleet of the Asian Cooperative, while exploring the Shaula system, was annihilated. Neither the AC nor Tellurian Legion fleets of that era carried defensive systems. Against the threat of future attacks Legion ships were fitted with considerable weaponry. Subsequent engagements with the kones revealed deficiencies, but our forces were shown to be capable of retaliation."

"An expeditionary fleet may never carry enough firepower to defeat a home defense network," Admiral Klein interjected.

"A valid point," Dr. Thoreau continued. "We continued to improve weaponry; however, the events at Oldfather indicate we have not improved enough. Admiral Runacres, your impressions of what transpired?"

"Captain Ketchie was one of my most capable commanders," Runacres said soberly. "Motherships under his command included *Borneo* and *Crete*, two of our heaviest-armed platforms. Evidence indicates that all ships were fighting when they were destroyed. We were vanquished in battle."

"How could they be so utterly and profoundly defeated?" one of the council members, an army general, asked.

"By a superior force," Runacres replied sourly. "Specifically, superior technologies. There are no better space pilots."

"Do we really know anything about this killer race? Anything?" another council member asked. "Where do they come from?"

"Oldfather has given us new data," Thoreau replied. "Admiral Klein, would you be so kind?"

Vice Admiral Klein, tall and elegantly tailored, stood and moved to a lectern. Her raven hair was streaked with white. Lights softened, and both side walls of the chamber illuminated into holographic screens.

"Mr. President, Admiral Runacres," the knife-featured intelligence officer began. "This is a distribution model of stable star systems. With every alien contact we refine the probability-of-contact regression model. Oldfather has given us another data point in space and time. Our first data point is Earth."

A green point of light expanded to a tiny globe.

"We must think in four dimensions," Admiral Klein continued. "Thirty years ago the Asian Cooperative Fleet was annihilated at Shaula, the first human contact with aliens—here."

A second point of light, a red sphere, expanded in the display.

"To date this was the only other data point for our computers to analyze, and the distribution solution for alien contact was hopelessly divergent. Now we have Oldfather."

Another red point illuminated.

"This event gives us a distribution base line adjusted for the universal expansion gradient."

The red points were connected with a curving, razor-thin bar of white light.

"Assuming the aliens are restricted to the same hyperlight constraints, that is, given gradient strength at any point, movement along gravitational field lines outbound from universal center is approximately one point one times faster than inbound movement and roughly ten times orthogonal movement, adjusted for galactic rotational angle gamma-prime and ecliptic offset theta."

"Admiral," Duffy interrupted, "some of us are merely lawyers."

"My apologies," Klein replied, thin lips tightening. "A bit technical, perhaps, but necessary to the discussion."

"There's a fourth data point, Admiral," Buccari interjected.

"Exactly," Klein said. "While Lieutenant Commander Buccari was isolated in the konish system, she discovered that Rex-Kaliph Two—Kon, the konish home planet—had come under murderous attack five centuries ago. If we bring that data point into the argument and advance it in time, we tighten our threat area considerably. Witness the distribution solution generated by a nexus of our most powerful processors."

A yellow spark blossomed, followed by a segmented explosion of colors; shades of reds and blues, like balloons within balloons, spread across a quadrant of the galaxy. Admiral Klein hit a button. The presentation zoomed in, enlarging the area under scrutiny. Reference grids indicated galactic and universal radials.

"The dark red zone represents a probability of alien contact greater than fifty percent. Here is the Rex-Kaliph system—Genellan—just outside the threat zone." She indicated the yellow point and highlighted the system's location, using holographic enhancement.

"Still a profoundly large territory," Dr. Thoreau announced. "It represents several lifetimes of searching, using existing methods."

"Hornblower system?" a panel member asked. "Where is Admiral Chou's discovery?"

"In the red zone," Runacres announced somberly. Klein nodded and pressed her panel; another point of red flared.

"Should we not . . . avoid areas of—" the same panel member asked.

"That would seem advisable, but permit me to show you what happens over time," Klein continued. "This is ten years hence. Rex-Kaliph, Genellan's star, enters the red area. Five hundred years ago, when Kon was attacked, the U-radial alignment to the gravitational gradient also placed that star well into the red zone. This region of the galaxy is moving through an arc that will realign the gradients, putting Genellan back into the zone."

"Earth is moving into the red zone," Runacres announced.

"As it was five hundred years ago," Dr. Thoreau said.

"Why wasn't Earth attacked five hundred years ago," the president inquired, "like the kones?"

"Five hundred years ago Kon had a mature technical civilization with commensurate electromagnetic signatures," Buccari replied. "Earth was just entering the electromagnetic age. We'd barely started transmitting, and what noise we'd made had not yet gone very far into space. We didn't show up on their scans."

"Exactly," Dr. Thoreau said, glancing at Buccari. "Our ancestors were providentially primitive."

"Now what?" Duffy asked.

"In less than a generation," Klein continued, "Earth will reenter this arbitrary danger area. Of course, at these scales and time frames, Earth should already be considered at risk. The point is, with each passing year our probability of direct alien contact increases until some time in the middle of the next century, when we will be roughly aligned with the aliens on this universal gravitational radial."

"We'll be hyperlight neighbors," Admiral Chou said, "for several decades. There's no avoiding contact."

"Precisely," Klein replied. "Since we've seen them twice on this galactic revolution, statistically the chances are becoming more likely that we'll see them again. Our best guess is that their home system or systems are here, higher on the galactic ecliptic than Sol."

A flat, white spheroid appeared at the far edge of the red zone. Silence held reign for several minutes. Dr. Thoreau cleared his throat.

"We must," Thoreau finally said, his voice firming, "expand our foothold on Genellan. A fleet-bunkering facility and an ordnance depot will be established in conjunction with the next settler transport. Admiral Runacres, do you have a status report on that convoy?"

"The uploading of the settlement transport is nearing completion," Runacres reported. "Admiral Chou will—"

"But King Ollant," Buccari interrupted, her voice breaking, "has given permission for only another thousand humans. And only if we transfer technology. The settlers and planet-based fleet personnel will easily exceed that limit."

"We will give Kon the secrets of hyperlight travel," Dr. Thoreau replied gently. "There is no choice. The kones will in time, on their own, deduce those fragile secrets. We might as well trade while we still have something with which to bargain. We need that planet. We need its resources, and perhaps most important, we need an ally."

"Whatever it takes," Duffy announced, his tone allowing no dispute. "Envoy Stark has been charged to secure the Legion's position. Commander Buccari, Ms. Mather's report suggests you are resisting settlement of Genellan. Do you have anything to say about our strategy?"

Buccari looked down at the table and exhaled. "No," she said stonily. "It will be up to those who inhabit the planet to determine its destiny. I am a pilot and a fleet officer."

"Very well," Duffy said, checking the time. "Now, Dr. Thoreau, would you present Admiral Runacres with his orders."

"Orders for the fleet," Dr. Thoreau announced. "Admiral Chou's Second Fleet will escort the next increment of settlers to Genellan. The strategic value of Genellan cannot be overstated. It is imperative that the Legion establish an enduring military outpost. Genellan represents humanity's greatest hope: an outlet for rampaging strife and overpopulation and the resources necessary for recharging our exploratory and defensive zeal."

Buccari exchanged covert glances with Admiral Runacres.

"After depositing the Genellan download," Dr. Thoreau continued, "Admiral Chou will proceed to the Hornblower system for rendezvous with the main battle fleet." Buccari concentrated on the words.

"The main battle fleet under Fleet Admiral Runacres," Thoreau went on, "will seek out the belligerent aliens and attempt peaceful contact. Pursuant to that objective, Admiral, your orders are as follows: Proceed first to system M796—designated Scorpio Minor—a class-one binary with Category-two probability of supportable life."

Thoreau looked up. "Admiral, I am sure you recognize this

system's proximity to Shaula," he said pointedly. "You will make every effort to locate and establish peaceful contact. If no extraterrestrial life is discovered, after cataloging the satellites of Scorpio Minor, you are to proceed to Hornblower, there to relieve and enhance the seed colony. After a rendezvous with Admiral Chou's units, the combined Tellurian Fleet will return to Sol system for refit and reassignment."

Return to Sol. Buccari's jaw tightened. She would not make it back to Genellan on this cruise, nor would her cliff dwellers. It would be another two years at least before she would see her son, and the cliff dwellers their families. It might as well have been a death sentence.

The juices never stopped in Edmonton's gut, a stomach always gnawing on itself. Night intensified the consumption, the erosion of surrender, of unhappy revel. Neon fluttered and strobed, and excited gases creating a lewd radiance easily outshining aurora borealis's timid flickering. Bars never closed. Laughter and dancing never stopped—nor did the sobbing. Broken wretches huddled in alleys, snoring in the humid warmth of cast-off energy. Steam rising from discharge vents lifted into the crisp chill the smell of urine and beer, vomit and rot.

Fighting gravity, profoundly worried, Carmichael staggered after Pulaski's peripatetic form, a burly dervish dashing in and out of bars. At times Carmichael could only see the glow of Pulaski's cigar jerking anxiously in dark alleys, and then the man would move through a shaft of light and Carmichael would detect his clenched teeth, his heaving lungs throwing off cigar smoke like a Punjabi locomotive. A half block ahead Pulaski disappeared into another seedy establishment. Carmichael looked around and was distressed to discover the hunters missing.

"Crap," he muttered, retracing his steps to peer into an alley.

Someone bellowed a curse. Carmichael returned his attention to the street to see Pulaski slamming shut the weather doors of a corner tavern. Pulaski crossed his arms and leaned forcefully against a street lamp. Except for the twitching cigar and its explosions of smoke, his face was invisible in shadows cast by his hood.

Chang, Godonov, and Lizard Lips appeared, all dressed in hooded spacer capes. Suddenly Bottlenose was at Carmichael's side, chirping. Relieved, Carmichael looked for Tonto.

"She's here somewhere, dammit," Pulaski growled.

"You guys frequent all the best places," Godonov wheezed. Lizard Lips and Bottlenose jabbered frantically.

"It wasn't this bad when we were in training," Pulaski said, removing his cigar and rubbing his face.

"Yeah, it was, Igor," Chang replied.

"Unbelievable. Even Ski's standards have improved," Godonov said. Lizard Lips punched the communicator and handed it to Godonov.

"Tonto found her!" Godonov exclaimed, looking up from the communicator. "Go!" he shouted at Bottlenose.

The hunter hop-waddled into the night, cape flapping. The humans, with Pulaski pushing ahead, followed their hound. Carmichael and Lizard Lips brought up the rear. Bottlenose led them through a cluttered lot, over a dilapidated fence, and into an alley.

The neon sign stuttered: THE SAS ATOON SALOO. The bar was empty, the patrons having been routed. A few brave souls stared wide-eyed through windows and open doors. Carmichael followed Pulaski past babbling misfits and into the establishment. Pulaski and Godonov confronted a panicked bartender. The drink pourer held an old double-barrel. Blue smoke curled in laminar layers below low lamps. The vid screen in the corner emitted only cold blackness. A steel guitar keened from hidden speakers.

"She'll be in the back booth." Pulaski sighed, looking around. "I thought this place burned down. Booch used to come here when she was pissed off. Shit kicking cheered her up."

"Get those monsters outta here," the bartender whined.

"Ah, shut up," Pulaski snapped. "You know who that is?"

"Yeah," the barkeep mumbled. "But you're scaring off the customers."

Carmichael walked across the wooden floor. She was sitting in a corner booth, head on her forearm. Tonto stood on the bench next to her, a wing draped over her back. The hunter looked up.

Buccari reached an arm around Tonto and buried her head in the hunter's soft fur. Tonto wrapped his other wing around the distraught pilot, masking her from view. Bottlenose, chirping sharply, jumped on the opposite bench and cocked his pickax head from side to side. Lizard Lips sampled the dregs in Buccari's beer bottles.

"Security's going to be all over the place," Godonov counseled.

"Yeah," Carmichael replied. "Get her out of here."

"Bingo time, Booch," Pulaski said softly, pulling Tonto away. The hunter moved as Pulaski hooked one of Buccari's arms and pulled her erect. Godonov grabbed her other arm.

"Time to go," she mumbled. "Goin' bug hunting. Gim' a fast sheep, for I intends ... hic ... to go in harm's way. Damn the torpedoes ..."

She looked at Carmichael and smiled. Her eyes rolled in her head, and she fell against Pulaski's chest. Pulaski hugged her tenderly. The burly man lifted her limp form and held her like a baby.

"She's going to have a bad morning." Pulaski chuckled. The unhooded cliff dwellers preceded them, scattering the shouting bystanders. A security siren sounded in the distance, coming closer.

"Hey, spacer, she'll want this." The bartender handed Carmichael a heavy object wrapped in a white-and-red ribbon. "She gave it to me as a tip. Got her name on it. Could've sold it for a fortune."

"Thanks." Carmichael glanced down at the gaudy Medal of Honor that Buccari had been awarded earlier that day. He shoved it in his pocket and tossed the bartender a hundred-credit note.

"Gawd-awful pretty fer a drunk," the bartender said. "Even wit' tha' scar."

"She's beautiful," Carmichael said, walking into the night.

SECTION FOUR

A TIME TO KILL

FORTY-ONE

DARKEST HOUR

"Scientist Dowornobb will not betray his king," Kateos snapped. She floated in the operation center between Tar Fell's cabin and her own. A holo-vid filling one wall displayed forces arrayed to do battle.

"It matters not," Tar Fell answered. "The information will eventually be disclosed. Scientist Dowornobb's obtuse nature only provides me an excuse to retain your excellent company."

"How soon before the Hegemonic fleet attacks?" Kateos asked. Her heart ached for her mate's tribulation, but her stomachs lifted into her throat in fear. She scanned the battle display with confused horror.

"Soon," Tar Fell replied.

"Should you not be at your battle station?" Kateos said.

"In good time." Tar Fell laughed. "You are anxious for me to leave, but I find our discussions stimulating. You provide insight into your philosopher-king. Perhaps his battle strategy follows his philosophy."

"You make a game of war," Kateos barked.

"Is war not a game, Ambassador?" Tar Fell inquired. "Is it not the ultimate extension of diplomacy, the inevitable endgame?"

"War is not inevitable," Kateos rebutted, steeling herself to the armada master's verbal counterthrust. She had parried many onslaughts since her impressment. Tar Fell had discussed diplomacy, history, philosophy, and economics, displaying a staggering breadth and depth of argument. Where would Tar Fell's zealous erudition travel tonight? At least her gas headaches were lessening.

"Ah, but war is inevitable," Tar Fell rumbled. "You must

accept the premise if you are to understand the game. Threat of force is effective only if predictably employed."

"I understand only that you use force," Kateos remonstrated, "where force is not required. King Ollant would have listened to your petitions. King Ollant would have given—"

"What I want is not the king's to give!" Tar Fell thundered.

"What do you want?" Kateos demanded, her anger rampant.

"To win," Tar Fell answered, softening his voice. "I want to win. Winning can never be a gift."

"What does it mean to win?" Kateos asked.

"First nation through the gates of technology wins control of trade," Tar Fell replied. "The Hegemony is already too powerful. Others must control the balance of trade, not King Ollant."

"Then I truly understand," Kateos sniffed. "It is simple greed."

Tar Fell shrugged. A soft tone seized the armada master's attention.

"I prefer to call it economics," he replied, making a deferential bow before floating through the hatch.

"Ollant means to do battle," Magoon remarked. On the holo-vid the squadron commander's visage was serene. Erect eye tufts belied Magoon's inner tensions. "He will be in weapons range within the watch cycle."

"Defensive formations are set, Armada Master," Krolk growled, his red-veined countenance flushed with combative juices. The Ransan's white eye tufts seemed to spring from his head like quills from a *kotada* rat. "Our ships are at the highest readiness levels."

"Adequate readiness levels," Magoon corrected. Krolk made a sour, burping retort, incomprehensible yet perfectly understandable.

Tar Fell observed the battle plot. King Ollant made no feints, no maneuvers. The Hegemonic fleet was arrowed straight at his defensive pincer, aiming unerringly for the focus of Tar Fell's strength. Ollant was putting all stakes on the table, pitting the experience of Hegemonic crews against Thullol-Ransan weaponry and numbers.

"He is courageous," Magoon remarked.

"Ollant has no choice," Tar Fell replied. "The longer he waits, the weaker his position."

"Our sting will dissolve his courage," Krolk said, gloating.

"Underestimate him not," Tar Fell rumbled. "Prepare for battle."

The Hegemonic battle fleet, accelerating to engagement velocities, pressed ever forward. Tar Fell's battle computers held their battle plan recommendations steady. Gaming outcomes were universally favorable. All the ships in his armada tensed for impact. Weapons systems allocated targets. Ship commanders sensed the approach of destiny.

"Ollant is insane!" Magoon reported over the command net. "I propose a slow retreat to keep his lead units exposed to maximum fire as long as possible."

Prudent tactics, Tar Fell thought, for coordinated crews experienced in fleet maneuver.

"He would break off the engagement," Krolk protested. "Let him advance into our trap. We shall destroy him once and for all."

Under the circumstances Krolk's was the correct answer, Tar Fell mused, assuming all ships maintained battle formation.

"Hold positions," Tar Fell ordered. "We fight where we stand."

At the last possible moment, less than four hours from contact, Ollant's squadron maneuvered radically, no doubt at great cost of fuel but with brilliant precision, vectoring directly into Krolk's flotilla, the area of greatest ship density. The king's reasoning was impeccable, Tar Fell granted. Where there were the greatest defenses, there lay the most valuable prizes—or the least experienced units.

"He's turning!" Tar Fell shouted into the command circuit, but Magoon's ships were already maneuvering. Hours crawled by. The armada master controlled his fury and watched the chess game unfold. He could only command his fleet; he could not fight ship battles. His subordinates adhered to orders. The adversary refused to cooperate.

Ollant's wheeling thrust drove deep into Krolk's formations. The Ransan's support lines, broadsided by Ollant's heaviest ships, were shattered within ten hours of first contact. Magoon's ships, in hot pursuit, exacted a fierce toll on Ollant's intrepid rear guard, but *Samamkook* and her companion battle cruisers, with velocity and point of attack on their side, ravaged Krolk's forces.

Ollant clenched his gauntleted fists. *Samamkook*'s main batteries discharged yet again, pounding *Rouue Massif* unmercifully. The Ransan ship was soundly built, the king allowed. And the battle was well fought—his own shields wavered before stubborn return fire. But she was beaten, the seventh of Tar Fell's ships to fall out of action.

A great tactical victory, yet Ollant grieved. Two of his valiant cruisers had been destroyed, and not a single ship in the king's line was without grievous battle damage. Other than glorious suicide, there was no choice but to break off the attack. Ollant stared into space, giving willful death and glory their due. Star Nappo, the fulcrum of konish astrology, pulsed white and blue against the infinite depth of the ebony vacuum. Ollant took no solace in its beauty. He had failed.

"Your Highness," Et Anitab counseled, "*Samamkook*'s primaries are deteriorating. Tar Fell's slowest cruiser can run us down. This ship must return to base for repairs and refit."

"Break off the attacks," Ollant replied.

Genellan was lost.

"The Hegemonic fleet withdraws!" Magoon reported. "They have committed to a gravity whip."

A burden lifted from Tar Fell's shoulders. Ollant's squadron with *Samamkook* in the van, heedless of punishment, had ripped through his armada, costing him seven ships, including the mortally wounded *Rouue Massif*. General Krolk had died bravely.

Tar Fell's cruel laughter rumbled across his command center. Technicians glanced nervously in his direction. Tar Fell did not care. The field belonged to his battered—but now battle-tested—armada. Genellan was still his, and time was on his side.

"General Magoon," Tar Fell roared. "Convoy the damaged units and dispatch them back to Kreta. All able ships make for Genellan orbit!"

"As you command," Magoon responded, sending formation signals.

Tar Fell floated to an observation bubble and located the blue orb that was Genellan. As *Penc* maneuvered for its acceleration burn, the aquamarine planet and its two moons moved steadily until they were dead off the nose. Light-years beyond Genellan pulsed Star Nappo, the brightest star in the konish skies, visible to kones in the southern hemisphere. A star of great good fortune, the Thullolian thought.

* * *

"King Ollant has been defeated," Scientist Mirrtis reported, entering Dowornobb's compartment under the domes of Ocean Station. Scientist H'Aare was on his heels.

Dowornobb looked up, searching the scientist's eyes. Horrible news, yet sweet. If the king's battle fleet had been repulsed, there was a chance his mate was unharmed.

"Tar Fell's flagship was not engaged," Mirrtis added.

Dowornobb exhaled mightily. The acrid emanations of his fear were displaced by waves of rancid relief. Dowornobb positioned himself on the chest lounge. He brought up his modeling programs.

"What now?" H'Aare asked. "There will be no rescue."

"I will do whatever it takes to bring my mate down from the battles," Dowornobb replied. "Even if it means giving Tar Fell the secrets to the stars."

"First you must have those secrets," Mirrtis rumbled.

"We are close," Dowornobb whispered.

So cold! Every sound was crisp and metallic, every color sharp and pure. Crimson on white, steaming blood melting unblemished snow, growing cold and black as it sank deep into powdery drifts. Using his thigh-length knife, Tatum levered a bloody winter-white pelt from a nightmare carcass, his gloves and snowshoes gore-stained. Nightmares had silky fur and thick hides. A good kill: ten skins, ten carcasses. Tatum hefted another animal by its leathery tail and gutted it with two practiced incisions. Entrails fell into a steaming pile, Tatum's vaporous breath blending with the heat of carnage.

"We got a load, Sandy," Schmidt said, words exploding through his mask in sinking white crystals. His fur-dressed hood hung low. Sun goggles covered the rest of his face.

Tatum threw snow over the remaining purple-gray carcasses. "Sure ain't going to spoil," he muttered, pulling his scarf over his nose and mouth and rubbing feeling into his nose. Only the absence of wind allowed them to stay outside. The tenuous warmth of exertion was an illusion. The dismal chill sucked away all energy. A dim sun low in the south cast sharp shadows with heatless light, giving dimension to treetops protruding from the drifted snow. He jammed his knife into a butchered animal and wiped it on a pelt, expunging crusty gore.

Tatum collected pelts and heaved their stiffening mass on top of the heaped toboggan. He joined Schmidt, looping a leather harness over his shoulder. Their breath blasting like locomotive exhaust, the brawny pair heaved into motion. They descended steeply to a hard-packed trail where Dawson, rifle in hand, was waiting astride a horse, its golden fur grown even longer, its nostrils streaming white. Tatum hitched the animal to the cargo, and Dawson led it down the hill. Tatum jumped on the toboggan's tail and used a foot brake to slow the sled on steep portions of the return.

Thin columns of smoke rose lazily above the snow-drifted palisade. An inversion trapped the smoke, spreading it laterally in a wispy haze that drifted languorously to the north. Tatum checked the skies. A high layer of cirrus clouds was forming. The sun was developing an ice halo; another storm was coming.

They came to the palisade gate. Great heaps of snow had been cleared from the entrance to reveal the mouth of a brightly lighted ice tunnel. Fenstermacher flipped them the bird and disappeared down the tunnel's bore. Toby Mendoza, in a Legion landing suit, appeared leading a robot lorry. It was too cold to risk using the electric-powered vehicles any distance from their battery chargers, and the fuel for the ATVs was being conserved for the generators. Dawson dismounted and helped transfer the hides to the lorry. When the transfer was complete, Toby Mendoza and the lorry disappeared down the tunnel.

"Let's get the rest," Tatum said, his words freezing in falling white bursts. He plodded up the packed trail, leading the horse.

"Winter's never going to end," Dawson moaned.

"Enjoy the sun," Tatum grunted, staring skyward, "while it lasts."

FORTY-TWO

UNDER WAY AGAIN

Runacres pulled his weightless body across *Eire*'s starboard observation wing. Observation wings were impractical devices yet pleasing to the spacer's sense of tradition. The next class of mothership would not submit to such impracticality. Runacres had given final design authorization for the lead mothership of the new Avenger class, which would start coming off the ways in five years. They were no longer motherships; the new ships were to be called battleships. Battleships, men-of-war, dreadnoughts—a rose by any name.

The darkened moon was above him, the brilliant limb of Earth's satellite dominating the celestial panorama. Through perfectly transparent carbon armor Runacres used a stationing scope to locate the elements of his fleet. Motherships *Eire, Baffin, Britannia, Corsica,* and *Tierra del Fuego* formed an equilateral four-sided pyramid, with *Eire* as the guide at the pyramid's apex. Motherships *Novaya Zemlya, Hainan, Iceland, New Zealand,* and *Shikoku* formed another pyramid, inverted and stacked symmetrically "below" the first. Fleet HLA auxiliaries *Tacoma, Halifax, Siska,* and *Jasper,* carrying fuels, stores, and repair machinery, took their stations in the cube defined by the pyramid bases, a stable and redundant grid matrix. Thus was arrayed the Tellurian Legion's main battle fleet on a mission to secure peace. The paradox of might—roses with thorns.

Beyond the moon's horn was the home planet. Runacres treasured his last look at Earth, a sublime jewel, at once an opal and a sparkling diamond against a bottomless backdrop of black velvet. It was winter in the northern hemisphere, the swollen polar cap largely in shadow. Blue oceans swirling with white clouds were aglint with the sun's reflected brilliance. He closed his eyes, burning the soothing images of mankind's first mothership into his brain. He pushed across the sponson and into the armored lock leading to the flag bridge.

"Admiral on the bridge," the tactical officer announced. Runacres flexed off the watch officer's station and sailed up the companionway, past the corvette group leader and operations watch officer.

"All units alpha-alpha, Admiral," Wells reported.

"Very well," Runacres replied, securing himself in his tethers and scanning the status boards. He looked down at *Eire*'s operational bridge. Captain Merriwether stared up at him. She lifted her gloved finger and brought it down, pointing forward. He nodded.

"Go forth and do battle," he whispered.

"Say again, sir," Wells replied.

"Jump the fleet, Commodore," Runacres ordered.

"Whatcha working on, Skip?" Flaherty asked, grabbing a squirt tube from the galley.

Buccari labored at the midstation console on the crew deck of the number six corvette, engrossed in technical files.

"OOD written qualifications," she replied, concentrating on the screen. "I intend to qualify this deployment. I expect you should be making some progress on this material yourself."

"One of these days," Flaherty replied, pulling himself forward. "First pilot qual burned out a few of my diodes. I'm in recovery mode." Her copilot disappeared through the overhead hatch. Behind her the EPL hatch hissed open.

"Corvette Landing Squad Thirty-six reporting for duty, sir."

Buccari refused to credit her ears. She looked up to see the big man at rigid attention, cherubic features devoid of hair. She closed her eyes and opened them. Chastain was still there, along with eight other braced marines: six men and two women, all big and strong but with the faces of children. Chastain had lost weight.

"Corporal Chastain," she said. "Welcome aboard."

"Thank you, sir," Chastain replied, brown eyes crinkling. "Sir, I was told that two cliff dwellers would be added to my squad. I've been given orders to take them to physical training."

She did not have to answer. Tonto and Bottlenose torpedoed headfirst from the overhead hatch, nearly decapitating everyone on the crew deck with their flailing flight membranes.

Lizard Lips followed more sedately. Godonov eased down in their wake.

Chirping and shrieking, waving ecstatic hand signs, Tonto and Bottlenose made abundantly clear their affection for the gentle giant. The rest of the crew peeked in at the cacophony. Chastain's marines were in danger of falling into full retreat. Buccari could only laugh. In the fluttering, screeching chaos she managed to squeeze Chastain's hand, to his great and expected embarrassment.

"A-a-tennn-hut!" Chastain suddenly bellowed. At the same time he hand signed to the hunters "Stop!" his facial and hand signals emphatic. The hunters, taken aback, froze in position, membranes in midfold.

"I warrior chief," Chastain said, hand signing his words with labored concentration. "You follow my commands."

Tonto and Sherrip looked at each other. Lizard Lips chirped something, and all three cliff dwellers hiss-smiled. With comical imperative, the two hunters joined the other marines, mimicking their postures. Godonov and Lizard Lips traded hand signs.

Hyperlight warnings sounded. Buccari took hold of the bulkhead.

"The family's getting back together," Godonov said, looping his foot in a tether. "Welcome aboard, Jocko. The hunters need you."

"Thank you, Mr. Godonov," Chastain replied, all business. "It's good to see you again—and Lieuten—er, Commander Buccari." He glanced at her, puppy eyes at once sad and happy, and then his gaze dropped, just like old times.

Hyperlight alert Klaxons clamored. HLA oscillations overwhelmed them. Taken by surprise, the hunters shrieked. Buccari controlled her vertigo and clung to her tethers. Wambling vibrations eventually dampened to gentle nothingness. At last the watch boatswain piped "Attention" over the general circuit. The wistful notes echoed into silence. The fleet was under way, committed to hyperlight cruising orders.

"Relieve the watch," the boatswain announced. "On deck the second section. Lifeboat petty officers on deck to muster. Relieve the station keepers. Now relieve the watch."

"I'm on the bridge," Buccari declared, pushing from the console and making for the EPL hatch. Out of habit she checked her watch uniform, fingers moving on their own, perfecting alignments and squaring creases.

"Skipper's departing!" Chastain shouted.

"Carry on," she said, pushing through the parting marines. She could not resist touching Chastain's shoulder as she floated by. She wanted to touch his face. "Carry on," she repeated.

As the hatch was closing behind her, she heard the cliff dwellers chittering with joy. Joy was what she felt at the sight of an old friend, a link to past.

"Commander Buccari."

Buccari's euphoria heightened. In the upper EPL bay with Lander Boatswain Nakajima was another familiar face: Pepper Goldberg.

"Pepper!" Buccari shouted, examining the dark-eyed engineering technician's crisp underway suit. "Excuse me, Petty Officer First Class Goldberg. Congratulations."

"Thank you, sir," Pepper replied. "I—I wanted to welcome you back to the fleet, sir. I know how tough your decision was to leave."

"Thanks," Buccari said. "I know you do, Pepper. They don't make decisions any tougher. So, uh . . . you've been assigned to Lieutenant Commander Pulaski's crew?"

"Yes, sir," Goldberg replied effusively. "Commander Pulaski's a fantastic skipper. We'd all kill for him. He's really something."

"I'll say." Buccari laughed. "I gotta go. My watch section's on deck. Good luck . . . Goldberg."

"You, too . . . sir." The engineering tech saluted.

Buccari returned the salute, pressurized her docking hood, and dropped through the EPL lock into the hangerbay. She arrowed across the maintenance voids, hustled over the quarterdeck, and darted into an up-bore. Her emotions were mixing uncomfortably, but she was certain of one thing: Her relief at being away from Earth was profound.

Kateos's relief at feeling solid ground was immense. The orbital lander settled into the Ocean Station landing gantry, its pressurization systems equalizing. Kateos stoically suffered through the transition. Her bladders and sinuses fluttered with magnificent accommodation to the pressure changes, and then she luxuriated in the warm, heavy air coming through the lander's ducting.

"Back to unbearable cold," Tar Fell grumbled.

"If you are so miserable," she asked, "why do you kill other kones for the privilege of being here? Why do you fight for Genellan?"

"I care not for this planet," Tar Fell snapped. "I care for what it signifies. My personal feelings and yours matter not at all."

The lock slid open. Surprisingly, Tar Fell paused for Kateos to depart first. She nodded demurely and entered the landing trunk. Scientist Dowornobb, attended by a brace of technicians and a platoon of troopers, waited for her. Against all social convention she ran to her mate, embracing him passionately, their love essence and tortured happiness filling the room.

"Ack, Scientist Dowornobb." Tar Fell coughed, covering his gash of a mouth. "As you can see, the king's ambassador is without injury. Now, enough of that. What technologies can you show me?"

Gently, Dowornobb pushed away, russet eye tufts lifting with livid emotions. The raw-sewage smell of his anger suffused the confined space; the air circulation systems, already laboring, whined into high gear.

"I am ready to begin experimentation," Dowornobb growled. "Will you provide me with the means?"

"Of course," Tar Fell replied. "And as a reward I will even allow you a few weeks with your mate. For your sake and hers, I hope you have something of substance to reveal."

Godonov and Lizard Lips followed the marines into the null-grav physical training compartment. Lizard Lips maneuvered adroitly, his atrophied flying spines wiggling like twin dorsals on a fish. Dozens of the ship's crewmen were in the sweat-smelly compartment. Spacers were required to exercise. Attendance and workout quality were tracked by robotic equipment networked with medical computers. Log files were maintained for all hands. Noncompliance with physical training requirements was a serious violation of fleet regulations.

The null-grav facility was popular because of the game rooms. The smaller half-gee facilities in the H-ring were used for workout regimens requiring a gravity load; this was considered drudgery. A wealth of team sports and competitive coordination activities had been developed in zero gee. Marines also used null grav for team training.

A tall, lean marine captain in PT gear was waiting.

"Let's go, marines," Chastain bellowed, saluting the captain. Shouting fanatically, the marines dove into the game room, shedding docking hoods and fatigues until they were stripped to PT gear. Telemetry monitors were attached, and player IDs were logged into room sensors. Godonov and Lizard Lips floated up to an observation window.

"Lieutenant Commander Godonov, sir?" the captain asked. "Captain Buck, landing company commander. Glad you could come down. We were hoping to get your help and the participation of . . . that one."

"His name's Lizard Lips," Godonov said, shaking the captain's hand, "and he would be greatly offended if he wasn't involved. I'm Nes."

"Jim," the officer replied with a warm smile. "Great. We've got a long way to go, and the brass is watching." He canted his head toward one of the ubiquitous vid-cams in the corner.

"About time," Godonov puffed. "What got things going? Not enough work to keep grunts busy on long cruises into bug territory?"

"No, sir," Buck said. "The commandant chewed ass. This is high priority now."

"The hunters won't let you down," Godonov said, watching the activity inside the game room. "They ain't pretty, but they won't quit."

Chastain had divided the squad into two teams, a hunter on each team. A ball materialized from a centering hole. Chastain pushed off and captured it, jackknifing off the far wall and propelling himself gracefully toward one of the netted goals.

"Our job isn't pretty," Buck said. "We have a war to fight. We need your hunters."

Another marine broke for the goal; Chastain threw a rifle pass, and the marine deflected the ball into the net. The hunters watched intently, waving rapid hunter signs. Their long jaws chittered nonstop.

"Now you have to teach them to communicate?"

"Precisely," Buck said.

"They understand some spoken commands," Godonov said. "Lizard Lips has a reading vocabulary of over two hundred words and understands Legion verb-noun syntax."

"That's a good start." Buck nodded.

"We can help, can't we, Lizzy?" Godonov said, hand signing. The cliff dweller shrieked his concurrence.

"Besides," Godonov added, "I'm way behind on my physical training."

FORTY-THREE

SPRING AGAIN

Samamkook's only remaining operational set of reaction engines catastrophically overboosted on orbital deceleration. Her skipper captured orbit by hard docking with a succession of convoy ships, using the other ships' retro potential to the limits of available fuel to slow the combined mass. Yard tugs assumed maneuvering duties when momentum loads were lowered enough for their smaller engines. King Ollant's decimated squadron returned to Kon orbit, limping into maintenance stations around the Northern Hegemony's orbiting shipyard.

From an observation bubble on *Samamkook*'s bridge Ollant watched soberly while new keels under construction were vacated from production docks, making room for damaged ships. Repairs could not be effected without sacrificing the efficiency of production. How would Ollant create a fleet that would answer the Thullol-Ransans?

"How soon to marshal another attack force?" Ollant asked his staff.

"Two moon cycles at a minimum, Your Highness," Et Anitab replied. "Three, maybe four squadrons at the most. Proficient crews, Your Majesty, may be the critical hurdle."

Ollant's mood darkened from mere misery to profound depression. He pounded his head, trying to make ideas come forth. What could he do to stem the flow of events? How could he gain some semblance of control?

"Your Majesty," Et Anitab reported, "General Talsali and General Et Barbluis have requested a joint conference."

Ollant lifted his head from his hands. He calculated why Talsali might be petitioning; the PDF commander would accurately assume that Ollant would be draining more crews from

PDF defense stations. But why would Et Barbluis call? The southern noblekone had no love for the Hegemony.

"Yes, of course," Ollant replied, rubbing his great face. He imagined he looked quite desperate as he positioned himself.

"Connect," the king commanded.

General Talsali's venerable image appeared, followed by General Et Barbluis's golden countenance. The ancient warriors were obviously burdened with duty. Ollant wondered how tired he must appear. Et Barbluis answered his fears.

"You wear defeat poorly, Your Highness," the southerner rumbled. "Pray you do not wear it often."

"Generals," Ollant replied, stiffening his back. "To what do I owe this assessment of my complexion?"

"Peace, Your Highness," Et Barbluis offered. "I mean not to offend but to provide succor."

Ollant stared blankly at the screen, striving to comprehend those simple words. Talsali broke the silence.

"The noble-governed nations of the south," the PDF commander explained, "while insisting on diplomatic participation in the negotiations for human technologies, do not support the Thullol-Ransa Compact's belligerent actions."

Ollant pushed forward, comprehension lifting the pain behind his eyes. He stared at Et Barbluis with breathless anticipation.

"The southern nobility has assembled three squadrons of fighting ships," the noblekone said, "with experienced crews. We are prepared to join forces with the Hegemony."

"Why?" Ollant, nearly struck dumb, asked. "The effect on the defense stations will be disastrous."

"Yes," Talsali replied. "Planetary defenses are in shambles. You must reconcile this disturbance soonest. In that we all agree."

"Your Majesty asks why," Et Barbluis said. "The future is in the balance. Tar Fell seeks to control that future. Tar Fell's motives are base; he would have power."

"Are my motives different, Your Excellency?" the king asked.

"Great power you already have, Your Highness," Et Barbluis replied. "How that power is wielded is not in doubt."

Ollant bowed deeply, noblekone to noblekone.

The great river groaned, a loud, wrenching resonance.

"What the . . . ?" O'Toole, huddling close to the campfire,

gaped. Tatum jumped to his feet. The granite-vibrating creak made it sound as if the very planet were moving under Tatum's feet.

Finally! Spring was near.

"Did you hear that?" Fenstermacher shouted, throwing down his fishing line.

"Did I hear what?" Chief Wilson replied sweetly, reeling in his line from the hole in the lake ice. "You mean that little noise that made us all wet our pants? Whaddaya think, you little dumb shit."

"Come on," Tatum said, sprinting up the wooded moraine defining Lake Shannon's northern limit. O'Toole was right behind him. From a vantage point on the moraine Tatum scanned the river valley below. Nothing looked different, but the direct rays of the sun were just lifting over the riparian cliffs. Fenstermacher and Chief Wilson chugged up to join them, their breath glowing in the morning sun.

"Another false alarm," Wilson said. "It's too cold."

They stood there, watching. Minutes crept by; the sun's rays flowed across the wide riparian valley. Fog sublimated from the tortured convolutions of ice. Small birds clicked and chittered in the trees.

"The river must burst at this same place every year," Fenstermacher said.

"Why do you say that?" O'Toole asked.

"Runs east-west," Tatum said. "The sun hits it direct."

"Yeah," Fenstermacher said, "and it's damn steep, so there's a ton of head pressure."

No human had yet seen the ice break up. Tatum, frustrated with waiting indolently for winter's end, had announced plans to camp out on the lake moraine. O'Toole had immediately signed on, and to the delight of everyone in the settlement, Fenstermacher and Wilson had elected to join them. The four men had camped in the cold for five days.

Tatum stamped his boots and rubbed his ears. As cold as it was, winter was undoubtedly in retreat. The sun's rays actually imparted a sense of warmth. There had been a week of earnest snowmelt, and the last storms had started with drizzle. Hardwood limbs swelled with hints of bud color, and sugar trees ran with sap.

"Can't wait," Fenstermacher chattered, silence anathema to his very being. "Cabin fever's worse than eating Chief Cookie's cooking."

"Feel sorry for Les." Wilson laughed. "She's got to live with you."

"River's about to break," Tatum said, stretching his lanky body. Stretching was one of the times he most missed his arm.

"Aah, it's a false alarm." Fenstermacher sneered, turning and heading down the moraine. "I got fishing—"

The river made a crunching noise. And then it exploded.

Chunks of ice rained around them like shrapnel. Booming echoes reverberated across MacArthur's Valley. From a hanging valley high on the western slopes a block of icy snow the size of an asteroid was let loose in sympathetic pursuit of entropy. The tiny humans pivoted to watch the thundering avalanche scrape the mountainside. The cascade of rock and snow gradually lost energy in the high valleys, but a scattering of rocks tumbled through the trees. Truck-sized boulders bounded off a high escarpment, falling directly into the lake. The monoliths crashed through lake ice with a series of hollow, overlapping *car-r-rumphs*.

"The lake!" Wilson shouted.

A spiderweb propagated from the penetration points; the concussion and the massive displacement of water had generated a discordant ripple that raced across the lake. The pristine white blanket of ice was transformed from planar flatness into a blue and silver moonscape of ice shards.

"Fishing gear!" Wilson yelled. Fenstermacher and Wilson started down the moraine. A loud grinding lifted into the air, stopping them in their tracks. Its rising intensity was compelling.

"The river!" O'Toole shouted. Everyone pivoted back to the river.

A salvo of rending ice failures zippered white and glassy down the length of the valley, emitting a series of majestic groans and snaps. The grinding was transformed into a high-pitched metallic ringing as the stresses on frozen liquid built with inexorable force. Tons of water, sensing imminent liberation after months of compressed imprisonment, squirmed and probed for weaknesses and found them. Great gouts of water, hammered by hydraulic pressures, spewed fantastic distances into the air. Rainbows coruscated through the valley, visual punctuation to terrible ground-shaking tremors. Islands of ice lifted ponderously from the river in a convoluted, arrhythmic ballet. The larger sections collapsed as they rose, rending the air with thunderous reports. Ragged fangs of ice lifted, twisting and warping until they pointed vertically into the air.

Water, bursting free, scuttled across the unbroken downstream ice. Up and down the river the tumultuous revolt of one physical state of matter against another spread, blasting an inarguable path.

"Hoooo-aaahhhhhh!" Tatum roared, a primal scream, his deep voice blending with the river's icy thunder. Fenstermacher's tenor joined in, followed quickly by the bass howls of Wilson and O'Toole.

Cries of joy. Cries of survival.

With the coming of spring the MacArthur's Valley council was determined to define its status with the New Edmonton regime. Stark would not relent. He not only refused to resume work on the hydropower construction, he ordered all technicians and marines to remain at NEd. The council sent a delegation south.

St. Pierre sat in the copilot's seat and watched the immense planet roll beneath the airplane. Johnny Rodriguez piloted the Explorer down the great river. Snow coverage thinned with each passing kilometer; large patches of taiga, muddy and brown, passed down their right side. Countless pools and puddles of snowmelt reflected the rising sun, turning the endless prairie into a yellow gem of infinite facets.

St. Pierre yawned. He was fuzzy-headed from a poor night's sleep. They had just lifted from the fuel-staging field, where they had spent the night fending off foul-tempered bears fresh from hibernation. St. Pierre had finally had to shoot one of the monsters dead before it did damage to the airplane or to them.

"Damn big planet, ain't it," Sam Cody said, putting his head and shoulders through the flight deck door.

"What it is," Rodriguez replied, "is a big damn empty planet."

St. Pierre nodded. Empty. That was the way he felt. He had not gotten over Maggie's death, and he was not certain he ever could. He had even considered returning to Earth, to his old job. His life might have purpose again. And companionship. There were few, if any, unattached human females on Genellan.

Except for Buccari. Sharl Buccari would come back someday. That thought, that hope, seemed to carry more weight than all the rational arguments for leaving.

"That son of a bitch better start our hydro back up," Cody snarled, breaking St. Pierre's self-pity. "Stark gives us any more crap about how *untenable* MacArthur's Valley is, I'll—"

"He's got to listen to us," St. Pierre replied. "He may have the technicians and the materials, but we know how to raise food. Maggie's and Leslie Lee's work with the gardeners would have saved their harvest. They would have planted the right grains."

"When has Stark ever listened to good sense?" Cody grumbled.

A frantic cry reverberated in the airplane's interior.

"Rodriguez!" Nancy Dawson shouted. "Turn back!"

"What?" Rodriguez shouted. "We mess around and we'll have to make another stop for fuel. I'm not going over the mountains light."

"Check the east bank," Dawson said, pushing Cody out of the way. She pointed. "Someone's walking next to the river."

"A bear," Rodriguez muttered, yanking power and lowering the nose.

"Bears don't make ruts in the ground," Dawson said. "Look at the tracks whenever it goes over sand."

St. Pierre followed Dawson's finger and saw the wiggling parallel scratches in the ground. He traced the broken lines until he saw the form on the river's edge, dark and large.

"Two people," St. Pierre gasped. "One's being pulled on a litter."

Rodriguez banked over the river and dropped more altitude. He came back again, right off the water, slowing. St. Pierre stared out his window at the dark form. Definitely a bipedal hominid—a human. The one standing put down the litter and waved with both arms. It threw off its hood, revealing long silver hair. The one on the litter did not move.

"It's Commander Quinn!" Dawson shouted. "And Hudson!"

Quinn stared after the plane, letting her hand drop. It had disappeared around the river's bend, descending as if to land. The retreating engine noises, carried by a chilly breeze, suddenly ceased. Quinn listened to the gurgling river. She bent back under the straps, bruised shoulders protesting, and started walking, head down. She listened to the river and to the sounds of the travois as its trailing ends alternately grated through rocks and hissed through sand.

"They're coming, Nash," she gasped, her shoulders straining against leather. "Hang on, Nash."

Hudson, strapped between two boughs, remained quiet. Quinn stumbled forward, onward. She was so tired. She dropped to a knee. Exhausted, she let the straps slip from her shoulders. She crawled to the river and drank deeply, then filled a wooden cup with crystalline fluid.

She heard shouts in the distance and looked up. People were running up the river's edge. Not bears, not nightmares or dragons, but people. She crawled to Hudson's side. She lifted his head and tried to get him to drink.

"They're here, Nash," she whispered, her voice gone hoarse. "Nash . . . we're going . . . to be all right, Nash."

She looked up. She recognized Nancy Dawson's red hair and deep voice. Quinn started crying.

"Come on, Nash," she begged, sobbing. "We're rescued. Don't leave me, Nash. I need you."

Hudson's blue eyes opened, shining brilliantly from his sun-blackened face. His tortured mouth, cracked and blistered, split apart with a weak smile.

". . . time you admitted it," he gasped.

"Oh, Nash," she gasped, putting her cheek on his.

Suddenly there were shadows about her.

"Get them to the plane," a voice said.

Quinn looked into the eyes of her friends. Dawson lifted her to her feet. The settlers, Cody and St. Pierre—she was proud she could remember their names—examined Hudson. Cody had food. He put small pieces in Hudson's mouth while St. Pierre got more water from the river. They lifted Hudson's litter and started trotting up the river, with Dawson supporting Quinn. They walked one foot at a time. She had been walking all her life, walking along a wide river. She dreamed as she walked of a beautiful planet, warm and bountiful.

Someone was talking to her. She saw the yellow airplane and remembered where she was. They carried her inside and laid her on furs. Hudson. Where was Hudson? She lifted her head. Hudson's head was next to hers. They were head to head in the aisle. Cody was leaning over Hudson.

"How . . . is he?" Quinn rasped.

"He'll be all right," Cody replied.

Relieved beyond comprehension, she fell back on the floor of the plane, feeling claustrophobic, surrounded by the hard, angular fixtures of civilization. Suddenly she was very tired.

Dawson leaned over her. Quinn remembered something very important.

"Oh, Nance," she slurred, eyelids too heavy to keep open.

"What, hon?" Dawson asked, brushing hair from her forehead.

"I . . . think I'm pregnant, Nance," Quinn mumbled. "Preg . . . nant."

Dawson, leaning close, squeezed her hand.

"Me, too," Dawson whispered.

Quinn smiled for both of them as she lapsed into sleep.

FORTY-FOUR

RECOVERY

Antiseptic smells assaulted Quinn's sinuses as she came fully awake. It was dark. A medical robot enclosed her like a sarcophagus. The robot responded to her movement, removing electrodes, and extracting IVs. Its top half clamshelled away. A thermal blanket deployed over her naked body. A medical technician, moonfaced and concerned, scurried in.

"Commander Quinn," he said, beaming. "Welcome home. Everyone missed you, sir. The whole settlement fell apart when you left, and—"

A fleet physician appeared. Dour and pinch-faced, she cast a reproving glance at the med-tech and waved him aside.

"Good morning, Commander," the doctor said, checking readouts. "You've gotten some much needed rest. Four days in fact, although—"

"Four days! Where am I?" Quinn asked, squinting at bright lights reflecting from polished steel surfaces. "Where's Hudson?"

"Why, the New Edmonton infirmary," the doctor replied, "and Mr. Hudson is in the next unit. He's doing fine. Not as well as you, but then again, neither is he pregnant."

Quinn looked sharply at the doctor. It was not a dream. The doctor nodded knowingly. Quinn stared at the ceiling.

"He will have to go back to Earth for catastrophic reconstruction and—"

Quinn peeled back the thermal blanket, lifted her legs over the unit's rim, and struggled to sit upright. She was dizzy—and naked. The smiling med-tech handed her a medical gown.

"You need more rest, Commander," the doctor admonished.

"I've been away from my desk too long," Quinn said, sliding to her feet. "Work's probably stacked up." She took a stumbling step, holding on to equipment like a toddler.

"Clothes, dammit," Quinn muttered, throwing the gown aside. The doctor nodded, and the nurse ran from the compartment.

"Where's Hudson?" she mumbled. Her head pounded.

She looked down at her belly. It was flat; her hip bones were prominent. *Pregnant!*

"Mr. Hudson is undergoing regeneration therapy," the doctor replied, bringing up his chart. "Severe infections, fever damage, muscle deterioration, and a long list of other problems, but he's responding well. I anticipate full recovery of organs and tissue. He's young.

"Catastrophic failures are another matter. He'll require complete replacements of left knee and elbow. Hip and left shoulder severely damaged. Beyond the scope of even a full mothership medical facility."

"He was going back to Earth for skin grafts, anyway," Quinn said.

The med-tech showed up with a clean utility jumpsuit. Quinn slipped it on. She would need maternity clothes. The thought panicked her.

"These are yours." The med-tech handed Quinn a pair of Legion field boots. A new pair of thermal socks was stuffed inside. The boots were scratched and deformed by abuse, but they fit like old friends.

"Take these," the doctor ordered, giving her a battery of pills and a squeeze tube. "I want to see you tomorrow morning."

Quinn did as she was told and limped down the metal ramp leading outside. She emerged in the shadow of a cannibalized PHM, trying to reconcile the missing time. A truck awaited. She collapsed in the seat and told the driver to take her to the admin building. The truck departed from the row of planetary habitation modules, exiting a concertina-wire-topped composite wall through a guarded gatepost. Stark and his walls.

Beyond the wall the cleared fields began. Spring planting was under way. She saw settlers sowing seeds and clearing weeds. And cliff dwellers! Cliff dwellers? Two guilders—gardeners—waddled across the field, occasionally stooping to smell dirt.

"Stop!" Quinn shouted. She clambered from the truck, every muscle in her body protesting its usage. She was not hallucinating. There were cliff dwellers. Someone shouted. A short settler carrying a big rifle came running, long, black tresses flowing behind her. It was Leslie Lee. The med-tech ran up to Quinn and gave her an enthusiastic hug, better medicine than any other she had taken.

"We were so happy to hear," Lee bubbled, her face illuminated with a beautiful white-toothed smile.

"And I'm glad to see you," Quinn replied, "b-but what are you doing here?"

"Envoy Stark agreed to restart the hydropower plant at MacArthur's Valley," Lee huffed, "if we helped NEd grow field crops."

"Stark shut down the hydro construction?" Quinn nearly shouted.

"He tried to shut down our whole settlement," Lee said. "No one's told you? Maggie St. Pierre and a marine were killed."

"What?" Quinn felt dizzy.

"Major Faro killed them," Lee said, childlike face hardening, "trying to implement Stark's stupid orders. Major Faro's dead, too. Nightmares . . . got her."

Quinn's consciousness reeled with overload.

"NEd lost almost its entire harvest to rain and fungus," Lee continued. "They should have planted rice. Wheat's got to be put in a lot earlier. Stark traded MacArthur's Valley—"

"Trade?" Quinn said, regaining focus. "Trade, my ass."

"We would have helped you, anyway," Lee said.

"I know you would, Les," Quinn replied, growing angrier. "I've got work to do, Les."

"Right," Lee said. "And congratulations, Mom," she whispered.

Mom! It was like getting hit with a board. Quinn sagged with the thought. Her anger was eclipsed by confusion. It must have shown.

"Nance can't keep something like that secret from me," Lee said. "But no one else knows, Commander. You okay?"

"Yeah, Les. Thanks," she said, reining in her emotions. "I gotta go."

She turned and made her way back to the truck, anger welling with each slogging step. She would face her personal problems later. Right now she needed to deal with Stark. She climbed painfully into the truck and tried to organize her thoughts. They drove onto paved roads through an arched guard gate and into the settlement. Construction on the settlement dorms was still behind schedule, but the art deco facade of the yellow admin building was complete and the grassy park around it had been landscaped to perfection. At its center a fountain sprayed gouts of water from the mouths of sculpted nymphs.

The infirmary must have given warning. The steps to the admin building were crowded with spacers and settlers. They were cheering! Et Silmarn was there, too. As the truck stopped, she was mobbed by well-wishers. She made a short speech and chased them all back to their duties, leaving only Et Silmarn and a tall dark settler. She remembered Reggie St. Pierre, the husband of the woman who had been killed.

Et Silmarn stumbled as he drew close. St. Pierre heroically attempted to steady the huge kone. Quinn tried to express her condolences. St. Pierre, gaunt and tight-jawed, thanked her.

"But why are you down here, Reggie?" Quinn asked. "They must need you in MacArthur's Valley. Are you also helping with the planting?"

"It's not clear the colony leadership is concerned with MacArthur's Valley's best interests, Commander," St. Pierre replied, his eyes dropping. "Sam Cody and I decided that one of us should remain. Sam's got a family to . . ." He stopped talking and rubbed his face.

Quinn reached out and touched the man's arm. St. Pierre looked up and tried to smile. Et Silmarn moved his ponderous bulk closer and patted St. Pierre gently on the back.

"Et Silmarn," Quinn asked. "You had fled to MacArthur's Valley with Kateos and Dowornobb. Has Tar Fell's attack been repulsed?"

"No, Commander," the noblekone replied, eye tufts drooping down grainy cheeks. "It-ah is worse than ever."

"That's the other reason I'm here, Commander," St. Pierre intervened. "We made a promise to the kones—"

"Your-ah envoy gave us a guarantee," Et Silmarn rumbled. "He-ah has reneged." Et Silmarn sighed heavily and closed his eyes.

St. Pierre finished briefing Quinn. She was impressed with his incisive intellect. She was infuriated with Stark.

"You are very tired, Your Excellency," Quinn observed, containing her fury. "Is there something you need?"

"Your technicians have provided fuel for my breathing unit and a small heated and pressurized structure, but I am not sleeping or eating well. I worry so much."

One of Stark's grease-headed assistants came through the door.

"Commander Quinn," he said unctuously, "Envoy Stark would like to see you."

"Governor Et Silmarn, Mr. St. Pierre," Quinn said, moving for the door, "would you accompany me?"

"Envoy Stark wished to see you alone," the assistant said, dodging out of Quinn's way.

Quinn stalked into the administration building, Et Silmarn and St. Pierre at her heels. The elevator was working. Quinn exploded onto the third floor, scattering a gaggle of Stark's assistants. She strode into the main room of the envoy's suite. Stark stood at the balcony. Colonel Pak and Clancy, the settlement mayor, stood nearby, consulting a console.

"Ah, Commander Quinn," Stark gushed. "It is good to see you well. You have no idea how anguished we were when we thought—" His color changed as Et Silmarn and then St. Pierre walked in. Quinn glanced at the dark visages of her companions and could not decide whose was the more terrible.

"—you had been lost," Stark continued.

"I'm back," Quinn said.

"The surgeon tells me you should not be up and about," Stark continued, regaining his control. "Please sit down. I insist."

She took a chair, her back and legs accepting the respite. Stark continued to prattle, trying to defuse the tense ambience with avuncular nonsense. Clancy fidgeted. Pak stood at alert attention, impassive, hand on his pistol grip. Two more thick-necked security agents wearing red berets moved through the door and took up positions.

"We have a great deal of work to do," Stark lectured. "This—"

"Mr. Stark," Quinn said, "I am removing you from your

duties. You and your assistants will remain in the settlement. At no time will you or your assistants have access to radio communications."

"Now, now, Commander." Stark chuckled. "You have had a terrible experience. You should think about what you are saying. I am in the middle of crucial negotiations."

"Envoy Stark," Quinn said, her voice growing louder, "you are relieved. You will report to your quarters immediately."

The agents sidled nervously, their hands moving to their weapons.

"Don't be a fool," Stark blurted, his facade shattering. "You exceed your authority. Captain Gray gave you your orders. And Colonel Pak is the senior officer here. He reports to me. If you think—"

"Shut up!" Quinn barked. She transferred her attention to Colonel Pak. His expression was fathomless, his posture, as always, formal.

"Colonel, do you question my authority?" she demanded. Pak's hand dropped to his side. Only the sounds of Et Silmarn's breathing unit broke the silence.

"I welcome it, Commander," Pak replied.

FORTY-FIVE

STALEMATE

"Can the chatter," Wanda Green shouted, gliding to the briefing console. "Scorpio Minor jump-out in three hours."

Eagle Squadron's nervous hum was clipped to silence. Buccari looked up from her console to stare at the faces of her squadron mates. They were sitting by rows: ship commanders, first officers, and second officers, three distinct generations of corvette pilots—a hierarchy. They were all frightened; some handled it better than did others.

Buccari's crew was unassigned; crew Six Bravo would be

sitting out the launch. Pulaski's crew would take the Six bird. She did not like riding the bench; it freed her mind to think, to worry. Images of her son—and other memories—intruded on her tenuous peace of mind.

Lizard Lips floated at her shoulder, using the communicator to ask questions—good questions but poorly timed. She waved him to his station against the bulkhead, where he immediately started querying his own terminal. The tense excitement escalated.

Commander Carmichael floated up from the rear of the ready room, his demeanor intense. Green suspended her briefing.

"Pilot change," Carmichael said. "Sanch-man is medical down. I'm putting Buccari's crew in the Three bird. Castro, you're flight lead."

"Aye, Skipper," Castro shot back, confidence flickering from her angular features. The senior corvette pilot turned in her seat and gave Buccari a sterile wink. Buccari felt an adrenaline surge.

"Take care of my 'vette, Booch," Oskar Sanchez said. The squadron ops officer rubbed an anemic face and forced a smile. Official word was that he was fighting an ear infection, but Buccari suspected something more serious. Sanchez's morose expression did little to allay her fears.

"Like it was my own, Ops," Buccari said, smiling back. Sanchez's disconsolate features softened at her glance.

Buccari looked up as the duty officer logged the changes, sending new orders to the crew areas. Buccari watched anxiously until her department heads mustered electronically, acknowledging the ship change. She consulted her briefing station and punched up the mission profile. It was a straightforward reconnaissance mission: stand off from the planet and investigate the primary moon. Castro was amending the flight-lead briefing on-line. Buccari read the additions and acknowledged.

"Okay, Mr. Godonov," Green announced, "science brief."

"M796 is a binary system," Godonov reported, floating to the front of the room. "Designated Scorpio Minor." Godonov triggered the wall display, illuminating a three-dimensional representation of the system. The screen zoomed in on the icon representing the secondary.

"System primary is a dead red," Godonov continued. "The

secondary is a remote and energetic G-star with at least five orbital bodies. Bravo Two is our focus."

The briefing image continued to localize until it isolated the icon for a planet with a single moon. Ecliptic lines and polar references illuminated, providing a reconnaissance grid. Mission vectors and range limits were schematically depicted. Buccari double-checked the grid reference with the nav system on the number three corvette. Godonov finished off the science briefing.

"Eagle pulls screen duty on the next rotation," Green announced. The ready room broke into boos and hisses. "So enjoy your recon assignments. Skipper and Pulaski have the equatorial orbit. I'm taking Chang around the poles."

"In your dreams, Art," Pulaski stage-whispered.

"At least Chang has a chance, fat boy," Green snarled sweetly, "even if on the ugly side of piss-poor." Pilots hooted at Pulaski's expense. Green's baleful glare snuffed the commotion.

"Castro," Green continued, "you and Booch have the moon."

"The moon platoon," Pulaski crooned. Castro gave her neighbor a bored glance. Green's eyes rolled in her head. Buccari stifled a laugh. The ready room's somber mood was lifting.

"Blackhawk is screen commander," Green patiently continued. "Sector screens and frequencies as briefed. You buttheads better know that drill by now. No emissions. Emcon I. As in silent, no bullshit on the air. Anybody squeaks, they answer to me." The XO floated squarely in front of Pulaski and glared.

"Any stupid questions?" she demanded.

His cherubic features bunched into an angelic smile, but even Pulaski acknowledged the gravity of the moment. The mission board was set; the brittle nervousness evinced earlier was tempered with professional focus and no little apprehension. Carmichael drifted to the front of the ready room.

"Eagles," he said, studying each of his corvette commanders. "This is the farthest fleet units have probed on this U-radial since Shaula. We're not expecting trouble—we're looking for it."

The ready room was silent. Carmichael had put their fears to voice. The whispering of the ship's circulation systems was distinct. A hatch clanged shut. Buccari looked around. Lizard Lips was alert, listening, dark eyes darting, maw cracked open to reveal rows of white teeth; even the cliff dweller felt the palpable tension.

"Follow your leads," Carmichael continued, gathering his flight gear. "And don't do anything stupid. Saddle up."

"Let's go, kiddies," Green added. "Tactical laser at flight leader's discretion. Heads up. This could be a hornet's nest. You best be ready—and quiet—or you'll be dead."

The pilots elevated from their stations without the usual banter and filed to the hatches, their thoughts and fears turned inward. The silence was deafening. Flaherty belched like a pig. Pulaski, not to be upstaged, lifted a leg and farted thunderously.

"Ah, tradition!" Green sighed, latching on to the overhead and fetching Pulaski a vigorous impulse with her boot, providing a graphic illustration of Newton's laws.

Eagle pilots streamed through hatches and dove for the crew chutes. Buccari followed Bart Chang down chute four and through a set of bladder valves. Pressure differentials sucked her along. Sequence locks cycled and spit her into the hangerbay crew manifold directly above the corvette stack. Buccari pushed down the number three crew tube.

Three tedious days later the two-ship section constituting *Eagle Five* and *Eagle Three* completed a reconnaissance approach to the debris-ringed moon. The dimly cast satellite hung suspended in star-glittered blackness. In the stellar distance beyond was its parent, a luminous planet. Both bodies were transformed into crescents of light by the orange sun-star. In the greater distance, beyond the local sun, was the system primary, an intense crimson flare.

"Not much," Godonov reported. "Just an iron-bound rock. I'll push out a monitor drone. No need to go any closer."

"Roger that, Nes," Buccari replied, checking tactical. Debris orbiting the moon gave the sensors fits, generating intermittent movement alerts. She increased range, desensitizing the resolution.

"One more dead satellite cataloged for the betterment of humanity," Flaherty offered. " 'Bout time for us buckaroos to mosey back to the corral, ain't it, Skipper?"

"Buckaroos?" Godonov protested.

"We passed our reconnaissance limit two hours ago," Thompson added. "Castro's not—"

"Last time I checked, us buckaroos were flying wing,"

Buccari replied dryly. "As in we follow, Commander Castro leads. Simple concept called the chain of command."

"Skipper!" Godonov shouted over the science circuit. "Burst intercept. Eighty percent indicator of intelligence, and it doesn't break. It's encrypted."

"You sure it's not a corona pulse, Nes?" Buccari asked.

"Looks solid, Skipper," her science officer replied.

"Laser-link to flight lead," Buccari ordered, tweaking the range on the tactical display. There was nothing definite.

"Radiating contacts in sector two!" Gunner Tyler shouted. "Fast-movers be coming through the moon ring."

"*Eagle Three* painting bogeys," Buccari broadcast on laserburst.

"Five has 'em, sector two," Castro responded. "Okay, Eagles, engagement spread. Buster in three seconds."

"Thought we were on a recon mission," Thompson said.

"Castro's crazy," Flaherty announced.

"*Commander* Castro, Mister!" Buccari snapped, silently agreeing. There was no percentage in a direct attack this far from their motherships. Where were the alien motherships?

"Taking combat separation," Buccari obediently replied over tactical laser. "Battle stations!" she announced over the intercom.

Flaherty sounded the maneuvering alarm. Buccari pulsed lateral thrusters, moving her ship away from Castro's corvette. She watched telemetry readouts. Split seconds before command acceleration, Buccari pushed her throttles to full military. The acceleration couch pressed into her back like a kicking foot that would not go away.

"Seven gees," Flaherty grunted. "Eight . . . eight point f-five. Accumulators draining."

"Bogeys. Three of them. Altering course to intercept," Gunner Tyler reported. An acquisition warning alarm burped. "We be targeted. Coming right at us they are."

"Should've beat feet back," Thompson moaned.

"Enough!" Buccari snapped. *This is stupid.* She checked tactical. The bogeys still showed as unidentified threats; course and speed readouts firmed up. Engagement warnings illuminated.

"Weapons status, Flack," she demanded. Targeting alarms yodeled steadily. A headlong attack at low fuel was insane yet exhilarating.

"Hot," Flaherty replied, disabling the alarm. "Real hot."

"Okay, Eagles," came Castro's voice, pitched high and loud. "We're going right through them. Energy control is slaved to my command. Break left after contact. Program firing decoys and jammers."

"Shit," Buccari mumbled, noting the telltale sequencing diodes on her tactical board. *You can have the damn decoys. Give me my guns.*

"Sir?" Flaherty asked, looking up.

"Nothing," she snapped. "Stand by to barrage-fire kinetics."

"Closure speed point eight. Doppler compensators engaged," Tyler reported. "Thirty seconds to cone."

"Roger cone," Buccari replied, gloved hands gripping the sidestick and throttle. Without warning her throttles retarded, inexorably, of their own accord, the engagement program taking control.

"Power back for energy accumulation," a synthesized voice announced.

Buccari jerked her hand in frustration. She used her eye cursor to interrogate the readiness of her ship and its weapons systems. Energy reservoirs on the directed-energy weapons—the laser cannons—climbed steadily to maximums. Every nerve ending in Buccari's body tensed with electric anticipation. She pushed air from her lungs and focused on tactical. A decoy launched with a thud.

"You have fire control on the kinetics, Flack," Buccari announced for the log, "and permission to engage."

"This is Lieutenant Flaherty," the copilot announced. "Solid acquisition. Flight deck has fire control."

"I wish," Buccari said under her breath, pulse quickening.

"Ten seconds to contact," Gunner Tyler reported.

"Hard lock on the starboard ship," Flaherty reported. "Solid locks—optical, radar, laser, and butt pucker."

"Five seconds," Tyler reported.

"Get 'em, Eagles!" came Castro's voice.

"Barrage-fire kinetics, now!" Buccari shouted.

"Pickle, pickle, pickle," Flaherty sang in a nervous falsetto.

Her corvette vibrated at an insanely high pitch as the ship's energy cannons, triggered by the battle program, unleashed their stored potential. The utter blackness of space flashed incandescent. Helmet filters *clickety-click*ed with active shielding as the engaging ships swept past each other at time-distorting velocities.

Despite the frenetic compensation of her active visor,

Buccari suffered moderate flash blindness. She clenched her eyes shut and willed the yellow and white images from her optical nerves. She opened her eyes again and frantically focused on tactical. *Eagle Five* was gone!

"Two breaking left!" she transmitted in the blind, spinning the corvette flatly about its vertical axis. "Lead, where are you?"

Eagle Five was no more—no transponder, no return, no Petri Castro, no corvette, no crew. Buccari punched the throttle to military.

"G-got ours!" Flaherty grunted against the acceleration. "F-flamed its bug-turd ass!"

"T-t-two be left," Tyler announced over the weapons circuit. "High, sector three. One is hurt."

"W-we t-took heat." Thompson choked. "Shield erosion sixty percent."

Buccari eased the power and increased the range on the tactical display. She checked relative bearing. There they were. For the moment opening distance, but the bugs were between her and the fleet. One of the alien ships lagged behind.

"Castro musta winged one," Thompson said, breaking the silence.

"They got the numbers," Flaherty said, "and they got position."

"And energy," Gunner Tyler added over the weapons circuit. "They have bigger guns. They ganged up on Five. The one we took out had discharged primary. We were hit by two pulses, but they be secondaries."

"Engineering, how do we look?" she asked, simultaneously checking her power board. Laser cannons were back to eighty percent. Engine instruments were in the green.

"Power plant's four-oh, Skipper," Chief Silva replied excitedly. "We'll get you wherever you need to go."

"Well, wherever we're going, we're going like a bat outta hell. I want everything you can give me," she ordered, overriding the battle program and grasping the heavy throttle. She punched in a squirt of attitude thruster and set her nose on a pursuit curve for the leading alien ship. "Stand by for full emergency."

She trained her helmet cursor on the weapons board and triggered buttons. The tactical hologram went blank.

"You shut off the targeting radar!" Flaherty blurted. "And acquisition. Wha—"

"You got optical," she snapped. "You remember how to bore-sight and jerk a trigger, don't you?"

"Gimme the laser seeker, at least," her copilot begged.

"When I tell you. And Flack, when it's time to dance, you may not have full power on the cannons, so don't start the music too soon."

"Golly, Skipper," Flaherty whispered over the flight deck circuit, "I love it when you talk romantic." Thompson giggled nervously.

But his laughter choked as Buccari shoved the throttle to the detent and disengaged the stops, simultaneously jamming the position lock and grabbing the acceleration grips. Her helmet snapped into the acceleration tether, her vision tunneled, and the corvette shuddered against the drag of its own internal inertia.

"Nine g-gees," Thompson grunted. "F-fuel f-flow surging. R-red line. T-t-ten gees. Arrggh! Twel . . . t-twelve."

Struggling with her vision, Buccari scanned the passive detector screens, laboring to pick up the lead alien, the apparently healthy one. An infrared scanner beeped and then localized. There it was, still tracking the inertial pipper. With her sharp attack angle and exploding acceleration the intercept solution was quickly pipelined.

"T-target angle be one-eighty," Tyler reported. "Coming at their rear."

Buccari pulled power. The drastic acceleration reduction felt like diving into a thick liquid. Energy-weapon accumulators had been sucked low by the emergency power dash. She watched potentials slowly increase to adequate firing levels.

"Surprised them, Skipper," Flaherty gasped, working his firing solutions. "That sucker's sitting on course and speed."

Acquisition warnings brayed. Her unsuspecting target suddenly veered to a new course, but it was too late. *Eagle Three*'s overtaking speed was too great.

"She's breaking," Flaherty reported.

"Okay, Flack, laser ranging," Buccari ordered. "Hold your fire until even you can't miss."

"Aye," Flaherty grunted, his reply trailing into an obscenity.

"The damaged one just went buster," weapons reported. "It was decoying. It's behind us."

"I like it better this way," Buccari said, unlocking the radars with her helmet cursor. "Now, Flack! Radar's back up."

The tactical display illuminated, revealing the situation plot.

Both alien ships were designated with threat halos. Their corvette's status was pegged at the highest order of imminent danger.

"Target be turning!" weapons reported. "We're lit up."

"She's all yours, Flack," Buccari barked, knowing that the energy depletion of a weapons discharge would prevent her from accelerating to escape speed before the other alien was within firing range. One chance to level the odds and then . . .

"Firing," Flaherty reported matter-of-factly. "In his kitchen."

The enemy ship was visible in the laser range finder, its bearing moving noticeably to port. In the blue-shifted blurring moment before *Eagle Three* streaked past, the enemy ship glowed and vaporized.

They were by. Cheers exploded over the intercom.

"Scratch number two!" Flaherty shouted.

"Can it!" Buccari snapped, staring desperately at the energy accumulation indicators and fuel. "We got big trouble."

She spun the ship, directing the nose at the onrushing alien.

"Ripple-fire decoys!" she shouted. "Lay a pattern of kinetics! Weapons, maximum jamming."

The corvette resonated with ordnance discharge. Buccari desperately scanned her reservoirs, knowing there would be insufficient recovery for even a minimum-range cannon shot. The alien moved in for the kill.

"Decoys!" she ordered, helpless. "Stand by for—"

The alien's energy blast enveloped them with blue-pink heat. The ship's electrical systems surged. Overvoltage warnings glared across the board, but the sharp power oscillations dampened quickly. Ozone warnings were triggered on the environmental panel and flickered out.

"Shields are fried!" Thompson cried, laughing to be alive.

"Bug fired out of range!" Flaherty reported. "She got fooled."

Buccari checked the scintillating tactical display. Though saturated with false signals and threat indicators, the alien ship was still decipherable. It had veered to parallel her course, holding at range limit and opening slightly, no doubt also desperately trying to rebuild its power reserves.

Buccari used precious fuel to goose her ship into formation with the alien, at range limit, setting up a deadlock. *Eagle Three* no longer had the power to escape but could still kill. Buccari set positioning parameters on the maneuvering controller and sat back, watching the sinister silver glint of her new lead ship.

"Skipper, what the hell?" Flaherty howled. "Why didn't you keep opening when you had the chance? We're out of fuel."

"They don't know that," she said.

Whichever ship accelerated toward the other would lessen its energy reserve. The ship holding the defensive position would have the advantage. She had maneuvered her ship into a deadly embrace, pacing the enemy craft exactly at the energy range limit.

"Why isn't it attacking?" Thompson whispered. "It's got more power."

"They don't know that," she repeated.

The two ships held position, arm in arm in the greater void, racing above the ecliptic of the system—a stalemate. Buccari scanned her instruments, desperately searching for inspiration. Her ship was fuel-critical. Combat maneuvers would exhaust the remaining fuel within a few seconds. Buccari stared into infinite blackness.

"Fay gay see mang?" an unholy baritone commanded.

Buccari jerked her head to stare at her copilot.

"Who—" Flaherty blurted. "Comm, where'd that come from?"

"UHF, sir," Tasker squeaked. "Over the radio."

"Jumping frigging Jupiter! It breaks!" Godonov shouted over the science circuit. "Chinese! Damn bugs are speaking Chinese. He wants to know your name!"

"The bugs," Thompson blurted, "speak Chinese?"

"Godonov, are you serious?" Buccari shouted.

"Fay gay see mang?" the voice boomed again.

"Give him your name, Skipper," Godonov replied excitedly. "Keep him talking. I've got all frequencies covered. I'll run your transmissions through a language converter."

"Golly, Momma, they speak Chinese," Thompson repeated softly.

Buccari tried to think. No ideas came forth. Was it a trick? She depressed the transmit button.

"Buccari," she replied, breaking regs and broadcasting. She forced herself to speak slowly. "Planet Earth. Who . . . w-what is your name?"

Long seconds of silence greeted her.

"Aw dig mang a'yerg," the booming reply rasped. *"Aw ulaggi. Boo-charr-ri da dug ho. Joy da, boo-charr-ri."*

"Name is Ahyerg," Godonov translated breathlessly. "I am Ulaggi. Buccari fights good. We fight again, Buccari. End of transmission. Keep 'em talking, Skipper!"

Before Buccari could respond, the alien's engines erupted, transforming her glistening adversary into a receding meteor. Buccari's visor clicked dark and then lightened in stages as she watched the alien disappear.

"Holy-bucktooth-moly," Godonov shouted over the intercom. "Wait'll you see these numbers. That plasma sucker was radiating all over the place. I ran a full spectral analysis. Got ion signatures on—"

"Tasker, send out a flash oprep," Buccari overrode, "and order up a fueler. We'll need a plug if they want us back this century. Nes, link data back to fleet. Fun's over; everyone back to work."

Buccari opened her scanners to full radius and checked the track of the alien ship. It was no longer accelerating, but its course was undeviating, down into the ecliptic and outbound from the sun-star to a rendezvous with its motherships.

Buccari concentrated on the needs of her ship. She sounded the maneuvering alarm, swung the nose of her corvette toward her own rendezvous coordinates, set the throttle to maximize velocity for the available fuel, engaged computer control, and punched the igniters. Programmed acceleration was no stronger than a whispering breeze.

Aliens, the killers of Shaula—they had learned the language of their victims. Were AC prisoners still alive? Were these aliens the Killers of Oldfather? If so, this was humanity's third contact with the marauders. This time there had been survivors. No, not survivors. Victors!

When would the next contact come? The inevitability of conflict was not in doubt. She thought briefly, achingly, of her son and realized with pain in her heart that she was where she belonged. Her destiny was to fight the aliens—the Ulaggi. She was ready. A sense of anticipation swelled within her breast; she was ready to engage, to exact revenge.

No, she wanted to kill.

FORTY-SIX

WE HARDLY KNEW YOU

Runacres had found them. He pounded gauntleted hands together.

"Damn fool pilot!" he shouted into his helmet, deafening himself with rage. His fleet stood at general quarters, fully grid-linked and ready to jump, waiting to make peaceful contact with a vicious enemy. Waiting, hoping, praying.

"Did you say something, sir?" Wooden asked meekly, still suffering from the admiral's temper.

Runacres glared knives at his group leader and stifled his fuming ire. Wooden's corvettes had made contact, and they had attacked! He debated relieving the group leader and Carmichael of their commands. He forced himself to be calm.

"Science, status on the probes?" Runacres demanded.

The science duty officer's image appeared on Runacres's screen but was quickly overridden by Captain Gray.

"Nothing since the ephemeral, Admiral," the chief scientist replied. "In our opinion they've jumped, Admiral."

"All corvettes are back on board, Admiral," Wooden reported.

"Three hours to scheduled jump, Admiral," Wells said quietly.

"Very well," Runacres replied, pushing off. Commander Ito stirred from the relative safety of a bulkhead station. "Lay another pattern of communication buoys. Commence HLA checks. We jump for Hornblower in three hours." He dove for the down-bore, his aide trailing.

Runacres departed the transport core at Level Five. As the Admiral entered the intelligence spaces, he heard a loud angry voice. He floated around a bulkhead and saw Carmichael in the passageway, helmet jerking at the end of its tether. The squadron commander's color was high. The big man confronted a short flight-suited officer still in helmet—Buccari. A half dozen disconcerted science and intel officers orbited Carmichael's hot burning sun.

"What the hell were you doing?" Carmichael raged through clenched teeth. "Attacking at range limit! Running yourself out of fuel! You were outnumbered and outgunned. What—"

"Dammit, I was following Castro's lead," Buccari snapped back. She pulled off her helmet, eyes flaring like green novas. "I was following my lead. Check the telemetry ... Commander!"

Carmichael's eyes softened. He opened his mouth to rebut her but then closed it tightly. He blew out a lungful of air and moved as if to touch her, his expression revealing some inner wound.

"Admiral on deck!" someone shouted.

Runacres glided up to the gathering and looked slowly around, his eyes resting on Carmichael. "Let's hold this *debriefing* in the proper chambers, shall we," he said.

"Sorry, Admiral," Carmichael said. The big man's chiseled face showed a peculiar strain, a visible display of stress. Carmichael was a combat-tested warrior. Something else was in this equation.

"You damn well should be," Runacres replied, giving no succor. "For those not already in violation of regulations, relax helmets," he added, removing his helmet and floating into the putrid-pink debriefing room.

Postflight lasted hours. Carmichael led the exhaustive questioning. Captain Gray joined them. Flaherty and Thompson were ordered in to assist Buccari and Godonov as the scientists re-created the events and provided technical assessments. Tactical playbacks and trajectory profiles were analyzed. Runacres could only shake his head at Buccari's power calls, given her fuel state. Pure genius or dumb luck.

"Quite a gambit, Buccari," Runacres said.

"Thank you, Admiral," Buccari replied, eyes darting at Carmichael.

"Not sure it was intended to be a compliment," Runacres said acerbically. "Let's go over the technical data again."

Captain Gray took over the debriefing, running science scans and electronic profiles. They replayed the alien's clear-voice transmission, its eldritch tone and arrogant tenor sobering all of them. Performance models for the alien ships were displayed on holo-projections. The computer-constructed emulation of the Ulaggi vessel represented an intimidating fighting machine.

"Still a lot of holes in the specs," Godonov temporized.

"Volumes compared to what we knew before," Runacres replied. "You did an excellent job under the circumstances, Mr. Godonov."

"Hell, Admiral," Flaherty snorted, "we parked Mr. Godonov's nose so close to the bugs, he could've checked 'em for hemorrhoids."

Buccari put her head in her hands. Carmichael stared at the overhead. Runacres made an effort to keep his demeanor appropriately stern.

"Fleet corvettes appear to be at a significant tactical disadvantage," Captain Gray said, breaking the bemused silence.

"If we hadn't run out of gas," Flaherty added, "we'd have flamed that bastard's ass, too. All they know how to do is attack. We—"

"Commander Castro's actions may be defensible," Buccari said, leaping in. "Had we attempted to evade, the Ulaggi might have run us down. By attacking, Castro created an acceptable outcome."

"You're rationalizing," Runacres said, making eye contact with Carmichael. "But there is one immutable fact."

The briefing room was silent, waiting.

"Our adversary may have more powerful weapons," Runacres said, "yet Buccari vanquished two of their ships. Legion units have finally inflicted damage on the aliens. Small compensation for Shaula and Oldfather but a victory nevertheless."

The room was silent.

"Now we've really pissed 'em off," drawled a voice at the hatch—Captain Merriwether's. No one had seen her come in.

Buccari was glad to see Merriwether. The flagship captain's presence dispelled the ragged tension in the room.

"Congratulations, Buccari," Merriwether said. "You just joined Carmichael in a select club—the only aces in the fleet."

"Living aces," Carmichael added, rubbing his eyes.

"No, sir, Captain," Buccari protested. "That's only four for me. One of my konish kills blew itself—"

"Bilge," Merriwether insisted. "You and Jack Quinn got fleet credit for that kill. Stop fighting city hall. Enjoy it."

"Mr. Flaherty, congratulations on your first two kills," Runacres said, shaking the copilot's hand.

"Thank you, sir," Flaherty replied.

"Flaherty was second pilot for Carmichael's kills," Merriwether added. "He's seen a lot of action."

"Right place at the right time, Captain," Flaherty replied.

"Shit magnet," Carmichael mumbled, giving Flaherty a half smile.

"Shit magnet, aye," Flaherty shot back.

"Admiral, all corvettes are recovered," Commander Ito interrupted. "Jump count is holding at a minute thirty."

"Very well," Runacres replied, putting on his helmet and pushing for the hatch. "We have a date with Admiral Chou. Carry on."

"Let's go, Eagles," Carmichael announced. "We have business."

She and Godonov followed their squadron commander to the down-bore. They dropped five levels to the midnight-blue decks of Level Ten. Flight deck crews waited in the ready room. Buccari stopped to stow her gear. Petri Castro's locker had been cleaned out. Buccari glanced into the ready room. Pulaski's seat cover had been moved over to the number five seat, and her name was now on Pulaski's old seat. She'd made the front row because Castro had died.

"Listen up," Carmichael announced. Buccari moved into the ready room, conscious of everyone's eyes darting to her.

"We lost *Eagle Five*," Carmichael announced. "Commander Castro and her crew died bravely. They went like warriors, in combat."

A soft, dispirited cheer went up.

"I want you all to remember this day," Carmichael continued, looking around, pausing to catch the eye of each crew commander. His gaze lingered on Buccari. She swallowed and glanced at her boots. Someone pushed a mug into her hand. A power bottle of an illicit amber liquid was passed around. It came to her next to last. She injected a ration into the mug and passed the bottle to Carmichael.

"Eagles, rise and remember," he finally said. "To those who go before us. To the crew of *Eagle Five*, our wingmates." He lifted the bottle toward the bulkhead, where the seat covers of *Eagle Five*'s flight deck crew were attached.

"Eagles," Wanda Green yelled. "Hip-hip—"

Mugs were raised, and three times Eagle Squadron

resounded with the full-throated yells of its pilots, not joyous but loud.

Buccari sucked down the whiskey, replacing her melancholy with intestinal heat. Her heart raced. She clenched her eyes shut, squeezing tears away. When she opened her eyes, Carmichael was looking at her.

Wanda Green grabbed Buccari by the torso harness and yanked her to the podium, pulling her into a big-bosomed hug.

"Booch took out two roaches," Green bellowed. "Eagle has another ace!" The ready room shook with triumph. Pulaski roared like a walrus, and the hunters added their own shrill accompaniment. Lizard Lips busily sampled the whiskey dregs. Buccari looked down at the deck bolts.

"Bart Chang, do the honors!" Green yelled.

Chang, at the duty officer's station, hit some buttons. On the status board Buccari's name, in garish crimson, appeared next to the *Eagle Six* primary skipper's slot. Two more bug icons, signifying alien ships dispatched to eternity, popped up next to her name, joining the three that were already there. Carmichael's name showed six trophy icons. Bart Chang and Oskar Sanchez had four apiece.

"Flaherty, get your ass front and center," Green ordered. Buccari's lanky copilot was manhandled forward by his squadron mates. Green and Buccari had to physically intercept his hurtled mass.

"Eagles," Green shouted, pointing to the board. "No longer a virgin, Flack Flaherty!" Chang illuminated Flaherty's two icons, and the ready room erupted in raucous cheers.

"Battle telemetry and tactical debrief after we jump," Green shouted, cutting off the celebration. "Wait until you hear Buccari's bullshit session with the bugs."

Pulaski yelled "Booch!" and another round of cheers lifted. The ready room chanted: "Booch! Booch!"

"Popcorn time," Pulaski bellowed.

Again Buccari caught Carmichael's sad brown eyes. This time he looked away.

FORTY-SEVEN

IN TRANSIT

In the numbing sameness of hyperlight there was nothing to do but one's job. Life was a routine, a haven of order and discipline.

"I stand relieved," Buccari said, saluting the oncoming watchstander. Another bridge watch logged, a small step closer to certification—a goal, a milestone, in an uncertain future. She collected her battle armor bag and pushed for the bridge hatch. It opened as she approached. Captain Merriwether came through.

"Captain on the bridge," Buccari announced, latching on to a bulkhead boss and arresting her motion. She assumed the vertical, as did everyone else on *Eire*'s bridge.

"Carry on," Merriwether declared. "Ah, Buccari, I was hoping I'd catch you." The mothership captain's expression was strangely sad.

"Sir?" Buccari responded.

"Ah, nothing." Merriwether laughed, not with joy. "Still standing bridge watches? Carmichael not keeping you busy enough?"

"He's keeping us damn busy, Captain," Buccari replied. "But I'd rather be up here busting my hump getting qualed than down in the ready room worrying about the next jump-out."

"Worrying? Your little kick-ass at Scorpio Minor has cranked confidence way up," Merriwether drawled. "The pilots I've talked to are actually looking forward to the next jump exit."

"That would make them fools," she replied. "I—"

"Lieutenant Commander Buccari, report to the group

357

leader's office," the sterile voice of her multiplex commanded. "Urgent priority. Lieuten—"

"Buccari," she said, terminating the call. "Excuse me, Captain, but I've been ordered to report to Captain Wooden."

"Good luck . . . Sharl," Merriwether remarked softly.

"Beg your pardon, Captain?" Buccari smiled.

"Let's not keep the group leader waiting," Merriwether replied, inspecting a deenergized tactical unit.

"Aye, Captain. By your leave, sir," Buccari said, saluting and pushing for the bridge hatch. As she floated through the command and control center, she wondered about her summons: Why was the group leader calling her directly? Where was Commander Carmichael?

She entered the group leader's underway compartments.

"Well, Buccari," Wooden said, eyes dark with fatigue. "You've done a remarkable job."

"Thank you, Group Leader," Buccari replied, suddenly even more suspicious. Why the past tense?

"Ah . . . you were on watch," Wooden said, avoiding her gaze, "or I would have called you in sooner."

"Sir?" she said.

"As you know," Wooden huffed, "Commander Sanchez has been taken off flight status, and with the loss of Commander Castro, Eagle Squadron is below qualification standards. I'm moving experienced skippers in from Grayhawk and Condor, and I'm transferring your crew to Condor. Commander Rowan is looking forward to—"

"Transfer! In the middle of deployment!" Buccari protested. Why? she wondered. But most of all she wondered why she was hearing this from the group leader and not from Carmichael.

"Crews are routinely exchanged between squadrons," Wooden replied. "I'll be cross-decking Mr. Godonov and the marines with you to continue attending to the cliff dwellers. Your team will remain intact."

"But Group Leader," she protested, "I would—"

"You have no option in this matter, Buccari," Wooden said.

"Aye, Captain," she replied softly. "Sir, I would just—"

"You're dismissed," Wooden said, returning to his console.

Head spinning, Buccari pushed for the down-bore. When she arrived at the ready room, someone else's seat cover was on her seat. Her crew had been removed from the board. Thompson was cleaning out their locker.

"We're Condors now, eh, Skipper?" Thompson said. "Flack's down in the hangerbay, checking out our new bird. *Condor Five,* primary crew. It's hot—a new kilo-mod. We're on for a 2130 shoot. Nestor's got the cliff dwellers on board. There's a steward cleaning out your—"

"What's the goddamn hurry?" she snapped.

"Only four weeks until jump-out. Commander Rowan's scheduled us for integration ops on the first watch. We'll be spending the next couple of days in simulation."

"We could've done sim work from *Eire.*"

"Orders, Skipper." Thompson shrugged. "They're posted."

"Yeah, yeah." Buccari sighed. "I'll be ready."

She pushed to the rear of the ready room, straight for Carmichael's compact office. Wanda Green and Sanchez looked up as she drifted in. Carmichael was not there.

"Sorry to see you go, Booch," Green said.

"Everyone is," Sanchez added.

"Could I see Commander Carmichael?" she asked.

"He'll be with the admiral for at least a couple of hours," Green replied. "I'll tell him you were by."

"Thanks," Buccari replied, pushing off, jaw tight. She left the ready room without looking back, no longer an Eagle.

She was a Condor.

Buccari made a standard approach to *T.L.S. Novaya Zemlya,* flying her new corvette by the numbers, slow and easy. *Novaya Zemlya,* "NZ" for short, was built more recently than *Eire.* She had a little more mass and a tad more beam at the hangerbays, but the familiar aspects easily outweighed the differences. Nevertheless, it was Buccari's first NZ approach, and she did not relax until the primary docking grapples reverberated against the corvette's hard points.

Commander Kyle Rowan, the Condor Squadron's commander, and Commander Zak Raddo, the executive officer, were there to meet them. She had her crew assembled on the crew deck when they came aboard.

"Welcome to Condor Squadron," Rowan announced. He was tall and spare with dark, deep-sunk eyes. "It's an honor to have this crew on our rosters. We've seen the battle telemetry on the Ulaggi engagement. And of course we've all heard of your skipper's exploits on Genellan."

"Hoot, hoot!" Commander Raddo blurted self-consciously.

Everyone on Buccari's crew stared at the XO as if he were naked. His swarthy complexion blushed purple.

"I brought the exec along to demonstrate our squadron chant." Rowan laughed. "You'll hear the 'Condor hoot' again."

"Hoot! Hoot!" Tyler roared, her already deep voice lowered another octave. Buccari's crew jerked with surprise. The hunters shrieked.

"Ah, Marigold Tyler." Rowan laughed. "Gunner Tyler's an old Condor; she's—"

"Don't be calling me old, Skipper," Tyler retorted, "or I be paddling yer tall fanny . . . sir."

"It's late," Rowan said after the laughter had died. *"Condor Five*'s in the simulators first thing in the morning. Let's get this truck secured and get everyone to quarters. *Condor Two*'s crew is standing by as escort. You have berths ready and waiting. Thank you."

Rowan departed. Raddo pushed over to Buccari and squinted nervously at the cliff dwellers. The hunters floated upside down, nostrils dilating, wing membranes slightly deployed to stabilize their positions. Godonov flashed some hand signs, and they backed away, chittering.

"Squadron's sim schedule's posted," the XO said. "You won't have time to scratch between now and the jump-out. You've got a standardization checkride, and your crew's been designated primary planet reconnaissance unit, 'cause you've got an embarked science officer and . . . because of your, ah . . . special marine detail."

"We'll handle it," Buccari replied.

"We'll help you handle it," Raddo said, smiling warmly. "Come on. I'll take you and your . . . friends to your staterooms."

"Let's go," Buccari replied, grabbing her duffel. Flaherty started whispering the Condor hoot. The others joined in one by one, the volume growing. The marines and the hunters in particular drove the incantation to a crescendo. The entire crew chanted as they flowed to the exit hatch, their individual chants being muffled and then disappearing as they pulled up and secured their docking hoods.

FORTY-EIGHT

PREPARATION

"Flotilla Two awaits your inspection, Armada Master," General Otred reported as Tar Fell boarded Otred's flagship. Flotilla Commander Magoon followed Tar Fell on deck. Otred was another arrogant Ransan but also an ex-PDF defense station commander and a proficient one. It had been Magoon's recommendation to elevate Otred to flotilla commander and to organize the armada into two flotillas. It was time; Squadron Six was approaching orbit, and Seven was lifting from Kreta.

"General Otred's ships," Magoon replied, "have demonstrated the best results of any squadron deployed."

"Faint praise, General Magoon," Tar Fell replied. "General Otred, are you prepared to fight? Are your ships and systems ready to engage the Hegemony? Are your crews ready to die?"

Otred, a short, extremely wide southerner, did not flinch. "I am wanting only two things, Armada Master," he thundered.

"Yes?" Tar Fell thundered back.

"My line assignment and your orders to attack!"

"Well spoken, General," Tar Fell said.

"Armada Master," Magoon ventured. "I have received word that Ollant's ships are intercepting our cruisers and ore loaders. He impresses any former PDF complement and returns them to General Talsali."

"A noble strategy," Tar Fell declared. "Order our ships to remain under the barrels of our defense stations or in PDF neutral zones unless traveling in squadron strength or greater."

"It will retard our training efforts," Magoon replied.

"So be it," Tar Fell replied. "Ollant will be hard pressed to sortie more than three squadrons this year. Our armada now numbers seven full-strength squadrons, and Ransan shipyards continue to lay new keels at greater rates than the Hegemony."

"There is rumor of southern intervention," Otred reported.

"This rumor concerns me," Tar Fell snarled. "Et Barbluis and the sinister pact of the nobility. If true, it will destroy Planetary Defense. Commoner-ruled nations would flock to our call, and we would have ten times Ollant's forces. It would be folly."

Tar Fell felt his eye tufts stiffen with incipient rage. His anger glands discharged, and his emotion bladders boiled.

"Armada Master," General Magoon said, involuntarily backing off, "I have received propitious information."

"Yes?" Tar Fell roared, anger simmering.

"Scientist Dowornobb is ready," Magoon said.

"Come, Generals," Tar Fell ordered, his rage flushed by excitement. "We are about to open the gates to the universe."

Ambassador Kateos was already in the command center, the expression on her face forlorn. She gazed at her mate with unshielded devotion. Scientist Dowornobb's image was displayed on the holo-vid. Tar Fell felt the power of the female's emotions, and suffered Dowornobb no little envy.

"Ah, good," Tar Fell rumbled, "the ambassador is here. Scientist Dowornobb, please proceed."

"How do I know you will honor your promise?" Dowornobb asked.

"You do not." Tar Fell laughed. "But fear not, scientist. I keep my word. Honor is not solely a trait of kings and northerners. Your mate has lectured me at length on the obligations of honor."

"Tar Fell speaks of honor, my mate," Kateos wailed. "Do not dishonor yourself. Do not reveal your secrets. They are for your king!" Kateos continued to plead with the holo-image. Tar Fell allowed the distraught female to unburden herself, relishing the exquisitely sweet perfumes of her sorrow. Finally Kateos's fire died. She floated head down, sobbing before the holo. Tar Fell moved forward.

"Ambassador Kateos," Dowornobb rumbled, his voice quavering, "have you finished?"

Kateos looked up and smiled at her mate. She nodded.

"Commence your experiment, scientist," Tar Fell ordered.

The vid-image split into four presentations: Dowornobb's image was in the top left; the top right screen was telemetric output; in the bottom two, one image backdropped by stars and one silhouetted against the planet, were four machines viewed from different perspectives. An orbital lander floated near one of the objects, providing scale. The machines were large and quite far apart.

"The engines before you are gravitronic grid generators," Scientist Dowornobb lectured, his voice growing stronger. The scientist's brow tufts stiffened with unconquerable excitement. "Permeating the ethers are gravitronic flux lines radiating on curvilinear paths from the origin point of the universe. These machines are capable of generating a gravitronic harmonic, a local resonance that flows into or away from the universal origin with nearly instantaneous physical translation. Lateral movement from the universal radial is possible, but—"

The scientist silently manipulated his panel. A quirky smile crept onto his bovine countenance. Dowornobb looked into the vid-cam.

"But I am talking too much," Dowornobb said. "A demonstration is more interesting. Please observe your screens."

Dowornobb fingered his panel. Fascinated, Tar Fell watched the orbiting grid generators, his eyes moving from one vid-square to the other. Tar Fell thought he detected an orange glow and a wavering. The machines disappeared.

"Where did they go?" Magoon demanded.

"Star Nappo," Dowornobb replied. "We think."

"You think?" Magoon laughed.

"It is a first step," Dowornobb answered defiantly. "Your scientists have verified my calculations. They have also delivered me interesting new specifications that support my hypothesis. I assume this information was provided by the humans."

"A step through the gates of the universe," Tar Fell replied, interrupting. "Scientist Dowornobb, I am impressed. The ambassador will be shuttled to the planet within the watch cycle."

"No!" Kateos shouted. "I choose to remain. The king's ambassador will remain on this ship. How else is she to conduct negotiations with the enemies of the Hegemony?"

"Kateos!" Dowornobb cried.

"Show him no more, my mate," she shouted, but the vid-link was interrupted.

"Deploy the fleet," King Ollant commanded.

Vid-images of Et Barbluis and Et Anitab saluted. The king's flotilla commanders turned to their chiefs of staff and issued movement orders. A long line of dreadnoughts activated propulsion drives and slid ponderously onto orbital injection trajectories for the planet Genellan.

King Ollant turned to the observation bubble on the bridge of the *Samamkook* and stared into star-slashed blackness. His battle-scarred ship took its position in the vanguard of the resurgent fleet—the Fleet of the Nobility. Kon and its moons fell behind.

Ollant was returning to Genellan with two flotillas. There were six battle squadrons: twelve battleships, twenty-four battle cruisers, and a convoy of fuelers and tenders. Ollant would not lose this battle, would not lose Genellan. In two moon cycles there would be a war to decide that planet's fate. Tied inextricably to the fate of Genellan was the destiny of the planet Kon, perhaps even the fate of the galaxy.

Irresistible forces were under way beneath domes of uncaring stars.

FORTY-NINE

NEW ARRIVALS

Ki perched on a sun-bleached log and watched the long-leg whelps frolic on the sandy crescent of beach, splashing in the crystalline water of the cove. A riot of moaning glory adorned the peninsula's tip, its leafy vine twining about fallen trees, its great white blossoms doubled in the lake reflection. The morning was advanced, with the moaning glory symphony reduced to desultory moans, plaintive and feeble. The sun's rays felt delicious on Ki's back and shoulders, tempting her to doze, but she did not. Her gaze swept the skies. An eagle had been spotted that morning, hunting the lake, by guilders arriving from the cliffs.

More cliff dwellers arrived every day: guilders and hunters. Fishers plumbed the lake shallows, building hatcheries behind cofferdams erected by stone carvers. Stone carvers also attacked the rocky ridge above the long-leg settlement, excavating caves and constructing terraces. Welling up from the rocks was ample spring water, but it was icy cold. Unlike the plateau, the rocks of the valley had no fire beneath them. These dweller caves would need many fireplaces.

But these caves also had the magic of the long-legs. Steam users laid conduits filled with a filament of pure gold. Already globes of luminescence burned white-hot, without wick or oil. But the source of the long-leg power was noisy and spewed noxious fumes. Steam users assured the adventurous valley dwellers that the noisy machine was temporary, that they would eventually have silent power, when the long-leg construction at the end of the lake was done. Steam users spent many hours studying long-leg construction methods.

Tall-red-hair shouted happily. Ki stirred from her thoughts, abruptly returning her attention to the lake. Had she been dozing? Tall-red-hair waded into the cove, pulling her hide shift up long white thighs. Thunderhead, screaming with joy, thrashed the water like a fish, easily eluding the long-leg female. Thunderhead swam well, much better than did the older long-leg fledglings. Ki had taught Thunderhead to dive and to ignore the panic in his lungs.

"Danger!" a hunter shrieked.

Ki jerked to bowstring tightness. The huntress heard the great eagle as it swooped around the peninsula headland, its wings cutting the air. Its fiery golden eyes locked onto the splashing fledglings. The tan and black predator came on, its talons spreading.

"Thunderhead!" the huntress screeched. "Dive deep for thy life!"

The long-leg whelp porpoised forward and was gone, leaving the other fledglings frozen with fright. Tall-red-hair screamed and bent to cover the children. Hunters erupted from the peninsula rocks, shortbows and crossbows twanging. Black-fletched arrows and bolts zipped the air, many thudding into the eagle's body. The eagle's attack wavered and broke. The raptor's great wings beat the air.

Long-leg death sticks exploded. Long-black-hair, sitting on the beach, fired first, and One-arm soon afterward. One-arm's shot blew the eagle's head sideways. The great bird fell into the cove with a tremendous, tumbling splash and was still.

Tall-red-hair and Long-black-hair scurried about collecting

fledglings. Long-black-hair grew distraught, looking frantically about. Tall-red-hair, hand over her mouth, touched Long-black-hair's arm and pointed toward the floating carcass.

To Ki's unending pride Thunderhead had pulled himself onto the eagle's breast, using hunter arrows for purchase. The child, balancing unsteadily on the precarious island, stood erect and screamed a low-pitched rendition of a hunter's victory clarion.

Warriors standing on the peninsula joined in raucously. The victory clarion completed, all the hunters sang tribute to the gods, raising to the skies the proud eagle's death song.

Construction at the MacArthur's Valley hydroplant had returned to full operation. A ringing saw blade made it difficult to communicate. At Quinn's direction Fenstermacher drove along the lake road, away from the noise. In the distance Quinn heard gunfire, not unusual in MacArthur's Valley.

"I appreciate your offer to assist with the administration of Legion affairs in MacArthur's Valley, Colonel Pak," Quinn said, "but I'm uncomfortable putting Legion security agents in responsible positions in both settlements. Everyone knows that Mayor Clancy is an agent."

"Was an agent! To everyone's benefit, Mr. Clancy has resigned from the agency." Pak laughed, his stern countenance transforming magically. Pak and St. Pierre exchanged meaningful glances. "I only offer to help. I would like to live in this valley."

"Of course," Quinn answered, burping. Her stomach was sour, and she woke up dizzy in the mornings. She wore baggy jumpsuits. "Reggie, you speak for the settlement council. What do you think?"

"It's time I made a confession," St. Pierre replied.

"Yes?" Quinn asked, suddenly nervous.

"I also came here as a security agent."

Quinn was thunderstruck. She could only gape.

"Crap!" Fenstermacher verbalized for both of them.

"Believe me," St. Pierre said wistfully, "my loyalties are with this settlement."

"I believe you, Reggie," Quinn replied.

"I trust Colonel Pak," St. Pierre said. "He and I didn't come to this planet to turn it into a police state. We came here to make the settlements safer places to live."

"St. Pierre deals in words," Pak added. "But I would add,

on Earth our profession, paradoxically, has a clearer purpose. We protect society against itself. Here living is surviving. There is as yet no self-destructive society. There is no state."

"Other than the state of nature." St. Pierre laughed.

"That I intend to enjoy," Pak said, "while it lasts."

Quinn started to reply, but with ear-ringing abruptness the metallic grinding of the sawmill shut down, its residual clanging echoing from the valley's walls. In the distance they heard the lodge alarm being roundly punished. The audio alarm on Quinn's admin unit beeped urgently.

"What is it?" Quinn said.

"Commander Quinn," the operator reported. "The fleet's back."

"You put forth an excellent effort, Hudsawn," Et Silmarn boomed in his own language. "Tar Fell enjoyed your debating prowess."

The noblekone held Hudson in waist-thick arms, bearing the human's lanky form effortlessly. Et Silmarn was not wearing a helmet; he rarely did in the admin building. Legion engineers had sealed off an inner sanctum and pressurized it with the hot acrid ether of a konish atmosphere. Hudson and Et Silmarn, together, occupied Stark's third floor suite, sharing it in a peculiarly tender symbiosis.

"That was no debate," Hudson muttered in Legion. "Tar Fell's got us between a rock and a hard spot." Hudson had just completed another a radio call with the contentious, imperious armada master. Tar Fell's demands had been disconcerting, but such was the nature of ultimatums.

"Under a rock-ah is more like it," Et Silmarn replied in Legion. Hudson could smell the sewage odor that signaled the kone's anger. He grimaced, but not from the stink. His pain never entirely went away. The Legion doctors wanted him immobile, imprisoned in their ineffective field tanks. No way. Cassy needed his help. There was too much to do. And now this. Now this.

Damn, and the fleet was back. Decision time. He so desperately wanted to see his baby born. He could not leave Cassy alone, pregnant and in the middle of a war. But he looked down at his useless legs. Who was he kidding? He was a useless cripple. He was adding to Cassy's burden. But, Lord, he wanted to see his baby. His baby girl.

Et Silmarn carried Hudson to the balcony and gently positioned him so that he could sit with a view of the broad, sweeping vista. It was a sunny, puffy-cloud day. Et Silmarn had become Hudson's legs. The kone was indefatigable, transporting the human everywhere. The odd duo had become a common sight patrolling New Edmonton, inspecting, teaching . . . leading.

"It's a good thing Fenstermacher can't see you carrying me around," Hudson remarked.

"Citizen Fenstermacher would not approve?" the kone asked, puzzled.

"He would compliment you," Hudson said with a laugh, "because your lips don't move when I talk."

"I do not understand," Et Silmarn rumbled, eye tufts drooping with bewilderment.

Hudson explained. As he did he searched the environs. NEd was surrounded with a sinuous contour pattern of dun wheat and variegated rice paddies. Beyond the cultivated acreage waved tall wild grasses of rippling emerald and yellow. In the nearer field of vision, settlement barracks were lined up like rectangular slabs along both sides of the central park. The austere buildings were mostly vacant, awaiting new arrivals. The first download of settlers had been moved from the dorms and established in agrarian hamlets along the ocean road. The settlers had learned to make adobe brick, as a stopgap because of the shortfall in composite-block production. Of necessity, settlers had also learned to kill grass dogs.

An electronic gong sounded—a high priority radio transmission.

"Urgent. Urgent," crooned a synthesized voice, the mellow tone belying the meaning of the machine-generated words.

"Yes," Et Silmarn thundered, effortlessly collecting Hudson and carrying him inside. Cassy Quinn's fresh blue eyes stared out from the holo-vid. Her face, framed with long silver-blonde hair, broke into a sunny smile as the duo moved within the vid-cam's pick-up. Behind her stood Chief Wilson and Reggie St. Pierre.

"It's about time you called in," Hudson chastised. "I'm getting kinda' tired governing this settlement for you. Oh, by the way, Admiral Chou's been asking for you. He dropped into the system for a visit."

"I just finished talking with the admiral," Quinn replied.

"I'll be taking off in ten minutes, and I'll be back in NEd before fleet units make orbit. I hope you haven't fouled things up too much."

"Et Silmarn and I moved NEd closer to the ocean," Hudson replied. Et Silmarn rumbled with laughter. "And I badgered the science weenies until they agreed to name the big moon Cassiopeia. They're going to name the little moon after our daughter as soon as you decide on a name."

"Admiral Chou will start downloading as soon as his motherships arrive in orbit," Quinn replied, struggling not to smile.

"I'm trying to be romantic," Hudson moaned. He wanted to touch her.

"Things are starting to happen fast, Nash," Quinn said, her face somber. Hudson knew what she was thinking.

"We're ready," he barked, dispelling his own turmoil. "We got a thousand more settlers to keep safe and secure. We'll handle it."

"I'm glad you're here, Nash," Quinn almost whispered, her lips tightening.

"There's another problem, Commander," Hudson reported.

"What's that?" she snapped, lifting her chin.

"The kones," Hudson replied. "They've detected Admiral Chou's arrival. Tar Fell demands to speak with Envoy Stark. Not to you, not to me. Specifically Envoy Stark. Until he does, he's refusing permission for more settlers to land."

"Shit!" Quinn groaned.

"Such unbecoming language," Hudson remarked.

"Guess what else?" Quinn replied sourly. "Admiral Chou's sensors have detected another fleet rising from Kon. King Ollant and Tar Fell are going to have another go at each other."

"Shit," Et Silmarn thundered, his expletive accompanied by a fulsome discharge. Hudson stared up at the angry giant and touched the grainy skin of his clenched fist.

"So our envoy made a pact with the devil," Quinn said. "Get Stark and call me back. Let's plan our strategy."

"Life grows more complex," Hudson said.

"One thing's clear," Quinn said. "You're going to be on one of those motherships when the fleet jumps. Stark, too, if I have my way."

"I'm not going anywhere," Hudson replied, "Mom."

* * *

"Armada Master," a crewman said. "We are receiving a transmission from the humans. Envoy Stark and Commander Quinn together."

"Yes," Tar Fell announced, feeling his power. Stark's downfall had little concerned him at first. But now that Scientist Dowornobb was being uncooperative, Tar Fell needed another source of hyperlight technology. The aliens wanted to land more settlers. A lever was at hand, along with a fulcrum.

Tar Fell moved into his communication area and sat before a comm screen. Displayed on split-screen were Envoy Stark and Commander Quinn. Tar Fell remembered Quinn as a younger, less weathered human.

"You have a request," Tar Fell broadcast. His armada had moved from orbit for maneuvers; there was an irritating two-second delay.

"Chancellor Tar Fell." Quinn spoke in high konish, her words clear and assertive. "We request permission to land one thousand settlers."

Brusque, to the point, with no effort at diplomatic maneuvering, so different from the envoy. Tar Fell wondered if terseness was the nature of the human female.

"I will permit the landing of one thousand human settlers," Tar Fell replied, responding in kind.

The humans waited anxiously as the signals carrying their words flew through the black vacuum. His reply received, the female breathed a sigh of relief. A poor negotiator; she was too obvious.

"On two conditions," Tar Fell thundered. The rising demeanor of the humans was crushed by the arrival of his words.

"And they are?" Quinn replied.

"Envoy Stark will be returned to his former status," Tar Fell rumbled. "I have need of his services, and I, uh, understand Envoy Stark's motivations."

The signal was received, and the female melted in her seat. Stark sat erect. The female composed herself.

"Stark is reinstated," Quinn replied. "Your other condition?"

"Envoy Stark, now that you are reinstated," Tar Fell replied, "my technicians will expect additional hyperlight specifications within the hour. Hold nothing back. That is my other condition."

The female turned and gave Stark a glance that would have been murderous in any culture, any star system. The envoy, apparently listening to the translation, closed his eyes and started speaking.

"It will be done, Chancellor Tar Fell," the translation began. "Please allow me to thank—"

Tar Fell terminated the connection.

FIFTY

HORNBLOWER SYSTEM

"Jump exit complete," Commodore Wells reported, his normally resonant voice tight with anxiety. "All units alpha-alpha."

"Contacts?" Runacres inquired, staring at the holo-vid of Hornblower Three. He studied screens, searching for aberrations, alert signals. There was nothing. No threat indications were manifest other than navigation alarms precipitated by the proximity of the planet.

"Negative targets. Board's settling out," Wells responded. "We're emitting. All sensors active. Communication buoys standing by."

"Launch communication buoys," Runacres ordered.

"Aye, Admiral," the tactical officer replied. "Comm buoys away."

"Any signals from the seed colony?" he asked.

"We have transponder only, Admiral," the flag tactical officer reported. "Transmission delay two seconds."

"Make course for standoff orbit," Runacres ordered, pulling off his helmet. "Alert Level Two. Grid Status One. Ahead full. Set the cruising watch. Battle armor, relax helmets. Stay alert, dammit!"

"Aye, Admiral," Wells replied, relaying the orders electronically. "Alert Two, Grid One."

"Corvettes away, Group Leader," Runacres ordered. "Deploy the screen. Let's get someone down on the planet."

"Aye, Admiral," Wooden replied, hitting mission launch.

Eire's watch boatswain piped "Attention" and passed the word.

"Lots of water," Runacres remarked. The planet stood proudly on the main vid, a lustrous teal-green, aswirl with clouds.

"Over eighty-five percent ocean," Captain Gray replied from science. "Temperate. Thick atmosphere, volcanoes, natural greenhouse."

Runacres looked down on *Eire*'s bridge. Merriwether's crew moved with nervous efficiency. The flagship captain strained against her tethers, her visored gaze jerking from one status board to another.

"What do your instincts say, Sarah?" he asked.

"Not liking it, Admiral," Merriwether drawled. "Something is very wrong. I'm counting the minutes until Admiral Chou arrives."

"Rendezvous window opens in ninety-three hours," Well replied.

"Four days," Runacres muttered. "At least four."

One by one the corvettes were shot into the void. She was next.

"Hoot, hoot," Flaherty grunted.

Acceleration pressed Buccari into her seat, dispelling her tensions; she was a pilot on a mission. Her corvette, *Condor Five*, lumbered down its launch guides and leapt into star-shot blackness. She hit the starboard stern thrusters, slewing the tail sharply to port.

"Clear angle," Flaherty reported.

"Mains," she barked, feeding in opposite momentum. She rechecked rendezvous coordinates and pushed the throttle to the standard acceleration stop. "Three gees."

Condor Five leapt forward. She held the 'vette's nose on a star and slammed in a vector. Condor lead was legging it.

"We're sucked," Flaherty declared. "We'll have to hammer it."

"Okay, Condors," Commander Rowan broadcast. "Buster, buster."

"Nine gees," Buccari grunted.

"Oboy! Hornblower, here we ... c-com—" Flaherty muttered, the words dying in his throat as Buccari shoved the throttle around the military detent. She grabbed the acceleration grip and labored to fill her lungs. The suffocating crush of power was sensual. Satisfied with her vector, she adjusted acceleration down to military. *Condor Six*, late on the power call, struggled to make formation. Trailing far behind the corvettes was the mission tanker, a fleet fueler, call sign Atlas.

Buccari noticed the corvette screen deploying ahead, forming a curved matrix across the fleet's forward vector. Transponder returns indicated units of Eagle, Grayhawk, and Kite squadrons taking positions in her penetration sector. A flight of Eagles held the center position. She linked to the screen matrix and was not surprised to see Carmichael's command code as screen commander. Eagle Squadron was shorthanded.

Her computer processed interrogations and provided the authentication signals necessary to penetrate the fire control barrier. She suspected Carmichael was observing Condor flight on his tactical screen. Feeling peculiarly deserted, she grew angry.

"Skipper, laser zinger from *Eagle Five*," Tasker reported.

"Go," she snapped, yanking power. She was closing smartly on her formation position. She engaged the station keeper, and the autopilot immediately started a gentle retro.

"Message reads: Eat my shorts, Hooter. End message," said the communication technician. "Any reply, Skipper?"

Pulaski.

"Negative," Buccari replied, feeling better.

Flaherty was tired of waiting.

It had taken over a day for Condor to make an orbit around Hornblower Three. Number Three and Four birds had assumed widely separated standoff orbits, maintaining direct laser comms with the approaching fleet. *Condor One* had established standard orbit on the polar trace, *Condor Two* on the equatorial. *Condors Five* and *Six* had descended to opposed landing support orbits, maximizing time over the seed colony's latitude. The fleet fueler was making its approach to orbit. Commander Rowan was SOPO, senior officer present in orbit.

Flaherty was tired of waiting, but his apprehension grew with each orbit. He was ready; the EPL was ready; the landing team was ready. Flaherty started another systems check on the Endoatmospheric Planetary Lander. *Condor Five* finished another mapping orbit. Other than the transponder signal, they had heard nothing from the seed colony.

"Datum's in the cone." Thompson made the routine call.

"Still nothing," Godonov reported from the survey lab.

"Any more biologics?" Buccari asked.

Flaherty's attention perked. Hornblower had an abundance of wildlife, including some nasty carnivores. Godonov's biological reports had been the exception to the nervous boredom.

"No change," Godonov reported. "Animal IR all over the place. Some huge stuff—elephant-sized returns and larger—in low areas near oceans. Nothing remarkable near the colony site. No personnel locators."

"Comm, send an oprep to Condor lead," Buccari ordered. "Orbit ten. No change. Request permission to drop in." Tasker acknowledged.

"Let's get this show on the road!" Flaherty grumbled into his helmet, his urge to land the EPL far outweighing his anxiety. He linked science screens and studied the data streams. Ten orbits had constructed a surface map of the target area. Ten times over the seed colony site and not a whisper from the colonists.

Plant life was lush, a jungle, even on the highlands where the site was located. Flaherty worked the spectrum analyzer, burning through the layers of cloud and vegetation. The colonists had not kept their landing sites clear. The settlement was overgrown. Flaherty found two locations that appeared to be lander scars grown over. He selected the largest for his touchdown datum and programmed a landing profile.

"What's wrong, Flack?" Buccari asked.

Flaherty looked at his commander. Buccari was busy at her console.

"What do you mean?" he asked.

"I don't ever recall you going more than ten seconds without shooting off your mouth," the pilot said. "You okay?"

"Pretty exciting stuff," Flaherty said soberly.

"Flackman's just maturing," Thompson snorted.

"That means I'm growing hair on my ass," he shot back.

"Sorry I asked." Buccari laughed.

"Condor lead's clearing us, Skipper," Tasker reported. "*Condors Five* and *Six* cleared for landing. Fleet site assessment: extremely dangerous but technically nonhostile. Primary source of danger remains indigenous life-forms. Senior science officer is landing team leader."

"Liberty call!" Flaherty shouted.

"Okay, Nes," Buccari announced. "We're in the window. Get your landing team on board. Mr. Flaherty's anxious to hit the beach."

"Roger," Godonov replied. "I copied all."

Flaherty jettisoned his tethers and arrowed for the flight deck iris. He dove into the axial passageway and jackknifed down the hatch into the crew decks. The survey lab hatch hissed open as he went by; Godonov and Lizard Lips dropped through on his heels.

The marines stood aside to let him pass. The hunters bounced off the bulkheads. Flaherty moved through the air lock and into the upper EPL bay. Chief Foster, in a silver lander suit, was waiting. Nakajima, concern and disappointment on her face, was there to assist.

"Checking good, Lieutenant," Foster said.

"Show time, Chief." Flaherty dove headfirst into the EPL's loading hatch and did a swimmer's turn off the fire wall. He darted around the cargo, went through the forward compartment, and pulled himself into the snug, single pilot position in the nose. Floating in the acceleration seat, he secured his torso harness and mated the service umbilicals. Flaherty exhaled. He was ready for prestart checks.

"Compute! Systems status—initiate," he barked. "Pilot Flaherty."

Ladder lights on the console sequenced, and a machine-generated voice replied: "Pilot Flaherty. Control check. Pilot has command."

"Launch sequence," he ordered. Screens displayed launch checklists. Items that had not been satisfied glowed with double intensity. Flaherty's retinal cursor and gloved hands flew about, satisfying the uncompromising demands of launch.

"All systems active and responding, sir," Foster reported. "Landing team strapped in. Hatch secured."

"Rog'," Flaherty acknowledged. "Final checks complete. Standing by to dump apple," he announced over the intership.

"Five-Alpha cleared to launch," Thompson responded. "Control set to button four. Report clear."

"Roger, copy all. Five-Alpha retros in two minutes. Counting down." Flaherty scanned the instruments, looking for anomalies, for nascent emergencies. Satisfied, he settled into his seat, anticipating launch.

"All checklist items satisfied," the computer announced.

The EPL bay doors yawned open. Harsh white light reflected from the planet's cloud-shrouded oceans, an immense light source permitting no shadows. His visor's glare protection activated.

Launch lights were illuminated.

"Mooring locks. Mooring locks," the computer warned.

Flaherty released the locks. Vibrations hummed through metal. The Endoatmospheric Planetary Lander lifted and moved outboard, pushed by a spidery gantry until it cleared the confined bay. Flaherty released the attachment fitting, fired a micropulse on the port maneuvering rockets to initiate a separation rate, and reported back to Thompson.

"You all set, Flack?" Buccari came up on laser.

"Piece o' cake," Flaherty responded, maneuvering until he could see the flight deck's shimmering view ports. "Site weather's ideal. Landing solution's in the can. I'll bring you back a souvenir."

"Don't do anything stupid," she admonished.

"You're just jealous," Flaherty replied.

"Damn straight," Buccari replied. "Okay, Five-Alpha's cleared for landing. Standard reports."

"Hoot . . . hoot," Flaherty replied, maneuvering away from the big corvette. Clear of *Condor Five,* he rolled the EPL smoothly inverted and lined up his thrust axis. The swirling blue and white planet filled his canopy screen. He retrofired mains, and the apple fell from heaven.

Chopping turbulence and elevated temperatures finally abated. The star ferry had entered an atmosphere. Brappa sensed the pull of a planet. The hunter huddled in a forward acceleration seat, breath rasping in his helmet. Sherrip was tethered next to him. His cohort's black eyes, fully dilated, darted behind his helmet visor. Next to Sherrip was the long-leg female, Soft-hands. She carried medical equipment. Giant-one occupied a seat near the rear loading door. The other positions in the compartment were occupied by heavily armed, green-suited space warriors.

"Big-ears inquires of thy condition," Toon-the-speaker chittered over the helmet-talker. Toon and Big-ears were tethered opposite, although Brappa could not see them; a big-wheeled machine piled with long-leg equipment squatted between them.

"My talons are most anxious to touch rock," Brappa replied. Sherrip chirped agreement. A panel of colored diodes flickered. Brappa had learned the long-leg numbers. The display indicating time increments until landing held the hunter's attention.

"As are mine," Toon answered.

Their star ferry tilted smoothly, the pull of gravity increasing each time. The flying craft was making sweeping turns; Brappa had felt similar forces on his own wings. Time counted down, approaching the oval icon representing nothingness. Ambient noise levels decreased.

"Big-ears says to prepare thyself," Toon screeched.

Brappa felt a sickening increase in gravity. They were tilting backward; vertigo swept him. Sherrip struggled against his tethers. Brappa grabbed the warrior's arm, settling him. Their craft shuddered violently. Engines erupted into life, eclipsing all other sensations.

The tilting motion swayed to a precarious halt. Brappa was upside down! The swaying motion reversed itself, accompanied by a horrible trembling beneath their feet. Brappa's sense of vertical was restored. The exploding cacophony and violent shuddering abruptly ceased, accompanied by a positive jolt that halted all movement.

The absence of motion was as disconcerting as the gyrations had been. Brappa dared to breathe. The floor was steeply slanted, with him sitting dizzily at the high end. Long-leg warriors leapt from their seats, furiously organizing equipment. Giant-one's voice thundered over the helmet circuits. The huge long-leg loomed from his station, bending to keep from bumping his head. Brappa clambered atop the equipment and surveyed the orchestrated chaos.

Big-ears removed his helmet and landing suit and signaled for the cliff dwellers to do the same. Brappa gladly did so, replacing his helmet with a lightweight headset. Brappa slapped and tugged at his body-formed armor and checked the load on his ultralightweight automatic. Long-leg warriors made similar preparations.

After an eternity the lander's main loading door slid upward. A humid stench assaulted Brappa's olfactories. With the hatch barely half-open, Giant-one ducked through, the other warriors on his heels. Brappa and Sherrip plunged into soft steamy daylight, leaving Toon, Big-ears, and Soft-hands to follow. Heat radiated from the lander's skin, but Brappa sensed a breeze coming off the planet. There would be thermals.

The sky was pale blue. The soil around the lander had been burned crusty and black. A wall of jungle loomed all around. The rippling of a soft breeze in the multitiered canopy was the only noise.

"Hunters!" Giant-one shouted. Sherrip and Brappa streaked to their squad leader's side.

"Up!" Giant-one commanded, thrusting his finger obscenely. Brappa ran at a long-leg and leapt. The warrior held his death stick in both hands. Brappa landed with both talons on the weapon, legs bent like coiled springs. The long-leg explosively boosted the weapon upward, catapulting the hunter. At the top of his arc Brappa unfurled his wings and pounded against thick air. He embraced a strong upwelling, relishing the heat dissipation afforded by his spread membranes. His armor fit well. Its elegant lightness did not hinder his climb at all. The death stick, though of considerable mass, was easier to take airborne than a hunter's bow—a good trade-off.

Brappa screeched his pleasure and wheeled about the scorched landing site, thermals lifting him above vine-draped trees. Sherrip answered his cry. Brappa looked down to see his cohort leaping from another long-leg death stick. The young warrior's wings cracked with a respectable timbre. On the ground the green-garbed long-legs trundled out the fat-tired machine.

"Giant-one asks for a report." Toon-the-speaker's voice was in his ear, chirping without stop, issuing endless cautions.

Brappa beat his wings until he was above a blanket of verdant foliage. A nearby tumble of broken structures marked the ruins of the long-leg colony. It lay in an area cleared of trees but already overgrown with creepers and vines. Sloping away to the south and rising to the north was a solid canopy of trees for thousands of spans in all directions. Far off to the south the verdure surrendered to a horizon of misty aquamarine, a great body of water. Other horizons were obscured by towering clouds. All this Brappa reported.

Brappa discerned a considerable watercourse meandering through the canopy to the southwest. A tributary to that drainage flowed nearby, and Brappa detected the muted sounds of a cataract. The complex weave of wildlife regained its voice, protesting their thunderous arrival. Swirling flocks of birds shared the upwellings, some large but none as big as a hunter. The other fliers fled in panic at his approach.

Brappa's perspective improved with altitude. His vision penetrated small portions of the canopy immediately below him, and the higher he went, the more ground he could perceive. Through all openings he saw fragmented movement, a slithering undulation, as if the humus beneath the canopy were flowing. He circled to the north and observed the same subtle wavering of the firmament. Sherrip screeched a signal. Brappa responded to the hunter's directions. To the south something crashed through the undergrowth, making directly for the landing site.

The heat was oppressive. Godonov's body exploded with perspiration.

"Whew!" Catta Burl gasped, backpacking her medical gear down the ramp. "I could use a cold beer."

Lizard Lips, twittering into his headset, waddled into the opening, alternately looking down at the ashy ground and staring into the air. Godonov followed the guilder's gaze into the sky and saw the wheeling hunters. He interrogated his chest-mounted science unit. The hunters' personal locators registered. He monitored the EPL's onboard sensors, checking the site analysis for toxins or infectious agents.

"What a dogshit site," Flaherty complained. Godonov tweaked down the pilot's frequency. The EPL pilot had to remain at the controls until the site was secured. "Move 'em out, Chief. Clear the blast radius."

"It's going to take a while, Lieutenant," Foster replied, working diligently on the off-load. "It's a damn jungle out here."

"Five-Alpha, team leader's up," Godonov broadcast, standing aside as Chief Foster and the marines off-loaded the lorry.

"Move 'em out, Nes," Flaherty replied. "I want everyone out of the blast radius ASAP in case I gotta get out of Dodge. Can't blow this hog outta here with all you vacationers standing on my skirts."

"Get out of Dodge?" Godonov inquired, looking about. Marines had taken stations around the site's margins.

"Yeah, yeah," Flaherty barked. "You heard me."

"Roger, pardner," Godonov drawled. "Okay, buckaroos. Let's mosey along, y' hear." Godonov was joking, but his stomach churned. Sweat ran in runnels down the small of his back.

The seared clearing was small. Trees had been cleared by the colonists out to a hundred meters on all sides, but implacable fronds and liana had grown back. The EPL had cratered a hole in the jungle, but not a large one. Tangled undergrowth higher than a man's height approached within forty meters of the groaning metal skin. Outside the ring the surrounding canopy soared majestically. The EPL's raging descent had atomized an avenue in the trees, cleaving the higher foliage like a hot scalpel.

Godonov and Lizard Lips worked their way outward from the EPL.

"Jungle's mighty thick," Chastain huffed, swinging a machete. Perspiration dripped from his nose. Something screeched, a piercing cry muffled by humidity and distance. The big man looked up.

"Start burning out the perimeter, Jocko," Godonov said.

"Yes, sir," the squad leader agreed. Chastain shouted orders. His marines positioned the robot-lorry near the crater's downwind edge. Within minutes a mobile laser blaster was pulverizing the overgrowth, clearing the oblong landing site out to the limits set by the giant vine-wrapped boles of the great trees. The lorry's dozer nose plowed the smoldering debris before it, slowly but inexorably expanding the tenuous limits of civilization.

Above the din of exploding vegetation Godonov heard a hunter's screeching signal. The science officer looked into the glaring sun. Both cliff dwellers hovered to the south. Lizard Lips frantically punched at the communicator. Godonov moved closer and watched icons appear on the screen. The guilder thrust the communicator at him. It read:

DANGER. UNKNOWN THREAT COMES FROM SOUTH. DANGER.

"Something's coming from the south!" the science officer shouted, grabbing Chastain. Lizard Lips signed more information to Chastain faster than Godonov could follow. Chastain's soft brown eyes opened wider with each sign. The huge man bellowed for terrain clearing to stop. The laser blasting ceased with an electronic ringing that died quickly in the stultifying humidity.

"Where?" Chastain shouted, his big hands signing the question.

Lizard Lips pointed emphatically downgrade, to the south. Godonov detected a noise like wind rushing through dry grass. It grew ever louder, coming from everywhere.

"Geez, you hear that?" a marine shouted.

"Nes, what's going on?" Flaherty asked over the radio.

"Something's headed our way, Flack," Godonov replied, glancing up at the lander cockpit. "From the south. You see anything from up there?"

"I see the same trees you see," Flaherty replied.

There was a shrill shout, almost a scream.

"That's human," Godonov whispered, the hair on his neck rising.

"Nestor! What?" Flaherty demanded.

"Quiet, Flack," Godonov whispered. "Get ready for take-off."

Chief Foster ran for the lander, working checklists over the radio. A frenetic rustling of underbrush lifted above the un-nerving wind-rushing sounds as if something were running amok, coming straight their way. Marines retreated from the forest's edge, bringing weapons to bear.

"Watch all sectors," Chastain boomed. "Move the laser! Aim it south and fan the beam!"

The big man stalked toward the thrashing jungle, assault rifle poised. Foster and Flaherty added to the confusion with their frantic preparations. Godonov turned down the volume to hear better and pulled his pistol. The robot-lorry trundled across the clearing. Fronds whipped about, getting nearer. A high-pitched gasping and sobbing grew louder—desperate noises. Something was almost upon them. The marines took aim.

Overhead, Tonto screamed a signal. Lizard Lips screeched and frantically signed: "No shoot! No shoot!"

"Hold your fire!" Godonov shouted.

The emergency beeper on his headset sounded. Godonov in-creased the volume. Flaherty was shouting.

"—coming out of the trees at nine o'clock!"

A face appeared, a tortured, beseeching face—a human face, oily hair hanging in lank tangles. And then a torso, a female, its sex apparent only because the creature's filthy clothes were in shreds. She staggered into the clearing and fell forward, the clinging tendrils of the jungle no longer resisting her headlong flight. Chastain was the first at her side, Godonov at his heels. Catta Burl was close behind. The woman was diseased; blood seeped from her nose. But it was her pale, swollen skin that most repulsed them; she was covered with scabs, rashes, and running sores. Her scent was rancid, her breath and body odor overpowering; she smelled of rot, of putrescence.

"Oh, man!" Burl exclaimed, probing beneath the victim's tongue. "She's one big infection."

"Get . . . in the lander!" the panicky female pleaded, push-ing Burl's hand aside. She was frantic, the dark irises of her eyes surrounded with bloodshot white. Gasping for breath, she struggled to her knees, her eyes darting over the ground. "Climb ... a tree. Quick ... only seconds."

The scratching was all around them, too loud for wind that deep in the damp stillness of the jungle. Godonov returned Burl's look of incredulity. Astounding Godonov with his quickness—and selflessness—Chastain snatched the leprous human in his arms and sprinted over the charred terrain. Godonov and Burl exchanged wide-eyed looks and leapt into a dash. Godonov detected movement on the ground.

"Everyone in the lander," Godonov shouted, looking into the sky. The hunters were too high. Godonov grabbed Lizard Lips and signed: "Order hunters to remain in trees. Ground has danger."

Lizard Lips nodded and screeched into his headset. All the while Godonov herded the cliff dweller toward the lander. The ground seemed to ooze. They were the last ones through the hatch. Chief Foster pulled them in and hit the release; the hatch hissed to at Godonov's sweaty back. It was an oven.

"Open the top hatch, Chief," Godonov said. "Let's get the hunters back on board and get some ventilation."

"Cargo hatch sealed," Foster reported over the intercom. "Mr. Godonov wants the dorsal hatch opened to retrieve the hunters."

"Roger. Get 'em on board," the pilot replied. "Wait! The ground's moving! It's like an oil slick!"

Lizard Lips screeched! The guilder slapped at his talons.

"What's going on back there?" Flaherty shouted.

"Hell, sir!" the boatswain shouted, flipping on a strong light and stomping his boots on the EPL aft deck. "We got bugs inside. You marines, give me a hand here." While the marines heel-danced, Foster shot a stream of caustic foam along the hatch rim. The sinus-biting odor dramatically increased the discomfort level in the sweltering compartment. Flaherty screamed for information.

Lizard Lips mewled pitifully and chewed on his own leg. As Godonov moved to the cliff dweller's aid, something stung his calf. He grabbed at the searing pain and looked down in horror to see a half dozen bluish-black insects bigger than his thumbnail swarming on his legs. Circular holes perforated his jumpsuit—perfectly round, like burn marks. He brushed the ones he could see to the floor and squished them with his boot. Something scurried up his leg. He slapped at it frantically.

"Take your pants off!" the bedraggled colonist ordered. Burl and Chastain had strapped the woman into a fluids unit, running IVs to both arms. "They get much higher and you won't be having children—ever!"

Something stung him behind the knee. Godonov needed no further encouragement. He unzipped his jumpsuit and peeled it and his thermals down to his boots, slapping and rubbing at his legs. His hands swept more vermin from his person. Chastain came over to help, stomping on the scuttling pestilence. But two insects had penetrated Godonov's skin, their heads burrowing deeper and deeper as he watched.

"How do you kill them?" Godonov asked, striving not to shout. He frantically checked his thighs and groin. "How do you get them out?"

"Anybody got a cig?" she wheezed.

"Goddamn!" Godonov shouted. "I got no time for a smoke. How do you get them out?" Shame briefly flushed his cheeks; the woman was obviously in greater pain than he was. Chief Foster and the marines looked up from their extermination efforts to watch Godonov's agonies. They began earnestly checking their own bodies for encroachment.

"You burn their butts," she gasped. "Like ticks."

"Ticks from hell!" a marine cried, pulling a pack of Legion-issue cigarettes. He flipped a stick to the woman and used his GP tool to ignite it.

"Caterpillars . . . with attitudes," the woman wheezed, inhaling deeply before handing the glowing fag to Godonov. "*Papalio mortalis*. Drillers, we call them. Carnivorous butterfly larvae. Feeding stage lasts a couple of months, and then they pupate for the winter. Come spring they'll turn into the prettiest swallowtails you've ever seen. Brilliant green and gold, bigger than your hand."

"Oh, shit," Godonov cried, trying to hold the cig steady.

"Just touch its ass. Don't burn it or you'll have to dig it out. It's going to hurt."

Perspiration streaming from nose to chin, Godonov applied glowing ashes to the thick insect burrowing into his calf. The entry point was swollen red. The insect struggled violently, aggravating the searing pain, but it backed out. Godonov swiped it to the deck and pounded it with the heel of his hand. It made a satisfying crunch. Chief Foster provided Flaherty with a running commentary.

"Doesn't take much for Godonov to drop trou, does it?" Flaherty chuckled, safe in his air-conditioned cockpit.

"Open the top hatch, Chief," Godonov grunted, swallowing an obscenity; he was too busy excavating the bug in the back of his knee. "Get those hunters inside." Under the stress of searing heat the second insect backed out and was dispatched. Godonov, checking his jumpsuit for more vermin, limped over to the cliff dweller and forced the creature to hold still while he scraped through its soft fur.

"What if the bugs climb the lander?" Foster asked.

"They're burrowers," the woman said. "They only climb on hairy things, things that bleed."

"Open the hatch, Chief," Flaherty ordered. "I don't see them climbing on anything."

The boatswain acknowledged and activated the hatch. All eyes lurched to the opening, but all that penetrated the EPL's confines was a shaft of hot white light and a fetid breeze.

"Corporal Chastain, post a sentry," Godonov ordered as he put his clothes back in order. Every tickle of sweat felt like another crawling bug. He concentrated on Lizard Lips.

"Aye, Mr. Godonov," Chastain replied, pointing to a marine. Chastain pulled down the ladder, and the marine, carrying her weapon, scrambled to the opening.

"Genellan cliff dwellers," the bedraggled colonist said, staring with fascination at Lizard Lips. "They're even uglier than their vids. Read your reports. You're Nestor Godonov."

"Yeah." Godonov grimaced, finding an embedded insect. Lizard Lips had all but eradicated it, along with some of his own fur and flesh. Frightened, the guilder looked at him and chittered nervously. Godonov hand signed his concern. Lizard Lips signed back his relief.

"His name's Lizard Lips. He thinks you're pretty ugly, too," Godonov added, stroking the cliff dweller's neck as Burl clamped a field bandage to the creature's leg.

"Won't argue with an ugly expert," the colonist replied weakly. Her breathing had stabilized. "Name's Morgan. Exobiologist. Welcome to Hornblower Three."

"Thanks," Godonov replied. "How—"

"Hunters making their approach," the sentry reported. A shadow covered the hatch, and suddenly Tonto and Bottlenose were perched on its rim, stowing their membranes. Both hunters excitedly studied the ground around the lander, intent on the crawling swarms. Lizard Lips screeched at them, mostly in hypersonic frequencies. They chittered back.

"So what happened to the other colonists?" Flaherty asked.

"Anyone else still alive, Morgan?" Godonov asked. He picked up the cig, sucked on it, and coughed.

"Three others." She coughed, fascinated by the hunters. "Conner, Smith, and Cheskov. At least they were alive when I left them. Cheskov probably won't last the night. I was the only one that could still run."

"Where are they?" Godonov asked.

"Could I have that cig back?" Morgan asked with a pitiful smile.

"Bad for your health," he replied, handing it to her.

"So's this planet," she said, grabbing the cig and pulling on it. "Got a tree fort over by the river—maybe three kilometers. On this planet, if you have warm blood, you live in the trees or in the swamps, at least during the larval run. Last year's run hit right after the fleet left. Drillers were our first big surprise."

"Did drillers kill the others?" Godonov asked. What were the other surprises? he wondered.

"Just Tohler and Rivera," Morgan replied, shaking her head. "The week after Admiral Chou left, the ground opened up. Tohler and Rivera died horribly. All of us were ravaged. We purged the settlement with extermination agents. Torched the ground. Even ran an acid moat around the colony. Put up chemical barricades. Salt does the job, but the rain kept washing the barricades away. And then one day they were gone, cocooned. Cocoons everywhere. The miracle of metamorphosis." She gave a short laugh that could have been a sob.

"What happened to the others?" Godonov asked.

"Not sure," Morgan replied, exhaling deeply and throwing her head back, eyes closed, mouth gaping.

"Here," Burl ordered, taking the cig and giving Morgan a slug of field nourishment. She sucked greedily at the power bottle.

"We were out on research," Morgan continued, nearly babbling. "A little over four standard months ago, I think. Tough to keep track of time. Six-day expedition—two out, two on site, two back. Up to the falls. Fantastic deposits. Immense quantities of free copper. Rich ores veined with turquoise, running right to the surface."

"What happened?" Godonov insisted.

"Lost radio. Came back early. Base was destroyed—

perimeter sensors wiped out, structures flattened. Worst thing was our DNA stills were destroyed. Couldn't engineer antibodies or antibiotics. This planet's a cesspool of viral and bacterial aggression. Everyone got sick. Look at me." Morgan started to cry.

"The other colonists?" Godonov persisted.

"Not a sign." Morgan sobbed. "Nothing, no bodies, no messages. Whoever ... whatever ... visited us took them. We never heard a reentry or a retro, but they left tracks. Boot prints and low-energy exhaust scars. Boot prints were man-sized but as wide as they were long. A few were longer than the others—much longer—and extremely narrow."

Flaherty whistled softly over the circuit. Godonov sat back and pondered the implications of Morgan's statement. Were they in a trap?

"How did you get past the bugs, sir—the drillers?" Chastain asked. "It was like you brought them to us. Where'd they come from?"

"They were coming whether I showed up or not." Morgan laughed cruelly. "It took 'em a little longer because you fried the local infestation. As soon as blood spoor hits the air, it brings them out."

"Brings them out from where?" Chastain asked.

"The ground," Morgan replied. "Drillers are everywhere. They well up out of the humus. They sense heat and smell blood, like a lot of things on this planet. You move fast enough, you can stay ahead of an upwelling, but you'd better find a tree before you run out of gas, because as soon as you stop, they'll be coming from all directions."

"How do you move around?" Chastain asked. "How do you get food?"

"They're dormant at night." Morgan yawned. "And there's no shortage of food. Edible mushrooms like lorry tires. Pick fruit off the trees all year around. There's an orchid that makes a nectar worthy of the gods. With spines that'll give you the devil's own rash."

"So we go after the others at sunset," Godonov stated.

"Yeah," she replied, the corners of her mouth turning down. "But you'll have other problems: vampires."

"Bats?" Godonov asked.

"Yeah, bats, too." Morgan shuddered. "But the vampires on this planet don't fly. They move like cats and weigh over two

hundred kilos. Some sort of marsupial. Nocturnal, eyes 1
dinner plates, prehensile claws like kitchen knives."

"Why are they called v-vampires?" a marine asked.

"Because vamps come out only at night and because of the
way they kill," Morgan replied. "Drain your blood and then
hang what they don't eat from a dead tree. Sun dries the meat,
and the carcass takes longer to spoil. Evolutionary resourceful-
ness. Vamps are pretty much the top of the food chain in these
parts. They got Lieutenant Samson the first night we landed.
Good thing they're dumb as stumps or we'd have all died a
long time ago."

"So h-how do you fight them?" Chastain asked.

"Flashlights." Morgan laughed softly. "Any strong light.
Scares them shitless. They go catatonic. Pow! Sitting ducks."

"Sounds easy enough," Godonov replied smugly.

"I haven't told you about the primates," Morgan replied.

FIFTY-ONE

RESCUE

Buccari signed off after listening to Flaherty's report. So
many mysteries to digest. She forwarded the survivor's debriefing and Godonov's science summary on laserburst. *Condor Six*'s EPL would be on the ground soon, augmenting the
landing team with another squad of marines and a medical
team.

She completed her commander's log entry for the watch
day. She was hungry and tired, but her corvette was scheduled
for rendezvous with the fleet fueler in less than an hour. The
ship would get serviced, and then it would be her turn.

Her thoughts returned to the day's events. She glanced at the
silvery lime of the planet turning below her. Killer caterpillars,
bats, vampires, and apes and monkeys. Buccari felt powerless.
She wanted to be on the ground, where all the action was, but

commanding officer of a corvette in hostile space.
as with her ship.
ides, she hated bugs.

ael's screen status flashed a positioning alert. He checked the disposition of the screening units. A section of Shrikes being relieved by two Blackhawk corvettes had pulled out of the matrix prematurely. The Blackhawks expeditiously closed the gap. Carmichael made a log entry and returned his attention to other matters, or tried to.

Buccari. He wished he could purge her from his mind, but she was always there. Closing his eyes made it worse. Her image became palpable. He could hear her throaty laugh. He shivered at the ghost of her penetrating glare.

"Skipper," his second officer said over the intercom.

"Uh, yeah," Carmichael replied, snapping to.

"Screen shift signal's in the air. Execute in thirty minutes."

"Very well." Carmichael exhaled, bringing up his maneuvering vid. "Let's look sharp."

Brappa sailed high on the powerful thermal, seeking cooler air. Powerful storms passed along the horizon. Bruised, flickering clouds towered into the heavens. Sherrip soared easily to the south, within signaling range. Brappa looked down on the stifling, malodorous jungle and screamed his joy of flight. This was a miserable planet.

Louder than the rumbling storm clouds, Brappa heard the double thunder of another long-leg star ferry. It would soon be landing, and it would be noisy. Yet that concerned Brappa little, for the hunters had a mission. The sun settled to the west. That concerned Brappa. Soon the afternoon thermals would dissipate.

The long-legs were trapped in the star ferry. Brappa and Sherrip had become the eyes and ears of the expedition, a great honor and duty. Toon-the-speaker had directed the hunters to search the jungle for injured long-legs in a tree domicile. Toon provided an azimuth reference and counseled caution. Brappa had seen the guilder's injuries; the burrowing insects were deadly. Toon also warned of other adversaries, large and carnivorous. Brappa was not frightened. Warriors did not shy from battle.

"It comes!" Sherrip signaled.

Brappa wheeled to gain Sherrip's perspective and saw the other silver star ferry growing large, descending on its landing track.

The landing retro of *Condor Six*'s EPL vibrated through the fabric of their metal prison. Godonov paused in his interrogations.

"The primates," Morgan continued. "Best thing about the vamps is they keep the primates away. The big monkeys—ghouls, we call them—are quick and smart. You won't scare them with a flashlight."

"Ghouls!" Flaherty muttered on the intercom.

"Vampires and ghouls." Godonov laughed. "Your biologists have a bent for the macabre."

"Good reason," Morgan replied without a hint of a smile. "Ghouls watch you night or day. They track you like hounds. They probe for weaknesses. If they perceive any advantage, they attack in teams. Always at least two, sometimes more. Males and females together. We've seen as many as twenty in a social group—or a hunting party, whatever you want to call it. You know when they're coming. Their growl changes to a horrible buzzing sound. Humming from hell."

"They sound intelligent," Godonov said. "They use weapons? Clubs?"

"No. No tool use as such," Morgan replied, "but they throw things: rocks, fruit, feces. Extremely unpleasant creatures; they prey on the other primates. Even on their own species—they're cannibals."

"How do you fight them?" Godonov asked.

"Bullets and blasters," Morgan replied grimly. "You hunt them and you kill them. That's all they seem to understand."

"What about the other primates?" Godonov asked. "The biological reports indicated you had trouble with pilferage."

"Yellows," Morgan replied. "Sort of blond chimpanzees with prehensile tails and flowing manes. And reds—smaller monkeys, cinnamon-colored. Both are omnivorous primates that band in large organizational groups. Bands of yellows sweep the forest like locusts. They hit our colony three times like a screeching, fluttering storm. Anything not tied down disappears. That's why we don't have a radio. Reds come through more frequently but in much smaller groups."

"Are they dangerous?" Burl asked. "Do they bite?"

"The yellows." Morgan shuddered. "If you get in their way, they'll rip you to shreds like a school of piranha."

"Shit!" a marine whispered.

"Yellows are the main staple in the ghouls' diet," Morgan continued. "Wherever you find yellows, you'll find ghouls. Ghouls stampede the yellows and reds to exhaustion—chase them in circles and harvest them as they drop."

Sherrip screeched a discovery. Brappa canted toward the hunter and also spotted the object; the lowering sun reflected from a glittering hemisphere, a light buoy deep in the trough of a heavy sea of twilight green. Brappa recognized energy collectors used by long-legs to trap the power of sun-stars. The curved section of solar cells atop a metal stanchion barely protruded above the treetops, hidden from longer range by a depression in the jungle canopy. Brappa pulled in his membranes and plummeted. Sherrip hung at his side.

As they descended toward the twinkling structure, a noise caught their attention—a shrill screeching, growing louder. And there was a softer, low-pitched sound, a fluttering of wind in the leaves, also growing louder. Brappa arrested his descent at the treetops. He combed the wind-ruffled canopy with his sonic receptors in an effort to determine the direction from which the alarming clamor was coming. Sherrip did likewise.

The noises grew louder, a frenzy of shrieking, an exploding bedlam, coming straight for them. Brappa and Sherrip beat down on the air, regaining altitude. The noises were too close. Suddenly the ether around them was filled with yellow animals exploding through the leaves, bursting incredible distances into empty air. The panicky creatures had long, curling tails and streaming white mustaches. Their distraught electric-blue faces were framed with flowing flaxen manes. There were hundreds, thousands, of the creatures, all propelling themselves through the verdant canopy in a frenzy of rout.

Brappa and Sherrip elevated on weak thermals, gaining a broader perspective on the spectacle. The soft afternoon sun reflected from bright yellow pelts roiling the leaves, a shimmering white-gold contrasting vividly with the stark verdure. Wavering constellations of yellow erupted into the sunshine and fell back like coruscating minnows in a sea of green, fleeing the rapacious denizens of the deep. Rolling eruptions undulated across the canopy, pointillistic ripplings of gold accompanied by the screeching of Furies. The frightened upwellings of nature gradually descended into distant foliage. Brappa wondered what invisible army of predators could create such havoc.

Brappa raised Toon-the-speaker on the radio and reported both the discovery of the reflectors marking the long-leg tree domicile and the tortured flight of the panicky creatures. Toon acknowledged, chastising Brappa for not reporting more frequently.

Brappa grew tired of the guilder's chatter. The hunter signed off and screamed his clarion. They still had a mission. Wheeling into the wind, Brappa pointed his head back to the stanchion of mirrors. The hunters descended once again, carefully, searching for clear air through which to penetrate the leafy overcast. Brappa searched vigilantly, wondering what lay beneath the jungle's inscrutable upper layers.

Lizard Lips punched on his communicator. Godonov took it from the cliff dweller and interpreted the icons: HUNTERS FIND TREE DOMICILE.

"I wouldn't let them get too close," Morgan said. "Conner is likely to shoot first."

"Yeah," Godonov replied, punching in instructions on the communicator. "I'm calling them back." Lizard Lips watched over his shoulder. The guilder screeched his agreement and chittered into his mike, listened intently, and then screeched some more. Lizard Lips punched something on the communicator.

"They aren't responding," Godonov said, reading the icons.

"What's the plan?" Flaherty asked over the intercom.

"I wish I knew." Godonov exhaled. There was an hour to sunset.

"Should we not take to the air?" Sherrip chirped nervously.

Brappa chittered for silence. He studied the cruel-eyed creature approaching through the canopy. The slope-shouldered beast glided stealthily along tree limbs, slipping silently through vines and creepers. Once the large beast leapt a great span between trees, barely disturbing the branches. A crafty hunter, it sniffed the air and approached obliquely from downwind, but it was still a dumb brute; of that Brappa was certain. Brappa signaled Sherrip to remain at his sentry post and, despite Sherrip's admonition, moved closer to the long-leg domicile. Brappa was a hunter on a mission, not a timid guilder. He had not come this far to be ruled by fear.

He looked down on the tree domicile. It was in the crotch of a great tree, four spans from the jungle floor. The stanchion that supported the beacon of solar cells soared into a dark, leafy shroud through which only muted twilight dappled. Wafting upward on dank, steamy currents was the unpleasant scent of the long-legs. The soiled white flanks of their structure might have hidden its occupants from sight, but it did little to inhibit their foul odor.

Brappa checked the stalking animal. Satisfied that it was still too distant to threaten him, he dropped lightly onto the log platform. The hunter crept forward and touched the white walls. They were unyielding and reinforced with logs. The stoutness of the structure had been tested; slivered claw marks and rough gouges marred all the surfaces. Reinforcing logs were splintered or gnawed. Broken light fixtures dangled from overhanging eaves. A water catchment covered much of the roof, although portions of the conduit and flashing had been torn asunder. Faint moans came from within. Brappa approached a shuttered view port.

A visceral alarm actuated. Brappa stopped and surveyed the tangle of branches, letting his senses govern. It was fast growing dark. A new scent wafted to his awareness, and a sound not of the trees—a humming sound. Brappa localized the sensory messages, a triangulation of instincts, and saw another of the round-shouldered beasts, much closer—above him and perilously near—slavering, poised to strike. The humming increased violently to a high-pitched growl. Sherrip squawked and unfurled his membranes. Brappa did likewise. He had underestimated the long-armed beasts. They, too, were hunters.

The canny creature leapt, arms and legs spread, fanged canines bared. Buzzing with rage, it landed heavily on the platform, arms flailing at a void. Brappa dove through vines and branches. Something yanked at his face. A clawed hand, irresistibly strong, raked his head, tearing at his communication device. The apparatus snagged; his head snapped around, and then he broke loose, twisting out of control. He cracked open his membranes and stabilized his trajectory. His communicator had been ripped away!

He pulled up from his descent to see Sherrip throwing open

his wings. Together the routed hunters swooped between dim trees. An object sailed past them. Another! Another! Something struck Sherrip with a sickly thud, and the hunter collapsed from the air.

Brappa pulled in his wings and plummeted after his stricken friend. Sherrip managed to right himself and extend his wings to slow his descent. His body glanced off a bough, upsetting his trajectory all the more. He hit the soft jungle on his back and lay there stunned. Humming came from all around.

Brappa grounded at Sherrip's side and frantically pulled the downed warrior upright, struggling to get him off the jungle floor. Sherrip was dazed; one membrane hung limply at his side.

"Move!" Brappa shrieked, shaking the warrior. "Thou must move!"

Sherrip's eyes came into focus. He pulled his arm up and stowed his membrane, opening and shutting his spindly hand. Brappa leapt for a vine and pulled himself from the spongy humus. Leaves were moving, their color changing from variegated patterns to a uniform blue-black; things scuttled upward, covering the surface like a rising flood. But slowly—the biters were lethargic.

"My hand! Climb for thy life!" Brappa screeched, reaching. Sherrip's survival instincts overcame his foggy brain. He clasped Brappa's hand. Heaving with all his might, Brappa pulled the other hunter to him. Both clasped the vine and climbed.

"Yeeoow!" Sherrip screeched. "I am bitten!"

"Climb first," Brappa called back, "or you will die!" He pulled them onto a thick bough. Sherrip frantically grabbed for his talon. Brappa moved to assist, flicking insects, some of which had gained a stubborn purchase, from his comrade's leg. Sherrip chittered in pain as he scraped and chewed, plucked and pulled, intent on expunging the devilish vermin. Sherrip pulled bugs from his skin and killed them with his teeth. Brappa also started eating the crunchy pests.

Brappa heard something. And then he smelled it.

The hunter slowly pivoted. The beast stood only a span away, long arm poised, wrist cocked, a stone ready to throw. Three more heavy-jowled creatures were visible, cutting off all escape except down to the swarming insects. Brappa rose to his talons and faced the creature. Even crouched to pounce, the densely muscled animal stood nearly half a span taller and was twice as wide as the hunter, its mousy fur tight over rippling sinews. Its face was a black mask of rage. It had drooping, rheumy eyes rimmed with scarlet and flaring nostrils circling gaping, sucking holes—horrible windows into moist, dripping sinuses. A bone-crusher jaw hung beneath hooked upper canines; it drooled in viscous streams.

Reconciled to combat, Brappa hissed ferociously, exhibiting his own powerful maw filled with jagged teeth. He unfurled his membranes and flung them out to their full imposing limit. The monster recoiled at the hunter's fierce demeanor, turning sideways and crabbing three quick steps. Behind him Sherrip hissed and postured with branch-shaking ire.

A piece of fruit exploded on Brappa's chest, staggering the hunter. Monsters jumped up and down and roared, many raising their own missiles. The closest one reared to its full height and bellowed. Brappa advanced, slowly drawing his death stick. The beast held its ground, roaring insanely. Filling his lungs, Brappa screeched back, his spitting, piercing howl rising into the hypersonic. Sherrip's voice joined his. The monsters recoiled, dropping stones and clasping their small ears. But the near one grew more enraged. It leapt, yellow teeth thrusting from gaping jaws, its long arms sweeping in a clawed embrace.

Brappa shot it through the nose, the muzzle blast strobing the jungle. The monster straightened and fell over backward, tumbling onto the jungle's surface, where it was slowly covered with blackness. The other beasts scattered into the darkening foliage. The humming stopped.

Brappa scanned the dusk. It had grown quite dark.

"D' you see that?" Conner gasped. "They got guns. Who are they?"

"*What* are they?" Smith coughed, dropping the binoculars and leaning his forehead against the mildewed wall, trying to recover his breath. The effort to stand was overwhelming. His joints throbbed. Every crevice in his seeping body alternately itched and burned. For the moment his discomfort was suppressed by fear of the intruders—ugly little beasts. Were these the pillagers of their colony come back? Perhaps the Killers of Shaula?

"Morgan must have ran right into their jaws," Conner wheezed, hopping on his good leg over to Smith's lookout. He grabbed the glasses and shoved them to the gun port. "They've come for us, too."

"What are they doing?" Cheskov gasped, struggling to his elbow.

"Climbing, I think," Conner replied, searching back and forth, high and low. "I lost them. Too damn dark."

"Should we turn on the security light?" Smith asked.

"They ain't vampires," Conner muttered.

"We're dead," Cheskov moaned, lying down.

"Not without a fight," Conner replied, grabbing a rifle. He checked the weapon's clip feeder and slung an extra ammo belt over his shoulder. He dragged himself to the corner near the trapdoor and collapsed behind a log buttress, propping his weapon into position.

Smith, fear overcoming all, put his head in his hands and slumped against the wall. He slid to the floor, trembling uncontrollably.

"Stop whimpering and get a weapon, Smith," Conner growled. "I'm tired of your act. You're in better shape than Morgan. You could have gone instead of her. For her sake, act like a man."

"We should just let them in," Smith cried. "Maybe—"

"Get a frigging rifle!" Conner barked, his voice cracking.

"Give . . . me a weapon, Smith," Cheskov gasped, pathetically struggling to sit. "I'll fight."

Smith, full of shame and horror, groped across the cluttered floor to the weapons cache and pulled two heavy automatics from the stack.

Something tapped gently on the door.

"What the hell?" Conner hissed.

"They're knocking at the damn door," Smith whispered.

"Quoth the raven, 'Nevermore,' " Cheskov whispered, taking the rifle. But he didn't have the strength to raise the barrel. Smith retreated against the wall and got ready to shoot. Something nagged at the back of his mind: a recollection, a pattern.

The tapping again: louder, rhythmic, familiar. Conner cleared his weapon and raised it to shoot. The knocking: *Tap, tap-tap-tap, tap . . . tap-tap*. Familiar. *Tap, tap-tap-tap, tap . . . tap, tap*.

"Don't shoot, Conner!" Smith shouted. "It's . . . a code! Shave and a haircut!" Smith staggered to his feet and, using the butt of his rifle, beat on the floor: *Thunk, thunk-thunk-thunk, thunk . . .* He stopped.

Bang, bang! came a pounding at the door.

"Two bits!" Conner whispered, pulling the barrel of his weapon back and pointing it into the air.

Godonov looked through the hatch at the darkening sky.

Morgan was unconscious, sedated. Catta Burl indicated that the colonist would be fine as soon as they got her to the motherships, but she was in no shape to go back into the jungle.

"Where are the hunters?" Godonov moaned. It had been an hour since their last report. Orbiting corvettes had a fix on the hunters' personal locators; they were still in the same place, three and a half kilometers to the southwest. What had happened? Tonto and Bottlenose should have been back at the lander long before sunset. Godonov's worry was laced with guilt.

"Local sunset, Nes," Flaherty announced. "Six-Alpha's ready."

"Tell them to hold," Godonov responded, trying to sound confident. The driller excavations on his legs throbbed with pain. "We'll go first. Open the door, Chief." Chastain took his position at the lander's hatch.

Lizard Lips squeaked with animation. He frantically pounded on the communicator and thrust it at Godonov.

I COME. I HELP. YOU NEED ME, the icons read. Godonov firmly shook his head. "No!" he signed, his hand signals crisp and unarguable "You stay!" He was not about to lose more cliff dwellers.

"Stand by," Chief Foster warned.

Two marines stood at the hatch with blasters on low power. Foster pulled the release. The hatch hissed into its overhead housing. A rainfall of insects pattered softly from the hatch rim. The marines recoiled frantically, raking the hatch apron with blasters.

"Stop!" Foster shouted. "They ain't alive. They were caught in the seals." Foster used compressed air to blow the opening clear.

Sucking up his courage, Godonov darted through the hatch and into the glare of the EPL's site lights, a cone of monochromatic whiteness. Unable to prevent himself, Godonov scrutinized his boot tops and pants legs for vermin. Chastain, stepping gingerly, led his marines onto the crusty landing site.

"Stop watching your feet," Chastain rumbled. "Heads up!"

The incandescent brilliance cast stark shadows that grew longer the farther one walked from the ship. It was less oppressive now that the sun had left the sky, but it was still hot and humid. Godonov lifted his eyes above the tall jagged horizon of the jungle and viewed the deepest, darkest hues of impending night. Bright stars, many in luminous clusters, twinkled in indifferent splendor.

"Get that laser going and clear a path to Six-Alpha," Chastain ordered. Two marines jumped on the robot truck and went to work.

Lights from Six-Alpha could be seen through the secondary foliage. Within fifteen minutes an avenue had been opened. The other EPL, a twin to their own, stood like a silver monument four hundred meters to the north. A chunky bullet slanted forty-five degrees; its collar of site lights threw down a sharply defined cone of incandescence. A two-hundred-meter gap of darkness separated the lander sites.

"Okay, Six-Alpha. This is landing team leader," Godonov broadcast. "We have a path clear to your position. The drillers are dormant. You are cleared to off-load."

There was movement at the lander's base. Marines scurried into defensive positions. Two humans moved through the dome of light and into the ribbon of blackness separating the EPLs. Godonov watched their silhouettes approach. A burly lieutenant and a noncom broke into Five-Alpha's circle of illumination, trotting up to Godonov's position. The officer's thighs bulged against the thick fabric of jungle shorts.

"First Lieutenant Kowolski," the officer said. "Let's go find our colonists."

"Yeah," Godonov replied, pulling up his science unit. "The hunters found the colonists' shelter at these coordinates. We've lost radio contact, but we've got their locators. I'm concerned—"

"Corporal Chastain," Kowolski ordered, "I want your men in tactical helmets—radios and night vision. Sergeant Carson's men will cover the landing zones. Let's get moving."

Chastain acknowledged and started shouting orders.

Godonov heard it first, a fluttering and then a screeching. It was far off but coming closer with each heartbeat.

"Listen!" Godonov shouted.

"What's that?" Kowolski asked, lifting his helmet.

"Get back in the landers!" Godonov said.

"What's the problem?" the marine officer asked.

"Something's coming," Godonov replied. The noise grew louder, coming right at them. Panic knotted Godonov's gut.

"Mr. Godonov's right, sir," Chastain said.

"What the hell's coming?" Kowolski asked, standing tall and surveying the darkness outside the cone of light.

"Yellows," Godonov replied, almost shouting. The low-pitched noise was thunderous, the screeching earsplitting.

"Yellows?" the officer snapped back.

"Monkeys, sir," Chastain shouted, lifting his rifle.

"Monkeys!" Kowolski shouted. "I'm not running from monkey noises. Form a defensive perimeter."

The words were hardly out of Kowolski's mouth when the jungle erupted with screeching shadows. As the black specters entered the stark cones of light around both landers, they flickered spectacularly into long-tailed streaks of vivid yellow, becoming golden darting meteors with faces of livid blue contorted in fear and rage, meteors with black lips drawn back from sharp teeth.

"Open fire!" Kowolski shouted, firing a big pistol into the onslaught. "Blasters! Area saturation! Fire! Fire!"

"What's going on?" Flaherty's voice, screaming over the radio, was frantic in Godonov's ear.

The marines laid down a fantastic barrage. Laser blasters hosed back and forth, cooking the small bodies into red jelly. But animals still got through, their yellow fur trailing contrails of smoke. The wretched comets were quickly dispatched with rifle and small arms fire, but then the laser blasters started losing their charge. The press of yellow fur was overwhelming. It was like shooting into a yellow, foam-crested tidal wave. A roiling current of screaming fur bounced and sprinted madly over the humans, cresting against the lander like a wave of golden water, splitting and flowing around it.

"Gotta close the hatches!" Chief Foster screamed.

"Give them ten seconds!" Flaherty shouted. "Everybody back inside!"

It was too late; the swirl of animals inundated them.

"Closing the hatches!" Foster shouted.

Creatures heavy with sinew covered them, blue faces contorted in fear and rage, snapping and clawing. Godonov beat away the first few and then fell to the ground, burying his face in the crusty dirt and covering his neck with gloved hands. With sudden horror Godonov realized that his face was pressed into the same dirt into which, only minutes earlier, a countless number of implacable flesh-eating drillers had burrowed. He jerked his face up, only to be kicked in the ear and clawed squarely in the mouth. Spitting blood, he drove his face back into the charred humus, praying for mercy from the planet's savage elements.

Animals pounced on his back and legs, sharp-clawed fingers tugging at his clothes. His flashlight was ripped from its lanyard. Metallic objects clattered around him. He lay on his science unit.

"Down!" someone shrieked. "Don't run! Get down!"

Futile gunfire sputtered to desultory potshots. Human screams commingled with screeches of the wild. The ground vibrated with the passage of frantic primates. Infinitely long minutes dragged by, an eternity of scuttling, shuffling, and screeching—howling animal voices, panicked, infuriated, insane. And the smell—a musky, fine-furred nightmare scent that would never be forgotten.

They were gone, and the silence was deafening. Someone groaned. Godonov lifted his head and looked to the side. A body, or what was left of a human, lay supine an arm's length away—Lieutenant Kowolski by the sewn insignia on his shoulder; there was no other way to tell. His face was gone, his bare legs and arms shredded. Chastain, hatless, one ear torn and bleeding, knelt nearby. The corporal still held his rifle, but his hands were crimson.

Another groan. Godonov looked around to see marines rising warily into crouches, some with weapons, an alarming number without. Several were horribly bloodied. Chastain staggered to his feet, a jagged cut across his cheek. He looked hopelessly about and then froze, staring wide-eyed into the jungle.

Godonov heard an unwelcome noise, a low-pitched, resonant growl, a buzzing. He pushed up onto his hands. Brushing cinders from his eyes, he squinted through swarms of settling dust motes coruscating in the bright cone of whiteness. Materializing from the haze, at the periphery of the landing site's surreal illumination, stood a long-armed, hulking form. Its massive, sloped skull framed sunken eyes that glowed coal-red. A prognathous lower jaw moved slowly up and down, modulating the rumbling growl. The dusty span between Godonov and the black-faced beast did little to mask the hideous display of teeth and drool. The buzzing increased in intensity.

"Mr. Godonov!" Chastain hissed. Godonov prized his stare away from the horrible animal. Chastain pointed into the darkness. Thirty degrees to the right two more Neanderthals sublimed from the darkness, two more sets of glowing coals. Godonov peered more intently and saw a third, a fourth, and a fifth horrible countenance skulking closer. Other shapes, silhouetted against glaring lights, slinked in the darkness between the landers. Ghouls!

Flaherty shouted over the radio, "We've got visit—"

The hollow, thundering discharge of Chastain's rifle masked the rest of Flaherty's warning. The horrible beast illuminated in the cone of light flailed backward and dropped like a sack of mud. Another weapon fired, but the gruesome apparitions had melted into the night.

FIFTY-TWO

RECALL

"Twelve alien ships, Mother!" Jakkuk snarled with malignant joy, staring at the solidifying images. The officer exulted in the hot effusion of blood to her brains. The animal within— her fear reflex, her *g'ort*—stirred as it had rarely stirred before. Jakkuk trembled with the unmistakably silky vibrations of dissociated rage.

"Yes," Dominant Dar hissed, hajil complexion flushing copper to bronze, an indication that she, too, felt the vicious sensations.

"F-fourteen heavy craft now c-confirmed in orbit, Cell Controller Jakkuk," the perspiring bridgemale amended, milky gray flesh draining. The male's stubby fingers fidgeted annoyingly. "Interstellars. Gravitron signatures correlate to emissions detected in system 1872."

"Fourteen!" Jakkuk repeated, her snarl descending to a basso roar. The bridgemales recoiled. Jakkuk snapped a glare at the nearest squat offender, her ire flaring. No roon was she! But that very self-awareness provided sufficient self-control to banish the tease of ecstasy. Her *g'ort* vanished, leaving a hole, a vacuum in her soul.

"What else, worm?" Jakkuk demanded, conscious anger inadequately replacing the exquisite subliminal rage of her *g'ort*.

"More than thirty-five screening vessels and pickets, Mother," the bridgemale replied with relief, instinctively attuned to the cell controller's emotional change. Jakkuk allowed her gaze to monitor the tactical holo. Images of the alien fleet solidified, fourteen large craft configured in a symmetrical gravitronic matrix floating in a constellation of escorts.

"A battle fleet," Dar stated, also returned to control. The fleet dominant posed regally, her thick braid of jet floating in a halo.

"Small wonder their trail is sharp," snarled Ship Mistress Kapu, the third hajil officer on the austere bridge. "They outnumber us two to one, and their detection systems have resolved our presence. There is no opportunity for ambush here."

"Honor is ours," another voice exhorted, monotonic inflections slithery and deadly. White-robed Karyai, the political, was the remaining presence on the bridge, languid at her post, blending into the alabaster luminescence, watching, observing, monitoring.

"Honor is ours, Karyai-lakk," Dar replied, silver eyes narrowing. "Yet battle is ill advised."

"Perhaps, Dar-hajil," the political replied, rising serenely. Karyai was tall even for a lakk, forcing the hajil officers to crane upward at the long features of the gray-faced mother. "Yet it is written: Engage and destroy the enemies of sisterhood."

"It is also written, Mother," the dominant replied, "dishonor not death with vain glory."

The political remained immobile for long seconds, and then her long gray eyelids slid slowly over orbs of pitch.

"Still engage," the political finally ordered, her steel voice betraying no emotion. "Engage not to do battle, Dar-hajil, merely to probe. If we cannot kill, then we will learn."

"To probe, Karyai-lakk," the dominant replied, nodding to Jakkuk.

Cell Controller Jakkuk pounded a fist against her breast and moved to her control station, her *g'ort* rising exquisitely. Ship Mistress Kapu and her bridgemales took action stations.

A contact alarm sounded—a rapid ringing—and then the braying countermeasures Klaxon. Runacres, grabbing his underway suit, dove from his underway cabin. He floated onto his flag bridge resplendent in nothing but his thermals. He stared up at the situation plot, hoping to see indications of Admiral Chou's transponders. Commander Ito followed him onto the bridge, carrying the admiral's boots.

"Unidentified contacts!" the flag tactical officer announced. "Sector three. We're targeted."

"Reorient the formation threat axis," Runacres ordered calmly, pulling on his jumpsuit. "Bring the fleet to general quarters."

"Aye, aye, Admiral," the tactical officer answered, triggering the signal. Runacres prayed that it was Admiral Chou, that it would only be another drill. His instincts shouted otherwise.

"General quarters," the boatswain announced. "All hands man your battle stations." GQ alarms clamored maniacally. Runacres reached into his battle locker and extracted his armor.

Wells and Wooden came on the bridge as Runacres sealed his helmet. The officers darted to their stations, displacing the watchstanders.

"Engagement radius in fifty-four hours, this course and speed," the tactical officer announced. "Refining radius. Fifty hours."

"Very well," Runacres acknowledged. He had two days to prepare for fleet action. Fast-movers and destructive probes could be in range in less than twenty-four.

"Confirmed unfriendlies," Wells reported as he pulled on his battle armor. Runacres jerked his gaze to the main status plot. Threat assessment processors declared the forming icons hostile.

"Reorienting screen axis," Captain Wooden announced.

"Weapons free," Runacres ordered, tethering down.

"Aye, Admiral," Wells replied.

Status boards illuminated firing zones. The fleet formation was too tight; there was excessive main battery overlap—wasted firepower.

"Formation two. Battle spread. Stagger the matrix," Runacres ordered. "Maintain gridlink. Clear your lines of fire."

"Formation two. Threat axis zero four eight hack niner zero," Wells announced, sealing his helmet.

"Sir," the tactical officer announced. "Contact resolution on six interstellar ships. They're painting us."

"Any communications?" Runacres demanded. "Are they talking?"

"Not in any way detectable, Admiral," Wells responded. "We're being scanned, but we're not picking up any patterned emissions."

"Very well," Runacres grunted. Six enemy capital ships. He had the weight of numbers. Was the advantage sufficient? Runacres called up unit commanders. Instantaneously the images of fourteen ship captains and Commodore Wells were displayed. Some were in the process of giving orders, but all quickly turned their attention to the flag summons.

"Prepare for combat," Runacres announced. "Stand by for orders."

The arrayed officers acknowledged. An interrogation signal illuminated. Runacres acknowledged, and the image of Bobby Foxx, hatchet-faced skipper of *T.L.S. New Zealand,* centered on his screen.

"Bring on the bastards, Admiral," the officer exhorted. "We owe 'em for Oldfather." Several ship captains hit their acknowledgment buttons.

"Our primary objective is unchanged," Runacres declared stonily. "Our mission is to make peaceful contact. Everything will be done to attain that objective! I say again: everything will be done to make peaceful contact. Is that understood?"

Acknowledgment lights illuminated with perfunctory alacrity. *Eire*'s interrogation diode illuminated. Runacres acknowledged, and Captain Merriwether's image took the center.

"We're still transmitting our brotherly love," Merriwether drawled. "I recommend we terminate those transmissions for several hours. Our message of peace will be all the louder when it resumes."

"Concur," Runacres replied.

"Transmissions terminating," Wells announced.

"Stand by for orders," Runacres declared. "Commodore Wells, issue the battle plan sequence."

His operations officer acknowledged electronically and proceeded to download engagement schemes and support permutations. The primary battle plan would not survive enemy contact, but at least his commanders would react in concert to the first magnitude of grievous disruption.

"Very well," Runacres announced, seeing all ships successfully linked to the active operation plan. "Today we turn a page in the history of the human race, nay, in the history of our galaxy! Stand at your stations. Hold your positions. We are here to make peace. Failing that, remember Oldfather." He signed off.

"Jump coordinates set, Admiral," Wells reported. "Earth Lima Two."

"Very well, Franklin," Runacres replied. "Captain Wooden, recall all corvettes. Set combat screens—high and low defensive arcs on the threat axis. Hold one-third of your assets in maneuvering reserve."

Smith moved to the door. Night had fallen.

"Okay." Conner gulped, struggling to position his weapon. Cheskov, mewling in pain, brought his rifle to bear. "Let 'em in."

Smith unlatched the door and slumped against the wall, his rifle at his waist, ready to fire on full automatic. The door, their last defense against the unholy terrors of the jungle, perhaps of the universe, swung slowly open, letting in a dank breeze. The oppressive, swampy stink was almost refreshing compared with their shelter's putrescence. Smith peered into the murk.

The jungle had a luminescence that was faint and without comfort. Smith could make out darker shadows of platform railings and vine-shrouded tree boles. His finger tightened on his trigger, overwhelming fear displacing resurgent hope. Why should they trust a simple knock pattern? How could such grotesque beings possibly represent rescue?

A short shadow moved into the threshold. Smith recoiled and knocked against a shutter support. Conner's blurry shadow stirred, his rifle trembling forward with unequivocal intent. The phantasmal shadow disappeared, and the humans froze, waiting.

The knocking again. *Tap, tap-tap-tap, tap . . . tap, tap.* Cheskov groaned and collapsed against the wall.

"Yeah! Yeah!" Conner squeaked, his voice broken with terror. "We hear you, asshole."

Smith banged out the first five notes on the floor, waiting for the mystery beings to respond. Instead of a two-tap response, something solid was thrown through the door. The object clattered across the floor, an ebony shadow immersed in velvet darkness.

"What was that?" Conner grimaced. "Did you see it, Smith?"

"Yeah," Smith whispered. "I'll ... check it out." Swallowing his fear, Smith painfully slipped to his knees and crawled, groping, to where the object had fallen. Just as his fingers discovered its form, he detected motion at the door. His brain analyzed the article's compact geometry. He could feel Conner tensing to shoot.

"Don't shoot, Conner," Smith gasped, staggering back to the wall. "It's a pistol! They gave us a pistol."

"What?" Conner said, disbelievingly. Smith staggered to the wall and flipped the light switch. Solar-powered lights came on strongly.

All three men inhaled audibly. At the door was a short, sinewy creature of appalling ugliness. Its double-lidded black eyes glared with fierce intensity; its red maw cracked open, revealing a long snout filled with glistening white teeth.

"Look," Conner wheezed, "on his chest."

Smith could not credit his eyes. The beast wore chest and groin armor of a familiar green hue; on the breast was stenciled in black: TLF MARINE CORPS.

"What the ..." Smith exhaled.

"Conner," Cheskov whimpered. "Conner, behind you!"

Smith and Conner turned. There, obscured in the cluttered corner of the shelter, beyond a surreptitiously opened trapdoor, was another knobby-headed beast, also garbed in marine-green armor. It slowly holstered a pistol, opened its gruesome mouth, and chittered nervously. It bowed, holding out its hands palms up.

"Sergeant Carson just died," Catta Burl said, applying a disinfectant to Godonov's torn lip. "The other wounded are stabilized. Alpha-Six's med-tech has everything under control. I can help you."

"You stay, Burl," Godonov ordered. "We're going in and coming out fast."

Kowolski and Carson were dead, and three others had been completely or partially blinded. Tonto and Bottlenose were missing, probably savaged by some jungle beast. Godonov examined his science unit and verified the heading to the hunters' locator beacons. Chastain stood ready with Privates Vegas and Hanks, awaiting orders. The remaining marines still standing were posted as perimeter guards.

"Why don't we wait for reinforcements?" Flaherty asked over the radio. "They'll bring down a crawler and just blast their way in."

"The settlers can't wait for a heavy-lifter to make orbit, nor can the hunters," Godonov replied, moving resolutely toward the edge of the floodlit area. He prayed the hunters were with the colonists.

"It's your landing party," Flaherty replied.

"Yeah," Godonov muttered. He grabbed a rifle.

Godonov checked out his night vision optics and secured a field lamp to his chest armor. Chastain stepped into the darkness first, the beam from his chest light shooting before him. Vegas and Hanks followed, with Godonov trailing in their footsteps.

"Mr. Godonov," Chastain said on the helmet radio, "field lamps or night vision gear? Can't use both."

Godonov pondered his options. Lights kept the vampires away.

"Lights," he ordered.

Fifty meters beyond the cone of light they confronted the seamless wall of jungle. Chastain hesitated, turning toward Godonov. The science officer signaled for the marines to spread out. Swallowing his fears, Godonov shouldered his way into the vine-tangled undergrowth. Chastain and Vegas went to his left, and Private Hanks stepped out to his right. They advanced slowly, trying to keep each other in sight. The black jungle quieted as they advanced. Herbal odors commingled with fetid rot and their own pungent redolence as the perspiring humans brushed and crushed the undergrowth.

Godonov estimated that they had traveled approximately a kilometer. Sweat poured from his body, and stinging insects hummed in his ears. He slung his rifle and checked his science unit, updating his position.

The buzzing noise started again, sliding higher in volume and pitch.

An assault rifle discharged to Godonov's left, its muzzle blasts lighting up the underside of the jungle. A human scream! In the strobing light Godonov saw dark shapes moving. A thrown object struck him squarely in the back, blasting the breath from his lungs and knocking him forward. As he fell facefirst into the brush, his chest light was covered. His science unit swung against its lanyard, and his rifle, still slung on his shoulder, banged against his helmet. The buzzing noise drew frighteningly near. As Godonov struggled to regain his feet, an irresistible force yanked on the lanyard to his science unit. Godonov leaned back on his knees and pulled his pistol.

The beam from his chest light revealed the savage countenance of a ghoul straining to rip away his science unit. It screamed. The warm, foul odor of its breath rolled across Godonov's face. Godonov fired point-blank, and the creature lunged backward into darkness. Automatic rifle fire sprayed the jungle to his left and right. Godonov wiped sweat from his eyes, holstered his pistol, and swung his rifle from his shoulder. He fired a short sweeping burst into random darkness.

"Cease fire!" Chastain shouted.

Godonov swept the area with his light. He could not see Chastain even though the marine's voice was only paces away.

"They got my light," Private Hanks shouted. The frightened marine, his face running with perspiration, moved closer to the science officer, taking desperate comfort in Godonov's leaf-chopped beam of light.

"They got mine, too," Chastain growled. "Vegas, how about you?"

Vegas did not answer.

The knobby-headed aliens dropped into the black void. Smith, burdened with Cheskov's limp form, followed the creatures through the trapdoor and down the square column of light cast from above. Smith held Cheskov to the ladder while Conner supported the man's weight with a rope from above. Smith's arthritic fingers protested at the abuse. His back muscles screamed, his joints throbbed, and the hammers of hell pounded in his head. His relief at making the yielding jungle floor was cathartic. Exhausted, he dropped Cheskov to the ground and leaned against the stout tree supporting their fort. He stared into darkness, wondering if he would ever see sanctuary again.

Cheskov lay groaning at his feet in the square of light from the open trapdoor. The hunters were invisible. Conner, clasping a crutch, wheezed to the ground. He unhooked their only flashlight from his belt and swung its beam around the azimuth, zigzagging high and low, the standard precaution before moving at night. A hunter materialized from the darkness, spindly hand shielding its eyes. It signaled impatiently for the humans to follow.

"Let's go," Connor wheezed.

His crutch-supported gait stirred the humus as he came over to help Smith hoist Cheskov. Conner needed his free hand for the crutch. Smith took the flashlight. Together, very slowly, the three humans, surrounded by impenetrable darkness, dragged themselves away from the lights of the tree shelter. Within a minute all vestiges of that beacon were swallowed by the jungle, leaving only their tenuous tunnel of portable light.

They had trudged five hundred meters when a ghoul's fiendish hum made Smith's backbone dance. Something whirred through the air. Smith's wrist snapped with the impact of a heavy object; the torch flicked aside, its beam careening skyward. Conner screamed to retrieve the light, but Smith was immobilized with pain. Cheskov's dead weight dragged both men to the ground. Smith looked up to see their precious light beam jiggling crazily, circling upward. The gloating growl of a large ghoul resounded through the jungle.

It was Thompson's watch, but Buccari slept fitfully at her pilot station. The irritating aural alarm in her helmet brought her reluctantly alert. Her tongue tasted like a rancid rag.

"Skipper, fleet is broadcasting an emergency recall," Tasker reported. "*Condor One* wants immediate status."

"Roger." Buccari grimaced, blinking at the bright planet below. She pulled the comm screen up and read the authenticated text—ALL UNITS: CATEGORY ONE RECALL—a simple message, repeated twenty times. Something was happening, something very bad.

"How much longer before Flaherty comes over the hill?" she asked, simultaneously interrogating the orbital parameters manager.

"Line of sight in twenty-two minutes," Thompson replied. The computer validated his response.

"Acknowledge and respond," Buccari ordered. "*Condor Five* holding orbit to retrieve EPL and surviving colonists."

Communications acknowledged. Within seconds Tasker came back: "Condor authorizes one orbit only."

"Tight," Thompson said. "We may have to leave them."

"No way," Buccari muttered, staring into space.

* * *

Brappa screeched his anger, drew his pistol, and took aim. The wily creature used the tree trunk as a shield. The light stick was gone. That was unfortunate for the long-legs, but at least now the irritating luminescence would not dim the hunters' night sight. Already Brappa's range of vision was accommodating to the darkness. Brappa distinguished beasts swinging in the trees, their halting passage infuriatingly leisurely. Brappa debated shooting at the brutes but decided to conserve ammunition. The ugly creatures seemed sufficiently repulsed by the hunters' signaling screams.

"Hark!" Sherrip twittered.

Brappa also heard the reports of long-leg death sticks; the welcomed explosions were difficult to localize in the baffling maze of vegetation. The hunters prodded the ungainly long-legs to their feet.

"This way," Brappa signaled. The hunters shepherded the stumbling trio, making their way slowly through nature's uneven tangle.

The buzzing noise sounded again, growing louder. It came from many animals this time, from many directions—too many. The hunters scanned the canopy and saw movement everywhere.

"They come!" Sherrip shrieked.

"They are here," Brappa hissed.

Brappa pulled his pistol. The warrior knew battle well. The outcome was no longer in doubt. Alone, the hunters might survive, but their mission was to bring back the long-legs. They could not leave their charges; therefore, they would die with them. Brappa screeched the death song. Sherrip did the same loudly and vibrantly. The buzzing diminished and then grew stronger. Brappa looked up and saw an animal dropping on them. He shot it as it fell. Sherrip fired and fired again.

Three buzzing brutes leapt from the vines, springing over the fallen long-legs. Brappa and Sherrip each killed one, but the third took Sherrip down before Brappa was able to dispatch it. Brappa leaned over his comrade. Sherrip pushed him off.

"We must fight," Sherrip screamed, but one arm remained at his side. To the accompaniment of the horrible buzzing, the stalwart hunter resumed the death song with a trembling voice. Brappa was about to join him in singing of their glorious death when flashes of white light flitted through the leaves. He heard the unmistakable voice of Big-ears shouting his long-leg name.

* * *

"Tonto!" Godonov bellowed over and over.

He heard their screeches and the unmistakable sound of their lightweight pistols. He also heard the gut-binding buzzing of the ghouls, mind-numbingly loud.

"Hold your fire!" Godonov ordered. "I hear the hunters."

"Me, too," Chastain roared. "This way. Shoot high."

The big marine plunged ahead of the light beam, diving into the jungle, his big automatic spraying the skies. The buzzing was louder than ever, a flood tide of vibrating insanity.

With neck-wrenching violence Godonov was knocked flat on his back, a great hairy beast tackling him to the ground. Sharp, implacable teeth gained a purchase high on his left arm.

"Shoot it!" Godonov screamed, grabbing for his pistol.

The ghoul viciously ground his jaw on Godonov's shoulder and then fell away, clutching his chest light. Private Hanks blasted the beast with a heavy-fingered burst. The animal screamed and fell, the light tumbling crazily into the underbrush. Both Godonov and Hanks jumped frantically to retrieve it, but in a heartbeat the light was flying through the air in the clutches of another ghoul. Hanks wasted a long, desperate burst trying to bring it down.

It was pitch black.

Godonov's shoulder throbbed with searing pain. Blood ran with sweat down his arm and back. He shook his head clear.

A hunter's pistol fired.

A loud grunt! And then a roar.

"Shit!" Private Hanks cried. "What's that?"

Some horrible beast was roaring, a ferocious baritone intermixing with ghoulish growls and banshee screams. It was a human!

"Chastain!" Hanks gasped. Godonov and Hanks stumbled after the noise. Branches and vines whipped and cracked furiously, as if elephants were thrashing in the jungle. The heavy thud of fist on muscle and bone sounded repeatedly. Godonov's eyes slowly adjusted. Shadows danced in front of him. Godonov jerked his rifle to bear, his finger heavy on the trigger. And then he distinguished Chastain's white face rising moonlike from the ground.

"Arrggh!" Chastain grunted, heaving something heavy into the brush.

Godonov remembered his night vision optics and dropped them in front of his eyes. He had no peripheral vision, but at least he could discriminate objects. The pink-purple shape in front of him screeched—it was Tonto. Godonov reached out and touched silky fur that was soaking wet with perspiration. Bottlenose moved into view. Something else was at his vision limits, white and blurry—he made out the colonists lying in a heap at the base of huge tree.

"You okay, Jocko?" Godonov asked.

"Bleeding a little," Chastain gasped.

"Me, too," Godonov wheezed. The heat was oppressive.

"They got us now," Hanks whined, his voice over the helmet radio obscenely loud.

"Listen," Chastain whispered.

"What?" Godonov mumbled, lifting his helmet to hear.

"The buzzing's stopped," Chastain said. The humming growl had switched off like a light.

"Where'd they go?" Hanks whimpered.

Godonov's heart pounded in his chest. He remembered something the colonist Morgan had said.

"Vampires," Godonov whispered. "Vampires keep the primates away."

Flaherty picked up the recall on a relay from *Condor Two*. "Damn!" he shouted, sitting up and staring down into the cone of harsh illumination defining his EPL, a vulnerable mote of civilization in a sea of steamy terror.

Two marines crouched in defensive positions. Across the landing site he could see the other apple surrounded by its own cone of illumination. The inscrutable jungle, vine-draped trees tall and foreboding, surrounded him, seeming to lean inward. The jungle absorbed the glaring spotlights, and clouds obscured the stars.

"You get that, Flack?" asked Jepson, the pilot of Six-Alpha.

"Roger," Flaherty replied. "When's your window close?"

"Forty minutes," Jepson replied. "I'll hang around as long as I can."

"Appreciate it," Flaherty replied. "Our partygoers may need the help. I got an hour before I turn into a pumpkin."

Jepson signed off.

"Okay, Chief," Flaherty said, switching to the intercom. "Let's warm up the barrels. Emergency recall."

"Aye, sir," Chief Foster responded. "I copied. Fuel pressures are up. Bringing tertiaries on line now."

"Roger," Flaherty replied, staring again into the dark jungle.

"Hey, Nes!" Flaherty said, keying his radio mike. "You read me?"

Nothing! Flaherty stared into the night, waiting.

"Five-Alpha. Team leader. Talk to me, Godonov," he tried again.

"Yeah," Godonov's transmission came back—a whisper. "Can't talk."

"Okay, buddy, I copy," Flaherty replied, hands moving furiously about his cockpit. "We've been recalled, Nes. I'm starting checklists. You need to terminate shore leave while you still have a taxi."

The double click of a mike button was Godonov's only response.

Vampires growled above them.

Smith's knees were buckling. His wrist was broken, but he tried not to slow down the others. He staggered after the big marine, the one called Jocko, trying to stay in his leaf-whipping wake as they crashed through the jungle. The big marine carried Cheskov. Conner was somewhere behind, being half carried by the other two marines. The little aliens had disappeared, but he could hear their pistols firing. Muzzle blasts strobed the jungle. They would soon run out of ammunition.

Far ahead Smith could see a glow, a white sparkling brilliance filtering through the vines and liana. The landing site! They were almost out of the jungle; his prayers would be answered. He would once again see other humans, eat real food, wear clean clothes.

He turned to see how far behind Conner and the others were. He heard them coming and pushed forward, fixating on the precious rays, the white shafts of purity penetrating the dark steamy jungle only meters away. He saw motes and bugs casting about in the gleam.

A brutal impact staggered him.

An implacable force penetrated the back of Smith's neck. His body was lifted violently from the ground, stopping his progress toward the light. The light receded as he flew upward. Yet there was no hurt, no pain at all, in any of his battered nerve endings. His sensory system collapsed into welcome grayness. His corporeal form flailed against a tree, but Smith's awareness was that of a disinterested observer. Smith knew he was dying and welcomed the escape. Darkness overwhelmed him. He would never see light again.

* * *

"Almost there, Flack," Godonov gasped. Hanks supported the colonist's limp form while Godonov made his report. Godonov's left arm hung lifeless at his side. He had lost his rifle. Sweat ran in his eyes. He had retracted the night vision optics; they were useless in the jungle with fronds and leaves covering his face. It was like opening one's eyes in pounding surf. But his natural night vision, abetted by recurring pulses of adrenaline, had grown acute with the passage of time.

"Roger," Flaherty replied, his tone annoyingly strong and secure. "I need you back real quick."

"That's high . . . on my list of priorities," Godonov panted, taking some of the colonist's weight. They staggered forward again, one uncoordinated step at a time.

Suddenly Chastain loomed in front of him. One of the hunters, Bottlenose, was with him.

"Where's the other colonist—" Hanks started to say.

"Shhhh!" Chastain hissed. "Bottlenose says they got him."

"Who—" Godonov started to ask, but immediately knew better.

"Vamps!" Chastain gasped. "They're all around us. Stay close. The hunters are out of ammo."

Bottlenose shrieked. Something big moved above them. Godonov detected movement. He pulled down his IR optics. Above them, staring down coldly, were a pair of saucer eyes, faintly crepuscular. A huge catlike body, only more muscular, tanklike, supported a wide, goggle-eyed gargoyle head. Godonov dropped the colonist and reached for his pistol. When he looked back up, the monster was gone. So was Bottlenose. A hunter screamed viciously. The underbrush exploded.

"Move!" Chastain ordered, pushing everyone before him. He juggled the unconscious colonist over his shoulder like a sack of sand.

Hanks and Godonov, dragging the other colonist between them, flailed into the underbrush and pushed through a thicket. A huge pair of eyes leapt straight at them, blasting them apart like tenpins. Godonov's helmet was ripped off, and the back of his neck grew warm with blood. Dazed, Godonov struggled to his knees, pulling his pistol.

Hanks screamed. The lights, refracted and shadowed by foliage, were not far away. In their faint glow Godonov saw the marine being dragged off. Godonov fired his pistol at a monstrous shadow, his rapid-fire muzzle blasts freezing the monster's image as he riddled its unspeakable form.

Hanks, shrieking, jumped to his feet with the frenetic nimbleness of panic and lurched blindly into the fronds.

"Big-shit trouble," Chastain said, pushing Godonov from behind. "The place is crawling." Chastain fired intermittent single shots from his rifle. "Muzzle blasts seem to hold them off."

"As long as the ammo holds out," Godonov said. "Let's move."

The hunters shrieked. Godonov, in agony from his wounds, reached down to pick up the downed colonist. Another black-eyed devil streaked from the trees. Godonov sensed it coming, his hearing suddenly acute. Knowing he was going to die, he turned to face his executioner.

Condor Six's EPL launched, its detonations blasting a shock wave through the trees. The flash of its exhaust was akin to an angry sun arising in the middle of the night. The jungle exploded with angular, stroboscopic light and pulsating shadows.

The beast coming for Godonov was illuminated in midleap, frozen in a beam of pure white light. The goggle-eyed monster fell from the black night as if it had been shot, landing on its face and spraying Godonov with leaves and dirt. The vampire made a frenetic dervish effort to stand, and then it went catatonic, back legs tangled beneath its muscular form. Godonov raised his pistol and shot it dead.

"Move!" Chastain shouted.

Forcing his own movement, Godonov swept his gaze about the surreal scene. Saucer-eyed monsters postured all around, some only a sweep of their horrible claws from the humans. The goggle-eyed terrors stared dumbly into the light, their pinkish-gray forms graven in the dark like horrible statuary from a fiend's nightmare.

"Move!" Chastain shouted again, spraying monsters with bursts of automatic fire. "Run for your lives!"

Blood and sweat pouring down his face, Godonov lifted the groaning colonist and stumbled forward. Chastain, with the colonist over his shoulder, crashed into the vines, boring a hole in the jungle toward the faint scattering of light. A hunter screeched. Godonov spotted a cliff dweller on the flank, moving wraithlike through flickering shadows.

The flare of light from the EPL was nearly gone. The vampires would be on the move. Godonov thrashed in panic through the vines. To his left Chastain's rifle threw out a burst of fire. A vampire shrieked. A great shadow slinked sinuously into his awareness, ahead and high. Clasping the colonist to him, Godonov fired twice before running out of bullets. He was rewarded with a primal scream. He pushed into the clinging vines, leaning desperately toward the glimmering.

"Team leader, come in! Nestor!" Flaherty transmitted again. "Come on, Nes! Talk to me." There was no response. He stared at the chronometer, his launch window inexorably narrowing. Recall notices arrived with unceasing urgency. He had secured the aural alarms, but the blinking override lights were merciless: FLEET RECALL. FLEET RECALL. He squirmed in his seat, anxious to leave the relentless tug of gravity.

"Gunfire's getting closer," Chief Foster informed him.

Helpless, Flaherty moved his anxious glance outside. All he could see was the stark cone of light and two wary marines. The planet was shrouded in darkness, a jungle, a mystery. Humanity, intelligence, civilization—whatever one wanted to call it—was a pinprick of light in a sea of atavistic darkness. This planet had no master.

The sentries moved closer to the boundary with the unknown, weapons poised. Flaherty watched as if sitting in a theater box. The radio in his ear provided a meaningless, panicked overture of commentary.

Actors entered stage left, falling awkwardly into the spotlight. The first was a marine, dragging his leg, fatigues shredded. The young trooper looked up into the harsh site lights as if seeing the sacred spheres of heaven. He returned his attention outward, searching for his comrades. Godonov fell onto the stage, supporting another human being in tatters, one of the colonists, and then Chastain erupted powerfully from the fronds, walking backward, firing his rifle from the hip. On Chastain's shoulder was another colonist, limp arms flailing with Chastain's movements.

Finally the hunters came. One was injured, his wing trailing on the ground. But both creatures struggled with a heavy object—a carcass easily three times their combined bulk. They dragged it into the light, leaping and tugging at its unyielding mass. Once they were clearly into the circle of light, their snouts lifted, mouths gaping for air and jagged teeth glinting in the pure light. One of the hunters, brandishing a long knife, ferociously leapt on the dead beast and with marvelous dispatch stripped the goggle-eyed horror of its pelt.

"Get them strapped in, Chief," Flaherty ordered, initiating final takeoff checks. "We're outta this hellhole."

Buccari watched the EPL approach. Hers was the only corvette in planetary orbit. Commander Rowan and the rest of Condor were already streaking out of the planet's gravity well, pulling away to rejoin the fleet. She checked tactical. Lagging behind the Condor flight but still far ahead of her position was the fleet fueler, heading back at its best velocity.

Condor Five was alone.

"Checklists complete, Skipper," Thompson reported. "Engineering has everything on line. Power reservoirs at maximums. Apple's in sight."

"Very well," Buccari replied. She lifted the throttle guard and checked tethers. "Order Flaherty and his cargo to remain strapped in. I'm setting a hard vector as soon as the docking collars close."

She did not want to be late for the party.

FIFTY-THREE

BATTLE OF HORNBLOWER

"Invoke the battle plan, Jakkuk-hajil," Dar ordered.

"As the dominant commands," the cell controller replied, settling into the insinuating embrace of the control pod.

Jakkuk relaxed and accepted neural interfacing. Her vision remained, but it was overwhelmed with hyperdimensional gaming matrices. Shutting her eyes, she established axonic links. Pancortex thought tendrils made contact. As usual Ship Mistress Kapu's intimate psychorhythms generated a nerve-tickling harmonic. At the other end of the sensory scale Mistress y'Trig, the cell's only roonish ship mistress, provided two personality receptors: one harsh, the other merely disconcerting.

Despite the racial dissonance, Jakkuk envied the roons their exquisite schizophrenia. Roons maintained touch with their *g'ort*—with their orgasmic fear—at all times. Occasionally it was difficult to tell one personality from the other. That was the danger of the roon.

There remained another roon with which to link: Destroyer-Fist a'Yerg, the attack commander. Attack command was suited for roons, whose rapacious natures were without remorse. With a'Yerg there was no mistaking the animal. Jakkuk strove to link with the destroyer commander, first confronting a'Yerg's hostile persona. The *g'ort* of a'Yerg was the strongest she had ever encountered. Jakkuk signaled for a bridgemale to open a circuit; the roon's psychic obstruction was infuriating. Jakkuk's anger throbbed into the command matrix.

"Do they continue with their broadcasts?" Dar inquired, a voice from another plane.

"Their simpering pleas for galactic cooperation have terminated," Jakkuk replied, cooling her anger. The electromagnetic ether was at last quiet except for the static of the stars.

"Perhaps they mean to do battle," resounded the slithery voice of the lakk, a voice from the highest plane. There was a cruel laugh.

As Jakkuk pondered, a sudden surge of roon *g'ort* swept her being—a'Yerg! Like a tuning fork held close, the intruding emotions sympathetically resonated with Jakkuk's own animal, awakening it ruthlessly. Curse the roon! Almost helplessly Jakkuk was linked to the destroyer-fist, their animal selves reveling in sensual fraternization. Jakkuk abhorred the diminution of her control and pulsed the cell control signal to profligate levels, asserting her telepathy with overwhelming intensity. A'Yerg's animal was pounded from her awareness. Jakkuk's own *g'ort*, stimulated by violation and not by fear, was left fluttery and weak. Without reinforcement, it flickered and died.

So it had to be.

Runacres returned to the bridge after a respite in his underway cabin. His eyes were scratchy; his nap had not been restful. The first day of the Battle of Hornblower dragged slowly into history. The fleets moved closer, with attack and screening units adjusting to the movements of the adversary. *How do you kiss a tiger?*

"Their motherships continue to move on an intercept course," Wells reported. "Thirty fast-movers are advancing at point six five but taking a circuitous route. On its present course the attack force will sweep past the screen at range limit and curl between us and the planet, using the gravity well for a whip, I suspect."

"Carmichael is adjusting to their attack profile, Admiral," Wooden reported. "However, Condor flight rising off Hornblower Three is vulnerable. Commander Rowan is asking for instructions."

"Condors will have to take care of themselves," Runacres replied.

"Peculiar tactics," Wells added.

"All the more effective," Runacres said. "Anything else?"

"The alien interstellar ships are holding in jump formation. They respect our greater numbers."

"They should," Runacres replied, pondering the developments. Why were the alien fast-movers maneuvering to his rear?

"UHF transmissions!" the tactical officer reported.

"Jupiter's balls!" Wells shouted. "Listen to this, Admiral."

Destroyer-Fist a'Yerg's animal screamed into the endless darkness, the yodeling battle cry of the roonish warrior. She screamed for her ancestors, screamed for her victims, for death.

A'Yerg's analytic being felt the tidal force of Jakkuk's telepathic escalation. Such desperate overgrasping! A'Yerg squelched her raging animal, allowing Jakkuk's angry presence to weave itself into her being. Nay, a'Yerg's mind deliciously embraced the intruding tendrils and intertwined them in her own dendritic fusion. Now was the time for killing. Cooperation would engender victory. She welcomed the union, relished it. Her sense of power blossomed, even if vicariously through the hajil cell controller. Ah, exquisite power, death-spewing power. And in death—new life. Her animal raged, and again a'Yerg gave her *g'ort* vent, screaming.

Fist a'Yerg's destroyer wing blasted across the alien screen, slanting ever closer, testing armament ranges. Energy beams flicked out at nine hundred *talers*. Her shields easily resisted the lancing beams, requiring only limited ion balancing. A'Yerg was content to exercise the aliens, who demonstrated no proclivity for offense. Like a game of *quors,* the battlefield was hers to arrange. The roon took note of alien ships rising from the planet, no doubt a planet survey returning from the pillaged colony. Her animal growled with satisfaction at the memory.

A'Yerg directed Destroyer-Hand y'Map to intercept. The energy potential of her force was so high, she could afford the excursion. Her orders were to exploit weakness, and this was too inviting a target to forgo. She logged her intentions and received no countermand.

Another roonish scream rent the galaxy—distinctively that of Hand y'Map. Good soldier she; the destroyer triad leader gave vent to her own savage animal. A'Yerg's *g'ort,* unhindered by rational inhibition, joined in the chorus, celebrating her sister's glorious assignment. Victory would be hers.

"They're going after the Condors, Skipper," Pulaski transmitted on the laser band. "Listen to 'em, would you!"

"Eye on the ball, Ski," Carmichael admonished. "Group will dispatch intercept. Screen's job is to protect the motherships."

Carmichael glanced at tactical and saw the Condors rising from the planet—only five. A fleet fueler followed.

There she was! The sixth Condor coming off the planet— Buccari's corvette. With a desperate effort Carmichael repressed the distraction. Another brace of hypervelocity probes approached screen sector two. He cleared Kite to intercept and then called a flight of Blackhawks out of reserve and ordered them to be used as a hot rotation for a division of Merlins. Carmichael had to keep fuel levels high and crews rested. He should have called his own number for rotation. His eyes burned.

Buccari's 'vette was rapidly overtaking the fleet fueler, its friendly icon winking blue on tactical. She expanded range scales and stared anxiously at the grand chess game unfolding before her. The two main fleets, surrounded by fireflies of fast-movers, fuelers, and other support vessels, moved ponderously closer. The alien fast-movers continued to slide around the fleet, holding their distance—testing. Carmichael maneuvered his screen assets, leapfrogging corvettes from position to position, anticipating the enemy's approach vectors, constantly changing defensive patterns.

With far more anxiety Buccari watched a detached section of alien fast-movers streaking at the Condors. Commander Rowan had driven his flight hard, gaining velocity at the expense of battle endurance, but the aliens had a tremendous energy advantage as well as a better gravity position. Once again she hit the maneuvering alarm. She hammered on five gees. Her survival depended on joining her squadron.

"Sh-shame to leave any fuel in that pumper," Flaherty grunted.

"Don't plan to," Buccari replied. She opened a laser connection.

"Atlas, *Condor Five*," she transmitted.

"Go, Five," the fueler pilot replied, her voice tight as a drum.

"Boost up to my vector," Buccari ordered. "I'm plugging."

"No way, Five," the pilot replied, "you're going like ratshit on a railgun. I'll spring this bucket's keel hopping your curve. Not to mention burn up my load. Someone else may need gas."

"Give it everything, Atlas," Buccari persisted. "That pumper can's history. You'll never get through. I'm removing your crew and taking all the gas I can suck down."

There was silence.

"Nothing heard, Atlas," Buccari barked. "You copy, Atlas?"

After another pause the fueler pilot replied, "Copy, Booch."

The icon for the fueler flashed an acceleration indicator. Buccari programmed her approach and laser-linked hookup telemetry. The fueler acknowledged. The computer indicated rendezvous in three hours.

"We're cut off," Thompson reported. "Those bugs are holding a hard intercept on Condor. I count six."

"Time for some hardball," Flaherty added.

"Their commander does not assume attack formation," Karyai said.

"Nor does she respond to Fist a'Yerg's demonstration," Jakkuk reported. Jakkuk transmitted a telepathic signal to all ship mistresses to stand by for maneuvers. Acknowledgments were immediate.

"A most conservative adversary," the political remarked. "She remains in matrix, ready to depart."

"As do we, Karyai-lakk," Dar replied.

"Perhaps a more emphatic diversion is in order," Karyai spit. "Attack the alien screen on the far reach. Let us test their mettle."

"Of course, Mother," Dar replied, authorizing the political's order. "Cell Controller Jakkuk, as ordered."

"As the dominant commands," Jakkuk answered, delivering the order.

Fist a'Yerg watched with ecstasy as Hand y'Map led her triads into a classic energy pincer, closing like a hammer and anvil on the hapless aliens. The alien flight leader was countering, but y'Map's destroyers would not be denied.

She also sensed Jakkuk's presence; the cell controller's psychokinetic signature was familiar to a'Yerg's mind. More emotional was the description that came to her, but emotions were filtered by the matrix. A'Yerg's *g'ort* sensed Jakkuk's telepathic intrusion also. Her animal surged playfully, cruelly attempting to control the controller. In vain; a'Yerg pushed her demon ego roughly into the shadows.

"Attack command," came Jakkuk's beckoning.

"Yes, Mother," a'Yerg verbalized.

Attack, came the telepathic signal. *Attack alien screening units. Probe and penetrate as able.*

A'Yerg turned her attention from the imminent skirmish back to the alien screen. The attack commander studied her more eminent target, analyzing her options, measuring, searching. It was time to attack. Puckishly, a'Yerg loosed her *g'ort* on the cell controller's dentritic link. A'Yerg sensed Jakkuk squirming with vicarious delight.

Condor Five was dwarfed by the gray bulk of the fleet fueler. Buccari matched velocities with the auxiliary and drove her corvette beneath its service blister, into the port refueling station. The clatter and the hollow thumping of grapples and service connections vibrated her ship. Mating locks and static probes signaled positive. Fuel transfer commenced almost immediately.

"Gotta be the all-time-record plug," Flaherty remarked.

"Outstanding execution, Atlas," Buccari broadcast. "Slave your autopilot to my command and start transferring crew."

"Atlas copies," the fueler pilot replied.

Her data annunciator verified control shift. Buccari brought up the fueler's autopilot and started feeding in course and speed programs. With the fueler under her control, she eased in a soft acceleration vector, pushing the limit of the refueling envelope.

And then she waited, trying to keep her mind clear, trying to anticipate, trying not to worry. Two hours elapsed as the fueler streaked through the heavens, transferring fuel to the corvette tucked beneath its ponderous thorax. Buccari anxiously watched her tactical display, analyzing the corvette battles unfolding before her.

Condor's engagement was about to start. She estimated action in less than ten minutes. Condor flight was getting squeezed. As she watched, Commander Rowan broke hard left, committing all five of his corvettes to counterstriking the nearest three aliens. A good move, but the energy levels of the attacking ships on his flank were so high, it would buy him little time. Buccari tweaked an intercept course into the fueler's autopilot.

"We're topped off," Thompson reported.

"Burp-p," Flaherty belched into the circuit.

"Okay, Atlas," Buccari said, "I want everyone but you and your number one to get their tails down here."

"You're the boss, Booch," the fueler pilot replied.

Commander Rowan concentrated on the tactical display.

Fire warning alarms *whoop*ed with dismaying persistence.

"Jamming ain't having much effect, Skipper," his copilot reported.

"Yeah." Rowan prayed that his maneuver had not come too soon. The enemy units were adjusting with alarming coordination, but at least he had forced the order of engagement. It was small solace. Even if he did damage to the first group, the second group would get to him before he could recharge his energy reservoirs.

"Engagement radius in three minutes," his weapons officer reported.

A head-on intercept.

"Okay, Condors," Rowan broadcast. "Number Three, take the bug on the left. Six, the one on the right. Two and Four will join me on the center bird. Fire kinetics at will. Slaving cannons, now."

The Condor pilots acknowledged. Rowan exhaled and executed the engagement program, then checked tactical. Coming down the gravity gradient, trying to cut him off, were six alien fast-movers, closing on intercept at mind-numbing speed. To his rear *Condor Five* had merged with the tanker and was transmitting refueling telemetry.

"Smart move," Rowan muttered.

"Say again, Skipper," his copilot said.

"Buccari's using the tanker's fuel to catch up," Rowan replied.

"She's hauling ass," the copilot said, taking note. "Too bad she won't make the first round."

"She'll make the second," Rowan said grimly, searching for options. Maybe Buccari was giving the bugs something else to think about.

"Engagement radius in one minute," weapons reported.

"Roger," Rowan replied. He hit the maneuvering alarm.

"Okay, Condors, let's earn our paychecks."

Buccari watched the icons merge. Suddenly there were only four friendlies, and *Condor Three* was flashing a distress signal. *Condor Six* was gone, its crew blasted to eternity. Only two aliens came off the engagement, so Rowan's ships had scored one. She clenched her fists as the second trio of alien ships ripped across the engagement area. Only two Condors broke clear. Icons for *Condors Three* and *Four* were gone from the screen. Three corvettes and their crews had been lost in mere seconds.

She was next. The five bugs arced off their targets, forming into a coordinated attack formation aimed right at her.

"Closing rate be point nine two," Gunner Tyler reported.

"Hot poop," Thompson blurted, "we're doing warp whoop-de-do."

"Okay, Atlas," she barked over the intership, "abandon ship, *now!*"

"We're coming, Booch," the fueler pilot replied.

"Hardly standing room," Thompson reported. "We got every set of tethers, every rest cell in the ship loaded with breathing bodies."

"Let's keep them that way," Flaherty muttered, working his targeting solutions.

"Engagement radius in four minutes," Gunner Tyler reported.

A minute went by. Chief Foster reported all hands transferred and secured. Buccari set the fueler's autopilot on full emergency acceleration with a ten-second onset delay.

"Breaking away," she shouted, hitting the maneuvering alarm. Buccari commenced an emergency breakaway, blasting away the fueler's grapples and scorching the receiving bay with a shot from her nose thrusters. As her corvette cleared, the fueler's main engines ignited. Buccari maneuvered hard, nose down, to avoid the big ship's engine bloom and simultaneously hit her own throttle.

"Always . . . w-wanted," she grunted, "t-to do that."

The fueler pulled away, accelerating. Buccari still had telemetric control. She put the big ship on a vector close enough to the three-ship bug flight to get its attention, set the acceleration at four gees, and locked its autopilot.

"T-two minutes," Tyler groaned.

Buccari let the tanker open to twenty kilometers and then took a position in its plasma wake, praying that the bugs had not detected her. She eased her acceleration to null, allowing energy reservoirs to build.

"One minute," Tyler reported.

"Decoys, Flack!" she commanded. "Standard pattern to starboard."

"Decoys, aye," Flaherty replied. The ship vibrated with ordnance release. She watched the noisemakers flash into the distance.

"Radar lock," Tyler reported. "Twenty-five seconds. My board be green. For the log, bridge has control."

"Lieutenant Flaherty has control. Cannons in full automatic," Flaherty confirmed. "Roger lock. Optics tracking. Optical lock."

"Fire when ready, Gridley," Buccari said.

"Aye, aye, Admiral," Flaherty replied.

It was over in the slow blink of an eye.

The fueler flared white, and then its ephemeral gas blossom was behind them. With a high-pitched frenzy *Condor Five*'s energy weapons salvoed. Buccari saw nothing through the forward viewscreen.

"Solid hit!" Flaherty shouted. Buccari checked tactical to see four hostile icons hammerheading their attack vectors, struggling to reverse course. Only four!

"Flamed another bug ass," Thompson shouted. "We're clean. Shields didn't even get warm."

FIFTY-FOUR

THIRD DAY OF BATTLE

It had been a most disappointing outcome. Fist a'Yerg pondered her tactical display—three aliens ships were still in the fight and racing up behind her attacking destroyers. Destroyer-Hand y'Map's remaining four destroyers were in pursuit. Clever fighters, those aliens.

The destroyer-fist designated a triad of destroyers to break off from the main attack to support y'Map with a flanking move against the rising alien fast-movers. That should be more than enough to squelch the distraction. A'Yerg returned her attention to the enemy screen, analyzed the defenses one more time, and issued the command to attack.

She let her *g'ort* have its head.

Runacres could only shake his head. Using the fueler as a diversion was tactical genius, although he pondered the fate of its crew. Three Condors were gone, but the three surviving Condors were still driving for safety. He prayed for them.

"Alien fast-movers have altered course," the tactical officer reported. "Three more bogeys are turning on Condor flight. Twenty-one bogeys are attacking screen center."

Runacres had already detected the course changes. Targeting information and threat assessments were updated in real time. Eagle Squadron blossomed with compound threat indicators. Reserve squadrons were moving. As the minutes passed, it became obvious that they would not get there in time to save the Eagles.

"*Condor Five*'s a hundred clicks out and closing," Buccari broadcast. *Condors One* and *Two* were deployed in battle spread.

"Welcome to hell, Booch," Rowan replied. "Got four devils on our tail and three more coming down. Engagement in four minutes."

"Tally ho," Buccari answered. She was in formation. Commander Rowan was calling the shots. His tactics were quickly defined.

"Let's see if we can get *Condor Five* in position to narrow the odds," Rowan called. "One and Two breaking right. Booch, after you take a shot, haul ass. Don't come back for us."

Buccari acknowledged and watched as Condor and its wing slid to a new vector, dropping decoys with abandon.

"Three minutes," Thompson reported.

The oncoming aliens maneuvered to intercept *Condors One* and *Two,* their trajectory projection overshooting and crossing Buccari's nose. She hammered her ship around to track the aliens.

"They be falling into our firing cone," weapons reported. "All systems hot. Reservoirs at peak. Radar lock. They be jamming."

Buccari eased her nose onto a lead pursuit trajectory and let her velocity vector cut the attack angle.

"Got 'em!" Flaherty reported. "Get me closer, Skip!"

"What!" Buccari snapped, slamming the throttle to the stops and punching the mains. She checked targeting. Flaherty was developing simultaneous firing solutions. She checked the power reservoirs for energy trade-offs. There were only seconds of excess available. She rolled the corvette to optimize weapon optics.

"G-good m-move," Flaherty grunted. "Optical lock on secondary cannon," he huffed. "F-firing p-primary . . . f-firing secondary."

The corvette vibrated with manic frequency, with both optical paths firing at full power. Energy reservoirs drained, and power warning lights illuminated. Buccari sucked back her throttles and stared at tactical. Only two bug icons remained.

"You got one!" Buccari shouted.

"Got two," Flaherty calmly replied, checking his weapons panel. "One's hurt, but it ain't showing."

Buccari watched tactical. *Condors One* and *Two* had set a return course for the fleet, recrossing the bug's attack vector. One alien ship remained in pursuit. Outnumbered, it held back, waiting for the four trailing bugs to join it. Its wingmate limped away.

"You're right, Flack!" she shouted.

"Unbelievable shooting, Five," Rowan broadcast. "We're heading home. See you back at the barn . . . and thanks."

Buccari acknowledged. She looked with trepidation to the larger battle. A wedge of alien fast-movers had penetrated screen center. Carmichael was sagging the screen, giving more time for the reserves to arrive, but overwhelming alien strength at the point of attack was telling. Decoy and jammer buoy returns shimmered the holo. It was a melee.

"Don't let him be hurt," Buccari prayed aloud.

"Alien interstellars coming from hyperlight!" the bridgemale shouted. "Between us and the alien fleet."

Jakkuk observed the presence of ten arriving units—close enough to be an immediate threat. The cell controller felt an exquisite blush of fear. She held her breath, trying to embrace the fleeting emotion.

"More alien ships," Karyai's slithery voice remarked almost with feeling. "Possibly a trap."

"Recall a'Yerg, Jakkuk-hajil," Dar commanded, her voice vibrant with climbing passion. "She has had enough amusement."

"As the dominant commands," Jakkuk acknowledged, sending out the telepathic summons. Jakkuk's *g'ort* ebbed with the press of her duty.

"Ready main batteries, Jakkuk-hajil," Dar commanded.

"All weapons stand ready," Jakkuk reported, sending out telepathic rejoinders.

"Do you jump, Dar-hajil?" Karyai asked.

"We watch, Mother," Dar replied.

Runacres tore his gaze from the battle and watched in fascination as the Condor birds scratched their way home. Buccari was magic.

"Eagle flight is getting pounded," Captain Wooden reported.

Runacres brought his attention back to the main drama and watched in horror as the alien attack force hammered his screen units. Screen command reacted well, but the weight of the attack was overwhelming.

"Hyperlight activity!" the tactical officer reported.

"Where away?" Runacres demanded, desperately scanning sensor returns. Admiral Chou or more aliens?

"Transponders!" the tactical assistant shouted. "Sector One!"

"Signatures authenticate!" Wells boomed. "It's Admiral Chou!"

Second Fleet! Runacres checked main status. Admiral Chou's ships presented themselves one by one, icons blooming as friendly units. Chou's ships were between his fleet and the main enemy force, arrayed in the standard grid matrix, an unsupportable combat formation, vulnerable to enemy fire. Runacres prayed they were not in range.

"Direct Admiral Chou to jump," he ordered. "Immediate emergency jump!"

"Aye, Admiral," Wells responded, working his panel.

Runacres watched status plots struggling to process the flood of confused data. Chou's units were surrounded with targeting halos and hyperlight anomaly ephemera. Alien acquisition radars were locking on.

"Second Fleet acknowledges, Admiral," Wells reported. "Admiral Chou reports termination coordinates Sol system, Earth Lima Two, per standard procedure. Jump countdown in final stage. Six seconds."

Runacres watched with fierce intensity, counting the interminable seconds, blood pounding in his ears. At jump minus three the aliens commenced firing their main batteries. Second Fleet retreated into hyperlight before battle damage telemetry was received.

"Recall the screen," Runacres ordered, breathing again.

Buccari switched to screen tactical frequency and listened. The back of her neck rippled with cold terror.

"Blackhawk flight is in," came a clinical report.

"Blackhawk, keep pressure on sector two," Carmichael ordered. Buccari exhaled with desperate relief. Carmichael was still in the game. "Merlins stay inside and cover us! We're taking a beating."

"*Eagle Five*'s gone!" she heard a voice—Pulaski's! He was *Eagle Four* now. Who was Five? *Please don't let it be Bart Chang.* And then, as if malevolent gods had read her thoughts:

"*Eagle Six* is hit bad!" Chang's deep voice announced. "Hull's ruptured. No power to cannons. We're going to the boats."

Buccari's stomach buckled.

"Lead's coming your way, Six," Carmichael broadcast.

Buccari localized *Eagle One*'s transponder and set a new course, aiming her corvette into the middle of the fray. It was hopeless. The screen was mangled, and the aliens were arcing back into Eagle's perforated sector like a meat-grinder blade.

"*Eagle Two*, this is One," came Carmichael's voice, sounding almost frightened. "You've got the screen. Pull it back to the red zone."

"*Eagle Two* has screen," Wanda Green acknowledged. "Jake, I'm receiving a screen recall! All units screen recall!"

"I copy," Carmichael replied. "I got business down here first. Take them home, Brickshitter."

Green acknowledged and began issuing consolidation orders, making a valiant attempt to retreat in good order. Slowly the screen pulled back, seeking protection under the mothership batteries.

Buccari streaked ever closer to the action. She watched Carmichael's and Pulaski's corvettes maneuvering toward lifeboat transponders. Rescue chatter filled the frequency.

The alien attack formation bore down.

"Skipper," Pulaski called, "we got unfriendlies up-Doppler, sector three, high. They're lighting us up."

"Got 'em, Ski," Carmichael replied. "I need you to hold 'em off for a sec. Go high while I give Six's lifeboats a push."

"You betcha, Eagle," Pulaski replied, his ship vectoring directly for the onslaught, spitting decoys and kinetic weapons at a furious pace. Alien ships adjusted their charge, concentrating their fire.

"Eagle, this is *Condor Five*," Buccari broadcast, her corvette only minutes from action. "I'm coming to help."

"Negative, Condor," Carmichael boomed back. "You've been recalled. Rejoin the fleet."

The alien force streaked for the Eagles. Pulaski drove into the teeth of their formation. Carmichael and the lifeboats were only seconds from engagement, but the lifeboat transponders were moving. The lifeboats were moving, either towed by EPLs or boosted toward the mothership matrix by Carmichael's corvette. Carmichael's ship separated from the rescue activity, his course set to aid Pulaski.

"I'm hit!" Pulaski yelled.

The leading edge of the alien torrent swept over Pulaski's corvette. His icon disappeared from the screen. Pulaski's corvette was gone. No transponders gave a glimmer of hope. Igor Pulaski was dead.

Carmichael's ship accelerated for the oncoming aliens, and the emptiness in her soul caused by Pulaski's death was replaced by a greater emotion—a nameless fear.

"It's too late, Jake!" she screamed.

"Get out of here, Buccari!" he shouted back, voice strained with rage and terror. Carmichael, his ship blossoming with threat halos, vectored for Pulaski's position. Buccari closed her eyes and jammed her throttles to full emergency.

Eagle One was engaging. The alien attack front, made ragged by Pulaski's counterattack, swung to meet Carmichael. The tactical display highlighted an alien coming under *Eagle One*'s fire. The hostile icon disappeared, but the concerted return fire of the alien's cohorts was telling. *Eagle One* glowed with impact flares. Shield collapse was indicated, but the ship somehow had not been destroyed. The wave of aliens swept by, leaving *Eagle One* tumbling, emergency transponders flashing.

"Get in your lifeboats!" Buccari shouted. "I'm coming in."

"No! Buccari! No!" she heard him shout—a desperate plea.

Boocharry! A'Yerg heard. The pilot was here. *Boocharry!* A'Yerg examined her holo display and deciphered the clues. Her destroyers had broken off all engagements except for the ships blocking their egress, and those vessels were all but destroyed. A'yerg noticed the single ship streaking up from the planet, running ahead of y'Map's pursuing units. Boocharry was the one wreaking havoc on her destroyers.

Boocharry! A'Yerg's *g'ort* flared magnificently. Boocharry! Jakkuk's recall would wait. A'Yerg signaled for y'Map to continue the attack and swung her triad of destroyers to intercept.

"Th-throttle back, Skip!" Flaherty shouted. "G-give the power accumulators some time. We can't kill 'em with insults."

Buccari's conditioning prevailed. She pulled the throttles back, steeled her nerves, and started planning her attack run. Many of the alien ships were moving away.

"Lifeboat transponders!" Thompson called.

Buccari saw the beautiful beacons. Her scalp crawled. She used thrusters to refine her course. She would need a hard retro to stay within the grappling envelope. Four bug ships were behind her, and three more broke loose from the pack and headed her way—seven to one.

"This little corner of the universe is getting pretty crowded," Flaherty said.

She hit the maneuvering alarm, pivoted ship smartly, and lined up the main engines with her retro vector.

"Start popping decoys, Flack," she ordered. "And give them a couple dozen heavies to dodge."

"Roger," Flaherty replied. A pattern of decoys was fired. Kinetics followed, rapid-fire *thunks* spewing slugs of depleted uranium on towers of fire into black infinity.

"Lifeboat transponders coming up," Thompson shouted.

"Seven gees," Buccari shouted, hammering the ignition. The corvette accelerated against its vector, slowing it down relative to the cloud of battle debris. Buccari saw two lifeboat transponders. *Eagle One*'s EPL did not get out. Buccari eased the throttles and engaged the maneuvering thrusters, playing her big corvette like a colt, sliding into a grappling approach for the nearest lifeboat.

"Bugs are coming fast," Flaherty reported. "I'm giving them another salvo of kinetics."

"Rog," Buccari replied, extending her nose grapple and twisting the corvette to acquire the lifeboat, now a flashing beacon on her viewscreen. More kinetics fired, their trajectories curving up and out. Buccari ignored the fireworks and focused on the docking computer. She designated the target and used verniers to bring the ship within the docking envelope. The computer did the rest. The lifeboat was snagged and secured to a grappling boom. One down.

The docking computer was already providing steering directions to the second lifeboat. She swung the ship hard and slammed the thrusters, jerking the ponderous corvette to its next rendezvous.

There it was, a strobing beacon. She designated the target, aligned her approach vector, and engaged the docking computer. The corvette started its approach. Thirty seconds to rendezvous. She exhaled and looked up, helpless to do anything but wait. She busied herself with status checks. Power accumulators were approaching peak.

"Four minutes to weapons radius," Gunner Tyler reported. "They be maneuvering to avoid missiles."

"Roger," Buccari replied, watching the lifeboat strobe grow

slowly closer. After an eternity the approach angle made it appear as if the lifeboat were accelerating downward. Flashing beacons disappeared below the corvette's blunt nose.

"Contact," Thompson shouted. "And grappled."

"Two minutes," Tyler reported.

Buccari eased in acceleration, gradually increasing it to four gees. Power reservoir indicators flickered off their maximums and started to fall. The corvette headed for home.

"Grid matrix!" Thompson reported. "We're in the grid."

"Roger," Buccari shouted, pulling the throttles back to null and hitting the grapple release. She pulsed the nose thrusters, and the lifeboats continued forward on a vector to the motherships. If the fleet jumped, the lifeboats would be carried into hyperlight.

Buccari maneuvered the nose of the corvette until it pointed at the nearest enemy: the flight of four that had been following her. The battle was coming to her.

"Thirty seconds," Tyler reported. "Bridge has control."

"Roger," Flaherty reported. "Bring 'em on."

Flaherty fired a decoy pattern and a salvo of kinetics.

"Power at ninety percent and climbing," engineering reported.

"Ten seconds," Tyler announced.

Flaherty unleashed another barrage of kinetics.

Buccari made a last check of tactical. Her corvette was a kaleidoscope of threat indicators. The lifeboats were clear. Maybe Carmichael would make it back—if he was even in a lifeboat. She shook her brain clear. She had to survive; she had to see her son again.

"Firing!" Flaherty snarled.

Energy-weapon discharge was overwhelmed by enemy fire. *Condor Five* shook like a rat in a terrier's mouth. Pink plasma patterns streaked across the viewscreens as flash shields slammed shut. Microseconds later the flash shields opened to reveal fuzzy, star-streaked blackness. Buccari blinked vigorously, trying to restore her vision. She struggled with thrusters, fighting to dampen out oscillations.

"Still alive!" Flaherty shouted.

"Shields . . . are gone," Thompson reported.

"Power accumulators are fried," Chief Silva reported. "She ain't gonna fire no more, Skipper. We're out of business."

"Fifteen seconds until next engagement," Tyler reported calmly.

"Roger," Buccari replied, covering her visor with her hands. Dead, she thought, removing her gloves and staring into space.

Buccari brought her gaze to the tactical display. Three alien fast-movers were closing rapaciously. There was not enough time to get everyone into the lifeboats. There was not enough room in the lifeboats for all the poor souls she had dragged to their deaths. She closed her eyes again and waited for the guillotine to fall.

"BOO-chaar-RI!"

"Skipper," Tasker shouted. "The radio. Some—"

"I copy," Buccari gasped, jerking her gaze into the black infinity of space. She saw only stars, taunting symbols of eternity.

"BOO-chaar-RI," the alien repeated. *"BOO-chaar-RI!"*

"Talk to . . . them, Skipper," Godonov said on the science circuit. "Translation program's going."

"Nes! I thought Burl put you under," Buccari shouted.

"Talk, Sharl," Godonov gasped. "I want to be awake when I die. Talk to them."

"Buccari here," she transmitted.

"Boo-chaar-ri," the voice repeated, rolling the syllables with sinister delight. *"A'yerg hei do. Lei sei, boo-chaar-ri . . . yu gwa aw yew."*

"It's Ahyerg," Godonov gasped. "You're dead . . . if Ahyerg wants."

"Go ahead, you son of a bitch," Buccari snarled.

Horrible laughter filled the universe. Buccari swallowed, forcing her heart back to its proper position.

"Lei yeng yet chi, Boocharry," the thundering voice proclaimed. *"Aw yeng yet chi. Ha chi Boocharry sei."*

"You win one, Buccari," Godonov translated. "I win one. Next time Buccari dies."

Buccari let her gaze fall to the tactical display. The alien attack ships streaked away.

The alien attack formation retreated, but the alien mother-ships moved ever closer. Relentlessly. Runacres pondered his alternatives. Even when outnumbered by twenty-four Legion ships to seven, the aliens had still engaged Admiral Chou's ships. They had belligerently attacked his corvettes and ignored his peace overtures. What could he do?

"Jupiter's balls!" Runacres exclaimed. "How do you kiss the devil?"

"We've got everybody we're going to get ... alive," Wooden reported dourly.

"All ships alpha-alpha, Admiral," Wells reported.

"Very well." Runacres sighed and stared at the aliens' formation, trying to understand their tactics. The aliens, still in jump matrix, approached at battle velocity. They would be in main battery range in less than four hours. Was he ready for a fleet engagement?

"They would respect us as enemies if we were to slug it out," Runacres said, opening his secure circuit.

"Only if we beat them," Merriwether replied. "I don't think we can, not without taking unacceptable casualties."

"Concur," Wooden nearly shouted.

"Concur," Wells said.

"Admiral!" Captain Gray's agitated visage came on his screen. "Admiral, they followed us through hyperspace."

"What!" Runacres exclaimed.

"The aliens followed us from Scorpio Minor," Gray reported. "Lieutenant Commander Buccari had another conversation with the same alien. Listen to this." He transmitted Buccari's chilling combat conversation with the Ulaggi attack pilot.

"If they followed us here," Gray announced, "they could follow us to Earth!"

Runacres debated his next move. Captain Gray was right.

"Jump countdown complete, Admiral," Wells reported.

"Konish planetary defense can handle them better than Earth can," Merriwether offered.

"Reset destination," Runacres ordered. "Genellan Lima One."

"Aye, aye, Admiral," Wells replied.

"Jump the fleet, Franklin," Runacres ordered. "Let's get out of here before we get hammered."

Hyperlight entrance for a human in a mothership was disconcerting, an insidious loss of physical reference. On the flight deck of a corvette, adrift in space near the margins of the grid, hyperlight transition was debilitating. Gravitronic flux made metal structures groan. Structures of flesh screamed—if they remained conscious.

The stars were gone. Only the ebony void of the hyperlight matrix remained. Buccari fought through the fog and concentrated on her ship and crew, keeping everyone busy with damage control. When the clamping vibrations of fleet tug grapples resonated through her derelict ship, the intercom was saturated with cheers. The imparted acceleration was exquisite.

Two OMTs maneuvered *Condor Five* into *Terra del Fuego*'s hangar bay, a bay littered with lifeboats and EPLs. No sooner had docking grapples secured her ship than emergency service teams and medical officers swarmed on board. Injured spacers and colonists were whisked off in isolation pods. All hatches on *Condor Five* were domed and umbilicaled to primary quarantine.

Buccari floated at her pilot station and performed her functions like a robot. She forced her brain to concentrate on checklists.

"Shutdown checklist complete," Thompson reported.

"All checklists complete," Flaherty reported.

"Flight log closed," Buccari announced. She floated in her tethers, not moving or speaking.

"You okay?" Flaherty asked.

"Yeah," she replied. "Get out of here."

Thompson and Flaherty left the flight deck.

Sobbing softly, Buccari wrenched off her helmet and squeezed her eyes shut. Tears poured over her lashless lids and floated from her ashen face—a mercurial constellation of pellucid pearls.

FIFTY-FIVE

RETREAT

Later. Bart Chang was waiting for Buccari when she cleared radtox. Floating gently across the quarantine station, they hugged for a painful eternity. And they cried.

"Popcorn forever," she whispered at last. Her leaden heart grew even heavier as she thought about the others. Pepper

Goldberg had been on Pulaski's ship, along with so many others. All were dead. Igor Pulaski was no more.

"Popcorn forever," Chang replied.

"Ski won't be happy until we chug some suds—" Her bursting heart overwhelmed her words and turned them to sobs. Chang held her tighter.

"Skipper took it damn hard," Chang said.

"He's okay?" she asked, looking up. She rubbed wetness from her eyes. Carmichael was alive. Bereavement loosened its claws.

"As good as can be, I guess," Chang replied. "You making it back really helped, but he's chewed up. He's—"

"He's here?" Buccari asked, her anguish mingling ambiguously with hope. "Is . . . he hurt bad?"

"Not so bad physically. Concussion, radiation poisoning, residual flash blindness, but . . . you know how he is. Eagle Squadron lost four ships and two crews. That's killing him."

"Yeah," she said, pushing off, her daring joy tempered. "I've got injured crew to see about."

"He wants to see you, Sharl," Chang said.

Heavily bandaged, Brappa stared agog into the repairing room where long-leg surgeons operated on Sherrip. Toon stood at Brappa's side, warbling with concern. Medical personnel gave the cliff dwellers as wide a berth as the narrow H-ring corridor would allow.

"We should have gardeners," Toon-the-speaker chirped. "A guilder would repair the hunter's membrane properly."

"Fear not," Brappa screeched, subconsciously flexing. Long-legs had once repaired his broken arm. "Brave warrior Sherrip will fly again."

"Hark," Toon chirped, "Giant-one comes."

The long-leg warrior, head bandaged and great pink face covered with a shiny poultice, limped to the window and stared in. He looked down and showed teeth.

"How fares Big-ears?" Toon signed.

"Come," Giant-one signed, returning the way he had come.

They followed the long-leg into another repairing room. Windowed tanks lined a wall. Giant-one went to a tank and looked in. Putting his hands together, he pointed at the window in the manner of cliff dwellers. Brappa and Toon peered in. Big-ears lay sleeping, naked, suspended in pale green fluid. His ravaged shoulder had been cleaned, and the bones had been realigned. Missing contours were outlined with a lattice-work of fine, almost invisible filament.

"They grow tissue and bone." Toon gasped.

"Our gardeners have nothing like this," Brappa said, looking into the adjacent tank. He saw one of the rescued long-legs, the female, her naked body covered with pox and pustules.

"Verily," Toon replied, snout pressed to the window.

Brappa felt a hand on his shoulder and looked up to see Short-one-who-leads.

Buccari retreated before the cliff dwellers' exuberance. Even Lizard Lips disdained any sense of decorum. Chastain, bandages, bruises, and abrasions covering every inch of bare skin, hunched his great shoulders and clasped his bandaged hands on his wide chest, as if restraining his joy.

"How are you, Jocko?" Buccari asked, grabbing his thick wrists and pulling him into a hug.

"Got more scratches and bug bites than I got skin," Chastain mumbled. He looked down at his boots, his abraded countenance radiating embarrassment. "They taped up the nastiest ones."

Buccari glanced quickly into the regeneration tank to monitor Godonov's peaceful repose. She checked the chart. Godonov's session was scheduled for a full week.

"I come back for regen when the serious injuries are taken care of," Chastain said.

"Marines always get last priority," came a deep voice from the door. It was Captain Buck. Tonto chirped and snapped to attention.

"Yes, sir," Chastain dutifully replied, coming to attention.

"At ease, Sergeant," Buck said.

"Sergeant, sir?" Chastain replied.

"You and your hunters did the job on Hornblower, Chastain," Buck said. "You and I have been ordered to train a company of cliff dwellers for integration into marine landing units. That's just to start."

"S-sir?" Chastain stuttered, looking to Buccari.

"I've got someone else to check on," she said, abandoning Chastain and the cliff dwellers to their new challenges. She was uncertain how she felt about expanding the cliff dwellers' military role, but other thoughts arose. She moved down the corridor to Carmichael's infirmary, where a med-tech waved her in. Rampant emotion overwhelmed rational thought as she put her hand on the hatch release; it was a mixture of emotions: joy that Carmichael was still alive, fear at confronting him, and anger at his unspoken rejection.

She pushed through the hatch and entered Carmichael's cabin. He lay on his back, rugged countenance flushed with acceleration and radiation damage. Thick dressings covered his eyes.

"Who's there?" Carmichael snapped. He was helpless and angry in his helplessness.

"Commander," she said.

Carmichael's tortured features softened. He pushed himself to a sitting position. "It's amazing how well I can see you," he said.

"Commander?" she replied, confused.

"Yeah," he sighed. "I wish I could see this clearly all the time."

"I'm not sure the flight surgeons would agree," she replied.

He laughed, but then he looked as if he felt pain. His chiseled face grew stern and then sad. "We lost some good people, Booch." He sniffled.

"Yes, sir," she replied, struggling not to cry.

Carmichael breathed deeply and regained his stern composure. "You disobeyed my direct orders, Buccari."

"Pilot discretion, Commander," she replied. "It's only way I could get your attention."

"My attention!" he snapped.

She said nothing. Her emotions were too embattled. So were Carmichael's. His stern demeanor collapsed.

"My attention is yours, Sharl," he whispered, his face soft again.

"Why did you transfer me, Commander?" she asked.

Carmichael tilted his head back, but said nothing.

"I can't understand . . ."

"I transferred you, Sharl," he at last replied, "because at Scorpio Minor I lost my objectivity. You were no longer just another pilot. We were at war, and I couldn't send you to your death."

"But Commander," she replied, confused. "You're concerned for all your pilots. Igor Pulaski died—"

"Please don't, Sharl," Carmichael begged, his deep voice almost a moan. He coughed and cleared his throat.

"Igor Pulaski would have followed you to hell and back," she persisted. "So would I. We all would. Someone has to lead—that's your job. It's our job to follow. Some of us will die."

"I'll live with Ski's death, Sharl," he said. His expression hardened almost frighteningly. "I could never live with yours."

"Dammit, Commander," she responded, anger flushing her cheeks. "You can't pick—"

"Sharl, I love you."

She could not breathe. Dizziness overwhelmed her. She closed her eyes and dropped onto the edge of his bed. His hand closed on hers. She returned his febrile pressure. He pulled her to him.

"No!" she gasped, making an effort to pull away. Carmichael's grip was like iron. He relented but did not let go.

"We're at war," she protested. "Our feelings have no—"

"I love you . . . Booch." Carmichael laughed sadly. "Damn, I wish I could see."

With her free hand she reached out and touched his face. He captured that hand, too, and held it against his cheek.

"I never want to lose you, Sharl."

"Jake," she whispered, yielding again to his pull.

"Lieutenant Commander Buccari to the flag bridge," her multiplex blared in her ear. "Buccari to flag bridge immediately."

"Buccari," she acknowledged, terminating the call. She tensed.

"Duty calls," Carmichael said, reluctantly releasing her.

"Yeah," she said, standing and taking a deep breath.

"We're jumping to Genellan," Carmichael said.

"What?" she blurted. *To Genellan!* She would see her son.

"Genellan," Carmichael confirmed. "Admiral didn't want to take the chance the Ulaggi would follow us to Earth, so—"

She did not give Carmichael a chance to finish. She jumped on the bed, grabbed his head, and pressed her lips to his. Carmichael's strong arms closed around her. He returned the kiss hungrily and passionately. At last she pushed away.

"You're crying," he said, wiping her cheek.

Buccari stood, fighting her passions. "I gotta go see the admiral," she whispered, her throat full.

"Wish I'd mentioned Genellan sooner."

"Get well, Commander," she said. "We have a war to fight."

"A war to fight," Carmichael repeated, suddenly somber.

"And a great deal to . . . talk about," she said as she left.

FIFTY-SIX

SHADOW OF THE MOON

Buccari, sitting at the controls of her corvette, anxiously awaited the transition from hyperlight. She struggled with a myriad of thoughts, memories, and checklist details. Had the Ulaggi followed them? Was Ahyerg waiting? Her blood ran cold. She forced disquieting images from her mind. Her concentration leapt uncontrollably. It would be nearing winter in MacArthur's Valley. Ion pressures in the number three engine manifold had been slow in building. Hardwoods on Lake Shannon would have lost their leaves. The lake would be icing up soon.

Flight-control links were solid. All tactical systems checked. Her Charlie would be almost three years old . . . Earth years. And Carmichael had said he loved her.

Gravitronic waves rippled through the fleet. Buccari closed her eyes and waited for the visceral undulations to dampen. She moved her hand to the throttle. General quarters alarms going off froze her heart. Was it just a precaution, or had they jumped into another battle? An emotion approaching panic warmed her neck and sucked air from her lungs. The signal to launch screen units brought her back to life. She waited her turn. She monitored the crew circuit. Her crew was chattering: checklists and bullshit. It helped.

"Think the bugs followed us?" Thompson asked.

"We'll find out soon enough," Flaherty replied. "Lead's moving."

Above them the interminable length of *Condor One* slid down its docking rails, a ponderous overcast scuttling before a storm wind. *Condor Two* was moving even before One had cleared the bay doors. The gigantic vessels trundled inexorably into the black void.

"We're up," Buccari barked. The bay director was pointing at her. She flashed her formation lights. "Counting down. Three ... two ... ugh!"

The third and last corvette remaining in Condor Squadron jumped down the rails. The star-sprinkled infinity accepted her ship, reducing all finite objects and grand concepts to insignificance. She hit the maneuvering alarm, counted to two, and slapped in the standard departure yaw. She looked ahead for *Condor One*. There it was.

"Mains!" she shouted, hammering the ignition. *Condor Three* leapt to its screen formation vector.

"Screen units away," Wooden reported.

"Multiple contacts!" the tactical officer shouted.

"God help us!" Runacres gasped.

Threat Klaxons blared. Arena boards blossomed with overlapping threat circles. Targeting radars kicked in, driving high-priority fire-control solutions. Runacres stared at the fantastic display taking shape before him. The threat environment was overwhelming.

"We're in the middle of a battle," Wells said.

"They followed us," Wooden said soberly.

"No," Runacres replied, shaking his head. "They couldn't arrive before us. Not with this many ships. Science, what are you getting?"

"Konish ships," Captain Gray announced. "Still analyzing data."

Runacres scrutinized the dispositions and mass distributions of the arrayed hardware. He quickly checked the battle computers; not surprisingly, the outcome simulations were not converging. The computer's only output was NO FAVORABLE OUTCOMES. ADVISE IMMEDIATE RETREAT.

"Small-scale hostilities in sectors three and six," the tactical officer reported. "Scout probes and interceptors. Main battle fleets are not yet involved. They are maneuvering on parallel vectors."

"Engagement radius with the nearest alien element is seventy-two hours away at battle cruise, Admiral," Wells reported.

"Hold position," Runacres ordered. "Maximum defensive posture. Maintain maximum jump readiness."

"Aye, aye, Admiral," Wells replied.

"And don't fixate on the kones," Runacres shouted. "The Ulaggi may be on our tails."

"It's that kind of day," Merriwether interjected.

Jaws clenched, Buccari checked tactical. She ran the range out to maximum and tried to interpret what she was seeing. She ran a threat analysis, using all known parameters. They were konish ships.

"No!" Buccari wailed. Tar Fell and King Ollant were fighting over Genellan. She scanned fleet distribution and determined the region of contention. With unshakable resolve she programmed a course and set the throttle to military acceleration.

"Nine gees!" she barked, hitting the maneuvering alarm.

"Skipper!" Flaherty blurted, his helmet jerking in response to each of her movements. "We're in the screen."

"Screen command," Buccari broadcast in the clear. "*Condor Three* is breaking formation on special assignment."

"*Condor Three,*" Commander Rowan replied. "Stand by."

"Negative," Buccari replied. "My intentions are to detach from screen assignment and proceed independently."

"Hold position, Three."

"I have new orders," Buccari broadcast, punching the ignition. "From a higher authority." Her corvette leapt from the screen.

"Buccari, are you crazy?" Rowan shouted for all the universe to hear. "Hold screen position."

"Screen Command, this is flag," came a very familiar voice. "*Condor Three* is authorized to conduct independent operations."

"*C-Condor Three,*" Buccari replied, grunting under the strain of building acceleration. "Th-th-thanks, Admiral."

Condor Three left Legion fleet dispositions behind and arrowed for the contested area between the accumulations of konish heavy ships.

"A-at th-th-this acceleration," Flaherty grunted after nearly three minutes of brutal hammering, "you'll be lucky t-to b-be conscious when you run out of fuel."

Buccari acknowledged Flaherty's advice and slowly brought the acceleration down to four gees and then to two. They had hours of acceleration sprint ahead of them.

"Tasker," Buccari barked over the comm circuit, "patch all frequency bands onto my broadcast channel."

"Aye, sir," the communication technician replied. "Ready, sir."

Buccari took a deep breath and closed her eyes.

"Chancellor Tar Fell," Buccari broadcast in high konish. "General Tar Fell. Minister Tar Fell. Whatever your proper title is. This is Lieutenant Commander Buccari of the Tellurian Legion. I request an immediate ambassadorial conference. Tar Fell, please respond."

Buccari listened desperately for any response. Nothing could be heard but the music of the spheres echoing indifferently in her helmet.

"Are we on all bands, Tasker?" she demanded.

"Yes, sir," Tasker replied. "Scanning all frequencies."

"King Ollant, this is Sharl Buccari," she broadcast, again in konish, trying a different tack. "Your Highness, I request that a representative be made available for an ambassadorial conference. Correct that. Your Highness, I *demand* a conference."

Silence.

"Chancellor Tar Fell!" she screamed. "King Ollant! Your Vows of Protection!"

Silence.

"A greater enemy approaches," she broadcast, forcing her voice into calmer registers. "That enemy may be here even now. The Tellurian fleet was just engaged in two separate star systems and was badly damaged. Our colony in the Hornblower system was destroyed. This alien force is probably the same enemy that murdered my people at Oldfather and Shaula. It is probably the same race that attacked your planet centuries ago."

She listened. Nothing.

"Confrontation in your system is just a matter of time," she cried. "Listen to me! We must not make war among ourselves! Listen to me!"

Nothing.

King Ollant monitored Citizen Sharl's beseeching radio calls. Hours passed. He struggled with his options.

"Citizen Sharl's corvette must soon be out of fuel," General Et Anitab reported.

Ollant remained silent.

"Her pleas are compelling," Et Anitab said.

"Are they also compelling to Tar Fell?" Ollant asked. "It

requires two to make peace. It takes only one maniac to make war."

"What are your orders, Your Majesty?" Et Anitab asked.

Ollant stared through the observation blister.

"Your Majesty," Et Anitab persisted. "Ship commanders await orders."

"Delay the attack," Ollant commanded.

"Tar Fell's forces continue to adjust to our maneuvers," Et Anitab persisted. "Our line of battle will provide an inadequate defensive posture should Tar Fell take the initiative."

"Delay the attack," Ollant whispered.

"The alien ship maintains course," Magoon reported.

Tar Fell, listening to the human's desperate pleas, watched the holo-vid. The icon for Citizen Sharl's ship vectored straight for the vanguard of his fleet defenses.

"As long as it emits no targeting radar, let it pass," Tar Fell ordered, intrigued. "Order all interceptors to remain clear."

Tar Fell scrutinized Ollant's approaching line of battle. The king's strategy was set piece this time—no marauding penetrations into the teeth of Tar Fell's defenses. But the king was delaying, allowing Magoon and Otred to maneuver against his buildups.

"I recommend a preemptive attack," Magoon announced. "General Otred's heavy squadron is now in position to dissect Ollant's flank."

"Yes," Tar Fell replied. "The king has lost his opportunity. Prepare to attack."

Tar Fell looked across the command center at the king's ambassador. Kateos hunkered next to the observation bubble, her face pale with fear. Tar Fell pushed off from his command station and floated to her.

"What make you of this, Ambassador?" Tar Fell asked. "One small ship between two battle fleets. Has Citizen Sharl gone insane?"

"Insane? No," Kateos replied. "She is a mother striking out to protect her young. You have never seen humans protect their young."

"We are not attacking her child." Tar Fell laughed. "This is committing suicide. Mothers do not commit suicide."

"The planet," Kateos said.

"The planet?" he asked.

"The planet is also her child," Kateos said. "The planet will certainly be lost to her if we wage war."

"She is selfish, then."

"She is in love," Kateos countered. "Citizen Sharl loves Genellan."

"Pah! A wasteland of ice," Tar Fell rumbled, turning to the observation bubble and staring at the planet—a perfect sphere of marbled hues, emerald and alabaster, dun and aquamarine.

"Your recommendation, Ambassador?" Tar Fell asked.

"Choose between infamy and greatness, Chancellor Tar Fell," Kateos counseled. "To my mind it is a clear choice."

"Armada Master, the human ship has penetrated our main battery radius," Magoon reported. "In the interest of prudent defense, General Otred requests permission to destroy."

Tar Fell looked down at Kateos. The female put her face in her hands. Tar Fell looked at the battle plot.

"The human ship carries an ambassador, General Magoon," Tar Fell finally said. "We will listen awhile longer."

Condor Three coasted into the shadow of Genellan's moon. Down-sun Buccari could see parallel lines of dim reflection: the Hegemonic fleet, an anemic constellation, compressed and of unnatural radiance. Tar Fell's fleet was up-sun and invisible to her eye, but that array of massive ships, more numerous and of larger unit mass than Ollant's, was painfully evident on her tactical display.

Her radios remained silent.

"All stop," Chief Silva reported. "Mains are overboosted, Skipper, but we'll cool 'em down for you."

"Very well," Buccari replied, breaking loose from her tethers.

"Fuel's below bingo," Flaherty reported. "We can get back, but only if Admiral Runacres doesn't change course."

"Rog'," Buccari answered. "Chief Foster to the EPL bay. Make ready battle armor and maneuvering unit." She checked tactical one more time.

"What?" Thompson and Flaherty shouted together.

"Flack, you've got the ship. When I give the order, I want you to head back to the fleet at best speed." She pushed off from her station.

"Uh, aye, sir," Flaherty replied, pivoting in his station. "Wha-what's your plan, Skipper?"

"For this ship to rejoin the fleet," she barked, pushing through the flight deck iris. "Stand by for orders, mister."

She moved through the fore-aft passage and dove into the crew decks. Chastain went rigid in his tethers, his expression alert but concerned. Tonto screeched, waving hand signs. She pushed through the after hatch, sliding into the upper EPL bay. Chief Foster was there. He had a suit of battle armor and a maneuvering unit waiting. She climbed in, levered the fittings closed, and performed pressure and system checks.

"I'm going for a walk," she announced.

"Pardon for saying, sir," Foster said. "You sure this is your stop?"

"Close the door behind me, Chief," she said.

"Aye, sir," Chief Foster replied, guiding her into the EVA lock.

The air lock closed silently, her battle armor sealing out all noises. Status diodes flashed. As pressure fell into the nonexplosive range, she hit the lock release switches. The outer lock slid open. She stared into space. Its cold breath crept around her. Resolutely, Buccari propelled herself from the womb of brightly lighted metal into infinite blackness. She tumbled. She activated stabilizers, and her twisting relative to the huge mass of the corvette ceased. Together, side by side, a mighty fleet corvette and its minuscule human pilot careened through space. She pulsed her maneuvering unit to open distance.

"Okay, Flack," she broadcast. "Take this 'vette back to the fleet."

"But Skipper," Flaherty protested, "what are you going to do? I can't leave. We'll stay with you."

"Mr. Flaherty," she replied, "shut up and report to the screen commander. That's an order. And Flack, do me a favor."

"Sir?" Flaherty replied.

"Use your verniers," Buccari said, moving from the overwhelming mass of her ship. "You light off your mains too soon and I'm carbon."

Flaherty gave a sour acknowledgment. Axial thrusters pulsed softly blue, and the corvette slid away, gathering velocity.

"*Condor Three*'s clear," she broadcast.

The ship's main engines blossomed with white fury. Her visor clicked shut and then cleared in stages as the flare diminished to the intensity of a moving star. And then *Condor Three* was gone.

She was alone. She activated her transponder beacon.

"We await your command to attack, Armada Master," Magoon reported.

"She is all alone," Kateos cried. "She wants only to talk."

"Words are cheap, Mistress Kateos," Tar Fell rumbled. "You of all kones, a translator for politicians, should know that."

"Yes," Kateos replied. "And yet the right words are precious."

"The right words, Ambassador?" Tar Fell asked. "How does one know when words are right?"

"When they are true, Chancellor," Kateos replied.

Tar Fell looked at the holo-vid. The pitiful transponder beacon, made mighty by its solitude, flickered dimly in the middle of the arrayed battle fleets. Tar Fell remembered the green eyes of the little dark-haired alien, the liquid sound of her laugh, the power of her being.

"General Magoon!" Tar Fell shouted.

"Armada Master!" Magoon replied.

"Hold your position."

Genellan was down. Buccari looked up at the moon. She was floating in the moon's umbra. The moon's backside was a deep, depressing gray, but in the reflected light of Genellan she could discern its mottled surface and shadowless craters. She desperately longed to see its surface bathed in the brilliant silver light of the star.

For solace she looked down at Genellan's ethereal limb and beyond. She stared, mesmerized by the cosmos.

"Citizen Sharl." It was King Ollant's voice. Was she dreaming?

"Your Highness," she replied.

"I will be at your position in three hours."

"Thank you, Your Highness," she replied, suddenly chilled. King Ollant was taking an immense risk. She waited for several anxious minutes.

"Tar Fell. I am waiting," she thundered into her helmet.

Nothing.

"Tar Fell," she persisted. "King Ollant has courage."

Nothing.

Buccari floated in endless star-spattered infinity. Her life support gauges registered an eight-hour air supply. Perhaps the balance of her life could be measured in the most finite of ways—eight hours. A unit of time comprehensible and sublime: a good night's sleep, a commodity not retrievable from recent memory. She yawned. She laughed at the thought that they might find her asleep. She laughed again at her conceit—a solitary human drifting in space, expecting kings and generals to attend to her arrogant beckoning.

A speck of golden light. It was a star, only different. Imperceptibly, it expanded. A ship—Ollant's. It approached so slowly that she wondered if it would arrive soon enough.

She forced her eyes to break their fixation and looked about. Her awareness suddenly resolved another point of light, with dimensions discernible to the eye, seemingly closer, moving faster relative to Buccari's orbital vector but coming from the direction of Tar Fell's fleet. Was it an attacker? No, it was only one ship.

The huge ships approached from opposite battle lines. Navigation lights and strobes were resolved on first one and then the other. And then there were individual features: sponsons and optics turrets. The king's ponderous battleship arrived first, coming to a halt relative to Buccari, two hundred meters away. Ranging lasers scintillated from the ship's angular chines. Radar would have cooked Buccari to a cinder.

The Thullolian ship kept coming, growing more detailed. Its maneuvering thrusters firing continuously, it expanded to fill her universe, growing impossibly larger until it occluded even the looming presence of the moon. It was huge! Its maneuvering thrusters fired gently, stopping it three hundred meters away.

Like an ant before two elephants, she waited for the next step. Nothing happened.

"King Ollant. Chancellor-General Tar Fell," she broadcast into the silence. "You have come far. The next step is small. Humble yourselves under the stars."

A hatch on the Hegemonic ship winked opened, a tiny orange rectangle on the ship's dark flank. Suited forms, miniaturized by distance, debouched from the entrance and took positions, maneuvering units sparkling like diamonds. A solitary form maneuvered straight for her, coming to a halt at her side.

"Citizen Sharl," King Ollant rumbled. "It has been a long time."

"Your Highness," she replied. "Again we meet under trying conditions."

"I would suffer much," Ollant rumbled, "for the honor of your presence."

"How maudlin," another voice rumbled in high konish—Tar Fell's. Buccari recalled the southerner's gruff timbre and thundering accent. Buccari and Ollant turned their attention to the Thullol-Ransan ship. Coming from the darkness were two suited forms. One halted at a hundred meters; from its size, Buccari assumed it was an interpreter. The other came forward with circumspection, maneuvering jets twinkling.

"Citizen Sharl," Tar Fell boomed, "do you strive for impartiality in this matter? Or are you merely a pawn of the Hegemony?"

"My first loyalty is to Genellan," she answered, lifting her arm and pointing. The planet, gibbous and brilliant, seemed to radiate its own luminescence rather than reflect the distant light of a sun. Genellan beckoned. Buccari twisted, rotating her vision so that the obscene, hulking forms of the battleships left her peripheral field of vision. She gloried in the planet's light, and she waited.

"A jewel," Ollant spoke, a lilting rumble.

"Yes," she replied, mesmerized.

"Belonging in no crown," Tar Fell grumbled.

"Nor belonging to any crown," Ollant replied, surprising Buccari with his sudden acquiescence. She favored the sovereign with a smile.

"I came not to stare at a planet," Tar Fell boomed. "Why, then?"

"For mutual protection," Buccari replied, turning from the planet to confront the konish giant. "There is at least one other race in this galaxy, Chancellor, a race of marauders. Both kones and humans have been killed by their weapons, murdered for reasons we have not been able to determine. We need each other's help or we may perish at their hands."

"Planet Kon is ready," Tar Fell replied. "Our planetary defenses will discourage these interlopers."

"Not if we fight among ourselves," Ollant offered. "Planetary defense stands crippled, to both our shame."

Tar Fell nodded.

"The Tellurian Legion," Buccari said, jumping into the silence, "will disclose everything about hyperlight technologies. There are no conditions, no secrets."

Tar Fell laughed.

"I have those secrets," the Thullolian rumbled. "Scientist

Dowornobb has been most productive, and your Envoy Stark is quite accommodating. I can reach the stars without you."

Buccari closed her eyes. There was nothing to trade.

"Tar Fell," she exhaled, making a final plea, "subject to King Ollant's concurrence and to ratification by the Tellurian Legion Assembly, I nominate you commanding general of the Konish-Human Expeditionary Fleet. It is my opinion that you must be given a duty—a responsibility—sufficient to your considerable ambition."

"To my considerable ambition?" Tar Fell growled. "You insult me?"

"Insult!" Buccari shouted, at the end of her patience. She maneuvered to Tar Fell and grabbed the behemoth's space suit. She pulled herself over its expanse until she reached Tar Fell's head. She banged her visor against the kone's faceplate and glared into the chancellor's surprised eyes. Tar Fell's eye tufts were iron hard.

"Citizen Sharl!" a familiar voice protested.

"Is responsibility an insult?" Buccari shouted, her anger vibrating into Tar Fell's helmet. "I offer you the highest of duties—the protection of your planet, of your solar system, against a common enemy that makes all our differences trivial. Leadership, Tar Fell! Leadership. I want your leadership!"

She pushed away, floating free in space. Her brain registered the familiar voice she had heard earlier, and she looked wonderingly out to the other kone hanging in the distance.

"Tar Fell," Ollant rumbled, bringing Buccari's attention back to the negotiators, "are these arrangements suitable?"

The king thrust out his hand in the fashion of humans. Tar Fell looked down at the proffered hand for eternal seconds and then brought his dark glare up to meet Ollant's.

"I accept Citizen Sharl's commission," Tar Fell said.

The Thullolian maneuvered toward King Ollant and clasped his hand. Buccari's heart soared. The bright planet blurred through her tears of happiness.

"Citizen Sharl's arguments are persuasive," Tar Fell rumbled, "but no arguments are as persuasive as those of the king's ambassador."

The Thullolian signaled. His translator floated forward.

"To fight the wrong war is folly," came a mellifluous rumble.

"Kateos!" Buccari shouted, pulling the visor-shrouded giant to her.

"We have so much to talk about, my sister, but first," Kateos said, turning to the Thullolian, "Tar Fell, I apologize for my evil thoughts. Your wisdom and honor are to be extolled."

"Pah!" Tar Fell proclaimed. "My intentions have always been for the good of my nation. You have only converted me to a higher principle. King Ollant, you have taught Mistress Kateos well."

"She teaches us all," Ollant acknowledged.

"Your Highness, I am your servant," Tar Fell rumbled, backing away and effecting a bow.

"You serve your planet," Ollant replied. "As do I. Let us reaffirm our Vows of Protection."

"So done, and solemnly," Tar Fell announced.

"There remains a war to fight," Kateos declared.

"Yes," Tar Fell said, turning to Buccari. "Citizen Sharl, in the impending conflict it will be my honor to fight at your side."

Hyperlight ripples faded. Cell Controller Jakkuk sensed the presence of alien consciousness and then detection systems validated her perceptions. She reveled in her fear. There were so many alien ships. Jakkuk's *g'ort* asserted itself with delicious substantiality and almost took control. Throttling her screams, Jakkuk soaked in the exquisite afterglow of the terror surge. Her control returned, but slowly. She did not hurry it.

"Aaaah, the humans have laid a trap!" Dar moaned. The dominant's animal was also ascendant. "Aaaah! How . . . many?"

"Yessss!" Karyai hissed. Even the lakk!

"Over n-ninety h-heavy ships," the terrified bridgemale groaned, recoiling at the emotional unraveling of his officers. His large eyes goggled with terror. "At least two hundred interceptors."

"Initiating battle—" Jakkuk started to report.

From the ship's bridge a bridgemale screamed, the undeniable scream of rapture-death. The gruesome squeal obliterated the spell. Jakkuk looked up to see Ship Mistress Kapu, eyes clenched, coupling organs exposed and bloodied, a mangled bridgemale dead in her savage embrace.

The bridge was silent, all eyes on an undeniable atavism: officers proudly disgusted, bridgemales frozen with terror.

"Clean it up," Dar commanded, her tone stern yet wistful.

Ship Mistress Kapu, shivering, expelled the bridgemale in a shapeless heap and glided to her bridge station. A walleyed bridgemale scurried after Kapu with clean garb. A clutch of drones edged nervously into position as a medico appeared to collect the egg mass. Her job done, the drones moved smartly to eliminate the vestiges of death.

"Jakkuk-hajil," Dar demanded, "have they seen us?"

"Not as yet, Mother," Jakkuk replied. "Our position is remote, and the star is an active emitter. Hyperlight emissions have diffused into background noise. They would have to know what to look for and where."

"Still, move the cell back," Dar started to command.

"Hold. This is not their home system," Karyai spoke. "Our ships have been here before, Daughters. In the time of a'Tka a roonish fleet despoiled this system."

"Ah!" the dominant sighed hungrily.

"The population was ravaged," Karyai continued. "For sport."

"For sport, Mother?" Jakkuk inquired.

"The indigenous life does not support our eggs." The political nodded. "Roons killed in frenzy. Records reveal a devastated planet."

"I have read of the devastation in the battle histories," Dar acknowledged. "Civilization here was thought to have ended."

"A resilient race," Jakkuk remarked, noting the density of the transmission spectra. Something struck her as puzzling. She adjusted her antennae and processed her findings.

"Karyai-lakk," Jakkuk petitioned humbly.

"Yes, Daughter," the political replied.

"The primary planet in this system is clearly the second planet from the star," Jakkuk stated. "This battle fleet is arrayed near the third planet, and signal characteristics would indicate at least two cultural modes."

The political sat mute for several moments, pondering. Jakkuk wondered if she had offended the imperious lakk.

"Depart the system, Dar-hajil," the political uttered at last.

"We shall return," Dominant Dar moaned.

"Of course," Karyai replied.

FIFTY-SEVEN

GENELLAN

Brappa stared breathlessly. The river valley that once had been his universe passed swiftly beneath. The yellow flying machine flew below dark scudding clouds, the window vibrating with its power. Engine noises masked the sonorous voices of the long-legs. Big-ears, shoulder bandaged like white armor, and Giant-one talked with the warrior leader, the one called Buck. Buck was to petition the elders.

"It eats the head wind," Brappa exclaimed.

"As in a dream," his cohort chirped. Sherrip, shoulders also shrouded with bandages, had his snout pressed to the window.

"This excites thee more," Toon-the-speaker derided, "than flying through the stars. It is only a machine."

"I see the ground moving faster than the wind," Brappa replied. "I have never seen the stars move. I understand what I see."

Brappa grew more excited as the river valley approached the plateau. He was almost home. His longing heart raced.

"The plateau!" Sherrip screeched.

Brappa dashed to the other side of the plane. There it was, the great vertical sweep of basalt shrouded in tendrils of steam—his home.

Brappa had earlier paid homage to his mother. Ki-wife-of-Braan had resided in the long-leg village all this time, tending the offspring of Short-one-who-leads. Ki was happy with her duty and proud. And now that cliff dwellers were living year-round in the valley, his mother would not be without her own kind. A colony of cliff dwellers removed from the plateau; Brappa could only shake his head at the changes.

The flying machine climbed and banked full circle, approaching into the wind, as hunters did. It slowed, lowering metal slabs from the back edges of the wings. The plane's landing path paralleled the cliff edge, fat wheels hovering above the flat rock of the plateau. And then it touched, bumping and jostling, mercifully stopping quickly.

Giant-one opened the door. Brappa dashed out, inhaling the fresh air. He screamed the clarion call of his family. Sentries answered raucously. Young warriors clambered above the cliff rim, raising pikes. Brappa ran past them to the precipitous edge and leapt into the void, his body rigid with exultation. The warrior's membranes deployed with a thunderous clap. Hunters elevated past him on the upwellings, screaming accolades, shrieking a welcome.

Gliss's cry rose above all the others. Brappa screamed back, his sonics bubbling with wetness. She was coming to him; she would wait no longer, and Brappa wheeled outward from the rocks to give her room. The huntress climbed hard, impatient with the wind's uplifting pace. Brappa struggled to maintain his position, his vigor heightened by cathartic emotion. Descending gently, he prepared to receive her. Gliss beat frantically at the air, not content to wait apart for the passage of another second. She hit like a crossbow bolt, a collision of emotion and muscle, grasping, clinging. Brappa encircled Gliss with his membranes. Their talons intertwined. Their heads came together in an irrepressible symphony of sonic passion.

They fell, a timeless plummet into the steamy chasm. The cliffside resounded with discordant well-wishing, screeches, and shrieks to the honor of their ancestors and the possibilities of the future, prayers to the rock gods and to the sky gods and to the gods of the beasts and fishes as well as to the gods of the great river. Brappa did not hear the prayers; he felt them.

Brappa embraced his mate with every muscle. He felt her warm body next to his and did not want to part. But his unerring instincts awakened and compelled him to spread his great membranes, halting their fall. She pushed away and twisted in the air, gracefully setting her wings and diving for their abode. Brappa followed his graceful huntress, swooping to her side between columns of rising steam. Together they landed on the worn wall of their terrace, between stone pots of fragrant blossoms.

Before him stood his offspring: two fledglings, shy and thin but nearly of a size to be sentries. Gliss shrieked the beginning of the welcoming ceremony, and the offspring bowed dutifully.

Brappa would not wait. Weeping like a babe, the hunter stepped forward and enclosed them all in his wings.

Brappa-the-warrior had come home.

It was a beautiful morning yet a sad day of farewell. Envoy Stark and his clutch of sycophants had already been escorted onto the heavy-lifter, certainly no cause for sadness. Tar Fell displayed no compunction to protect Stark. The Thullolian considered the human envoy an expedient tool, nothing more. Artemis Mather was designated Legion envoy pro tempore, although Admiral Runacres made it extremely clear that Commander Quinn was in charge.

Yes, a sad day of farewell; now it was time for Nash Hudson to depart, to return to Earth for another painful reconstruction. Buccari's sadness was salted with abiding impatience; she still had not seen her son.

"Why am I always getting my ass busted on this planet?" Hudson groaned. "I look like sausage. Even uglier than you, Dowornobb."

"It-ah is your dream," Dowornobb responded, "that-ah you would be as handsome as I am."

Kateos castigated her mate with a vibrant whisper, but Dowornobb and Hudson laughed together, the kone's happy thunder eclipsing all.

"They'll make you beautiful, brown-bar." Buccari laughed, trying not to cry. Quinn, full-term pregnant, cried hard enough for both of them. Quinn's sorrow was deeper.

A hot sun beat on the runway's apron. In the distance, ocean swells lifted by a turning tide crashed heavily on the beach, drowning out construction noises. An offshore breeze, fragrant with salt and seaweed, blew away diesel fumes and human shouts. Three heavy-lifters and six EPLs were on the flight line. Another EPL, on final, coasted in for an unpowered landing.

"Sharl, promise me," Hudson said, feigning sobriety.

"Promise you what, Nash?" Buccari replied, taking her eyes from the rolling apple.

"Promise you'll take care of Cassiopeia. She's helpless."

"Asshole," Quinn sob-snarled, letting go of his hand.

"Hardly the way I want to be remembered," Hudson said with a smirk.

"I asked Envoy Stark to drop in on you every day," Quinn

said, thrusting her finger at his nose, "just to see how you're doing."

"Arrggh!" Hudson cried. "I'll get you for that."

"You already did," Quinn said softly, giving him a last kiss. Her silver hair scintillated in a mischievous breeze. A med-tech activated Hudson's stretcher and guided it onto the heavy-lifter's elevator. As it lifted, all they could see was Hudson's good arm waving over the edge.

"He should have left with Admiral Chou," Buccari remarked.

"Hudsawn refused to leave as long as we were in trouble," Dowornobb said. "A true friend."

"He wanted so to see his baby born," Kateos moaned.

"I wish I could go with him." Quinn sniffed, hands on her swollen belly. Hyperlight and pregnancy did not mix.

"They need you here, Cass," Buccari said. "You've got to get ready for another five thousand settlers this year and another ten thousand next year. NEd will be a metropolis in five years."

"A fortress city, you mean," Quinn said grimly.

Breakers pounding the shore offered small solace for their fearful thoughts. A tractor towed the EPL from the runway.

"I wish you could stay longer, Sharl," Quinn said.

"Me, too," Buccari sighed.

"Do you know how long you'll be gone?" Quinn asked.

"At least the winter," Buccari replied. "Dowornobb and I will be working at the Ransan shipbuilding facility orbiting Kreta, one of their moons."

"Booch!" came a shout, a very familiar voice. She whirled. Two tall spacer pilots strode across the mat, one wide, one lithe: Carmichael and Chang! She forced herself not to run to Carmichael like a schoolgirl.

"Where is he?" Chang shouted. "We dropped in to see the Nashman."

"Already on board," Buccari replied, staring into Carmichael's deep brown eyes.

"Sucker's hard to catch!" Chang said, heading for a boarding ladder. "I'm going up, Commander. I don't want to miss him again."

"Right behind you," Carmichael replied, staring down at her.

"You'll have the whole transit to visit," Buccari said.

"We're not going back to Sol," Carmichael replied. "I've cobbled together a corvette group for the mothership cell that's staying behind. Commodore Wells designated me group leader."

Buccari's joy blossomed.

"I better go see Hudson," Carmichael said, striding away.

"I may not see you before I leave," Buccari shouted after him. "I'm in a hurry to get to MacArthur's Valley. I've scheduled an EPL."

"Carmichael's Taxi at your service." Carmichael saluted as he walked backward. "Somehow Eagle Squadron got tasked. Load up. We'll be right down."

Buccari turned to see Kateos, Dowornobb, and Quinn staring at her. She blushed and forced a wide smile from her lips.

"That one means much to you," Kateos rumbled.

"He was my squadron leader," Buccari replied inanely.

"A very old friend." Quinn laughed.

"He's a good pilot and an excellent leader," Buccari explained.

"I hear words," Kateos replied. "Your eyes are more eloquent."

Buccari reveled in the EPL's touchdown but agonized over every second during rollout and the tow back. By the time the apple came to a halt, skin temps were stabilized, unlike her nerves. The boatswain raised the cargo hatch, and Buccari stepped outside to a beautiful autumn day, crisp and clear. Cloud shadows dappled the taiga plain. An eagle soared overhead. The western mountains heaved heavenward from northern horizon to southern, sucking Buccari's breath away.

Much had changed. Quinn had driven the Legion engineers hard to complete the MacArthur's Valley rollout, enabling them to transport the heavy equipment for the hydropower project. For thousands of meters the taiga was scraped away, leaving large gashes and mounds of broken tundra. The dark runway stretched to the northwest, curving smoothly to a distant crown and then falling over the horizon, as if never ending. Heat shimmered from its unnatural surface.

There was no buffalo musk. The fall migration was well advanced.

"About time you got your fat spacer ass back."

She whirled and grabbed Fenstermacher by his hide jacket, pulling the wiry Survivor into an exuberant embrace. Reggie St. Pierre stood nearby, handsome features cut with an uneasy smile.

"Easy," Fenstermacher whined, hugging back with equal enthusiasm. "I got a reputation to consider. Les doesn't take kindly to my . . . fraternizing with officers. Reggie and I are here to escort—"

"Reggie," Buccari said, breaking loose. "I'm so sorry. Is there—"

"Thanks . . . Sharl," St. Pierre answered, jaw tight and sad eyes averted. "It's better if we just . . . not talk about it. I'm glad to see you."

"Oh, I'm glad to see you, too," she replied, wanting to console him. St. Pierre smiled tragically. She stepped forward to embrace him. He returned the embrace with unexpected intensity.

"Helo's waiting," Fenstermacher said impatiently.

"Yeah," Buccari said huskily. St. Pierre's hold loosened. Buccari tried to fathom his emotions, and her own. She looked up. His dark eyes stared down into hers.

Someone cleared his throat. She turned to see Carmichael, silver and bulky in his lander suit.

"I've got to leave," Carmichael said, his expression unreadable.

"Oh," she said, smiling at St. Pierre and pushing away.

"I have three days to organize my corvette group before the jump," Carmichael continued. "By the way, I'm listing you on the muster sheet."

"You'll let me be one of your pilots?" she asked.

"There's a war to fight." He laughed, but not with his eyes.

"I'll be begging for flight time," Buccari replied.

"Begging. I like the sound of that," Carmichael mused.

"We still have to talk," she said.

"I'm looking forward to the conversation," he replied.

"Gear's loaded, Sharl," Fenstermacher interrupted. "Everyone in the valley is waiting to see you. Helo's waiting."

"Oh, Commander," she said, "this is Winfried Fenster—"

"Jake-Ace and me're old buddies," Fenstermacher said.

Carmichael laughed, shaking hands with the wiry little man.

"And this is Reggie St. Pierre," Buccari said. "Our newspaper publisher."

"And mayor of MacArthur's Valley, too," Fenstermacher added. "Sam Cody retired to his estate, Sharl."

Carmichael and St. Pierre shook hands firmly, measuring each other. They were both tall men: Carmichael broad and rugged, St. Pierre intense and handsome. St. Pierre nodded, his smile tight. Carmichael did not smile.

Bart Chang ran up and bear-hugged Buccari, breaking the tension. Buccari said her final good-byes and watched the corvette pilots walk to their lander. Carmichael turned and waved. She waved back. He disappeared inside. She suddenly felt short of breath.

"You love him, don't you?" St. Pierre asked softly.

She looked up at the tall, dark man; his expression was at once sad and caring. She nodded.

"Come on!" Fenstermacher shouted, trundling the lorry closer.

"Let's go," Buccari said, jumping on the lorry. Her emotions were in turmoil, but of one thing she was certain. "I want to see my son."

"I'm in a hurry, too," Fenstermacher huffed. "Gunner Wilson and me are going fishing. You wanna come, Sharl?"

She smacked him in the back of the head.

The transfer of Buccari's gear to the helo was quickly done, and within minutes she was staring out the window at the long azure expanse of Lake Shannon, its blue crystalline surface limned by crimson- and yellow-leafed hardwoods. The autumnal splendor was in turn surrounded by the deep green and teal of firs and pines. Snow levels had fallen, and the blue-tinted glaciers were frosted with a fresh mantle of virgin white.

The helo flew down the lake. Buccari observed more changes: A crust of man-made structures met the shore at the lake's southern end. Among them was the hydroplant, a buff multiple-story cube squatting over one of the larger inflows. It was not attractive.

"Swing by the hydro," she shouted to the pilot.

Forest had been cleared. A road ran down the lake from the settlement cove to the hydro. Buildings had been erected along the road.

"It looks like a town," Buccari said.

"It is," St. Pierre shouted back. "The hydro construction supported some incidental enterprises. Most of the cabins are closer to the hydro than they are to the palisade. We've constructed the Legion admin office there and a new communication center. The only major drawback is that it's farther from Longo's Meadow, but with the helos it doesn't matter that much."

The helicopter looped back along the lake, toward the

settlement. Buccari looked out into the wooded rills and feeder valleys. She saw Tookmanian's church, luminescent in a coat of whitewash. Its finished steeple rose proudly. She also saw cabins in groups of four ranging down the valley flank.

"How many people now?" she asked.

"Almost three hundred," St. Pierre said, "counting Legion personnel. A lot of marines and construction crew have remained. We've even had a few southern settlers wrangle their way up here."

"Need more women," Fenstermacher shouted. "Hydro's turning into a cowboy town. It's pretty rough. Cliff dwellers won't go near it."

"Cliff dwellers?" she asked.

"They've joined us," St. Pierre explained. "They started a colony above the settlement. We helped them clear land. They terraced and irrigated it. They cleared land down by the lake, too."

"They took over the old quarry," Fenstermacher added.

The changes were too much to comprehend. Buccari sat back as the helo made its approach to the back corner of the palisade. She saw golden horses stomping around their paddock. Around the perimeter of the helo landing zone a gathering had assembled: her friends, hair and fur whipped by rotor wash. More came running across the common.

Buccari jumped from the helo and into a field of welcoming arms, Nancy Dawson and Leslie Lee foremost. Dawson, tall and big-boned, her explosion of red hair spilling into the breeze, was immensely pregnant. Buccari pressed against the swollen belly and was rewarded with subterranean movement.

"Twins!" Dawson groaned, but she was smiling. The only person with a broader smile was Tatum, standing close, arm around his golden-haired daughter.

"More goddamn redheads," Fenstermacher snarled.

"Tall, dumb ones." Chief Wilson laughed, trading mock glares with Dawson. Standing next to Chief Wilson and Terry O'Toole was someone she vaguely remembered: Colonel Pak, the security chief. He wore expedition fatigues and carried a fishing pole on his shoulder.

Tookmanian, Mendoza, and Schmidt ran to get her gear. Adam Shannon, jet-haired and grown even huskier, stared at her with a wrinkled sunburned nose. Leslie Lee led little Hope by the hand. Sam Cody, Mrs. Jackson, and ranks of settlers cheered. Buccari waved, but her gaze darted about, searching. Her emotions built to a frantic pitch.

"Behind you, Sharl," Lee said.

Buccari turned. There he was, standing next to Great-mother. The huntress chirped sharply. Her son had grown so much. His blue eyes were dark, shining mirrors of morning sky. The boy stepped forward and bowed in cliff dweller fashion.

Buccari fell to her knees. Charlie ran into her arms.

EPILOGUE

THE FUTURE BRINGS

Heavy clouds scudded over the taiga plain, abetting dusk's dominance. Also pushed by the biting northerly, a hunting eagle glided low across a snow-dusted esker, awesome pinions stirring the thin mantle of white powder. The giant raptor descended smoothly into a tundra swale, hunger compelling it to ignore fatigue. The raptor's eyes, golden and cruel, followed a tenuous line of tracks scarring the windblown whiteness. Driven by instinct, the black-and-tan eagle was governed by nothing but nature's truth.

From afar the tundra appeared flat, a white-mottled prairie, but the taiga plain was pocked with dells and downs, particularly along the river cliffs leading to the valley of the volcanoes. At one point bedrock broached the permafrost, forming an irregular butte. Its modest elevation presented an unencumbered view. In season buffalo dragon inhabited its rock tumble, but the yodeling terrors had gone south with the migrating herds. The growler packs, too, were gone, either after buffalo or into the wooded valleys in search of elk and deer. At this time of year there was little to fear except the weather.

The butte was a sacred place, a place to die. Aged hunters, warriors without caring family, sometimes came here to a final resting, their bones mixed with dragon kill and growler carrion.

Craag-leader-of-hunters came not to die but to think. For thinking was an arduous task, and the butte was also a place to discover, a place to meditate, a place to listen to one's heart. For Craag was worried about life. He needed time to ponder one thought at a time.

There was cruelty under the stars, but Craag was undaunted. Bear people had wantonly murdered his ancestors. It did not surprise him that there could be other beings who would wantonly kill bear people or even long-legs. Smaller fish were eaten by bigger fish. Yet Craag was perplexed. The gods of nature were sometimes cruel, but they were never evil. In nature death had purpose. What was the purpose of this war in the stars? Why should his hunters be instruments of death in an unnatural war?

Was there a choice?

His world had changed when the long-legs had come with their fighting spirit and technical magic. Cliff dwellers had moved from the cliffs to live in the long-leg valley. Now the bear people wished to be allies of the cliff dwellers. A world turned upside down.

The hunter leader lifted his long snout and opened his mouth to taste the wind. The eagle's scent came to Craag and cleared his mind. The warrior nocked an arrow. He had a death stick in his belt, but Craag chose to fight his valiant foe as a hunter in the ways of his father and his father before him.

Craag leapt onto the highest pinnacle of the butte, spread his great membranes, and shrieked his clarion call. The eagle's head turned, scanning upward. Its eyes fixed on Craag's silhouetted form, and the great hunting bird pounded cold air to gain altitude.

Craag prayed for his ancestors. Craag prayed for their simple world. In vain, the warrior acknowledged—the past was gone.

The eagle screamed. Its talons swung outward. Craag sang the eagle's death song. And took aim. The gods this day would have their sacrifice.

Craag prayed for a future.

Don't miss where it all started...

GENELLAN: PLANETFALL

1995 DelRey Discovery of the Year

Genellan—a beautiful, Earth-like world where intelligent cliff-dwellers waited in fear for the day the warlike bear people would return...

Genellan—the only refuge for a ship's crew and a detachment of spacer marines, abandoned by a fleet fleeing from alien attackers...

Genellan—where Lt. Sharl Buccari tried desperately to hold on to the threads of command over both the civilians and the marines in a furious attempt to keep her people together...

At stake: the secret of hyperlight drive, the key to interstellar flight...

GENELLAN: PLANETFALL

Book One of Genellan
by Scott G. Gier
Published by Del Rey® Books.
Available in bookstores everywhere.

COMMENCEMENT

The Sting was what made Ronica McBride special——as well as the years the interstellar government. the Com. had invested in teaching her how to use it.

Newly graduated and ready to use her Class A talent——making her the most valuable resource in the Com——Ronica McBride should have had the worlds at her fingertips. But instead she was lost on an unknown planet. without any idea of how she had gotten there . . . and without her Sting.

As Ronica struggled to find a place for herself on the wilder-world. accept her loss of talent. and regain her missing memories. she began to discover that everything the Com had taught her was a lie.

COMMENCEMENT

by Roby James
A Del Rey Discovery

Published by Del Rey® Books.

At your local bookstore now.

WHEEL OF DREAMS

Kiera was desperate. The dreams that had threatened her soul had grown more sinister in the short time since her beloved mother had died. She might learn the secrets of the magic awakening within her—but only if she could escape her abusive father and find the witches rumored to inhabit the cities of the Blasphemers. So when her cruel father sold her to a mercenary from the north, she went with her new husband willingly enough...or so it seemed.

WHEEL OF DREAMS
by Salinda Tyson
A Del Rey Discovery

Published by Del Rey® Books.
Available soon at your local bookstore.

✎ FREE DRINKS ✎

Take the Del Rey® survey and get a free newsletter! Answer
the questions below and we will send you complimentary
copies of the DRINK (Del Rey® Ink) newsletter free for one
year. Here's where you will find out all about upcoming
books, read articles by top authors, artists, and editors, and
get the inside scoop on your favorite books.

Age _____   Sex ❏ M ❏ F

Highest education level: ❏ high school ❏ college ❏ graduate degree

Annual income: ❏ $0-30,000 ❏ $30,001-60,000 ❏ over $60,000

Number of books you read per month: ❏ 0-2 ❏ 3-5 ❏ 6 or more

Preference: ❏ fantasy ❏ science fiction ❏ horror ❏ other fiction ❏ nonfiction

I buy books in hardcover: ❏ frequently ❏ sometimes ❏ rarely

I buy books at: ❏ superstores ❏ mall bookstores ❏ independent bookstores
 ❏ mail order

I read books by new authors: ❏ frequently ❏ sometimes ❏ rarely

I read comic books: ❏ frequently ❏ sometimes ❏ rarely

I watch the Sci-Fi cable TV channel: ❏ frequently ❏ sometimes ❏ rarely

I am interested in collector editions (signed by the author or illustrated):
 ❏ yes ❏ no ❏ maybe

I read Star Wars novels: ❏ frequently ❏ sometimes ❏ rarely

I read Star Trek novels: ❏ frequently ❏ sometimes ❏ rarely

I read the following newspapers and magazines:
 ❏ *Analog*   ❏ *Locus*   ❏ *Popular Science*
 ❏ *Asimov*   ❏ *Wired*   ❏ *USA Today*
 ❏ *SF Universe*   ❏ *Realms of Fantasy* ❏ *The New York Times*

Check the box if you do not want your name and address shared with qualified
vendors ❏

Name _____

Address _____

City/State/Zip _____

E-mail _____

gier/genellan

PLEASE SEND TO: DEL REY®/The DRINK
201 EAST 50TH STREET NEW YORK NY 10022

DEL REY® ONLINE!

The Del Rey Internet Newsletter...

A monthly electronic publication, posted on the Internet, GEnie, CompuServe, BIX, various BBSs, and the Panix gopher (gopher.panix.com). It features hype-free descriptions of books that are new in the stores, a list of our upcoming books, special announcements, a signing/reading/convention-attendance schedule for Del Rey authors, "In Depth" essays in which professionals in the field (authors, artists, designers, sales people, etc.) talk about their jobs in science fiction, a question-and-answer section, behind-the-scenes looks at sf publishing, and more!

Internet information source!

A lot of Del Rey material is available to the Internet on our Web site and on a gopher server: all back issues and the current issue of the Del Rey Internet Newsletter, sample chapters of upcoming or current books (readable or downloadable for free), submission requirements, mail-order information, and much more. We will be adding more items of all sorts (mostly new DRINs and sample chapters) regularly. The Web site is http://www.randomhouse.com/delrey/ and the address of the gopher is gopher.panix.com

Why? We at Del Rey realize that the networks are the medium of the future. That's where you'll find us promoting our books, socializing with others in the sf field, and—most importantly—making contact and sharing information with sf readers.

Online editorial presence: Many of the Del Rey editors are online, on the Internet, GEnie, CompuServe, America Online, and Delphi. There is a Del Rey topic on GEnie and a Del Rey folder on America Online.

The official e-mail address for Del Rey Books is delrey@randomhouse.com (though it sometimes takes us a while to answer).